Secrets & Lies

Carey Anderson

DEDICATION

I would like to dedicate this book to my sister from another mother. My very special T. She's one of the most hardest working women I know. She's always grinding and making things happen. I hope you find the time to sit back, relax, and join me on this little journey though my imagination. I love you sweetheart, I always have and I always will. I cant wait to see you again. Until we're together again, I'm sending my love virtually. I love you dimples!

Cover Design by Cover Couture

Photo Credit: Stephreedmckenzie / iStock
Photo Credit: Studioportosabbia / iStock
Photo Credit: KariHoglund / iStock

Join me on Facebook – www.facebook.com/careythewriteranderson

Twitter - @CareyTheWriter

Blog - http://careyanderson.blogspot.com

Website – http://www.careythewriteranderson.com

Editorial – Treasures of Joy Editorial

Sometimes two people no matter how hard they try, they cant make it work. Often times we want to blame the other person. Sometimes there are variables unseen that interfere with the harmony we seek.

ACKNOWLEDGMENTS

I would like to acknowledge all of my supporters. I know I say this time and time again. I would not find the strength to continue without your continued support.

I would also like to acknowledge my Beta Readers who take time out of their busy schedules to read my doodles and let me know if I'm talking out of the side of my neck.

Also to my Rough Riders, you all pick up right where my Beta Readers leave off. You all are amazing and I could never thank you enough for your support as you also take time out of your busy lives to not only read my work, but you tell others about me. Thank you so much.

To my loyal readers, the ones who have made yourself known and the ones who are silent. I thank you from the bottom of my heart.

He took a step forward into my personal space and there was no more wall to back away into. I felt so powerless, and I was truly disappointed in myself. I tried my best to control my breathing. "Alaina I love you, and no matter what you will always know that's the truth. I messed up. I messed up big time. I couldn't blame you if you never forgave me, but I'm hoping that you do." When he leaned in to kiss me, I turned my head and he kissed my cheek then he started sucking on it.

So many thoughts ran through my mind and I was so angry for allowing this to happen. What happened to all of my anger? What happened to all the pain I promised him when I saw him again? You see, Royce is my soon to be ex-husband of ten years. We met in high school when he moved to my school. He was the all-star athlete whose military father moved his family to my neighborhood. Royce was, Royce was the guy from the movie.

Chapter 1

Alaina

"Alaina raise your hand," Mr. Perez called out. I did as I was told, "Royce you're going to work with Alaina on this project."

I bucked my eyes and immediately I was in shock. I wanted to standup and run out of that class. Royce smiled at me and I thought I was going to DIE! My life up until this point has been standard. Nothing that completely knocked the wind out of me or made my life anymore noteworthy than any other persons.

I'm you're average teenager, average brown to dark brown skin. Shoulder length dark brown hair, average height, and average build. Average brown eyes, average features, average intelligence, and average personality. When my English teacher had us write about ourselves there was nothing I could say about myself that was beyond average. I titled my paper the Average Black Girl from Richmond California. My English teacher loved my paper and she gave it an A for Average. I smiled so much at her little joke. With everything in my life being so average, I knew within myself that this moment just transported me outside of my average world and something about the moment made me become less than average.

Royce walked over to my table and sat down next to me. "Royce Chambers, it's a pleasure to finally meet you."

"Alaina Barton, nice to meet you as well." I quickly had a pep talk with myself, I told myself not to act nervous or shy. Too bad that little talk with myself didn't do anything for me.

"So it looks like we're going to be partners this semester. Can I get your phone number so we can talk after school?" Then he flashed that beautiful smile at me. His teeth were so straight and WHITE! I don't know why I wanted to sit there and count each one. Can you say a little twisted?

Wait he just asked me a very important question, focus Alaina. Don't blow this by being the normal dork that you always are. "How about I get your phone number? That way my dad won't have a heart attack when you call my house."

Royce smiled, "overly protective father huh?"

"I don't know about overly. My dad loves me and cares about what happens to me." But he really is.

"I get it; if you were my daughter I'd surround you with an electric fence. None of these horny teenagers would be allowed to look in your direction." Then he took out a pen and wrote down his phone number. "I don't get home from practice until 7:30; can you call me after 8?"

Did he just flirt with me? I told myself to calm down. How would I know if he's flirting? Nothing like this has ever happened within my average life. "8 it is." I put his number in my folder for this class in my binder.

Royce smiled at me as I stood up, "We have the same class next, can I walk with you?"

My eyes bounced around the room, "I guess so." I didn't know he noticed me.

Our one-minute walk down the hall was one that I will never forget. You should've seen all the eyes that looked at us as we walked together. Being your average girl at John F. Kennedy High School, not too many heads turned at any of my average girl existence. Walking down the hallway with Royce changed everything. Royce looked down at me with a smile as he asked me about my grades.

I shrugged and told him they were pretty average; average is my answer for everything. When I was little, I used to worry about being pretty when I grew up. As I got older pretty seemed like such a hassle, so I settled on average. I don't consider myself to be ugly, but I don't really stand out in a crowd. I don't mind that so much anymore, but when I was younger, it really bothered me. Probably cause my cousins made pretty seem like everything else was useless if pretty wasn't attached. In class, Royce sat in the desk next to me and asked me a ton of questions about myself. You could see people watching and trying to figure out why we were even talking. My friend Chareca watched as she smiled at us and silently cheered us on.

Suddenly I went from average existence to on Royce's radar. Royce and his friend Kenneth came to have lunch with Chareca and me one day, and then they never left. Chareca and I had a blast with Royce and Ken. Sometimes it seemed like we spent our entire lunch laughing and carrying on.

"Chareca, you so pretty. Why you don't have a man?" Ken asked her with a smile.

"I'm accepting applications if you're applying." She smiled back at him.

Ken chuckled, "application submitted."

"Application in review."

"Wait a minute! Just like that? He uses some lame line on you, and you go for it?" Royce asked blinking at Chareca.

She hunched her shoulders, "I liked it, so I don't care."

Royce looked at me, "this isn't fair. Can you even date?"

"Not exactly," I said feeling disappointed. My dad feels dating is for marriage, and since I'm sixteen and not looking to get married anytime soon there's no need for me to date.

"What does exactly mean?" He leaned forward, "tell me you've thought of a loophole."

My face started stinging with embarrassment. "I... I... I..."

"Wait a minute, does this mean that you're interested Royce?" Chareca said defending me.

"What do you think? My friend doesn't do this with everybody." Ken said in his friend's defense.

"Do what?" Chareca smiled while she folded her arms.

"THIS!" Ken said pointing around the table. "When have you seen Royce with any girl as much as he's with Alaina?"

"Like that's supposed to mean he's more interested in her than he is in getting good grades." Chareca waved Ken off.

Ken smiled at Chareca, "why does your dismissal turn me on?" Chareca's cheeks turned red and we all laughed. "I haven't found a loophole, but I'm allowed to do things with Chareca."

"Sounds like a loophole to me. So what's up for Saturday?" Ken said not beating around the bush.

"What makes you think we want to see you guys on Saturday?" Chareca put her hands on her hips.

"Girl! I love your sass, it makes me want to take you over my lap

7

and spank you." Ken raised his eyebrows at Chareca.

Chareca gasped, and then she started laughing. "Freak!"

"Yep! I am completely, and I'd like to show you how freaky I can get."

"Sssshhhh! Man, people can hear you." Royce said looking around.

"So!" Ken stared at Chareca.

"You don't want people getting the wrong impression about Chareca do you?" I asked.

"You've got a point, give me your number; I've got a lot of things I want to tell you in private."

"Your application is still in review."

"I plan to be your boyfriend by tomorrow and your lover by Saturday." Then he winked at her.

Our lunch went on like this for the rest of the period.

In the morning, Chareca told me all about their telephone conversation. She said Ken wasn't kidding about wanting to be her man. She said he came out guns blazing. He told her that he's liked her for some time, and since she wasn't picking up on his subtle hints, he's now taking the direct approach. I asked her if she even liked Ken and she said yes. She just never thought he would be interested in someone like her.

That Saturday was the first of many "outings" for us. I loved spending time with Royce. I didn't feel average when I was with him. I felt pretty, sexy, and smart.

Despite his best attempts, it took quite a while before Chareca allowed Ken in. The day that Chareca finally gave in shocked me; we said we were waiting until we got married.

Ken's mother worked on Saturdays so we normally hung out at

his apartment. After a couple of months, the expectation began that Chareca and Ken would disappear into Ken's room and that was the norm. They would go in Ken's room, while Royce and I would kiss and make out on the couch. Royce and I were kissing when we heard; "Ooohhh!" and a series of moans come from Ken. Sometimes you could hear the bed when they made out in there, but never any moans. Royce and I stopped kissing as we looked at each other like we couldn't believe what we were hearing. The moaning stopped and we resumed our kissing session.

A little while later, we could hear Ken again. I asked Royce if he thought they were really having sex. He shrugged and then we got back to our own lip action. They spent all day in that room until it was time for us to go. They came out to use the bathroom, and at one point Ken took food in, but they acted as if we weren't there. When it was time to go, Ken's bed was completely tore up and he had no jokes to offer, just stars in his eyes for Chareca. Chareca was completely focused on Ken, she didn't pay Royce and I any attention. Royce and I exchanged looks.

Ken and Chareca have always been affectionate, but this time they were sharing long passionate kisses. They were telling each other that they loved each other. They looked at each other like they were drunk. They stayed in their own world the whole bus ride as well. When we got off the bus, Chareca smiled at me as we walked down McDonald Ave towards Nichol Park towards the ramp. "Did you guys do it?" I was dying to know for sure.

Chareca smiled innocently at me, "yes."

I started screaming and jumping up and down. "Why? Why didn't you say anything? What made today the day?"

She kept her head down, "I wanted more. I think we've made out in every possible way we could make out."

"Do you like it?" I had so many questions to follow this one.

"Yes," she looked so embarrassed. "Please don't tell anybody about this."

9

"Chareca, I wouldn't tell your personal business like that."

We walked at a snail's pace as Chareca told me everything. She was now beyond sprung, but it didn't take a genius to see that Ken was too. After that, we didn't really see Chareca and Ken too much anymore. As soon as we got to Ken's place he and Chareca would disappear, we'd hear Ken's moans and the bed, and then that was it.

I was afraid that Royce would start pressuring me to do it now that Chareca and Ken were doing it. To my surprise and delight, Royce never pushed me to go further than our usual make-out sessions.

Two weeks before graduation Chareca called me before school and she told me her front door would be unlocked and to come early. When I opened her front door, I called out to her. Chareca's little sister told me that Chareca was in the bathroom and she wanted me to come in when I got there.

I knocked on the bathroom door as I opened it. I was expecting to see Chareca working on her hair like she normally did. I'd come in and then she'd ask my opinion about her final styling options. This morning she was sitting on the edge of the tub with a towel over her mouth as she cried into it with a pregnancy stick in her hand. Immediately I felt so bad for her, I didn't even make her say it. I hugged her and I told her it was going to be ok. Chareca helplessly cried on my shoulder.

When we got to school Ken was smiling at us as we approached until he saw Chareca's swollen red eyes. Fear spread across Ken's face and he turned pale. Chareca marched up to him and plunged her face into his chest as she cried out loud. Ken put his arms around Chareca and he asked her if she was sure. She cried as she said yes, and in that moment I was so thankful for my virginity that Royce had recently began asking for. It wasn't easy to tell him no, but it was for moments like this that I didn't want no parts of sex. My dad would be so disappointed in me. Royce and I walked away to give them some privacy to talk things out.

Even though they dated for two years, Chareca's parents seemed shocked when she and Ken told them they were pregnant a week after graduation. To my surprise, Ken proposed to Chareca, and she happily accepted. They got married quick, fast, and in a hurry. Ken said he didn't want to miss anything with his child like his father missed with him. His father was in his life, but he never lived in his home. Ken did not want his child to grow up like he did.

Even though some of her family tried to put an ugly spin on their marriage. Chareca was excited and all in to the planning. Their wedding was small and her sister and I were her bridesmaids, Royce and another one of Ken's friends were his groomsmen. Fortunately, their families blended well together.

I didn't tell my dad that Chareca was pregnant for fear he would flip out thinking that her situation was contagious or something. I graduated as a virgin, and I was quite proud of my achievement. Chareca moved in with Ken and his mother. Ken's mother was so happy to have company and another girl in the house. Ken started school in the Fall. Everything seemed great at first.

As a graduation present, Royce's father bought him a car. It was a nice car at that. Not some broke down bucket. A brand new, nicely loaded car. Royce was so excited; he'd wait for me around the corner to take me out or to Chareca's.

I almost died the first time he passed me the key to his car to teach me how to drive. I was so nerved up it wasn't even funny. Royce was a good and almost patient teacher. I got the hang of driving his car really fast. I got my learner's permit, and then my dad let me use his car to get my license. My dad didn't question how I became a good driver overnight. He never took me driving. He didn't seem concerned with my driving until I got my permit. It seemed like he forgot that I might want to know how.

Royce got into Cal Berkeley, being an army brat definitely had its perks. I got a job at a bank as a teller. At first we spent as much time together as we could on my off days and in-between his classes. Slowly however, his calls became less and less to the point that week's would go by without a word from him.

I was with Chareca and Ken's mom at their place watching a movie when I asked Chareca if Ken's heard from Royce. She said they talked all the time. I told her I hadn't talked to Royce in weeks. Chareca and Ken's mom promised to give him a hard time the next time they heard from him.

Royce

"Hello?" Chareca said answering the phone.

"Hey how you doing, is Ken home yet?" I poured a bowl of cereal.

"He's not here yet." Then she took a deep breath, "why haven't you been calling my friend?"

I frowned at the phone. "I've been busy, why you all up in my business?"

"Look Royce, I could beat around the bush with you, but that's not my style. Alaina loves you and if you're going to be that guy who uses being in college as the reason to mess around you might as well break up with her now. She's been turning down the advances of other guys as she waits on you."

I froze, "what other guys?"

"Don't act concerned now. What do you think is going to happen while you're out chasing tail? You think my best friend won't find someone else?"

Some guy could push up on Alaina, but I know she's the faithful type. I've been dating this girl for the past two plus years and her legs won't open. She said she was waiting for marriage and I can see that she means it. Some guy pushing up on her doesn't mean he gets anywhere with her. Truth be told I've been dating, but I didn't share that with my best friend. I can't trust him not to slip up and tell his highly emotional wife. It was one thing while we were all dating in high school. Ken suddenly became the faithful type when Chareca opened her legs to him. He said his experience with Chareca was unlike any experience he had ever had. He was immediately sprung and in love. I hoped Chareca would talk some sense into Alaina about all this waiting, but when Chareca popped up pregnant, I knew not to even think about trying anymore. "I'll call Alaina, thank you for the heads up. Tell Ken I'll call him back later."

I took a deep breath then I called Alaina. She answered on the second ring. I tried to beat around the bush and ask her how she's been. She wasn't going for it. Alaina demanded to know what was going on. "I love you Alaina, and I'm not trying to hurt you. Before I do something that I will regret I think we need to take some time apart."

Alaina didn't try to mask her tears, "why? Royce what did I do wrong?"

"Nothing, you're perfect. It's me, it's all me. I want to be the man you deserve but right now, I'm too distracted. I don't want you waiting for me so that you can start living your life. When I come back to you, I promise I will be all the man you need me to be and more. I just need some time." Alaina hung up in my face as she cried.

****

"Well! Well! Well! If it isn't Mr. Baseball." A female voice said as her arms spread around my waist from behind me. "How come you haven't called me?"

I turned around and smiled at Vanessa. "You haven't given me a chance to call you."

"When am I going to see you again?" She asked anxiously.

This girl is greedy; she keeps going and going and going. As much as I can dish out, she gladly takes that and then begs for more. I had no idea a woman could be this insatiable. Vanessa definitely made my head swell so big. "Well if you gave me a chance, I was going to call you tonight."

Vanessa squirmed with excitement; she started clapping her hands, "PERFECT! I'll make dinner. Bring your appetite, and then I need you to bring your appetite." Then she kissed my lips.

Vanessa seems to be every guy's dream woman. She is beautiful, smart, and her body is mind blowing. She's crazy for me! When Ken met her all he could say was *whoa*! **WHOA**! Ken said he didn't think it was a good idea to introduce Chareca to Vanessa. He said she's very protective of her best friend and her claws would definitely come out at just the sight of her. I agreed, and then I asked how Alaina was doing. Ken said she was fine, she got promoted to lead teller. I asked him if she got really depressed about our breakup and started eating and packing on weight. I know it's wrong, but that's what I was hoping for. Ken laughed and said the exact opposite. He said she has been walking with Chareca and then that walking turned into more exercise. "Your girl is looking pretty good these days." I tried to act like it wasn't bothering me. "Is she dating?"

"Here and there, although she has gone out a few times with this last guy. You want her back?"

"What? No! I have upgraded to a better make and model. I just think about her sometimes."

"Vanessa is beautiful, but I don't see you out with her all that much."

I exhaled. I couldn't believe I was about to say this out loud. "Vanessa is a freak!"

"You've said that."

"Too much of a freak."

"Yeah right, is that possible?"

"Sometimes I've got to turn her down. She act like I'm supposed to be ready at all times." Ken looked at me sarcastically. "Seriously, she be pawing at my junk in public. At that party we were at last week she gave me head in the middle of the party."

Ken's eyes got so big as he covered his mouth, "no shame!"

"None! That mess wasn't cool!"

"Why did you let her?"

"I was drinking, and caught off guard. She went straight to deep throat and she's good at it. Got me walking around feeling violated like I'm a girl."

We were quiet for a long time. What guy complains about getting it good? "To tell you the truth, you might want to follow up with Alaina. She's getting older, and I think she's really liking that guy."

Chapter 2

Tavio

"Hi Tavio!" The ladies said as they walked past me. This morning's announcements were about my stats from last night. I smiled as I made my way to my next class.

Some people offered their congratulations while others let their jealousy consume them.

My dad would take my sister and I to the park every Saturday. On the days it rained, we were in the garage. We played every game imaginable until we couldn't. In my family, we're very competitive, so we'd go in hard. It didn't matter that my sister was a girl; she played just as hard as me. When our little brother came along, years later, he fell right in line with us. It didn't matter that he was littler than we were. He was expected to give his best just like we were.

My sister and I are the resident athletes at Richmond high. We got all the sports teams covered football, basketball, baseball, even soccer. Even though I will admit, I'm only good enough to be on the team. Unique my sister dominates on that field as well. She's on the volleyball team and track.

I'm not a dumb jock though. My grades are part of my competition. It's my goal to beat myself in everything I do. I will admit that I relaxed for a little bit. A couple of my teachers gave me good grades just because they liked me. When my momma found out about this, she went completely off. She rewired my thinking and reminded me to stay in the game. If it didn't challenge me, it wasn't worth my time.

So with my grades, and schoolwork, I barely had time to squeeze in time for a girlfriend. Tempest was my stand in for maintenance really. I didn't have time to date her. She'd come to my practices and games with her friends and cheer me on. Most times after practice, she'd sneak in the locker room or something. She's pretty and she's built, but we never had some earth shattering conversation or bond. I steal moments away from everything and everyone to talk to Eva. She was my elementary crush, junior high school girlfriend, and until she moved my one and only true love. She challenges me in everything and I love her for it.

Our plan is to reunite after college, marry, and have a family. We wanted to go to the same school or close by each other. However, we agreed that the logistics of trying to make that work added too much stress. So we vowed to keep in touch and to see each other when we could. I'm not going to bore you with the details of my day to day.

"Spellman! You're not following your diet plan."

"My weight is fine; I'm in the range coach." I was tired of having this conversation. Part of the reason I train so hard and work so hard is because I love to eat. I'll be good for the most part, but I'm not gonna lie. Food is my true weakness, my vice to bring me to my knees. As much as I love to eat, I barely cook. I'm more of an eater than a cooker. My bulk helps me on the field; I will never be an easy win.

"That is not the point. I can tell when you've slacked off. Your performance is not up to par. Cut it out, draw on your discipline. When these recruiters come and take you out to eat, they will watch everything you choose. You're being judged from the moment you stepped into our school all the way through the pros."

I didn't say anything; I let him have his whole speech. I have no intentions of going to the pro's, Olympics, or any other sport. I may run with a ball now cause I need them to pay for my education. I plan to find my way into the corporate side of the Pro's. I don't know how yet, but I won't be killing myself running around with a ball in my hand hoping for love and adoration from my team. Maybe marketing, heck if I know. I'm not killing myself like this to end up crippled and possibly broke.

When my coach got tired of talking, he sent me out to do more laps. Fine by me, those potato skins were worth it.

Eva

My head popped up as soon as I heard the phone ring. "Hello?"

"Beautiful," Tavio's voice sang through the phone.

"What is that? Do the greeting right."

He cleared his throat, "hello my beautiful African Queen."

I smiled as I bowed my head, "my King." Then I sat up, "how much time do we have?" Tavio buys calling cards so that we can talk across the country. He called me once on his parent's dime and he was on punishment for a long time when his parents got their phone bill. So now he buys calling cards when he can and then we get to talk.

"Twenty minutes, and you eating up my time with formalities." He pretended to snap at me.

"You know the rules. Now I want to know what's wrong with you."

"Huh?"

"Huh? Don't act surprised. You know our time is limited and you trying to pick an argument so we don't have time to discuss what's wrong with you."

He took a deep breath, "I miss my Queen."

"What happened?"

"Tempest told me she loves me. I felt like a jerk for not saying it back. She don't have any reason to love me. She don't even know me."

"What are you going to do? The road to me is years away from now." Tavio knows I date, but we don't talk about it. I guess I like to torture myself by making him talk to me about her.

"If I got to break up with her I will. I don't love that girl and I'm not going to pretend."

"If that's your resolve, stop beating yourself up about it. It's not like you're going to change. It is what it is." I got comfortable as I leaned against the wall. "You got what I need?"

He sucked his teeth, "yeah I got it."

I laughed, "un un! Don't act like you don't want to give it to me."

"You better know that I love you! I wouldn't do this for anyone else."

"I know you love me, now show me how much." I smiled giddy with anticipation.

I could hear papers rustling in the background and then he cleared his throat. "Yesterday we went to the Richmond Marina. We stretched; well more like you stretched and I watched you bend over. As usual before we ran I took a sample of your full lips softly caressing mine. I told you I loved you and you said the same. Then we began our run around the marina. Passing other families out for their family bonding time after dinner. Owners and their pets, kids learning to ride bikes and skates. We stopped on the pier to catch our breaths before we began our journey back. Baby you're so beautiful to me that I don't know what you said. All I know is I loved watching you say it. Before we started back I sampled your nectar again. I swear I could spend all day on your lips. After I drank my fill and used your butt as my personal squeeze toy, we began again. When I wanted to stop, you wouldn't let me. When we finished I laid out on the grass. You laid on top of me claiming that you didn't want the bugs to crawl all over you. We both know how you like to pretend like you could dominate me. You kissed me and I forgot I was exhausted and that we were in public. I had to convince you that we had to stop because there was an older woman trying to watch everything with longing in her eyes. So you drove us back to your house. Your grandmother was knocked out. We quietly made love in the garage."

I started laughing, "made love? Really? Why you being so proper?"

"Get over it, that's the mood I was in."

I laughed some more, "ok. Keep going."

"That's it; I had to go take a shower. When I was relaxed I couldn't get my groove back."

I laughed, "the shower was that good?"

"We could try right now." I could hear his smile.

"Ok, let me lock my door."

****

"I heard you on the phone last night." My sister Rickie cut her eyes at me. I didn't say anything. "I don't understand why you got to test limits."

"She never said I couldn't get calls, besides he calls later because he's on California time."

Rickie huffed, "when are you going to stop stringing him along? He likes you and you run around here like you don't have a man."

"Rickie, it's complicated." I don't discuss my relationship with my big sister. I don't discuss my life with her at all. All she does is judge me and try to make me feel bad about stuff she doesn't know about.

She doesn't know that technically Tavio and I aren't together anymore. Or about all of our plans for the future. I honestly think she's jealous. Nobody has ever loved her and cared for her like Tavio always has for me. She was the only person happy about our move across the country to Florida. My grandmother lost her house that she lived in with her husband and raised all her children in. The bank gave her pocket change to pick up and move away from the only home I've ever known. My grandmother's sister told us to come live in one of her rental properties. We had nowhere else to go. Daytona Florida is not like Richmond California. The people move slower and the way they talk is hilarious to me. I had no idea that people here had country accents. Tavio says I'm starting to get an accent. I don't think so, but he likes teasing me about it.

Due to all the humidity my hair finally grows and apparently pretty fast. I've always kept my haircut short because my hair would never grow longer than touching the top of my neck. Once it hit that length it would stop, so I cut it. No sense in walking around with awkward in between stages hair.

The only thing to like about the humidity is how it affects my hair. At first I kept cutting my hair and fighting with it. I finally gave in by default and now even though it's not long I've got some hang time happening back there.

Rickie got our mother's pretty hair and skin. Her hair is thick and grows like a weed. I honestly think she grows it long to rub in my face because mine won't grow like that. I got our mother's shape though. Big legs, thick thighs, round butt. Tavio's story made me laugh cause I don't run. I don't like to exercise really. I'll walk, and that's all I do. Even when he and I went on the track, he would run. I'd walk around the track cheering him on.

Rickie gets up early every morning even on the weekends. She works out using the videotapes our grandmother bought us and she works out until her shirts are drenched in sweat. Then she makes breakfast for us. She's had a whole morning by the time I roll out of bed. She has to do all that though. Her simple curves would get lost in any kind of thickness. Then she'd just be round.

I could sit here going round for round with why my sister and I fuss. My grandmother says our relationship was perfect until I turned four and told Rickie no. Ever since then we've been fussing. I love my sister and I know she loves me; we just get on each other's nerves. Especially since we've moved out here to Florida we've had to have each other's backs.

Most people don't like the girls from CALIFORNIA! We've been called stuck up and everything else. One time we fought our neighbors because the momma got mad at our grandmother about the garbage cans. How were we to know there were designated spots? Instead of talking to my grandmother about it, she came out the house cursing and screaming. Her three kids came out having her back. Rickie and I went out, had I known we were about to fight I would've came prepared. I'm not going to lie; I was not winning until Rickie helped me. That girl hit like hammers, and she got me with the first one. Slammed me around and then Rickie came to save the day. As soon as everything stopped spinning I was able to help.

Now my grandmother and Ms. Carol are good friends. They fuss all the time but they look out for each other.

Rickie and I made our way to school. We're in the same grade. Ok so let me tell you how that happened.

Our mother was in love with our father. She's the baby girl of my grandmother's kids. So she was still at home when she got pregnant with Rickie. And a year later she was pregnant with me. I remember our father, but I choose not to think about him. What can I do about a man who chose to leave his girl and kids? My sister on the other hand took it very hard when he left us. One day our mother didn't come home. Rickie took it very hard and she ended up getting held back a year. My grandmother says I'm the fighter, even Tavio says that's what he loves about me.

"Eva! You hear me calling you!" James called after me.

Rickie blew air, cut her eyes at me, and then she hurried on to class. "I didn't hear you."

"What you got for your man?" James stood in front of me confident in my lust for him.

"I've got to go to school today. I don't have time for this." I turned to walk away.

James grabbed my backpack, "ain't nobody stopping you from being a nerd. But I demand a proper greeting when you see me." Then he pulled me in to kiss him.

I frowned and backed away from him. I spit on the ground. "I TOLD YOU ABOUT THAT JUNK! CHEW SOME GUM OR SOMETHING! I hate the taste of cigarettes."

He picked me up, "I love it when you yell at me!" He put me down and then he made me kiss him again. "Since you on a nerd mission today I'm picking you up after school."

"My sister..."

"Convince her to come with us. I know somebody if she want her own hook up."

"My sister don't like thugs."

He smiled at me, "every good girl wants a thug."

"No they don't. Just like every thug don't want a good girl. You need to let stereotypes go. I'll see if she'll come with me. But if she says no, I got to go home with her."

James' smile dropped, "tell her she better." Then he walked back to his car.

At lunch I sat next to Rickie, I smiled real big at her. "No!"

My smile dropped, "you don't even know what I was going to ask."

"I don't like James, I don't want no parts of whatever he's talking you in to."

"Oh come on, live a little."

She shook her head, "nope."

It was going to be a waste of breath to plead with her. "Can you help me figure this out?"

"Just go to the store for grandmother. It shouldn't take too long whatever you two have to do."

"Ok," I swallowed hoping this was going to work.

I told James to wait around the block from our house. I told my grandmother I needed snacks for my homework. She didn't question me about it. I ran to James and he drove to the park. He parked in the corner in the back of the parking lot by the trees and bushes.

I prefer Tavio's muscular thickness to James almost skinny thinness. Both of them act like my stuff is the best they've had. Tavio loves me and I could feel it whenever we made love. With James it's just sex even though he tries to act like it's more for him.

Tavio

"Are you going away to college?" Tempest asked.

"Berkeley, you?"

She straightened my cap and tassel. "No, I was just wondering if this is where we end?" She looked in my eyes.

"Only if that's what you want. It doesn't matter to me."

My statement wounded her, "it doesn't matter to you?"

I exhaled, "can we talk about this later?"

"Why? It's not like it's going to matter to you then either." Then she turned on her heels and huffed away.

I shrugged again and then I checked my reflection in the mirror. I'm more than halfway to the man I want to be. That much closer to the point where I can marry Eva and live happily ever after.

When I crossed the stage my family and friends cheered me on. I emailed Eva pictures from graduation after looking at hers. I missed her so much.

****

Tempest smiled at me with nervousness in the corners of her eyes. "I like your place, it's nice."

I closed my eyes as I started to dose off, "thanks."

"Tavio, I need to tell you something." The uneasiness in her voice robbed me of my peace. I stared at her, "I'm pre..."

I sighed out loud, "are you sure?" Of course she was. Of course that's why she asked if I was leaving. Of course! Of course!

"Yes, my momma kicked my butt already. I'm still pregnant."

"So you're keeping it?" I couldn't really feel anything.

"Yes, are you mad?"

"Disappointed in myself, who am I going to be mad at? You didn't get yourself pregnant." Tempest started crying, "why are you crying?"

"I love you, and you've never seen me. Most times I think you're imagining her while you're with me. You don't know anything about me and you don't care. I just told you my momma kicked my butt and that went completely over your head. Why do I have to be pregnant to see everything for what it is?" I didn't say anything, "thank you for not asking if I did this on purpose."

"Are you... How far are you?"

"Four months."

"Why you wait so long to tell me?"

"I was hoping I didn't have to. I waited until my momma was drunk to tell her." She cried some more. "I got a job; I'm determined not to be on welfare."

"I'll do everything I can on my end. I'll get a job too."

****

I wanted to sleep but I needed to do laundry so that I could have something to wear to work tonight. I couldn't put off laundry any longer. I cursed the sky when I only had four quarters in my coin jar. I loaded up my clothes, detergent, etc. into my car. I needed to go to the bank for a roll of quarters. While I was there I might as well put my cash that I was saving in my safe deposit box.

Although Tempest has been cool about this baby and accepting what I give her, there's a voice in the back of my head that screams gold digger. So I keep my bank accounts at minimal balances. Instead of having my checks deposited directly into my account I take my check to the bank, cash it. Keep what I need on me, give Tempest money or bring her what she needs, and I put the rest in my safe deposit box.

I looked at the teller line and my boy from school wasn't here. I never have to wait in line when he's here. He always takes me next. He justified this with his manager by telling him I'm a team member. Of course on the day when the line is ridiculously long he's not here. I waited in line like a normal customer understanding why our customers get so irritated about the wait. When the merchant teller opened her window, she got the line moving. She was kicking out customer transactions as if she was playing a video game. "May I help the next customer?" She called out.

I happily hurried to her window. "Thank goodness for you. I thought I'd be in this line forever."

She smiled, "how may I help you today?"

"I need a roll of quarters and I need to get into my safe deposit box." I said as I signed my withdrawal slip. "Ben's not here today?"

She read my account number upside down and backwards for that matter. "I have no idea, I just work here." Then she opened her drawer. "Here's your quarters, and then I'm going to have you meet me at the end of the counter so we can get you in your box."

There was a reason she was quick. She told the waiting merchant customer she would be right with them. She checked my signature and information on my box card then she buzzed me into the vault. Her fragrance danced in my nose as she led the way into the vault. I told her I didn't need to go into the room. I barely opened the lid I shoved my money in, then we locked the box again. She escorted me out of the area and then she hurried back to her window. I wanted to ask her about the fruity smell that she was wearing. I imagined Tempest wearing the same thing. Before I asked I caught myself. I think that's kind of a personal question. Since I wasn't sure I turned on my heels and left.

I went to the Laundromat in El Sobrante. Since it was early I had free range of the washers. I sang a song of thanksgiving and then I loaded four washers at once. I worked on homework in between washing and drying. Folding took longer since everything was ready at once. Feeling accomplished about my day I swung by my parent's place. My mom was gardening in the front yard. I bent down and kissed her. "How's the baby baking?"

"He's cooking, I took diapers and wipes over like you told me to."

"Good, and you need to have some at your place too." I could see disappointment in her eyes.

"Thanks mom," I looked around.

"I told you about these girls. I'm just surprised it wasn't Eva."

"Eva's not like that."

"You so sprung on that girl you don't listen. I hope this time apart opens your eyes. She's going to have a fit when she finds out about the baby."

"How do you know she doesn't know already?"

"I already know how she's going to respond. You won't be able to hide it from me neither. Mark my words."

****

"Congratulations! It's a boy!" The nurse said laying my son on Tempest's chest.

I looked at his little body with so much pride. That's when it hit me, "I'm a father! I'm a daddy! I have a son!" I took a step back as I watched Tempest and the baby bond. He's definitely mine, look at that head.

I asked Tempest if my mother and sister could come in now. She excitedly said yes as she kept kissing the baby. Unique was pacing in the waiting room. I told them to come, both of them cried as soon as they saw him. My mom said it was like looking at me all over again. Lil T cracked his first smile at my mom. She was in love!

Eva

I stared at the positive test as I cried. This cannot be real; I just got adjusted to the swing of things over here in Atlanta. Rickie stayed in Florida with my grandmother at a school nearby, James picked me up on

27

his way back to Florida. He paid for my plane ticket back out here. I knew he was too drunk to be trusted that night but he was kind of insisting so I went along with it. James is not my future, this is not my plan. Tavio would never forgive me for this. I cried myself to sleep last night, and I've spent all morning staring at the test. I'm not doing this, James will have to give me the money. I called his number, "who dis?"

"Eva! Jerk!" I could not STAND him for nothing in the world right now. The mere sound of his voice enraged me.

"What's wrong with you?"

"You don't know how to use rubbers!"

He breathed irritated air, "what?"

"I'm pregnant! How could you do this to me?"

"To you? How do I know it's mine? I don't know what you do when you're out there switching around those college guys."

"James you out here so much they think you're a student. When could I possibly hook up with someone else?" He was out here so much, and whenever he came I missed curfew at my dorm. I've spent the night in his car, and we've gotten rooms. I could be studying or walking out of a class when I look up and there he is. I never knew when he would pop up. Had I known that he was going to be here so much, I never would have given him my class schedule.

"Don't mean nothing, I'm not always there. I highly doubt that baby is mine. You need to call the real father and get off my phone with that nonsense."

"James!" I screamed into the phone, "please don't do this to me! I need to get this taken care of as soon as possible. I can't allow this to go on."

"See! That's how I know it's not mine. Any girl who gets pregnant by me always wants to keep my baby. I'm the one who has to make them get rid of it."

"I can't have a baby right now."

"You too good to have my baby?"

"I'm in school, I don't want any body's baby right now."

"Yeah, yeah, yeah. Females who really don't want babies don't rely on no rubbers to keep them safe. You always think you're smarter than somebody else. You just trying to get my money."

"I don't think I'm smarter than you. Please don't leave me hanging like this." I cried.

"Here's your first hard knocks lesson, tell them other fools to strap up. I'm not giving you one red cent. Guess you just going to have to come home and have your baby. If I think it look like me, then I'll take care of you." Then he made a kissing noise over the phone and hung up.

I couldn't believe it! No, actually I could believe it; I didn't want to. The only man I've ever been able to count on was Tavio. TAVIO! He said he's been saving up his money so he could come see me. I sat there trying to think of a story that would convince him that I needed the money more than he needed to save it.

After two days I decided I would tell him, that I got fired from my job and I was behind on my dorm fees. I was prepared to cry and falsify documents to support my claim. To my surprise when I told Tavio I needed the money he didn't ask for an explanation, he asked me how much I needed, then he told me to pick it up in the morning at Western Union. He called me back that night with all the information so I could pick up the money in the morning. As soon as I had the money I went down to student health and made arrangements to have this situation taken care of.

****

"That guy was looking for you again, what's his deal?" My roommate Katrina asked me.

"He has issues and he's not my problem anymore, I'm done." Turned out that my only issue wasn't that he got me pregnant. I had to take extra antibiotics and I was humiliated! I did heed his advice and got on the pill even though I was off the disappointment of so-called men. I'm at school to focus and get my education. Not for these orgies and ridiculous experiments that these idiots are all about.

"So I should continue to tell him that you're not here?"

"Tell him I switched schools and you don't know where I went. This is a pretty big campus. It's not like he can comb every class looking for me."

"As long as you remember to tell Chauncey that I'm out with a study group whenever he calls." Chauncey was her uppity boyfriend. I swore he was white because he's so proper. She assured me that his skin was a beautiful hue of brown that she said she wanted to drink like it was maple syrup. She would go on and on about how pretty his skin is. One day she showed me a picture, and I caught myself before I drooled. He looked like a male model. His skin was a beautiful brown like Tavio's but Chauncey's was smooth like he never had a zit ever in his life. His hair was jet black and nicely faded. It looked like he definitely walked around with a brush in his hand massaging those waves. He still sound too uppity whenever I answered the phone to tell him she wasn't there. I doubt she was cheating on him, she just liked her freedom.

"You got it. Do you think we will be roommates next year?" I asked as I grabbed my bag for class.

"My father has already spoken to the housing committee to make it so. Consider it a guarantee." She gave me a thumbs up.

Chapter 3

Alaina

I smiled as I told my work friends how Cleavon showed up at

Chareca's baby shower baring gifts. Cleavon was mister personality in a room full of mostly females. Ken stared at Cleavon when he said he was there for me. No doubt taking him in to make a full report.

Even as we waited the nine grueling hours while Chareca labored. In the calm moments Ken would sneak questions in about Cleavon. Little Cara Mia was born and I was exhausted. I kissed Chareca and the baby then I hurried to my car.

As a belated graduation gift my grandparents on my mother's side helped me get a car. My father felt a brand new car wasn't practical for a first car, but my grandparents didn't care. I gripped the steering wheel as I watched Royce walk in front of my car without even seeing me. I thought about running him over, but I didn't want to risk damaging my new car.

When I got home I crawled into bed. I was so thankful that I happened to have the day off cause I needed to sleep.

I awoke to the sound of my father knocking on my door. "Are you sick?"

"No," I croaked.

"You know I don't allow you to sleep the day away, are you decent?"

"Yes daddy," I turned my body towards the door.

"What's going on with you? I don't allow you to sleep the day away." He looked angrier than his voice let on.

I cleared my throat and sat up. I took a deep breath, "Chareca and her husband had their little girl early this morning. I was at the hospital with them."

Shock and surprise spread across his face. "When did she get married?"

"This summer," I watched him as I saw him start the calculation.

"Please don't do the math dad. She's happily married and they have a little girl now."

My dad rubbed his head, "children are a lot of work."

"We're not all bad, right?" I smiled.

"Baby girl you are the exception." He kissed my nose then he walked back towards the door. "I'm going to make dinner, any request?"

I smiled bigger, "SPAGHETTI!" I yelled as I threw my covers off my shoulders.

He chuckled, "one day you'll tire of my spaghetti."

"Never dad," I assured him as he walked out. I plopped backwards and fell asleep again. When I woke up I could smell food. I drug my tired bones out of the bed to the kitchen where my dad was cleaning up before he sat down to eat.

That vein was throbbing in his forehead, which meant he was thinking and he was going to have a talk with me about something. It was too late to run away, he was making my plate. I took a deep breath and then I sat down. My father prayed over our meal and then he picked up his fork. He perfectly twirled his pasta on his fork and then he held it just above his plate. He exhaled and then he asked me why he wasn't invited to the wedding. I looked at my plate as I shook my head. When I looked at him I could see that pain there. I sunk a little in my chair. I apologized but I didn't offer an excuse. He told me he would've liked to have been at the wedding. Chareca and I have been friends since we were little. Our parents even double dated from time to time.

I knew he would've gone, but like I said he would've flipped out once he found out about her pregnancy. Plus stuff like that always made him think about my mother. Pain and confusion always hit him like a piano suddenly dropping on his head. Then he talked about his wedding and how nervous he was. He stammered all over his vows, which made everyone laugh. As he went down memory lane, torturing himself with my mother's memory, I could hear her voice as she recalled their courtship, wedding day, PG version of their honeymoon night, when they were pregnant with my brother, and how they tried for years after and then finally when my sister and I came along. Both of them wanted a little girl desperately to complete their family. I used to cry when I thought about my twin sister who passed away when we were little. I imagine those overwhelming feelings of loneliness I get are in part the grief from losing her. I know my life would be totally different if she were still here. My life would be different if my mother was still here too.

I ate a little and then I mostly listened as my father went on and on about the only woman he ever loved. Suddenly he stopped talking and then he looked at me. "I know you're getting to be about that age where you think you want to settle down. You're a young adult so I can't exactly stop you. I'm begging you to wait, wait until you know yourself."

"I know myself dad." I said lowly.

"Really? Then tell me who you are. What do you stand for? What do you have to offer someone in a relationship?"

I hate when he's in these moods. "I'm your daughter, I stand for honesty, love, and integrity. I only have love and faithfulness to bring to a relationship." He stared at my eyes for a minute. I knew my comment hurt him, but he had me backed against the wall. "I'm your daughter daddy, I'm not her."

"You remind me so much of her." Tears defied him and filled his eyes.

"I'm all you, I look like you, act like you, you raised me."

"Don't ever..." He snatched his words back out of the air. He got up quickly from the table. He took his plate to the sink, and then he hurried out of the kitchen retreating to his bedroom.

I sat there digesting that he was trying to tell me not to be like her. Not to be like my own mother.

33

****

"I'm waiting for the next excuse you're going to use." Cleavon said turning his ear to me.

"I don't need an excuse. I'm going to be with my friend and the baby. You don't have to be everywhere I go."

"I'm your man, yes I do."

I folded my arms and huffed. "No you don't." I exhaled slowly, I did not want to take him with me to Chareca's. "Fine, I won't go then."

"You embarrassed to be with me?"

"No. I just don't think we need to be everywhere together."

"You don't want to go nowhere, you don't call me."

Am I talking to a female? "Cleavon I call you."

He raised his eyebrows, "did you call me yesterday?"

I looked at my watch, "my lunch is almost over. I don't have time for this."

"Ok so where do you want me to meet you?"

I really wanted to go be with Chareca and the baby. "Meet me at Taco Bell at 6:30." In that moment I made up my mind that I wouldn't be there.

He frowned, "I thought today was an early day? Why so late?"

"I'm going to help balance the ATM's." I gave him a quick unaffectionate hug then I hurried back inside the bank. I called Chareca to tell her I was still coming.

At 4:30 I ran to my car and drove high speed to Chareca's place. I parked in her mother in-law's space in their garage since she wouldn't be home until later. I laughed uncontrollably for two minutes straight. I told Chareca how much Cleavon is driving me crazy. "He acts like a fricking female, he's too clingy and controlling. He wants dibs on my free time, but I have no clue what he does when I'm at work." I went on and on about how much he bugs me. Then Chareca asked me why I was still with him. I had no clue so I shrugged. I've never broken someone's heart. Cleavon tells me how much he loves me all of the time and it just seems mean.

I played with Cara Mia while Chareca and I discussed our plan. Next fall we'd enroll at the local junior college together. Her mother in law would keep the baby during the day. Meanwhile Chareca wanted to go walking with me and work her way up to running.

We were working on our plan when Ken and Royce excitedly burst into the door. My eyes immediately started to sting when I saw him. Royce had on basketball clothes like that's what they were getting ready to do. "What's up Alaina, I didn't know you were coming over today." Ken flashed Chareca a look.

"Did I forget to tell you she was coming?" Chareca said sarcastically.

"I need to make a reservation to come over now?" I stood to go to the bathroom.

Royce's eyes ran all over me, but he didn't say anything. I went to the bathroom feeling like I had the victory. When I walked out of the bathroom Royce was walking out the door and Ken ran into his bedroom. Chareca grinned at me, and then Ken came out. He kissed his girls and then he said he would be back. When Ken was gone Chareca and I laughed hard. I asked her why Royce didn't even say hi. She said communication goes both ways. I told her he broke up with me, and broke my heart. He's obligated to speak first and for me to give him a hard time.

I was playing with the baby, when we heard, *ALAINA!* coming from the street outside. I swallowed then I looked at Chareca in disbelief. She looked out the window and it was Cleavon, he was walking up the street screaming my name. "No he didn't!" Chareca started laughing.

"He doesn't know where we live does he?"

"No, I pointed to this area one time when we drove by. See! I knew there was a reason why I didn't tell him the right block when I told him where I lived."

"ALAINA!" He carelessly screamed through the street.

Chareca laughed, "he is crazy!" Then she opened the kitchen window. She stood back so he couldn't see her. "SHUT UP WITH ALL THAT NOISE! I'M CALLING THE POLICE!"

"ALAINA BABY PLEASE!" He frantically looked around trying to locate Chareca's voice.

"Aw! The crazy guy is pleading."

An older gentleman from across the street stepped on to his porch with his pants pulled up above his navel and wife beater T-shirt on. "Son! Come here!" As Cleavon approached him he looked him up and down. "You on drugs? What's wrong with you?"

"I'm looking for my girlfriend." He pouted.

"From the looks of things she don't want to be found. Can't say I blame her all that much based upon this. Now I'm going to be as nice as I can be about this. You got five seconds to get in your car and drive away. If you don't, I'm going to let my dogs loose on you." He pointed behind himself to the two big dogs waiting on the porch like they were waiting for instructions.

Cleavon hurried back across the street to his little car and then he drove away slowly. Chareca laughed as she said Mr. Bowman don't play. I did not like what I just saw. I made up my mind to call in sick tomorrow to avoid that fool. I'm not gonna lie, I was disappointed when Ken came home alone.

Royce

Alaina looked good, too good. Breaking up had definitely done her some good. I guess my mom was wrong about Alaina. She said Alaina was going to put on weight as soon as I told her I was done with her. I had to get away. I drove to Vanessa's, I'm just going to breakup with her. This isn't working for me. I won't stay for dinner. I worked on my speech and I had it down to a science. I knocked on the door and then it slowly opened.

Vanessa's roommate opened the door just enough so that I could see that she was only in her underwear. I coughed and then I asked for Vanessa. The door opened more and Vanessa was equally undressed. "We were playing a friendly game of I never." Vanessa said gently pulling me in the door. "Neither one of us has ever had a threesome. Royce have you ever had a threesome?" I shook my head no as my eyes bounced between them. "So I say we share this experience between the three of us, are you down?" I shook my head yes. "Nobody tells anyone about this, what happens here stays here, deal?" I shook my head yes.

****

She was walking almost running looking behind herself. Alaina almost ran me over. "Where's the fire?" I held on to her cart.

She hid behind me, "my ex is stalking me. Please help!"

Then a guy came jogging past our aisle, he stopped then he walked towards me. "Alaina, I can see you." He seemed irritated.

"Baby, is he bothering you?" I looked back at Alaina.

"Baby?" He immediately got angry and started hitting his chest. "Don't try to play this game with me, you don't even know her! Now move out the way and mind your own business!"

I stepped forward and pushed Alaina back, "this is your only warning. Turn around and leave otherwise I will break you down right here in front of everybody!"

I could see the fear in his eyes as he was all talk and not about to do anything. "Forget you Alaina! You play too many games!" Then he tried to mask the fact that he was retreating in fear.

I looked at Alaina who was watching the direction that he walked away in. "Who does that? You break up with them and they tell you no, that they're not allowing you to."

"Guess your loving is better than you thought," I smiled.

"Yeah, but not good enough." Then she straightened up. "Thank you for getting him off my back." Then she started to walk away.

"Um, I think we should shop together the rest of your shopping trip. What if he pops out of a corner cause he really doesn't believe that I know you?"

"Good point," she said looking uncomfortable.

"What are you here for?"

"I'm making macaroni and cheese for a barbecue today. What are you here for?"

My mouth filled with saliva, "the same one you made for Ken and Chareca?"

Her face lit up with excitement, "how do you know about that?"

"I came over the next day, and Ken told me I had to try a taste. Then I had to scrape the pot for the crumbs cause there was only a swallow left. What I got to do for a pan for myself?"

"That's not going to interfere with your post season dietary plan?"

"Naw! I'm pre-law; I've scaled back a lot on the baseball activities. I hope to attend Stanford Law."

"I thought you wanted to be the star athlete? What happened?" She asked as she slowly walked putting items in her cart.

"The reality of seeing how many people put everything they have into trying to go pro, and when they don't get picked up their entire worlds come to an end. I've got to be smarter than that."

Sure enough, I spotted that punk following us. When he saw me see him he threw up his hands and walked out of the store.

I forgot what it was like to talk to Alaina, when I spoke she listened. She wasn't trying to cloud my thinking with sex, she wasn't even offering it. I missed her terribly. Being with Vanessa has its perks, but she definitely needed to slow her little fast butt down. Most times she's out maneuvering me. The addition of her roommate was a fun idea, but sometimes I feel like they spend the time they should be studying trying to come up with new ways to shock me. I kind of miss the old-fashioned way of making love. One man, one woman, in one bed. Getting lost in each other and sharing the moment. If I'm not having sex with Vanessa she's talking about it. I think she's more turned on by the idea of me being a star athlete than she is about me. It seems like she's building her portfolio or something.

I can't believe I just told Alaina what I've only told my parents.

"You'll be a wonderful lawyer, your powers of persuasion are amazing." She smiled at me.

"Back to this Mac n Cheese, you going to hook me up or what?"

She smiled at her cart, "I think I can give you a personal portion. Do you still live in the same place?"

"Yep," I couldn't contain my smile for nothing.

"I need an hour and a half to go home and whip this up. Your place is on my way to the barbecue. I can drop it by if you like."

"Perfect, I'll wait for you."

Alaina

I had nervous energy as I moved around my kitchen. The way Royce kept looking at me kept making my leg tingle. I had to look away, I couldn't handle it. I don't understand why he broke up with me just to look at me like that later. Could he actually realize that he made a mistake and want me back? Yeah right, I bet those college girls are all over him. I'm the unpopular square sitting over here on the side.

I told my dad I would bring him a plate back from the barbecue and then I drove to Royce's apartment. I was so nervous, what if he made a move on me? I told myself not to think of it, cause I couldn't say for sure how I would respond to that. I left my purse and the rest of the food in the car. I tucked my purse under the seat, but I didn't take it with me so he wouldn't think that I had any other intentions other than dropping off this dish.

Royce was shirtless when he opened the door, he smiled at my dish. I told him I forgot to get a disposable dish for him while I was at the store. I told him he could bring the pan to my job when he was done with it. Royce stepped to the side so that I could enter his small studio apartment. I put the pan in the oven and I told him it was still warm so he could dig in or wait until later. As I stood to walk away from the oven, he stood in my way. He told me he liked my perfume. I thanked him; he said it made him hungry. I laughed and then I walked around him. As I headed for the door Royce grabbed my hand. "Alaina, I'm so sorry for what I did to you. You've always been too good for me."

I was surprised, "how am I too good for you?"

"You are way more disciplined than I could ever be. I know you have a picnic to get to, but I was wondering if you could find the time to talk to an old friend?"

"Talk to?"

"Yeah, catch up. Find out how you've been. What's new with you. I told you about my latest development I'm curious about yours."

"I don't have anything to tell."

"Not even about this guy?"

"Oh," there wasn't much to tell. However, if Cleavon motivated him to want to talk to me, I'll take it. "I guess, I got to get going. My purse is downstairs and everything else," I hurried towards the door.

"So I guess we'll talk later?"

"Sure why not?" I hurried out the door.

I screamed as I hit the steering wheel all the way up to the park. Our group appeared to be the only group in the park at this hour. I spotted my coworkers and their families spread out over the benches next to our grill. "Alaina! You brought it?" Ben said too excited to look at my dish. I had been bragging about my Mac N' Cheese for some time. Ben told me to put my money where my mouth was. "Now that you are here we can sit down and eat."

I said hi to my other coworkers as they hurried to the table with their plates like they were starving. The guy with the baby looked familiar, but I couldn't remember why. He looked like he was stuck trying to figure out how to maneuver getting his plate and the baby. The little guy was so cute in his little jeans and expensive shoes. "You look like you could use a hand." I smiled at him, he exhaled. "Can I hold him for you while you go get your plate?"

"You wouldn't mind?" He said as he handed the baby to me.

"Not at all, he's too cute."

"Thanks Alaina," he said as he stood up.

I stifled my gasp at the knowledge that he knew my name. Now I was going over all the possibilities in my brain about who he could be. The baby was a happy baby, and when you stood him up he liked to bounce.

Ben sat next to me, "here's the moment of truth. I'm putting a fork full in my mouth, this is your last chance to tell me to stop before you're embarrassed."

"I have nothing to be embarrassed about, I'm sure you will like it." I said smiling at him.

His friend sat down and reached for the baby. "I can take him." When I handed the baby back he started fussing and demanding to come to me. "What did you do to my son?" He joked.

Ben slapped the table, "it's my fault for doubting you! Tavio, taste the Mac N' Cheese."

His friend put a fork full in his mouth then he frowned at me. "Are you married?"

I smiled, "no."

"This tastes like a man trap." Then he got up to go get more.

"A! Don't take it all!" Ben yelled as he hurried back to the dish.

Pretty soon everyone was going back for more until it was all gone. Ben said from now on he was calling me the MAC!

I kept the baby with me as I walked around. He was the cutest little thing. His dad eventually came to get him so he could change him. When I gave the baby to him he smirked at me. "Now he smells like a girl. What fragrance is this?"

I laughed, "cucumber melon."

"His mom not gonna believe he was hanging with you, and not me." He smiled, "I guess I have to blame your food." Then he walked away with the baby who kept looking back at me.

Most of my coworkers are college students who work at the bank because of the flexibility. Then there's the older ones who've been with the bank since the beginning of time and are looking forward to retirement. I'm the only one who's there to make a living.

I made a plate for my dad and then I said bye to my little boyfriend.

****

"Can you blame him? If I had never lost my mind I would want to be everywhere you were as well." Royce said rubbing my hand with his.

All night he's been flirting with me, touching me, and hinting that he wants me back. "Why did you lose your mind?"

Sadness flashed across his face. "The grass looked greener from where I stood."

"So what's different now?"

"Alaina, I miss you. I want to get back together."

"So you can break my heart again? No thank you." I moved my hand, then I sat back in my chair.

Royce leaned forward then he took a deep breath. "I'm serious about us. I'm in love with you Alaina." I gasped and sat up, "I don't want to sneak around this time. I want to meet your father. I want him to meet my parents."

"Why?" I was trying to slow my heart rate down. My heart was pounding so hard I thought it was going to fall out of my chest.

"I want to marry you. I want you to be my baby momma, I want to build a life with you."

I gasped again as my head swished around. "Huh?"

Royce laughed at my lost expression. "There's only one Alaina in this world. I want you forever."

"Is this some kind of trick?"

He shook his head, "no. I get it. The first time we make love will be on our wedding night. I'm in if you're in." He laced his fingers into mine.

"You're proposing?" I felt light headed.

"Not yet, I want to get back together for now. However, I plan to propose soon."

"I don't know what to say."

"All you have to say is yes." Then he leaned in to kiss me.

I drove home on a cloud. Royce wants to marry me. **ME**! When I walked in the door my dad was watching television on the couch. He took one look at me and then he turned around. He turned the television off, and then he patted the couch next to him. He kissed my forehead when I did. He asked me who the guy was. I got nervous as I asked him how he knew it was a guy. He laughed at me as he said he was young once. I bubbled forth and told him everything. I don't know why I thought he would be mad. He wasn't overly happy either, but he didn't yell at me or go crazy like I thought he would. He told me to be careful and to pay attention to everything. He said who I marry will affect everything about my life.

Chareca and I went crazy over the phone. She said she should've known that all the whispering Royce and Ken had been doing meant something. Chareca suggested looking at wedding dresses. I couldn't breathe thinking about it. I told her I would let her know when I was ready. For now I was happy to have my boyfriend back.

Royce

Reunited and it feels so good! I whistled as I got out of my car. Alaina and I were back together and my future was looking up. As soon as I walked in the door I stripped and got in the shower. I could hear someone knocking at my door while I showered. If she stands out there long enough she'll get the clue and leave. As I put on lotion my phone rang. "Hello?"

"Royce, I was knocking and knocking."

"I was in the shower." I said unenthusiastically.

"What's wrong with you?"

"There's no easy way to say this, but I think we need to go our separate ways." Vanessa gasped, "I'm not the man for you."

"Why?" Her voice shook like she was angry.

"I can't keep up with you. You need someone who's in to getting sucked off in the middle of a party. I need my lady to conduct herself like a lady in public. When you brought your roommate into the mix it was interesting. Again you like performing for an audience, and that's only cool every once in a while. I kept telling you to stop having her in the middle of our time. She's approaching me when you're not around. Making me look like I'm creeping on you or that I'm with her. You picked her not me, she don't get to claim me. Everything is too complicated, and I'm not the man to live out this fantasy with."

"Royce, if you're feeling some kind of way you discuss it with me. You don't breakup with me." I imagined her standing at a pay phone with her shoulders hunched and her free hand flat with her fingers spread out as she talked. I told her that her hand gave her away when she was upset.

"When was I supposed to be able to get a word in? You're always on! If all I wanted from a girlfriend was kinky lude sex then you would be perfect. I'm not looking for just sex though."

"I can change," she cried making me feel like garbage.

"Please don't change a part of yourself that you love. You love being a freak, you shouldn't change that for anyone." Then she hung up on me.

****

"I'm just saying if you want to end up with a fat wife marry her!" My mom crossed her arms.

"Mere what's wrong with a fat wife? Maybe if you ate something you would finally mellow out and stop all this useless bickering," My father said.

"Royce doesn't secretly have a thing for fat women like his father." She rolled her neck.

"Secret? It's no secret that I love a woman with confidence no matter what she looks like. You act like a woman should be shunned for embracing herself for who she is."

My mom's eyes filled with tears. "You want to do this right now?"

My father put his hands up in surrender. Neither one of them wanted to look at each other. I moved my rice around my plate. "I love her, and if she starts putting on weight, I'll walk with her. I was just telling you two so that after I make my intentions known to her father we want everyone to meet."

"Royce, why her? She's not good enough for you!"

"What makes Royce so special? Alaina is a nice girl, I don't think he's good enough for her." My father bobbed his head to say he stood by what he just said.

My mom and I stared at him, "you are out of your mind! Our boy is going to be a lawyer! He's going to have money and every success that comes along with it. Alaina is not what I envision on his arm."

I exhaled, "I don't want your vision either. You don't have to live with the types of females you point out for me. I'm ready for this part of my life to be over. I'm marrying Alaina because I love her and she loves me. She's been good to me, loyal, and faithful. Something you two have yet to get right." I looked at both of them like, *yep I said it.*

"I already told you I'm all for you and Alaina making it work. Marriage is not easy son, but I think you'll have a good chance in front of you with someone like Alaina. She seems to appreciate you and support you. I have no doubt she will take care of you as well." Then he got up and walked out of the kitchen.

"I don't appreciate you? I don't support you? And I know I take good care of your no good two timing behind!" She called out after my father as he walked out of the door. Her eyes filled with tears, but they wouldn't dare defy her by dropping. "What you want to get married for? Didn't I always tell you to avoid it? You're so hard headed! Why should I waste my breath on you!" Then she stormed out of the kitchen and slammed her bedroom door.

After a show like that who would want to get married? I got in my car and drove to Alaina's place. I sat in my car trying to sort out my feelings. My parents weren't always like that. We used to have a standard and loving military family. One day something changed in my dad. Then one day we found out about his first woman on the side. From then on there was always someone. She was always full figured and in love with him. Financial reasons are the only binds holding my dad to my mom and she knows it. I don't know why he gave up on her, on us. One day he didn't care anymore. Well he didn't care about our mom. I don't understand what another woman could give you that would make you ok with seeing your children live like this. I kept taking deep breaths as I sat in front of Alaina's place in my car. She must've seen me cause she came out and sat in the car with me. She asked me if I wanted to talk about it. I shook my head no. Alaina reached over and hugged me. I squeezed her back, this is what I need. Not some overly dramatic exercise. Just tender love and affection.

Alaina's father stood in the doorway watching us approach. He was sizing me up the entire way. We shook hands after I entered. He invited me to sit on the couch. Then he gently touched Alaina's arm and asked her to give us some time alone. Alaina gave her father pleading eyes as she complied with his request. Our conversation was pretty standard father and future son in law flow. He asked a question, I carefully answered making sure my answer was to the point and not confusing. Eventually I heard Alaina laughing, she was on the phone. When Mr. Barton smiled like the interrogation was over, I put my hand out signaling that we weren't done. "I need your blessing on my plan."

"Oh?" He looked at me sideways.

"I would like to marry your daughter."

"Why?"

"Simplest answer, I love her and I want her forever."

"You think she wants you?"

"I know she does."

"What makes you think you're good enough for my daughter?"

"I know I'm not good enough for her, but I plan on trying my best to measure up. I..." Then the front door opened and a guy I've never seen before walked in. Mr. Barton seemed surprised until he saw who it was. They warmly embraced.

"Who's this?" He said looking me up and down.

"This is Royce, Royce this is my son Wesley."

I stuck my hand out to shake his hand, "he's here for Alaina?"

His father smiled, "yes."

"No! No! ALAINA!" He yelled.

Alaina rushed in to the living room with concern on her face until she saw her big brother. She screamed and ran to him. "What are you doing here?"

He kissed her forehead then he cut his eyes to me. "Who is he?"

Alaina put her arm around my arm, "Royce is my boyfriend."

"What? Start over!" He looked at his father, "I thought we agreed that she wasn't allowed to have a boyfriend?"

"She came to me after the fact." His father continued to smile. "Alaina honey, let us start our conversation over."

"No! Wesley can't be trusted." She squeezed my arm.

I pecked her lips, "it's ok."

"How you gonna kiss a man's baby sister in front of him like he's not standing here?" Wesley looked around, "where's the gloves? Me and him about to box!"

"Wesley come on, you don't...."

"It's okay, go ahead," I said.

Wesley smiled as he walked out of the kitchen door. "You still never said what brought you by today?" His father said handing us gloves.

He looked at his father, "it's over!"

"No son, don't give up on your wife."

"Not much I can do, she's moved on." He put his hands up to signal he was ready. We circled each other, "I punked out and it still wasn't good enough. It's over," he swung at me to test me out. I swatted his punch, and then he lunged but just enough to see what I would do. "I got a spot on the marina."

"Already?" Mr. Barton sounded surprised.

"I had the money, I..." I tagged him in his chest telling him to pay attention and stop acting like I wasn't nothing. "Oh you got a little power." He smiled like a crazy person.

We actually started sparring and he was pretty strong himself. I tagged him and then Alaina opened the door asking what we were doing. I looked at her to tell her it was alright and he clocked me. I stumbled two steps ready to unleash fire when Alaina ran in the middle of us.

"STOP IT!"

"This is how men figure each other out and bond." Wesley said pulling Alaina back to him.

"How could you learn anything hitting each other?"

"It's quite simple. You see your friend here is very guarded. He's probably been hurt quite a few times. He doesn't come right out and tell you anything. He gives you little pieces to see how much you can handle. He's going to be constantly testing you to see what you'd do. That's not necessarily a bad thing, but I wouldn't call it good. This is what you want little sis?"

"Wesley, I love him." She sounded like a little girl.

Wesley laughed, "yeah but sometimes love isn't enough. Ask Malcolm and 'em."

"Who?" All of us looked at him.

He started cracking up. "Never mind wrong story." He laughed some more. "Anyways, I guess he's fine for now."

****

I felt like someone was looking at me, I looked around the restaurant until I spotted her. Vanessa was staring at us with the most hurt look on her face. I looked at Alaina and Chareca, they were busy talking. Ken had just taken the baby to wash her hands. I could tell Vanessa was torn. I shook my head no at her and then she turned her eyes away. I hadn't seen her in months and although I know I chose this celibate lifestyle, I was pretty pent up. I whispered to myself to calm down. Vanessa had on a V-neck T-shirt, sweats, and sneakers. The unsexiness of her clothes turned me completely on. I turned my eyes and I told myself to get it together. The only thing missing from my relationship with Alaina was the sex. Other than that I had everything I needed from her. When Ken came back we packed up and left. Vanessa continued to stare as we walked away.

We hung out with Chareca and Ken for a while, and then I drove Alaina home. "What do you think our sex life will be like once we're married?"

"I have no idea, I expect you to teach me things and to be patient while I learn."

"You know we could practice somethings while the big day approaches. We don't make out like we used to."

"Practice leads to the real thing. I've waited this long, why not see it through?"

"We could practice, at least oral."

Alaina looked embarrassed, "are you asking because you need something?"

"I need you, but if you're uncomfortable then we can wait."

Alaina took a deep breath, "I love you Royce. I appreciate that you've taken the time to choose me. I don't want to ignore what you need. I don't know what I'm missing. I can only imagine what the other side is like, and I can't wait to experience everything with you. I'm just nervous about it all, I don't want to have sex until we're married. Honestly if we dance too close to the fire, all I'll focus on is that we're close to the fire. I don't know how much I'll enjoy everything."

I picked up her hand and I kissed it. "I can wait."

I purposely pointed the car at my place even though my body was screaming for me to go to Vanessa's and see if she would take pity on me and provide me with some sort of relief. I literally shook my head and told myself to get it together. My heart jumped into my shoes when I drove past Vanessa's car in the visitor's parking in my lot. I stood next to the door staring at her car. She got out of her car and stood next to her car. I turned on my heels and I told myself to go into my apartment. I wasn't going to do this.

When I walked inside I left the door cracked and then I sat on my Futon watching the door. I felt like a little kid who was waiting for their father to come in the room with the belt. Five minutes later Vanessa walked in the door and she shut it behind herself. She looked like she was having the same inner struggle that I was. We stared at each other for a long time not saying a word. Watching the inner struggle in each other.

When I didn't move, Vanessa dropped her purse by her feet. She kicked off her shoes. Then she slowly took off her sweats and then her shirt. She stood by the door in her panties and bra.

She was waiting for me to do something. Normally she would've taken control and whether I wanted this to happen or not my body's reaction to her was the only confirmation she needed. I shook my head as I tried not to stare, but her body was even more beautiful than I remembered. I took off my shoes and socks. I stood up and took off my shirt and t-shirt. She pointed at my pants. I slowly took them off. I stood there with a tent in my briefs as I stared back at her. She wiggled her finger for me to come to her, I didn't move.

If I go across that floor to the point of no return what does this mean about Alaina? Even saying her name mentally caused me to deflate. I rubbed my head and looked around the room. Vanessa stared at my briefs, and then she wiggled her finger again. I stood in front of her, when she reached for my briefs I grabbed her wrist, I told her not to touch me. If we were going to do this, we were going to do this according to how I wanted to do it.

Vanessa seemed turned on by my take-charge attitude. The tent was back and it was now too late to turn around. I was so happy that she had condoms in her purse, cause I had thrown all mine away. Dirty and hard was the tempo all around my place. I made up for all of my lost time.

Chapter 4

Tavio

"What's up MAC!" I said to Alaina at the window next to Ben.

"Hey Tavio where's my boyfriend?" She smiled as she wrote something down.

"With his mom and her boyfriend. They trying to create they own Brady Family."

"I thought you and lil T's mom were together?"

Ben started laughing cause he was there when Tempest and I were hugging each other trying to get Lil T to hug her. On that particular day he wasn't feeling his mom and it was killing her. So I was playing nice and hugging on her. I haven't touched Tempest since the possibility of this guy came up. Why would I keep her hanging on when he wanted to give her something real? They've been dating pretty strong now. "I'm about to go see my girl. She's in school in Atlanta, I go out to visit her whenever I can."

"That's so nice, I always wondered how long distance relationships work."

I shook my head, "it's agony. Trips like this make it worth it."

"The call center must pay you really well."

I shook my head, "it's cool plus I work graveyard shift so I get shift differential too. You interested in coming on grave?"

"Maybe," she said then she walked away.

"She's going to have a wedding soon. She's going to need all the help she can get." Ben volunteered.

"Good for MAC!" My heart sped up, "I'm gone. I'll catch you when I get back." I smiled real big then I reminded myself not to run.

On the plane I wrote poetry, short stories, my hand kept moving. Oddly enough I was writing for my son indirectly. When I got home I would decide which ones go up online on my blog. When I got off the plane I tucked away my writings for Lil T. This is the trip that I tell Eva about my son.

When I exited the plane Eva was there happily waiting for me. Our eyes connected and she got excited. I've missed the curves of her face, the sound of her breath. I picked her up and swung her around, while she squeezed my neck. We did our standard I miss you's, hugs, and kisses. Then we went down to the carousel. "Is it too late to cancel your rental car?"

"Why?"

"We're going out to dinner with Katrina and Chauncey tonight. They're outside waiting for us."

I've met her roommate Katrina before, but who the heck is Chauncey? "That's only for tonight, I'd prefer to have a car at my disposal. They can follow us to the hotel."

"But why? If you could save the money from renting the car today and only come back for it tomorrow, if you'd even need it at all."

"Are we supposed to be under their power all day? And how am I supposed to get back to the airport to get my rental? Besides, when I made this reservation the person over the phone told me that this weekend was busy and the only reason they had a car for me is because of a cancellation that just happened. I want my own car even if I don't use it."

"Fine Tavio! I'll tell them we'll meet up with them later." Then she stomped away.

That wasn't the way I wanted our visit to start, but I shook it off and got my luggage at the baggage claim.

As I was talking to the girl at the rental car counter Eva stood to the side watching. I guess the girl smiled at me one too many times for her liking cause she came up to me and put her arms around me. I didn't say anything I just smiled at her obvious jealousy. The girl at the counter didn't stop flirting with me. She even upgraded my rental to a luxury car claiming that they somehow gave my reserved car to someone else. Then she pointed out the survey amongst the many papers she gave me. She said if I gave her a high review for her service she'd make sure she made it worth my time. Eva gently punched me in my stomach signaling it was time to go.

I thanked the girl then we walked out to the car that had been pulled by the curb for us. We walked around the car inspecting it for anything. We pointed out the small scratches and dings, and then we sat in this car that seemed to cradle our bodies. Eva apologized for over reacting. I didn't say anything, I just knew that now wasn't the time to bring up my son.

Hopefully after I broke her off a few times she'd mellow out and then we could have a calm and rational conversation. I put my bags in the closet of my room and then I smiled at Eva. As I walked towards her, she put her hands out. She said we didn't have time and she wanted to hurry up and meet up with her roommate. That's when the argument started. I didn't save my pennies to fly all the way here to run around after her roommate. I was here to see her and be with her.

Eva

He must be crazy if he thinks all I want to do is lay up in this hotel under him all weekend. After all this time I finally met Chauncey and despite his proper tone he's actually a nice person. I want him and Tavio to meet. I think he would be a good connection for Tavio later on in his career.

We will eventually have sex, but sex isn't on my high priority of things to do these days. I enjoy sex with Tavio, but I only see him maybe once every three to four months. If I focused on sex then I would be in trouble like a lot of these girls up here. Some of them are only with their boys to have a regular sex buddy. Then some are just so turned out that they don't care if their partner is same sex or not, they just need somebody to get it on with.

Don't get me wrong I'm anxious to sleep with Tavio, but I feel like we need to put sex in its proper place. We need to make these connections for our future and then get to the fun part. All he's hearing is that I want to get out of this room. He can have tunnel vision sometimes for real. "Tavio, let's just go have the day and then we can have the night and the rest of the weekend."

"Why are you pushing for us to spend time with them. Since when you become little miss joiner?"

"What's wrong Tavio? I thought we could enjoy the day."

"I traveled all this way and I am not feeling the love right now."

I exhaled, "baby!" I walked up to him and put my hands on his butt. "I can't wait for tonight. I just want you to meet some people with some connections while you're out here. Just a little networking and then we can get to our time"

"I can network at my school, I don't need to come out here to meet people."

"You'll never know too many people, please do this for me." Then I kissed him.

A quick blowjob and we were on our way. Katrina and Chauncey were in our room kissing up against the wall when we walked in. "Sorry, I didn't think you two were here." I said standing in the doorway.

Katrina laughed, "it's not like we have some sort of system developed. Our men don't live out here." Then she got really excited, "ok. ok. Let's introduce them!" She pointed to Chauncey, "this is my boyfriend Chauncey."

"And this is my man Tavio," I said.

"Hey I like his title better. Next time introduce me that way." Chauncey smiled, "it's nice to meet you." He stuck his hand out to Tavio.

"Tavio, nice to meet you."

Katrina excitedly put her hands out. "I don't know if you're aware of what is happening here. The four black people that's about to run the world are in this room. DIG THE ENERGY! GIVE IN TO THE MOMENT!"

We all laughed, "well I would certainly like to be one of the people to run the world. I'll settle for being able to pay my bills," Tavio said.

I shot him a look to cut it out. "We are going to run everything! I am very excited about this."

We sat in our room talking about our future plans. Katrina and Chauncey come from connected families. Katrina's family loves me because their daughter does. Once we got along, she told me horror stories about her previous roommates from the years prior. Whenever they come out they invite me to do everything with them. They look out for me just like I was one of the family. Katrina's brother Colby always looks at me, but I talk about Tavio all the time. I think I've made it pretty clear that I'm not available and I'm not interested.

Tavio shot me a look when Chauncey chirped his car just like the rental car that he got.

Chauncey took us to a fancy restaurant. As we pulled up to the valet Chauncey said dinner was on him. Tavio looked around like he was uncomfortable for a minute. Chauncey kept talking to him and encouraging him to order drinks and whatever he wanted. They didn't even card us. Katrina guided us through the menu, and everything was superb. Tavio really enjoyed the food, he had so many drinks he showed no shame. He used the roll from the table basket to sop up his au jus from his plate. Chauncey said Tavio was reading his mind as he did the same thing.

When our waiter asked about dessert, Katrina said no. Tavio looked at Chauncey like he was telling him to say otherwise. Chauncey cleared his throat and told the waitress to bring the dessert cart. Katrina's eye twinkled as she smiled at Chauncey. When they brought the cart she wiped drool, then she told Chauncey he better still love her when she gains twenty pounds. Chauncey looked at Tavio and said it was just more cushion for the pushing.

Tavio ordered a chocolate soufflé, chocolate mousse, and a raspberry sorbet. I ordered vanilla bean gelato, and Tavio told me to try something I never had before. I told him I never had any of his desserts but I wanted vanilla instead of raspberry.

We took separate cabs to the hotels since no one was ok to drive. Tavio and I laid on the bed, we started kissing and then he fell asleep.

Tavio

Ok, ok so her friends were a lot of fun. You have to admit that a name like Chauncey automatically puts your guard up. His fancy car, and obvious money make you want to hate this dude. Chauncey and Katrina are down to earth people who happen to have money.

I kept trying to find the right moment to tell Eva about Lil T, but I couldn't find it. I took a deep breath and I stroked Eva's face. "Let's talk about our future." Eva said and my stomach dropped.

"Ok, how far are we talking?" This was it.

"Next five years. I was thinking that when I finish school we should move to Boston. I think you can connect with Chauncey, and Katrina's family said they have a job already lined up for me." Her eyes were big already. "Do you still want to get married?"

"Yes, of course."

"Would you be ok with being one of those couples who doesn't have kids?"

"We can't be that couple." Here was my chance.

"I know that we always talked about kids." Then her voice shook, I looked at her and realized that she was probably crying before she said anything. "I just don't know if I could go through that. I don't even want to try. Every time I think about being pregnant I go into hysterics. Maybe! Maybe once we're established we can adopt."

"You don't want to have my baby?" I wiped her tear.

She kept opening her mouth to talk but nothing was coming out. "I know it's selfish, but I want to keep you to myself. You are the only person that's ever belonged to me. You are the only person I'm allowed to be stingy with." She took a deep breath but she started crying harder. "We can have a good life! The fact that both of my parents walked away from me doesn't mean that I'm worthless." She cried harder. "It doesn't mean that I'm worthless!" I hugged her, "what if I decide I don't want to be a mother after they're already here? My dad left, ok. Dad's leave! Whose mother leaves them? Neither one of them wanted me. I can't do that to someone. The thought of having a baby sends my head spinning. Please don't hate me Tavio." She cried harder as she looked at me.

"We can talk about this later. We don't have to make definite decisions right now. Let's save this conversation for later."

Eva

I sat on my bed feeling restless. I put tissue between my toes and I took out the nail polish. I carefully and slowly painted each toenail as I tried to clear my mind.

This trip was weird. I started freaking out about having babies after Tavio and I took a walk through the mall. Maybe I never noticed it before, but he seemed very tuned in to little kids everywhere we went. A woman dropped her baby's blanket as she hurried past and he saw it falling, caught it and got it back to her.

He was looking at the little kid's clothes when I went in the fitting room at the Gap. It seemed like all the little kids and babies in the mall were looking at Tavio and smiling. Although I don't think it's possible, what if Tavio showed his butt once I was pregnant like James did. He still comes up to this school from time to time looking for me.

During the summer, I basically lay low for the couple of weeks I'm home. Then I go out to Boston to work for Katrina's family. Rickie said James just had two babies and one of the mother's is only fourteen. I was so angry all I could do was stare at her. Every time I think about James and what he did to me I get so angry. He did have one point, if I didn't want to have a baby I shouldn't rely on rubbers to save me. I never thought of getting on the pill because I focused on the importance of protecting myself with condoms.

Now that I'm only with Tavio I guess I could relax about the condoms, but I don't know what he does when he's home. It's not like I haven't noticed that he's always quick to come here. I know he has his own place, why hasn't he flown me out to California? I figure Tempest is still hanging on, and maybe things have gotten deeper with her. He never said they broke up, one day he stopped talking about her. Even recently she's been there when I've called him.

It seems like the babies were drawn to him and he to them. It freaked me out, and who knows. Maybe this was the weekend he was going to propose. He seemed like he was thinking about something all weekend. I guess I'll call in a couple days and calmly tell him I don't want to have a baby. I don't really want to adopt either. You never know who's messed up kid you're getting. You have a 50/50 chance if you ask me. Your kid could be messed up just because they come from you. Or they can be messed up because they come from other people more messed up than you.

What do I know about loving a kid? My parents ran away from me. They ran and never looked back. I have to think real hard to remember what my mother looked like. If it weren't for the pictures, I'm sure I would've forgotten by now.

I blew air on my toes on my left foot, then I prepared my right foot. Boston is kind of far and Tavio didn't say yes or no to moving there after graduation. This trip he was the man of little words. He was listening and thinking mostly. I know he's never lived with snow, and maybe that could be a setback for him. I'll promise him that I'll make it up to him. Even if he says no at first, I'm going to Boston.

As soon as I get a place I want to send for my grandmother. I know she says she's fine living in her sister's place, I know it doesn't feel like home to her. She's used to being able to do what she wants when she wants to. To have to ask her little sister at that for permission before she makes any improvements to her place is disheartening to watch. I don't care if I end up in a one bedroom, she can have the bedroom. I just want her to be with me where she can feel comfortable again. Since Rickie likes it so much out there in Daytona she can stay. If Tavio comes I know he would want my grandmother with us, it would be a no brainer to get a two bedroom until we can afford a house.

I blew my nails. This shade of orange calmed me, instead of energizing me like it's brightness should've. It made me feel good cause I wasn't feeling as horrible and a little less restless.

I picked up the phone and called Tavio. His answering machine picked up. "You know who you called, now leave a message… BEEP!" I took a deep breath. "I was thinking about you. I wanted to apologize for losing my mind during this trip. I guess we have some things to sort out. I've been thinking a lot about our future. And well… The future isn't so far away any more." I exhaled, "call me back when you get this message. I can't stop thinking."

Katrina walked in as I hung up the phone. "Why do you look like death? You should be on cloud nine like you normally are when Tavio leaves."

"I freaked out and I told him I don't want to have a baby."

She fell on the bed, "he wants you to have his baby now?"

"No, I'm talking about the future. I told him we could adopt, but

I really don't want to do that either. I'm just being honest."

"You shouldn't tell him that if you don't mean it."

I felt bad, "what's the plan for you two?"

"After graduation we're going to announce our engagement to our families. Two years to plan. Meanwhile settling into our careers and new lives. Marriage and then we'll start trying on our honeymoon. We'll have two kids, best schools and education. Annual family trips, you know pretty standard stuff."

I sat there looking at her with big eyes, "do you have a plan B?"

"Of course, if after two years we have not conceived then we will adopt and keep moving forward. Both of our doctors have given us clean bills of health. You never know what could happen when you're trying to have a baby. Your kid could come out with special needs, or anything. If that happens we'll re-evaluate our business plan to make sure we're totally plugged in to our child's needs. I…"

I cut her off, "I never even put the special needs idea into my brain. That seals it! I can't have a baby. I'd be the one stuck with the baby who would be a forever child. I don't really have patience for kids as it stands."

"So in other words, don't call you to babysit?" Katrina laughed.

"Not if you want them to have a trauma free childhood."

Katrina patted my hands, "you say that. And watch, you're going to end up being the best mother ever."

Tavio

"Pppsssttt! Lean in." Ben said to me over the counter. He and Alaina leaned in from their side of the counter. Ben looked around to make sure no one was listening. "We want to work in the call center. I've got eight hours this week, and next week isn't looking any better. I got bills to pay." Ben said trying to control his temper.

"What about you MAC?"

"Car note, and hello a life. Management might take it seriously if it were their money, but since they're all salary they could care less."

"Now you know it would be hard to move both of you over at the same time. The powers that be don't like moving talent from the branches to the back office."

"Help me Obie Wan Kenobi you're our only hope." MAC said pleading.

"Resumes?" Both of them slid them to me as if they knew that was going to be my answer."

"I'll make dinner for us once we get the jobs," MAC volunteered.

"Ooh! I'll bring the wine!"

"You haven't even gotten the jobs yet."

"You said you have a good relationship with management there. We have every faith you can get us in."

****

"WHAT KIND OF WINE IS THIS?" Alaina said holding her glass up high in the air.

"Can you believe my parents will spend three hundred dollars on a bottle of wine that they forget they even have, but won't give me twenty to buy books! It's almost like I turned eighteen and they shoved me out the door."

"So you're saying this is expensive stuff that I will never be able to afford," Alaina asked.

"When Royce becomes that high power lawyer you will." Ben said taking another sip of his glass.

Alaina smiled, "he wants to marry me you know. Little Miss Average is going to have a not so average life."

"Miss Average?" Ben slurred, "look at this spread! What's average about all of this? I've never had barbecue chicken so tender, juicy, and slightly spicy. Cornbread and Collard Greens on point girl!"

"Tavio why are you so quiet? You think my food is nasty don't you?"

"No! Your food is delicious. I'm thinking about Eva." I said holding my fork like I have all evening. I've been avoiding the conversation since I came back. She has this whole future mapped out for us. I can't move to Boston, my son is here. She dropped the bomb on me right before I left saying she doesn't want to have kids. We always talked about having kids. She was in tears telling me she doesn't want them. She doesn't know about my son."

"HOW DOES SHE NOT KNOW? He's with you all the time!"

"When he's here, I call her back when he's sleeping. I can't choose between my son and my girl!"

"Who would you choose if you had to?"

"My son of course, but I'm hoping she wouldn't make me choose."

"Well if it doesn't work out with Eva, someone asked me about you the other day." Alaina smiled.

"Who?" She had my attention.

"The new hire, she saw me talking to you in the vault after you went in your box."

"THE GIRL WITH THE BODY?" I ran my hand over my face.

Alaina shook her head yes as she laughed. "I'm all over that!"

"If that's your type." Ben said, waving us off as he took another drink.

"What is your type?" I asked as I thought about it. Outside of MAC, he never seems interested.

"I'm focused on school right now. Women will be throwing themselves at my feet once I have my career going."

"Are you gay? Blame it on the wine and come out to us right now." I was only partially teasing.

"Just know that you are not my type Tavio." Ben said then we heard a car drive in the driveway next to the house. "My roommate is home. Finally you can meet him."

"I've already met him," MAC said as she approached her glass for another taste.

Ben's roommate was cool actually, and the four of us sat around drinking the most expensive bottles of wine I have ever tasted. These wines were so smooth that I didn't miss the hard stuff with our meal. Alaina gushed over her unofficial planning as she called it. I sat there bored as she went over details I hope to never be involved in when it was time for my own wedding.

When it got late, Alaina called her brother to come get her. Ben offered his bed and he would sleep on the couch, but she insisted on calling her big brother cause she didn't want to have to justify staying to her boyfriend who was already not happy about her coming over. Alaina's brother Wesley was so cool that he ended up staying for a long time kicking back with us talking about life. We told Ben that his wine made everyone open up too much and share things that as guys we don't just sit back and pour out hearts to each other and especially when we don't know each other.

Wesley told me to pay attention to the fact that something is telling me not to be completely open with Eva. I did admit that although I didn't ask her what she needed money for, it sits in the back of my mind like I should ask her about it. Just to ease my conscience. I'm sure it was for books or something, even though the sound in her voice was a little more desperate. She hasn't been the same since then either.

****

"Congratulations you two. What are your schedules?" I said hugging Alaina and Ben at the same time.

"I'm a little blowed. I got days!" Ben said.

"I think only me and another person got grave. Everyone else got days and weird schedules at that."

MAC was smiling so big her dimples were about to cave in to the other sides of her face. "Congratulations Alaina, we're going to miss you smelling up the training room with your perfume." One of the trainers joked.

"I guess you'll have to come out to the floor to smell me from now on." Alaina laughed.

"How do you know Tavio?" The trainer asked her like I wasn't standing there.

"He used to come in the bank all of the time. Why?"

"He's got quite the reputation around this office for being a flirt. You're going to be on the team he leads, watch out for him." Then she winked at me.

Alaina looked at me, "you never told me you were a lady's man."

"Cause I didn't know that was my reputation."

"I believe it, at school all those girls be hanging on wishing to be assigned to work with you. You can try to act like you didn't know it was true if you want, but we know the truth."

Eva

"Come in," I said to the person knocking on my door. I was studying at my desk, and in no place to take a break.

I turned around as Colby walked in the room. He stopped after his second step when he didn't see his sister. "Katrina told me to meet her here."

"You can wait here, but I think she needed to meet with her tutor so who knows how long she'll be." I returned to my homework.

Colby walked over to Katrina's bed. He looked at her side of the room, then he stood there staring at me. "Why is your side of the room so cold and uninviting?"

Katrina had artwork and pictures of her family up. She had little girlie things all over to make her side of the room look like a home. My side was plain and neat. "Cause this is temporary housing. Why would I invest emotion into it?"

"Cause you live here for now, even if it is temporary."

"If it's only temporary I don't see the point. When I buy my house, I'll make that place so warm it could never be mistaken for cold." I went back to my work.

"You approach everything like that don't you?"

"What makes you say that?" I continued writing.

"Take me for example. I know you know how handsome I am, you've seen me watching you. You don't take me serious because I'm Katrina's little brother." I stopped writing and looked at him. "I guess because you could never see a future with me, you don't waste time flirting with me or any of the things your eyes tell on you about."

I looked him up and down, this was a setup. "In my limited experience men are disappointments and a waste of energy. Colby you are handsome and you know that. You don't need me to say it or act on it. I see the way those girls run all over themselves for your attention during the summer." I turned back around.

"All except you." I could feel his eyes on me.

I shrugged, "I guess that makes me different."

I could hear him moving closer to me, but I didn't move. His hands started kneading my arms and my shoulders. "You are different that's why I can't stop thinking about you. It wouldn't hurt you to smile at me from time to time." Then he bent down and kissed my neck.

I jumped out of my chair, "don't do that! What is wrong with you?"

He grinned at me, "I like you Eva. If you stopped running from me you'd realize you like me as well."

"I have a boyfriend."

"All the way in California. I heard you telling Katrina that you have an open relationship. How you know it's ridiculous for either of you to expect the other to wait until you see each other once every six months."

"Three to four!"

He moved in closer, "yeah that makes a difference." He kissed my lips. "They're as soft as I imagined them being." Then he backed up. "I wanted to let you know that I want you."

"No thanks," I said as my heart pounded.

He stood up straight, "I'm handsome, I have my own money, I'm getting my education, I don't have any children, I'm available and I've chosen you."

"Yeah, but for what?"

"Sex slave and everything else underneath." Then he laughed while sweat beads actually broke out on my forehead during my internal struggle. "I want you Eva, when you decide you're ready. Come to me." Then he walked back to Katrina's bed. He sat on her bed and grabbed one of her magazines. He flipped through it like anything in it could actually be of interest to him.

I frowned at him then I sat down. Why was I sweating so hard? Probably because pre-James I would've actually been opened to his idea. However my reality now is that Tavio is the only man I can trust. And even that isn't easy.

Katrina walked in the room less than two minutes later. Colby stared at me while his sister talked his ear off about some class she was taking. I closed my books and decided to go for a walk.

Chapter 5

Alaina

"Grave?" Royce said like he was annoyed.

"We talked about this. If I work nights, I'll make that much more. Besides when we officially move forward with the wedding I can plan during the day. When you're not in class you can spend time with me. You can study at night while I'm at work."

"What does your father think about you working at night?"

"He doesn't like it, but what can he do or say? I have to work."

I fidgeted with my dress, I don't remember it being this short when I tried it on it the store. "Stop fidgeting. You chose that dress, deal with it."

"What's wrong with you?" I was trying to hold back my irritated reaction to his tone.

He exhaled, "my mom picked a fight with me as I was walking out the door. She may not be here tonight. I'm trying not to be irritated but it's not working."

I rubbed his head then I kissed his cheek. "I'm sorry she did that to you."

"No matter what, please never forget how much I love you."

"As long as you remember the same." I kissed him again.

We walked into the restaurant hand in hand and then he took me to a banquet room. Everyone yelled surprise as we entered. I looked at Chareca as I repeated "surprise" and then I looked at Royce who had dropped down to one knee. He held out a ring and told me that even though I was too good for him he wanted to spend the rest of his life trying to get on my level. Then he asked me if I would do him the honor of becoming his wife. When I said yes, he picked me up and hugged me. Chareca and I hugged as we excitedly celebrated. My dad and Wesley congratulated me as well. The rest of the night I was floating on cloud nine. I kept looking at my ring in amazement. I was going to actually marry Royce Chambers. My average life was turning out not to be so average after all.

Royce

Vanessa was screaming my name as she exploded all around me. We rolled over and she proceeded to explode again and this time she took me with her. Vanessa orgasms back to back sometimes. She said she's only experienced this with me. This go around in our relationship is different. She isn't as aggressive as she was before. Sometimes I can see that it's killing her not to come after me, but she waits for me. I remember that she likes freaky stuff, so we'll still do adventurous things, but not the embarrassing stuff that she was in to. When Alaina goes to work at night, sometimes I go over Vanessa's. One time Vanessa asked me how Alaina took it when I broke up with her. We got distracted by our waiter and I never went back to the conversation. I never told her or gave her the impression that Alaina and I broke up. I have the best of both worlds right now. The love and loyalty of a disciplined woman like Alaina, and the mind blowing sex from a woman like Vanessa.

Vanessa got up and went to the bathroom. I watched her softness walk. She came back with a warm towel, and then she licked her lips as she cleaned me. I smiled as sleep pulled me in. "Do you think I should get breast implants?"

Her question was so random that it jerked me. "Your body is perfect! Why would you want to change it?"

She smiled, "thanks. I would like to be a little bigger though."

"Why would you risk your health for something that's only a want? Please don't do that for me or any other man. You're not flat chested, and I think your body is amazing. But you gotta be happy with your body."

"Well I know I'm bigger than that girl you were with that time." I looked at her cause I didn't know who she was talking about. "The girl you dropped to come back to me." I didn't say anything. "I mean she was cute, but not cute enough to think she could have my man."

"Vanessa! What we just shared was fun, why are you wasting our time talking about another female?"

"You've been distant lately. Are you getting bored with me?"

"I've got a lot going on. I told you about my parents and how they fight. Plus, I've finally decided on my major."

She sat up excitedly, "AND?"

"I'm going to go into corporate law."

"MONEY!" She screamed excitedly, and then she jumped on

me.

We had a good laugh; she asked me what made me decide. I told her that I've been researching what aspect of law I wanted to go into. Alaina and I decided the other day that corporate law was the best fit for my talents and me. Living here in the Bay Area the fields were always ripe for harvesting.

Alaina

"Alaina why didn't you call me the moment that it happened? Your grandfather and I are very excited." She smiled really big at me. "We've been saving for your wedding since you were born." She clapped her hands excitedly. "Anything you want sweetheart! What's your wedding plan?"

"Chareca and I have been looking around and we found some really cost effective ways to have a beautiful wedding." My grandmother's smile dropped. "We found a lot of things we can do ourselves and we came up with a schedule so that we can reasonably get it done. We…"

"Stop it!" My grandmother raised her hand. Then she pointed at my folder, "are these discount dresses in here?" I stammered. She waved her hand, "look baby." She tried to make her voice as tender as possible. "Your grandfather and I talked about it last night. We sent the full payment for your car this morning. You can have the wedding of your dreams. I want to take you to New York to go to this FANCY dress shop and find your dress."

I adjusted in my seat trying to get my words together. "I… I…"

"NO!" Tears filled her eyes, "you've been a trooper through all of this. You lost your sister, you lost your mother! You didn't fall apart and lose your mind. You've been a trooper through all the craziness. We can do this? Show you how much we appreciate you!"

Chareca wiped tears from her eyes. I never told her about my sister, but she understood the gravity of my grandmother's speech. "Thank you," I barely got out through sobs.

"Who do you want to go? I'll start looking for hotels."

"My dad, Chareca, Wesley, and my friend Ben." I wiped my nose.

She took a deep breath. "Moving along. Tell them you need them to take time off from work. They'll need three days. Flight out, all day at the shop, and flight back."

****

"Don't tell anybody I did this for you." Tavio said clicking around his computer. "Have you heard the latest on the gossip mill? You're my work wife." He smiled.

"What's a work wife?" I was trying to gauge how offended I should be.

He exhaled, "basically all this. I take care of you. You take care of me. This..."

"Why didn't you tell them I'm like a sister to you?"

Tavio smiled, "my sister don't walk around smelling like melons. Look, it's not a big deal. The rumor is unfounded, you're engaged, and I'm dating Nadia. People only know what they see."

I didn't understand what my perfume had to do with anything, but whatever. "How are things going with Nadia?"

He leaned back on his chair, "she's cool for now. She can't cook." Then he rubbed his flat stomach. "Food is important."

"Can Eva cook?"

"Enough, she got in the door before I knew to have such requirements."

"Excuse me Tavio, I have a work question for you if you have time for that."

Tavio and I looked at Mandy; she always got something smart to say. I walked over to my desk and shut down my computer. I waved bye to Tavio and then I went home. I called my grandmother who hardly ever sleeps. I told her I got confirmation of the days off. Everyone else was already set to go.

****

My dad kept kissing my forehead as we waited at the gate to board our flight. When my grandparents walked up their hellos were awkward with my dad. Wesley broke the ice by introducing Ben. My grandfather asked how he fit in. I told them that Ben is my fashion conscience. When my grandfather cut his eyes at Ben he announced that he was not gay. He reminded them that there are plenty of fashion designers who were straight.

Ben kept everyone laughing as he recalled the scrutiny he underwent from his family as they watched him to make sure he was telling the truth.

On the plane I tried not to remember a time when my family wasn't awkward when everyone truly loved each other. All of that was when my mother was here. All of my grandparents were excited about the marriage of my parents. They had been friends and were so excited when my parents expressed an interest in each other. My parents wedding was a big deal for all of my family. My mother said her baby shower for Wesley was huge. She said the hospital was packed when he was born. She said everyone celebrated my brother's birth and constantly came over with gifts to see him. Wesley was and still is so spoiled. When Wesley turned four they started trying, he was eight when my sister and I were born. My eyes stung with this trip down memory lane. I put my head down and I told myself to get a grip. Cara Mia did so good on the plane people were surprised to see that a baby was on our flight and such a long one at that. We checked into our nice hotel and then we went out to dinner. We got in the bed early so that we could get up early the next day.

When I called Royce after we found my dress, I told him I was so excited about my dress but I couldn't tell him anything about it. He asked me who was in my room and I told him it was Chareca, Ben, and Wesley. He was irritated when I said Ben was coming with me. I told him I would be back tomorrow and I couldn't wait to see him.

Royce

My mother was hovering the entire time I was talking to Alaina. She asked me if Alaina got her dress, and when I said yes she asked what it looked like. I told her I had no idea. When I told her that Alaina chose Turquoise, Silver, and White as our wedding colors. She said she hated it, and told me to tell Alaina to change it. My mother got so mad at me because I didn't care about the colors of the wedding. Besides I knew she was just trying to start a fight between Alaina and I. I wasn't going for it cause I could see what she was doing. She is going crazy because she has no control over our wedding and the planning. I told her that Alaina's grandparents were paying for our wedding and they kicked up our wedding to classy from low budget like we were planning.

Instead of getting married in a little gazebo off of a small reception hall. We're now getting married on the grounds of the Berkeley Claremont Hotel, and our reception will be on site as well. All I want is a say in what I wear and my life as Alaina's husband. All this wedding planning and picking is not for me. When I got tired of my mother's questions, I left. I told my sister that Alaina would pick out bridesmaids dresses next and she'd call both of my sisters when it was time to do that.

I got in my car and drove over Vanessa's. Her roommate still shoots me wanting looks and tries to push up on me at times. One day she'll figure out that her aggression turns me off.

Vanessa was in her room sitting at her desk with her legs folded as she worked on her paper. She had her glasses on; her hair was pulled into a wild ponytail. Like she got irritated with it and snatched it into that style as a punishment. Thinking about the wedding filled me with excitement and extra energy. When Alaina and I finally have sex we will be complete. As time passes I ask myself what I'm going to do with Vanessa. I actually care about her too. Now that she's learned to back down and let me be the man, our relationship has picked up steam. I don't know what I'm going to do, but I tell myself I have time.

I bent down and kissed her. She immediately started talking about the paper she's working on. She was trying to put her thoughts together and she was pulling her hair out. Watching Vanessa's mind work once she was in a zone was fascinating. She has to be the smartest woman I will ever know. I have no doubt that once she sets her mind to do something, not only will she do it. She's going to be running things in no time. I helped her with her paper and then we fell asleep. We didn't even have sex.

When she snuggled into me in the middle of the night my eyes popped open. I don't spend the night with her. I always go home a lot earlier than this. That way I would always be home when Alaina called or popped by. Vanessa looked so happy and content in her sleep. At first I admired it, and then it irritated me. I quietly crept out of her place and went home.

Alaina

"You should be smiling, you won!" Tavio said not understanding my dilemma.

"I know but, but… I need to think about this." I looked at my name on the board. It was under Tavio and other teammate's names. "Who are you bringing?"

"Good question, I guess I could bring Nadia. Or I could bring this other girl. I got a couple of days to decide." He searched my face, "why wouldn't you bring your fiancé?"

I motioned for him to follow me back to his desk away from the crowd of people who were still celebrating our sales goal win over another team. "Royce and I would have to share a room. That would be too much temptation."

Tavio frowned, "why wouldn't you want to share a room..." His eyes stretched three times their normal size. "You two haven't done the do?"

"Ssshhh!" I put my finger up to my lip, "don't spread my business."

He leaned in, "you've never had sex?"

"Shut up Tavio!" I don't know why his question annoyed me.

He sat there staring at me with his mouth hanging open. "I didn't know virgins existed after middle school. I thought high school was all about getting broken in. You just proved me wrong," he chuckled.

I slapped his shoulder, "don't tease me. After my wedding this will not be an issue."

"No wonder Royce is all pent up like that. I don't know how he does it. You're liable to end up pregnant on your honeymoon."

I had a flash back of the extremely embarrassing, uncomfortable, and painful pap smear I endured to get put on birth control early to switch up my period, and to make sure they were more than in my system by the time of our wedding. "Whatever, you understand why I can't invite him on this trip? I can't bring Chareca cause Ken will tell Royce."

"Just bring Ben or your brother."

"I can't share a room with Ben either. He may be my brother from another mother, but he's not my brother. Wesley has to work."

"So come alone then. I'll bring Nadia and you can be our third wheel." Then he smiled at me, "you could even come watch us and learn some pointers."

"Ha! Ha! That was so funny I forgot to laugh."

Royce

Shoot! I was trying to think of a way out of it. Vanessa wanted me to go with her to her cousin's party in a couple of weeks. Vanessa was really excited about it. I told her I would make sure I could get the night off. I went to my parent's pet store and straight to the back. I don't know why, but I really wanted to go to the party with Vanessa. She wanted to celebrate her A on that paper I helped her with. I needed to figure out what Alaina was going to do before I could say yes or no.

"Hello?" Alaina said.

"You getting ready for work?" I tried my best to sound nonchalant.

"Yes, but I was getting ready to call you so thank you for beating me to it. Next Thursday my job is sending me to Monterey for a conference. I will come back on Sunday morning."

I turned my eyes up heaven ward and said *THANK YOU!* Then I focused on our conversation. "Sounds like fun. I was just calling to tell you I love you and that I was thinking of you."

Chapter 6

Tavio

"What you doing next Thursday through Sunday?" I asked.

"My sister's throwing a party Friday night, I was just about to invite you to come." Nadia's voice smiled from the kitchen.

"I can't, I was going to invite you to be my plus one. I won a trip to Monterey. I guess you can't go."

Nadia's head popped around the corner. "You wanted me to go! That's so special. I was going to…" Then my phone rang. Both of us stared at the phone. "It's probably her." She sucked her teeth.

"I'll let the answering machine get it. You were saying?"

She sucked her teeth again, "never mind."

"Nadia don't act like that, I was clear about where I stand."

"I know, and I've been clear about Stan. This is just so weird you know? You've got your baby momma, and your girl, who am I?"

"You're Stan's girl."

She shook her head, "I don't know where I belong anymore."

Eva

I slammed the phone down when Tavio didn't answer. Rickie's engaged and instead of being happy for my sister I tore into `her. It was like I wasn't even myself. She called me all happy and excited and I immediately got pissed off as soon as the words crossed her lips.

I needed to talk to Tavio and not his machine. I got up and started pacing the room, I couldn't think. Katrina came in the room all happy about her perfect life and I needed to vent. I fell to my knees as I cried. I told her I was going to have to drop out of school. My sister was going to be getting married and my grandmother could not be on her own in Florida.

Katrina hugged me and asked what I was going to do about school. I wanted to finish, but I needed to find a job. Katrina kissed my forehead and then she told me not to worry. She picked up the phone and called her mother. She told her about my situation.

With our heads smashed together we talked to her mother over the phone. She told me to check into transferring to the University of

Boston as soon as possible. She said she would review the openings at their various companies to see which position would be a good fit. She warned me that the position would be entry level and I would have to prove myself and work my way up just like anyone else. I tearfully thanked her. She told me to call her and let her know what I found out about my transfer options.

Tavio called me back hours later, I was so irritated that I told Katrina to tell him I wasn't there.

****

"So you're going to move to Boston." Tavio said, but I couldn't decide for his tone.

"Yes, I know it's a little early. Thank Rickie for that."

"Why does it make you angry that she fell in love?"

"That doesn't make me angry. I just don't understand how she could call herself trusting someone she just met."

"She didn't just meet him though, you all went to school together."

"Who's side are you on? Rickie always hated on you calling me. She was always against us. Now she's getting married?"

"You're just jealous," he laughed at me.

I screamed and then I hung up in his face. I'm not jealous of my sister. I just know now she's really going to judge me. She always thinks her way is better than mine. Just cause she found a loser to marry her doesn't give her any extra credit. I paced the floor trying to calm down. When I couldn't, I called Tavio back. I asked him to see if he could transfer to Boston. He didn't even try to think about it. He flat out said no. We argued until he hung up on me. I waited for him to call me back. I started pacing then I gave up after an hour and a half. I called my grandmother who knew nothing of my plans. So I broke everything down to her. At first she tried to object, but I told her it wasn't up for negotiations. I'm going to stay with Katrina's family until I have enough saved for a place. As soon as I have a place she's coming out. Rickie's wedding would happen this summer.

Tavio

"You two want to come with us?" Mandy said motioning towards the beach.

I looked at Alaina to say. When she said yes I followed. "I want to go on record for saying that alcohol, water, and black folks don't mix. Proceed at your own risk."

Alaina removed her sandals, dug her feet in the sand, and moaned. "This feels so good, you should try it."

Now that she told me, I can see how naive this girl really is. She shouldn't moan like that, but I know she doesn't know better so I'll give her a pass, "No."

"Sit down, sit down." Mandy pointed to the rock next to hers. She put her hand up like she was about to pledge. "Honest moment, do you two secretly hook up?"

Alaina slumped and I started laughing. "Not you too Mandy. I'm engaged and he has his many. He's like a brother to me."

Mandy smiled at me, "you two ever kiss?"

"No!" Alaina laughed. "He's like a brother to me."

"Un huh, and both of you came unattached," she smirked at us.

"My girl had a family function."

"Why you didn't bring one of the other ones?" She pointed her finger at me.

I took another gulp of my drink. "Mandy! Leave them alone.

While you're all up in their business I'm standing over here bored. Entertain me," her man demanded.

Mandy quickly got up and walked a few feet away using the darkness to shield her embarrassment as they started kissing.

Alaina was tipsy, as she finished her drink. "How come whenever people question us I'm the only one speaking on us being family?"

"Cause we're not family. Good friends, yes. Family, NO! You can claim Ben as family."

She bumped me, "I'm such a brat that you don't want to be my brother?"

"MAC with the way you cook I could never be your brother. You cook up too many man traps for me to stupidly fall for that brother zone which is worse than the friends' zone."

"But we are friends," she slurped on her glass.

"Yes we are," Mandy and her man were no longer visible. They walked further along the beach. "You sure you ready to get married?"

"Yes, I love Royce so much."

"I love Eva but things are changing. We're both changing a lot. Lil T has changed my vision for my life. I can't even bring myself to tell her about him."

"You need to stop punking out and just tell her. It's not like you guys are really together."

"How you figure? We're real, just separated by distance."

"Not when you hold back the most important part of your life from someone."

"So Royce knows everything there is to know about you?" I looked at her.

"Not everything, but most things."

"Tell me something he doesn't know," I moved in closer.

Her eyes were red, she was completely drunk. "I can't think of anything."

"He know about your crush on me?" I laughed at my joke.

She started laughing, "how do you know about that?"

I sat up straight, "huh?"

Alaina laughed hard, I was about to ask her again when someone approached us. They said the bus was here to take us back to the hotel. Mandy and her man came with sand pouring out of their backwards shirts. Alaina laid her head on my shoulder on the bus. I smiled at her; my drinks were filling my head with thoughts that I tell myself to never even consider. When we got to the hotel I took Alaina's room key and then I led her to her room. As soon as we were in, I sat her on her bed. "You like me?"

"You like me!" Then she laughed.

I laughed a little then I told her to focus. "You like me?"

"T-Bone! You're great! You're great!" Then she laid back on the bed.

"Stop playing, I'm trying to talk to you." I stood over her.

"I'm too drunk Tavio. Liquor really is the devil."

"Since when are you religious?"

"I grew up very religious until my mom died," she sat up. "My grandparents were so mad at my dad cause they thought it was his fault. They broke his heart and when they found out the truth they've been so sorry but it was too late to take it back. All that they said, all that they did." She looked sad, "Royce doesn't know that I was born a twin. I don't tell people about her cause it hurts too much."

I sat on the bed next to her. "How old were you?"

"We were almost three. They try to tell me I was a baby, but I remember her." Then she started crying. "Change the subject!"

"I don't know how to come clean with Eva. I'd rather break up with her then know she's rejecting my son like I know she will."

Alaina patted my leg, "it's for the best Tavio." Then she left her hand on my thigh.

"MAC?" She gave me the most clueless look, which made my body calm some. "You like me?"

"I sure do," she smiled then she pinched my cheek. "You are adorable!" I kissed her, I thought she'd reject me but she was too drunk. "That was nice. Thank you." Then she continued to smile with droopy eyes. "You're coming to my wedding right?" She shifted gears like she wasn't a part of the kiss we just shared.

"I will if you kiss me again." She smiled, and then she kissed my cheek.

I took a deep breath; I was getting drunker by the second. I kissed her forehead and I told her I'd be back in the morning.

In the morning I brought Alaina medicine for her head in the morning then we had breakfast. She remembered nothing about our kiss. She was completely normal and I was dying.

Eva

Katrina's house was huge and everyone had their own lives. Katrina said I probably wouldn't see everyone all at once very often. She wasn't kidding. Katrina came home with me and helped me get settled in the guest room. I thanked her parents over and over. Then Katrina showed me how to get to school and we went over my bus routes to work from school and the house. Katrina assumed that I would use her car, but I don't know how to drive. I didn't have the time or resources.

I haven't seen Colby all that much which is a good thing. I've been trying to avoid him as much as possible.

After a couple of months I had enough saved to find a place to stay. When I called my grandmother I told her to start packing because I was looking for a place for us.

I was annoyed by the whole application scam. I'd apply for a place and then the apartment would be awarded to someone. I finally found a two-bedroom apartment over a garage. The owners were retired and liked the idea that my grandmother would live with me. Colby and his parents helped me move my boxes. I bought a blow up mattress to use until my grandmother brought the furniture including my old bed. Colby stood quietly to the side while his parents told me how proud they were of me. Mrs. Singleton said she's been receiving good reports about me at work. She told me to keep my eyes open and decide where I wanted to go next. She hugged me and kissed my cheek like I always see her do with Katrina. My grandmother has always been my only parental figure in my life. Even then she always felt like a grandmother not a mother. You would've thought Mrs. Singleton personally gave me a million dollars by how much her words lifted my spirits.

The next night I was sitting on the floor next to my phone waiting for Tavio to call me back. The doorbell rang, I took a deep breath. I knew who it was, and why he was here. I didn't move. Last thing I wanted was for Mr. & Mrs. Singleton to be mad at me for sleeping with their son.

My body fizzled letting me know that I was overdue for a tune up. I called Tavio again, he didn't answer. I screamed lowly, this is not my idea of fun.

Chapter 7

Alaina

My eyes popped open and I laid there wondering why I keep having dreams like this. I keep having dreams where I'm kissing Tavio. I tearfully confessed to Chareca, and she said it was just wedding jitters. She said she kept having dreams that she was kissing Billy Dee Williams, Denzel Washington, and any other handsome celebrity right before her wedding. She made me feel better, but every time I woke up I felt guilty. I picked up the phone, and I called Royce and he was wide-awake. I asked him what he was doing and he said he just got home from a run. I asked him if he wanted to get together for breakfast. He said we'd have to go right away cause he had study group. He's been working hard at school so that he could relax this summer with me after our wedding. We'd only have to work and then get into the swing of him being in school in a couple of months.

Royce leaned in at the table as he said we only had three more weeks. His grin was big as he raised his eyebrows at me. I did my best to pull back my excitement but I still laughed loudly at the reminder. Next weekend, Royce was moving into the apartment that we would share as husband and wife. We were upgrading from his studio to a one bedroom. I already had everything that I planned on moving packed; now we were just passing time. "Can you believe we're about to do this?" Royce smiled excitedly at me.

I shook my head no, "I can't. You sure you want to be my husband?"

"Positive! You sure you want to be my wife?"

I kissed his soft hands, "absolutely."

"Why do you want to marry me?" He smiled waiting for my answer.

"When you could've had anyone you picked me. Although you left me for a while, you decided that what we have is special and you've been patiently waiting for me for this moment. I don't know any man who would do that for the woman they love." Royce held on to his smile, but it changed a little. "I am nervous about our wedding night, but I trust you to be patient with me. I can only imagine all the things we'll do, how amazing everything is going to be. I can't wait to lay with you and give in to the things that come naturally."

"So you're only worried about the sex?"

"At first, I've waited a long time for this. You've always taken good care of me; I look forward to taking good care of each other. Why do you want to marry me?"

"You're loyal." He watched my eyes.

"That's it?" I released his hands in fake protest.

"That's the primary reason. My parents aren't loyal to anyone. My dad says you're too good for me all the time. I'm his son and he's looking at you like you're the answer to my family's prayers."

"Your mother doesn't think that way," I deflated.

"My mother is a special case. I don't pay her any more attention than I have to. Just so you know, I'm looking forward to the sex as well. I'm boldly going where no man has gone before."

We laughed and enjoyed the rest of our time together, telling each other how much we were going to miss each other for the last two weeks before the wedding.

Royce

Alaina's speech about waiting on her killed me. I drove to Vanessa's rubbing my head and telling myself I had to tell her, or break up with her. The problem is that we've been so good. Vanessa and I haven't argued in months, sex with her seems like it has only gotten better. The only complaint I have about her is that she is not Alaina.

Vanessa is smart, beautiful, and an amazing person to know. I'm dreading breaking up with her. I get so nerved up about breaking up with her that all I want to do is sleep with her. I don't want to be without her.

I bet that's what's making this stinking sex even better. In my mind it's like each time is breakup sex. I used my key to her front door, the apartment was still. Her roommate's door was open, which meant she wasn't home. Vanessa was in the bathroom. I hurried in her room and stripped down to nothing. I pulled her covers back and then I got in the middle of it. I posed in the bed waiting for her to come out. Vanessa came in the room rubbing her nose as she sniffled. She jumped really hard when she saw me. Her eyes were red and she was crying. I sat up completely alarmed. My gut tightened, please don't tell me you're pregnant, was all I could think. I sat up as she hurried to the bed.

She buried her head in my shoulder as she cried; she said her mother was in a car accident. I was relieved it wasn't what I was thinking. She said her mother was ok, but she's in a lot of pain. She cried saying she doesn't know what she would do if something happened to her mother. I told her to stop entertaining the worst ideas. I asked her if she was going to go home. She said she was going to go after finals and spend as much time as she could without losing her job. She told me she was going to miss me. I told her I was going to miss her more. I asked exactly when she left, and she said on Friday in three weeks. I exhaled; she was leaving the night before my wedding.

Alaina

Tavio has been mister no nonsense since we came back from Monterey. I don't know what's wrong with him. He sends me away from his desk, and he's been keeping his conversations short with me. I made Salisbury steaks, with garlic mashed potatoes whipped to the ultimate creaminess, and broccoli for dinner. I made him a plate, but he's not getting it until he tells me what's wrong with him. He pulled up next to me in the garage, and his face held no expression when he looked at me. He used to make funny faces at me or something. Now he's just blank.

"Tavio what's wrong? What did I do?"

"I didn't say you did anything."

"But you haven't said that I haven't done anything either. What's wrong?"

"Nothing Alaina."

"Oh come on, I know when something's bothering my big brother."

"I'm not your brother."

"You know you're my brother from another mother."

He looked at me, "when you were drunk you said you liked me."

I gasped, then I started laughing, "No I didn't, why on earth would I say that?"

"Do drunk people lie?"

"I don't know what you think you heard, but…"

"We kissed…" I stood there with my mouth hanging open. I didn't know what to say. I guess those weren't dreams, they were memories. "It was an accident, and I was going to talk to you about it, but somehow we ended up drunk again. I wasn't going to say anything, cause I know you were drunk. I was drunk, and it didn't mean anything. I've just needed some distance to let it wear off." He looked at my hand, "what is that?" He reached for my hand.

"I… I don't want to give this to you now." I raised my hand slowly.

He grabbed my hand and took the plate from me. "Stop playing woman, you know me and food."

"We can't be friends anymore." My stomach started to hurt.

"Alaina, listen to me. It didn't mean anything. I'm never going to tell anyone."

"I'm just like my mother!" I grabbed my chest.

Tavio looked up from the plate. "No you're not. Wait, yes you are? Being like your mother is a good thing right?" He was distracted by the plate. "YO! Garlic mashed potatoes! Where's the gravy? Please tell me there's gravy." I took the cup out of my pocket and handed it to him.

Tavio got excited and then he leaned in and kissed my lips. A quick peck. I looked at him and he did it again. I stared at him and he put the plate and cup on the roof of my car, and then he came in for a real kiss. I backed away from the kiss, and I said a faint *don't*. We stood there staring at each other for a long time. Tavio was trying to gauge whether he should listen or move closer. When Tavio backed away I put my eyes on the floor. "Why?"

"I can't be the only one with the memory swishing around my brain. I'm sorry, I was out of line for that. Give me a little bit and I'll shake it off."

"You better not tell Ben, or Chareca, or anybody!"

"I haven't and I won't. Thank you for the food."

I was a mess my whole shift, reversing fees that I shouldn't, typing the wrong notes on accounts. In the bathroom I hit my head on the wall and told myself to get it together. I can't believe I told him I liked him, and I actually kissed him? I cried a little as I kept telling myself I was not my mother. I could be faithful! I will be faithful to my husband and everything will work out fine.

****

My bridal shower was embarrassing and a lot of fun. All of my friends, cousins and aunties together in one room and getting along. It's been years since everyone has gotten together. All of the side conversations where everyone was catching up felt great.

The Aunties and older cousins and friends left all of us *youngins* as they called us, went downstairs in my grandmother's house, the liquor was pouring and then we went over the items I got. I even got a few more risky items. My cousin said she couldn't give this piece to me in front of our grandmother. It was a crotchless teddy with the breast exposed. She said I wouldn't be ready for it right away. She said it's probably a one or two-year anniversary get up.

My cousins and friends overloaded my brain with tutorials about everything. I got tired of closing my mouth so I left it hanging open. One cousin gave me a double vibrator and then explained how to use it. I had no idea such toys and gadgets existed. All of them said I could call them any time if I ever had any questions. I made them promise because I couldn't comprehend all that we spoke about. I didn't know what I liked, how could I tell Royce.

They suggested things that my mother told me were bad a long time ago. All of these happily married women were telling me it was normal, I didn't know what to think. I kept looking at Chareca in surprise whenever she had two cents to add to the conversation. I felt so overwhelmed. "Don't worry baby, most of this will come back to you later. What you need to know for your wedding night is to relax and take your time. It's probably not going to be magical, give yourself time. You don't know what to feel, or how to feel it. Take your time and you don't let him in until you're ready. Don't let him rush you, **take your time**." My cousin said then she rubbed my shoulders.

On the way home I asked Chareca what her first time was like. She smiled and said, "take lots of deep breaths. It was uncomfortable but good. We had been messing around all day so I was ready. It's not like Ken expected it to happen when it did. My experience was different than yours will be. Royce has waited all this time for you. He's going to be anxious and pent up, but it will get better."

When I got home I was actually scared, I paced around my room for a little bit then I called Royce. He picked up just before the call went to his answering machine. "Were you sleep?"

"No, just walked in the door. How was your girl party?"

"It was nice, I need to be honest with you." He didn't say anything, I took a deep breath. "I'm nervous, a little scared out of my mind. I don't know what to expect. Everyone keeps warning me that you're going to be *pent up*. Does that mean you're going to get impatient and hurt me?"

He was quiet for a minute. "Alaina I want your first time to be special. I want you to enjoy it as much as I will. I promise to do my best to make it good for you."

I exhaled loudly, "please don't hurt me Royce. Since you promise not to hurt me, I will do my best to relax."

Royce

I tried to sound as patient as I could while talking to Alaina. I came home to change and grab a few things to spend the night at Vanessa's. I'm trying to give her a proper send off since she's leaving next week. I've done my best to avoid having her call me, cause that number has been disconnected and Alaina and I have a new number. If she comes by my place for any reason, I don't live there anymore. I at least want her to go to her mother on a happy note. Although I know she won't be happy with me when she returns. I sometimes wish there was a way to split me in half and I could make both of them happy. I hate having to choose. I'm in too deep with Alaina, I love her too much. Vanessa feels like my soul mate, if I believed in them she would be it.

I pretended to be sleepy and then I got off the phone with Alaina. I grabbed my things and then I ran out the door. When I got to Vanessa's she was in the kitchen making a cup of tea. She asked me if I wanted one, and I said yes. She had the couch setup to watch a movie and cuddle. "What do you think about getting a place together for next school year?"

"Why would you leave this place, it's nice."

"You're here all the time and I would like the space to be able to enjoy you in any section of our place that I see fit when the impulse hits me."

I rubbed her butt, "you and your impulses."

"I think we should continue moving forward."

"Let's talk about it when you come back."

"As in you don't want to, or let's make a plan when I come back?"

"As in you're about to leave. You need to focus on your mom while you're out there. I know you'll be at the library trying to find a place for us. Focus on your mom and when you come back we'll discuss whether we think it's a practical idea or not. I like living on my own though, I have my space when I need it."

"Can I meet your mother when I come back?"

I was trying to stay calm, inside I wanted to flash on her and ask her why she was ruining this moment for us. But she doesn't know she's ruining our moment with plans that will never be. I counted backwards in my head. "My mom is a trip, she don't like nobody. My last girlfriend was genuinely sweet to her and bent over backwards for her. My mom still found fault with her. Her last resort was that she didn't like her because she felt that she was going to end up fat."

"What does your mother look like?"

"Tall and thin, she eats a very clean diet. Makeup is always on, hair always done, always pulled together. The only time she wasn't pulled together was the first time she got pneumonia. Appearances are very important to her."

Vanessa looked at me with her freshly washed face, "you've never sat with your mother like this? I mean I wear makeup too, but it comes off at some point."

"She's the last to go to bed, and the first to wake up."

"What's your dad like?"

"He's a tortured soul, he wants out so bad he can't stand it. I think it's something about his retirement or something. I don't exactly understand it, but in his case it truly is cheaper to keep her. My parents can't stand each other so they're always arguing and carrying on. What are yours like?"

"My mother is my best friend, she's the first person I tell everything that happens in my life. She and my father just weren't a good fit. They realized it before they went completely sour. My father says he loves my mother for giving him me, and she says the same. My mother and I went together to my father's wedding. We were at the hospital when my little brothers were born."

"Your mom and your stepmom get along?"

She shook her head, "very well actually. I know it's not the standard way of doing things, but my parents have made it work for my sake."

"Why are you such a freak if you grew up like that?"

Vanessa started laughing then she hit me with a pillow from the couch. "Excuse you! This is college! This is where you learn who you are and what you're made of. You're supposed to experiment to understand what you like and what you don't. I spent my childhood in books. I'd read Judy Blume when my mother was looking and then I'd sneak her adult books at night. I got to college and lost my mind. I wanted to try everything to make an educated choice about how I wanted to proceed."

"Are you done experimenting?"

"No, but I've learned that there is too much of a good thing. I lost you and I don't want to go through that again." Then she kissed me.

KILL ME!

Alaina

As I took my next call I saw Tavio walking over to me. He looked upset so I watched him as I spoke with my customer. He leaned against my desk as he watched me service my call. When my caller hung up I put my phone on not ready and then I typed notes. "What's up T?"

He took a deep breath, "there's no easy way to say this, so I'm just going to say it. I need you."

"For?"

"Tempest has to go into work early today, and I have two classes this morning. Lil T needs to hang with Auntie MAC if you can help me out."

"What time will you be done? I have to go to the final dress fitting for my bridesmaids, my wedding is Saturday."

"My classes will be done at 2."

"My appointment is at 1, I guess he could come with me."

"Thank you Auntie MAC! I'll make it up to you." He looked around at the people who were trying to pretend like they weren't listening to our conversation. "Tempest will be outside when we get off."

When we got off work we walked outside to the parking lot together. Tempest was waiting in the visitor parking with a sleeping Lil T in his car seat. We hugged hello. "Your big day is coming up isn't it?"

"Saturday," I got butterflies at the thought of it.

"That is so good, maybe if things keep going like they're going I may have a wedding of my own soon." She said with stars in her eyes.

Tavio frowned, "things are serious between you two?"

"He loves me and I love him." She was so proud.

"What's the hurry? Honestly I think we're too young to be getting married."

I looked at Tempest, she started wiggling her neck. "Age is a copout. When you're in love and it's real it doesn't matter if your eighteen or forty-eight. When it's real you'll make it happen right away."

"What do you know about real love?" He folded his arms.

"I know that I was in love with you, you were so in love with your ex that you couldn't even see me. My man does and feels everything for me like I feel for him. I know what it feels like when a man doesn't love you, and he loves me. That has made it easy to fall for him and to fall so hard." Then she looked at her watch. "I got to get going."

Tavio got his little man out of the back of Tempest's car and then we walked to the garage. I could tell Tempest's words hurt him, but I didn't say anything. I followed Tavio to his place. He put Lil T in his bed, then he told me I could sleep with him and he'd get a little sleep on the couch. I gave him my keys so he could move the car seat to my car and then I laid down with the baby. Lil T's face keeps changing, at first he looked mostly like his dad. Right now he's looking like a complete mixture of both of them. As I drifted off to sleep I heard his phone ring softly. When his answering machine picked up it was a girl. "Tavio? I haven't heard from you in a minute. Why aren't you taking my calls or calling me back?" She sounded upset and like she couldn't believe he wasn't home. "We need to talk, my grandmother's going to be here soon. Call me back!"

I got up and Tavio was sitting up on his couch staring at a book. "Was that Eva?"

He exhaled irritated air, "yeah. She moved to Boston cause her sister's getting married and she needed to move her grandmother in with her. She lined up a job out there, and she thinks I'm supposed to pick up and move out there to be with her."

"Why wouldn't you?"

"Lil T for one, my family is out here for two, and I don't want to live in Boston. She never asked me if that was what I wanted. She made all these plans without discussing it with me. She thinks she's going to tell me how things are going to go and I'll just be happy with it. You going to follow Royce all over this country on a whim of his?"

"Well seeing as I keep postponing school, Royce is going to be my main provider. If he says we have to move we have to move."

Tavio stared at me for a minute. "You are so beautiful." I put my eyes on the floor; I wasn't expecting him to say that. "I can't believe you're getting married in a few days."

"Thank you, I know. I'm going to be a wife and one day a mother. I get nervous, but I'm excited."

"I don't want to cast a shadow on your relationship, but I want to tell you the truth." I glanced at him then I looked back down at the floor. "You may be ready, but Royce is still young. He's going to mess up, and so will you. Because of the type of person you are I know you'll fight to work things out. Make sure that when you're interviewing for the role of an affair that you come to me first."

I looked at Tavio and smiled, "you are so silly."

"I'm not moving so what else is there to talk about?"

"Talk to her T, You owe her an explanation."

"I'll think about it. Now go lay down before I get up off this couch."

I turned on my heels and went back to the bed. As I was falling asleep Tavio came in the room getting his stuff for his shower. I smiled in my mind watching him move around his room. Tavio wasn't like Royce, Royce is on the thin side, I think Royce is a little taller, but Tavio is stocky. Tavio got in the shower and I laid there lost in my thoughts. Right before he left he came in the room and kissed Lil T who was sleeping, and then he kissed my lips. I didn't say anything I just looked at him. I silently prayed that he stopped cause I couldn't ask him to stop doing what I wanted him to do. Tavio said he'd come to the dress shop as soon as he was finished.

****

Cara Mia got so excited when she saw Lil T; the two of them play very well together. Chareca stood on the pedestal exhaling loudly, "I'm so happy finals are over." She started school this past fall like we planned. I decided to focus on my wedding, and next year we'll be adjusting. I promised myself that I would enroll after our one-year anniversary. "This is a perfect way to start the summer. After Saturday we're going to be two old married ladies." Chareca smiled real big, "my best friend is marrying my husband's best friend. Can you even imagine?"

"YES!" I laughed so hard.

"Now Alaina, I'm sure everyone's been pumping your head with exaggerated stories about married life and sex. I'm going to tell you as straight as I can." My grandmother paused, and then Chareca leaned in. "Sex is not like you read about in books or the way you see it portrayed in movies. The fantasy is that your sex life will be good from your first experience to the last. That your husband will be all over you, and that you won't be able to get enough of your husband. Immediately you'll be in sync with each other's bodies. Or that you'll never argue, fuss, and fight. That's what everyone wants but it's not what most people get. You get what you get. Your husband may not have an insatiable appetite. You may not even like sex right away. He's going to make you cry, and you're going to make him feel like less than a man at times. Now I know you and Chareca are close, but there should be no one closer to you than your husband. There are going to be things about your marriage that you can't and really shouldn't share with anyone. You only share your very personal business when you absolutely have to, and it should always be with someone who's mature and you know for a fact that you can trust. I know you two love each other," she pointed between Chareca and I. "But the fact of the matter is that she's married to your husband's best friend. You two can't make the issues in your marriage issues for all four of you. Remember to pull back."

"I think Chareca does a good job of that." I smiled at Chareca, "she doesn't tell me all of their business. They don't even really fuss in front of us."

"Thank you, my mom had this same conversation with me before my wedding."

"I'm not trying to bring you down or anything, but look at your parents. We all thought things were one-way cause we were on the outside assuming. Your father went through a lot with my daughter. He wasn't even the one to break the news to everyone about her truth. He endured our accusations in protection of her memory. I wish he'd let us apologize." She tried to pull back her tears.

I looked at Chareca who turned to the mirror to fidget with her dress. I was now irritated. How my grandmother going to tell me not to tell my business, but she's telling my business to Chareca. "Grandmother this topic is killing the vibe in here. Let's talk about something else."

"My point is that I want you to be realistic. I should've had this conversation with your mother."

I turned my head and I looked at the kids quietly and happily sitting in the chairs playing with each other. The rest of my bridesmaids came excited and ready to try on their dresses. I was so happy my cousins were here, my grandmother needed to focus on someone else and stop bringing my mother up.

I know how to keep secrets, I've never told a soul about the kiss. Or my crush on Tavio, I will forever claim him as my brother until the grave. I will never admit to anything else. As my cousins were coming out of their dressing rooms we were discussing lunch and where we wanted to go. My grandmother informed us that she was treating. We were still trying to think of somewhere cost effective when Tavio walked to the back of the store where we were. Everyone kind of stopped talking and looked at him. Chareca smiled and said hello cause she was the only person who knew him. "Everyone this is my mentor and friend from work, this is Tavio. At work I tell everyone he's my big brother."

"I'd kill myself if my brother was that fine," my cousin said.

Tavio blushed, "this is his son." I pointed to Lil T who still hadn't noticed his father.

"Tavio are you involved?" My grandmother said dissecting him.

"Yes," then he smiled at her. "It's nice to finally meet you. Alaina tells us about you all the time."

"I'M SORRY I'M LATE! TRAFFIC WAS CRAZY!" Ben said coming into the back frazzled. "Hey Tavio, I didn't know you were coming here. How did you beat me?"

"I took the back roads, I should've known you were going to be here." Tavio teased Ben.

"Don't start with that gay stuff again, if Wesley believes me why don't you?"

"My baby Wesley?" My grandmother asked.

"Yes, the other night we were…."

My grandmother cut Ben off. "Oh he's Wesley's friend." She exhaled hard, "ok. Ok. That's good. You're coming to the wedding Saturday?"

"Yes, with my date."

Ben and Chareca kind of held the same expression as they held their tongues.

****

Everyone sat around engaged in their own conversations as Ken and I looked at our watches. Royce was late to our rehearsal. Finally Ken said we should rehearse cause time was getting away from us. And all Royce really had to do was stand in the front. My father and Wesley looked like they were ready to pounce. As we all walked out of the hotel Royce sped in front of us. He was sweating and upset. "I'm sorry! I'm sorry! I had to run paperwork to the San Jose County office and I thought I had enough time to get here on time. Traffic is a mess out there. I didn't want to stop at a payphone and delay any longer. I got here as fast as I could!"

"We're just glad you're ok. I was worried something happened to you, cause I know my son wouldn't ever be late on purpose to something so important," his mother said.

"Alaina, are you ok?" He walked up to me and put his arms around me.

"Traffic?" I watched his eyes.

"You can check the evening news. Why would I lie about not being here? This is the moment leading up to the most important moment of my life. I'm so sorry!"

I wanted the tension to be over and I knew my father and brother wouldn't relax until they thought I did. Holding on to being angry wasn't going to make anything different. I let it go. "Next time get off the freeway and find a payphone."

Royce kissed my lips and he mouthed that he was sorry again. We went to the restaurant for the rehearsal dinner, and then I kissed my groom goodbye. As I got in the car with my dad to take me to my grandmother's he exhaled deeply. "You sure you want to do this? You're so young and it's not too late to back out."

"I love Royce very much. I'm sure."

"My mother is disappointed that she hasn't really had the chance to spend time with you before your wedding."

"Aunt Meg said the same thing. I'll try to see everyone after the honeymoon; they've all had weddings they should know how this goes.

Royce

My father didn't say anything he just watched me. He's the only person to always know beyond a shadow of a doubt when I'm lying. Truth is, I spent the day with Vanessa pretending to make all these plans for when she came back. By plans I mean conversations. She still thinks we're going to talk about moving in together. I wanted to tell her the truth, but I couldn't stand to face her once she knew the truth. I didn't tell her next year I would be at Stanford. My number was already changed, and I avoided anything that would make her have to pick up the phone to call me. Alaina and I's new place is in the El Sobrante hills; my old place was on the border of Berkeley and Oakland. I was going to completely disappear into thin air. I hated to think about how heartbroken she was going to be when she realized the truth. My selfishness could not let on that there was anything wrong.

When we got to the airport her flight was delayed and I silently cursed to myself. I did my best to seem relaxed even though inside I was dying as time kept ticking away. As soon as she boarded her plane I ran out of the airport to my car. On the radio the traffic report provided me with the alibi for my whereabouts.

No matter how I try to lay I can't get comfortable. My conscience was eating me alive. I took large breaths and I finally got three hours of sleep before I had to be up. Ken came over, bright and early. "Happy release day!" He threw confetti in my face at the front door. "You should be so backed up that I bet Alaina gets pregnant tonight."

I frowned at the dots on the ground in front of my front door. I got the broom and started sweeping. Ken was so busy reminiscing that he didn't catch half my grumbles and irritation from lack of sleep. We went to the barbershop, and then we had breakfast. "How do you remain faithful to your wife?"

Ken laughed, "that's easy. Chareca is crazy, she'd kill me. Then once she revived me, my mother would finish me off. Look don't doubt yourself. I was worried about the same thing, but I look at my beautiful feisty wife, and our gorgeous daughter. What we have, I could never have with someone else. Just because some other female may be pretty and cool, she's never worth the risk."

****

I smiled at my sisters and cousin and Alaina's family as they walked down the aisle. There were so many people looking at me and smiling, I focused on the edge of the aisle where Alaina was going to appear. I saw a guy and a girl slide in at the back of the rows, whoever they were they were late! Everyone stood as Alaina and her dad walked down the aisle slowly towards me. My heart sped up as I saw her. Alaina was beautiful and she looked so angelic. She focused on me only watching my face for a response to her. I licked my lips to try to contain my excitement. She was beautiful and I felt like the luckiest man alive. When they got to the top of the aisle Alaina's father reluctantly passed his daughter to me. I couldn't stop looking at her, Alaina looked so beautiful! She squeezed my hand and then her cousin began. He went on and on and on. At times my mind floated off into thoughts of work things and most important **TONIGHT**! I was relieved that there was a light at the end of the tunnel when we got to the vows and ring exchange. I promised with all my heart that we would be together until the day I died.

When I kissed Alaina our kiss went on for a long time. The cheering from the onlookers reminded me that we had an audience. Everyone stood up as we walked beyond the rows and on to the grass on the side. The wedding party joined us and we took pictures. Our guests were escorted inside the hotel while family came in for family photos. I kept hugging Alaina and kissing her, we did it. We were married.

When we went into the hotel we went into our banquet room and everyone cheered us again as we entered. We had our first dance and then we took our seats at the head table. We were served our dinner while everyone else lined up for the buffet. People came over as they could to congratulate us. I lowered my eyes to my salad when someone approached us. "Congratulations Alaina." I looked up cause I didn't recognize the voice.

"Royce, you remember Tavio. My friend from work." Alaina said happily.

"The one who calls you MAC, right."

"Nadia doesn't feel good, so we're going to go." His eyes cut me as if I was supposed to recognize the name.

"Oh, tell her I'm so sorry to hear that. Thank you guys for coming, even if you did slide in right before I walked down the aisle."

"Thank you for starting late, I would've hated it if I missed you walk."

"Thank the hair and makeup folks for that, it wasn't my doing." Alaina smiled. "Here she comes, I'm sorry you don't feel well." Alaina said standing up to hug the girl.

I looked at the girl who had HATRED for me in her eyes as she approached my wife to hug her. I immediately felt sick. It was Vanessa's cousin Nadia. The world is too small! I froze in place as sweat broke out on my brow. Tavio searched my face for recognition of Nadia, but I could tell he didn't see it. Nadia had tears in her eyes as she hugged Alaina. "I know how long you've waited for this and how excited you are. We've only talked about this since you two got back together." Her voice shook a little showing she was trying to hold back emotion.

"Thank you, this is Royce the object of my affection all these years."

"Please tell me you have a twin brother or a cousin who could pass for your twin? You look just like this guy I met at a party not too long ago."

"I've been told that I look like a lot of people. I haven't met most of them. You never know."

"You never know," she repeated through clinched lips.

"Let me get you home." Tavio said taking her hand in his. Then he nodded at us and walked away.

I sat there trying to catch my breath. Alaina was oblivious to what just happened. I needed more information about her *Friend.* I told myself to calm down and relax knowing that no matter what we would have tonight without drama.

****

I carried Alaina over the threshold and then I kissed her. She tried not to look scared. She asked me to unzip her and then she scurried away to the bathroom to change. I got naked and I laid in the middle of the bed. I waited, and waited, and waited. I don't know what was taking Alaina so long in the bathroom, but I dozed off lightly at first. And then hard. The lack of sleep the night before, and the long love making session with Vanessa earlier that day finally caught up to me and I was out.

I woke up as the sun was coming up. Alaina was sleeping next to me. She looked very pretty in her gown and she smelled great. The excitement of the morning was with me. I told myself to calm down cause she was completely nerved up about this part. I started kissing on her neck and when her hand became alive rubbing my head I kissed her mouth, morning breath and all. I took my time and we made out for a long time. Alaina completely tensed up as I started to work my way in. I had to stop and get her to relax. This whole experience was very wearing on my self-control. I wanted to go in, but I knew she was scared and over thinking everything.

It took so long to get in that I blew not too long after I was finally in. I tried to keep my eyes open but all of that self-control drained me and I was sleep again. Alaina woke me up and said we needed to go have breakfast. I asked her if she was ok, and she smiled and said yes.

I was kicking myself internally. I knew that was weak. I know I'm so much better than this. After we ate I told myself I was going to make it up to her. Alaina said she was trying to wake me for a long time and then she finally fell asleep, so she was tired. I told her to lay down and I was going to go find us some ginseng.

I got in my car and went to the house where the party was. Nadia was getting out of her car. She saw me sitting in my car and she came hollering and screaming. I asked her to get inside. She sat down angry with her arms folded. "So Alaina's friend is the guy you were talking to Vanessa about?" I watched her eyes, "does he know you're married?"

Nadia started crying hard, "YOU CAN'T BLACKMAIL ME!"

"All I'm saying is that me and Vanessa are done. She's going to find out soon enough. I'll tell her everything and a few things that sound like the truth. He won't ever look at you again; your relationship will forever be ruined. Or you can just keep quiet. Let all of this run its course. I won't let on that you ever knew anything."

Chapter 8

Tavio

Nadia smiled at me, "now just because I'm going to MAC's I mean Alaina's wedding with you does not mean it's ok for you to start getting ideas."

"Wait a minute, I thought we were going to the justice of the peace right after."

We had a good laugh, and then my phone rang. When I didn't move towards the phone Nadia cut her eyes at me. "Just talk to her. Tell her about your son, you're done with her anyways."

"I'm not done, I'm looking for the words."

"So why not tell her you need to talk."

I shuddered, "as a man I will not utter the very words I hate to hear."

Nadia laughed, then she went in the bathroom. I looked at my machine that said I had a new message waiting for me. I didn't want to spend today and tonight thinking about Eva. I decided to listen to the message when I got back. After lots of complaining on my part Nadia was ready just in time for us to be really late. She told me to relax because weddings never start on time. I was relieved to see that she was right, but we hurried and made it to our seats just before Alaina and her father started their march.

Alaina looked so beautiful, her dress, her hair, and her makeup were perfect. Even though it was an overcast day, the weather was still perfect for the perfect bride. Nadia and I smiled really big at Alaina who was focused on Royce only. I told myself to get over the jealousy that I felt in the pit of my stomach. One day it would be my turn and MAC and Ben better be as excited for me. Alaina's voice shook as she said her vows; I imagined tears in her eyes as she promised her heart to Royce. One day I will have this.

I was so busy paying attention to the ceremony I didn't notice how stiff Nadia became. Her eyebrows were frowning and she stared ahead like she was dumbfounded. I asked her what was wrong, and she said she thought she was going to be sick. When Alaina and Royce walked past us, Nadia sat down and held her stomach while she shook her head. I looked at her trying to understand her sudden change. As we walked inside Nadia held on to her stomach as she mumbled to herself. We sat at our table close to the front just behind the family with Ben and his date. She was tall and thin, very model like. I had never seen Ben with a girl and although he continued to tell me he was not gay, I kind of needed to see him in a relationship with a woman before I'd believe him. Showing up here with a date was a step in the right direction.

I got Nadia a ginger ale from the bar in hopes that it would settle her stomach. We hadn't even eaten yet. We were told to sit and then the wedding party entered the banquet hall, and last but not least the happy couple. Nadia stared hard at Royce. She looked like he stole her puppy. She broke out in a slight sweat and then she put her hands on her head to try to calm herself. I asked her if she wanted to go, and she apologetically said yes.

I couldn't read Royce's expression when he saw Nadia. He

didn't say anything right away, he kind of watched her. In the lobby Nadia marched over to the payphone and made a call. She growled when she slammed the phone down and then she walked angrily next to me. When we got to my car I asked her what was going on. She said she needed to talk to her cousin. She said she called her cousin to ask her something. She forgot that her cousin went home to visit her mother. She said when she got home she was going to call her cousin first thing in the morning.

That night Nadia and I had angry sex, she was mad for her cousin, and I don't know why I was angry. Maybe it was the whole we need to talk conversation I needed to have with Eva.

Eva

I was standing at the bus stop slightly freezing my behind off. Then Colby pulled up to me and unlocked his door. I couldn't move fast enough to get in the car. He asked when I was going to get my license. I told him I got my permit and I hadn't had time to pick a driving school because I've been focused on work. Colby pulled over and told me to get out. When I did he tossed his keys to me. He asked me not to kill us both. I thought I did pretty good for my first time driving. Colby said I did good, but the sweat beads on his forehead suggested that I freaked him out more than he was ready for. I was surprised when he came the next morning to let me drive to school. He started picking me up from work as well.

Once I felt confident behind the wheel and he was no longer silently freaking out. I took my driver's test. I didn't pass the first time; I missed by a couple of points. I was so disappointed, but I was so nervous I could see why I failed. The second time I passed, I thanked Colby over and over for his help. Next thing on my agenda now is to save up for a car.

****

I grunted as I hung the phone up again! Lately I rarely catch

Tavio home. I have a better relationship with his machine than I have with him. "What's the matter?" My grandmother asked as she took her seat in her favorite recliner.

"Tavio didn't answer again. I need to make sure he has his ticket for Rickie's wedding. It's a couple of weeks away."

"I think it's so special how you two have kept in contact after all these years."

"I guess," I mumbled as I sat back in my chair. I can't handle Tavio flaking out on me. He's always been someone that I can count on no matter what anyone else has done.

My grandmother looked at me sending my sadness. "Ooh! Guess what I made?" She said excitedly as she stood.

"What?" I could feel myself sinking into depression.

"Apple cider donuts!" She smiled real big as she walked into the kitchen.

I frowned, "where did that come from?"

"Your friend Colby took me to an orchard. They had them there, and he bet me that I couldn't make them just as good. He's going to learn to stop doubting me." She placed the plate of homemade donuts in front of my nose. She knew I was going to decline but the smell of them stole my attention.

"When did you go with him?" I picked up a donut and pulled it apart with my fingers. I already knew I was in trouble.

"Remember when I came home with all those apples?" She smiled at the memory. "We picked them ourselves. They had these there and I fell in love."

"They're good," I said reaching for another two.

"I'm trying to mind my own business but you know that Colby

boy likes you."

"He told you that?"

"Only after I made him fess up. He comes by whenever he's out of class. He takes me around and shows me different places out here. He sits with me and his ears always perk up whenever you come up. Why don't you like him?"

I sighed, "I only have eyes for Tavio."

"You haven't seen that boy in years. Why are you holding on to the memory?"

"Grandmother, I see Tavio every three to four months since I started school."

She bucked her eyes, "you do? Why didn't you mention him?" I shrugged, "I don't know. I want him to move out here with us."

"As in, stay here with us?" I shook my head yes. "Were you going to get married?"

"Probably not right away."

She took the plate back to the kitchen. "So how was that supposed to work?" I could hear irritation in her voice. "I can go back to Florida if you plan on living in sin." She had her hands on her hips and she was wiggling her neck.

"Why would it matter? Aunt Henrietta wanted to rent her house out again. It's not like you could've stayed there."

"I don't care! Little girl I don't care if you're paying all the bills or not. The only time a man better be living here is if he's your husband!"

"You let my dad live with us."

"No! Not un! He spent the night a couple times, but he ain't neva lived with me!"

"You don't want me to be with Tavio?"

"I don't want you giving away the milk."

"Grandmother, I'm not a virgin." She gasped, "I haven't been since high school."

She looked at me like she wanted to hit me. Then she stormed out to her bedroom and slammed her door.

I rolled my eyes as I finished my donut. I thought about trying another one when my grandmother came out the room. She walked up to me and gently put her hand under my chin as she tilted my head up towards her. "You are beautiful baby, don't let no one make you resort to accepting their leftovers. Stop calling that boy; if he's coming he'll call you. Whatever's going to happen will happen."

****

I was so happy to finally see Tavio after all of these months without him. I kissed and squeezed him tight. Rickie seemed surprised to actually see Tavio. I guess she thought I was lying about us still being together. My grandmother wasn't mean, but she kept watching Tavio. I knew she was going to be full of opinions on our flight home.

Tavio left the day before we did, but my grandmother did not disappoint. "He's hiding something."

"How could you know that? You don't know him like I do." I knew she was right, but I was hiding my own secret.

The entire flight she kept going on and on about it. Colby picked us up from the airport with a girl in his car. He said Katrina got a flat tire that she had to go get fixed so she called him a few minutes ago to ask him to pick us up from the airport.

My grandmother gave Colby's friend the fakest hello I've ever heard. Colby looked completely uncomfortable as I engaged his friend in conversation. At one point my grandmother looked at me and asked why I was talking so much. I told her I was so happy that Colby found

111

someone so it was only natural that I'd ask questions. Colby hurried us out of the car, he almost threw our bags inside and then he left.

My grandmother said I sounded so jealous. I ignored her and then I took a hot shower. I was sitting on my bed in my pajamas looking at pictures from the wedding. Tavio looked so handsome, and in most of our pictures we were smiling or laughing. I chuckled at the picture where we were laughing so hard as Rickie, Tavio, and I shared stories about us running around doing dumb stuff with his sister Unique. My grandmother was not happy to hear any of it. I was enjoying my walk down memory lane when there was a soft knock on the door. I assumed it was my grandmother and said come in. Colby quietly walked in, I gasped and scurried into my bed under the covers. He stood there staring not saying anything for a long time. "What?"

"You have fun on your trip?" He didn't close the door all the way so I assumed my grandmother was near.

"Lots. Why are you in here?"

"Did you breakup?"

"No!"

"Then why were you all in my business tonight?"

"I was just being nosey, dang! You can't take a joke?"

"A joke?" He watched me, "my feelings are a joke to you?"

"That's not what I meant. Don't blow things out of proportion."

"Put a jacket on, Katrina asked me to pick you up."

I looked at the phone, "she would've called."

"She was on the phone with Chauncey when she asked me to bring you over." He said impatiently.

Something wasn't adding up but I said I'd be right back and I went in the bathroom and put on a bra. I put on sweats over my pajama bottoms and a jacket. I put on my flip-flops and then I followed Colby out of the door. My grandmother was smiling as she stared at the TV while eating her popcorn.

"I think we need to get to know each other. I've gotten to know your grandmother and she's a lot of fun."

"Maybe you two can double with us when Tavio comes out." I laughed at my joke.

"Stop it! You like me that's why you keep making all these not funny jokes about my life. You actually think that's going to change how you feel about me."

"Please! I don't..."

He cut me off, "spare me your denials."

I gasped and stared at him. He's getting on my nerves. When we pulled up to his house Katrina was on the phone outside pacing. I did think that Colby was lying, but I let it go. If I thought he was lying why did I come with him?

Katrina was yelling and crying as she paced. When she saw me she hung up her phone and then she threw her arms around my neck as she cried. She said Chauncey had an affair. The female saw her car outside the salon and she punctured her tire. Katrina said she made it home before she realized there was something wrong with her car. I asked how she knew all this, and she said Chauncey called her in a panic cause the woman called him telling him that Katrina was going to have an accident cause of what she did to her tire. Chauncey's been confessing everything over the past few hours and she felt so stupid and betrayed.

I asked Katrina what she was going to do and she didn't know. I stood there watching her go off and then feel all kinds of regrets. Chauncey kept calling and she said he'd probably try to show up in the morning before she went to work. I told her to come spend the night with me that way we could go to work together in the morning and she'd at least have that time without him bothering her. When we went inside I was stopped by her mother. She wanted to know how the wedding went. Katrina said she was going to pack and she'd be back. I talked to her mom for a little while, and then I made my way to Katrina's room. She was on the phone crying with Chauncey no doubt, I could tell she needed some privacy so I went out of the room.

The sound of music coming from Colby's room caught my attention. I poked my head in and he was standing in the middle of the room staring off into the distance. When I moved his eyes caught me and he told me to come in and shut the door. I walked in but I didn't shut the door. Colby walked over to the door and then he shut it. When I started to say something he walked up to me and kissed me. I felt like I was about to be in trouble. So I slowly backed out of the room.

******

I'm tired of it! Whenever I call Tavio he's never home. Our phone conversations have gotten shorter and shorter. I decided to pop up out here in California. I've had his address since he moved to his place. His parents still live in the same house since we were young, and I know his class schedule. Flying out here, I knew that the likelihood of Tempest being at his place when I got there was high. I didn't care about all of that. I needed to know what was going on with us. Whenever I try to make a plan with Tavio we end up arguing or getting off the phone.

I spent two hours trying to find his place in Berkeley. The sudden one way streets and pedestrians with no regard for your vehicle as you drove made me crazy. I exhaled when I finally found his little building. I knocked hard like I was the police just in case he was inside sleeping. When there was no answer, I went back to my rental car and waited. After another hour, I decided to go to his parent's house and hopefully catch him there. No one was home there either. So I went back to Tavio's and waited some more. As I waited, a car pulled up with a couple in the front. The guy parked and then a girl got out of the car.

As she walked up the steps to Tavio's front door, I realized that it was Tempest. She knocked and then she went back to the car. I was going to assume that the guy was a family member or friend probably dropping her off until I saw them with their tongues down each other's throats. I was confused as to why she was here. Then another car pulled up, it was Tavio. He waved and then he pulled into the driveway of his building. Tempest got out of the car, and then she started grabbing stuff out of the back seat. Tavio hurried back over explaining that he got held up with something. He had a backpack with what I assume were his books. He was probably studying somewhere. A little head popped up in the back of the car and my heart stopped beating. I sat there paralyzed as I watched the baby climb out of the backseat. Tavio smiled big at the child as he talked to Tempest. She handed him the bag and then she got back in the car with a smile. Tavio smiled down at the child breaking my heart. When I opened my car door, Tavio looked at me and his smile dropped. I stood next to the car staring, I told myself to hear him out. Maybe I was assuming the worst. I grabbed my bag out the back seat of the car. Tavio held on to the hand of the child but he didn't move. I locked the car then I crossed the street towards them. "What are you doing here?"

"You are impossible to get on the phone. I figured this was the next best way to reach you."

"You figured?" He stared at me.

I looked at the little boy, he looked like Tavio but a little different. "Who's child?"

Tavio took a deep breath, "let's go inside." Tavio picked the little boy up who looked at me but he was no longer smiling. He was watching my face for a reaction. When we walked inside his small one bedroom apartment, I appreciated how neat everything was. Tavio wasn't a neat freak, but his place was tidy. He put the little boy down and he ran to a chest that he opened and it was full of toys. "What if I would've been gone for my two days off?"

"I would've gone to your parent's place." I put my bag down. "He's yours?"

"Now you know why I can't move to Boston."

"Why can't you?" I waited for his answer.

"You can't be serious."

"I'm very serious. He can come out on summer vacations and stuff like that." I said even though it was killing me as the words came out of my mouth.

He pointed to his two chairs, and very small, dinner table. "Have a seat." When I did, he grabbed my hands in his and he looked me in my eyes. He slightly squeezed them as he said; "I will never do that to my son. He didn't ask to be here. I owe him to be here for him when he needs me."

I started shaking my leg as I looked at the little boy. "But I'm in Boston."

"I know."

Tears fell from my eyes, "don't do this to me. Tavio please! Why would you have unprotected sex with Tempest?"

"I was always strapped up. I don't know what happened, but my son is here. She's engaged and moving on with her life. We weren't in love and she said it took her being pregnant to get it."

"To get what?"

"How in love I was with you."

"WAS? WAS? What do you mean was? You don't love me anymore?"

"I'll always love you and have love for you, but you don't want kid's period. You try to pretend to compromise for my sake, but you don't want them. I can't be that selfish just to have you in my life that I would force you two to be together. Both of you will be miserable and I couldn't live with myself."

I tried to pull my hands away but he wouldn't let me. "You are a coward! You were trying to phase me out. Why wouldn't you just tell me the truth? Why didn't you come to me?"

"I didn't know how." He said gently still not letting me go.

I started crying and the baby stopped playing and looked at me. He told the little boy it was ok. "How could you do this to me? I trusted you with everything in me! You know I've never had anyone! You are all I have!"

"Next trip out I was going to come clean, I swear. Children are forever, and even if little T wasn't here, the fact that you don't want them is a big problem for me. I want to get married and I want to have more children. We always wanted children, and then one day you changed the plan without talking to me. One day you became more ambitious than you were family oriented. You want to rule the world, while I want to do well enough to provide for my family's wants and needs. I don't know what happened, but our plans changed."

I cried harder, James happened. I wanted to tell him, but I couldn't let it come out. I sat there crying and crying letting my tears reflect the pain in my heart. I couldn't believe he was breaking up with me. Tavio has always been in my life, what am I supposed to do now? Who am I supposed to be? Tavio asked me what I wasn't saying and it couldn't move past my throat. I never told anyone, only student health, James, and I know.

Tavio

Eva's tears were killing me. I ordered pizza, but Eva was too upset to eat. I told her to take the bed as I made up the couch for little T and I to sleep on. I could hear Eva crying in my bed, heartbroken tears that I could never fix. Little T asked me why Eva was crying and I told him because she was sad. He tried to think about it, but then he went back to playing with the suds in the tub. I watched my son and I told myself that this was worth Eva's tears.

My son would always need me, where she could outgrow me and I'd have no excuse for abandoning my child. No matter how I sliced it, Eva doesn't want him, she doesn't want children period. I want more kids; I have to have more kids. When I can afford them of course. Although I just got promoted to Supervisor from team lead at the bank, the money is laughable. The money provides a roof over my head and food in my son's stomach. However, these pennies did nothing for where I need to be. School is going well, and I can't wait to be done. I figure when I graduate little T will go to preschool and then I can move to a daytime position. IF! If I don't decide to go to graduate school. The bill for grad school is pretty hefty and I don't know if I'll need it. I plan to discuss it with my mentor next time we meet. Tempest's man is alright, but the closer that their wedding day gets the more I seem to have little T with me. I'm fine with it, and my mom and sometimes Alaina help when I'm in a bind.

I was laying on my couch with little T who knocked out as soon as his head hit the pillow. Give him a bath and clean pajamas and he's out cold. Eva came out of the room and sadly walked into the bathroom. I watched the light under the door. She stood in the middle of the floor staring at me with puffy eyes, and then she shook her head and went back to my bed. I heard her cry a little more and then I could tell she fell asleep by all the snoring that came from the room. Back in the day, that was how I knew she fell asleep on the phone. She would start snoring loud. I went to sleep best I could.

When I woke up in the morning, I carefully got off the couch and I went into the room. Eva was laying in the bed staring at the wall when I came in. I asked her how long was she out here? She said she was stuck out here for three more days, cause she didn't really have the money to change her ticket. I told her she could be sad on her time, I wanted to make the most of her trip out here. She exhaled like she was the most depressed person in the world. Eva patted the bed so that I would sit down. When I did she put her arms around her neck and cried. She said she couldn't believe that I would ever pick anyone over her. She said she needed a minute to get it out and then she'd try her best to suck it up. "All my life, it's always been your love for me that kept me sane. When my sister was losing it over our parents, you and Unique would come and play with me. I hated all the running around you guys did, but you always made me laugh and smile. I didn't have time to be sad because you always made me happy." She sniffled, which seemed to make more tears come out. "I hated everything about the idea of moving to Florida. If it wasn't for your plan that we would be together, I don't know where I'd be. Probably on drugs somewhere completely washed up."

"I doubt that," I shook my head. I don't think her grandmother would've allowed it.

"I'm saying I never had to imagine life without you. I can't compete with a baby. She won and she's not even playing the game anymore."

"Eva, she didn't get pregnant on purpose. Tempest knew all about you, her world turned upside down when she found out she was pregnant. Her mother beat her up and then she kicked her out. She stayed here for a little bit, but there were never any pretenses of love between us."

"So where did we go wrong?"

"When you decided without me that careers were more important than having a family. I know college life is expensive and I always saved just so I could get out to you. That day you called me for the money was the first time you seemed different. You've been different ever since then. You put up a wall even from me. I should've told you right away. I handled that wrong. Once you started talking about no kids and you already had your mind made up… I knew then that we weren't going to make it. Why have you become anti-children?"

"Forgive me for knowing that I plan to work hard, and that I wouldn't have the time to give a child all of the attention that they need. Forgive me for not being selfish and wanting to have them anyways and then have to live with the guilt of knowing that they're being raised by a nanny. I wanted to be your baby, I didn't want to share." She cried some more.

"What would happen when your work became too time consuming and you didn't have time for me. I mean I plan to work hard as well, but my priority will always be my family. Or what if you died, what would I have? Memories, but no physical aspect of you. I'd be all alone to grieve. No grandchildren to look forward to, nothing. My life would either live and die with you, or we'd become strangers from working so hard and never having time for each other. Eva, we're not on the same level anymore. Before we hurt each other anymore than we already have let's end as peaceably as possible."

She looked at me, "how can you live without me?"

"I won't." I rubbed her head.

She leaned in and kissed me. Then she looked at the doorway, "is he sleep?"

"Yes."

"Close the door," then she laid back on the bed.

Eva

I said goodbye to California in my heart. I kept taking slow deep breaths as my plane took off, as it stayed in the air, and when it landed everything felt final in my soul. I took another deep breath and then I tried to convince Katrina that I was ok. She kept staring at me like she was scared. I forced a laugh and I did my best to put on my best face even though I was dying inside.

When we pulled up to my place, Colby's car was parked in the driveway. Katrina frowned and asked why he was here. I joked and said he was secretly dating my grandmother. When we walked inside my grandmother and Colby were in the kitchen. The place smelled delicious, my grandmother was yelling at him, "smoosh! Smoosh! Smoosh!" as Colby had his hands in a bowl trying not to look disgusted. They were laughing so hard and having a good time. She said she told him the best way to mix dressing is with his hands. Colby said he had doctor's hands so he had to be delicate.

My grandmother said they decided to make me a turkey dinner with everything that they could find at this time of the year. I looked around the kitchen at all the prepared dishes and I asked her who was going to eat all this food? She said that Katrina's parents were coming over, and Katrina's boyfriend. Katrina looked surprised; she said no one told her anything about all of this.

I excused myself as I went to my bedroom. I decided to take a shower and wash not only my flight off of me but everything. Tavio is no longer my man. He's no longer the man in my life. I now have no one but my grandmother. I got in the shower and I washed everything, my hair, under my nails. Everything that could've soaked up any part of Tavio was scrubbed. When I came out the bathroom, my grandmother called out that everyone was here and dinner was ready. There was a table in the middle of the living room and chairs. I quickly put my things away in my bedroom. I took a deep breath. I can make it through this.

Everyone was already seated, and of course the only available seat was between my grandmother and Colby. Katrina gave me a concerned smile and put on a happy face. I told everyone about all the places the Tavio's took me. Little Tavio is a cute kid, but he was a lot of work. Strapping him in and taking him out of his car seat, bringing his stroller even though he wanted to walk. His cranky fits when he got tired. Tavio is very good with his son, he didn't yell at his son once. My father was always yelling at Rickie and I. I liked seeing Tavio with his son, but I recognized how much work he had to put in and I'm focusing on advancing at work. Mrs. Singleton has told me numerous times that she's received positive reports about my performance. Then she tells me about new positions that will be coming up. She explains what each department does and why the position would be a good skill set to have. I'm not stupid; I apply for each one she points out. Then I hold my breath.

Once I stopped talking, I noticed that everyone was focused on their plates. You would think they've never eaten before. Mrs. Singleton dropped her fork and pushed her chair back. "Mrs. Pearcy you have taken me back to my roots. I haven't eaten like this since I was a child and my grandparents would visit. Everything is superb! I cannot eat another bite."

"She speaks for herself," Mr. Singleton said as he shoveled another fork full of food in his mouth. "I forgot food could taste so good."

"Charlotte you don't cook for your man?" My grandmother asked.

"I don't have time to create masterpieces. Our cook doesn't cook like this either."

"Oh yes, the cardboard with a side of celery," Mr. Singleton said as he dipped his biscuit in her gravy and then he took a savory bite.

"I keep telling Eva to join me in the kitchen, but you know how she is. She's always working, always focused on her grades."

"Is that a bad thing?" Mrs. Singleton asked.

"It can be. I have no doubt that Eva will be a success; she has drive and determination. Do you think it's a coincidence that she somehow fits in with your family so well? Eva and her sister Rickie love each other, but they fought all the time. Rickie was always in the kitchen with me. Always looking for a better love than what she knew within herself. Eva used schoolwork to escape her life. One day if she doesn't wake up and pay attention life will pass her by."

Mrs. Singleton looked thoughtful, like she was trying to see if she should be offended or not. "You're saying that she needs to have a balance *right*? There's nothing wrong with being ambitious and career driven, but she needs to balance that with life *right*?" Katrina was cleaning up my grandmother's words.

"Exactly! Charlotte, everyone won't be as fortunate as you to have a husband and children who understand."

"Understand?" Mrs. Singleton adjusted in her chair.

"A husband who understands and takes it when you're too tired, and children who despite missing you aspire to greatness for your approval." Mrs. Singleton cut her eyes at her husband. "You've got wonderful kids and a good husband. I'm just saying, I understand working hard. Just don't forget what it's all for." My grandmother sat tall like she just checked the whole table.

Mrs. Singleton looked at each of her kids and then her husband; none of them would give her direct eye contact. I was completely embarrassed; I apologized with my eyes. There's just some things my grandmother wouldn't understand. "Oh I see. You've been talking to my children and you gather this information from them? Mrs. Pearcy, I like you, and you know what? If you can manage it, I'd like to fund Sunday dinners like this for us as a family on a regular basis. I also feel the need to put you in your place old woman. I know what era you come from, that same era that my parents came from. The wife stays home, takes care of the children, and caters to her man's every whim. So what if he runs around on you and even fathers children outside of your union. You stand by your man and you hold everything together with a fake smile and nightcap of whatever liquor or cake to get you through the pain and disappointment of your life. Thank you for talking to my children and spending time with them. They miss having a grandmother type in their lives and you can fill that void. Why? Because you remind them of my mother. My mother was like you, loved her man's dirty draws. She turned on her family to defend him no matter what. My father was a hard worker and he made sure my mother never had to work. We did, but as his wife she didn't have to ever work outside of the home. He paid for her silence. He paid for the blind eye she turned to the abuse that happened in my home. I decided for myself that I would not live like that, and I was fortunate enough to meet a man who has never uttered that he was threatened by my ambition and he let me fly as high as I wanted. Rey knows I love him, but a house like you had, we will never have. The abuse that you allowed your children to suffer because you loved your man. The guilt you carry because the abuse continued to pass on from your children to your grandchildren. I've read the books, and I can quote you the statistics, but I doubt you will follow me so why waste my breath? Your granddaughter is not allowing her past to define what she will achieve for herself. Instead of applauding that, you're most likely encouraging her to find the achievements in a future husband and settle like you did. She has a beautiful mind and as long as she wants, she will never have to settle. Stop frowning on her success and making her feel like something's wrong with her for not letting some guy run all over her." Then she turned to her husband, "Rey she's right, we'll schedule a vacation right away." Mr. Singleton put his hand over hers. No doubt applauding her for holding back and not going off on my grandmother like she could've. "I will look to have more balance in my life, but you need to do the same Mrs. Pearcy. Eva is a great girl; she's young and doesn't need to be worried about a husband right now, if ever. You're not always going to agree with the choices your children make, but she doesn't have to make you happy because her mother didn't."

My grandmother was angry but she started it. "I didn't consent to any abuse!"

"Grandmother please calm down, she was speaking matter-of-factly just like you were. Neither one of you know each other's lives first hand."

My grandmother looked at me, "un huh."

"Come on Mrs. Pearcy, you dished it out, you can take a little." Mrs. Singleton grinned.

It was silent for a little bit as my grandmother tried to check her emotions. "This meal has been perfect; please tell me there's dessert?" Chauncey asked with a big smile that made everyone relax.

"It's not much; I just made a banana pudding. Have you ever had banana pudding?" She said calming down by the second.

"I don't think so." He was trying to remember.

"It's not that hard to remember, either you have or you haven't. I bet after you taste it you'll never forget you've ever had it." She bragged.

Colby leaned towards me, "what's wrong?"

"Nothing." I said returning to the conversation at the table.

"I don't believe you."

"So what!" I huffed.

Tavio

Now that Eva knows, it feels like a huge weight has been lifted off of my shoulders. My biggest darkest secret has been revealed and now I'm free to be me. Nadia snuggled in to me. "What do you want to eat tonight?"

I got excited. "You're actually going to cook?"

She sucked her teeth, "dream on! I order and you pick it up on your way out." Then her phone rang. Nadia slowly stretched as she reached over and grabbed it. "Hello?" She listened closely, and then she slumped. "Of course you can come here. I have a friend here, but he's going to be leaving in a little bit. You can come over now, it's ok honey. I know."

When she got off the phone, I watched her face. "It's my cousin; she's going through a hard time right now."

When her cousin got to the house, she had that same look like Eva. She was defeated and even though she wanted to fight, it looked like there was no point. "How could he vanish into thin air? We were going to move in together and everything. Then he just disappears." She cried, "I thought we were in love."

Nadia rubbed her cousin's back, "he's evil!"

"I'm moving back to Boston, I can't function out here."

"You're going to let some coward run you off? What about us? I thought you moved out here to be closer to us too?"

Vanessa shook her head, "I can't do this! What if I ran into him somewhere?"

"Then you curse him out! And beat the mess out of him. You don't run away."

"I need my mom, I already told my roommate I'm leaving, and I'm transferring schools. I was going to quit my job, but I was able to transfer. I just got to pack my few things and ship them back home." Then she looked at me, "why would he make me believe he loved me and then vanish into thin air?"

"I don't know. Maybe there was something he couldn't tell you. Maybe this was the easiest way."

"For him, he didn't spare me any heart ache. He saw me off at the airport; he told me he loved me and everything." Then she wiped her eyes, "I tried to call him from the airport once I landed and I knew there was some kind of mix up. I called his house phone over and over, and the recording kept telling me that the number was disconnected. I panicked, but what could I do I was all the way out there? When I get back, his apartment is empty, and there's no phone." She turned towards Nadia, "what I look like even gracing someone like that with the sound of my voice? It's done, it's over. I'll live even though it hurts like crazy right now, cause I don't understand what I did wrong."

I didn't know what to tell her, I felt bad for her though. Part of me wanted to call Eva and check on her. I hated that she was somewhere hurting on account of me. No matter how I tried to sum it up, someone was going to get hurt. Eva could move on and rebuild, my son's whole definition of life itself is based on the love I give him. I couldn't knowingly put him in a situation where he would be hurt. I left earlier than planned to give them some space, get some food, and get over to work.

Alaina would be coming back to work in a week. It has been so different around the office without her there. Some of them fools actually told me they were surprised that Alaina wasn't actually marrying me. They figured I was really her fiancé and we were lying about the whole thing. The imaginations of some of these people is ridiculous. We may chat a little at work but the truth of the matter is that Alaina talks to Ben way more than she talks to me. They don't know Ben so they... I told myself to stop thinking about Alaina, she's **married**.

Eva

"This is Eva, you're going to take over her daily reports." My boss said, "Eva just got a new position that she'll be transitioning to in a few weeks. So we're dividing her task amongst the team. It's going to take four people to do what she does on the day to day. You've got some pretty big shoes to fill. Eva this is our new hire Vanessa. She's a transfer from our California office. Can she sit with you to begin learning your reports this morning?"

"Of course!" I said looking the girl over.

"Perfect, Vanessa when you're done here come back to my desk." Then she looked at me. "I know you normally zip through these reports with no problems, can you try to slow it down for her?"

I winked at Vanessa, "I'm sure she can keep up."

"Thanks you two," then she walked away.

I took my jacket out of the extra seat in my cubical so she could sit. Vanessa was average tall, pretty face, brown skin, just past her shoulders length hair. Her entire outfit was very cute, and her figure was nicely stacked. I hope she isn't one of those girls who thinks too much of herself. Her attitude determines how well I train her. I know it wasn't right, but ask me if I cared. "Were you in a similar position in California?"

"Kind of, the California office is a much smaller satellite office." Then she swallowed. She forced a smile in front of the pain in her eyes.

It was the same kind of pain I felt everyday these days. I smiled at her and then I brought up my reports. I walked her through the basic steps, and so far so good. She wasn't stuck up and she got all my quickwhitted jokes and she offered a few of her own. After a few hours our boss came to get her, I guess we lost track of time. At lunchtime, I stood up, trying to think of where I was going to go. I still didn't know the area all that much. Vanessa came over with her jacket and asked me where I was going for lunch. I shrugged cause I didn't know. She smiled and then she told me to come with her. Vanessa talked fast and excitedly when we got in her car. She relaxed and spoke in her natural voice; she was down to earth and cool as far as I could see. We went to her mother's house, which happened to be close by. We had a quick lunch of sandwiches and chips. Her mother was really nice and loving. She kept hugging Vanessa and kissing her as she hobbled around the kitchen being nothing but adorable. If I actually had a mother that was worth something, I imagine she would have been more like Vanessa's mother than Mrs. Singleton.

As we left Vanessa's place her mother told me she liked me, she told me to come back soon.

Chapter 9

Alaina

"Just relax," Royce said as he got on top of me. I took a deep breath and tried to do as he said. When he started to enter me, he pulled back. He licked the tips of his fingers and then he rubbed his spit on his hands and a little on me. Then he pushed himself inside of me. At least it doesn't hurt as much anymore. Royce started kissing me as he moved and used his hands to tell me to move. "Come on baby!" He grunted in my ear. I started humping him back and he started moaning out loud. The more I moved the louder he got. I was tired of feeling like a failure. Tired of feeling like something was wrong with me because none of this did anything for me. I rolled Royce over and I got on top of him. Royce smiled as he said, "YES!" He put his hands up like he was surrendering to me. It felt a little different up here, but this wasn't for me. I used my imagination until Royce grabbed me and rolled us over again. The veins in his neck popped out and his eyes bulged as he came. I kept moving until he was done.

Royce kissed me as he caught his breath, he looked at my face. I don't know what he's looking for when he does that. His face turned sad, and then he put his arms around me. This is the part I like. Royce cuddles with me, kisses me, and tells me how much he loves me. He always falls asleep after a few minutes, but I live for it.

When Royce was completely knocked out, I got up, I took a bath, and then I stood in the mirror looking at myself. I'm my father's child, I see him in my face. The older I get the more I see my mother as well. The resemblance to my mother bothers me. I've been trying so hard not to be her, that anything that reminds me of her I shut down. Everyone is so excited about me being married that they assume that Royce rocks my world on a regular basis.

We have sex about three times a week unless he gets really bogged down at work and school. Then we have sex more often. There have been times when I've gotten going and then I don't know what happens. It's like I fizzle out or something, I've tried to look up orgasms, or even simple climaxes. Sometimes I feel like it's going to happen, I'll get close. Then suddenly something happens. I don't know what it is, but I can't get there.

Royce has tried everything he can think of to try to help me, but it's no use. He's the only person I can talk about this with. I'm so embarrassed I can't tell Chareca. I pretend like our sex life is hot and heavy to everyone else. It's so embarrassing to say I don't know how to feel. That I don't know what I'm doing or what I'm supposed to do. I don't know what I'm supposed to feel or how I'm supposed to feel it. Standing in the mirror, I promised myself that whether or not I felt anything is irrelevant. I didn't want my husband to get bored with me, so I was going to try harder. I wasn't going to tell him anymore that I wasn't into this. I was going to fake it until I make it.

****

"Who is she?" I asked Royce annoyed with the female who was openly staring at us in line.

"Who?" Royce said as he lifted his eyes from me and then he spotted her. He clinched his jaw. "She's my ex from college roommate."

"Why would she be looking at you like that now behind something that happened so long ago?" I watched his face for a sign. When he lies, he flares his nostrils. It's not obvious, but I picked up on it when he's trying to sugar coat his mother's critiques of me. Now I watch for it, but I've never told him I know when he's telling the truth or not.

"When we became official, I suddenly broke up with my ex. It was pretty ugly actually. I don't blame her for looking at me like that. You're right it was a long time ago. Do you want to meet her?" He looked at her again.

"Why would I want to meet her?"

"Maybe you don't believe me and you need to verify my story."

"Stop being silly," I smiled at him.

"May I help who's next?" The popcorn girl asked.

"Yeah, let me get a tub with extra butter." Royce said not looking at me.

"No you don't, he can have a medium with a normal amount of butter." I told the girl.

"Gee, thanks mom!" Royce said then he kissed my cheek.

Mister all-star has been gaining weight lately. He tries to act like it doesn't bother him, but I know it does. It's like all his mom's negativity about my weight bypassed me and clung to her son. I'm so determined to prove her wrong that I make sure I get my exercise in as much as possible.

Royce isn't like Tavio; Tavio is a big guy naturally. He's still fast and agile with his thick build. While Royce is slowing down cause he's not meant to carry the little bit of weight he's gained. Royce isn't bad but he no longer has the washboard stomach that I loved. When I started cooking lighter, you know doing my part to help, he started complaining, and then I'd wake up to the smell of whatever delicious midnight monster of a snack he'd make.

Royce smiled at me as I eyed the nachos. I wanted them, but if I got them, he would pick something else up and then think it was justified. I told myself to be strong, and then he told me to take in the aroma of the fake processed government cheese. He told me he knew I wanted it. I shook my head no as my mouth filled with saliva. He pointed to the counter at the jalapeños, and all the other fixings that I like to use to dress up my nachos. When I started to weaken, he told me we would just put the nachos on the tray to see how it made the tray feel. We both started cracking up. He told the girl to give us two slurpees and a hot dog. When I started to protest he kissed my cheek and told me not to fight it cause my nachos were going to be so good to me. I stood there like he was making me get those doggone nachos. He told the girl to give me extra government cheese. He sucked my cheek and then he patted my butt and told me to get moving cause I was holding up the line. Before we got to the register, he picked up two boxes of candy as well. When I cut my eyes at him, he told me we were sharing. That girl was watching everything we did.

Royce and I sat on the aisle with our mountain of gross, fattening, and delicious snacks. That girl came in our theater and she looked around until she found us. Royce and I were looking at her. She sat a few rows ahead of us where she could easily turn around and watch us. That was dumb, we paid money to watch this movie, and that's what we were going to do. She could waste her time looking at us if she wanted to. That was on her.

I was in to the movie; it was very suspenseful and well written. Royce put his arm around my chair and I continued watching the movie. He moved in closer to me and then he sucked on my cheek. I looked at him and told him to cut it out cause I was in to the movie. He started kissing on my neck while his hand went down my shirt. That's when I noticed we had an audience. She didn't even try to pretend like she wasn't looking. I don't know why Royce feels like he has to put on a show for an acquaintance of his ex, but I wanted to watch the movie.

Royce was all over me and he knows he's barking up the wrong tree. I chose to ignore him instead of fight with him. His mouth did feel good, but I was watching the movie. Royce pulled my knee to open my legs and then his hand went under my skirt. Right when I was about to tell him to stop his hand felt unlike it ever has before. I looked at him and he kissed me. His kiss seemed even more passionate and then my body stiffened and then I couldn't sit still. Royce covered my mouth, I guess he knew what was about to happen and I was just catching on. I screamed into his hand, but it happened at the same moment that something happened on the screen. So everyone ahead of us was making noise in response to the movie. My hips took on a mind of their own as they moved to the rhythm of how he was strumming me like I was a guitar or something. When he released my mouth, I immediately put my head on his shoulder. My heart was pounding and I felt *relaxed*. He put my hand on him as he reached for a napkin. I was stroking him for a minute when he grabbed my hand and mumbled a curse. He grabbed his pants and then he hurried out of the theater. I thought he had to pee suddenly. The girl was still in her seat, so I sat back. As I licked my fingers I realized what Royce's curse was about. I had jalapeño juice all over my hands. Shocked I grabbed my purse and hurried out of the theater as the credits started to roll.

I stood outside the men's bathroom. I didn't know what else to do. I watched his friend look me up and down and then leave. After a while I opened the door and called out to Royce. I could hear water running as he whimpered that it burns. I bit my lip, I told him to get some wet paper towels and we'd figure out how to fix this at home. Royce looked so wounded as he walked slowly and carefully to the car. I drove us home and then he put an ice pack on his crotch. After talking to an advice nurse I got ointment for his irritated skin in the morning. It took a whole week for Royce to be able to laugh with me about the irony. I told him we didn't need those nachos, but he insisted. No those nachos didn't kill me, but if he just would've left well enough alone we might have been able to celebrate my first and only for a long time climax.

Royce

"What is that wife of yours feeding you?" My mother frowned at me as she scanned me.

"We happen to feed each other."

"Clearly she's not eating the same things she got you eating. This is ridiculous Royce! What's happening to you?"

Irritation burned in my stomach, "where's Dad?"

"You know better than to ignore my question as if I wasn't just speaking. I raised you better than that!"

I exhaled, "school, work, you name it. I've got a lot on my plate. I haven't had time to exercise. I'm going to work on it as soon as I pass the bar."

"You should at least get a workout with that girl. What good is she if she can't get that part right?"

"Stop it! You are talking about my wife! Alaina and I are fine. You need to be worried about where Brooke disappeared to or Rachel and her boyfriend."

"STOP IT!" Rachel ran out the bathroom with toothpaste all over her mouth and her toothbrush in her hand. "I've gotten my fair share of mother love for the day. It's your turn. Take it like a man Royce."

"You just don't want her to know your truths," I smiled.

Rachel put her free hand on her hip as she pointed her toothbrush at me. "Why should I care what either one of them says. Dad knows better than to judge me with all the crap he does. And she sticks around dealing with it like a weak pathetic excuse. I don't care what they think or have to say."

Rachel backed up and moved away from the table as my mother banged her fist on the table. "All of you are some of the most disrespectful brats a parent can have. I am not responsible for you getting fat, you being a married man's whore, your sister's indecision for what team she's batting for, or your brother acting like he doesn't have family. You all need to take responsibility for your own failures and mess ups! I..."

"You're the only one who cares, Dad doesn't care. He just wants us to be happy. You're the one who puts pressure on us to live up to your standards." Rachel snapped back.

"I know for a fact your father feels some kind of way about you messing around with a married man!"

"Yeah, he don't like it. But what can he really say to me? Don't do as he does?" Then she looked at me. "Royce, Dad hasn't been here in over a week. He comes home when he feels like it now. If you want to talk to him, page him or catch him at the store. Why would he come home to her?" Rachel slammed the door.

I thought my mother should've been hurt, but she was angry. She marched up to the door banging on it. She told Rachel she was kicking her out. Rachel laughed and said she'd move out when she felt like it. I decided to bow out and go find my father. My mother was going to be in her feelings from now until...

As I walked towards the store, my father pulled up. I told him I went by the house looking for him. He said I should always check the store first. I asked him why he stopped going home. He looked me up and down. "What's going on with you?"

My parents know how to make you feel uncomfortable. I gestured towards the building. "School, work, it's a lot."

My father looked me in my eyes, and then he told me to follow him to his office. He closed the door and he told me to have a seat. "Who is she?"

I frowned, "the only she in my life is my wife." I held up my ring hand as a reminder.

My father looked at me like I was an idiot. "Who's the female who held you up the night before the wedding?" I didn't say anything I just stared at him. "So you going to sit there and act like I don't know you. I don't know when you're lying or trying to get over on someone? I knew you were lying and I know it was a female."

"Why don't you and mom get a divorce? What's with all the torture?"

"Oh so this is supposed to be a sharing experience? You want me to tell you something just so I can help you? It's none of your business what happens between me and your mother."

"Just like it's none of your business what happens between me and my wife. BUT! It affects you. All these affairs and you two never taking each other seriously. She picks arguments with you just to feel like you're engaged with her."

He sat back in his chair, "I know. That's why I don't even talk to her no more. All I'm going to say is that your mother is not an innocent victim in all of this. When I decide to let her in on everything you all will know about it."

"Meanwhile you torture her?"

He shrugged, "your mother and I are just a technicality." I sat back shaking my head. " You love Alaina?"

"More than life itself," I said sincerely. "She's not like mom. She takes care of me, and she does everything she can to try to make me happy."

"Have you stepped out on her?"

"Not since we've been married. I don't ever want to hurt her like that."

"So that girl from our lunch date, you told her to stand down?"

My dad came out to have lunch with me one day by surprise.

135

This girl from my class has been relentless about pushing up on me. I was nice about it at first, but now I'm just blunt. I tell her to leave me alone and everything. She's not ugly, but I honestly don't ever want to feel what I've done to Vanessa ever again. "Of course! She's real stupid, she don't care."

My father watched me, and then he gestured towards my body. "This has guilt written all over you. You need to come clean and then move on. Your wife loves you, and she'll work with you through anything. Don't let what it is that's eating you up stop you from moving forward with your life."

****

I was looking through the accounting reports irritated cause I couldn't find my difference. I was about to scream when the door to my office opened as he knocked on it. It was my brother Brice and he had the biggest smile on his face as he opened the door. "FOOL! What happened to you?"

"I've been eating good and living with a good woman what you think?"

We hugged very tight, "yeah but you ain't been married long enough for it to be ok for you to let yourself go. Did Alaina blow up too?"

I smiled, "no. She's still as sexy today as she was the day I proposed if not sexier."

"So what's up? Is it cool for your brother to come by to have dinner with you two?"

"Let me call home, Alaina still works nights so she may have started dinner already." I called Alaina and she said it was perfect.

Brice hung around the office cracking everyone up. When we got to my place Alaina was too excited to see my brother. Brice is always a ton of fun, and they've always gotten along. When it was time for

Alaina to head out to work, she hesitated and actually considered calling in to work to hang out with us. She remembered something she needed to turn in tonight, so she had to go in. I walked Alaina out to the car as usual. We kissed our normal kiss good bye and then when I walked back inside Brice was looking at our wedding pictures with a smile. When he looked at me, he said I'm not technically fat yet, but I definitely let go. "How's your sex life?"

"WHAT? You don't ask a married man how his sex life is with his wife." Brice waited for my answer. "She tries but she's not into it."

"You smothered her?" He asked with a straight face then he laughed.

"No! You fool!"

"What are you holding back for?"

"I'm not! I've tried everything I can think of. I only got her there once and it was totally by accident. I tried to replicate it and it didn't work."

Brice looked at me like he understood, "public place?"

It's like he's reading my mind, "Yes!"

"It sounds like she's all in her head. She have a history of abuse?"

"Naw, don't you think I've asked all that? No abuse, and no man has ever touched her."

"She's all up in her head then. It's your job to get her to relax. I say you trick her."

"How?"

He leaned in as he smiled, "make her some spaghetti with some special oregano." He waited for me to catch on. Then he pulled a plastic bag out of his pocket.

"Weed? Aw man! Come on! I can't fool with that! Besides I don't cook, not like that. I'm the microwave king."

"Will she eat it if you make it?"

"Yes, but..."

"But what? I know you want to see her eyes roll back in her head one good time cause you're hitting it just right. She needs to relax, you only gotta do it once and then she'll be free."

"It's illegal."

"What's the difference between this and when she tries to trick you into eating healthy?"

"Good intentions," I laughed.

"The quest for an orgasm is good intentions."

"I don't know," I wanted to try it but I wasn't sure how she'd respond.

"I know you want to try it. Tell you what, you can blame it all on me. We'll make dinner tomorrow night. You can plead not guilty."

"That could work, she don't work tomorrow night." Brice smiled big at me, "have you done this before?"

Brice held his big smile and shook his head yes. "All I got to say is get ready."

Then there was a knock at the door. Alaina's father and brother were coming over to take a look at my car. It's been making a weird noise and Wesley thinks I need a new timing belt, whatever that means. We all sat out in the cool El Sobrante night air talking about life and things.

When Alaina got in the bed, I knew I had a couple of hours before I had to get up and get to school. I put my arms around her and kissed the back of her head. Alaina stirred in my crotch, I told myself to calm down and to wait for tonight. I was happy when she dosed off and fell asleep. I kissed Alaina before I ran out the door. I told her that Brice and I were making dinner tonight. She said a sleepy ok as she rolled over.

All day I was giddy and distracted. All day I tried to remember what it was like that time in the movies. It's hard to remember cause I always seem to remember the burning part more than anything else. I told myself to calm down cause there was always the possibility that it could not work and Alaina would forever be mad at me. Even if Brice didn't give me permission to blame him I was going to. Brice came just before quitting time for me. I couldn't help it I was excited and more energetic than I've been in a long time. Dad looked at us and smiled. In the grocery store I kept bouncing around. Brice kept telling me to chill out. I couldn't, he had no idea of what this night was going to mean to me.

Brice was carefully taking each item in the grocery bag out, explaining why it was important to our meal. Alaina came in the kitchen with the phone on her ear. "Hold on, he's here. Let me ask him. Just a minute." Then she took the phone off her ear. She kissed my lips, "can we keep Cara Mia over night? Chareca's...."

"NO!" I surprised myself by barking. Brice stretched his eyes at me to tell me to chill out. Alaina stared at me in surprise. I took a deep breath. "What I mean is, Brice is showing me how to make spaghetti then he's getting out. I got that wine Ben gave us out of the closet breathing in the corner. You can pick any chick flick you want I just want some alone time with you."

Alaina held back her smile, "all you had to say is you're missing me. You don't have to be so dramatic." Then she put the phone to her ear. She started laughing hard, "you heard that? I know girl, guess he has some ideas." She winked at me and then she walked out of the kitchen. As soon as she was out of eyesight Brice told me to calm down before I end up blowing my cover.

I took a deep breath; it's been three years almost four. I was well over due for tonight.

Alaina

I took a deep breath and told myself not to worry about the mountain of cheese that Royce was sure to put on the spaghetti. I was going to run in the morning with Chareca anyways. I talked to Chareca and then I decided to get in the shower and put on some comfortable sweats while Brice was here. I rinsed my hair and then I imagined it loc'd up in dreads. When I mentioned it to Royce he had a fit. He said he didn't like them. So I don't talk about it. I'm glad I listened to Chareca and mentioned it to him. Cause I had already made the appointment to get them started. I told myself it didn't matter. He doesn't understand my vision though. He's thinking big bulky locs like Whoopi Goldberg, and I was thinking much smaller than that. So my compromise has been braids, he at least tries to tolerate them.

When I emerged from the bedroom, I told them that dinner smelled great. Brice was packing his to go plate. Royce was lighting the candles on the table that he set for us. He had soft music playing and he was too excited. I looked at the kitchen shaking my head at the mess. He said he would take care of it later. I knew that was a lie. There was a salad bowl, French bread, and plates of spaghetti.

Royce told his brother to get out as he poured the wine. Brice laughed and then he gave me a hug goodbye. Royce told me to sit as he hurried his brother out of the door. As he came to sit the phone rang. Royce shot up and ran to the phone. He turned the ringer off, and then he told me this was our time. I felt so special.

I tried the salad and it was delicious. Royce watched me try everything. The spaghetti had a different taste to it. It definitely wasn't my daddy's spaghetti but it was good. Royce watched me eat with the biggest smile on his face. The wine complimented the spaghetti perfectly. I was so glad we waited to drink it. When I finished my plate Royce took it to the sink then he told me to pick a movie. When I acted like we were going to watch it in the living room he had another mini protest as he said he wanted to watch in the bedroom. I wished he would just say what he wanted to do. I licked my lips cause that wine was stronger than I remembered when we shared one with Ben. Royce kept watching my eyes, "good wine huh?"

"Stronger than I remember." Then he took me by the hand and led me to the bedroom.

He took the movie from me and put it on. I don't know why I was just standing there looking around like a fool. I felt, I felt, I felt *interesting*. I could still feel the grapes bubbling on my tongue from that delicious wine. Royce looked at me and smiled, then he told me I needed to get comfortable. He took off my top and my pants. He smiled at my underwear, "you're always matching. Thank you."

Then he kissed me, and he tasted like wine. This was a kiss like way back when we first dated. Back when it didn't feel like he was holding back anything from me. Once he stripped me of everything I laid on the bed and under the comforter cause it was a little cold. I told Royce to strip for me. He smiled and pointed to the TV, he asked if I was going to watch my movie? I waved him off. He turned off the movie, and then he went in the living room and turned on the stereo again. I don't even know what was playing but I was enjoying the show.

Although I try to tell Royce all of the time that I love him, and I don't care that he's gained weight, he always acts self-conscious about his current body. He won't walk around naked in front of me anymore. He's always got to be covered. Even though we don't have lots of money to splurge I think another bottle of this stuff is worth saving for. Royce even did a little dance like he used to for me. When he kissed me, he was relaxed and not holding anything back from me. He kissed every inch of my body and he let me touch him all over too. The feeling from the movies was back, the tingles and he hadn't even touched me there yet. I started to think about it, but Royce distracted me.

We were on our sides and I put my leg up on his hip, I kept kissing Royce and enjoying his touches. When he pushed in we both exhaled at the same time and then we looked at each other. My normal mechanical way of being didn't apply here. Royce was open to anything I did to him at this point. I pushed him on his back I looked down at him. He started to reach for the cover but I kicked it away. Everything felt so good and so open I didn't want it to change.

Royce kept looking in my eyes and telling me he loved me. I told him the same as I did what came naturally and not methodically like I normally do. This time it was as good to me as it normally is to him. The urge to move faster took over and my body told me to go Go GO! Royce who's normally quiet except for the occasional compliment or slight cheer was so gone that he kept moaning out loud which turned me on more and more. He was liking everything I was doing to him and it felt glorious. I could feel everything building and I couldn't stop, even if I wanted to. Royce was calling out my name and then I started calling his as my body tensed up in the sweetest sensation that made me go crazy. Royce's eyes bucked as I kept yelling and going. I didn't want this feeling to end. My legs started shaking and then everything started shaking on me. Royce rolled us over and he kept going while every movement made my explosion happen over and over again. Royce exploded and then he collapsed on me a little. He tried to hold himself up as if he thought he was going to smash me or something. I couldn't stop moving everything was still exploding within me. Royce grunted as I felt him come alive inside me again. When I rolled us over I was cold as if I was wet. I figured it was sweat and I couldn't stop myself. He kept going and going, when Royce couldn't go anymore, he used his hands until I finally passed out.

In the morning I looked at Royce as if I was still drunk, he smiled at me and caressed my face gently. He told me how much he loved me and he thanked me for last night. I was so excited it finally happened we were both free and it felt great. When Royce started to get up he searched the room for his T-Shirt. I told him to go to the bathroom; it wasn't like we had roommates or something. He ignored me and then he moved to the edge of the bed where his clothes were in a pile from his strip tease. He put on his T-shirt, and then he put on his pants. He went to the bathroom and then he got in the shower.

The bed was still wet from all of our love juices. I scooted close to one of the puddles and smelled it. It smelled like Royce and I. My body got excited as I thought about everything that happened last night. How free we were and how natural everything felt verses the way it's always been. Royce came out of the bathroom in his robe. He walked into the closet, lotioned and dressed in there. I sighed because we were back to the shame. I walked in the closet as he pulled up his pants. I walked up to him and kissed him with everything in me.

Royce smiled and said I needed to stop acting like I could go again. He was pulling back from me already. I wanted him to stay present with me in this closet. If it meant I had to go when everything was sore so be it. I didn't want to lose the feeling we had last night. I kissed him in desperation. Royce kissed me back, but he didn't get lost with me. He was starting to act like his normal self, and I don't know what I did to make him close up like this again. He went to the kitchen to eat breakfast. I sighed and started taking the bedding off of the bed. I tried not to cry as I told myself we at least had last night.

****

"Well, I think you need to decide what you're going to do. Cause I need to plan the rest of my life. Ken and I want to have another baby. Either I'm getting pregnant in the summer or the Fall." Chareca told Ben.

"Seriously? Either way that means you'll be pregnant in the Spring delivering in the summer or later. I won't have my assistant for some time. What am I supposed to do without you Chareca, you're my right hand." Ben said falling out into his chair.

"I can manage your appointments and schedule. You will have to manage your hoes on your own."

"This isn't fair! Alaina doesn't have any kids yet. Why can't you wait for her?"

"Royce and Alaina don't dictate what Ken and I do. Cara Mia will not be an only child."

"Oh come on, Chareca give me one more year! Please!"

Chareca looked at me then she looked at Ben, "NO! Get on my nerves and I will quit right now."

"Why you always threatening to quit? You know how much I need you," he pouted.

"I'm sure you could lay with these models without my help."

"I could but it would be like. *Oh I slept with him.* After you get done with them, they look at me like I'm the most romantic **God** they've ever laid eyes on. Come on, I know the difference without you. I'm not stupid."

"Decide what you're going to do." Chareca crossed her arms.

Ben grumbled and then he looked at the calendar like he was trying to work something out. "If you get pregnant in the summer you could still work. That means you'll deliver in the spring." He drummed his hands on his chair. "Chareca, you complete me. I'll find a way to work around whatever you and your husband decide to do." He grumbled. Then he thrust himself up, "I'm going into the studio. I'm not available if anyone needs me."

"What about my wine?" I called out.

"I'll call you when the shipment arrives." Then he waved me off as he walked into his studio.

Chareca chuckled then she sat in the chair at her desk. She smiled evilly, "you're not off the hook. What you need all this wine for?"

"I just really like it, a bottle a month is a reasonable request in my mind."

Chareca studied my face, "Alaina I've known you since we were little. You can say it's personal. That won't stop me from prying but I'll be a little more sensitive about my approach. You're acting like this wine is going to save your life."

My sudden outburst of tears surprised me too. "I can't talk about it. I just need it ok!"

Chareca popped out of her chair and hugged me. Then Cara Mia and lil T came running wanting to know if I was ok. I pulled back my tears and I told them I was fine. I looked at the time; Tavio was going to be done with his appointment shortly. It was the perfect excuse to get away from Chareca before she got on my case real bad. "Come on T," then I looked at Chareca. "You'll tell me how much I owe?"

"Ben's paying for it," she watched me.

I took little T's hand and then we left. "MAC why were you crying?" He looked at me with sad eyes.

I rubbed his cheek, "I'm ok baby. Let's go find your dad; I'm sure he's rushing to get to his little man."

We met Tavio at the Ferry building. He had on a suit and he smiled real big at both of us. "Let's have celebratory popcorn." He moved towards a vendor.

"What are we celebrating?"

"My slow ascension to my goals! I'm starting part time, but I'm on the right path." He smiled at little Tavio. "You have fun?"

"Yes, but MAC started crying when Ben walked away from her."

"Real tears?" He asked me.

"I'm a girl, it happens." I looked at my watch. "I need to get back. We're having dinner with Wesley and his girlfriend."

"Ok, we can have dinner before I take you home." He said to little Tavio.

"Ok," he sighed as he slumped.

Tavio's alarm went up immediately, "what's wrong?"

"Nothing," little Tavio looked at the ground.

Tavio was about to press him for an answer. I told him to wait until I was gone.

We walked quickly through the downtown San Francisco streets. Little Tavio looked out the window as Tavio and I made small talk. We were sitting in the four seats that sat two by two facing each other. Lil T was on his knees looking out the window, while Tavio and I talked.

An older gentleman came and sat in the fourth seat next to little Tavio. He smiled wide at Tavio. "I need to shake your hand young man." He reached out to shake Tavio's hand. "This is a real fine family that you have here." Tavio blushed and I grinned really big at him. "Look at you in your Sunday blue suit. Your woman looks good; clearly you don't beat on her. And this is a real nice young man. Do you have any others?"

Tavio started to say something, "no. Junior's an only child for now." I chimed in.

"The world needs more good kids like this one. I had to put my dog on some kids the other day; they tried to break into my house. They didn't know I had a dog cause I keep him inside until the night. He goes out in the dark, does his business then I bring him back in. He took a bite out of one of them too." He shook his head in agreement. "Do you know they momma come looking a hot mess talking about she called the coppers cause my dog bit her son. I said to myself thank you Jesus she called the cops! The coppers, they came too. Two big and mean looking coppers. As soon as she showed the boy's leg where my dog bit the boy, I showed the coppers where the boy busted out my screen breaking into my house. They were good coppers, they took the little punk to the hospital and they said he was going to the kid jail." He pointed his finger at little Tavio, "you got yourself a good kid right here. Make sure you stay on him and raise him right. He's going to be someone important." Then he stood up to get off of the train. "We need more black people like ya'll! Take care!" Then he got off the train.

Tavio and I laughed a little. "He didn't let us get a word in did he?"

"He was a cute old man." I tried to hold on to my smile. The closer we got to my stop the less I wanted to smile.

"What's wrong? How's the interviews going?"

"So far so good, I have a final interview **tomorrow** then they'll make their decision. I'm trying not to get my hopes up, but it would be nice to work a normal 8 - 5 like the rest of the world and have my weekends back."

"Ok, so what's wrong?" He watched my eyes.

"Nothing. I got a case of the blah, blahs I guess." Then a high school looking kid stood up to get off the train. He had short locs. I couldn't help it I stared at his locs with complete hair envy.

"When are you going to get yours?"

"Royce don't like them."

"So," Tavio said rolling his hands.

"He has to look at me. I wouldn't do that to him." I adjusted in my seat here we go.

"You don't wear certain things because he don't like them, you can't wear your hair the way you want cause he don't like it. Please tell me you have just as many opinions about his clothes and life period."   .

I looked at Tavio, "look! Just because you do all your bed hopping and barely slow down long enough to remember anyone's name doesn't mean you know anything. You haven't had a steady relationship yet. Who are you to tell me anything?"

Tavio was quiet for a minute. "You can sit over there with all your sass that you save for me, and wouldn't dare show him all you want. MAC you dang near disappeared on me. It don't matter if I'm married or not, you know I'm telling you the truth. You do everything that Royce wants; I bet you even wait on him to tell you when it's ok to have sex."

I gasped, HOW DID HE KNOW? "Shut up!" I said through clinched teeth as I nodded towards the baby who wasn't paying us any attention.

"He don't know what we're talking about. If you act like it's something then he'll know. You just mad cause I read you," he chuckled.

"I'm not doing this!"

He turned towards me, "all I'm saying is that if you disappear MAC. Eventually so will he. Be yourself."

When I got home, I showered and then I walked into the closet to pick a dress. Royce walked into the closet. He stopped and stared at me. I smiled at him and he smiled back. He picked out his clothes for dinner, and laid them on the bed. He sat next to his clothes and took his socks off. I decided that I wanted to try to assert myself. I stood in front of him and then I kissed him. He returned my kiss but he wasn't focused on me. When I lifted his shirt, he told me he was about to get in the shower. I smiled and said I could use another shower. His smile dropped, he said he needed his space in the shower.

Normally I would stop and act like his rejection didn't bother me. Today I wanted him to push his feelings to the side like I do for him and do this for me. I started kissing his neck and rubbing his ears. He sucked on my cheek then he nicely asked me to stop. He said he needed to shower and get ready. The fact that his body hadn't responded to me said he wasn't into this at all. I wanted to cry out of frustration. "I appreciate it Alaina, but you'd only be doing it for me, and I'd rather wait. I don't want a quickie right now." He kissed my forehead then he went in the bathroom.

I dressed and then I waited. At dinner Wesley and his girlfriend were late, and they came in all smiles and goofy. I was so jealous I could've spit nails at them. What's wrong with me? So what if I can't get there, I still enjoy the intimacy with my husband. I guess if I don't get there he feels like it's a waste of energy unless he wants to exert it. I was drinking my wine hoping for a physical miracle in this glass. Wesley looked at me and his smile changed, "Alaina. You're starting to look more and more like Mom."

I could've died, kick me when I'm down. I rolled my eyes, "WHATEVER! NO I DON'T! You look like her, I look like my daddy!"

"Our Dad!" His nostrils flared.

I looked at Wesley, he knows what I meant. "Right!"

Wesley went from happy to pissed that fast. His girlfriend and Royce looked completely lost. "Get up!'" He threw his napkin on the table.

"Wesley, I was agreeing with you," I waved him off.

"I will drag you out of here! GET UP NOW!" He was standing and about to embarrass me.

Royce was already looking around to see who was watching our table. I got up and marched out of the restaurant. I took us out by the cars. "Calm down Wesley! I didn't mean anything by…"

Wesley was so mad; I imagined his hands going across my face. My big brother has never hit me, but in this moment, I knew he wanted to even though he wasn't going to do it. "WHAT'S WRONG WITH YOU?"

"I didn't mean anything like you're thinking. I don't like thinking about her. I don't want to hear that anything about me is like her."

"WHY? SHE'S OUR MOTHER!"

"She was selfish and evil!"

"You're so above having a selfish moment. A moment of weakness!"

"A moment? Come on Wesley we both know it wasn't a moment."

"You have some pent up feelings towards me because of what happened?"

"NO!" I wrapped my arms around myself. "You're just as much of a victim as I am. As Alaysia was!"

Wesley gasped like I hit him in the chest. "ALAINA!" He yelled into the night air. "WHY TONIGHT? WE COULD TALK ABOUT HER AND ALL OF THIS ANY OTHER NIGHT!"

"MY SISTER DIED BEHIND HER SELFISHNESS!" I screamed as I bent over.

"OUR SISTER!" He turned his back to me and took two steps away. "Alaina you need help."

"Help for what? I'm fine!" I swallowed my emptiness.

"I can't do this with you tonight. You've killed my whole vibe." He walked back towards the restaurant angrily. I followed behind him. Wesley asked our waitress for the check and she pointed to Royce. "How much do I owe? We're leaving!"

Royce looked at me like he didn't understand. He handed the billfold to Wesley. Wesley slapped his credit card in the billfold, and then he nicely asked the waitress to process his card quickly. "Are you ok?" His girlfriend asked him.

"No! We're leaving!"

"We didn't share our news." She reminded him lowly.

Wesley shifted his weight from leg to leg. The waitress gave him the billfold and he signed his receipt. He dropped it on the table. "The night is ruined! Come on baby let's go." He said gently to his girlfriend. She gently touched his hand and looked at his face. He exhaled, "you're going to be an auntie." Then he walked out.

I started crying and Royce got up quickly as he told me it was time to go. He was so embarrassed. We rode home in silence. I changed my clothes to get ready for work. "What was that?"

I waved him off, "family stuff."

"I'm family," I could tell by his tone he wasn't letting it go.

"Let it go," I said walking into the living room. My plan was to take a nap before it was time to go. Apparently Royce wasn't letting it go.

"You've got all these secrets no wonder you can't be free with me! I'm trying to help you."

"You're trying to help me? Mister can't let his nakedness see daylight! If you're that embarrassed about your body go join a gym. You've got all these rules about everything and I try to work with you, but you're ridiculous!"

"Oh so you bust one nut after how many years and suddenly you're an expert? I've been having sex, and good sex at that, long before you!"

"Clearly you didn't learn anything if your wife feels like this!"

"Your inabilities are not my fault!"

"Of course they are fat boy!" Royce was so mad he marched back into the bedroom and slammed the door.

I grabbed my keys and purse then I slammed the front door when I left. I knew our neighbors were going to be mad. He'd be kicking himself if I got in a car accident on my way to work.

I slept in my car until it was time to work. When I got home, I was going to sleep on the couch. Royce came in the living room and told me to get in the bed. He put his arms around me and fell asleep as if we hadn't argued. Just like he always does.

Royce

I got up to get in the shower and Alaina was laying there staring off into nothing. I felt bad about last night; I was on defense from not understanding what was happening with her and Wesley. I laid back on the bed and then I kissed Alaina's cheek. I told her I was sorry for making her upset. Alaina exhaled like she was still irritated. I kissed her neck, and when she didn't flinch at my mouth on her neck, I started sucking on it. "Stop Royce! Why would you even try to have sex right now? This is not about your feelings!" Then she sat up irritated. "Why are we doing this? You're not happy, I'm not happy! Why should we keep going?"

I didn't see that coming, I screamed! "WHAT ARE YOU TALKING ABOUT? WHO BREAKS UP OVER AN ARGUMENT?"

"We're not even arguing over what we're mad about! There's too many unresolved issues!"

"Unresolved? What are you talking about? This is the first I'm hearing that you're unhappy!"

"No it's not, you just don't pay attention."

I took a moment to get my thoughts together. I took a deep breath and then I sat up and put my emotions in check. "Why are you unhappy?"

My sudden calmness startled her. "Whenever something happens with someone else you always have to make it about you. Last night you should've left me alone. Let me cool down, but you turned my argument with Wesley into an argument between us."

"We've been married for how many years now? You know everything there is to know about my family, but I know nothing about yours."

"Please you know everything you need to know. Besides I know I don't know everything."

I took a deep breath, "so what are we supposed to do, compare notes?"

"Why are you so afraid of what people think? That time in the movies was to prove a point to someone else. That was the last time. You..."

"You are my wife! I'm supposed to screw you in public like you're a hoe or something? I do recall getting burned by that whole exhibition scene." I got off the bed, "I feel like this, when you have something real you don't need to put on a scene for others. You're my wife; you're not supposed to be on display for anyone but me. If you can't deal with me wanting what we share to be private then go file for your divorce. If you're going to be childish and talk about divorce over an argument then go now, before there's kids in the middle of our battle."

Alaina tried to pull back her surprised expression. "It's not childish to need excitement."

"What does excitement have to do with why you're all pushed out of shape?" I gave her a minute to answer, she was quiet. "I'm not going to have a conversation like this with you again. Next time you bring up divorce or splitting up you better be on your way to file. If you want to talk to me or you feel like you need some attention just say that. This unnecessary dramatic scene is what I'm not going to do. You have no idea how many hearts were broken so I could live in yours. I'm not perfect and neither are you. Either do something about it or shut up!" Then I got in the shower. I was telling myself to calm down.

Alaina walked in the bathroom. I thought she was going to use it. I looked up at her standing on the toilet barely looking over the shower. She had my big gulp cup in her hand. She was still mad, she told me, "you shut up!" Then she threw ice water on me.

Alaina

I ran out the house as fast as I could. Although I know he wasn't going to run out the shower after me, I didn't chance it. I went to my dad's. My plan was to lay in my own bed and clear my head, make up with Wesley, he tried to pay me a compliment, and I tore into him. That wasn't right. Royce will be fine once I go into my goodie box and put on something nice for him. When I pulled up to my dad's house there was a car I didn't recognize in the driveway behind his. I parked next to the curb and then I used my key to open the door. There was an overnight bag by the door. The smell of breakfast cooking hit my nose as I walked in on my dad in his robe, drawers, and socks. He was kissing some woman who smelled like freshly sprayed perfume as if she spent the night. She was fully dressed and it looked like she was on her way to work. I cleared my throat since they obviously didn't hear me come in the door. Could this day get any worse? The woman looked at me as my father started kissing her neck. "Baby it's Alaina." She tapped him.

I threw my hands in my jacket pocket, "baby?"

My dad looked so guilty as he tried to straighten up. "Baby girl, what are you doing here?"

"I didn't realize I needed to call first! What's going on? Why is she calling you baby?"

"Baby girl this is my girlfriend Marlene."

"Girlfriend?" I felt like I was going to be sick.

The woman stood there looking stuck like she didn't know what to do. She turned around and turned off the stove. "Yes." My father said letting go of his smile.

"Why would you need a girlfriend?"

"Baby, I'm going to go. I'll see you tonight?" She waited for his answer.

"Yes of course sweetheart, I'll see you tonight."

"What's going on!" I yelled.

"Little girl, you better remember who you're talking to. Sit down and I will be with you in a minute." He said sternly to me. He turned to that woman and smiled as he walked behind her to the door. She picked up her bag and said something lowly to him. They lightly chuckled and then he did it. HE KISSED HER! I shot out of my seat! My father cut his eyes at me and I didn't say anything. He shut the door and locked it. He whistled as he walked back to the kitchen. He made his plate then he sat at the table. He looked at me and then he shook his head. "You couldn't possibly think I'd never have anyone." Then he put a fork full of food in his mouth.

I was so angry I started shaking. "How long have you been seeing her?"

He shrugged as he moved his head while he thought about it. "Off and on for years. Look, I wasn't going to put it in your face. I kind of figured you'd react like this. I'm not old and decrepit, I have needs too."

"You're a hypocrite! You told me to push back my needs to remain chaste and pure. The whole time you were sleeping around!"

My father drank some of his coffee, "*so*."

"So? So? So, you're a hypocrite!"

He shrugged again, "*so*."

"How dare you demand of me what you weren't even doing?"

He frowned at me, "I'm your father. Not your equal. I didn't have to keep Marlene from you, and you still better have worn white on your wedding day."

"Hypocrite!" I stood up.

"So what," he said calmly.

"Were you cheating on my mother?"

His eyes turned evil, "no." His controlled anger made me move closer to the door.

"Both of you tried to raise us with all these morals that neither of you upheld."

"We are not equals Alaina; I can raise you to be better than me. Better than your mother, whether I'm doing it or she ever did! As long as you don't become her, you're fine."

I walked out the door slamming it. I expected him to call me back inside. He didn't even look out the window. I drove around crying and crying. Once I knew for sure Royce was gone, I went home. I got clothes for work tonight then I left. I wandered around all day, and then I slept in my car until it was time to go to work.

When I got off work, Royce's car was parked next to mine. As I approached the cars, someone grabbed me and I screamed. It was Royce, and he looked annoyed. That annoyance turned into anger as he went off. He wouldn't let me get a word out. He told me to leave my car and that we would come back later for it. I sat in the car like a little kid who was in trouble.

He asked me where I went all day. I told him about my morning. He had a guilty look on his face as I told him about Marlene. Apparently I'm the only person who didn't know about her. I dug into him asking him how he could know something so important about my father and think it wasn't important to tell me. He calmly said it wasn't his business to tell. It was easier to be mad at Royce than to deal with everything going on in my head and in my heart.

No my father and I aren't equals, but if he can't lead by example why was it imperative that I follow the rules he laid out for me? Wesley sure as heck didn't follow them, why do I have to be the only one? Times like this, when I need to talk the emotions out. Have mutual understanding for all that I'm going through, I wish my sister were here. Who knows, we'd probably be the twins that ended up hating each other instead of being close as adults.

Although we were always hugging and kissing each other as far as I can remember.

When we got home, I laid on the bed with my shoes and everything on. I know Royce hates it, but I lacked the energy. Royce undressed me and then he snuggled up next to me. When he kissed my neck I expected him to keep going, but instead he started talking. He told me about the first time he found out about his father cheating on his mother. I could tell it wasn't easy at times to talk on this level. I recognized the struggle and I kept thanking him for sharing with me. That encouraged him to keep going. At times, I found myself finishing his sentences as he looked for the words to express his thought. I've never felt so understood ever!

Although I laid on this bed too emotionally spent to think of anything else. I apologized for taking everything out on him. Royce accepted my apology, we made slow love. When it was getting really good to me, I asked him to turn on the light. I wanted to look at him as he took me over. Why did I ask that? Why did I stop us? He quickly and abruptly finished and acted like he didn't know what I was asking for.

Chapter 10

Tavio

I returned to my place from dropping little Tavio off at preschool. Nadia pulled up fast and anxious. We barely made it in the door. She was on me fast and hard. Then she went in the bathroom and washed up. She kissed my forehead and said she was blissfully late for work. I tried to fight off the feeling of being used. It didn't used to be like this. I guess when I wasn't looking for more, this situation was fine.

I thought about calling Eva like I do every morning or late night. I miss my friend even if I wasn't much of one. I turned on my notebook to blog and get some work done. I don't remember falling asleep, but the phone woke me up. I cleared my throat, "hello?"

"How are you?" Eva said quietly.

I sat up and focused my eyes. "I've been worried about you. I've wanted to call you, but I figured you hated me so I didn't want to bother you."

"I do hate you, but I miss my friend more." I smiled, "so Unique is going to have a game in Florida. She reached out to Rickie since she was going to be out that way. Are you going?" Her tone was cold, I wasn't used to it.

"No, this is the first I'm hearing of it."

"Good, then I'll go."

"Why wouldn't you go if I was going to be there?"

"Tavio, I'm not ready to see you or be around you. I'll fall back into old habits, and I'm the one butt hurt when it's all said and done."

"You don't think I'm hurting?"

"You broke up with me!"

"So you'd rather ignore our indifference, try to stick it out making each other miserable and postponing our breakup."

"I'm still in love with you," she said in defeat.

"I'm about to punk out." She chuckled a little, "I still love you. None of this changes any of that. I think about you multiple times a day. I'm over here bouncing around without you. You were my future, now the future's just a dark and scary place. I love you Eva and I'm sorry it couldn't be different."

"So... If our paths should cross how should we react to each other?"

"What would you like?"

"We've already had the best breakup sex. Oh and by the way, you went out with a **BANG**!" Both of us started laughing hard. "I don't think it would be fair to either of us to go there again. Cause if we did we might as well be together for better or for worse."

"And I don't want a for worse with you. I don't think I could handle it."

"Me neither," she said quietly.

"So then we'll be cool if our paths should ever cross again, but we know we can't cross that boundary."

"Right."

"I still love you Eva that's never going to go away."

"You promise?" She sounded like she was trying to regain her composure.

"Yes."

"I love you too, and it's never going to go away. Goodbye Tavio."

"Goodbye Eva," I smiled. "But you still going to call me right?"

"Maybe once a year or whatever."

I smiled, "ok."

Eva

Vanessa, Katrina, and I have been like the three amigos. Turns out that Vanessa is a lot of fun and she's just as driven and intelligent as Katrina and I. She doesn't compete for men or anything like that.

She told Katrina and I her heart-wrenching story about the guy that ran her out of California. Appears they dated for like a year and then they broke up. She said she was heartbroken, but she kind of understood. She said at the time she was going overboard with the idea that all men wanted a freak. She said she loved this guy so much she didn't want to wait for him to ask her. She wanted to be his everything. She said he was kind of a prude, but he was right she needed to pull back some. She said she was experimenting to the maximum and she was kind of relieved that he wasn't in to it. She said when he came back to her she mellowed out and allowed herself to be free. She said that looking back she can see now that she was settling but she loved him so much. When I asked her how she was settling, she said he didn't like to take risk. His idea of frisky was doing it on the couch. She said she wanted adventure and passion. She said he was fine otherwise, but now she knows she needs more.

I told her about Tavio and how he was down for anything that I was down for. I told her he was the only guy to take me *there*. James was *fine*. Looking back, I don't know why I even messed with him like I did.

By far, Vanessa was the most experienced amongst the three of us. Sometimes I would even gasp at the things she's done. Every so often, we get a room at a hotel to get away from our families. The stuff Vanessa told us that weekend made me miss sex, not enough to go out and have some though. Katrina was asking specific questions, I knew she was planning on trying something. The next night she spent the night with Chauncey. That next weekend he was proposing ahead of schedule. Vanessa and I high-fived Katrina when she blushed over how good she got her man.

Just like that, we were planning Katrina's wedding, which was going to take place right after our graduations. Katrina said their schedule for children wouldn't change, but Chauncey couldn't wait to marry Katrina any longer than he absolutely had to.

Our trip to Florida was a much-needed break from everything. Our parents informed us that they were having Sunday dinner with or without us. We told them to enjoy their dinner. Vanessa and her mother have joined us for Sunday dinners as well. Vanessa asks me why I don't give Colby a chance. I told her like I tell him, I just can't. With Tavio and I's breakup Colby has made it known to everyone that he's interested in me. His parents seem perfectly ok with it. I just can't do it, I don't know why. I just can't! Vanessa tells me to stop playing with the future doctor and to give him a try. She smiles and says he's a freak, she said she can tell by the way he is. I shrug it off. I don't know, I just can't do it.

After we checked into our hotel, we went to Rickie's place. Rickie and her husband's place was nice and modest. Rickie made their apartment a nice little home, where if it weren't for my grandmother my walls would still be barren in our place. Rickie and everyone hit it off; her husband was at work so we made our way over to the hotel that Unique was staying in.

Unique met us in the lobby. She was tall and muscular, her body was always built but she still was very feminine. Rickie and I got so excited when we saw her. We screamed with excitement and we hugged in a circle really tight. Unique introduced us to a couple of her teammates and then we went to the lounge area. Unique wasn't twenty-one yet, but she said drinking wasn't her thing anyways. The three of us told stories about our childhood that kept everyone in stitches. Unique was so much like Tavio, you automatically loved them and they blended in nicely everywhere. I was focused on Unique as she spoke when Rickie cursed and fell back in her seat. Everyone looked at her and then the shadow over our section caught our attention.

James stood there smiling at me like he just knew I would ever think positively of him. "Ladies." He said to our section. I gritted my teeth trying to hold back my hatred. "Why you sitting over there girl? Get up and give your man a proper greeting, I've been looking for you for a long time."

I looked at everybody, "let's go!" I stood up.

"Hold on! Where you supposed to be going?"

Everyone stood up, "where's security? This pest isn't going to go away without an exterminator!"

"Pest? What you afraid I'm going to tell your business?" He said loudly.

My face started stinging, "come here!" I said through my teeth. I led James by the receptionist desk where we could be easily seen by everyone just in case he tried something. Far enough away so that they wouldn't hear my business. "GO AWAY JAMES! IF YOU DON'T LEAVE ME ALONE, I'M CALLING THE POLICE AND TELLING THEM THAT YOU'RE HARASSING ME!"

He smiled, "what did you have? A boy or a girl?"

"I didn't have a baby." I folded my arms trying to hold back the emotions and hatred that flooded my brain.

He tilted his head to the side, and then he stepped in my face and grabbed me by my hair. "I know you know better than to lie to me. You lied about being pregnant?"

If I screamed my sister would come running and then everyone else would come. The girl behind the counter looked scared and stuck, she didn't move. "No, I didn't lie."

"Well then what happened?"

"I'm going to call the police!"

"They gotta catch me first and you'll already be dead! Answer me!" He jerked my hair hard.

"I got rid of the baby!" I cried.

"How? I didn't give you the money, and it's not like you could afford it."

"I got a loan and I went to student health."

James got mad and threw my head towards the floor, "I ought to kick your butt right now! How you think it's ever ok to raise an eyebrow to anything that belongs to me?"

"You said it wasn't your baby!"

"Well we both know better don't we! You was supposed to come home to your man." He stood over me angry like he wanted to hit me. "You still out there?"

"No, I switched to Berkeley."

"California?"

"Yes!" I got up off the ground. I looked at the girl behind the counter. "Can you call the police? Why are you standing there watching him man handle me?"

"You pick up that phone and I'm going to blow your brains out!" Then he looked at me, "you think California is going to save you from me? You belong to me! This summer if you're not home looking for me, I'm going to kill your grandmother, and your sister. Got it?" He looked me in my eyes.

"Got it," I said lowly.

"After I kick your butt for killing my baby, I'll let you get pregnant again. I don't care if you're still in school or not! You're coming home, and I'm gonna take care of you."

"Why? You got like two or three other kids!" I spit at him.

He reared up like he was going to hit me, and I braced myself. He smiled like he liked my reaction, "stop listening to rumors and worry about what I tell you." He looked me up and down, "you better be happy that I'm too tired right now. Next time you need to show your baby daddy some respect and stop trying to front in front of your friends."

"Everything ok?" Unique said looking at my hair as she approached us.

"We were just catching up on old times, and how I'm going to bless her with my child soon."

Unique looked at me, then she came and stood next to me. "You ready to go, we got a long drive ahead of us," she said to me.

"Ok," I said wondering what all did she hear. The girl behind the counter was still looking scared.

"James, was it?" Unique said and my heart dropped.

"And you are?"

"Linda, Linda Yee."

"Bring her to hang out with us when we celebrate your graduation." Then he looked Unique up and down, "alright then Linda. I'll see you soon." Then he walked out the door.

"You guys we've got to go for a ride on the freeway. Otherwise he'll know we're staying here." Unique told her friends, then she looked at me. "You were pregnant?" She wasn't really asking me. She was letting me know she heard everything.

Tears came to my eyes cause I knew it was pointless to ask her not to tell Tavio. "Can I explain?"

"It's not like it's any of my business. I think you should focus on making sure Rickie and her husband are safe."

Unique gave me a hug and then she and her friends walked out with us. They got in one car and we got in my rental. I told Rickie what he said. She waved it off saying she lives in Orlando now. She said he would be tearing up Daytona looking for them.

The rest of the trip I was on edge. We got to the airport extremely early so I called Tavio expecting him not to be home. My heart dropped when he answered. "What are you doing home?"

"Why would you call me and expect not to talk to me?" He was in a good mood.

I started crying hard, "has Unique called you?"

"No, what's wrong?"

"I messed up ok."

"Ok."

"He was just a space filler. I was passing time with him until we could be together."

"Ok." His tone was even no emotion.

"When I told him I was pregnant he did it on purpose apparently and then he denied me. He made me beg him for help and he refused me. His plan was for me to come home and depend on him. That's when you sent me the money."

"Why didn't you tell me?"

"I couldn't! No one knew!"

"You should've told me. Instead you let him harden your heart."

"While you let yours fill up with a son that wasn't from me!"

"What difference does that make? You let him turn you off to kids because you didn't want to have his. What about ours? I don't care about what happened with him and I wish you would've had enough faith in me to come to me with this. We would've been fine. I could've been there for you."

"How? You were busy keeping your own secrets. You know what it doesn't matter. I wanted you to hear it from me and not your sister," then I hung up.

****

"Ok so, that's my cousin Maurice the one I've been telling you about." Vanessa pointed at a very handsome guy. "He has a good job, good credit, no kids, recently single."

"But is he a good guy?"

"He's the best! He's always looked out for me and protected me."

"Does he like black women?"

Vanessa laughed, "that's his mom." She pointed to a chubby very brown skinned woman. "All of her boys love her very much and say they want someone like her."

I looked him up and down. "Doesn't mean he'd like me." I was looking for something about him that reminded me of Tavio. I don't even feel bad about it. Tavio's a good guy. If anything about this guy reminds me of him he's good.

I took a deep breath and approached the group of men with Vanessa. They all said hello to her and gave her hugs. Then they looked at me. Vanessa explained that I was her friend and she's been telling me how fine all the men in her family were and she wanted me to see for myself. One by one they introduced themselves. Each one flirted which made me blush. A family of charmers I see. I know Vanessa pointed out Maurice, but I got goose bumps when Kiev touched me. I think it was his eyes or something. Whatever it was I smiled at him, which seemed to kind of catch him off guard. I followed Vanessa through the house to the kitchen where we were enlisted to help prepare and serve. Kiev came in the kitchen and volunteered to help as well. All the women smiled but didn't say anything.

Kiev stood at the sink next to me smiling at the greens as he washed them. "You're in school?"

"Yes."

"How much longer you got?"

"I graduate this summer, are you in school?" I asked.

"No." He kept smiling, "where you moving to once you graduate?"

"I'm staying out here. I've already moved my grandmother out here."

"We have Sunday dinner at her place every Sunday." Vanessa's mother interjected into our private conversation.

"Aunty!" He said like she embarrassed him.

The other women laughed at her, "oh I'm sorry. I was just trying to help.

That's when I realized that all conversations had stopped so that they could listen to us. Kiev and I didn't say anything else. We looked at each other and smiled from time to time.

When it was time to eat, everyone helped bring all the food out. We took our seats, and I held back my smile when Kiev sat at our table. Vanessa brought Maurice to our table and a few of her other cousins came as well.

They all asked me questions about living in California, and Florida. Like are there really alligators roaming around freely? And are there earthquakes every five minutes of everyday? I laughed and had a good time answering their questions. Then I asked them questions in return.

Maurice asked me why I was single. I told him I was very picky about who I let in my heart. I don't open it freely. When he asked me why not? I asked him if he let everyone who found him attractive in just because they did. He smiled and said he considered each person who presented themselves. There it was, that playboy vibe. I was completely turned off now. I exhaled and said, *I don't take disappointment and rejection easily*. Maurice thought he was being charming by asking who would reject me. I told him I'm not a good fit for a lot of people. I told him I have rejection issues that go pretty deep. I don't trust easily and I'm not open to a lot of nonsense. Kiev nodded and Maurice caught it. "How's the divorce coming Kiev?"

Kiev looked irritated, "you're an idiot!" He got up and walked away.

Maurice and a couple of the other cousins laughed, I shot Vanessa a look and she looked at Kiev with sad eyes. I excused myself and I went to the bathroom. When I came out the bathroom, I didn't see Kiev anywhere. I didn't return to the table. I hung out with Vanessa's mom while Vanessa remained with her other cousins. I kept looking for Kiev and I didn't see him anymore for the rest of the night.

****

I've been trying to be cool, but I want to ask Vanessa so many questions about Kiev. I was disappointed when she said that Maurice asked about me after her family's get together. It had been a few weeks and I was about to let it go, when Vanessa asked me if I would consider someone who's been married before. I got butterflies immediately! I got them under control as I said a nonchalant *divorce wasn't an issue.* Vanessa asked me if I ever would consider someone who was more artistically inclined, instead of corporate driven. That's when I slumped, I hadn't ever thought of my man not trying to be the next entrepreneur on the top one hundred list. I was quiet for a minute then I told her I didn't know. That was my honest answer. Then I asked her why she was asking. Vanessa sighed then she moved her hands. "Kiev has been asking about you. He seems to think you two had some kind of connection. Kiev is very dear to me and I don't want another female to hurt him."

"Whoa! You think I would hurt him?" I blinked my eyes to make sure I was hearing her right.

"E! Don't get all-sensitive, we're just talking. However, I'm being honest about what I see."

"See? You don't see nothing." Then I pushed my salad around my plate.

"Look at how you string poor Colby along? The doctor is ready for you and you always play the game. Maybe you will get with him or maybe you won't. I don't want that for Kiev. He's been through enough."

"Shouldn't that be our decision?"

She exhaled, "Kiev is already gone. I just don't want to see him get hurt again."

"He's not a child," then I picked up my glass of water. "Now tell me about him like you did Maurice. Why do you adore him so much?"

"He's one of the bigger cousins who always looks out for us. He actually cares about what happens to us. He was the only one kicking a fuss about the situation when my cousin Nadia got married. He tried to protect her, but in the end she told him to let her go." Vanessa said like it was a painful memory.

"What am I missing? Fill me in."

Vanessa looked around the food court, "stick around my family long enough and you'll find out." She was quiet for a few more minutes. "Anyways, I need to change the subject so I'm going to. My father and stepmother want to take my mom and I out to dinner Saturday night. Do you think it will be too much of an interference for Katrina if I ask her if we end our evening with a free meal with my parents?"

"Please! With all the money she's dishing out for her wedding she should welcome a free meal. Ask her when we get back to the office."

We talked about other stuff but I was on cloud nine. Kiev was interested in me, and he's the first guy since Tavio that I've been interested in. His protectiveness over his family was definitely a Tavio feature and a good one to have.

When we got back to the office Katrina and Chauncey were lip locked in an extreme tongue-wrestling match. I couldn't tell you who was winning, but they were both completely into the kiss. I cleared my throat as I looked around but not at them. I reminded her that her mother had already told them to cut the madness out. She said her office was a place of business and not their personal make out headquarters. Chauncey bit his lip as he reluctantly pulled away from Katrina. They were locked in a love stare that was sickening to watch.

Vanessa and I said our goodbyes as we laughed at those two. Then she went to her department, and I went to mine. I couldn't stop thinking about Kiev all day. He asked about me, he asked about me! I kept telling myself to stop jumping the gun. Maybe we'd never work out, but I couldn't stop thinking about his lips. I wondered what his body looked like. Tavio has always been thick, but his stomach is a solid six-pack. His thunder thighs were always muscular and shapely. It was like any supposed fat turned into muscle as soon as he gained it. I could stare at Tavio naked all day and that wouldn't be enough. Kiev is tall and slender; I wonder if he works out at all? I hate to work out; right now, I'm on the good graces of good genes and youth. Last time I saw my mother she wasn't fat, but I was a very little girl then. Who knows what she looks like today, heck if she's even still alive. Both of my parents could be dead for all I know. My dad was on the thin side too. I don't know much about the women in his family. They knew about us and didn't care. Would it bother me if Kiev didn't have any muscles? I don't even know. I shook my head; I can't focus on the physical aspect. What does an artistic soul mean? Does that mean he doesn't work? He has no income? That would be a problem for me. I never imagined myself with someone who wasn't knee deep in corporate America. I took a deep breath and I told myself to relax. To go with the flow, and to stop letting the thought of this man make me think about my parents; people who have never been concerned with me so why should I concern myself with them?

Tavio

Her eyes were searching for me, even though she was trying to act normal about it. Every time I come in the Post Office she's all smiles and eyes. Nadia has been hit or miss for the past couple of months. She doesn't seem to have much time for me anymore. I asked her if Stan was back but she quickly says no and then changes the subject. If her boyfriend comes back, we always said we'd go our separate ways. So I don't see what the big deal is; without the illusion of Eva, MAC being married, and now this distance between Nadia and I. I feel so lonely when I don't have my son. Good news is that I get to have him more now that Tempest is married. I still have way more downtime than I want. I spend time with my parents and my brother. I'd love to be in a real relationship right now. I'd love to be working towards something real. "I can help who's next." She called out as she smiled at me.

"That would be me." I said hurrying to her counter.

"What can I do for you today?"

"I have a question about my PO Box, can I show you?" I held up the key.

"Sure, meet me in the lobby." She said as she closed her computer. When we met, she smiled. "What's your question."

I looked her up and down, "I have so many. But you're asking about the box aren't you?"

She blushed, "what's your question?"

"Can I have your phone number; I'd like to take you out on a date."

"Boy, you don't even know me. I could be really crazy!"

"Or you could be perfect, only one way to find out for sure." I winked at her.

"How old are you, if you don't mind me asking."

"22, how old are you?"

She put her hands on her hips, "30."

"Ok, so now that that's out of the way. Can I have your number?"

She looked surprised which made her blush harder. "What's your question about your box?"

"Oh right," I waved her on to follow me. I showed her that my box door needed a little oil cause it seemed to be rusty. We went back to her window and she filled out a maintenance slip for me. Then she gave me a separate piece of paper with her number on it. What kind of name is *Breezy*? I shrugged maybe it was her nickname or something.

When I pulled up to the house, my little brother was outside with a girl. They were doing that can't look at each other directly in the eye cause they'll blush too much stuff. I remembered junior high school like it was yesterday. "Dakarai, who's your friend?"

"Jessica this is my big brother Tavio, this is Jessica." He said pushing past his blushing expression.

"Nice to meet you," I said to her then I looked at my brother. "You are bold! You talking to her right here when momma could come out at any minute and flash on you."

"Momma's met Jessica already." He smiled at me.

"WHAT?" My face dropped. I pointed to the street sign across the street. "She would've hung me up on a pole for bringing a girl anywhere near here."

"Yeah, but you still brought Eva and her sister around."

I cut my eyes at him, "why do you remember that? And I had to bring them as Unique's friends."

Dakarai shrugged, "I guess she's changed."

"Is this your girlfriend?"

"Yes," he said through clinched teeth.

"Does she know that Jessica is your girlfriend?"

"YES!" He said again through clinched teeth. I was embarrassing him but I was appalled at the blatant favoritism.

"MOMMA!" I yelled as I marched towards the house. Dakarai and Jessica started laughing. My momma opened the door with concern all over her face. "Why Dakarai get to have girlfriends over?"

She pointed towards them, "They're standing on the sidewalk talking."

"I couldn't stand on the sidewalk and talk to nobody."

"You got the nerve to question me? Mister Father at eighteen years old!" Dakarai and Jessica started laughing louder. "Dakarai is a good kid and I don't want him sneaking to do anything and repeating your one deadly mistake."

Embarrassed I walked inside, "it's not fair momma."

"Why are you worried about what happens with your little brother. He's a good kid and he's not as sneaky as you." Then she looked at me, "what's up with you?"

"Nothing," I tried to shake off my feelings.

"Un huh!" She eyed me.

"Seriously."

"Un huh."

"Man momma ok!" I sat at the table, "I want to get married, I want to be settled already."

"BOY!" She waved me off, "you're barely out of this leg of college. You're a long way from settling down. You need to focus on your career and your son."

"You were married and had me and Unique by the time you were my age."

"Yep and you can't be me no matter how hard you try." Then she smiled at me. "It was different only twenty two years ago. The goals you have set out for your life require a little more dedication and focus. Your father and I's focus was on getting married and having you and your sister. Your brother got thrown in the mix later to switch things up on us and reset the clock."

"I want little Tavio to come home to a family with me as well."

"You're not trying to compete with Tempest are you? Cause you know it can't be easy over there."

"Not competing, but I don't want him to miss out."

"As long as he has you, he's not missing out on anything. Right now that boy needs you, he don't need a stand in hogging up his father's time and attention. Little Tavio will be older when you marry and have more children, but that's for the best. He'll be old enough to understand that you're not replacing him, and that no one can take his place in your heart. Hang in there son, and focus."

****

"I've been dying to ask you, what kind of name is Breezy?"

"Funny you should ask Tavio."

I started laughing, "Tavio is a name."

"And so is Breezy. My mother liked it, that's the name she gave me." We took a couple more steps towards her front door. "Look, you're a cute kid and all, but I don't have time to play this game. What do you want from me?" I smiled an evil grin. She chuckled a little, "that can't be all."

"Well I don't know you well enough to say that there's much more to you. This is only our third date. Besides, I have a ways ahead of me before I'm ready to settle down."

"Look let's not waste each other's time here. My clock is ticking and I doubt that in five years we'll be married with a baby." She paused to check for my reaction. I stood still and held my breath. "So in my mind this has the potential to go nowhere that I need it to go. My clock is ticking and I can't beat around the bush about what I need."

"So you're telling me I'm not good enough for you?"

"I'm saying that you're not ready for what I'm ready for." Then we stopped walking, "so here's my proposal." She put her hands on my collar and acted like she was straightening it. "How about you come in for a night cap, and when we're done you go your way and I'll go mine. No strings attached." Then she kissed me.

I was in to the kiss, but my mind wouldn't stop thinking. I told my Johnson to calm down while I tried to think this through. She was honest about her agenda; she's looking for a husband and a father to her child. I don't know that she isn't above trapping a man to make her fantasy life a reality. My gut is telling me to back away, even though my Johnson is screaming for relief. I backed up, "there is nothing I would like more then to take you inside and wear you out, but I can't do it. If I break you off you will be sprung and then there will be no husband or no baby cause you'll be chasing me down. I think we should end our night here."

"Are you serious?"

"Yes."

"You know that whole speech was so you wouldn't think I was a hoe."

"And I don't think you're a hoe."

"But I want you to come in."

"Yeah but I shouldn't…"

She turned around and started walking towards her door. "Whatever little boy, if you don't bring your tail in here!" She took out her keys.

I turned and started walking towards my car. Her "little boy" comments were going to get old real fast. She called out to me, but I got in my car and left. When I got home, I called Mona a fellow student from the college. We gave each other noncommittal and unattached sex. My momma was right; I need to focus on my career and my son.

Eva

"Happy housewarming!" Katrina said with a big box in her hands.

"Thank you," I said reaching for it.

"Nope, I got this one. You can make yourself useful and get the boxes out of Chauncey's car." She said as she happily hurried to my kitchen. I walked out the door and Chauncey was taking boxes out of his car. "What is all of this?"

"You told her she could decorate the downstairs bathroom." Chauncey smirked.

"Yeah, I was thinking a little rug and a couple of towels."

"Katrina never functions that small." Then he took his boxes inside.

I smiled as I looked at the buckets of paint and boxes of things in this car. Katrina went all out. I made the mistake of telling her that I wanted an ocean theme throughout the place to remind me of my years in California. She shook her head at me when I suggested painting all the walls blue and hanging the occasional shells around. I agreed to let her decorate one of the bathrooms but from the look of it, she's doing all three bathrooms.

My townhouse is three bedrooms and two and a half baths. This place was one of Mrs. Singleton's many rentals that she decided she didn't want to keep on the books anymore. She asked me if I was interested before she put it on the market. I excitedly said yes and then we started working on the deal. The deal was sweet and it moved unbelievably fast. One day I was saying that I would like to buy something after graduation and the next thing I know I own a beautiful townhouse.

With Katrina's wedding a week away, I thought she would be too distracted with her wedding to focus on my place. She said this was the perfect distraction for her. Colby walked in the door carrying things from Chauncey's car. He was in worn looking jeans and an older looking t-shirt. Katrina said he was on her painting crew, she said he's the best painter she knew. Colby thanked her for the compliment, and then he asked her where she wanted him to start. She explained which paints she wanted where in each bathroom and then she told me to come to the kitchen with her. She had black and white pictures, black frames, and white matting for each. The pictures were of beaches, sand, seashells, lighthouses, starfishes, etc. She had us put together potpourri in pretty dishes.

Colby started with the half bathroom downstairs, since it was so small. He had it painted in no time flat. While he worked on the half bath, Chauncey was taping and prepping the other bathrooms for him. Once the walls were dry, Katrina took out Chauncey's power tool. She told me we were installing a towel rack next to the sink. She drilled, attached, and then placed everything where it should go. The bathroom seemed like a hotel bathroom when she was done. I loved the sandy browns in that bathroom. The seashell boarder was so pretty, and it was the constant theme through all of the bathrooms. The bathroom upstairs was more mauve and maroon. My bathroom in my master suite was a light almost electric blue, all of the hardware in there was stark white, and the accessories were black. It was so beautiful! I immediately smiled and thanked Katrina. She asked about the rest of the place. I told her we were bringing everything from the apartment over. "Please put your current furniture in the third bedroom and let me do your bedroom."

"That's going to be my office; there isn't enough room in there to have both."

"Yes it is, if I show you will you let me?"

"Katrina, you have a wedding to focus on."

"That's already planned; this will give me something to focus on besides my jitters."

"PLEASE LET HER DO IT!" Chauncey begged.

We all laughed as I said okay. Katrina told us to be quiet as she backed away into the bedroom. She slowly turned around in the middle of the floor as she used her hands as if she was talking. Colby and I laughed at her. Katrina said this was going to be my retreat. She asked me what colors I wanted. I asked if my bathroom needed to match. She thought about it for a minute, and then she said she'd find a way to make it all work, I told her I liked Green, Purple, Silver, and Turquoise so she could pick from there and make it work.

We ate pizza in the middle of my living room floor and drank mixed drinks from the stuff Colby brought over in celebration. Vanessa was out on a date, so there was no telling when we would see her. Katrina kept writing stuff down as the ideas came to her. She told me she'd have my bedroom done by Wednesday.

Tuesday night, I walked into a fully decorated and furnished bedroom. The walls were lavender with a purple accent wall. There was a big four-poster bed in the middle of the floor with draping all around it. My furniture was black and my comforter and pillows were Silver and turquoise almost like the blue in my bathroom. There were little green accents strategically placed in the room that you would only notice if you wanted to.

I started crying as soon as I saw it. Katrina asked me if she made my room a retreat, and I whole-heartedly said yes. That bed begged to be laid on. The lounge chair at the foot of the bed asked me to sit on it. I couldn't wait to live in this bedroom. My grandmother smiled but it wasn't a complete smile. I asked her what was wrong and she said nothing, she was ready to move in.

Katrina's wedding was a blast; her parent's money was well spent. My grandmother took my car home so she could do some more packing and I told her I might come home with Vanessa. Without my grandmother's disapproving eye we took advantage of the free bar. Colby kept bringing me drink after drink. When it was time to go, Vanessa said she was going to catch up to me later cause she had a hook up. I didn't see whom she was talking about, but Colby volunteered to take me home. "How come you still live at home?"

"It's just easier right now. Once I decide on a location for residency then I'll think about investing in rentals until I find the place I want to call home. Your place is really nice."

"It sure is; your sister turned my bedroom into a retreat."

"I didn't see the finished product."

"You want to go see it now?" I smiled at him.

"Um! Sure! I mean sure! I mean yes, if you want me to see it."

I giggled, "of course I do. I appreciate everything you've done for me."

I couldn't get the key to go into the hole, my hand kept moving, so Colby took the key from me and opened my door. Colby smiled as he walked around my room looking at everything. He said he always thought Katrina should've been an interior decorator. Then he said maybe that will be her second go to after she's done with Corporate America.

I took off Colby's jacket and laid it on the chaise. I looked around and then I sighed. My grandmother was going to be blocking for real. This room may never see sex. Then I smiled at Colby. He was standing with his hands in his pockets leaning against the doorway. I reached for my zipper as I watched his eyes. Colby told me not to tease him. I unzipped my dress and asked him if he wanted to help me break in my new bedroom. I expected him to say yes, but I wasn't expecting what I got. Colby was good, powerful, and a FREAK! Vanessa called it; I silently thanked her for being right. Dare I say he was better than Tavio? No, he was completely different. I'll never love anyone like I loved Tavio, so nothing could ever compare. Colby was just different.

In the morning, Colby kissed my forehead. "Thank you for finally coming around. I was starting to lose hope." I smiled, but I didn't say anything. "Our families are going to be so excited when we tell them that we're together."

I hadn't thought about this night meaning we were together.

Tavio

I stood up with a smile, "thank you for the opportunity."

"Mr. Spellman I see wonderful things in your future. You have a certain charm that just can't be bought." My new boss said.

"Thank you, I got it honestly from my father."

"It's going to take you far. I'll see you on Monday."

"I'll see you on Monday." When I got to the Bart station, I did a small leap for joy. I have been in contracts for my current firm for a couple of years. I've made it clear since I started that I wanted to eventually one day be an actual agent. Our agency handles athletes all over the country. When I was in contracts I was part time, but I got a chance to learn everything from the ground up. My mentor has been showing me the ropes. She told me to pay attention to each contract that came across my desk, and to ask questions constantly.

We went over deals and why some deals were negotiated lower than others. She said she loved my eye for details and all of the questions I had. Monday I start my junior associate position. The pay is ten times better than at the bank, even though it's still only part time. My only reason for hanging around the bank is to still see Alaina on a regular basis.

Ben has opened his own studio and he employs MAC's best friend as his assistant. He's doing really well, and I see him all of the time. I got Alaina a job on the daytime team that I'm on. Having Alaina follow me to this department didn't help the rumors about our supposed affair. A while ago, someone saw Alaina's husband up here when she was still on the night shift. He put her in his car and drove away. People swore that Royce was finally catching on to our affair and he came up here to fight me, not knowing that I was on days. People and their imaginations! Although I know better than to allow my mind to rest too long on that married woman for fear of what I might think of…. We are not having an affair, we don't mess around, MAC is a faithful kind of woman.

When I got home I called MAC's desk. "This is Alaina, how may I help you?"

"It's time to grow my hair out," I smiled.

MAC quietly screamed into the phone, "YOU GOT THE JOB?"

"Yep, and now that I've got my foot in the door I can finally start working on my locs."

"I'm so jealous!" I could hear her pen tapping on the desk. "I'm so happy for you."

"Thanks, it's about time. This whole pay your dues is no joke. I was starting to feel like this might not happen for me." My mentor said that once I landed an associate position then it would be ok, to change up my look. Right now, I look very corporate and while that's the look I needed to get my foot in the door. When it comes down to acquisitions my clients needed to feel like they could relate to me. When you look out on a soccer field, tennis court, baseball field, basketball court, football field, etc. you see the players expressing their individuality. "So what are you going to make me for dinner?"

"See if Ben is available for dinner on Saturday or Sunday. Chareca and I can cook at his place, and I'll invite my brother and his girlfriend."

"What about your father?"

Alaina breathed hard into the phone, "I'm still not talking to him! AND I SWEAR TO GOD TAVIO IF YOU DON'T WANT TO BE RESPONSIBLE FOR ME FLIPPING OUT ON THIS PHONE AND LOSING MY JOB YOU WILL NOT DO THIS TO ME RIGHT NOW!"

I put my hands up like she could see me, "fine."

MAC exhaled, "are you going to bring a date?"

"I have to?" The thought irritated me.

"It would look good if you did."

"Who cares what it looks like? I don't want to give some female the wrong impression like I'm sharing a part of my life with her."

MAC was quiet for a minute, "do you think our friendship is healthy?"

"DON'T START!"

"Does our relationship stop you from having something real with someone else? We're just friends."

Her tone, her comments, all of it rubbed me the wrong way. "I'm getting off the phone now. You really do know how to kill a good vibe."

"I'm trying to be real and unselfish, Tavio you're a good guy and you deserve to be happily involved with a woman who appreciates everything I know you're capable of giving."

"How about this, I know I'm a good catch and when I'm ready to settle down I will. It'll probably happen around the same time that you forgive your father for being human." I could hear her getting angry, she was breathing hard on the phone. "I'll call you back once Ben agrees to Saturday or Sunday. Take care Alaina."

Eva

I was irritated as I looked at my grandmother. She was serious, seriously asking. "Did they put you up to this?"

"No, and I haven't mentioned it to them yet. But I figured that it makes sense. You're always at Colby's and their luck has dried up in Orlando. I would love to have both of my babies close by."

I know she wasn't trying to kick me out of my own townhouse, but it surely did feel like it. "Fine! I'll rent this place out to you guys. I'll look for something else."

"Why would you look for something else, you're always at Colby's why not make it official?"

"Because I need my own! When Colby gets on my nerves I come here. Now you want to take my retreat from me. FINE!"

"Maybe if you stop retreating you two could talk things out and finally get engaged. I don't know how much of this sinning I'm supposed to tolerate," she huffed.

"STOP IT! STOP IT! You don't care what I do as long as it's with Colby. My ex couldn't live with us, but Colby could just about. You practically threw my things into his condo. Colby can do no wrong!"

"He's a good man!"

"So are other men, but you'd never give anyone else a chance."

"NO! Not un! I'm not going to do it with you today child. Colby is a good man! He loves you! He's a doctor! I don't know who you think you're supposed to find better than him. Case closed! I'm not trying to discuss other men with you like it's an option. PLEASE! Now your sister is pregnant and her husband lost his job. Of course they're moving in here. You're going to welcome them with open arms. Do whatever you need to do to find her husband a job, your sister too. I'll take care of the baby for her when it comes. We are a family and we pull together when we need to. That's it; nothing else is up for discussion. You might even want to get started on a family of your own. You know to speed things along." I gasped at her and she laughed.

"I don't want to have children **EVER**!"

My grandmother stared at me, "more lies. You're just scared. You're going to have babies and you're going to be a wonderful mother. Stop this nonsense."

I stomped my feet in irritation, "I'm not a child. You can't…"

She put her hand on her hip, "why are you still here? Get going! You heard what I said. I'll call your sister and let her know that everything is good for her to come out. They should sell everything they have and then come on."

"Oh, so I don't get to keep my furniture?"

"You are some kind of selfish today aren't you? You can afford the mortgage and expenses here until your sister and her husband get on their feet. You don't need that big bed no more since you spend all your time sinning at Colby's. It's just stuff and you can let it go. This is your sister, same mom and same dad sister. Everything you've been through, she went through it too. She needs you, and one day when I'm gone, she'll be all you have. You're the one with the fancy high profile job, driving fancy cars, taking first class vacations. I can't believe all the places you've been to over these past few years. You are not hurting for money and your sister is destitute. Stop being selfish!"

"Why should I be punished for applying myself in school, for making good connections? I've worked for everything that I've gotten. I wasn't given anything."

"Charlotte helped you."

"She pointed me in the right directions, but I had to make it happen. She's been overseeing my progress, but she hasn't given me anything."

"She helped you, and now it's time for you to help your sister. Point her in the right direction. Let her see that it can be done. You can work until the cows come home, at some point you have to ask yourself what is it all for if you are too stingy to help anybody."

Chapter 11

Alaina

"You can ride over with Ken, Chareca and I are going to the grocery store then we're going to cook. You and Ken can give Wesley a chance to get there." Then I stood on my tiptoes and kissed my husband. I had a feeling he'd be annoyed about the whole thing. That's why I presented it the way I did. I know Tavio is looking forward to this meal. He foams all over himself when I sneak leftovers to work for him. He has no shame about it either. Regardless of anything else, he eats my food first.

Royce looked down at me, "I want chicken wings." He was daring me to dispute them.

"Chicken wings don't really go with our menu tonight." I tried to smile sweetly.

"You are my wife! Your man wants some chicken wings now hook me up!"

I kissed his lips again, "ok."

When I turned to walk away, he patted my butt. "You're my woman, everybody needs to remember that!" He called after me.

I don't know why he said that but I went with it and hurried out the door. In the grocery store, Chareca was all bubbly and giddy about the night she and Ken had. "Ok! Ok! I know we don't normally talk like this, but if I don't say something to somebody I'm going to burst." I looked at her completely euphoric expression and I felt sad. I couldn't even say why. "Ken is so excited to be trying. Last night he came home all smiles and winks at me. He made a phone call and then he told me that his mother was going to watch Cara Mia for us. We only went to a Holiday Inn not too far away. He bought roses and sprinkled them on the bed. He laid me down and gave me a naked massage… GURL!" She started kicking her legs. "It was so good; I bet last night got me pregnant! It had to!"

I swallowed my jealousy, *"congratulations."*

Chareca stopped her celebration and looked at me. I turned my face cause my eyes were watering up. Chareca grabbed my shoulder and turned me back towards her. "What's wrong?"

"Royce and I don't have nights or anything like that."

"Well last night was special, but you two have good times?"

"No," I put my head down. I was so embarrassed.

"Never?" Sadness was all over Chareca's face.

"One time."

"Once?"

"Once!" I kept my eyes down.

"ALL THESE YEARS! ONLY ONCE?"

I put my finger up to shush her. "ONCE! Quiet down."

She put her hand on her chest, then her eyes filled up with tears. Chareca grabbed me and we cried together. She rubbed my back as she cried with me. "I'm sorry! You've been married all these years and it hasn't been great. I'm sorry, I'm so sorry."

"It's my fault though; I don't know what I'm doing wrong."

"Who says you're doing anything wrong?"

"Royce says that no one's ever not responded to him so it has to be me."

Chareca got mad, "each woman is different. It's not one size fits all! I knew Royce was lacking, and he's trying to put it off on you."

"I don't think that's what the issue is."

"How would you know? Have you ever seen a dick outside of

Royce's?"

"No, but I don't think that's what it is. It has to be me."

"Why does it have to be you?"

"Cause I'm the newbie, or at least I was. I don't know what to ask for."

She interrupted me, "you were new how many years ago? You know, you just let him tell you that it's you. He's getting his regardless. Can I help you with this?"

"How can you help me?"

Chareca had no idea, but her eyes screamed at me. "I don't know, but I can't let you go out like this. You were so excited about getting married. You waited until you got married, this just isn't fair." Then we hugged as I agreed.

When we got to Ben's place Tavio and lil Tavio were already there. Cara Mia grabbed the deck of cards; she was excited to show little Tavio how her mom showed her how to shuffle the cards. They were going to play I Declare War on the balcony. Ben and Tavio were already drinking and talking about who knows what. Chareca and I said quick hellos and then we took over Ben's beautiful kitchen in his loft. When he bought his loft, the first thing he did was have his kitchen renovated even though I would've been perfectly happy with the kitchen he bought the place with. He had tons of counter space and a middle island for more counter space. He had every modern appliance we could think of. The best part is that whenever we came over to cook, he'd give his housekeeper a heads up and we didn't have to worry about cleaning up after ourselves. Chareca would make sure everything was an organized mess of course, but we were free. I seasoned Royce's chicken wings and then I put them in the refrigerator to marinate with the steaks while we made everything else. We were having steak, new potatoes, macaroni and cheese, salad, and greens. Chareca kept whispering ideas for me to try. She told me to do things with Royce and to pay attention to how they made me feel. She advised me to have more of a voice in what I liked and what I didn't. We were sipping on the Sangria Ben made as we cooked and talked. Ben and Tavio came in the kitchen with their glasses in their hands.

"Guess what Chareca; Gia confirmed that she can do my show." He did an excited dance.

"OH MY GOODNESS! THAT IS SO GREAT!" Chareca said giving Ben a sloppy high five. Tavio and I waited for someone to include us in their celebration. "Gia is one of the hottest and newest faces on the runway scene. Singer turned model on the top 20 list. Everyone wants to work with her, but she's hard to get."

"How did you get her?" Tavio said taking another sip.

Chareca smiled really big, "I have my ways. When will you do your run through?" She asked Ben.

"We can go over the calendar on Monday. You guys are here for Tavio." He said giving Tavio pleading eyes.

"Don't take over my time with your business talk." Tavio said waving them off.

Chareca and Ben were talking at the same time as if they could hear each other while they spoke. They hurried to Ben's home office. I smiled at Tavio, "it must be nice to have your dreams come true."

"MAC, when are you going to start making yours come true?"

I shrugged, "I guess I don't really have any outside of being a wife and one day a mother. You all have the dreams."

"MAC is dreamless?" He smiled a slightly tipsy smile at me.

"I don't know what I want to do. I never got around to going to school. You all knew what you wanted to do in high school."

"It's not too late to start dreaming."

I took another drink; his comment irritated me. "What's the point in dreaming? I'd rather be grounded right here knowing what I need to know and being happy doing it."

"Why are you irritated?"

I exhaled, "you're drunk. Leave me alone Tavio."

He put his fingers in his hair, "how long do you think it has to be before I can start loc'ing it?"

I shrugged, "I guess if you go without a few haircuts you can start with little twigs and grow from there."

"Where should I go?"

"I don't know," I didn't look at him.

"Oh come on. I know you know. You've researched them to a science. You know who I should go to, and what length my hair should be to start them. Don't play dumb."

I set my glass down and I walked over to him. I put my fingers in his tapered hair and I started moving his hair around. Tavio smiled and closed his eyes. He slightly moaned as I touched him. His moan hit me like a lions growl strikes fear in its prey. I liked his reaction to my simple touch, but I knew it was the Sangria making him act this way. Normally he looks me in my eyes to the point of making me uncomfortable.

"Depending on how your hair grows you should have at least half an inch of hair in a month. There's a shop in Oakland that you should go to for a consultation. It's a husband and wife, and they do beautiful locs. I'll give you their info."

Tavio looked me in my eyes, "you could always go with me."

"Royce doesn't like locs, he barely tolerates braids. The whole time I have them he's asking me when I'm going to take them down."

"When does Alaina get to do what Alaina wants to do? No wonder you won't allow yourself to dream."

I took my hands out of his hair; I exhaled and walked away. What was I supposed to say to that? That it's not true, or that he's wrong? I went to the sink and washed my hands. "Once we put the steaks on the food will be ready. We'll wait until everyone gets here to do that."

Tavio walked up behind me and put his arms around me. I froze, "It's ok MAC. One day you're going to be free." Then he softly kissed the back of my neck. It felt like lightning shot through my body. I gasped as I tried to understand what that feeling was. Tavio walked out of the kitchen unaware of what he just did to me. I held on to the counter wondering why it was hard for me to breathe. I felt warm and tingly all over so I crossed my legs hoping that the tingles would stop. I was stuck for a long time. I blame that Sangria. When Wesley and his girlfriend came, she hung out in the kitchen with me while Wesley and Tavio sat on the couch watching something on TV. Wesley downed his first glass of Sangria like it was fruit punch, he said it was really good. When his girlfriend Trisha brought him another glass, I told her to tell him to slow down. Trisha said everything smelled delicious. I showed her the food that was staying warm in one of the ovens. She said she couldn't wait to taste my food. She said that Wesley told her that he's always enjoyed my cooking. "Are you two going to get married?"

Trisha smiled at my sudden outburst and then she chose her words carefully. "Not right now, we plan to take inventory in a bit and see how we feel. It's not like William was planned, and we've both been married before. So we're in no hurry to do that again."

"I didn't know you were married before."

"Yep, crashed and burned; fortunate not to have any kids during that disaster. Wesley has been good to me, but we aren't in any hurry to jump right in."

"You don't think a child is a bigger commitment than marriage could ever be?"

"Wesley and I will always do what's best for our child. The commitment to our child is bigger than if we stick together or not. We don't have to be married to co-parent."

"I guess I just figured since you've been married before you'd know whether a person is worth the risk or not."

"Just because Wesley is nothing like my ex doesn't make this situation a hurried experience." She smiled, "William happened off script. However, I don't want to rush things just because we messed up."

I was about to say something else when Royce and Ken loudly walked in the kitchen. "I am here! FEED ME!" Ken said smiling ear to ear.

"I don't smell chicken wings!" Royce said walking in the kitchen.

I jumped cause I completely forgot about his chicken wings. "Cause I wanted to make sure they were fresh."

"I bet you got the mac n cheese ready though." He looked at me out the side of his eye. "Her husband don't get no love," he told Trisha.

Trisha looked at me with no expression. "Royce go in the living room with the men." I pushed him in the direction of the living room. Trisha didn't say anything she just watched me. Chareca came back and we finished the dinner. She excitedly told Trisha and I all about the models they were going to use for Ben's show. They were so excited about Gia though. Chareca brought Ben's laptop in the kitchen and she showed us Gia's portfolio. Gia is absolutely BEAUTIFUL! Chareca said she is very down to earth and very intelligent. She said having Gia in their show just took everything over the top.

At dinner the conversation was nice, when I put the chicken wings on the table, Royce moved the wings close to him. I asked everyone if anyone wanted any, everyone said no. Then Royce asked me why he couldn't have the wings to himself. I didn't know what his problem was but I was not amused by his possessive behavior. Tavio praised my macaroni and cheese, which made everyone else join in. Everyone except Royce, I didn't understand what his mood was about. Wesley noticed it and he got quiet, he kept looking between Royce and I. Tavio and Ben decided to ignore Royce. While Chareca and Ken disappeared after shooting each other looks across the table. Tavio raved over the food and then Ben, Trisha, and Wesley joined in. Royce quietly gnawed on his wings. "Did I tell you, I'm going to start my locs?" Tavio told Wesley.

"Serious? I was thinking about loc'ing mine."

Trisha sucked her teeth, "don't you need a more corporate look for work?"

"That's what I'm saying, plus I think of dirt when I see them," Royce blurted.

"So let me understand what you're saying." Tavio adjusted in his seat. "What's the difference between locs and braids?"

That's when the debate began. Tavio, Wesley, and I against Royce and Trisha. Ben sat in the middle thoroughly entertained and drunk. When Chareca and Ken quietly slid into the table announcing that it was time for dessert Cara Mia looked at her parents. "Mommy, your shirt is backwards!" Cara Mia tisked at her, "you said I'm supposed to pay attention."

Ken sat there laughing looking at the table while Chareca was dying. "Yes you're right, now SHUT UP!"

Royce was a little huffy as he drove home. "Your little boyfriend the reason you want to loc your hair?"

"Royce don't act like that. If anything I talked locs up until he had no choice but to love them."

"I hope you don't think I'm supposed to get them things too. I hate locs!"

"Why do you hate them?"

"They're dirty! They look a hot mess!"

"They're not dirty, I happen to think they're beautiful."

"What difference does that make? I'm the one who has to like what I see, and I'm telling you I don't like them."

"Fine! Then let me be honest with you! It's not 1992 anymore. You can let the curly top go. Just cut it off!" I didn't mind his curl activator generated curly top, but I was being petty.

Royce reached up and touched his hair. He was starting to thin on his temples so he let the curls grow a little longer to cover that. I didn't care about the reasons why, I wanted it gone. "Gurl! Quit tripping, you fell in love with my hair like this."

"We aren't high school kids anymore. Embrace your grown man style."

Royce exhaled, "won't my face look fuller with my hair low?" His insecurities were on his shoulders.

I felt bad about pushing him. "No, but if you feel like it's an issue you could let your beard grow in and then contour it."

"Contour?"

"Ask your barber, he'll know what I'm talking about. I think you'd look distinguished with the low cut and neatly trimmed beard."

He rubbed his chin, "distinguished? I could try that." Then he smiled at me, "thanks."

I took a breath, "meanwhile I want to cut my hair."

"What? Why?" He reached over and put his hands in my hair.

It was shoulder length and pressed straight. "I want something different too."

"I like your hair like this." He ran his fingers through it. "Don't cut it please."

"You get to change but I don't?"

"Only because you're telling me to, I like that you haven't changed since high school."

"Fine!"

When he walked into our place, I sat on the couch, picked up the remote, and turned on the television. "You're not coming to bed?"

"Not tired," I waved him off.

"I can help you with that."

I sucked my teeth; I was in no mood to be in that bed. "Not in there you can't."

He frowned, "what's wrong with the bed?"

"I'm tired of the bed. We don't have kids or roommates why we gotta be in the bed all the time? In the bed, under the covers, with the lights off! I'm tired of that."

"So I'm supposed to treat you like some trick and freak you on the couch? You want to be treated like a whore?"

"YES! GAWD! Thank you! I thought you weren't going to get what I was saying." I folded my arms and waited for his response.

Royce looked so stuck, like he wanted to laugh, but he was too shocked. "Yes?"

"YES!" I took my shirt off, smiled at him, and leaned back on the couch. He stood there staring so I took off my pants too.

Royce grabbed himself, "stop playing Alaina. Come to the bed."

I shook my head, and then I took off my bra, when I started pushing my panties he gasped. He walked away, I exhaled, I knew he wasn't going to do it. I changed the channel, enjoying sitting in my birthday suit flipping channels. Royce came in the living room in his t-shirt and shorts. He swallowed then he begged me to come to the bed. I said no, and then I told him I was really excited about breaking in the couch. He looked at me and he knew I wasn't kidding. He ran back to the room and came back with a blanket covering him. He hit the light switch and jumped on me.

It was good, I was in to it. Right when I thought I was feeling something, Royce got a cramp in his leg. He got mad and said it made no sense to be humping on the couch like some teenagers. He said I must want to show off cum stains on the couch when we had company. He got up still hard as a rock and limped back in the bedroom. I laid there staring at the ceiling. For the first time in years, I got on my knees and prayed. I asked God what was wrong with me and to help me. I told him that he created sex for a man and a woman, a husband and a wife to enjoy. I waited until I was married; I didn't play how close could I get to the fire and still this was what I got. I want to enjoy sex just like everyone else. I stayed in there on my knees praying for a long time, begging to be fixed.

****

The doorbell rang and Royce and I popped up. I got dizzy from moving too fast. I looked at the clock and it was 8:00am. I asked Royce if he was expecting anyone and he said no. I started to lay down again and they rang again. Royce got up, put his robe on and marched to the front door. I doubt he even bothered to see who it was before he opened. He snatched the door open and I couldn't hear anything. I expected Royce to tell them to go away and then he'd come back to bed. *Alaina*, he called me. It sounded like he was smiling. I put on my robe and walked towards the living room. It was my Granny Shane and my Auntie Sara. "Why aren't you two up? You see how late it is." She said as she put her arms out for me to come hug her.

"Momma I told you they both work and this is really early to pop up at someone's home."

"Come in, come in." I said bringing them to the couches.

"Would you like some coffee or tea?" Royce said moving

195

towards the kitchen.

"Do you have any chamomile tea?" Granny Shane asked.

"Of course! You gave me a whole bucket that I've been making my way through from the wedding."

"The wedding? How many years ago was that?" She was trying to remember.

"Almost six years," I smiled.

"You playing, that bucket don't even last me six months. Yes, Sara and I would love a cup, if it isn't too much trouble." Royce went in the kitchen to put the pot on. He prepared everything and then he went to the bathroom to brush his teeth. "So," she slapped her knee. "I could beat around the bush, but it's not my style. Why aren't you talking to your father?"

Auntie Sara shook her head, "real smooth momma." My granny shushed her.

"Cause he's a hypocrite and I don't want to deal with him," I folded my hands.

She searched my eyes, "you're mad about his girlfriend?"

I sunk in my seat, "everybody knew about her except me?"

"Yes," she watched me.

"Momma!" Auntie Sara blurted.

"What? She asked me a question and I'm answering her."

"You're going to make this worse. Calm down." Then she looked at me. "He didn't feel you were ready to know about his friend. Your dad was a young man when your momma died. Did you think he would never have anyone?"

Royce walked back into the kitchen. "Does he know

everything?" My Granny asked.

"Only what he needs to." Then I looked at Sara, "I understand that. He's supposed to lead by example. He lied to me for all those years."

"He didn't lie, he just didn't tell you."

"Omissions are lies auntie."

My Granny shook her head, "this isn't fair. First, your momma did what she did. My son took the high road and dealt with the blame for all those years. Your daddy let them blame him for your momma's suicide. He let them point the finger at him." She started getting angry as she cried. "All the time knowing it was her guilt that consumed her. Then he finds someone to love and lives in secret all these years trying not to trigger any craziness with you. When does my son catch a break? Wesley was a horrible teenager! He was confused and hurt about everything. The person who deserved his rage is nowhere to be found. My son deserves to be happy too!"

"Then he shouldn't have lied to me!" I said as respectfully as I could.

"He didn't lie to you." My auntie said.

"An omission is a lie!"

"Royce!" My Granny called out like he wasn't right there in the kitchen. He stood in the middle of the kitchen with sweat on his brow. "Do you agree that an omission is a lie?"

"Um! I mean! Um!" He took a deep breath. "I can see where Alaina's coming from. But Bill has a point too."

"Royce you are a lawyer, you can do better than that. Yes or no."

"No," then Royce went back in the kitchen.

I stared at the back of his head; if they weren't here I would've jumped up and smacked him upside his head. "Doesn't change the way I feel. He didn't have to hide her. He could've been honest."

"But you understand that he wasn't trying to set that example for you." My Auntie said.

"Right, so he lived as a hypocrite. Granny, Auntie, I really don't have anything to say to him. I appreciate you coming by EARLY and waking us up. However, if this is all you came for you're wasting your breath."

My Auntie started laughing. "Sara did she just politely kick us out?" My auntie shook her head yes while she laughed. "Don't make me take you over my knees. I haven't had my tea yet."

Sara looked at my lamp table in the corner. She stopped laughing and smiling. She picked up the picture of Alaysia and I. We were babies and smiling at each other. "Since you all want to come with hard questions this morning. Why did it make them feel better to try to convince me that I was a baby when she died? I remember playing with her, I was not a baby."

My Granny looked at me, "I guess you'll have to talk to your father for that answer."

Royce made us breakfast to go along with our tea. They stayed until about four. I know Royce was in that kitchen listening hard. I never told him my mother-committed suicide. All he knew is she died young. I went completely off the handle when he tried to question me about it. I got on him so badly that he walked out the door and didn't come home until later. I was sleep on the couch and when he tried to wake me, I went off. This is all according to him; I don't remember any of it. Tavio said I called him crying but I wasn't making any sense. He said he came by and I was still talking crazy. He put the blanket on me and tucked me in on the couch before he left. All I know is that in the morning I was hung over and in no mood to discuss anything.

Royce

Alaina's been sad lately and I can't even pretend like I don't notice it. Maybe she's upset that I've gained another ten pounds. I want to throw the scale away; I'm tired of watching the numbers go up and up and up. I've thrown it away twice and Alaina's gone right out and bought new ones. She said she needs the scale for herself and if it bothers me that much not to step on it. My sister Rachel said she loves my new look, and I've noticed women looking at me. I guess I do look handsome like this. I just can't seem to get the motivation together to get this weight off. I was blaming school and then studying for the exam, but all of that is over now.

Ken and Chareca miscarried; Ken said that Chareca was so depressed that sometimes she couldn't get out of bed. He said one day Alaina and Chareca's sister came over and got in the bed with Chareca. He said they spent the day there. He said ever since then Chareca's been getting better. It seems like the energy transferred. "Maybe we should surprise them with a weekend away. Can you afford it?"

"Depends on where we go and if my mom or Chareca's parents can watch Cara Mia."

"I've got a credit card let's get in the car and drive. You cover the gas, and I'll cover our rooms. Deal?"

"They'll ask too many questions."

"If you can get a sitter, we'll pack their clothes. They'll think we're going out to dinner and then surprise we're on a road trip."

Ken smiled, "ok. Let me make some calls." He whipped out his phone and called his mom. He didn't get the complete question out of his mouth before his mom was screaming yes and how romantic the idea was. Alaina and Chareca were in Chareca's car so I told Ken to tell them to come home so we could go out to dinner. Then I hurried home, I broke out the secret card. I was doing a pretty good job as I packed our bags.

As I grabbed our daily vitamins, I looked at Alaina's pills. In that moment I decided it was time to have a baby. That would delay school a little more for Alaina, but it's ok. I packed everything up and then I turned on the timer for the lights. As I drove to Ken's I told myself that this would work. I needed a week to make sure she was off schedule and would have to start all over on her pills. I decided my mission that I chose to accept was to be on her every time she inhaled. That also meant that I would have to endure her runs from the bedroom to try to escape me. Even though I've applied at quite a few corporations, they were waiting to hear whether I passed the bar before they really indulged me. Money was right around the corner. I'm not normally a count my eggs before they hatch type of guy, but I need this.

Therefore it has to be. When I got to Ken's his mom called the girls into her bedroom, which gave him the opportunity to pass me their suitcase. I took it down to the car and put it in the trunk. I stood at the bottom of the stairs breathing; it wasn't too long ago when these stairs were nothing to me. I told myself I'd get it together while Alaina was pregnant as a gift to her. She loves me, even in this body. I don't know how I would feel if she blew up.

My mother always said it was going to be Alaina, now she swears that Alaina is making me fat on purpose. One time they got into an ugly argument about my weight. I had to pick Alaina up and carry her out of the house cause she wasn't backing down and my mother continued to provoke her. My sisters, brother, and father were all smiling at Alaina and secretly hoping I would let her go. I saw it in all of their eyes. They had no reaction, no instinct to protect their mother. I was the only levelheaded person in the room at that time. Alaina felt so bad for going off so badly on my mother. I told her it wasn't her fault and I thanked her for defending me. I haven't seen my mother since then. I thought about how hurt she'd be to finally have a grandchild and not be allowed to see it. It would serve her right for talking about my weight like I was some diseased or less than valuable person because I gained weight.

She liked my haircut and beard until she heard it was all Alaina's idea. Then she accused me of hiding behind my beard. Pretending to be something I'm not. I shook my head. This was my romantic and sporadic get away with my wife. Alaina is going to be so excited; spontaneity turns her on if nothing else. She doesn't like predictability.

I took a deep breath then I made it up those stairs. I took a minute outside the apartment to get my composure. Then I went inside. Chareca was telling Ken's mom that we would watch a movie together after we came back from dinner. As we walked to the car, I asked Ken if he wanted to go North, or South, or East? He said East would be good. As we drove on the 80 East bound freeway, Alaina asked why were we going to Sacramento for dinner. I told her we needed an adventure. She smiled really big and then she went back to the car conversation.

When we got to Lake Tahoe, Ken said this was perfect. When we pulled up to an Inn, we told the girls we would be right back. They happened to have two rooms overlooking the lake. They were on opposite sides of the Inn, which was perfect for us. We went back to the car, got our bags, and set them down in our rooms. Then we walked across the street to the restaurant.

It was busy and lively in there. Our waitress called all of us Suga and she was so lively she made our dinner even better. The food was delicious and I devoured every bit of it. Then she threw in complimentary desserts. Chareca and Alaina shared their desserts, which was crazy to me. I enjoyed every bite of mine. We extremely over tipped our waitress then we escorted our very tipsy women to our rooms. Ken and I high fived before we went our separate ways. When we walked in the room, Alaina and I started kissing. I needed her to not think about asking for those pills tonight, and the only way to do that was to completely distract her. I turned the wall switch off, and then Alaina moved us across the floor. She opened the curtains and the moonlight bounced off the lake and gave us a nice nightlight to make love by. It was dark enough for me and light enough for her. For the third time ever my wife was here in the moment with me. I got so excited about her finish that I was barely down ten minutes and I was ready to go again.

We made love all night long; I amazed myself with my stamina. Alaina was in to it and it felt even better. We were losing ourselves in each other. I had her calling my name and everything.

In the morning, I pretended to be sleep as I heard Alaina tearing up the suitcase looking for her pills. "Royce! Wake up! WAKE UP!" I moaned like I was irritated, "where did you put my pills? Are they still in the car?"

"They should be in the suitcase." I turned over.

"I searched the whole bag they're not there. Do you think they may have fallen out? Should I call the front desk and see if they found them?"

"Whatever, I'm tired and drained." I rolled over and pretended to be sleep.

Alaina called the front desk and then she left. When she came back, I asked her where she went. She said she went to retrace our steps because she thought I could've dropped them along the way.

****

"Babe! It's here! It's here!" I jumped up and down looking at my offer letter from my new employer." I held the piece of paper in my hand that contained our future.

Alaina waddled in rubbing her barely there stomach with a smile. "Is it as good as you hoped?"

"I knew I was taking a risk when I countered, but BABY it was worth it! LOOK AT THIS!" I excitedly held up the letter. Alaina smiled as she read. She kissed my lips and then she told me that she was proud of me. I smiled really big at her. I know she's been stressed about everything since she found out she was pregnant.

A few months ago Alaina called me in tears from the doctor's office. She was so upset she couldn't even drive. Foolish of me to think she'd be happy about having my baby. Her mind went straight to all the reasons that we weren't ready. Of course she had good points, but I didn't care about that.

I told her I was excited. This was my first time getting someone pregnant and it was perfect. I refused to be sad about it. Alaina stopped talking then she asked me if I did this to her on purpose. I didn't expect her to ask me that so I got quiet. Even though I deny it, she doesn't believe me. I've been the doting husband as much as I can be. Dealing with her mood swings and sudden tears. Whenever someone mentions her mother she gets mad lately. It's not her normal annoyance either. Those arguments are vicious so I've learned to leave it alone.

I'm excited about the expansion of our family. And I'm relieved that we will be able to afford it. "I'm happy for you," she smiled at me.

"Happy for us!" I took her in my arms. I sucked on her cheek, and then I lightly kissed her.

"For us, I've got to get back to my food." She said as she pushed me away.

That was my cue to leave her alone. I held on to my smile. I called my Dad and I told him the bank met my counteroffer. I could hear how proud he was. Then he asked when we were going to look for a house. I told him we'd go as soon as we agreed to a location. It's been awhile but Alaina wanted to stay in Richmond to be closer to her dad, while I want to move to Walnut Creek for better schools. Maybe I should ask again while she and her father are on the outs. My father said he would gift us money towards the purchase of our place. Then he asked to speak to Alaina. She was in the living room in the corner of the love seat with a blanket and a book. She looked like she was going to be annoyed by my interruption until I told her it was my father. Then she got that smile my sisters get when they talk to my dad. I sat on the couch watching her talk to my father. She was all smiles and cheeses. I wonder if our little girl will be like that with me. I'm hoping this one is a boy though. I want a junior, and finally she can let go of Tavio's son. He will no longer be needed to fill a void. Sometimes I swear she spends more time with that little boy than he spends with his own father. That little boy don't like me no more than I him. I will not be sorry to see him go.

Alaina handed me the phone and then she went back to her book. When I got off the phone, I put it back on the charger. "My dad wants us to hurry up and buy."

Alaina put her book down, she hates when I interrupt her. "You haven't started the job yet. Don't you have to have so many years in the job?"

"Depends on how we work the deal. Right now, we need to decide where to live. I want to put Walnut Creek back on the table."

"And I want to stay near Richmond."

"Why? What's holding us out here?"

"My nephew, my family."

"They can visit us in Walnut Creek."

"Visit?" She sucked her teeth. "I'm going to need help with this baby."

"That's what you have me for."

"Please! Just like everything else you promise to help with you won't. I'll be up at all hours of the night. You'll expect me to stay home when the baby is sick. I wanted to wait."

"For?"

"To be ready. To be ready to be a mother. I know you heard my Granny the other day. You know my mother killed herself! Then you thrust me into parenthood without discussing it with me. You have no idea what it's like to be me. You don't ask! You used to talk to me! You used to want to know what made me tick. Now you run around here acting wounded until you did this. Does it make you feel like a man to have control over my body like this? You couldn't control me sexually so you decided to take this route? You…"

I walked out of the living room. Pregnant women are, pregnant women are… I needed to go for a walk. I grabbed my wallet and keys off the nightstand, and then I headed for the door. Alaina was calmly reading her book again as if she didn't just tear into me. "I'll be back!"

"Whatever!" She said like she didn't care.

I stood in the doorway looking at her. "For your information, I happen to be ecstatic that you're pregnant. If you need to blame me, then blame me. We're married and whenever you have sex the possibility is there that life could come from that single union. Look at Ken and Chareca; they weren't planning for Cara Mia. They were kids and somehow they embrace their life change better than we are at a more mature age. I didn't know the details about your mother's death because you refuse to talk about her. How was I supposed to know what happened? For the record, I'm not happy about our sex life. I wish you knew how to let go and just live in the moment with me. Making love to you is all that I dreamed about. How do you think it makes me feel when you're not into it? You ever think about the fact that you don't talk to me anymore? You run around giving Chareca, your brother, that little boy everything. By the time you get to me, you're all talked out. How long are you going to stay mad about being pregnant? Is our child going to know about this? What kind of mother are you going to be? You're mad at me fine. Be mad at me for loving you; be mad at me for our piece of forever. Don't take it out on our child." Then I walked out the door.

Alaina

For a minute, I was looking for Royce so I could run him over. I felt relieved that Tavio was home. I said a quick prayer hoping that he was alone. I knocked on his door and waited. "WHO IS IT?" He said in a deep voice. Then he looked out the window next to the door. He had on dark blue sweat pants and no shirt. "What's wrong?"

"Is this a bad time? I need to talk."

He stepped to the side, "come in."

Royce would never walk around shirtless. I told my eyes to stop looking. Tavio went to his bedroom then he came back with a T-shirt on.

"I'm sorry for barging in on you."

"It's ok; I was going over stats and rosters. You want a drink?"

"Sure, what you got?"

"I got that Henny, or Jack, I don't have Coke but I got Pepsi. Or I could open a bottle of wine."

Awkward.... "Tavio, I have news."

He leaned on the counter and smiled at me, "what's up?"

"I'm pregnant," I gave him an embarrassed smile.

His head bobbed, he closed his eyes and spun around. "So orange juice then." He snatched his cabinet open. He slammed the glass on the counter. He snatched the refrigerator open, and then he sucked his teeth. "Are you sure?"

"That I'm pregnant? Yes, why are you mad?" I watched him.

He slammed the refrigerator closed. "I'm not mad." He roughly sat my glass in front of me on the table. "What did you want to talk to me about? I know it's not my kid." He tried to joke.

"I don't know I think that kiss in Ben's kitchen did it," I smiled.

"What kiss?" He searched my eyes.

He was drunk; I knew he didn't remember or realize that he did it. "I could make something up, but I need a moment to be serious."

"Ok," he said pouring himself a double shot of Hennessy and then sitting across from me at the table.

"How are your parents?"

"They're good. Dakarai's about to graduate soon, they are too excited about being empty nesters again. If it wasn't for little T I doubt I'd hardly see them once Dakarai goes to college."

"Were you planned?"

"My birth?" I shook my head yes, "never gave it much thought. I assume so. Why?"

"You can't tell anyone! I need to vent."

"Of course."

"My mother committed suicide because of a guilty conscience. I can't talk about what she felt guilty about right now." Tavio rubbed my hand letting his eyes speak his sympathy for me. "I'm not ready to be a mother!"

"What does Royce say?"

"He's too busy being excited about all of it. He just keeps trying to plan things, but he hasn't asked me if I'm scared. We never discussed parenting styles, because I know we're not ready."

"But you've been married awhile; I guess I thought you weren't having any kids with him."

"My husband? Of course, just not yet; just because we got married young doesn't mean we have to be young parents. He just got his offer letter from the bank. We don't have anything saved yet. We live paycheck to paycheck. Now he's talking about buying so we can be in further debt."

"He doesn't know about your savings account?"

"How do you know?" He smiled at me but he didn't respond. "You're not supposed to look me up."

He laughed, "like you don't keep tabs on my money." He rubbed my hand again, "I'm sorry about your momma. How did your father explain your mother's death?"

I took a deep breath, "at first he said it was an accident. But my grandparents said things didn't add up and they wanted answers. They wanted to know what happened to their daughter. Then he had to tell them it was a suicide. She was depressed before she died so they just knew my father was mistreating her. They weren't there, he did everything he could. Then all of my mother's secrets came pouring out. My sister's death was the event that set everything in motion."

Tavio froze for a minute, "you lost your sister and your momma?"

"My twin, you really shouldn't drink when I tell you stuff. You never remember anything. We've talked about my sister before."

"Or maybe you should stop waiting until I'm drunk to tell me stuff. Heaven only knows how many juicy things you've said while I was inebriated." He picked up my hands and kissed them. "Alaina, you're going to be a great mother. I can't tell you what being a mother is like, but I wasn't ready for little Tavio, obviously. You adapt to the things that happen in your life. I can't imagine life without my son now. Take several deep breaths and celebrate your child. You know your grandparents will support you, and you can add my parents to the list. My momma was just asking how you and Royce were doing. Stop trying to control life, it happens."

"But Royce did this to me on purpose."

He shrugged, "maybe he did. Maybe he didn't. He's your husband who loves you and is all into the idea of a family with you. Now what you could do is milk this whole scenario. You could come out with some nice pieces of jewelry."

I exhaled slowly, "please don't tell anyone about what I told you."

"Of course not."

I leaned in to the table then I rubbed his head. "Your locs are coming along nicely." I chewed back my jealousy.

He shook his head, "you like my twigs?"

Then I stood up, "they're coming along nicely. They're going to look really nice when they get long."

"They look nice now." He flipped his short locs at me.

"They do," I picked up my purse. "Guess I'll go home and apologize to my husband."

"You should, besides I got work to do."

I walked around the table and I hugged him. He kissed my forehead as he rubbed my back. "It's going to be ok."

"Thanks," I made myself let go then I walked out.

I got back before Royce. I went back to my spot on the couch and started reading again. He came home a few minutes later. I immediately apologized for my attitude and for blaming him. Royce looked relieved that I was in a better mood. I asked where he went, and he went to the store to talk to his dad.

Royce

Alaina rolled her eyes at me as the nurse weighed her. She informed me that we as a family were going on a strict diet after the baby was born. I didn't say anything, I just stood there. If I argued, I was an insensitive jerk. The doctor came in our exam room followed by a different nurse who was bringing the ultrasound machine. The doctor talked to Alaina and asked her how she was feeling.

Alaina told her about the crazy dreams she keeps having. They're always about me. Sometimes she's beating me and she doesn't know why. One time she ran me over and she was mad when I didn't die. She woke up screaming when she killed me. In that dream, she caught me cheating on her and she said she lost it. I think she's responding to the women who respond to my new look. I've gained so much weight that my wedding band doesn't fit anymore. Every time she looks at my empty hand, she gets mad. I don't see the point of investing in a new ring when

I'm going to lose weight and my ring will fit again. I'm faithful to my wife! Those girls may smile at me just to make her mad, but none of them would stick around after I unleashed the blubber. Besides, I don't want to hurt my wife like that.

"Do we want to know the sex of the baby today?" The nurse asked as she put goop on Alaina's stomach.

"YES!" We said in unison.

The doctor sat over to the side writing information down as the nurse called it out. "There's your baby's head, it's sucking its thumb." I grabbed Alaina's hand. "I hope you two ordered a baby boy cause that's what you're getting."

"Yes!" I celebrated.

"Whatever," Alaina fake pouted.

Suddenly the room got hot and I couldn't catch my breath. "I'm having a son!"

"Baby please sit down." Alaina was almost off that table.

"I'm ok, just excited." I sat down and caught my breath.

I called my dad, then brother and sisters. Everyone was excited this was our first grandchild. Then I called Wesley and Alaina's grandparents. Alaina's Granny Shane said she gets to throw the shower since Alaina's other grandmother took over the wedding. I didn't care; I'm having a son.

Chapter 12

Tavio

I couldn't do anymore work when Alaina left. I couldn't think anymore. It felt like she walked in here and sucked up all of my positivity. Royce is an idiot and he's forever making a mess of everything. As I sipped my drink, I asked myself why I was holding on to that no paying job at the bank. I decided that when Alaina goes on maternity leave I'm quitting.

****

"What am I a rabbit? What's this supposed to be?" Alaina asked with attitude.

"If you don't want it, I'll take it?" I reached for my veggie platter.

She blocked my hands, "no. I'm saying next time hook your girl up with some cold cuts as well. This will be my afternoon snack."

"Can I get a carrot?" Mandy asked.

Alaina put her elbows out like she was protecting gold. "Back off! Pregnant lady selfishness right here."

Mandy laughed then she looked at the picture on Alaina's desk. "Your husband is FINE! I would've gotten pregnant the night before the wedding."

Alaina frowned at her, "Mandy was that you I saw climbing out my window the other day?"

"I was just kidding, goodness."

"Don't kid like that about my husband."

"Fine, now I can finally have Tavio to myself."

Alaina narrowed her eyes, "you know Tavio is off limits too. If you're hard up for a man go mess with Bart. He's the only one available in this department."

We looked at Bart who had on headphones while working. He was a big dope with no people skills. We laughed when Mandy frowned. "Wait a minute, you got your husband. You just want me to continue bringing you food. Why I don't get to have nobody?"

"Please! Your body is probably begging for a rest. You could stand to go awhile without sex."

"Don't hurt yourself trying to keep tabs on my sexual escapades."

"Speaking of the devil!" Mandy said smiling really big.

I turned around to see Royce walking towards us. Alaina shot out of her chair and hurried to him. "What are you doing here?" They hugged quickly, no doubt being mindful of corporate policy.

Royce shook my hand, "we have a meeting upstairs with a few of the legal teams. I've been planning this pop up since last week."

"Royce this is my friend Mandy. She was just drooling over your picture," Alaina said.

"Respectfully of course."

"I don't know how you do that respectfully, but whatever. Did you drive out here?"

"No they drove us over, can you wait an hour for me? We can ride home together."

Alaina smiled real big, "of course."

"So is this what you do all day? Stand around talking to Tavio."

That was my cue to walk away; a lot of the people in the office were looking. I didn't even listen to what Alaina said to him. I went back to my cubical. I looked at the calendar counting down the days until I was out of here. My boss wants to fill my position with Alaina. However, Alaina doesn't want to commit to the responsibility with a newborn at home.

Royce knocked on my wall, "hey. You cool?"

I turned around in my chair and I pointed to the guest chair, "have a seat." Royce sat down; he was looking around my cubical. "You have something you want to ask me?"

"It just dawned on me that we've never had the opportunity to talk."

"And you think about this right now?" I watched his eyes.

"Yeah, let's schedule a man date."

"This weekend I have my son."

"Perfect!"

"Get my number from Alaina." Then I turned around and went back to work.

Royce went back to Alaina's desk, I could hear them talking and laughing. When he left, Alaina came to my cubical. "What did he say to you?"

"He wants to have a man date with me."

She frowned, "man date?"

"His words not mine."

"You're going to be ok with this?" She looked concerned.

"As long as we remain close stuff like this is going to happen."

****

Tempest opened the door with a very pregnant stomach. "How you feeling?"

She rolled her eyes, "very pregnant. Can you come in for a minute? We want to talk to you."

"Sure." I said hello to the other kids and little Tavio. I followed Tempest into the back room of the house where her husband was playing a video game. "What's up?" We shook hands.

He turned off the game, and then he looked at Tempest. "You were serious?"

She rolled her eyes at her husband. "Look! You are no help around here, and I can't do this no more."

"Tempest don't be ridiculous! Don't do this!" He said frustrated.

"You two want me to come back?"

"No! Look! I'm tired! With another baby on the way I can't continue to do it all on my own. Tavio, I need you to take little Tavio full time. He can come visit here on the same schedule that he goes to see you."

"I don't want little Tavio to move out."

"Too bad! I'm…"

"TEMPEST! SHUT UP AND SIT DOWN!" Her husband was standing and angry. Tempest sat down huffing. "Now you're right, I could stand to step things up around here. But you can't send your son away and think he's not going to feel some kind of way about it." He looked at me, "Tavio, I don't want your son to leave. You remember how she is when she's pregnant; super emotional and irrational."

Tempest put her hands up, "I'm tired, and I need help!"

"I'm sorry! I'll help out more, don't do this." He said as he sat next to her and rubbed her back.

"How about we do this, I'll take my son with me. You call me when you want to see him."

"Naw man, that's not necessary. We just need to bring her emotions down some." He said rubbing her back.

"She's only going to get worse. I appreciate the fact that you want my son here. But I can step up and help out more."

Tempest's husband looked pissed, "you did this on purpose." He stood up and rubbed his head in frustration. "Look I had a stepfather growing up. Little Tavio is always welcome where ever I am! This is his home the same as its mine. He's my son just like lil Tyrek."

"I understand, and I appreciate that. Right now your woman needs you and I can help lessen the burden a little."

"Tavio is not a burden." He spit at Tempest.

Tempest didn't say anything; she knew that if she said anything in front of me I was going to take my son. I don't know if it's me or the lack of "support" but like he said she did this on purpose. We all agreed to make the transition as transparent to little Tavio. We said bye to Tyrek and his parents then little Tavio and I went out to breakfast. He told me about his week at school as I went over the logistics in my mind as I tried to figure out how I was going to make this work. We went home and I told little Tavio to put on his basketball gear. We went to Alaina's to pick up Royce. Wesley pulled up at the same time as we did. "Hey I thought today was my man date?" Wesley started cracking up.

We laughed together, "who says that?"

"What's up little man, you dunking yet?"

"Not yet, but I got hops," lil Tavio said proudly.

"I can't wait until my son is this big. There won't be a ball he doesn't master." He chuckled, "guess I'll have to be there for my nephew too." Wesley shot me a look. When Wesley opened the door, the smell of food slapped us in the face. Royce and Alaina were laughing in the kitchen. "Hello?"

"Wesley?" Alaina's head popped around the corner. "Oh and the Tavio's are here too." She smiled, "I keep telling you about leaving the door unlocked."

"Do you want us to come back?" Wesley asked as I stood there wanting to leave.

"No, please take him out of my kitchen. He's trying to eat everything."

"What you making us?"

"Dinner will be ready when you get back. I decided that tonight's dinner is going to be about little Tavio so we're having ravioli, risotto, salad, and spinach."

"No biscuits?" Wesley asked being funny.

"We're having dinner rolls. Smarty-pants, now go! Go have fun!"

"Can't, Ken's not here yet." Royce said.

"We're only missing Ben and Brice at this point." I chimed in.

"He had a date, I asked."

"So, I didn't know this was a group date. I thought you were going to wine me and dine me. You know buy my affection," I joked.

"I get it; it was a wrong choice of words."

A few minutes later Royce's brother and his best friend Ken got there. Wesley rode with us, and we followed them to the park. Royce said he wanted to play flag football; the three of us against the three of them. I looked at Royce for a minute. He was heck of soft; he probably hasn't worked out in years. His brother and his best friend at least looked like they snuck in a workout from time to time. I hope he's not underestimating my size just because I'm a big guy. Royce kept looking at me, and watching me. This game may start off as flag, but somebody was going to get hurt. Wesley got excited when little Tavio took off with the ball. I smiled so proud; my boy is agile. The game was going good, even though Royce kept getting winded and trying to play it off by talking about anything to catch his breath. Ken asked him if he needed to take a break and he refused saying that he was fine. During our little halftime break we drank water. Brice asked me if I played football in high school. I told him I played everything in high school, and I've been teaching my son all the games. Brice was actually pretty cool; he and Wesley hit it off too. Royce stood on the side watching. Ken was talking to little Tavio about the basketball game that was on last night. They were so engaged in their conversation that they paid us no attention. "So you still play?"

"I'm teaching my son, I stay pretty active."

"You need to get in shape, you're about to have your own son to teach."

Royce looked annoyed by the comment. "Your sister is too stubborn for her own good. Couldn't you convince her that it's a good idea to move closer to her job?"

Alaina told me that he wants to move to Walnut Creek and she refuses. He's even taken her to look at a few houses out there. She said the houses were nice, but she wants to be close to her support system. I reminded her about her little speech that she gave me about not wanting to move to Boston. She sucked her teeth and then she admitted that it was different once you were faced with the decision. I personally think he wants to move away from me. Like there's anywhere he could move her that would interfere with our friendship. "What's wrong with Berkeley?"

"Cost more."

"You work in the city, why would you want to go further away?"

"Either way I'm on Bart. When I'm not working I would like to run to the grocery store in Walnut Creek. I'm over the waterfront."

"Pick your battles Royce, you can move to Walnut Creek later. Give that girl what she wants." Wesley said halfway smiling.

"Berkeley might as well be Oakland."

"Your problem is that you're always trying to control stuff. Let go and give that woman this one."

Brice chuckled, "least I'm not the only one who sees it."

"WHAT?" Royce barked at his brother.

"Alaina does everything you want her to do, when you want her to do it. I'm actually kind of proud of her for *FINALLY* putting her foot down."

"I thought I was the only one." Wesley said, "Alaina don't complain so I don't say anything, but you got some serious control issues. She can't even wear her hair the way she wants. You got something to say about everything with her. If you don't get it together, the meanness she's been displaying while she's pregnant will continue. She's going to get tired of doing everything you want and you pretend to do what she wants."

Royce's eyes darted to me, "she complains about me to you?"

"Royce! You don't ask another man a question like that. Be cool!" Brice said.

"That's what this is right? A whole setup to ask Tavio what he knows about you?" Wesley teased him; "I told you from the beginning I'm watching you."

"What you want to ask me?" I asked directly.

"Not so much ask you, but I just wanted to let you know that I don't think it's a good idea for Alaina to work with you on the day to day anymore. She never told me you sat steps away from her desk. I know you probably got some kind of a little crush on her, but she's my wife. As you see she does what I tell her to do. I'm letting you know man to man that you need to back up."

Brice and Wesley looked at me; I smiled. "So you feel threatened by me. Thanks," I laughed. "You wait until we're years into our friendship to pay attention. It's too late, doesn't matter where you go, or what you do Alaina and I will always be close. If it wasn't for me calming her down you wouldn't have a wife to be huffy about right now. You need to sit your Twinkie eating butt down and get a grip."

Brice and Wesley hyped up what I said. "Break's over!" Royce said walking out on to the grass with the ball. Wesley shot me a look telling me to look alive. I smiled as I told myself not to get too excited. I've wanted to hurt Royce since he married Alaina. I told myself to be cool.

It was our ball; Wesley and little Tavio ran out wide. I held on to the ball a little longer knowing it would tempt Royce to come for me. He sensed the setup and came for my flag. I threw to Wesley who moved the ball to our first down. Royce was watching me and I could see his brain calculating everyone. It was our fourth down and we were right outside our in zone. Little T hiked and then he threw to me. Brice was supposed to be on me but Royce was coming as well. I caught the ball and ran. As soon as I hit our in zone I stopped and spiked the ball. Royce was attempting to stop but his body was still moving. I turned in a circle making him just miss me. He fell face first down on the grass. I continued my celebration dance. Brice told Royce to get up so that they could try to block our kick. Royce moaned then he rolled over slowly. Grass and blood were all in his mouth. Brice and I jumped back. Wesley asked what happened Royce started to say as he took his tooth out as blood poured out of his mouth. Wesley pointed to the sprinkler that Royce perfectly landed on. Immediately I knew Alaina was going to be mad. All that food was going to get cold.

Royce's front tooth was completely out and the right fang next to it was loose. Wesley whipped out his phone and called Alaina. He asked her where their dentist was located and then he told her to meet us there. Wesley told Brice to follow us cause Royce was focused on the pain in his mouth. I drove to the dentist office and as we parked Wesley looked at me. He asked me how I knew what dentist they went to? I told him I referred them. I knew the office was open on Saturdays and they didn't close until four and it was just after two. They rushed Royce past the normal cleaning rooms to the doctor's room in the back. I sat next to my son and then I exhaled. Alaina was going to be mad at me, there's no way Royce wasn't going to blow this way out of proportion. I was deep in thought when I realized Wesley, Ken, and Brice were staring at me. As soon as I looked at them, they started laughing. Brice and Ken reenacted the fall. Brice made it look like Royce was reaching for me when he fell. Everyone straightened up when Alaina arrived. Brice told her what the doctor told us. Alaina asked what happened, and so Ken told her best he could without laughing. Wesley and Brice watched Alaina as if they were looking for a reaction from her towards me. One of the assistants took Alaina to the back. "So," Brice looked at little Tavio. "Why do you call my sister MAC?"

"Cause she makes the best macaroni and cheese I've ever had."

"You don't like your mom's?" Wesley asked him.

"No! Hers tastes nasty, Tyrek likes it though."

"That's your little brother right?" Ken chimed in.

"Yep! I can't wait to tell him my dad made Royce bleed."

Eva

Rickie kept hugging me real tight, almost like she was holding on to me with everything she had in her. I kept staring at her little stomach. I couldn't believe she was pregnant. She was going to be a mother, I was scared for her. "Eva, I am so thankful for everything. We had no idea of what we were going to do, and then this happened." She pointed to her stomach.

"You didn't get pregnant on purpose?"

"No, I mean we wanted a family just not right now when we were struggling to take care of ourselves."

"Are you scared?" I stared at her stomach. Life was growing in there.

"Terrified! This whole thing makes me think about our parents. They were younger than we are now when they had both of us. I will never subject my baby to that kind of stress and turmoil. I'm determined to be better than them." Then she looked around, "your place is really lovely Eva. We will do everything we can to get out of your way as soon as possible. Thank you for the suggestions. We applied everywhere you told us to, and to any other place that said it was hiring. As soon as we can manage we will be out of your way." She said looking around nervously.

Seeing my sister trying to hide her tears and shame melted every bit of resentment I had about this whole setup. "Rickie, don't worry about it. I need you all to stay. I thought Grandmother told you the plan?" She shook her head no, as she looked down. This place is three bedrooms, the baby will have the other room, and you two will take my room."

"What about you?"

"I'm going to stay with my boyfriend for now. I may buy something else, but I'm not worried about it at the moment." I smiled, and then I saw the calculations running through her brain. "Once you two are on your feet you can pay me rent."

"We have a little money from the sale of everything; we can pay you rent now."

I stopped her from talking she was breaking my heart. My sister's non-mooching attitude made me want to do everything for her. Then I remembered how I felt when Mrs. Singleton helped me out. It was my turn to help someone who truly needed it and who wasn't trying to get over on me. "Right now, we need to find you a doctor, and get your nursery setup. Your husband will have a job shortly. You need to rest." I said rubbing her hand. "Grandmother said she's going to keep the baby for you when you go back to work, but I don't want you going back any sooner than you're ready to go. You need bonding time with the baby. No child deserves what we got, and I already know you're going to be a better mother than what we had."

My sister sat on the couch, leaned her face into her hands and started crying out loud. I was happy our grandmother and Rickie's husband were out running errands. They barely landed a couple of hours ago, and you could see both of their minds going. They seemed so sad getting off the plane and stressed about everything. I automatically assumed that they were looking to get over on me. I didn't consider how stressed they were on their end and maybe all that they had been through. I rubbed Rickie's back as she kept crying and crying. "Everything just keeps happening, it was like a domino effect. I don't regret the decision to get married. I love my husband and I wouldn't give him up for anyone. We had to give up school to work, which was fine. You saw our place we were doing fine. Then suddenly I lost my job and it's been so hard to find another. I was housekeeping, babysitting, anything and everything I could think of to make a couple of dollars as I looked for a job. Then Quincy lost his job, we lost our place. His family acted like we were lepers that they had to show kindness to. We've slept in our car more often than I want to talk about. With all of our hustling to survive I couldn't get down to the clinic on schedule, I got my pills a couple of days late. Then…" She started crying harder.

"Why would you sleep in your car when I'm a phone call away?"

"We're not looking for charity, if it wasn't for the baby we would've continued to tough this out until things started looking up. We went to the library and looked up jobs out here and started applying. I'm so sorry Eva, our problems should never be yours."

I put my arms around my big sister, "everybody needs help sometimes. I was going to drop out of school to take care of grandmother when Katrina's mom helped me. She helped me get a job in her company, but that was it. She's been watching me, but she hasn't given me anything. I had to work and go to school, while your grandmother insisted that I fall for Colby," I smiled.

"You don't like your boyfriend?"

"I love Colby, he's great. Even though his mother owns EVERYTHING, he's not some spoiled little rich kid. He's good to me, and he and grandmother are buddies. He's great."

"But?" Rickie looked tenderly at my eyes.

222

Now I started crying, "what's wrong with me? It's been years since we broke up and all I do is think about Tavio. I wonder what he's doing now. How old his son is, how his career is going, everything. I miss him so much!"

"He's fine, his career is going good. He bought a house in Richmond, his son is in school. Why don't you call him?"

"Last time I talked to him we argued. I can't face him."

"Because of James?"

"Unique told you?"

"Uh! No, I was there that night. I didn't hear what you were saying but it didn't look good. Ever since then Unique asks how you're doing but she won't call you. What happened?"

"James got me pregnant on purpose trying to force me to come home. I didn't tell Tavio about it, but he gave me the money to fix everything."

"But you weren't together?"

"I was embarrassed and ashamed. I didn't tell anyone about it, but now I don't want children ever. I changed Tavio and I's whole life plan behind my own trauma. He didn't tell me about his son probably for the same reasons as I withheld mine. Tavio still wants the dream, and I don't."

"Colby doesn't want a family?"

"We haven't discussed it. He's just so happy to be with me."

Rickie rubbed my back, "you love him?"

"I do love him, he's so sweet and good to me. I'm just not head over heels you know?"

"Does he know?"

"Mostly, upfront and honest is not my strong point." I looked at my sister's very old school and mismatched suitcases. "We should take a picture of this moment. This is when everything turns around. After you get used to the snow, you're going to love Boston. It's so pretty out here. Let's put your bags away and then do some window shopping."

I showed Rickie her new bedroom. She started crying again. We moved all the furniture out of my old office into the garage last weekend. I asked Rickie what color she wanted to paint the nursery. Worry about the cost flashed across her forehead. I told her we'd start thinking of concepts.

Then we went downtown to go window-shopping. Rickie's eyes got so big when we went into the baby section of one of the stores. She said she couldn't believe she was going to be a mother. She said she was excited and scared all at the same time. I asked her if she had anything for the baby yet, and she said she only had a baby book that she wrote every nuance down in. As we sat and drank our hot cocoas someone approached us. COULD THIS DAY GET ANY WEIRDER? "Hi." He said watching my eyes for a reaction to him. "You're Vanessa's friend aren't you?"

"Yes, how are you? Long time no see." I stood to hug Kiev. "This is my big sister Rickie, she just got here this morning. Rickie this is Kiev Vanessa's cousin." She smiled and said hello.

"I didn't want to interrupt, I just happened to see you and I wanted to say hello since you disappeared all those years ago."

"Are you an oil painter?" Rickie asked as she scanned Kiev's clothes.

He smiled, "right now I'm doing what pays the bills. I make copies of the classics. Sometimes they're oil, or acrylic. Personally I love chalk, I like to get into everything with my hands and feel every stroke. Shadows tell so many stories and set the tone for a scene. You paint?"

"I took an art class in school. I'm a terrible artist though. Do you have your work on display anywhere?" Then she took another sip of her cocoa.

"Not consistently, but I have small opportunities to shine here and there. Matter of fact if you're going to be out this way Thursday my work will be on display downtown. At the Expressions Art Gallery on first street. Bring your families and come see my work."

"Sounds like fun," Rickie looked at me for approval or rejection.

"What time?"

"Doors open at 7pm. Hope to see you all there. It was nice meeting you, I'm going to get going."

"It was nice meeting you too." Rickie had a goofy look on her face. We watched him walk away. When he turned the corner she looked at me. "What's the story?"

"Huh?" I took another sip.

"There was obvious tension, what's the story."

"There is no story. Like he said we met years ago, and that was it. This is the second time I've seen him in my life." I adjusted in my seat. "I was feeling him when I met him, but then Colby and I happened. My head isn't right anyways, I'd only hurt him."

"How old is he?"

"I don't know."

"He's definitely *mature*."

I laughed, "*mature*?"

"He's older than us, I just don't know by how much."

"Is there anything wrong with an older man?"

"Nope, Quincy is your age." Then she smiled at me, "are we going to the art gallery?"

"Um, let me talk to Vanessa first. She's very protective of him. If she thinks it's a good idea then I'll make sure Colby can go."

"Good answer," Then Rickie took another sip.

****

Colby walked in the bedroom and stopped in his tracks. "You look beautiful!" Then he came in for a kiss. "Give me twenty minutes and I'll be ready." Then he hurried into the bathroom.

I looked in the mirror; I hoped my outfit didn't scream that I was fishing for attention. My jumper was olive green, so I accessorized with the gold bangles, earrings, and necklace that Colby surprised me with just because he thought of me. Colby's always sweet like that. He writes me little love notes and then leaves them in weird places for me to discover them randomly. Sometimes I feel like Tavio told him what to do to make me feel special. Tavio used to write short stories, poems, and love letters to me just so I knew how much he loved me. Colby came out of the shower in only his towel. I looked at my short hair, "I'm thinking about shaving my head. What do you think? Too masculine?"

Colby studied my face then my head. "Nope, I think you have the right head shape to pull it off. Go for it!" Then he kissed my lips.

"You already got me, you don't have to agree with me anymore." I called out to him while he was in the closet.

He walked out with his clothes. "I'm not kidding, I think it takes a certain amount of confidence to rock a baldhead with pride. You are gorgeous with or without hair. Your hair doesn't define you."

I smiled big, "I'm going to do it! My hair never grows right anyways. The only time it got some length to it was in Florida. I'm kind of curious to see my hair in its natural state anyways."

"Sounds good to me. So who's showing is this?"

"Vanessa's cousin Kiev. I have no idea of what we're walking in to. I don't know if he's any good or not." Then my work phone rang. I took a deep breath then I answered it. Pearl from the California office was calling. She quickly apologized then she quickly explained yet another issue they discovered in that office. I've been doing my best to try to resolve everything remotely. With all the issues that's coming up they're going to need to send someone out there. I don't want that person to be me.

Colby was now dressed and waiting on me. When we got off the phone I wrote down some notes and then we left. We picked up my grandmother, Rickie, and Quincy. As soon as they got in the car Quincy started going over all of the applications he submitted today. Even though I told him to relax, he said he had to keep going until he found something. He said he has a baby on the way as if we didn't know. Colby did a good job of getting Quincy to relax and he took him off topic. That good doctor bedside manner was showing. As we got out the car Colby told me we had to leave by 8:30 to make our reservation at 8:45. Then he smiled at Quincy and said that he wanted to treat them to a delicious meal as a welcome to Boston gesture.

When we entered the gallery there were people everywhere. Most of Kiev's pictures were black, grey, and white. I put my arm around Colby's as we walked around. Rickie and Quincy were talking about the different pictures and it seemed like my grandmother was in a hurry to see them all. Colby asked me what I thought of the beach landscape picture. I told him it made me think of San Francisco's Ocean Beach. It was normally overcast there whenever we went even though we didn't go very often. Colby said he wanted it for his home office. I liked the idea and suddenly the picture became perfect. I wrote down the number for the painting. My grandmother came over excited, she told Colby she found a piece that she had to have for the baby's room. She pulled him by his free arm away from me like she was a child eager to show her parent something. Colby grabbed my hands and drug me along with them.

The drawing was of a grandmother rocking a baby with a bottle in a rocking chair. The eyes of the grandmother were loving as she stared down at her baby. Colby smiled and said she had to have it. As I turned to look for her, I saw Vanessa dressed to kill in a dress that showed off the body she killed herself in the gym to have. She brushed all of her hair back and it was bone straight showing off the precision of her expensive hair cut as her hair stopped in a straight line at her shoulders. She had on big dangly earrings and simple makeup. The guy she was talking to couldn't stop staring at her shiny lips. She looked amazing! I tapped Colby and I pointed to Vanessa. He nodded and continued his conversation with my grandmother.

"Hey sexy!" I said interrupting her conversation.

"Hey sexy yourself!" She looked me up and down. "You are working that jumper!" She snapped her fingers at me. She introduced me to her man du jour. He seemed nice enough, but I wasn't impressed. She always dates the wrong kind of guy for her. I guess she's trying to get all of her fantasies out of the way now. "Did you see anything you'd like?"

"Yes, Colby's going to buy two."

She smiled, "the young doctor's going to buy two huh?" She looked at her friend. "You hear that? TWO!" She raised her eyebrows.

"Nessa, these pictures ain't cheap!" The guy shrugged.

"And neither am I," then she took my arm. "I might come back."

I couldn't help it, I laughed out loud. "You are so bad."

"I know, aren't I." Then she pulled me towards a woman who she told to come over. "This is my friend Eva, Eva this is Kiev's girlfriend Faye."

My heart sped up, I guess I couldn't care whether he was single or not. "Nice to meet you." I said, as I looked her over.

Faye's hair was all over her head in a very curly Afro. Her glasses sat on the bridge of her nose like they made her educated guesses for her. She was a little shorter than me and even though she wasn't bragging, I couldn't miss the curves she possessed that I wished I had. She was the same milk chocolate tone as me. She was beautiful without one stroke of makeup. "Oh this is the Eva I've heard so much about." She looked at me like she was looking into my soul.

I looked at Vanessa as her smile dropped, "from whom?"

"Kiev told me he ran into you the other day." Then she looked me up and down. "Did you come alone?" I looked at Vanessa again; Vanessa was now looking for her cousin. Vanessa went to the left and I walked towards the right where I left my grandmother and Colby. Faye stayed put watching me walk. She's weird! I stood at a painting gathering my thoughts. Kiev was talking about me? I tried to push back my smile. Faye stepped in front of me, "let me apologize. I just don't believe in playing those female cat scratch games. Kiev and I talk about everything, I know you met once ."

"Ok, but you're awfully forward. I'm not here alone to answer your question."

She smiled, "so this is it. Show me what you're made of." I cringed at her challenge. "You like my man?"

"We only met once. I was intrigued by him, but we never had a chance to talk or anything. I can't say I liked him cause I didn't know him."

She smiled at me, "I like you. Thank you for your honesty. Physical attraction is only natural, and I know why any woman would be attracted to Kiev. He's so majestic and he pulls you in."

"Majestic, nice adjective." I smiled at her.

"Have you said hello yet?"

"No I haven't seen him."

She stretched her hand out towards mine, "come on. Let's find him together."

I took a deep breath, I didn't give her my hand but I walked alongside her as she talked about some of the pieces as we passed them. When we turned the last corner, Colby and my grandmother were talking to Kiev already. Kiev was taller than Colby and very lanky, he had his whole artist look. His hair was wild all over his head, but his beard was low and neat. His shirt hung off his shoulders nicely. He had on nice jeans with rips all through them, and boots. His hands were rough and like he made a living using them. Colby extended his arm towards me as he told Kiev that I was his lady. Kiev's eyes stabbed me like he wasn't expecting Colby's statement. I saw my grandmother register Kiev's expression while Colby was looking at me and smiling. Faye smiled at Kiev, and he returned her smile. "Eva, I see you've met my girlfriend."

"Yes, Vanessa introduced us. I see you met my man. Colby this is Faye, Faye this is my grandmother."

Faye smiled and then she shook their hands, then she looked at me. "Isn't this a tight knit family. Does your grandmother go everywhere with you?"

"I'm sorry, Faye is very blunt. It can take some getting used to." Kiev said to our group.

"Seems like someone should've fixed that for her a long time ago." My grandmother said cutting Faye with her eyes.

"My family tried to beat it out of me, but this is who I am, love it or hate it." Faye said watching my grandmother.

"You better be happy you're not my grandchild."

"All the beatings in the world would not have changed who I am." Faye said then she looked at Kiev who shot her a look telling her to cut it out.

"My man Colby is going to purchase two of my paintings. I was telling him that there are other pieces in my collection that I believe he would love based on his selections. Now that I know he's with Eva it only seems fair to offer a discount."

"Absolutely not! You are very talented and I plan to tell others about your work. I can support your work and show my appreciation by purchasing my pieces at full price. Just keep creating." Colby said watching Kiev's eyes.

Kiev put his hands up, "if you insist."

Colby looked at me then he looked at Kiev again, "how do you know Eva?"

"I told you how we met," I was getting embarrassed.

"I'm talking to him." Colby said, then he looked at Kiev waiting for him to speak.

"My Uncle's BBQ a few years ago. How long have you two been together?"

"A few years now," then Vanessa walked over. She had concern all over her face. She was looking at Colby trying to read him. "Your cousin is very talented. We're going to look around some more then we'll be out of your hair." Colby moved his arms to tell me and my grandmother to go to the left. I did as I was told.

"Let's go!" My grandmother said beyond angry.

"No, we still have time before our reservation, besides I want to look around some more." Colby said as he walked calmly looking at the other pictures.

"Why would you bring us here?" My grandmother snapped at me.

"Don't do that, Eva hasn't done anything wrong." Colby said in my defense.

"I can see as clear as day that that little boy likes her. We don't need to be here for that. I don't want that picture no more! Don't buy anything here." My grandmother was getting all worked up.

Colby stopped walking and he looked at the worry on my grandmother's face. He put his arm around her to calm her. "I'm going to buy those pictures. Look around, this brotha is talented and one day he's going to be BIG. We need these original pieces in our collection. He hasn't done anything wrong either. Can you blame him for liking Eva?

She's a brilliant and beautiful young lady that you raised very well. I'm not threatened by his little crush. She's with me. If you think he's a better catch for your grandbaby then please let me know right now. Otherwise, why would you care? Eva came directly to me and asked me if I wanted to come. She hasn't hidden anything about this guy from me. She even told me about their attraction. I don't see any reason to be concerned. Everything is out on the table."

I could see my grandmother calming in Colby's arms; he definitely knew how to handle her. "Well I don't like his girlfriend! She's rude!"

"She is an acquired taste, but isn't that his problem and not ours?" He rubbed my grandmother's shoulders. "Come on, let's see if we can find anything else we like. We are getting in on the ground floor."

"Ok," my grandmother said as if she wasn't just angry.

Colby looked at me and smiled, "how did you do that?"

"Once I learned how to calm you down when you're angry I became a better doctor altogether." Then he kissed my forehead.

"You saying I'm high maintenance?"

"You know you are." Then he patted my butt and told me to come on. I stayed with Colby the rest of our time in the gallery. I saw Kiev a few times from across the room. He gave me a pained smile as he watched Colby and I. Before we left the gallery Colby picked out two more paintings.

Tavio

"You didn't even go to your son's baby shower?" Mandy asked me.

"Nope, I saw everything when Tempest brought it home."

Mandy was telling me about all of her plans for Alaina's baby shower here at the office. Once she said that they invited Royce I knew I had to hold back and not go overboard cause mister sensitive would take anything I did the wrong way. So I put money in the pot to buy the stroller that Alaina registered for and my office planned to buy for her.

As I spoke to my boss, I told her that the demands of my main job were ramping up. I told her I was going to have to leave this job a lot sooner than planned. "Tavio, I need to tell you something."

"Shoot," I said not having a clue as to what she could possibly have to say to me.

"Payroll got a wage garnishment letter from the child support office for you. The reason they reached out to me is because the information was all over the place and they needed to verify that it was you. I mean you're the only Tavio in the entire bank, but some of the information was flat out wrong. No birthdate, no social, just a bunch of craziness."

I felt like she punched me, "child support? For who, for what? I only have a son."

She pushed the letter across the table, "you didn't hear of this from me, but you need to contact the district attorney's office to get this straightened out."

I picked up the letter looking for a name. "Breezy Collins" has named me as the father of her child. My breath became fire as I looked at the letter in disbelief! At least I didn't have to search my mind to remember this woman. What kind of a name is *Breezy*? How could I not remember the woman I had enough sense to walk away from. I never touched her, barely kissed her. This is ridiculous! "I never slept with this woman. We went on a few dates, and I knew better."

"Contact the D.A.'s office and demand a blood test. Then you can move on."

When I got to my desk I called the number on the letter. I was transferred to a clerk after sitting on hold for fifteen minutes. The person I spoke with was very apathetic towards me. I realize I'm not the first and I won't be the last man to call in claiming that they have wrong information, but she could've at least gave me the benefit of a doubt. I wasn't rude, cause I know she isn't personally responsible for this situation. She told me I should come down to their office in Martinez, which was on my way home, to pick up the paperwork to contest paternity of the child in question. I left a little early, I didn't even say goodbye to Alaina like I normally do or walk her to her car. My car flew to that office. There were men everywhere looking lost and annoyed. The receptionist told me to take a number and then someone would give me what I needed.

I sat in the chair bouncing my leg looking from person to person. My anxiety was shared with each person I made eye contact with. I've never not taken care of my son; I always make sure he has before I have. It is an insult to me as a man to be here. The room fell silent as a girl walked in the door. Her hair was done, fingers painted, dressed in designer clothes and shoes, her body was banging, the stereotypical gold digger. She walked up to the receptionist desk like she owned the room. Most of the men looked at her in disgust, the others drooled. She waited at the receptionist window and then a guy came from the back office. He looked annoyed, "I've told you that we sent the letter. We can't make the employer respond any faster. You know how this process works, it takes time."

"I need the money now! I can't wait!" She screamed.

"None of this will get you any more money faster. Maybe you should talk to the father and see if he can help you."

"He's not going to help me. He's mad that he has to pay anything at all. This is ridiculous! His salary is a matter of public record. Why do you have to wait for confirmation, just increase my child support. He owes me!"

"Or you could get a job and stop wasting his money on those ridiculous clothes!" One of the men in the waiting room interjected.

"You need to mind your own business! Nobody asked you nothing!" She snapped.

The men in the waiting room seemed to start cursing this girl all at once. The guy from the back looked like he wanted to send her away. But seeing how the waiting room became alive he was forced to take her to the back. One guy was saying that she reminded him of his baby momma, and how they weren't even sure that his daughter was his because she cheated on him so much.

I was getting lost in their stories when a familiar voice called my name. I looked up to see Mona standing by the door waiting for me. I got up and followed her to her desk. The room was full of cubicles with short walls so you could see who was where at all times. The cubicles along the walls and windows had high walls like mine at my office. I sat in the chair next to Mona's desk. She started typing, "what are you doing here?" She said lowly.

"I don't even know, this came into my office. I never slept with this girl. Matter of fact the night when she was throwing it at me, I called you when I got home."

"Whoa! Well then that was a long time ago." She smiled, as she glanced at her wedding picture on her desk.

"Right, how do I make this disappear?"

"First thing, you can't let on that you know me. I'm not supposed to handle any cases where I know either parties involved." I nodded in agreement. "Fill out this paperwork. Then I'll get the paternity test setup." She clicked on her computer. "She says that you admitted to her that you're the father, and then refused to see the child."

"That sounds just like me." I shook my head.

"In this line of work I can't even go by that. There's been guys who seem like the most standup and genuine persons until you get your hands in their pockets. Some guys who had all these character witnesses to say what type of person they are. Then you find out the truth. I'm not saying that you're like that. I've just learned to let everything play and not to pass judgment on anything. There's nothing worse than a mother who is supposed to be paying child support and she acts like she should be exempt because she gave birth to the child. We get all kinds in here."

I filled out the paperwork at her desk as she worked on other things. Little miss gold digger cursed everyone out just because she could, and then she stormed out of the office like someone would chase her. The guy who has been dealing with her yelled in frustration. I heard him telling someone that she made a lot of money on the cases she had in their office and that she was just greedy.

That night I helped little Tavio with his homework. When he went to bed I sat at my desk trying to understand why a woman that I only had three dates with and barely even kissed would try to tell the world that I was the father of her child? When I drove by the last place I knew she lived someone else lived there. That was probably a good thing cause nothing good would've come out of me confronting her.

Eva

I grabbed Colby's hand as the butterflies in my stomach flew up through my throat, and out of my mouth. Colby's friend and barber Lamar turned on the clippers and I squealed excitedly. "Say goodbye to life as you knew it!" He said as he slowly moved the clippers towards my head. "It's not too late to change your mind." He taunted me.

"Never! Do it!" I said as I squeezed Colby's hand.

He started at the back of my head. Every stroke felt like pressure releasing from my scalp. When he was done I looked in the mirror I was completely naked. My eyes popped out, my nose, my lips. I looked at Colby, he was watching my eyes. "What do you think?"

"I'm going to have to get used to it, if you like it I love it." Then he kissed me.

I kept smiling at myself, I kind of loved it. I was going to have to get used to it myself. However, I feel so free! Next up on my list of things for me is to get a tattoo.

When we got in the car, I put my makeup on while Colby drove. When we pulled up to the light I put one more stroke of lipstick on then I smiled at Colby. He bucked his eyes at me and came in for a kiss. He told me I was beautiful. I fixed my lipstick then I smiled harder in the mirror. When we pulled up to my townhouse I took a deep breath. I told Colby to protect me cause my grandmother was going to hate my hair, or I should say head. I opened the door and went straight to the bathroom. I called out that Colby and I are here. My grandmother and Rickie were in the kitchen, and everyone else had yet to arrive. I stalled in the bathroom for as long as I could. I could hear Mr. & Mrs. Singleton's voices as well as Chauncey's laugh. My grandmother knocked on the door and asked me if I was ok. I told her I would be out in a minute. I stood in the mirror taking deep breaths. "I am not my hair! I am not my hair!" India was going to be my silent soundtrack through this dinner. Once my grandmother got over the initial shock she'd have to live with it.

I slowly opened the door as my heart was pounding out of my chest. I could hear movement as they brought dishes to the table. Quincy was the first person that I saw and his eyes stretched wide as horror etched itself across his face. He sat frozen in his chair as he stared. Mrs. Singleton was smiling until she looked at me. Her smile dropped as well as she stared at my head like it was something from another planet that she was trying to understand. Vanessa and her mom carried dishes from the kitchen. Vanessa's mom didn't even notice at first. Vanessa stopped walking and then she smiled at me, with a smile of approval. Katrina had the same reaction as Vanessa. I took my seat at the table next to Colby, he was smiling at everyone as the unforgivingly stared at me. Rickie was walking at a normal pace that quickly slowed as she looked at me. Her look was a combination of what did you do and horror. My grandmother was focused on the salad bowl in one hand and the warm dinner rolls in the other. She sat down at the table and then she looked at everyone as we sat in awkward silence. When her eyes finally landed on me she immediately reacted. "WHAT HAPPENED TO YOUR HAIR?"

I ran my hand over my baldhead, "I cut it off."

"WHY? Did you get a bad perm?"

"I've wanted to do it for some time, this seemed like the right time."

She pointed her fork at my head, "you wanted to do that to your head?"

"Yes."

"You look like a man! Are you trying to tell us something?"

I tried not to deflate in front of her. "She does not look like a man. Plenty of women in Africa have and still wear their hair like this. I think she looks beautiful!"

"Colby, you already got her. You don't have to pretend anymore. She looks ridiculous! Fortunately it will grow back."

"For the winter months I plan to let it grow just a little. However as soon as the Spring weather rolls around I'm going to look like this."

My grandmother hit the table with her fist, "WHY? I DON'T LIKE IT!"

"But I do!"

Colby put his hand over mine, "we like it. That's really all that matters."

"What about your job? You think they're going to allow you to walk around with your hair looking like this?"

Mrs. Singleton cleared her throat, "her head, I mean hair has nothing to do with her job performance. Her look doesn't detract from the mission statement of our company. If anything it encourages our values and vision for the company."

"I love it!" Vanessa blurted, "only a woman confident in who she is and what she stands for could rock that hair style. We are going to take this style of yours out!"

My grandmother kept staring at me and whenever I looked at her she rolled her eyes at me. Every time she did it, Colby kissed my cheek, hand, or whatever was available to him. Rickie kept looking at me with big eyes, I know she doesn't like my new style, but at least she's trying to be nice about it.

"Well seeing as the vibe is already awkward in here, we thought we might lessen the tension some. Chauncey and I are officially four month's pregnant."

The energy shifted in the room, and Mrs. Singleton screamed in excitement. I mouthed thank you to her.

As we cleared the table, Vanessa told me she was serious about going out. I tried to hurry out with Colby and his parents, but my grandmother called me into the kitchen. "I don't like your hair and you're going to let it grow out. Why would you wait until you're almost thirty to start acting like a teenager again?"

I kissed her cheek, "you do realize that I'm grown don't you? You've told me more than four times that you don't like my new look. Fine, I think I've gotten the message. I happen to love it, and my man loves it too. We are done with this conversation. You may bully me about a lot of things, but my self-expression will not be one of them. Good night Grandmother, I will talk to you later." I turned on my heels and walked out of the kitchen. I felt so strong and so powerful. Colby was waiting in the car. That night I was the Goddess and he was my willing servant. We even took out the swing in our bedroom as we had the time of our lives. I felt so free and so powerful!

Tavio

"I hate my mother in-law! I really don't want her anywhere near my son." Alaina said before she gulped down her water. "As I opened my gifts she kept interjecting stuff. Kind of talking low but loud enough for everyone to hear. She kept saying I was going to make her grandson fat too. When we played the belly game at the shower she thought it would be funny to take heck of string saying that's how big she thought I was."

I frowned, "I've never been to a shower. What are you talking about."

"There's a game we play. They take string and they measure how big you are around. Then the guest have to guess by looking at you how much string they need to match. The person who guesses the closest wins. Chareca only took a foot of string."

"Willingly throwing the game?" I couldn't believe it. I'd never throw a game, I have to win.

"She's my girl and had my back. Royce's momma gonna take enough string to knit a scarf!"

"You didn't kick her out?"

"Everyone was tolerating her until my Granny Shane came out of the kitchen. She heard Royce's mom say something and she kicked her and anyone else who felt some kind of way about it out. Once they left the vibe was peaceful at my shower. One good thing that came out of that though, is their mutual dislike for my mother in-law got my Granny and my grandmother talking. Both of them vowed to be at the delivery and to be on guard to keep her away from me and in line."

"My momma and Unique said they had a great time. They didn't mention anything about her getting kicked out."

"That's because they're the sweetest." Alaina started bouncing in her seat with a wicked grin. "You should've seen her face; I read the card aloud from Royce's father. He bought all of the furniture for the nursery. He said as soon as we close escrow he was having some work done to the house, but the first room to be ready is going to be the baby's room."

"That was nice of him."

"Yeah, it was his idea to have the shower earlier so that it would be one less thing to do later on."

I drummed my fingers on the table. "You know I brought you out to lunch to tell you something."

She looked at her fork, "I know. That's why I keep talking. I know I'm not going to like it."

"Be happy for me."

"You already barely work here as it is. I'm not going to be happy about you abandoning me."

"Our working relationship isn't the only relationship that we have. We hangout outside of the office."

"Yes, but with everybody else. At work and on lunch is the only time I get to spend one on one time with my other best friend. How am I supposed to monitor your loc growth and live through you. Every time Royce does something with you he gets hurt, mamed, and embarrassed. Eventually he's going to say we can't be friends anymore."

"He is your husband."

She stared at the table, "and I do what he tells me to." Then she smiled at me. "Although, I at least got him to compromise to move to Berkeley. I know he hates it, he has no enthusiasm about our house. Where I am ecstatic!"

"That just goes to show that sticking to your guns isn't the end of the world."

"Or that as long as his dad is on my side I can have whatever I want. I think my father in-law tries to make up for his wife being such a witch. He had us over the other night and he pulled out all the stops for me."

"He's officially moved out and everything?"

"Yep, after Rachel told him what his wife was saying to me at the shower, he said that he's filing for divorce. He doesn't care about the money any more."

"How does Royce feel about all of this?"

She shrugged, "he won't talk to me about it. He just keeps eating. All he said to me was that he couldn't expect them to continue pretending for the rest of their lives." Then she looked at me, "what do you think about the name Jerrell?"

I thought about it for a minute, "sounds like superman's pop's name."

She started laughing. "Leave it to you to come with something crazy like that. I like the name."

"Royce doesn't want a junior?"

"I want my baby to have his own name."

"What does Royce say?"

"It doesn't matter, I'm putting my foot down." She smiled, "I don't want to cry so we're not going to talk about it. You better not forget about me! I need your friendship. You and Chareca are my only sanity these days. My dad has become more and more persistent. He wants to know his grandson."

"Explain to me again why you're fighting with him?"

"He lied to me, he held me accountable to a standard that he wasn't upholding himself."

"Hear me out," I put my hands up as a peace offering. "You've never lied?"

"He's the parent, he's supposed to lead by example."

"I can remember when I was growing up, there were certain things I felt a certain way about the way my parents handled them. The older that Tavio gets the more I realize how hard it was. You're always going to want better for your children than you have or your parents could provide. He messed up Alaina, you can be mad at him all you need to be. But forgive the man, don't keep his only daughter away from him anymore. He has to be going completely crazy."

"He's not, trust me. He's still with that woman, and apparently they're all out in the open with everything now."

"I know he is."

"How?"

"You are only my friend, and I can't imagine my life without you in it. I wouldn't care how mad you were at me. I would hound you until you forgave me."

Alaina blushed, "ok. I wasn't expecting you to say that."

"I love you and I'm going to miss you."

"I'm going to miss you too."

****

I laid on the bench and lifted the bar. Wesley stood over to the side watching me. Something was on his mind and I was waiting for him to get to it. He watched me do my set, then he handed me my water bottle when I sat up. "Did Alaina tell you? Royce's wrist is sprained."

I spit out my water as I started laughing. Wesley gave in and laughed himself. "I didn't do it on purpose."

"Why do you think he keeps challenging you?" Wesley watched my eyes.

I lowered my eyes as I shook my head in agreement. "I know."

"At least you're not denying it. Finish your reps and then let's go have a talk." I finished my workout and then we walked over to the cafeteria. We ordered our protein shakes and then we sat at a table off to the corner. "My son has sickle cell anemia."

"I'm sorry to hear that."

"Do you know if you carry the trait?"

"I've gotten tested for everything that I could think of, it's never come up. As far as I know, no one in my family has it."

"That's good to hear. My sister is very precious to me." He looked at my eyes, "how long are you going to hang around in the background like forbidden fruit? Royce isn't completely dumb. You think he doesn't know how you feel about his woman?"

"You're pleading for Royce?"

"No! Heck naw! I've got some serious words for that fool next." He adjusted in his seat; "let me clue you in on what you're dealing with." The server delivered our shakes. "Alaina ever tell you about our family? Our sister?"

My stomach locked up on me. "She told me your mother took her life and that your sister died. She mentioned how it affected your grandparents."

"Alaina is so angry with our mother that she's trying so hard not to be her, and here she is on the cusp of repeating history." Wesley rubbed his hand over his face. "Although our parents were in love our mother had this whole other life that no one knew about. We were being raised in a God fearing home while the whole time our mother cheated on our father. She cheated with a man who carries the sickle cell trait. He passed his disease to me and I passed it to my son. Alaina nor our father carry the trait." He watched my eyes to make sure I followed him. "When I was about two or so they called the whole affair off. After our mother had the twins her affair began again. They would meet up at different hotels. This particular meet up I was put in charge of my little sisters and told to go walk around the hotel. Alaina was always calm and mild, while Alaysia was more like our mother in her wild spirit. She wandered off and I tore up that hotel with Alaina in my arms looking for

Alaysia. The hotel staff found her floating in the pool. I didn't know what room my mother was in. When my mother came, one look at that man and I knew the truth. All of the truths came spilling out. Our father still protected our mother as much as he could. Nothing anyone could do would bring our sister back. The next few years we dealt the best we could with as much of the truth as we were given. Alaina used to call her mirror reflection Alaysia. She would talk to her and play with her. I honestly think if our parents could've convinced her that there was no Alaysia they would have opted for that. I had no idea until a few years ago that Alaina carries so much hatred for our mother. I didn't think about the fact that she would have as many pinned up feelings as I used to. My teenage years were difficult, and I was angry about everything. It took my grandfather sitting me down and pointing out how much I was hurting my father and my sister and neither of them deserved my wrath." He looked at me, "I'm giving you some background. Letting you see how your relationship with Alaina is deeper than you realize. Alaina is playing with fire; she carries the genes of a conflicted woman. She can't even see it behind hating her so much."

I sat back, is he trying to tell me to walk away? "This is a lot to process."

"I think you should know what you're getting yourself into."

"What does that mean?"

He took a big sip of his shake. "I'm trying to look ahead and see how this story ends. I honestly didn't think they'd be together this long. I really didn't think she would have children with him. Why do you think I befriended you and Ben all those years ago?"

"Because of our charm and natural good looks of course." I smiled.

"You fool, ya'll ugly!" Then we laughed. "I wasn't sure which one of you it was going to be. I knew it was going to be one of you. Now I respect that you've kept your friendship honest. This baby opens up too many emotions for my sister. She's so much like our mother, without the outright defiant attitude like Alaysia had. She's not going to stay with

Royce. He's too emotional, and guarded. He holds back all the time, meanwhile calculating. Perfect for his job. Not perfect for my sister."

"You think I'm perfect for her?"

"No! No one could ever be good enough for her. I'm not telling you to wait either. She has our father's loyalty gene, so she could end up stuck to this loser longer than you could afford to wait. I'm giving you the courtesy that no one has ever given me. Background information."

Eva

I was holding my breath, please don't say it! Please don't say it. "Eva, Vanessa, Paul, and Lucas pick your teams. Come up with a travel schedule and plan of attack. I need that entire office evaluated. I need a reason to keep the California office open."

"Outside of the prestige that comes from having a physical presence in California?"

Mrs. Singleton looked at Lucas; she was trying to control her anger, she pointed to the board. "Did we not just go over the numbers? It is expensive to maintain these offices just so we can say we have real estate there doesn't work for me. We could move those jobs to almost any other state in the US and the work would offset the expense. Say one more dumb thing and you'll be the first person waiving his pink slip." Vanessa and I exchanged looks across the table. Neither one of us wanted to go back to California. It would be different but we were going back to the Bay Area. The place I grew up in, and for Vanessa the place where her heart was broken. "You all have two weeks to plan. I will review your proposal at that time. We need to get the ball rolling. I expect you all to deliberate immediately." Then she stood up.

The rest of the teams exited the conference room leaving the four of us in a stare down. Paul and Lucas were going to pull the whole they have families and very hands on teams that the need to monitor. It's not our fault that we have seasoned staff that perform according to the standards we set out for them. I DON'T WANT TO GO TO CALIFORNIA! TAVIO IS OUT THERE! How can I go to the Bay and not see him? Would Colby hate me if my clothes fell off at the sight of Tavio. After our stare down we arranged a meeting to discuss. Vanessa and I met in the garage by our cars. "Stallone's?"

"Yes!"

Stallone's was our go to spot when we couldn't think of anywhere else to go. As we sat down Vanessa said, "for all I know he's not even out there anymore. He could've moved anywhere."

"I know Tavio is still there. Rickie talks to his sister all the time." I took a deep breath. "Doesn't matter, this is business we can do this."

We sat there for hours talking each other up. Vanessa looked up and smiled as strong arms caressed me from behind. I leaned back to kiss Colby. I asked him what he was doing here. He said he came for food in between rounds. He had to go back to the hospital but he wanted to see me. I told him Vanessa and I needed to go to California for work, but we hadn't worked out the details yet. Colby asked me if he should be concerned. I kissed him and said no.

Chapter 13

Alaina

Jerrell looked up at me as he ate. I thought looking at Cara Mia or my nephew William melted my heart. Looking at my son was a complete trip. Everyone had me so nerved up about the delivery, but it wasn't that bad. Royce was right there from the beginning to the end. He even got emotional holding his son for the first time. He kept kissing me, telling me he loved me and how thankful he was for our son. He's been so mesmerized by our son that he hasn't even tried to fight me on the diet that I enforced. He makes me sick actually; weight has been falling off of him faster than it has off me. I guess that's a good thing cause I didn't have as much weight to lose as he does. His clothes started hanging off of him and I had to drag him to the store so that I could figure out his new size. Normally I bring clothes home for him, but I couldn't guess his size by looking at him. We only got a few things because he's still losing weight and it didn't make sense to buy a lot of stuff.

When Jerrell finished eating I handed him to his father. Then we got out of the car. Royce is too excited for this doctor's appointment for my liking. It's my six-week checkup, but I don't feel ready. I've actually enjoyed my six-week break from Royce's nonsense. Chareca rubbed my head when I told her pregnancy didn't improve our sex life. I was looking online and there were testimonies from women who said that after having their baby they couldn't get enough of their husbands. I don't want sex more now than before. I know it's messed up, I just don't know what's wrong with me. Every time I think about sex I think about how dirty it feels. Chareca suggested a lubricant before the pregnancy and it helped a lot. I just don't know what's wrong with me.

"Mrs. Chambers, how are you feeling?" My doctor asked as she sat on the stool next to the table I sat on.

I exhaled sadly, I don't know where the tears came from but they poured out of my eyes. "I'm sorry."

My doctor gently rubbed my knee. "It's ok sweetheart, you're in a safe place. Let it out."

Why did she say that? I grabbed my dress off the chair next to the table. I covered my mouth as I sobbed from my heart. "I've been married seven years and I can count on one hand how many times I've enjoyed it. I only know my husband and I don't like it. I could do without sex for the rest of my life. I've thoroughly enjoyed these past six weeks and I'm afraid you're going to tell me it's ok to go back to what I'm not ready for."

"Honey it's ok, plenty of women feel the same way you do. Some are afraid about loss sensation and things like that. You're going to be ok."

"No I won't! I've tried! I've tried very hard to find one way or another to make things work and I just can't. The past six weeks I didn't have to worry about trying and it felt great. If I go out there saying it's ok, I go back to searching for a feeling. Any feeling!"

"It sounds like you're blaming yourself?"

"I was the virgin, he said he never had any complaints before. It has to be me!"

"Mrs. Chambers every woman is different. Just because he knocked it out of the park with someone else doesn't mean he's going to ring your bell."

I reached for tissue to blow my nose. "I guess."

The doctor stood up and opened the cabinet. She took down a folder and then she grabbed papers. "Bear with me, I need to ask you routine questions and then we can continue." She asked me questions like; did I have thoughts of hurting my baby? How happy have I been? When I feel sad what do I think about? She gave me pamphlets about postpartum depression. What to expect after the baby was born, and a list of support groups in my area. She spoke with me until she made me laugh. Then she did my six-week exam. She told me that I was physically ready, but it was up to me to tell my husband when I was truly ready. She asked me what type of birth control I wanted to use, and then anger spread across my body. Somehow my pills were *lost*. I wasn't going to give him the opportunity to do that to me again. There were too many choices and not enough time to go over the options right there in her examination room. I took pamphlets on my options with me. When I walked out into the lobby with red eyes Royce kind of sunk in his seat. He kissed my forehead and then he held my hand while he carried the baby in his carrier in the other hand.

When he got in the car I told him I wanted to go see my daddy. He paused for a minute and then he asked me if we should call first. I took a deep breath and said no. Her car was in the driveway just like before. This time Wesley's car was there as well. Royce carried the carrier as I walked slowly to the front door. My heart was pounding as I took out my key to open it. I could hear the television and they sounded like they were having a good time. William was in the middle of the floor on a blanket playing with his blocks. My daddy was sitting on the couch with his back to the door. He was watching Wesley's face as Wesley smiled at me. My daddy twisted in his seat and looked at me. He looked sad and relieved. He told us to come in. His girlfriend stood up looking very comfortable in her cotton shorts, bare feet, and tank top. She asked us if we would like something to drink as she walked into the kitchen. Royce asked for water for the both of us.

My daddy stood up and rushed me. He squeezed me so tight I moaned from the pressure. He kissed my cheek as he kept squeezing me and rocking me from side to side. "Hi dad," is all I could get out when he looked at me.

"I'll get to you in a minute. First let me see my newest grandson." He said moving the blanket back. "He looks like me!" My daddy said as he unbuckled the baby and took him out of his seat. My daddy held Jerrell like a professional. He sat back down and got comfortable holding the baby. I picked up my nephew and sat on the couch next to my dad. I was showing him the baby as Wesley took pictures of us. Then he shoved the camera into Royce's hand and told him to make himself useful. Royce and my dad's girlfriend stood to the side as we took family photos.

Royce

AND ROYCE IS BACK IN THE BUILDING! Fifty pounds down and I can see my old face in the mirror. How did I forget how FINE I am!

My mother has been so energized about my weight loss, that she's volunteered herself to go walk with me. The whole time she's complaining about my father and all of my siblings, I'm not excluded from this list. I tune her out most of the time.

I think about Alaina and our son. I'm so in love with our little family. I can't wait to see what our next child looks like. I can't wait until we're a family of six. All of our personalities and family bond. Alaina and I going to parent teacher conferences. Family vacations, the whole nine yards. You would think my momma who was so concerned with my wife blowing up, would've been happy for me that my wife didn't even look like she gave birth to my child. Her first grandchild. Nope she blames Alaina for my weight gain and I don't say anything. It's just easier to let her say whatever. "Who's watching the baby during the day?"

"The baby stays with Alaina."

My mother stopped walking, "shouldn't she be back at work?"

"She was cleared to go back to work, but I thought she should stay home with the baby."

"Why would you let her trick you into being the sole breadwinner while she lays up and probably gets pregnant again? No! un un! Send her back to work before she traps you with another baby."

In order to trap me with anything that would require her letting me next to her. Alaina's hollering not ready! My balls are so blue they've turned purple. My wife has been loyal and patient with me; I can ride this out with her. "Alaina is in no hurry to have another baby right now."

"What does she do all day? She go shopping?"

This was getting old, "what do you do all day?" My mother jumped as she looked at me. "Dad doesn't even come home to you. How's the divorce coming along? Maybe if you put the same energy that you put into pointing out my wife's flaws into your marriage he wouldn't be divorcing you."

"Royce!"

"Naw mom, why are you fighting the divorce? You don't want to be married to dad anymore anyways. You're just being difficult because you can be."

"You are as ungrateful as your father! I can't believe this! Go ahead and be dumb Royce! You have no idea of what women are capable of and the scandalous things they do. You go ahead and be stupid and learn on your own." Then she stormed ahead of me.

I followed her until we got back to our cars. She hurried into her car and sped away. I guess she thought I was going to follow her home. I was over the extreme outburst for the day.

I went to my father's store. He pulled up at the same time that I did. He got out of the car with a smile, "I was just at your place visiting with my grandson. Alaina said you were with your mother."

"Yep," I said taking deep breaths.

"Go home to your family, don't let her get in your head. Misery loves company."

"Am I stupid for making Alaina stay home with the baby?"

"What do you mean by making?" He leaned against his car to listen to me.

"Mr. Chambers! Mr. Chambers!" A little voice said. "I'm going to get a puppy!"

My dad smiled really big at the little boy, "today is the special day? That's great son." My dad waved hello to the little boy's father. "Today's the day huh?"

The man shook his head like he was exhausted, "yes. He wouldn't let me sleep. It took some pretty crafty procrastination to get him to wait this long."

"Make sure you show me which one you pick." My dad said to the little boy who was excitedly running to the door.

"Ok! I will!" The dad shook his head smiling as he entered the store behind his excited kid.

My father's smiled dropped as he returned his attention to me.

"What do you mean by make?"

"I told her she needed to focus on getting better."

"What do you mean by better, she looked fine a few minutes ago."

I exhaled, "she won't let me next to her. I think her plate is full trying to figure out how to be a wife and mother. I make enough money that we can afford for her to stay home. How is she supposed to juggle a job, our family, and me?"

"What did you do?"

I shrugged, "I didn't do nothing. She had the baby and now she starts literally fighting me if I try to touch her."

"Son? Do I look stupid? I didn't think I looked stupid, but I guess I do."

"I didn't do nothing, when she was pregnant we were fine."

"Sounds like you weren't paying attention."

"Dad, why do you always take her side? Why don't you think it could be something she did or didn't do?"

"I'm your father, and I know how sneaky you are. You will always fight against your inner mother traits."

"I'm not like her."

"You're the only one of her kids who can stomach her, why is that?"

"Because she's my mother, and the only one I have. How can you fault me for having a relationship with my mother no matter how difficult she is?"

"Because! You're the only one who hasn't opened your eyes and seen everything for what it is. Your mother is selfish, and manipulative."

"What are you talking about?" I felt defensive. I could feel the inner struggle, I didn't want to think about it.

"I can't point it out for you, you've got to see it on your own. I loved your mother and I took her all over this world. There used to be a time when we were so in love and then one day that all changed. Go home; go help your wife with your son. Rub her feet. Tell her how much you love and appreciate her. Do something to make her feel special. You can't expect her to just open up to you the way she used to when everything has changed."

"But nothing has changed, I'm still the same."

"You've never given birth so you need to ask her instead of assuming. Go talk to your wife, go pamper her." Then he walked inside his store.

When I got home, Alaina had music playing loud and she was dancing in the middle of the living room with our son in her arms. Her hair was in two French braids, and the straps on her dress had fallen just off her shoulders. She was singing the song to him and they were having their own love fest and I felt like I was intruding. When I closed the door Alaina jumped. She walked over to the stereo and turned the music down. She said she thought I wasn't coming home until later. I shook my head no as I looked her over. I wanted to pick her up and take her to our bedroom. Instead I tugged on her dress and I told her it was cute. She grinned at me and then she walked away from me. I went in the kitchen and threw everything in the blender for my shake. I shook my head real fast trying to let the bad things go away. "What are you doing?" Alaina laughed as she walked in the kitchen.

"Nothing," I looked her up and down. "Look, if I can't hit it then you can't walk around here looking like that."

She half grinned half frowned, "like what?"

"Your dress is short showing off your legs. The material looks soft and I can easily flip it up out of the way. That dress makes your breast sit up nicely. I don't understand why I can't sleep with my wife in the first place. Then you want to walk around here looking like a chocolate drop and I'm supposed to contain myself."

"You want to talk about this?" She watched my eyes.

"Wasn't I just speaking? Duh! Don't ask dumb questions!"

Alaina exhaled, "don't go there with me Royce! I will walk away and leave you in here to figure it out for yourself."

"Whatever!"

"I don't trust you, and until I can decide on a birth control that you can't sabotage when you feel like it, I'm not messing with you."

"You don't trust me?"

"**NO**! You did this to me on purpose."

I hit the counter, "I'm sick of you blaming me! We are married and babies happen when you have sex. Why is that so hard for you to accept? I had to accept it right away, but you hold on to the dumbest stuff. You just want me to run around here kissing your butt, begging you for what you should be giving me without hindrance."

"Funny how I've been extremely careful for six years and the one time I let you catch me off guard here I am."

I looked at her, "this better not be about Tavio!"

Her eyes bucked, "what?"

"You're going to withhold sex from me because I said I don't want him coming to my house?"

"He has nothing to do with this."

"Good! Cause I don't want you hanging around him anymore."

"You can't tell me who I can hang around and who I can't!"

"Yes I can! And I just did!"

"You have to control everything! How I wear my hair, when we have a child, how I dress, you even control whether I get to go back to work."

"And you control where we live, what we named our child. You aren't powerless!"

"Right, and you will not run my friend off!" Then she turned on her heels and stormed out of the kitchen. I heard her stomp up the stairs and slam a door. I looked across the room into the family room where the baby was sleeping in his pin. I took a deep breath putting my head down. I needed to calm down cause I was messing this whole thing up. I made my shake and swallowed it down. I was still pent up! I grabbed my keys and I left. I drove over to the gym I've been eyeing not too far from our house. I went in and signed up for a membership for Alaina and I. I went over to the weights and started lifting. I was yanking weights off the ground and doing whatever would make me sweat. "Royce?"

I looked up and I saw Mandy, "oh hey. What are you doing here?"

"I work here," she smiled.

"You don't work at the bank anymore?"

"I'm still there. I work here on the weekends."

"Doing what?"

One of the guys in the gym walked by slowly grinning at Mandy. She ignored him and focused on me. "I'm assisting my boyfriend. He's a personal trainer, the head trainer here. He gives his trainees workout plans and then I spot them and help them along. You interested?"

"Sounds expensive, can you hook me up with a discount?"

Mandy smiled, "of course. You're married to my girl. It's the least I could do. You want to see the different plans he offers?"

"Sure," I followed her to the desk. I told my eyes not to look at her walking around in her skintight pants and sports bra. Her back was to me, no one would know if I looked. I caught myself staring.

"Baby, this is Royce Chambers. He's married to my friend from work. I told him about your program and he wants to sign up."

Mandy's man looked me up and down. "What did you use to play?"

"Baseball mainly, but I dabbled in all sports in high school and in college."

"Have a seat, tell me what your health goals are." Mandy gave him his checklist and other papers.

By the time I left the gym I was covered in sweat, and feeling so much better. I was tired but a good tired. When I got home Alaina had changed her clothes and she had the diaper bag by the door as she dressed the baby. "Going somewhere?"

"The doctor told Chareca to take it easy so we're going to go be with her and Cara Mia." Alaina said without looking at me.

I walked up to Alaina and I put my arms around her. She stopped moving. I sucked on her cheek, "I'm sorry! I was too pent up to talk rationally about anything."

"Ok," she said lowly like she didn't believe me.

"Can we try our talk again?"

"I'm getting ready to leave."

"Chareca could wait," then I caught myself. "Or I can wait until you come back."

Alaina melted in my arms a little, "or we could wait for you to shower and you could come with us."

I smiled, "you'd wait for me?"

"Of course," she tried to keep her sappy look off her face. She was weakening.

I held her out in front of me; I looked her in her eyes. "Alaina, I'm sorry. I don't know how to feel about you rejecting our family. I'm excited about Jerrell and I can't wait to have more children with you, when you're ready of course. It hurts my feelings when you seem so angry about our family. We've been married for seven years now, this is the next step in our relationship."

Her eyes filled up with tears, "you're taking over everything. I feel like I'm drowning."

"I'm sorry, I will do better. I got us a membership at the gym up the street."

Alaina bucked her eyes; "Wesley put me on his membership at Nae's Fitness and Health Spa in Albany."

I smiled, "oh I see. Is his gym better than mine?"

"Yes, they have a daycare and classes. They have a healthy cafeteria, on site masseur, trainers, and nutritionist. They have an indoor pool, and basketball courts."

"But Mandy works at mine," I countered.

She smiled, "she told me she worked in Berkeley. I didn't realize that was the gym."

"Well keep both I don't care. I like the trainer at Mandy's gym, so I'm going to go there."

Alaina

"Earth to Tavio, hello?" I waved my hands in front of his face.

"Sorry," he was in heavy thought about something.

"What's wrong? You've been spaced out."

"You remember Nadia?"

"Of course," I said increasing my speed two levels.

"I saw her at the store the other day. She was acting like she couldn't even speak when she saw me. Then a couple of days later I get a Direct Message from her. In the message she's talking like she wasn't weird when she saw me. She wants to see me."

I increased my pace, "you want to see her?"

"One day she just disappeared, I'm curious to know where she went." He shook his head, "but that little voice inside is telling me to let it go."

"All I can say is listen to your gut."

"This is coming from the woman who married Royce Chambers." He laughed at me.

"Forget you! Regardless of everything else I know my husband loves me."

"He sure does," Tavio laughed. I didn't bite the bait and ask him what he meant by that. "I've been dating Sabrina and things have been cool. I don't know if I want to go backwards like that."

"I..." a woman marched up to Tavio.

"Tavio Spellman! HOW DARE YOU DENY OUR CHILD!" She screamed at him and everyone in the gym stopped what they were doing and looked at us. I had no idea who she was or who she could've been. "How can you look at yourself in the mirror?"

Tavio stopped his machine and he jumped off so fast. "YOU ARE CERTIFIABLY CRAZY IF YOU THOUGHT I WAS GOING TO ACCEPT THAT BULLET! GET AWAY FROM ME BREEZY!"

"What about Danyale?"

"Who is that?" He grabbed his towel.

"Our daughter!"

"You are crazy! Are you supposed to be on medication?" He said as he walked away. Security guards started towards them.

"DON'T YOU WALK AWAY FROM ME!" She screamed as she tried to grab his clothes.

Tavio put his hands up, "Breezy please don't piss me off. I'm trying to be nice to your crazy behind."

"What seems to be the problem?" The first flashlight cop said.

"He's been running from me for years. He won't pay child support for our child. He got the courts to lie and say he's not the father of my child, but he's the only person I was with."

"I never touched her! I haven't seen you since I left you standing in front of your house. You are a special kind of crazy!"

"Why are you over here bothering her?" The second flashlight cop asked.

"I was on the treadmill minding my own business when she approached us."

"Ma'am, we're going to have to ask you to leave."

"He leaves me with a baby to raise by myself and you're making me leave?" She started crying really hard.

"Let's go!" Tavio said to me.

As I started walking behind Tavio, the girl rushed me and grabbed my ponytail. I fell backwards and Tavio lost it. He pushed the girl down and he caught himself before he backhanded her. The flashlight cops ran over, and pulled the girl away from me. She was kicking and screaming. Talking about she was going to sue Tavio for putting his hands on her. Tavio helped me up and asked me if I was ok. I said I was ok, "you gotta walk out the door sooner or later! I'm going to be waiting for you."

"You wanna threaten me right now?" Tavio lunged at her, but one of the flashlight cops sacrificed himself and jumped in front of Tavio. The force from Tavio's charge knocked the flashlight cop backwards like a tumbleweed. He tumbled a good thirty feet backwards. You heard everyone gasp. The girl looked like she finally realized she should be scared, and she ran behind the other flashlight cop. "Get her out of here before I handle her!" Then Tavio grabbed my hand and pulled me to the cafeteria. People kept looking and whispering about us. I watched Tavio waiting for him to explain. He took a deep breath and then he closed his eyes and said something to himself. "I was still in school when I took that dizzy broad out on a couple of dates. She was talking about how she was thirty and looking to get married and start a family. I knew I wasn't ready for any of that so I told her to have a good life. I left and never looked back. Then almost a year ago I got a notice that she was coming after me for child support. I barely kissed her! I got a DNA test to prove I was not the father of her child. The results said there was a 1% chance I could be the father." He was angry thinking to himself.

"That must have been a powerful kiss," I smiled.

"My kiss never got you pregnant." He smiled at me.

"SSSSSHHHHH! Not cool! That was a long time ago."

"I'm just saying," he immediately relaxed.

We sat in the cafeteria for a while. I looked at my phone. I had to go get the baby from my grandmother. "Baby boy all packed?"

"Yep, I really appreciate this. I'll have to bring little man something back."

"Don't worry about it," I said holding back my excitement. Tavio is going out of town for a few of nights, so little man is going to sleepover at my house. I didn't even ask why he couldn't stay with his mother. Tavio asked me when his parents told him they were going to be out of town. Unique was going to spend the final night with little Tavio at his house. I told Chareca I would pick up Cara Mia for her since she was getting down to the wire in her pregnancy, and she was very tired. They were having another girl and they were excited. "When I pick him up from school, we'll swing by your house and pick up his things."

When we walked outside the girl was out there. However her certainty about jumping bad had wavered. She stood inside the open door to a car. Tavio told me to get in his car. He drove around and pulled up behind her car. He got out and she quickly got in her car. He wrote down her license plate number. He took a picture of her car with his phone. The girl got scared and drove away slowly. Tavio hurried back inside his car and then he followed her. Then she stood on the gas, Tavio followed long enough for her to speed as fast as she could. I watched his face as he went off. "She wanna see crazy, I can show her crazy!"

Lightning struck my stomach as I watched him in protective mode. His locs were sprouting like weeds; they were now touching his shoulders. I wanted to reach over and touch them but in this moment I didn't think it was appropriate. Tavio took me back to my car then he followed me to my grandmother's house. When I got out of the car, I thanked him for watching over me and protecting me. He looked at me funny then he blushed. I got so tickled I laughed hard, I told him to do well on his trip then I walked towards the house. My grandmother opened the door with Jerrell in her arms. She was trying to get a look at Tavio's car. "Who was that?"

"Tavio, you remember Mrs. Spellman who was at my shower?" My grandmother was looking like she didn't remember. "You remember his sister Unique." Everybody remembered Unique; at first her name got their attention. Then she's such a people person that everyone fell in love with her.

"Oh yeah, that's her brother?" I shook my head yes as I reached for the baby. "Doesn't explain why he was outside just now."

"We were at the gym and some crazy girl showed up. He was

making sure I made it here safely."

My grandmother eyed me for a long time, I started getting irritated. "Does your husband know about him?"

"Of course he does, we do stuff with him all of the time." She gave me a yeah-right look. Anger shot through me. "I'm not your daughter. Maybe if you would've gave her the side eye, I'd still have a mother!" It just came out. I couldn't even hold it back.

My grandmother gasped then she looked at me like I was crazy. "Now I know you know better than to talk to me like that. This is your only pass Alaina, if you ever talk to me like that again I will forget that you are my motherless grandchild and I'll hurt your feelings."

I swallowed air and then I walked to the couch where the baby's diaper bag, seat, and jacket were. I was now irritated when just a few seconds ago I was happy and laughing. The mood change irritated me and I was trying to pull it together, but it was irking me. I need to take a break from my grandmother. I don't know how I thought spending this much time with my mother's mother was going to work. "I'll call you." I mumbled as I stood to leave.

"Alaina, no. Don't leave like this." I took a deep breath and begged my tongue not to say anything I couldn't take back. "I didn't mean to imply that you are doing anything. I was honestly asking you a question like I'd ask anyone."

"Ok," I said standing to leave.

"Royce mentioned to your grandfather that you have been in a slump." She raised an eyebrow.

I closed my eyes and started counting backwards. "Did he mention how he forced Jerrell on me before I was ready? I've already discussed this with him. I needed the space to figure out a different birth control method. I was just about to give in, but now that I know he's been running his mouth he may never touch me again."

"Alaina, you can't leave your husband hanging like this. Your husband is a very handsome young man. Have you ever stopped to think about the women who throw themselves at him? Are you trying to lose him?"

My eyes filled with tears, "no. I love my husband."

"You have to consider his needs as well as your own."

By the time I left there, my grandmother had me feeling so guilty and selfish. I went to the store and bought stuff for dinner. I cleaned up around the house and then I made dinner. I hadn't told him about little Tavio spending the night tomorrow night. I bathed the baby, fed him, and then I put him down for the night. Jerrell is such a good baby. He sleeps through the night and some of the mom's in my new baby support group have two year olds who don't sleep through the night. The first time he slept longer than normal, Royce popped up around three something in the morning and ran into the baby's room. I didn't know what happened so I ran behind him. Royce was hovering over Jerrell listening for his breathing. Even though he verified that Jerrell was breathing he woke him up anyways.

I cleaned the kitchen after I put Royce's food in the microwave. I watched a little television and then I made my way to the bed. I was trying to wait up, but I fell asleep.

Royce

I don't even miss sex all that much anymore. I've stopped trying to get next to that woman. To deal with my frustration I've been putting that energy into my workouts. Sometimes I actually work out with Mandy's boyfriend. Usually he and I talk about when I used to play sports. I understand that he does this to paint the picture for me that I've done it before and I will do it again. His little pep talk came in handy when I plateaued for a few weeks. I've still got a lot of weight to lose to get back to my former self. However, everyone has finally started to notice my transformation. Most of our legal team are all married, but these little assistants running around the office pump a brothas head up for real.

I just wish Alaina could find it in her heart to forgive me. If I knew our son was going to cause all of this I would've waited to have him. Even though I can't even imagine life without him. My mother says that Jerrell doesn't look like me. He has my nose, my eyes, but he looks more like Alaina's father than anyone else. He has his own look really. If I didn't know for a fact that I caused his birth I could see my mother's words plaguing me.

"Earth to Royce! Hello! Hello?" Mandy snapped her fingers in front of my eyes. "If you're not going to focus we can go home. I mean I have better things to do with my time."

I smiled, "my bad." I replanted my feet and then I grabbed the bar.

"1! How's Alaina? 2!" She counted for me.

"Good!" I grunted!

"3! She don't miss us? 4!"

"Yes!" I grunted.

"5! Tell her to come visit again. 6!"

"Ok!"

She counted then I stopped at the end of my rep. I picked up my water bottle as she adjusted the weights to get hers in. I pretended like I was looking at my bottle as I watched her flex and unflex. Her breast jiggled ever so gently as she started to sweat. I miss breasts, Alaina won't even let me touch them.

One time she got engorged waiting for the baby to eat. She was in pain and her breasts were huge. I offered to help her and you would've thought I suggested something totally perverted. I'll be happy whenever I get my wife back. I know it's not a big deal to her, but sex is important to me. Mandy said she's ready to have a baby but her boyfriend wants to wait. So while she waits she helps him build his clientele. Part of that is walking around here just about naked parading her body in front of these men and women. So the women will say they want to look like her so that they can get a man like hers. And so the men will continue to work out to get a woman like Mandy. I don't understand why he lets her walk around like that. I'd snatch Alaina up if she tried to show off in that way. I'm a man; I know what men think about when they see women dressed a certain way. I might actually go to jail behind my wife though. Alaina is beautiful inside and outside. I love everything about my wife. When I'm not on her yuck list we normally have fun. She gets my dumb jokes and we make each other laugh.

"Royce! What is wrong with you? Why do you keep spacing out like that?" Mandy asked.

"I'm just thinking."

"It can't be good for lawyers to space out like that."

"I'm not at work so it's ok."

"How's the baby?"

"He's good, almost three months. He's gotten a tiny bit more interesting. I can't wait until he's bigger. I'm taking him camping, fishing, everything."

"That's so nice, will your daughters go too?"

I shrugged, "if they want to go. I don't see why not."

Mandy smiled real big, "that's good. My dad was never around. I always imagined that he would take me places and show me how to do things. Your children are very fortunate to have you."

"One day you're going to be a great mother."

"What makes Alaina a great mother?" She watched my mouth like my next words were important.

I didn't know if this was a trick, but Alaina is a great mother so I spoke the truth. "She's very loving with our son. It's not just the basic feeding, clothing, and bathing him, which she does. She caresses our son, she plays with him. She celebrates his minor accomplishments. She keeps him on a schedule, which has already worked out to our benefit."

"How so?" She leaned in like I was going to tell her the secret to life.

"He knows when it's time to go to bed, and he starts getting tired on schedule. We all know what time he's going down and it makes things easier."

"I guess that means you know exactly when the adult time begins." She snapped her fingers happily. I turned my eyes trying not to reveal any of our business. "Right?"

"Right," then I looked around. "I'm tired can we stop here?"

"That's up to you, but it won't take long to finish."

"Naw, I'm tired. I'm going to call it quits. Surprise my wife by coming home at a decent time for once." I needed to get out of that gym.

"Walk with me to get my bag and I'll walk out with you." Mandy said as if she just knew I was following her. I like walking behind her anyways, her build is more muscular than Alaina's but I still liked to look at her butt in that spandex. Then I remembered the way she just looked at me. I told myself to look away. "Still walking home?" She asked pulling my attention back to the room.

"Yes," I said following her eyes to the window. It was raining, not just raining it was pouring.

I took a deep breath, "I can give you a ride. You're only a couple of blocks away right?"

"Naw, I'll walk." I said trying to get up the gumption to do it.

"Nonsense. Your pores are open; you'll catch a cold for sure.

Then I'll have to sit at home and wait for you to heal."

"What do you mean?"

"I only get paid for working on the weekends. I come during the week to help you."

"Your boyfriend is ok with that?"

"He doesn't care. Come on," she said leading the way to the door. We lightly jogged to her car and she chirped the doors so we could get in. Her car was little so my knees were up against the dashboard. She sat there laughing for a good twenty seconds and then she said her boyfriend does not have my problem when he sits in the front. I pointed her in the right direction to my house. "Royce this house is beautiful!"

"You think so?" I personally think the house I had my eye on in Walnut Creek was better looking. "Alaina has a plan to do a bunch of remodeling on it. We're saving for phase one right now."

"Phase one?" She looked at me with big eyes.

"Yes, we're putting dual pane windows all over the house. That's going to make the house more energy efficient. Then we're going to update the kitchen. A few other things she wants to add here and there. Lastly she wants to remodel the exterior of the house and have it landscaped."

Mandy's eyes were big, "sounds wonderful. Alaina's a very lucky girl. I never lived in a house. This is better than anything I could even imagine. "You're such a good provider Royce, I hope Alaina understands how lucky she is."

I blushed, and suddenly that car was burning up. Mandy and I seemed like we were too close. "Alright, I'm going to see you later."

I got out of that car fast, I don't know what's happening but I told myself to get a grip. When I walked in the door the music was up loud and I heard little voices singing along to Kris Kross singing, *Jump! Jump!* I expected to see Cara Mia when I walked into the kitchen, but I saw Cara Mia, little Tavio, Ken, and Alaina having a little dance party. I stood there trying to hold back my laughter as Alaina and Ken did the Kid N Play while the kids looked on. Alaina's back was to me, when Ken saw me he pointed to me and told me to take the bridge. The kids got quite the kick out of me rapping that I was the *miggidy miggidy mac daddy*. Jerrell was in his swing helplessly watching the show. When the chorus told them to jump jump, Alaina jumped and everything moved when she did. I looked at Ken who was focused on the kids. I shot her a look and she frowned but she stopped jumping. When the song went off, I turned down the music and then I asked Alaina how come she didn't tell me that we were having company? Then she claimed she told me when I got in the bed. I rolled my eyes cause I could've been sleep for all I know when she supposedly said something to me. "Tavio is spending the night tonight and tomorrow night. Cara Mia's coming over until her dad gets off work."

Everyone looked at me; Alaina thinks she's so slick. This is her way around having this kid's father in our house to have his son.

"Ok, baby girl. Let's go home to mommy." Ken said to his daughter.

"Ken can I show you my spelling test before you go? I got a good grade," Tavio said excitedly.

"Of course you can little man. As black men we need to celebrate each other's triumphs."

Ken and Cara Mia followed lil Tavio out of the kitchen. Alaina was packing up food to send home with Ken. She stopped as soon as they were out of sight. She walked up to me and kissed me. I wasn't expecting her to do that so I stood there speechless. I forgot what I was about to fuss about. "Did you come home early because you're missing me?" I shook my head yes. "Good because I miss you too." Then she kissed me again. I couldn't tell if I was dreaming or not so I slapped my face as hard as I could. Alaina covered her mouth, "why did you do that?"

"Just making sure I'm not dreaming." Alaina came in for another kiss, but I cut it short when I heard them approaching. Alaina looked a little annoyed but she didn't say anything.

"Alright Royce and Alaina, thank you so much for everything." Then Ken opened the door. "Whoa! You walked home in this?"

The kids joined Ken in his exclamation about the weather. "I got a ride from my trainer. I was going to though."

Ken smiled at me, "looking good. Keep up the good work."

"Thanks," I said then he left.

Alaina took my food out of the microwave and then she put it on the table. She put their food on the table as well. Little Tavio watched me like I was watching him. Alaina was all excited chatter and she kept engaging us in conversation until I stopped outright watching the kid.

After dinner I told Alaina I would wash the dishes so that they could start their movie. The kid was more interested in entertaining my son than watching the movie. He kept getting in his face making funny faces. I was going to tell him to stop when my son erupted into excited laughter. Alaina smiled at them like she knew it was going to happen. Her hair was lose all over her head and as she looked down at our son who was sitting in her lap her hair fell forward. I wanted to take her upstairs and leave the kids, but I waited. Jerrell's laugh was contagious and you had to laugh right along with him. At eight o'clock Alaina stood up and told Tavio he had thirty minutes to shower, and brush his teeth.

With the baby in her arms they walked up the stairs and she gave him instructions on where to find fresh linens and toothpaste, mouthwash, and soap. Tavio took himself in the bathroom and shut the door. Alaina went in our room and started breast-feeding the baby. I was going to get in the shower in our room, but then I realized she wasn't going to be finished before that little boy came out, so I waited. When that little boy walked out the bathroom he had a towel wrapped around his waist, no shirt, and his dirty clothes folded in his hands. His little arms and chest were all cut up. He looked at me and smiled oblivious of my jealousy. I watched him walk into the guest room. He put his dirty clothes in a bag. He took out his deodorant, put some on. Then he took off his towel, no shame about the fact that he was naked in a strange house. I turned my eyes and asked myself why I was jealous of a little kid.

By the time Alaina came out of our bedroom Tavio was dressed and repacking his things. She handed Jerrell to me then she asked me to burp him. Jerrell looked at me with the face of a satisfied little boy. I put him on my shoulder as I watched Alaina tend to this little boy. She tucked him in, tickled him, and then they talked for a little. She reminded him that we were right across the hall if he needed us. Jerrell burped and then he passed out on my shoulder. I put his pajamas on, and then I turned on his video monitor and night light. When I walked out of the nursery Alaina was still in the room with Tavio. They were still talking. Tavio was smiling up at Alaina as she smiled at him and rubbed his forehead. I needed to get in the shower, but she was coming out when I was ready. In the shower I took my time and made sure I got every crevice.

When I walked out of the bathroom in my t-shirt and shorts Alaina was laying in the middle of the bed in a long nightgown. She smiled at me. I smiled at her and then I hit the switch on the wall. Alaina leaned over and turned on the light on her nightstand. Fine, the light could stay on a little longer. I kissed my wife like my heart has been begging me to. Alaina responded to my kiss, when I touched her breast she moved my hands away. I told myself not to focus on that and to stay in the moment. Everything was technically fine; everything was exactly like it's always been. Everything was, was boring. Alaina was doing this for me, she wasn't into it. Normally it only bothers me a little, but tonight it bothered me a lot.

Alaina

"How's my little man doing?" My daddy said as he took Jerrell out of his carrier.

"He can sit up on his own now. Set him on the floor and see." I said excitedly.

My daddy sat him down and Jerrell sat up looking at us like we were crazy for being amused by such a minor ordeal. My daddy laughed and said he loves the expressions that Jerrell makes. "To what do I owe the pleasure of your company?"

I shrugged, "Jerrell and I wanted to see what you're doing for dinner. Royce is always at the gym these days, so we don't feel like sitting at home waiting for him to get there when we're already sleep."

"He's at the gym that much? You would think he'd look like Wesley if he's there that much."

"He's losing, it's just not falling off his body at a rapid pace anymore."

My daddy watched my face for a minute. "What's wrong baby girl?"

I was going to lie and say nothing. "Jerrell is my only reason to smile these days."

"When are you going back to work?"

"Royce wants me to quit, but I'm on leave because I want to go back. He says daycare would cost too much."

"You don't want to stay home with your son?" He watched my eyes.

"Does that make me a bad mother if I say no?"

"Not at all, everyone isn't meant to stay home. Tell me something, when are you supposed to go back to school?"

I exhaled, "this is supposed to be my time but things didn't work out that way."

"You want to come out to dinner with me and the boys?"

"Sure," I sat on the couch.

"I'm eligible to retire tomorrow. I've been eligible for some time now. I hadn't done it yet cause I needed to fill my days with something. Maybe I could watch Jerrell and William during the day. At least that way I could see my baby girl daily."

"You would do that for us?" I was speechless.

"Of course! I'd do anything for my kids."

"Maybe I could work part time and go to school. What do you think?"

My dad smiled, "discuss it with your husband and then let me know how it's going to go."

I got up and kissed my dad's cheek, "thank you daddy."

Then in a very loud manner Ben, my brother, nephew, Tavio, his father, son, and brother walked in the door. "No girls!" Wesley said coming to give me a hug.

"Sorry, I didn't mean to intrude."

"How you doing sweetheart?" Mr. Spellman said as he hugged me. "We need a pretty face in this mix."

We went out to dinner and I had a lot of fun with the men. My dad finally asked Tavio why he and Ben call me MAC. He made it seem like my macaroni and cheese is the best culinary dish invented. Ben was his hype man as they went on and on about the first time they had it. Ben told the table that if you wanted to see Tavio get excited about anything all you had to do was attach food.

Mr. Spellman said Tavio has always valued food since he was a baby. He said when Tavio was a baby he had to keep a hand on his mom's bosom to make sure his dad didn't steal his milk. He said Tavio could not wait to eat table food. Mr. Spellman and Dakarai were a lot of fun to hang out with. I had no idea he knew my father. Wesley said they all get together often and watch games together and sometimes they go play. Wesley said Ken comes when he can as well. When Wesley walked me to my car I asked him why they didn't invite Royce and his father. Wesley said in the beginning Royce did come. He said once Royce started getting to busy with school they invited Tavio and Ben. He said Royce always had an excuse for why his father couldn't make it. I had no idea that they did any of this at all.

When I got home, I was excited about the idea of going back to work and possibly finally going to school. I looked at the time and I thought Royce would've been home by now. I put Jerrell to bed and then I got ready for bed. At a quarter to ten I picked up the phone and called Royce. Royce called me back around ten thirty and he said he was talking to his trainer and that he was on his way home. When Royce came home he went straight to the shower. I sat up in the bed waiting for him so I could discuss my plan. When Royce came out of the shower he seemed annoyed that I waited up. "How was your workout?"

"Like you care!" He snapped at me.

I stared at him; I was trying to understand where the mood swing was coming from. "Of course I care. You've been working really hard, and I appreciate you taking on your health for the benefit of all of us."

"Whatever!" Royce got in the bed all huffy and then he laid with his back to me.

"What's wrong with you?"

He exhaled then he laid on his back. He stared up at the ceiling, "my workload is picking up at work. Other lawyers at my level have assistants, but my boss acted like I was being ridiculous for asking. Her compromise was that I have to find a level one assistant; instead of at least a level two like everyone else. This could blow up in my face. I'm trying to think this through."

"That's why you worked out so long?"

"I guess," then he looked at me and smiled. "I'm sorry for

snapping at you. You didn't deserve that."

"I have news," I smiled.

He sat up and looked at me, and then he smiled. "You're late?"

"NO!" I hit him with my pillow. "Wouldn't you just die!"

He grabbed me and started tickling me. "Never! I will always be happy about our family expanding."

Once I caught my breath, I decided to avoid the baby conversation altogether. "So my dad is thinking about retiring. He said he would keep Jerrell for me when I go back to work or if I go to school."

"You're not going back to work." He said dryly.

"Royce, I know you want me to stay at home and have a bus load of your babies, but I want to work. Or I want to go to school. Or I want to do both. Everybody went to school except me. I want…"

"NO! You need to tend to our family and take care of the house. If you want to study something study why you can't get into making love to your man. I've tried everything I can think of to help you and nothing works. You figure out what's wrong and then we can consider all this other nonsense you're talking about."

****

When my old boss called to check on me I was extremely emotional. So she asked if she could have lunch with me when her boss came out for a visit. "Alaina, he is adorable."

"Thanks, he's such a good baby too." I said smiling at Jerrell.

"Let's get to the reason why we wanted to meet with you out of the way." Kelsey my bosses' boss said. "I know I'm over stepping every boundary known to man by saying this but I think it has to be said." She waited to see if I wanted to know and of course I was hanging on to her next words. "I understand that having a family is great, and being in love is wonderful. BUT! I need you to wake up, look at the day and age we live in. The days of mom and dad making things work through anything are almost unheard of today. Divorce is the new norm for marriages, and it's not uncommon for a person to marry two and three times. I know you love your husband, but you are giving him too much power. He gets to tell you when you can work and when you can go to school? Both of those things that benefit your life. They define how you will provide for yourself and your child in the future. We like you Alaina and you're a wonderful asset to the bank. I wish you would reconsider leaving the bank. I would hate for you to lose your seniority by trying to be the faithful and loyal wife. You've earned every day that you have under your belt."

"Kelsey I knew you liked me, I had no idea that it was on this level. You'd risk your job to set me straight." I smiled at her.

"If I felt there was any real danger of being this honest with you I wouldn't do it." She smiled back at me.

"To be honest I don't feel right about leaving the bank either."

"Alaina I want to tell you about a new part time position that I have. The hours are very minimal, however I think you would be perfect for the position," my boss said.

I happily listened as she explained that the position mainly consists of daily reporting. I would handle the department numbers for reporting to upper management. My boss said I would have a laptop and I would only have to come in once every six months or so. I felt like this was a sign and an answer to my prayers. When does your boss and their boss come out to beg you not to quit your job?

After my lunch with them, I went by Laney College in Oakland. I started the paperwork for school. I was nervous about it for a minute until I thought about it. Royce leaves early in the morning to catch Bart to work in the city. Whenever he finishes there, he goes to the gym until the late evening. As long as I left nothing out, how would he ever know that I was in school?

Royce

"Royce!" She pushed my hand away. "Stop it!"

During our legal call today my bosses' boss gave me the biggest compliment on my advisement to one of our internal partners. "It's time for lunch." I said looking her in her eyes and then I walked away. I sat at my desk and then I watched Mandy lock her computer and tell another assistant that she was going to lunch. I waited ten minutes and then I locked my computer and then I left. Every time, I say this time is the last time, but I love the way her body responds to me. Knowing that I turn her on, that she doesn't have to rely on a lubricant to get excited about me lets me know I still got it. I went to our restaurant and I walked into our usual booth in the back.

"I ordered for you."

"You know what I like." I smiled.

Mandy kissed me as she threw her leg over mine. "Meet me in the bathroom in two minutes."

Our waiter brought our drinks to the table. I told him I would be right back and to set our food on the table when it was ready. I took off my blazer and I laid it across the seat. Then I went to the bathroom that showed occupied and I knocked on the door. Mandy opened the door, and I bent her over. Hearing and feeling her appreciation for me makes me go harder. Mandy covered her mouth in an attempt to conceal the sounds of our sex session. We stayed in that bathroom for a while, and we had worked up quite the appetite by the time we returned to our table.

The rest of my day went by smashingly well. I hung out for quite a while after work clearing out my inbox. I got excited when I saw the time. I hurried over to the Bart station to make my way to the gym for my workout with Mandy. I was standing on the platform waiting for my train when I heard someone call my name. "MAC said you lost quite a bit of weight, I almost didn't recognize you," Tavio said.

"That sounds like a compliment so I'm going to say thank you." Tavio looked me over just like I was looking him over. "I can't believe you actually wear your hair like that to work."

Tavio stared at me for a minute, "if I had never met your dad and your brother, I would swear you were raised by an emotional female. I don't get you or what's exactly wrong with you. You got issues! There's nothing wrong with my hair, and it actually helps my career. My clients don't see me as just an agent. Why am I wasting my breath explaining any of this to you?"

"My wife said she hasn't seen you in a while, is that true?"

"Why would you question me about what your wife told you?"

I walked up on him, "I know about your little crush on my wife. I've known for some years now. A smart man would know better than to ever look in Alaina's direction. My wife is loyal and faithful. The fact that you've resorted to wearing your hair like this just to give you two something to talk about is ridiculous and desperate."

Tavio exhaled, "out of love and respect for MAC I won't break you down right here in front of your peers. If you ever step in my personal space again I will take you out. If you're so secure in your relationship why would you need to think anything of me? If you don't get out of my face right now I promise to kill you in the next ten seconds." His eyes turned red and had glazed over that fast.

I was expecting him to back down at least a little, but now he's looking completely crazy. I took a step back, "stay away from my wife."

"Nope! Not going to do it. MAC and I are close as you know better than anyone else. You're the only idiot to be threatened by our friendship. You may control everything else about her life, but I am the one aspect you can't touch no matter what you do." Then he grinned at me, "why don't you go back to trying to challenge me on any field or court you can think of like you used to do? I guess you got tired of getting hurt. A smart person would've learned then that you will never be a match for me."

I put my hand up to mimic him talking. "Yakidy yak! We both know Alaina is faithful and loyal. One day you'll get some sense and move on." Then I walked away.

Chapter 14

Tavio

I called Alaina as soon as I got to my car. I comically replayed her husband's attempt to buck up at me. Alaina didn't see the situation the same way I did. I still laughed at the whole situation the whole way to Unique's place. She asked me what was so funny, so I told her about Royce at the Bart station and she laughed with me. I reminded her about my barbecue on Saturday.

During the car ride home Lil Tavio turned off the radio. "Dad, how come one day I started coming to your house more than my mom's?"

"Because I wanted you with me, you don't like living with me?"

"I do, I just wondered if my mom asked you to take me."

"Why would you think something like that?"

He shrugged, "I don't know."

"Why can't I be selfish with my little man? You excited about the barbecue on Saturday? Your brothers and sister are coming."

"Is Cara Mia coming too?"

"Of course, what would our barbecue be like without your best friend?"

"Is Sabrina coming over tonight?"

"No, she's out of town on business. She'll be there on Saturday. You miss her or something?"

"No, she's always around. I'm just happy to have a break."

I laughed, "what you know about a break?"

"That's what they say on TV when the girlfriend gets on your nerves, you need to take a break and then it's not so bad."

"You're pretty smart for an almost nine year old."

Eva

"This could possibly be grounds to quit my job!" Vanessa was pacing and almost foaming at the mouth. "I mean how we get stuck with majority of the travel? Just because we don't have husbands and children! That doesn't make this fair!"

I glanced out the window of my office at the surrounding city, like I do from time to time to calm my nerves. "I understand."

Vanessa stopped in her tracks, "you understand? What's up with you? You've been acting weird lately."

"I'm an aunt and there's another baby due shortly, things are getting weird. You haven't noticed?"

"You and Colby getting the baby itch?" She smiled as she sat down.

"OH GOD NO! At least not on my part. I don't want to have a baby ever. Do you?"

She stared out the window, "I wanted a family with my ex. I wanted to do all the things we talked about. I guess I've been doing everything but thinking about my future. I wouldn't be opposed to having a baby later on. That would mean I'd have to deal with a lot before then, and I'm not ready to deal."

"Are you talking about the ex in California?"

"Yep, I thought the thought of losing my mom in a car accident was the biggest pain I would've ever had to deal with in my life. Then he abandoned me, I've been treating men like the disposable toys that they are ever since." Then she thrust herself out of the chair and walked to the window. "I do have family out there. My cousins Nadia and Nadine are good people and they'll be excited to see me. My old roommate is definitely on the list of people to see out there."

"Yeah and Unique, you remember her don't you?"

"You ask me that every time she comes to town. Of course I remember her. You can show me where you grew up before you moved to Florida. We could make this trip worth our time. And when our trips take us out there without each other it sounds like we have enough to keep us busy between the down moments."

"Truth be told, I'm going to go out there on a mission to wrap this up ahead of forecast. I don't necessarily want the California office to close, but I won't be crying if that's the final decision."

"My roommate said she saw my ex, she said he got fat. I would be lying if I said I didn't want to see him drowning in failure."

"All these years and you've never said what your roommate's name is."

She smiled, "Nefertiti Childs. I always called her Kid since she said I couldn't call her Titi. Poor thing I turned her out too."

I raised an eyebrow, "how did you turn her out?"

"College was a wild and experimental time for me."

"Well nothing's changed then, you still experiment," I smiled.

"Kid and I had a threesome with my ex." Vanessa smiled like she was embarrassed.

My mouth fell open, "please tell me everything. Was it awkward? Did you hate it? Did you love it? How did it affect your relationship with him? How did it affect your relationship with her? Did you do it more than once?"

"I thought it was every man's fantasy to have two women in the bed with him. My ex was into the idea at first, but he couldn't handle it. Kid admitted to getting too emotionally involved after he and I broke up the first time. I loved it; it was the best of both worlds for me. I got to watch and participate. His body was beautiful, and it's a shame that he let it go to waste. Looking back, I know now that's not how you treat someone you want to be with. At the time I thought I was beating him to the punch of all the freaky things he was going to ask of me."

I was searching for words to ask my next question. "So you watched him be with her only?"

Vanessa looked me in my eyes and grinned, "no. It was all experiments in my mind. Research for my likes and dislikes really."

"Have you done that since?"

"No, there's no need for further research. I'm not curious anymore."

"What about Kid?"

"She lives in San Francisco with her partner and their two kids."

"You turned her out too?"

"No, she was on the fence long before us, we may have helped push her in that direction though."

"You're right, you were wild. It's not going to be weird seeing her?"

"Nope, that was college."

Tavio

I went over Alaina's around eight o'clock in the morning. She said I just missed Royce who went on a morning hike with his mother, and then he'd go to the gym for a few hours. This fool spends an awful lot of time away from home. You would think that he would be at his goal weight by now. He could still stand to lose another eighty pounds, and those little cuts on his arms are the least he could show for all of his *labor*. Jerrell gets so excited when he sees me. We do our normal so excited to see each other thing, then he gets angry when I leave. If I didn't need Lil T's help he could've stayed with Jerrell but we needed to get going. We loaded up all the marinated meat that Alaina prepared for us and then we went back to my house.

Mr. Barton, Wesley, and William got to my house first. Wesley said he did not want to risk me burning the meat. I figured grilling wouldn't be difficult, but they seem to think that since I don't cook I would make a mess of the meat on the grill. We put the brisket in the smoker immediately. Mr. Barton said that the meat needed every minute it could get to come out just right.

My parents came over next and my momma put her feet up inside while the four of us drank beers and talked around the grill. Lil T and William were running around being kids when Sabrina arrived. She had met my dad before, but this was her first time meeting everyone else. I was standing in the living room when Sabrina walked in the door. "I'm so sorry I'm late!" She announced as she walked in.

"It's ok," I said giving her a hug and quick kiss. "My parents are here, as well as Wesley and his father."

"One moment, let me go put these cupcakes in the kitchen and I'll be right back." Sabrina hurried to the kitchen.

My momma sat on the couch unimpressed, "Mrs. Spellman. It is so nice to finally meet you."

"Nice to meet you as well."

Then there was absolute silence. No girly chatter or friendliness, just gut wrenching silence. "Come say hi to my dad and meet my friends." I led her to the backyard. Wesley frowned immediately when he saw Sabrina. "Everyone this is Sabrina these are my friends. Mr. Barton and Wesley."

"Hello," Sabrina said evenly. "So, what do you all have cooking out here?"

"Meat," Wesley said like she asked a dumb question.

"Tavio," my momma called out from the house. "Send your girlfriend to come help us get these sides together. Your sister is here with the groceries."

"I guess I'll see you in a little bit." Then she walked back into the house.

My eyes immediately went to Wesley, "walk with me, talk with me, my friend." One of the features I like best about my house is the size of the backyard. Every time I think of putting a pool back here, I think about how impractical it would be. Richmond probably gets hot enough for a pool a total of a week annually. That's a generous estimate at that. Even with a huge pool, and a pool slide back here I'd have plenty of space to play football and anything else I can think of. Wesley and I walked to the far side of the yard. "I'm not going to beat around the bush with you. Proceed with caution with that one. She used to date a friend of mine, she's a good friend of my ex-wife's, one night she tried to use alcohol as the reason she was flirting with me. This was a long time ago, but I'm telling you how she was then."

"So why you seem angry today?"

"Cause she acted like she didn't know who I was."

"She could've matured and she feels embarrassed about how she behaved then."

"Watch her is all I'm saying."

Then Tyrek, his junior, and the rest of his kids walked out of the house. The kids joined Lil T and William. Tyrek talked with us for a little bit. As soon as Lil T took out the basketball Tyrek senior jumped out of his chair to challenge my son. They were having a blast on the court playing while the rest of the boys watched in amazement. Even Mr. Barton watched in amazement as my son took on a grown man and gave him a real run for his money.

When Alaina got to the house she called me to come help her at the car. Jerrell got excited when he saw me as if he hadn't seen me this morning. I asked Alaina where Royce was, and she shrugged. She said when she told him she was coming over he told her to have fun. She looked upset, then I told her she needed to do what the man told her to do and have fun. Then I looked at the one tray of macaroni and cheese. My smiled dropped as I asked where the rest was. Alaina told me to stop playing cause her tray could feed forty people. Then she started complaining about how expensive it was to make that one dish. I smiled at her and told her next time I wanted two trays and all she needs to do is open her mouth and say how much she needs to cover the cost. Alaina called me a spoiled brat and that she'd think about it. Cause she was thinking of retiring her macaroni and cheese apron. So I told her I'd end our friendship the day she retired. Our relationship was built on her macaroni and cheese.

"Sabrina this is MAC and Jerrell. MAC and Jerrell this is Sabrina."

"It's nice to finally meet you, I've heard so much about you." Alaina said putting her arms out for a hug.

Sabrina looked uncomfortable as Alaina hugged her. I saw my momma and Unique exchange looks. I guess Sabrina's not dazzling them in here. Then Alaina and Tempest hugged and started chatting like old friends. At least I could say that everyone else was putting forward their best foot to be cool. "I brought a macaroni and cheese dish, I didn't know it was your specialty. No one told me," Sabrina said.

"Sucks to be you, I came today because Tavio said MAC was

bringing the mac." Tempest joked.

"You guys are too much. Sabrina I'm sure your macaroni and cheese is delicious. Tavio was complaining that I didn't bring enough so, your addition will be perfect."

"I brought a jello mold too, does anyone have the market cornered on that?" Sabrina snapped.

All of the women stopped what they were doing and looked at Sabrina. No one said anything, they all slowly went back to what they were doing like they were giving her a pass. Unique opened the refrigerator, "who put all these cupcakes in here? I need space for the potato salad."

"They have whipped cream icing, they need to be refrigerated. Where should I move them?" Sabrina asked me looking completely annoyed. My baby was sinking.

"Give them to me. I can put them in the refrigerator in the garage." After I put the cupcakes away, I couldn't stand to watch the scene in the kitchen any longer. I went back out to the backyard.

Ken and Cara Mia came out of the house and Cara Mia took off to play with all the boys. Ken said you could cut the tension in the kitchen with a knife. He said he excused himself and came outside. Once all the meat was ready we told everyone to come outside with the side dishes. As we were setting things in their places I asked Alaina to bring the salt and pepper out to the table. Now I didn't see anything wrong with my request, but Sabrina was upset. I stopped looking at Unique cause she kept shaking her head NO at me. When it was time to make my plate, the pressure was on. They put out Sabrina's macaroni and cheese first. I got some and a few others, but there was less than a third of the dish gone. Her macaroni dish wasn't nasty. It just wasn't what everyone came for. Like if I had never had MAC's I would think this was good.

It got a little violent though when I realized everyone was sneaking into the kitchen to get the real deal. When I went in more than half the tray was gone. I couldn't hide the pan so I got a mixing bowl and put the rest in it and then I hid the bowl in the garage in my refrigerator. Tempest's evil behind came outside busting me out. "Where's the rest of the macaroni Tavio?"

I kept my eyes on my plate; "there's plenty on the table over there."

"YOU KNOW I DON'T WANT NONE OF THAT! I'M ASKING YOU ABOUT THE GOOD FOOD!" She blasted me. Wesley busted up laughing making it hard for others to hold back their laughter.

I couldn't believe she said that, Sabrina got up in anger and embarrassment and took her tin foil pan back in the house. "You're trying to get me in trouble."

"I don't care about all of that. Hand over the mac n cheese and nobody will get hurt."

"I choose death!" I said looking her in her eyes.

"I will cut you! You think I'm playing!" Then she looked at her husband, "please tell him I'm not playing!"

"You know how pregnant women are." Her husband shrugged.

"AGAIN?" Everyone blurted in unison.

"Look! I am married and I can have as many babies as I want. Stop changing the subject, where's the food?" Sabrina came back out of the house looking all wounded. Tempest smiled at me letting me know she would continue on with her nonsense if I continued to hold out on her. If I played my cards right I could still get some tonight. If I held on to my food, I could jeopardize it all. I sat there debating with myself. There was always tomorrow to get some, I didn't have to get none tonight. Tempest cleared her throat. When I stood up everyone laughed at me.

Tempest and I fussed in the garage about how much I was allowing her to get. I was only trying to give up five cheese-covered noodles and she wanted too much. After we had each other cracking up about our fight I asked her if Sabrina was that bad. She said point blank that she didn't like her, but it wasn't up to her to choose the right person for me.

MAC helped me clean up while Sabrina talked my father's ears off about who knows what. I asked Alaina if she wanted to take anything home to her husband, and she quickly replied no.

When everyone was gone and Lil T was tucked away Sabrina pouted about the disaster that today turned out to be. She said her family loves me, and it was a shame that mine didn't feel the same about her. I told her to give it some time. "Truth moment." I hate when she starts a conversation off that way. "Your friend MAC, where was her husband?"

"I don't know actually, he was supposed to come."

"Why does her father and brother have to be here? It was already uncomfortable enough being here with your ex who seems to get along fine with your mother and that sister of yours."

"That sister?" I looked at her to give her a chance to clean up her statement.

"Well what am I supposed to say? She doesn't like me."

"It's not like your cousin was all that fond of me either, but you don't hear me making comments like yours."

"My mistake, let me correct it." She cleared her throat. "All I'm saying is that it was uncomfortable for me to be in the same room with your ex's and your mother and sister. All of these women that you're still close to."

"Chareca and I never dated," I smiled.

"That's not funny!"

"Look, I'm with you. With the exception of my sister and you, every woman in that kitchen is a happily married woman. Focus on that part instead of this nonsense."

"Nonsense? Everyone acted like my food was trash just because MAC or whatever her name is didn't make it. That was so rude."

"In the future, just don't make macaroni and cheese and you won't get your feelings hurt." I laughed Sabrina didn't. "Come on you're going to let today spoil tonight? I haven't seen you in a week, I know you miss me." I watched her eyes. When they dilated a little I knew there was a chance to end the night on the proper note.

"I guess your family doesn't like me, that's a hard pill to swallow, I wanted them to love me like mine loves you."

I put my arms around her and rubbed her back, "you'll have plenty of time to redeem yourself."

Then I kissed her, she was trying to hold back her eagerness to kiss me but it wasn't working. "But!" I kissed her lips and she melted, "how are we going to move forward if I don't get along with your family?"

I put my finger up to her lips; she was doing more thinking than I wanted to do. "SSSHHH! Right now I'm only concerned with reuniting our bodies." Then she melted into our kiss. Sex with Sabrina has been good, but it didn't start out that way. She was of the mind that she needed to pull out all these tricks initially in hopes of blowing my mind. She was trying to be all about me, and that's just not the way I get down. Don't get me wrong I love the tricks, but I don't believe in being gotten until I've gotten you. I could see surprise all over Sabrina's face the first time I hit that spot that had her climbing up the walls. She's been quite sprung ever since. They always try to make it seem like men are the only ones who get turned out by sex. I'm happy to note at least in my life that's not true.

Eva

When Vanessa's cousin Nadia came in with her husband, Vanessa got excited and hurried over to them. Nadia's husband was a little shorter than her and a lot older. He wore glasses and it seemed like he wore them just so he could squint at you through them. Even though he was acting like he was too good, Nadine and Vanessa still warmly greeted him and welcomed him in. Vanessa whispered something to her cousin and they laughed. Nadia's husband stood there with his nose up in the air like he was too good to be here. I didn't understand why Vanessa and Nadine seemed to cater to this man who acted like they were beneath them. It wasn't my business so I kept quiet. "Nadia this is my friend Eva." Vanessa introduced me, "and that's her husband Augustus."

"Nice to meet you." I said shaking her hand. Nadia was very pretty. She had beautiful brown eyes, high cheekbones, and full lips. She was a perfect milk chocolate complexion and her body was banging. All the right curves in all the right places. She had all of her hair sleeked up into a bun on the top of her head and simple diamond earrings that danced in front of my eyes as they caught the light.

"Hello, it's nice to finally meet you, Vanessa talks about you all of the time."

Nadia smiled, "same here." We hugged hello. Then she looked at her husband who openly stared at my lack of hair. "Are you ready to go eat?"

"We're starved," Vanessa volunteered.

"I made reservations at the Equinox, I hope that will do for tonight." He said like he was doing us a favor.

I looked at Vanessa who signaled to me with her eyes to be cool. Vanessa and I rode with Nadine while Nadia and her husband led the way. Their car was as expensive and pretentious as he is. I asked what the story with Augustus was and they said we'd all talk about it tonight after Augustus left. Nadia called and said that Augustus wanted Nadine to park in the valet parking as well. When we walked into the restaurant, people were hurrying to cater to Augustus. They told him his special table was waiting for him. They sat us down and immediately took our drink orders while they brought his right out. Augustus took a sip and then he nodded that it was good. He didn't bother to look at his menu while Vanessa and I looked over everything. Our waiters brought out enough appetizers to fill the table. It looked like they brought out one of each item on the menu and a couple that weren't. Our drinks were refilled without request, and when the waiter came to take our order. He spoke with Augustus first, he told him about the chef's specials that were not on the menu. Everyone ordered one of the specials and then they paired wine with our meal. Everything was delicious! Augustus sat at the end of the table like he was tolerating us at best. He kept looking at me with a glimmer of disgust on his face. That made me smile even bigger at him. If it bothered him to look at me I wanted him to have to stare at me. I kept telling stories where he would have to look at me.

When dinner was over Augustus told them to bring us tea before serving our dessert. He told everyone to drink it to aide in our digestion. The tea was very delicate and it had slight notes of honey, lemon, cinnamon, and peppermint. It wasn't too warm, it was, it was perfect. Our desserts were brought out in this big production. Flames and big reveals for our delicious creations. Augustus didn't even look at the check, he put his credit card in the billfold and sent the waiter away. I offered to pay my portion but he waved me off like I was being ridiculous. Nadia gently told Augustus that she was going to ride with her sister to our hotel and then she'd come home from there. Augustus told her to keep her phone on her and not to stay out too late. To me it looked like a child asking her father for permission to stay out past curfew, but I don't know their situation. When Nadia got in the car and we drove away she exhaled loudly. Her quiet and gentle demeanor was gone. Now she had a personality and she was fun. We hung out in Vanessa's room. Once an hour Augustus would call Nadia and ask her when she was coming home. She'd make her voice all sweet and gentle as she said something like we were in the middle of a story or something and then he'd callback.

I couldn't take it; I had to ask how she ended up married to a controlling old man. Nadia said he saw her walking past a restaurant as he ate in one day. She said she and her sister would walk to their mom's job after school daily. Her mom was a single parent and they lived in a not so good neighborhood. She said one of their friends was a latch key kid and someone followed her home and raped her. When their mother found out about that she had the girls walk to her job and wait for her until she got off. Augustus started going to that restaurant all the time until he figured out where they were going. Once he figured out which store their mom worked in he bought so many big-ticket items from their mom that she was always excited when she saw him.

One day Augustus told their mom that he wanted to marry Nadia. Nadia was only fourteen at the time. Nadia said he would always look at her and ask her if she liked certain things but she didn't realize he was looking at her like that. Nadia said it kind of felt like an arranged marriage like that.

Their mom made him wait until Nadia was fifteen and a half before she let him marry her, and that was after he promised her lots of money. He moved the three of them out to California and he has always paid for everything. I sat there staring at Nadia waiting for her to tell me she was pulling my leg or something. She just kept talking; they said it caused a lot of problems in their family.

Kiev tried to save Nadia from this old man, until she told him it was ok. Nadia said they were so broke and things were only about to get worse. She knew that if she married Augustus her mother would never have to stress about money again. And she hated seeing her mother so stressed about things she couldn't do anything about. She said it isn't so bad; she's been all over the world. She's been taken care of very well. I couldn't help it; I had to ask her what the sex was like. She said it was fine, not great, but not horrible. She said Augustus is in really good shape and he takes really good care of himself. Then she smiled and said of course she's had better. I looked around the room as her sister and cousin smiled at her. She said at one point she convinced her husband to allow her to work so that she could feel a sense of accomplishment and what it felt like to earn a dollar. She said she got a job as a bank teller and she met some interesting people. She said she dated a little here and there and she even found herself in love with one guy. She said it got so deep that she considered divorcing Augustus to be with this guy. I was on the edge of my seat listening to find out what happened next. She said she had to stop being selfish and think about all that she would be costing not only herself but her mother. Even though her mother moved back to Boston, Augustus still paid for everything. She said maybe when he dies she'll get a second chance at love.

I asked her if he ever found out about her affairs. She said not exactly. She said when he had a hunch that something was going on he made her basically give up her freedom. She said she doesn't mind so much anymore, cause she now appreciates how he takes care of her. Money is never an issue and she can have anything she wants. She said she was living the life that other people only dream of ever living.

So then it was my turn to share. I hadn't thought about my parents in years. Coming back to the Bay was only ever about Tavio and his family. I hadn't thought of the possibility of mine. I have cousins out here, from my grandmother's other children's kids. None of them call my grandmother to check on her. None of my aunts or my uncle even said goodbye when we were homeless and had to move. I pay them about as much attention as they paid us. I told them about how my ex was my everything and that sometimes to this day I wonder where we would be if I hadn't messed up everything. We all sat quiet for a minute thinking about yesterday and all the things that could've been.

That night I had a dream that Colby broke up with me, and Tavio wouldn't take me back. No matter how hard I tried, I promised him I would give him as many babies as he wanted. Yep it was a nightmare and I was so happy to wake up and be distracted by work. In between meetings with the management out here, I kept thinking about Kiev. It's good to know that at some point in his life if not now he stood for decency and right over wrong. Get it together Eva, Colby is wonderful! He loves you and you love him. Stop thinking about all these other men.

****

It was the last meeting of the day, and Phyllis was giving me a rundown of her direct reports and about their various teams. She handed me her printed out Visio created flowchart. I was glancing at the names when one caught my attention. *Clifton Pearcy*! I stared at the name, which was my uncle's name. My grandmother's only son. What are the odds that he would work for an affiliate of my company? I listened a little more closely as the manager explained what her different teams did. When I asked what the team my uncle was on did, she explained that they worked the mailroom and routing for a lot of the company. I told her on our next trip out I wanted to visit the mailroom.

After work, Vanessa and I drove back to our hotel exhausted from our final day of meetings. I was excited to have dinner with Unique, and even more excited that I was going home tomorrow. I missed my niece and Colby. As Vanessa and I approached the table Unique stood up excited. She said she was so happy I finally came out her way. She smiled as she stared at my head. She said she wanted to be shocked, but my haircut fit me. I asked her if that was a dig or a compliment. She said it was a compliment to my strength and ability not to care about what other people think. As we were talking Vanessa's old roommate that we've heard so much about joined us. She introduced her roommate as Kid, even though her roommate corrected her and introduced herself as Nefertiti. Most of the night Unique and I were in our own conversation while Vanessa and Kid caught up. Unique asked when I came back if I wanted to see Tavio. I asked her if he hated me. She smiled and said as far as she knew he didn't. I told her she could invite him, but if he declined then I knew that was my answer.

Tavio

I took a moment to grab air; I was staring at the offer letter for my newest client. His contract was so fat it completely knocked the wind out of me. I had a few client relationships that I was nurturing but this was the first one of this magnitude. My hand shook as I called Aaron at his family home. He answered on the first ring. "A man, how are you doing?" I tried to make my voice sound disturbed and unexcited.

"Come on man! I caint take too much more, are you holding the offer?"

"Yes," I showed no emotion. "I'm sorry man, I'll fax it over so we can go over it together."

I could hear him deflate over the phone. "Alright man, and are you sure this is the best we can do? Is it too late to shop around some more?"

I hit send, "it's on its way. And I'm sorry to tell you this is the best we can do for now."

There was silence outside of Aaron's heavy breathing. His machine buzzed and then it started running in the background. "I don't know what I'm going to do, this has always been my dream. I don't………….. TAVIO! TAVIO! TAVIO! YOU TRICKED ME MAN! AAAAA!" He yelled in the background. Whoever was there with him started celebrating with him. "WE DID IT! WE DID IT!" He screamed at the person. I waited with the biggest smile as he celebrated for five minutes. Then he came back to the phone. "This is the best we can do!" I could hear his smile through the phone.

"That's just your contract with the team. Like I said, we have endorsement deals, and everything else setup. I'm going to link you up with a financial advisor. It's up to you how you manage your finances, but I would hate to see you squander it all. Build your nest egg you understand me?"

"Yes, yes I understand! Thank you Tavio. I appreciate all of your support over the years. I never would've made it this far if it wasn't for you. Thank you for everything!"

I told Aaron to stop acting like a girl, and we could talk tomorrow.

As soon as we hung up, I called Alaina and I asked her what she was doing. She said she just finished her paper and she was about to make dinner for her and Jerrell. I told her to put something other than sweats on and to come out with me to dinner to celebrate. I told her I'd tell her what we were celebrating when I picked her and Jerrell up. I got off Bart and I went straight to her house. I know Royce doesn't want me in his house, so I respect that Alaina is enforcing that. However, the street and sidewalk are city property and he doesn't control that. Alaina brought the car seat out and Jerrell held her other hand as she walked slowly. "The house is coming along nicely."

"Thank you, it's almost the palace I always envisioned it to be."

"Royce bugging you about another baby yet?"

"He's been doing that since this one came out. I'm not ready to have another baby yet. Besides he'd actually have to spend time with me to make that happen."

"Well you basically only really need two minutes to make a baby happen, and in Royce's case I'm sure sixty seconds is a stretch." I laughed Alaina didn't, "sorry."

"I don't make jokes about Sabrina so don't talk about my husband."

"There's less scope for the imagination with Sabrina."

"Please! The girl looks like a Who from Who Ville! She has no chin and a pointy nose."

"Sounds like you've been sitting on that observation for some time," I stopped laughing.

"I don't say nothing because I don't want to hurt your feelings. You like her and that's all that matters."

"Sounds like you like Sabrina as much as I like Royce."

"I don't know Sabrina not to like her. She was acting a little spoiled at the barbecue, but maybe she was having a bad day that day. What are we celebrating?"

"Before we get to that, she keeps mentioning moving in together."

Alaina looked at me, "do you want to?"

"Lil T says he tolerates her for me. I'm getting older and eventually I would like to have more kids. There's plenty of women available if all I'm looking for is someone to sleep with. It seems like the options seem to disappear when I think about having a baby. She's the closest I've come to a decent option in a long time. Besides sleeping around gets old when all you want is a wife of your own."

"Sounds like you're tired of waiting for the fairy tale?"

"I guess."

"It sounds like a catch 22 honestly. You don't want to settle, but you're considering settling. No one can help you with that one my friend except you."

"I understand what you're saying, but I need to hear your experience. What made you settle for Royce?"

Alaina jumped like I pinched her. "I didn't settle for Royce! We got married because we were in love."

"I'm not saying you didn't love him, but you did settle for him."

"You're making me mad! I did not settle for Royce. We were in love and we took it to the next level, that's all."

"Alaina, I love you and I say this as a person who has deep respect and admiration for you." I braced myself for her to punch me in the arm. "When it comes to Royce you get stupid. And not just a little stupid, I'm talking dumber than the dumbest dumb person." Alaina gasped and started punching my arm as I laughed at her. "Love is supposed to make you stupid, but I personally think you take it too far. You don't challenge Royce like you should. You let him run everything about your life. You are a young, beautiful and vibrant **YOUNG** woman. Why can't you wear a stinking V-neck t-shirt? You don't smell like fruit anymore either."

She punched me again, "I don't know how this became a get on me session because you don't know what to do with your funny looking girlfriend. You're on the fence cause you know she would make funny looking babies. You're not cute enough to save any children coming from her. I married my husband because I loved him and I couldn't wait to be his wife. When you're married there are certain sacrifices you make for your mate. You wouldn't know anything about it because you've never compromised for anyone."

"What are you talking about? I've compromised plenty."

"How?"

"I gave up the love of my life because she decided she didn't want to have children."

"How was that a compromise? Sounds like you held to your guns."

"I compromised my life's plan so that she wouldn't be you. Married to me pretending like my wants were her wants and not happy with her life." Alaina looked out the window and she didn't say anything else on our way to Unique's. When I parked the car Alaina was still looking out the window. "You not coming in?" Alaina shook her head no. I grabbed her shoulder, "are you crying?"

She wiped her face, "no."

"Alaina that's not fair, don't cry. I'm sorry! I was just messing with you!" I kept pulling on her shoulder.

"Don't pick on me because you're mad about your life." She wiped her face.

"I'm sorry, you're right I was picking on you. I'm just tired of waiting for my life to be the way it's supposed to be. I'll have this conversation with Unique. Please stop crying." I leaned over and kissed her cheek.

"Tavio!" She looked back at Jerrell who was sitting quietly looking at us. "You can't do that. One of these days Jerrell is going to be able to tell Royce and Royce will blow things out of proportion. He won't understand that you were just kidding."

I wiped her tears, and then I kissed her nose. "I don't care. You forgive me?"

Alaina got out of the car and started walking towards Unique's place. I got the baby out of the car. He smiled up at me like he knew his dad was an idiot.

I invited Unique to come out to dinner with us. Then I told them about my client's gigantic deal that I landed today.

"Guess who's coming out here in a week?"

"Coming out here?"

"Eva, she was out here before, and she's coming back."

Alaina smiled, "we were just talking about her."

"What about her?" Unique looked at me with a smile.

"I was just rehashing our breakup is all." I shot Alaina a look to tell her to shut up.

"Do you want to see her when she comes out?"

"She doesn't want to see me."

"Both of you said the same thing. She's open to seeing you if you're open to seeing her."

"I have a girlfriend."

"Alaina and I can come," Unique said happily.

"I... I... I mean if you need backup sure, I'd love to be there. I've got Jerrell."

"I already asked my momma to keep the boys for us." Unique smiled, "I kind of figured you'd want to go too."

Eva

I was holding my niece and enjoying her new baby smell as she smiled at me and tried to control her hands so she could touch my face. My grandmother snapped pictures of us. I never knew I could love a little person so much. To make things more interesting little Quinn has Quincy's deep chocolate hue, Rickie's beautiful hair, and my face. She couldn't look more like me if I gave birth to her myself. Grandmother hogs her though. She only really gives Quinn back to Rickie to feed her. Other than that, Quinn is always with her. I had to whine and complain to have this time with my niece. Even still she's all in our business snapping pictures. Quincy came home excited about his day. He got a job in the hospital administration office. He excitedly told us that he got a promotion today. We all sang his praises. "Eva, I can start paying you rent." He said excitedly.

My grandmother shot me a look. "Quincy you and I will discuss it outside of mixed company."

"You know what I told you." My grandmother said to me like she was checking me.

"I do know that I am grown, and regardless of how much you throw your weight around here this is my house. I will do with it as I please."

"Oh I see you drank a double dose of bald headed courage juice today!"

"WHAT??" Rickie yelled as she laughed out loud.

Our grandmother started laughing, "don't forget that I am your grandmother. You need to show me respect at all times."

"Well then you need to remember that I am grown and you've got to give respect to receive it." I gave the baby to Rickie. "If it weren't for me you would've been homeless! I didn't have to change my life plan to accommodate you. You move out here and act like you're running things. Suddenly I can't pick my own boyfriend, or make any other decisions for my life. I'm not a little girl, I am a grown woman who can make her own decisions."

"You're a dumb kid who is only going to mess things up! I set you up real nice with the Singleton kid. You were going to let that young man pass you by."

"So what if I mess things up! It's my life!"

"Like you were going to in Florida!" She crossed her arms and tapped her foot. "You think I didn't know about you and that little thug? Why you think I sent your goofy behind away to school?"

"I chose to go to Atlanta." I heard myself say, but everything was replaying in my mind.

"Did you now?" She smiled at me. She was right, she kept encouraging me to apply to schools away when I didn't want to go too far away. "That fool was running around telling everyone about the things you two did. Now of course I thought he was lying until our little conversation where you told me about you and that boy from California. That just proved to me that I've always done the right thing by you two."

I had nothing to say to that.

****

"Eva Graham, this is Yolanda Culpepper. She's the manager of the mailroom and she'll be our guide on our tour of the mailroom today." Phyllis said.

I don't know why I felt nervous about seeing my uncle whom I hadn't seen or heard from since we left. Yolanda explained the daily process to me, she showed me the van that certain employees were cleared to drive to go pick up the mail. They showed me the mail processing room, where they had machines that sorted the mail and ones that opened certain types of envelopes. I never knew working in the mailroom could be so detailed. I don't know why I thought they got the mail and sent it on. When we stepped on the mailroom floor everyone was busy at their stations working. I spotted my uncle's big shiny head immediately. He was talking smack while he worked. Someone nudged him and told him we were here, and he quieted down. He looked at us and then he went back to his work. He didn't even recognize me, but I shouldn't expect him to. We walked around the floor and when we got to my uncle I asked Yolanda what he was working on. "This is Clifton and he's one of our senior persons, he's been in this department about twenty years."

My uncle turned around and looked at all of us. "How ya'll doing today?"

"Oh we're good, we're just touring the facilities," Phyllis said.

My uncle didn't look at anyone long enough to see me. He went back to focusing on his job as we continued our tour. As we were finishing up, my uncle and a colleague of his came over to say goodbye to us. "It was nice meeting you Mr. Pearcy." I said watching his eyes.

"You as well, I'm sorry I didn't catch your name."

"Eva, Eva Graham," I said shaking his hand.

He didn't get it, "well it was nice to meet you."

I don't know why I was disappointed, "you too." Then I took two steps, I turned towards him. "You know what, I used to have an uncle named Clifton. He looked a lot like you. I guess there's more than one Clifton Pearcy in the Bay Area."

As my words settled on him, his smile dropped. "Eva?" He said with stretched eyes. "Pearl's baby?"

The mention of my mother's name irritated my stomach. "Grandmother's baby." I corrected him.

"Eva!" He said excitedly.

"Ok, listen to me." I took a step back. "We can't do this here. What time are you off?"

"3:30."

"I saw a Starbucks a few blocks back, meet me there." Then I walked away.

I sat in that Starbucks shaking my leg with anxious energy. I was debating with myself about what I was going to say. How badly I was going to go off on him. He's been in that mailroom for at least twenty years which means he was working there when we lost our home. It wasn't that he couldn't help us, he didn't want to. My whole life would be different if we never moved away. I'd be married to Tavio with babies of my own. A totally different existence. Not that I was completely hating my life right now, but I'm just saying. There would've been no abortion. No trauma!

When my uncle walked in he hurried to the table. "Eva!" He reached for my hands over the table. "Look at you! All sophisticated and important! How have you been?"

I tried to control my tone. "HOW COULD YOU LET US BE HOMELESS AND STRANDED? HOW COME YOU HAVEN'T CHECKED ON YOUR MOTHER IN OVER TEN YEARS? YOUR MOTHER! YOUR NIECES! WHAT KIND OF MAN ARE YOU?"

"You've spent all this time with my mother and you don't know the answer to that question? You and Rickie had a place to go, she wasn't supposed to take you. We didn't know where she went. We looked for you all for years."

"Who is we?" I was dreading his answer.

"Your parents! Your aunties! All of us! Your momma and your dad have been clean for the past nineteen years. They got married, she didn't tell you any of this?" I shook my head no. My uncle rubbed my hands that were now clasped on the table. "Your father left because he and your momma had habits. Your grandmother laid into him good one last time. He left to get himself together, to get clean. Your momma couldn't take living with your grandmother anymore, but she wasn't living right. Your grandmother kicked her out. Your father found her and convinced her to get clean. They've been trying to get you girls back since your father has gotten clean. Your grandmother has fought it every step of the way. It seems real convenient that her house that was paid for suddenly had a mortgage that she had to default on. She packed you girls up and disappeared into thin air." Then he leaned in with glassy eyes, "your parents have been looking for you."

I leaned back, "this is some BULL!" I stood up and walked around my chair, and then I threw myself in my seat. "Are you telling me that my grandmother kidnapped us?"

"I wouldn't use those words," he tried to calm me.

"What words would you use? Did she have permission to take us?"

"No, but…"

My tears burned like acid! "You have no idea what I've been through. What Rickie's been through! We thought our parents abandoned us!"

"I know baby, we were trying to settle things amongst us. And then bring you two in once it was settled. Do you wanna see your momma?"

A fireball hit me, "NO!" I stood up, "I can't! I can't even! I can't do this! I can't! I can't!" I picked up my purse. "Please don't tell anyone we're related. Next time I'm in town I'll call you. I can't do this right now! I need to think!" I hurried out the door.

When I got to my room I cried, I cried harder than I've ever cried about anything in my life. My grandmother is the root of all evil! I called Colby who happened to be in his office. "What's wrong?"

"Being out here in the Bay, it's bringing up all this stuff about my parents. My brain hurts right now."

"I love you," I could tell he didn't know what else to say.

"I love you too."

"I can't wait for you to come home. I know that doesn't sound like much, but you're coming home to a full body massage."

I smiled, "thank you baby. I'm going to meet Unique and Tavio for dinner."

"Ok, call me if you need me."

I laid down until Unique called and said they were downstairs. I threw water on my face and then I made my way down to the lobby. Unique said Tavio was at the table waiting. She looked at me and asked me if I was ok, and I told her it's been a long day. As we approached the table Tavio was sitting with a girl. They were chatting probably about nothing serious, but I recognized the look in his eyes. It was the way he used to look at me. I told myself to check my feelings at the door. When Tavio looked at me he genuinely smiled, he looked at my hair and I was staring at his. "Oh my God! Look at you!" I said reaching for his locs as he came in for a hug.

He rubbed my head, "look at you. I love the head!" Then he kissed my cheek. "This is Alaina?"

"It's nice to finally meet you," Alaina said.

I noticed her wedding band, "when did you get married?"

"I've been married almost eight years."

Tavio smiled, "she's not my wife. I'm not married. Are you?"

I exhaled, "no but I've been with my boyfriend for some time."

Tavio watched my face for a minute. "What's wrong?"

"Nothing I had a long day."

Tavio and Unique stared at me because they knew better. I tried to hold it in, but my emotions got the best of me and I erupted into tears. When I told them what my uncle told me Tavio and Unique started cursing. My friends understood the emotional pull of the whole situation. Unique and Alaina were crying with me as we sat drinking our drinks. "Well at least we understand why you scalped yourself."

Unique choked on her drink and Alaina told Tavio to stop. I sat back as I started cracking up laughing. I told Tavio I hated him so much.

******

The whole plane ride I kept trying to think of what I was going to do. When I exited the plane I was completely surprised to see Colby waiting by the gate with balloons and flowers. I ran to him and I cried in his arms. He took a cab to the airport, so he drove my car home. When we got home I climbed into bed with my clothes on. I know Colby hates it and especially when I have plane germs all over me. I couldn't think I just wanted to sleep.

I awoke to Colby sleeping next to me with his arm around me. I stared at his face for a while. Even when I was running from him I knew he was handsome. I love the way he loves me. It's always dependable and reliable. He never shoves himself down my throat. However, in this moment I can't deal. I needed to talk to Rickie, but I hadn't decided what I was going to tell her yet. I slowly slid out of the bed. I quietly grabbed my purse and then I tiptoed out of the room. I got in my car and I went to the house. I couldn't tell if Rickie was home. When she answered the phone my tears were back. I asked her to pack up the baby and go for a ride with me.

Quinn looked so pretty in her little jumper. I kissed her and then strapped her into her carrier. Rickie asked me why I was being scary. I took her back to my place. Colby was walking down the stairs shirtless wiping sleep from his eyes. I apologized and then I told him that Rickie and I needed to talk in the office. I told him that anyone other than Quincy doesn't get to know we're here. He doesn't know where we are or when we're coming back. Colby stood there watching me as I shut the door. Rickie sat in one of the chairs facing the desk. I sat next to her and grabbed her hands. Rickie's eyes got big, and then I poured out every detail to her. I even described how shiny uncle Clifton's head was. Rickie chuckled a little but she went right back to crying just like me. Rickie asked how could she see how much we were suffering and not say a word? She let us believe that our parents didn't love us, that our parents abandoned us when she knew they were fighting for us. Hugging my sister as we cried took away that lonely feeling. This didn't happen to just me, I wasn't alone. "What did she do with the money?"

"What money?" I didn't know what she was talking about.

"The money from the refinance. He said the house was paid for and then she suddenly had a mortgage."

"She most likely spent it. That was a long time ago."

"With all the penny pinching she does I doubt it, but you're probably right." Rickie took more Kleenex and then she blew her nose. "I want to talk to them."

I knew she was going to say that. "Rickie, I don't know if I can. I feel so defeated right now."

Rickie sat up and looked at me. She wiped her tears and then she patted my hands. "It's ok, you were strong for us when I was weak. I can do this for us little sister."

"Can you come to California with me the next time I go? My job pays for the room and car. I'll buy your plane ticket."

******

I held onto Colby as we heard Katrina screaming all the way down the hallway. Colby's face was blank as he stared down the hallway towards Katrina's room. Mr. Singleton was rocking in place like he couldn't figure out what to do with himself. Chauncey's family was in the waiting room as well. Vanessa shook her head and said she couldn't do it. Her mother laughed and said each mother has gone through it and that as soon as it's over you start forgetting about the pain. Rickie laughed a "yeah right" laugh. I felt so bad for Katrina, she read all the books, and she did tons of research. She took class after class. All that studying and she's still screaming in pain. If I wasn't against babies before, this was sealing it for me.

Chauncey's mother came out after the long silence. Her face was wet with tears, "she's here!" She announced to the waiting room. Everyone cheered; Colby asked how Katrina was doing. Mrs. Lee said Katrina and the baby were good. Colby announced that we would be back after the crowd settled down. I was happy he said that cause I was tired and my eyes were crossing from lack of sleep.

It was early Saturday morning, the sun hadn't risen yet it was so early. Colby drove us home and then he invited me to shower with him before getting in the bed. That was his nice way of telling me to wash the hospital off before I got in our bed. That was the thing; no matter how tired he was when he came home he always showered before he got in our bed. I put on a little lotion and then I happily slid under the covers.

Colby stood over me as he pulled the covers back. I gave him a get serious look. Colby said he needed a cap off. I whined telling him I was tired. He turned on music and started dancing in front of the bed. I told myself to go to sleep, but my eyes wouldn't shut. I watched him do his striptease as I laid there pretending that he wasn't turning me on. Colby's rhythm is always smooth and right when you think you got it he switches it up on you. I actually asked him if he was a stripper at some point in his life. He said no, but he knew a stripper who taught him well. I sat up cause now I couldn't sleep thinking of what he had in mind.

To my surprise he only wanted to make love, no tricks, or toys needed. It was a nice send off into my deep slumber. Neither one of us woke up until midafternoon. Colby rubbed my back, "when can we get started on ours?"

My eyes searched the room, "our what?"

"Our family," then he gently touched my nose.

"I hope you mean buying a puppy or a kitten cause I don't want to have children." I should've said that nicer but it spilled out of my mouth.

"Eva, I know today's scene was scary but every pregnancy is different. Our scene could be totally different."

I sat up, "Colby I don't want to have children ever!"

"Ever?" He sat up with me.

"Never ever! I've told you this before."

"No you haven't!"

"Yes I have, you just weren't listening to me."

"Why?"

"Lots of reasons! For one I didn't have parents while I was growing up."

"You had your grandmother."

"Lot of good that did me. Look! If I was a stick in there and make the best of it, come what may type of person, then I would've kept that baby in college. I had to choose, and I chose me. I've been choosing me ever since. No one sticks around like they say they will. You're wonderful today Colby but tomorrow you could go through some trauma or change and become a totally different person. There's only so many levels of vulnerability that I'm willing to sink to. If we broke up today it would hurt me. Knock the wind out of me, but I wouldn't be out for the count. Eventually I would rise again to face another day. Eventually I would move on with my life. Having a baby would make it impossible for me to grieve which would mean I'd have to lock my feelings up inside to raise your child that you stuck me with. I would become bitter and dead inside for sure."

"So you don't even want to marry me?"

"I wasn't thinking about marriage. I actually like things the way they are now. When you get tired of me, you go your way and I go mine. I would hope that we would part on good terms."

Colby jumped out of the bed fast in one angry motion. "So you're telling me, while I'm over here pouring my heart into us thinking that we're building towards something else you're waiting for the other shoe to drop? Who does that?"

"I do!"

He gently put his hands on either sides of my face. "Eva, baby! I love you! I love us together! I'm not going anywhere, I don't want anyone else. You are it for me!"

"That's what you say today Colby, but who knows how you'll feel next year. Or five years from now?"

"Look at me! My name is Colby! Colby Singleton! I am not Tavio Spellman! I will not let you push me away like what we have doesn't matter to me. I want you! I need you! I want a family with you!"

"You want more than I can give you Colby. All I have to give you is right now, today. Tomorrow you may not want me."

"You're pushing this off on me, you're saying that eventually you're going to want to trade up. Eventually you're going to want someone else."

"No, that's not what I'm saying."

"Yes it is! No one will ever love you like I do. I'm perfectly happy with you being who you are."

"As long as I'm willing to have your baby and sign my life away to you. No one gets to hurt me like that! NO ONE!"

"When have I ever given you a reason to doubt me? Give me one example! Just one!" I was quiet thinking for a long time. "I can help you out with that. I've never given you one because I'm not going anywhere."

I pulled my face away. "You don't get it! YOU KNOW WHAT! FORGET IT! FORGET ALL OF THIS! I'LL MOVE OUT! I DON'T

NEED THIS!" I stormed in the bathroom.

"EVA! BRING YOUR BEHIND BACK IN HERE NOW!" I had never heard that level of bass in his voice. I slowly walked out of the bathroom and I stood in the middle of the floor. "This is what you want? I tell you I love you, that I don't want anyone else. That I want us forever and you break up with me?" I refused to cry, I looked around the room. "Seriously Eva?"

"You want too much from me. There's no convincing me. At least Tavio knew it and accepted it. You like bumping your head against the wall."

"I would throw my head through a wall for you, and you just don't get it. I bought this place for you, for us. I was perfectly fine at home stacking my money. Everything I've done has been to make myself worthy of you. And this is the thanks I get. I can't stop you from leaving, but one day you're going to remember that once upon a time someone loved you for real. No puppy love, no conditional love, none of that. You ran from me! You're leaving me!" Then he walked past me and went in the bathroom.

Tavio

"Tavio! No!" She said firmly to me in the middle of my conversation with HER friends. I looked at her like she was crazy. "Anyways..."

"Sabrina, I'm leaving. Ask one of your friends for a ride home." I got up and started walking away.

"What? No! I'm sorry!" She tried to stop me from walking.

I pulled my arm back; she tried to grab me again. "TOUCH ME ONE MORE TIME AND SEE WHAT I DO TO YOU!"

Sabrina gasped and froze in place. I got in my car and left. As I crossed the bridge I realized I left a plate of untouched food on the table.

I sucked my teeth cause I was looking forward to my cajun shrimp over creamy herbed polenta. I tried to think of a drive through and the thought irked me some more. I called my momma to see if she was cooking. I could hear noise in the background, she said they were entertaining guests and I was welcome to come by. I didn't feel like being around a bunch of people. I called Ben and he and Chareca were fussing about his upcoming show. Does everybody have plans these days? I called Wesley and I was so relieved when he answered. He said he was kicking back with his son and I was welcome to come by.

When he opened the door the smell of food hit my nose. I asked him what he was cooking as I followed him to the kitchen. He said Alaina made him a pot of Jambalaya yesterday and he just took the pot out of the refrigerator to heat some up. He told me to have a seat. "MAC made that whole pot for you?"

"That girl has got too much energy. She's in school, working, and taking care of my nephew, but she got time to make all this food."

"Oh right cause mister lawyer is working hard at the bank and the gym."

Wesley shook his head, "I'm just waiting."

"Waiting for what?"

"When my little sister calls me crying cause she's finally figured out that he's cheating on her." I didn't say anything cause it was obvious to me too. "Why you think she don't see it?"

"She loves him, and she's loyal." I said watching him take the plates out of the microwave. He set my plate in front of me and my mouth filled up with saliva just off of the smell. "I don't know that she would call you once she figures it out. Aren't you the one who told me she suffers from a defective loyalty gene?"

"Yeah, but man! That's my little sister! The only one I got left. She can't stay married to Royce. He don't deserve her."

I put a fork full of food in my mouth. Wesley smiled at me. I let the spicy flavor sit there for a minute while I mentally worshiped Alaina. "HE DON'T DESERVE TO EAT LIKE THIS!"

Wesley laughed, "everything comes back to food for you doesn't it?"

"I'm basic, feed me and you got me."

"So what ruffled your feathers young buck?"

"Sabrina got on my nerves! I left her stranded in Corte Madera with her friends."

"You breaking up with her?"

"One day, this is not going anywhere. She's rude and disrespectful. I just don't feel like bouncing around right now. I'm getting too old for that."

"Who you telling, I'm older than you and I'm about to throw all the towels in. William's momma decided that she likes having babies and I'm not going to infect more kids with the possibility of the disease we're both carriers for. William's version of the disease is very mild, but he'll have to be on guard all of his life. I can't knowingly do that to another child. So we're done. She's already moved on."

"Already?"

"WOMEN ARE SO COLD BLOODED! For all these women who say they can't find a man, I need to know where they call themselves looking cause my ex's seem to find them easily."

"Lil T's momma found Tyrek and shoot he married her. That man so sprung he wishing my son was his too." I laughed, "naw Tyrek is cool though. Thanks to him our blended family don't seem so blended. We feel like a family. He's not threatened by me, I don't invade his space. He and I can hang out like old friends even. He's good to my son, and I can't do nothing but be grateful."

"I hope William is that fortunate, only time will tell. Just remember how Tyrek conducts himself so that when I kill Royce and my little sister is free to marry, you can remember to keep Royce's family in my nephew's life."

I laughed hard, Wesley didn't.

Eva

Quinn had all of us working on that flight. The cabin pressure was bothering her, then she didn't want to sit still all of that time. By the end of the flight, Vanessa was rethinking her resolve to ever have a child of her own. Normally we all go out to dinner when we arrive at our hotel, but Vanessa was tired and said she was turning in early.

As soon as we got to our room Rickie picked up the phone and called the number I gave her for uncle Clifton. "Hello may I speak to Clifton... his niece Rickie..." then she rubbed my hand as I held Quinn looking at her. She smiled, "hello uncle.... yes this is Rickie.... the Rickie.... yes.... yes.... listen... if you're going to be home would it be ok if Eva and I dropped by? Yes... yes.... ok, hold on..." she took the cap off the pen on the desk and wrote his address down. "Ok.... we'll see you in a little bit.... bye." She grabbed her diaper bag and told me to come on.

I slowly followed behind my big sister like I was in trouble or something. I'm not going to cry! I'm not going to cry! I told myself. When we got to the rental car, Rickie put the address into the navigation system and I strapped the baby in. The only noise in the car was from the navigation telling us which way to go. A lot of things about Richmond had changed, but then a lot of things were the same. As we drove under the underpass on 37th I remembered walking to seven-eleven when we were young.

Memories about everything were hitting me. I was trying very hard to remember my parent's faces. I could see different aspects of them, but I couldn't clearly see their faces.

When we pulled up to my uncle's small house he came hurrying out the door. He hugged me first then he stood still smiling at Rickie, he called her his baby girl and told her to come give him a hug. She hesitated for a minute, and then she gave him a courtesy hug. I got the baby out of the car and then we walked in the door. Three women were sitting at the kitchen table. I remembered two of them Rickie and I looked at the other woman. She said she was uncle Clifton's wife. "Clifton, she looks just like Pearl." My aunt said about Rickie. Fortunately they didn't tell me I looked like anyone. They kept looking at my head but they didn't say anything. My aunts and uncle explained everything to Rickie like he told me. Rickie asked questions though, I was just sitting there. I didn't have the energy to argue or pay attention to one more thing. In a matter of a month my whole world has fallen apart.

When the doorbell rang, Rickie looked at me and I stared at her. I don't know why I was prepared to run out of the room but I was. My heart was pounding so hard you should've been able to see it from across the room. It sound like a lot of people were coming in the door. They were whispering for a minute. And then a little girl peeked in the dining room. "My momma says you guys are my big sisters." She smiled while she inspected us. "What happened to your hair?"

"I cut it off."

"Why?"

"Because I wanted to." She looked just like me.

Two teenage boys walked into the dining room. Both of their eyes went to my head and then to us. All three of them looked like us. Then our father walked in. At least my memory didn't exaggerate how tall he was. He looked sad and nervous but he didn't say anything. Then our mother walked in, tears were already pouring out of her eyes as she entered the room. She looked from Rickie to me to my head to me again back to Rickie. "Get up and give me some hugs!" She extended her arms.

Rickie and I hugged her, but I didn't know how to feel. Rickie looked guarded as well. Our father and brothers came over for hugs. "This is my daughter Quinn. My husband had to work otherwise he'd be here."

"We got a married daughter, and a grandbaby."

"I'm an auntie!" Our little sister Brenda said.

"Are you married too?" Our father asked.

"No, just broke up with my boyfriend actually."

"I'm sorry to hear that," He said.

"So, this is a nice family. How long did you wait to start over with a new family?" I asked.

"Junior is twelve years younger than you Eva, and we weren't trying to replace you."

"You let us believe you walked away from us like we didn't matter." Rickie said.

"You can thank my momma for that."

"Take responsibility for your actions. You were strung out and that's how she was able to take us," Rickie charged.

"I got hooked a little after Eva was born. I introduced your father to drugs. I was running from the pain. I didn't realize that I took him down with me. My father used to mess with me, my mother knew and she didn't care. Everybody knows about it. It's not some family secret that no one knew about. Everyone knew! None of that excuses what happened in your life, but it's what happened. First she kicked your father out and then she kicked me out. She wouldn't let us back in the house; she called the police on us. She got restraining orders to make us stay away. And right when we were about to get you back she disappeared. The house was empty and she was gone. I don't know what she told Aunt Ethel, because we called her asking if she heard anything and she always told us that she hadn't heard from my mother."

Rickie cleared her throat, "so let me say, first off that it's nice to meet all of you. I have no memories of either one of you in your right minds."

"How much could you remember, you were a little girl." Our father said dismissively.

"Oh we remember you. Eva doesn't remember you like I do. She was able to have a semblance of a normal childhood as long as the kids from down the street were close by. I on the other hand remember everything that happened and everything that was done. It may have been wrong how grandmother did you, but she wasn't completely wrong."

Our mother got a little nervous. "Babies, let us talk to your sisters in private." She said sounding like a loving mother. Even though Quinn was sleeping on my shoulder I started rocking her with my nervous energy.

Our father took a seat next to our mother and started rubbing her back. "You can only ask for forgiveness for your transgressions. They do not define who you are today. Draw on the principles to help you remain focused in this moment. We've discussed this and this is your opportunity to make this right. You can do this." He said lowly to her as she cried a little.

"Rickie, I'm sorry doesn't go far enough. Nothing excuses what I did to you. The hardest part of sobriety is living with what my disease did to you two. Especially you Rickie. You don't ever have to forgive me, and I won't blame you for that. I was sick baby, that's all I can say."

I looked at Rickie who looked disconnected and unmoved by her tears. "I wet the bed for years. Most of my hair fell out. I couldn't focus and they held me back a grade in school. My little sister is the only reason I'm whole today." I didn't understand what she meant. "Eva wouldn't let me stay down when I wanted to die. She drug me outside to play with her friends. When I told myself no one would care if I lived or died and I convinced myself to kill myself, my annoying little sister kept following me around the house and harassing me to come play with her."

I whispered, "I didn't know you wanted to leave me. That

would've destroyed me."

"I was only passing on the destruction she handed me." Rickie looked at our mother. "What if Uncle Bump wouldn't have saved me?"

"Uncle Bump?" I had no idea of who she was talking about.

"Our father's brother. She gave me to her pusher. Our uncle died freeing me. She sat there getting high not concerned with what was happening in that room. I ran home covered in our uncle's blood. You were outside playing. Grandmother cleaned me up after the police came. The pusher was arrested after I pointed him out, but our mother was nowhere to be found. Grandmother saved us! And you have the nerve to act like she did you wrong."

"We got cleaned up! It's in the past." Our mother cried, "I deserve a second chance."

"According to whom? Did you ever stop to think about what being with you would have done to me? No! You washed your stank off and probably prayed that I didn't remember. I remember you beating her up. I remember you punching Eva."

"She did what?" I looked at Rickie as I went into a full body rock.

"I'm not proud of the things I've done. Losing my brother was the bottom of the barrel for me. Your mother and I have had to dig deep to be here right now. Rickie, you don't have to forgive us. You could hate us forever and you would have every right to. We just want the two of you to know that today we are in our right minds. We love you very much, and our door is ALWAYS open to you."

I looked at Rickie who looked so crazy. I've never seen this expression. "How about I take your number. This is too much to cram into one night."

******

I looked around my little one bedroom apartment and smiled.

I've never lived alone before and something in my soul said this is what I need. Colby has tried repeatedly to *talk some sense* into me. No matter how you approach it, children aren't negotiable for me. And without children I don't see the point of marriage. Not that Colby was offering marriage without children. I had movers bring over the furniture I used to use before I bought my townhouse. I rented the living room and dining room furniture. I wasn't going to stay here too long. I was looking for something else to buy. I figured once we figure all this California stuff out I'll have the time to really look and find something that felt like me.

I sat on the floor and painted my toenails. The number of coats depends on how much thinking I had to do. Sunday dinners have fallen apart since Colby and I broke up. Colby won't tell anyone why we broke up, he's convinced that I need time and then I'll suddenly be in to the idea of a family. If he only knew what we saw in California he would gladly run. I haven't processed all that I took in that night.

I don't know who to be mad at. Our parents blame our grandmother, and we haven't told our grandmother about them. Rickie has been doing great though. We talked all week about stuff from when we were little. I have no memory of physical abuse. What kind of mother would I be? Rickie's a good mother to Quinn, but still. Colby will be a good father though. He'll be just like Tavio, an excellent father. Being his wife wouldn't be any different than being his girlfriend. And I loved being his girlfriend. The sex was out of this world, when he said sex slave he wasn't kidding. I completely trust him and I was open to everything he introduced. I don't know if that translated to mean anything further.

I took a deep breath, I couldn't think about Colby anymore. I missed him, but this would pass just like my feelings for Tavio did. When I see him now he's looking at me but he doesn't see me anymore. He looks at me the same way he looks at Rickie. Like I'm an old friend, not like he still carries a torch for me or anything. That girl that he kept calling MAC has him by the nose. Her goofy behind doesn't even see it either. That's a train wreck of emotions I'm happy to not be a party to for once.

Once my toes dried I got dressed and I met Vanessa downtown for dinner and drinks. "Now that you're free, how far off the deep end are you willing to go?"

"I'm not even willing to approach the precipice of your life style." I laughed as I took another sip of my wine.

Vanessa laughed and then her phone rang. "Hey you..." Her face dropped, "um I kind of forgot.... I'm downtown at Stallone's, but I'm not alone...." She took a deep breath, "you know what! Screw it! We're all grown! Come on over.... You'll understand when you get here.... Un huh... Un huh!" She hung up her phone and then she set her eyes on me. "We're all grown!"

"What is that supposed to mean?"

Vanessa waved me off as she tried not to be irritated as she drank some of her drink. I was about to get on her when Kiev approached our table. He smiled real big when he saw me. He smiled big as he said, "we're all grown. I love your haircut." Then he took his seat next to me.

"Where's Faye?"

He shrugged, "she don't like me no more. Where's your man?"

"I don't have a man anymore," I blushed.

He smiled bigger at me, "I guess our opportunity has presented itself." Then he looked at Vanessa. "Thank you for forgetting about our dinner plans."

"You're not welcome!" Vanessa was angry.

Kiev kept staring at me and smiling. At the end of dinner, Vanessa paid the bill then she stood up and walked out. She didn't say goodbye or anything. Kiev walked me to my car, I asked him where he parked and he said he caught the bus. I offered him a ride home. I hadn't spent any time in this part of Boston. Kiev asked me if I'd like to come in. I wanted to go, but I told him I'd take a rain check. He wrote his number down then he kissed me. He was trying to get me to change my mind. I grabbed my steering wheel and used it as my anchor. I finally backed up and I told him to call me.

Chapter 15

Alaina

Chareca and Ben were fussing about some fabric that he got in. He wanted to use it to make pants and she wanted him to use it to make a blazer. They went back and forth as I sat there watching my baby through the glass play with Cara Mia. It has been almost three months since Royce has even tried to sleep with me. He's hardly ever home even more now. "I have a question." Ben and Chareca stopped talking and looked at me. "Do you think a man can love his wife and not try to sleep with her?"

"MAC?" Ben swallowed, "you're making me uncomfortable."

"I mean, I know I'm just this average unnoticeable black girl. You know average brown skin, average bosom, average looks, average body, I mean I could go down a list of the things that make me just your average girl from Richmond California. My life became not so average when the guy of my dreams noticed me. The guy of my dreams wanted me, he wanted to kiss me, he wanted to touch me, he wanted to be with me. I came alive in his arms. The man of my dreams asked me to marry him. He wanted to be my husband! He wanted to put *ME* the average girl from Richmond on a pedestal when he could've had anyone that he wanted and he chose me. I'm pretty sure by now that it's no secret that there is one-way in which I'm not average. I've tried everything I could think of to change it. No matter what I do, I don't work! At least an average enjoyment of sex would probably bring my husband back to me right? FIX ME! FIX ME PLEASE! PLEASE BRING MY HUSBAND BACK! I PROMISE I WON'T GIVE UP! SEND HIM BACK!"

Chareca and Ben rushed to me. Chareca hugged me while I cried into her arms. Ben stood in front of us. "All my life I've known I was different. I mean I look at clothes and I see stitching, and fabrics. Because I've always taken a severe interest in my appearance and the clothes that my mother and sister wore. Everyone assumed that I was gay. They didn't just assume they insisted that I had to be gay. So much that I thought I was gay. Something inside wouldn't let me say it though. I mean I would stand in the mirror and say, Hey Ben! You're... and it wouldn't come out. So I'd call myself a sissy, I'd call myself any name I could think of. I told myself every mean thing I could think of. I mean I tried to look at men as if there could ever be something that burned inside of me to want to touch one. My knee jerk reaction is to cringe when I see a naked man. I am broken fix me!" He stared at me.

"What are you talking about?" Chareca asked Ben.

"I am no more gay than MAC is average. Stop telling yourself that crap! The narrative in your head plays over and over."

"SHUT UP BEN! YOU'RE GAY! WE'VE DISCUSSED THIS!" Chareca yelled.

"Shut up Chareca! I'm not gay! MAC, I'm not gay!"

"I SWEAR TO GOD BEN YOU BETTER BE GAY! I'VE CHANGED MY SHIRT IN FRONT OF YOU!"

Ben smiled real big, "I know!"

"BEN!" Chareca got up and started hitting Ben! "I'm telling my husband!"

Ben's smile dropped, "Chareca! Don't unleash your husband on me. He's freakishly strong and he has the worst temper."

Chareca wiggled her neck at him, "I know!"

"Ok! Ok!" He put his hands up and then he looked at me. "I'm sorry MAC, Chareca is stealing the mightiness of my speech." Then he sat on the coffee table in front of me. He took my hands into his. "Listen MAC, you may say you're average. That's just a part of your greatness. You are the best thing that has ever happened to Royce. You are too good for him. You're so busy blaming yourself, what if Royce doesn't know what he's doing? What if the problem isn't you? I mean it's no secret that you were a virgin, what if you lack the knowledge to call him on his stuff? I had this one girlfriend," then he looked at Chareca who frowned at him. "*Friend*. I had this one *friend* who I met when I thought I knew it all. I had a one-size fits all approach at the time. My approach didn't work for my *friend*. I had to dig deeper and try different things. That relationship required open communication, and something different." Then he looked at Chareca, "I know Ken sees the models I date. How could he believe I'm gay?"

"They're on your arm for events, he never sees them creeping around here. None of us do." Then Chareca looked at me, "do you understand the point of his story?"

"How would I know?"

"Ask for something different. It's your relationship too."

"Like what?"

"Where do you always have sex?"

"In our bed."

"Initiate sex somewhere else."

I started crying, "I tried that and he made me feel so bad."

"Royce is a fool!" Chareca blurted, "I try not to say anything cause I know you love him. It's not right for you to be sitting over here feeling like this while he allows work and the gym..." She looked at me like I was crazy. "The **gym**!" She crossed her arms and rolled her eyes. "All his other stuff to keep him away from home. You said he only comes home to ask you if you're pregnant. Like he's subliminally implanting the idea that the way to get him back is to have another baby. He ain't home for the one you got. He better be thanking God he got you and not someone like me. I would hurt his feelings! I agree with my friend GAY Ben! Royce is missing the mark."

Ben stared at Chareca, "seriously though. I'm trying to come out to my friends and you're forcing me backwards. That's not right!"

Chareca raised her fist, "cause my husband will **kill** you."

"Why did you change your shirt in front of him?"

"The baby spit up all over me, I had a spare shirt. Now that I think of it, you got quiet. I should've known then." She slapped his shoulder while Ben laughed.

"That wasn't my fault, and milk does a body good!" Chareca screamed and slapped his shoulder again.

We laughed while the baby slept through our noise in the play pin. I thanked my friends for making me laugh and getting out of my funk.

Royce

"I guess when one blast from the past pops up, two more are sure to come. I hope the next person is even better." A voice said from behind me.

I turned around to see Kid, she wasn't a kid anymore. Her lips were dark and her face looked dried out. She looked like she's seen some rough days, and maybe today things were looking up. She wasn't that bright eyed and bushy tailed Kid like she used to be. "Hey Kid, how you doing?" I was trying to gauge her tone.

"What happened to that athletic body you used to have? I used to love to watch your stomach flex and unflex!" She closed her eyes and smiled at the memory. Then she shook like she was orgasming at the thought of it.

"I'm not a teenager anymore." I tried to make my voice even to mask my irritation and embarrassment.

She looked me up and down, "you got that right."

"What do you want?"

"When was the last time you seen or spoke to Vanessa?"

I stood there staring at her trying not to let my emotions show. I wanted to ball up and hide at the mention of her name. "It's been years, why?"

"Can you believe after all these years she's been coming back to the Bay?" She faked surprise.

I could hear my heart beating in my ears. "So?"

"SO! So you know you want to see her. And let me kill the suspense for you, she looks even better than when she was a teenager. My girl works hard to keep her body in check, her hair was on point, she's still bad!"

How did I miss it, I thought Kid was always checking for me. She was in love with Vanessa and her way to Vanessa was through me. No wonder she took it so hard when I wanted out. I smiled at Kid, "is she now?"

"Yep, and she asked me if I've seen you around. I told her about the time I saw you at the movies all over some girl. I normally see you once every three years or so, but the fact that she asked about you just the other day made me come over here."

"Now you can tell her you've seen me."

"You want me to give her your number for old times sake?" She smiled.

"She doesn't live out here?"

"No, but she's going to be visiting a lot over the next few months. Maybe we could all go out to dinner."

"You think she'd want to have dinner with me?"

"She'll have dinner with us. Vanessa was in love with you. I honestly think she still is. She hasn't had a serious relationship since you either."

"Kind of like she needs to clear the air with me first?"

"Yes."

"What if I wanted her back, where she live at now?"

"She went home to Boston. I mean her job has an office right there in Emeryville. She could probably transfer out here. We could be one happy family."

"Where she work at that you think she got pull like that?"

Kid smiled, "like I'm going to tell you the name of her company. If you want Vanessa you have to go through me. You'd be a fool not to want her."

"I'm just saying she couldn't just walk on a job like that unless she's pretty high profile."

"She didn't just walk on, she worked her way up. She transferred from here out there. She's made some interesting friends out there too. "

BINGO! I don't need Kid to find Vanessa. "I don't know Kid, I don't look the same. She might look at me and run the other way."

"You're definitely missing the six pack, but you're still handsome. It's not like you can't get it back."

"That was a backwards compliment if I ever heard one. Ok so I can work on my body, but how will you get rid of your ugly?" Kid got mad immediately. "I'm still handsome, and you said Vanessa is still gorgeous. I don't know what happened to you. I barely recognized you. You look all dried out and lifeless. I mean what would you bring to the threesome? Musk?" I touched my nose to say she stank.

"FORGET YOU ROYCE! You will NEVER see Vanessa

again!" Then she stormed away.

I openly laughed at her for a long time. As soon as I stopped laughing thoughts of Vanessa flooded my brain. Vanessa could never get enough of me, where Alaina wants anything but me. I'm sure she's relieved that I haven't even asked her for sex in a month.

I opened my work phone and I scheduled a two-hour meeting so that I could spend that time figuring out when I would bump into Vanessa.

Alaina

"You look like you're ready for another one." Chareca smiled at me as I held Kendall in my arms.

"She's so precious, and I love babies. I will have more later, but for right now I can't. I'll just love up Kendall like I did with Cara Mia until Jerrell came."

"Why can't you?"

"I keep telling Royce I want to get our house in order first. All of the renovations are almost done."

"And the real reason is?"

"You can't tell Ken!" She shook her head yes. "I'm in school." I covered my mouth in embarrassment. "I'll have my AA soon and then I need to decide where I want to go from there. Royce didn't want me to go to school period, and I don't get why it's such a big deal."

"Because Royce is a controlling brat. He gets on my nerves. Ken hasn't talked to him in ages either. Ken spends more time with Wesley and Tavio."

"I know, he's been working really hard. Then he's at the gym a lot."

Chareca rolled her eyes, "whatever. I know that's your husband and I'm overstepping my boundaries here, but I got to say something and you're the only person I can say it to. What about you? Don't you need time with him? Have things gotten any better?"

"No," the buzzer sounded. I hopped up and ran, "SAVED BY THE BELL!" I sang out loud. I could hear Chareca laughing. Unique had on shades and her hair pulled all back. "Hey sexy! Take the elevator up to the top, seventh heaven baby." Unique laughed.

Chareca called out to Ben letting him know that his three o'clock was here. Chareca knows Unique but they've never hung out. Unique has a formal event and she mentioned how frustrating dress shopping is because of her shape. She's tall and very toned; she wanted to look delicate for her event. I suggested that she have something made, and then I asked Ben. He was trying to say he was too busy to do it, but Chareca told him he would do it. He told Chareca to stop bullying him.

Ben walked into the living room with his sketchpad and fabric swatches. He sat on the couch watching us say our hellos. Then he got his tablet and started messing with it. Chareca told us to sit on the couch. "I'm trying to find pictures of you off season. You lay pretty low it seems." Ben said as he clicked away.

"I do, my personal life is my personal life. What exactly are you looking for?"

"I'm looking for your natural style, not what you will tell me you like, but what you've picked out in the past. You all continue talking, I'll get back with you in a minute." He said flipping through all of the images of Unique on Google.

I gave Kendall to Unique to hold. Kendall was smiling at Unique as she made her laugh out loud. It was so cute I took out my phone and started snapping pictures. "When are you going to have any of your own?"

"I'm still looking for mister right and not mister just for right now." Then she looked at me, "another one bites the dust."

"That's his loss!" I reassured her.

Unique exhaled, "I know. Now I have to find a date for this thing too. It's turning out to be too much hassle. In the end, I could take Tavio, but I'd rather not take my brother you know."

"This is the picture!" Ben interrupted us. "You liked your look in this picture?"

It was of Unique in a linen type shirt and a khaki skirt. She had on ankle boots and her hair and makeup were simple. She looked amazing, but very plain. "Yes, but…"

"Listen, I'm the professional." He took out his sketchpad and started drawing. "I don't stitch until we agree on the design." I love to watch Ben work. Once he gets going his eyes move around everything. A simple curved stroke becomes elegance. "You have beautiful arms and shoulders. We're going to show them off." He held up a picture of a ball gown, the skirt wasn't extremely full. The straps were just off the shoulders. He drew her standing like she was in the picture. Her hair was down and beautiful.

Chareca looked at Unique like she already knew she loved the design. Unique held the sketch with big eyes. "It's like you took a picture of me in the future. You have an amazing gift Ben."

He smiled, "this is what I do for a living." He took his fabric swatches and sat next to her. He held different ones up next to her face and Chareca kept saying no. "Look at her chocolate skin! This is her night, she needs to standout. She's the MVP and she needs to look like one."

Ben exhaled like Chareca was making him tired. "Look at the pad she's going to stand out. The dress shouldn't be loud in color. She will make more of a statement almost muted in color. Besides, look at this picture." He pointed to his tablet. "The girl likes to wear earth tones, we can't have her feeling uncomfortable. Here!" He held up an almost cream swatch and then he said gold accessories. He wrote everything down next to the sketch. He asked her what her shoe size was. Then he designed her shoes. He said he had a shoe designer friend who could make her shoes custom for her dress. Then he drew a picture of Tavio and what he should wear to compliment her. As he took her measurements Unique was awkward. "I'm not intentionally feeling you up," he joked.

"Don't believe him, this is how he gets over." Chareca said.

"Stop telling all my secrets." Then he looked at his schedule, he asked Unique when she needed the dress by. He told her he'd have to squeeze in her dress and the vest for her companion for her event. Unique thanked him, and then she left to meet up with someone. "I was expecting Tavio in heels. I couldn't remember her specifically, seems like I didn't really see her or interact with her whenever I was around his family."

"She looks just like him," Chareca said.

"Nope, that is a beautiful young lady. Now I know why Tavio never had his sister around me." Then he started tapping Chareca. "Can I ask if I can be her escort?"

"You're grown why would you ask me?"

"Cause you keep telling me I'm gay, do you think she thinks so?"

"I don't know what the girl thinks."

"MAC you know her, you think she would go for me?"

"I don't know, she normally goes for the basketball player types. Stranger things have happened."

Royce

I called the Emeryville office, I asked for Vanessa. When they transferred my call and Vanessa answered my stomach tightened and I caressed the phone. I kept the phone on mute as she asked if anyone was there. It was Vanessa, alive and well. When she hung up, I sat at my desk stuck for a minute. I rubbed my solid stomach embarrassed about my appearance. Last time I saw her I had the body of an athlete. She used to tell me how much she loved it. I wanted to blame Alaina for my new shape, but I knew better and I let the idea go.

I called a florist in Oakland and I had the most expensive arrangement sent to Vanessa's office. I told them not to attach a card. I left the office early and then I sat on the couch in almost the corner in the lobby of her office building. I looked over paperwork in between watching each person get off the elevator. It was getting close to the time that I needed to head over to the gym. As I put my phone away I saw my flowers first. Vanessa's smile was huge as she walked with a bald headed chick. Some people take self-expression too far. Vanessa's hair was pulled back in a ponytail. She was dressed simply nice but that turtle neck sweater and slacks highlighted everything I missed seeing. Vanessa was so busy admiring my flowers and talking that she didn't pay me any attention. She looked as good as Kid said she did. I sat there for another thirty minutes trying to talk myself out of what I was thinking. I couldn't walk away now.

When I got to the gym I took my time getting dressed. I was trying to think of a way to approach Vanessa. It didn't matter how I set it up in my brain Vanessa was going to go off on me. When I approached the machine I decided tonight I was going harder. I was into my workout remembering everything I could about Vanessa. I was in a zone, sweating harder than I've ever sweat before when I realized Mandy was standing in front of me. She asked me why I didn't tell her I was leaving? I told her I had an appointment. Then she surveyed my scene. I know she wanted to ask me where the extra motivation was coming from, but she stood still for a minute. She walked away to get free weights. I was sitting trying to catch my breath when I lost my air. Alaina was walking towards me with a big smile on her face. I looked in the mirror and Mandy didn't see her yet. "Hey stranger." Alaina kissed my lips.

"Hey yourself, where's Jerrell?"

"Your dad is at the house with him. He suggested that I come workout with you for once so I could get a good look at you."

"Alaina?" Mandy said looking flushed.

"Hey girl," Alaina gave Mandy a hug. "I haven't seen you in forever. How have you been?"

"I'm good, it's been awhile. How's the baby?"

"He's good, he's getting big."

"Big? Sounds like it's time to get started on number two," Mandy smiled.

Alaina chuckled, "I'm not ready for number two yet. It's ok if there's a little gap between the kids."

"You want them to bond and be close don't you?" I said trying to hold back my irritation with the topic. Mandy knows how annoyed I am with Alaina's need to wait.

"Wesley and I are close, it depends on the kids not the gap in their ages." Alaina watched my eyes.

"My brother and sisters were right there with me. We had a blast together growing up. You dang near grew up like an only child. That's not what I want for my son."

Alaina put her hands up, "chill out. I didn't come here to fight."

"What did you come here for?"

"Duh! To spend time with you. You pay for my membership I figured I should use it at least once."

"I thought Wesley's gym is better than mine."

Alaina exhaled, "I love it when that vein starts throbbing on your forehead. That's your jealous vein." Mandy started laughing and I turned my head cause I wasn't expecting that response.

"What are you wearing?" Mandy continued to laugh.

"Workout clothes, you don't like them?" Alaina twirled in my sweats and my T-shirt, which completely swallowed her up.

"You too cheap to buy real workout clothes?"

"Alaina is a married woman. Your man may not have a problem with you walking around the gym naked, but I do."

Mandy's jab at Alaina back fired. "This material allows your skin to breathe while you sweat. Her clothes soak up the sweat and then she's going to get soggy."

"I rather she be soggy than naked. Besides Alaina shows consideration for me by covering up. She knows what I will tolerate and what I won't."

"Wow!" Then Mandy picked up her water. "It was good seeing you. Are you leaving early tomorrow too?" Mandy put her hand on her hip.

"From where?" Alaina looked at me.

"She's talking about work. Don't ask me dumb questions; you have access to my calendar. You can see what meetings I have and the ones I don't."

"Work?" Alaina looked between us.

"You know she's my assistant."

"I didn't know that, I was wondering who you got back then."

"Yeah but she gets on my nerves most of the time."

"Mandy girl, tell me the truth. Do those girls up there throw themselves at my man?"

"There's quite a few that be checking for him, but everybody knows he's married. Besides I let the ones who don't seem to care know that he's taken." Then Mandy started walking away.

"Thanks," Alaina called after her. She looked at me trying to read my mood. "Why are you mad?"

"She gets on my nerves. She's a good assistant, but she don't listen to her man. Her little dig at you pissed me off. I appreciate that you respect me as your husband and man." I kissed her lips. Electricity hit the back of my thigh. Alaina smiled as she turned her head to look at the equipment. "It's been a minute since I've done that huh?"

I caught the sadness in her eyes as she looked down at the floor. "You've been busy, it's ok."

"Did you need to work out tonight?"

"If you're done, I could go tomorrow." She said lowly.

"I just realized what my problem has been." Alaina looked at me with a smile. "I've had the worst attitude lately." I stood up. "Let me go get my things out of my locker. I'll be right back." As I walked out of the locker room Mandy looked at me. I raised my fist at her and she blew me a kiss. I held Alaina's hand as we walked down the street.

"Why did you leave work early?"

"I took a late lunch with one of our in-language lawyers. He's an outside counselor." That was true, but it happened last week.

When we got to the house my dad and Jerrell were wrestling in the family room like Jerrell and I often do. My dad looked at me like he could see through me. "So it looks like you found him."

"Of course!" Alaina said letting his words slide off of her.

"Were you alone?"

"I was on a machine." I don't know why he's trying to bust me out. He cheated on my mom, if anything there should be a guy code here or something.

"Ok, well I'm out of here. Jerrell, next time I will beat you!" He smiled.

"Nope," Jerrell smiled back with Alaina's smile.

"Alaina maybe we can make this a regular appointment." He said to her while looking at me.

Alaina smiled, "that would be nice."

My dad patted my arm, "you truly are your mother's child."

Fire turned in my stomach, what was he trying to say?

****

My mom crossed her arms, "why would you ever ask me something like that?"

"It's a simple yes or no answer."

"I want to know where the question comes from."

"I've been thinking is all? I don't understand what happened with you and dad. One day we were a family and then the next we weren't."

"I don't have time for this. I have an appointment to go to." She grabbed her purse off of the chair.

Rachel came out of her room with a smile. "Mother! Mother! Mother! Why won't you answer your golden boy's question?"

"Shut up Rachel! It's a dumb question!"

Rachel folded her arms in her doorway, "you afraid to lie anymore? Go ahead and answer him. Royce just wants to know if you ever cheated on dad? That's an easy answer unless," she smiled big.

"Pack your stuff and get out Rachel! Your father and I are divorced! Get out of my house!"

"Nope, not leaving until you sell."

"I don't have time for this!" Then she hurried out of the door.

"Your answer is yes. She still sees the guy too. He's ended up everywhere we moved to. When we got to California and he showed up here that's when dad got fed up. That's when dad started stepping out too. He didn't want to be without us."

"Dad said I was just like her."

"He said something similar to me when he found out about my man. Look, it's your life and your relationship. I'm not telling you to cheat, but make sure you're fair if you do. My man has always told me the truth. I'd hurt him if he thought it was ok to lie to me."

"Does his wife know about you?"

"She'd be dumb not to. We travel and everything else together. I'm respectful of his relationship though."

I laughed, "how is the mistress respectful?"

She didn't like my laugh; "I don't bring him drama with his wife. On the occasions where she and I have been in the same room I was cool."

"Why are you ok with being a mistress?"

"Some cultures call it a second wife. There's not enough men in the first place, and the one I fell in love with happened to meet her first. Their relationship doesn't take away from what we have. I'm not trying to be first, everyone can't be. As long as I'm loved is all I care about."

****

"Do you have any questions?" My boss asked me.

I couldn't erase my smile, "none! Thank you!"

My boss stood up and walked out of the conference room. I walked over to the window and looked out at the city. I love working in the city. I don't love the commute and the sometimes characters on the

Bart train. Moments like this, I enjoy them. I looked down on the city looking at all the people looking like organized ants as they moved here and there.

I picked up the phone and dialed my florist. I had them send another bouquet to Vanessa. This was my second and last time sending them. I'm not trying to freak her out and have her call the police on me. I had them say, "you're still beautiful!" I've gone to that lobby a few times and watched her walk out of the building. She doesn't wear a ring, but that doesn't mean anything cause I don't wear one either. I've followed her to the same hotel a few times and it makes sense that she would stay there. It's close enough to the office. I stroked my beard taking in the fact that just the sight of Vanessa has kicked up my dedication in the gym. Now I'm not just there to watch Mandy, but I get a good burn in during and after my workout.

Rachel's words have been replaying in my mind. Vanessa is going to be angry when she sees me. I'm hoping she'll give me a chance to speak. I don't know what I'd say to her, but at this point I'm willing to drop to the ground and punk out just for an evening alone with her.

I called information and I had them connect me to a florist close to home. I had a similar arrangement sent to Alaina. In the card I wrote, *get a babysitter.*

My boss just gave me a huge promotion. My bonus will be based off my new salary so Alaina can finish all of her upgrades to the house and we'll finally have our palace. As a thank you to me she needs to get pregnant right now. I don't see the point in waiting any longer. She can still shop for furniture while she's pregnant.

Tonight I'm going to take my wife out to dinner. Tell her about my promotion and make her feel special. Then I'll tell her it's now or never.

When I walked out of the conference room I didn't look at anyone. I went to lunch. I walked over to the Powell street mall. I was going to get a suit, but I decided on a nice outfit for tonight.

"Where did you go for lunch?" Mandy asked lowly.

"Shopping, why?"

"It's Thursday," she said like I was supposed to understand what that meant.

"So?"

Mandy immediately got irritated, "what's going on with you lately? You've been absent minded, so uncharacteristically flaky." Then she chuckled, "you wouldn't be crazy enough to cheat on me would you?" She poked her eyes at me.

I exhaled, "you live in a sick and twisted world. You are not my wife, I don't owe you anything." Then I pointed to my shopping bag on the other side of her chair.

"Royce don't play with me, I will mess your world up!"

I stood up, "conference room now!" Mandy stood up; she walked to her desk and grabbed a pen and paper. Then she followed me as usual to the conference room. As soon as I shut the door I looked at her. "Sit down!" When she did I sat on the table next to her. I stroked her face then I grabbed it so she couldn't pull away. I didn't squeeze too hard. Just enough to get my point across. "Don't you ever in your life think it's ok to threaten me. I will mess your whole world up! Not only will you lose your job, your man, I'll make sure your mother is unemployed as well. You don't deserve my loyalty, because you aren't trustworthy. Alaina trust you with her most prized possession and look what you've done. Maybe you don't know my wife like I do, but she will come for you." Then I released her face.

"You'll lose your job and your wife!"

"I'm a lawyer I can find another job or start my own firm. I will never lose my wife. She's loyal and dedicated to me. She'll be hurt, but we will come out on top."

"All I was saying is that I felt so dumb waiting for you and you never showed up." She searched my eyes. "What's going on with you?"

"Nothing."

"I fell in love with you because of the father and husband that you were. I got carried away and I never should've made this happen. You're changing and I don't like it."

Her comment made me nauseous. "Love?"

She gave me an irritated look, "you think I would cheat on my boyfriend for just anyone?"

"I don't know what you do."

"You're being really mean! Stop trying to hurt me right now." Then she stood up and walked out.

I went over to my coworker's desk and asked her for some of her ginger cause my stomach wouldn't settle down. As soon as I felt calm come over me Alaina called. "Royce?" She sound like she had been crying. I immediately looked at Mandy like she better not have defied me.

"You get my flowers?"

"Yes, they're beautiful. I can't go out tonight. I'm sick, Jerrell is too."

"Since when?"

"Yesterday, that's why Jerrell was in the bed with me." She sniffled, "he seems to be better today. I feel like death warmed over. Can you come straight home? I need your help," she sniffled again.

I looked at my bag and I felt disappointed. "Of course, what should I bring home?"

"Something for you and Jerrell to eat."

I left my bag at work. I went to the grocery store walking around from aisle to aisle getting soup, crackers, fresh fruit, I didn't remember her symptoms so I got almost one of every cold and flu medicine. I was putting my bags in the car when someone called my name. I looked up and the bald headed chick was looking at me. Vanessa was approaching fast. She held so much pain on her face. She slapped me as hard as she could. Then she turned to walk away. I grabbed her arm as I shook my head to shake off the sting of her slap. "Vanessa?"

"Get your hands off of me!"

"Vanessa please! I'm sorry!"

"Don't you think I know you're a sorry excuse for a man! How could you do that to me?"

"Vanessa I haven't been right since then I am so sorry."

"You think I have?" She tried to get her arm free.

"Please let me explain, although it won't take back what I've done. I need to plead my case."

"I wouldn't give you the satisfaction!"

"I'm not asking for me, I owe you an explanation. You were good to me, and I did you wrong."

Vanessa snatched her arm and then she wrapped her arms around herself as she cried. I felt horrible. Her friend came and told her to come on. I gave her my business card and I asked her to call me. She tore the card in half then she put it in her pocket. I stood there watching them get in their car and leave. I stood still feeling like a first class heel. I needed to make this up to her.

When I walked in the door with all of my bags Jerrell exclaimed, "dad!" As he came running full speed. A greeting I experience rarely because I normally get home when he's sleep. I hugged my son and then he helped me by dragging the bag I gave him into the kitchen. Alaina looked like death just like she said. She thanked me for coming home and then she went to bed. I warmed up soup, but Alaina had no appetite.

I played with Jerrell then I put him to bed. I fell asleep watching television. In the morning, I kissed Alaina's cheek then I went to work. I was in my groove, as I reviewed a document. My phone rang and I answered without looking at my caller ID. "This is Royce."

"Royce," she sounded like she was still crying.

"Yes," I swallowed.

"I couldn't get it together this morning. I'm working from my room. I have a meeting at 9, can you be here at 10?"

"Where?"

"My hotel. Come to the Westin in Emeryville room 511." Then she hung up.

I told my boss I was going to log in later and I packed up my work laptop and left without saying a word to Mandy.

I was so nervous the entire Bart ride to my car. I drove cautiously and slow. Was she calling me over to kill me? Not that I didn't deserve it. I took several breaths before I got out of my car. I knocked on the door at 9:45am.

Vanessa opened quickly and then she went back to the desk to her laptop. I always knew she was going to be running stuff. It sounded like people were reporting to her. She was giving direction and listening. I sat on her bed and watched her. She's still so beautiful, Kid's description of her did Vanessa no justice. The only change is that her hair is longer. I watched her twist it up behind herself, like she was going to war. When she ended her call she put one finger up to me, and then she called someone. She told them to call her cell if they needed her cause she was going offline.

When she hung up she closed her laptop then she looked at me. Her expression was cold and unfriendly. "Explain."

I put my briefcase on the floor and then I tried to get comfortable. "I was engaged when we got back together. I got married the day after you left." She had no reaction, "I'm sorry Vanessa, I didn't mean to hurt you like I did. I..."

"Well your intention wasn't to make me feel good. Are you still married?"

"Yes."

"Where's your ring?"

I looked at my empty hand. "I had to take it off."

"Trouble in paradise?"

"Yeah, me."

"Oh?"

"My guilt about what I've done to you has consumed me. I tried to push you out of my head, but it didn't work. I started eating to dull the pain. You remember how I used to be. Now I'm embarrassed and making a mess of everything."

"Children?"

"A son, he's two."

"Let me see a picture." I took Jerrell's picture out of my wallet. Vanessa started crying when she looked at it. "Cute kid, he doesn't look a thing like you." She handed the picture back.

"Thanks? He looks like her dad more than either of us."

She stared at me for a minute. "I HATE YOU! You have no idea how much you hurt me! I trusted you! I was in love with you!"

"I'm in love with you!"

Her eyes bucked at me, "you're disgusting! What about the woman who was worth breaking my heart for?"

"I'm in love with her too."

"I don't accept your love. It's too painful!" Then she scanned me, "you've cheated on your wife haven't you?"

For the first time I felt regret for my selfishness. "Can I explain?"

"It's a yes or no answer."

"Yes I have but it's not that simple."

Vanessa laughed as she wiped her eyes. "There's layers to your selfishness? God!"

"My wife doesn't like sex."

Vanessa started laughing, "that's exactly what you get. What she do, fake it until you got married?"

"She's very old fashioned, she was a virgin when we got married. In the beginning she tried very hard. One day she gave in, when we had our son she gave up."

"How did she give up?"

"She wouldn't let me touch her for months. Then this woman came along responding to me and showing me that it's not me."

"I'm pretty sure it's you," she smiled.

"I deserve that."

"All hatred aside, I'm pretty sure it's you. She don't know how to stand up to you is all."

"What are you talking about?"

She laughed at me. "I took you outside of anything you knew. I was out there, but you were on the opposite side of the spectrum. The way you keep pulling on that jacket I'm sure you're always hiding. Take it off!"

"What is taking my jacket off going to prove?"

"Do it!" I did, "now take your shirt off."

I looked her in her eyes, "NO!" Besides the fact that the last time she saw my body I had a six-pack, this wasn't going anywhere. She's too angry.

"Fine! Get out!"

I stood up putting my jacket back on. "Thank you for letting me tell you the truth."

"Well I don't feel sorry for you," she came around the desk.

"I didn't expect you to, I just figured that you're the one person I owe the truth to."

"Me and your wife," she held back her smile.

"Yep, that's what death beds are for." She chuckled, "how about you? Are you married? Any children?" She held up her empty hand. So I held up mine, "doesn't mean anything."

"No husband, no kids."

"Boyfriend?"

"There is someone in my life if that's what you're asking."

"Is he special?"

She exhaled, "he is what he is."

"I still love you."

"Get out!" She pushed me out the room. Then she slammed the door shut.

I exhaled; I started to walk away when I noticed that I left my briefcase. I exhaled again, and then I knocked on the door. "My bag." I said as soon as she opened the door.

I walked to the bed and picked up my bag. She was standing

there with her poker face on, but I noticed her hand. It was flat like she was trying to be strong. I looked at her hand then I looked at her. She asked me what was wrong with me. I hurried over to her and kissed her. When she didn't push me away I dropped my bag and I put my hands all in her hair. I pulled her into me as I continued to kiss her.

Alaina

"How you feeling?" Royce rubbed my foot as he went to the closet.

"I feel so much better," I sat up and stretched.

Royce came out of the closet in sweats, with his sneakers. "I'm going to take Jerrell to the park."

I got excited, "he'll love that. What time will you be back? I can have food ready."

He sat on the bed next to me. He smiled at me and then he kissed me deeply. "That's not necessary. We're going to be gone all day. Go do something girly and we'll be back late tonight."

I frowned, "girly? Toy trucks and trains have been my world for the past year. I'm not sure I remember girly."

Royce sat in front of me looking at my face. "You are so beautiful!"

I gasped as I blushed, "flattery will get you everywhere."

He put his hands under the covers and between my legs, "I want in."

I blushed, "since when you act like this?"

"You don't like it?" He gave me a knowing smile.

"I mean, it's alright," I giggled.

"Maybe I can't wait," he said coming in for a kiss.

As we were kissing the phone rang. He told me to answer it as he put on his shoes. It was Unique and she asked me if I could go with her to find stuff for her new condo. Royce kissed my cheek and then I heard him go in Jerrell's room. I told Unique I would be right there. As I was in the shower Royce opened the shower door. He was completely naked. I was confused; my husband hasn't stood naked before me since we were newlyweds. He snatched my loofah out of my hand and then he kissed me. It felt like the water was encouraging this. This whole experience was brand new. When we connected Royce felt different. He picked me up and put my back up against the wall. Everything tingled and then it sizzled. For the first time in years I finished. Royce watched my face then he smiled and worked me harder. When he finished he put me down, washed up, and left me in the shower with weak legs. For a minute I wondered if Royce switched bodies with someone else. That whole scene kept replaying in my mind. That was **FANTASTIC**!

Unique ran all over the Bay looking at stuff, taking pictures, and then comparing them to the other items we picked. I couldn't stop thinking about Royce all day. I love my husband!

Royce

"I'm pregnant!" Mandy said.

Everything in my body went limp, "what?" My head immediately started hurting. I don't believe this.

"It's not yours. We've always been protected." She smiled, "I want to find some cute way to tell him. I can't believe this is finally happening. I've wanted to be a mother ever since I was a little girl." She had the most fulfilled smile on her face.

"Congratulations?" All I wanted to do was go home.

"I hope you understand that we can't continue." She disregarded me like I was nothing.

"Yeah, yeah, yeah! I understand, I would think that goes without saying." I couldn't think of anything other than getting out of this booth. I didn't care where she went or how she got there; I just needed her to get away from me. Mandy was too excited to let my horrified reaction to her affect her. I dropped money on the table for the bill and then I hurried out of the restaurant. I didn't wait for Mandy; I hurried down the street feeling my anxiety and then relief that it was over between us at the same time.

At my desk, my hands wouldn't stop shaking. This was too close to home. Things have been good. I haven't had sex with Alaina since that morning in the shower. That's because I've been taking my son everywhere on the weekends. On the weeks that Vanessa's in town, I spend as much time with her as I can. My workouts have increased in intensity and FINALLY the weight is falling off me like it always should've. I was feeling really good about myself until this reality check.

I was lost in my thoughts when someone grabbed my arm. "Royce!" It was my sister Brooke.

I hadn't seen her in years. "Whoa! What are you doing out here?"

"I just got off work, on my way to pick up the kids from school."

"Instant Mom's job is never done huh?"

"I guess, so how's the life of the lawyer?"

"Guess you would know if you came around. You've barely gotten to know my wife and our ninth year is fast approaching."

"I would've met her if you would stop trying to have me around your mother."

"Why would you let her stop you from being there for me? Rachel and Brice come around from time to time."

"It's not like you come to see me, or keep in contact with me. If it wasn't for our cousins and the rest of your mother's family out here I'd have no one."

"Why are you saying that? You isolate yourself. You need to come and meet my son, maybe he could meet your kids."

"Step kids, I haven't adopted anyone." She corrected me.

I looked at her, "ok. Well we've never met your partner either. So, what if I get something together with just us kids. We'll bring our families and just hang out."

She looked around, "I don't know."

"Oh come on when was the last time we all were together? Probably when we were all at the house for dinner. Mom and dad were still married and everything…"

She cut me off, "they got divorced?"

I smiled at her, "give me your number. You need to get caught up to speed. Some people go away to college and never come back." I smiled.

Seeing Brooke did make me feel better and that helped me redirect my thoughts. It was business as usual back at the office except for that stupid smile Mandy had plastered on her face. Mandy always wanted a family of her own, its selfish of me to be bothered by her advancement. However, I'm not going to lie. Ending things with her removed a lot of the guilt I was feeling about my life. I can't feel guilty about being with the women I love. I feel like my old self again. I have the love and loyalty of Alaina. While I have the love and satisfaction of Vanessa. I know she feels guilty about us, and I don't like that part. I just don't know how to fix this. If Alaina knew she would not be ok with this. I have to figure something out. I stroked my beard trying to think of something. Maybe Vanessa could transfer her job back out here, when she does we could have a family. I know she's always wanted one. It wouldn't be totally ideal, but I can't think of her having anyone else's child and she's getting that itch. I stayed late, but I decided to go straight home instead of stopping at the gym.

When I got home Alaina was making dinner, singing and dancing, while Jerrell sat in his high chair cheering her on. Alaina startled when she saw me walking into the kitchen. She screamed at the top of her voice and Jerrell looked like he was about to run up out of his high chair. "WHY ARE YOU HOME SO EARLY?"

"I was thinking about what you said, and you're right. I need to spend more time with my family. You don't want me home or something? You got a secret boyfriend stopping by in a little bit?"

"Ha! Ha! Very funny." Alaina kissed me. "Welcome home, you scared me is all."

That night, I made love to my wife. It wasn't great and it wasn't fantastic, but I knew I was the only person who was doing it.

Alaina

"So you had a good time?" I asked Unique who couldn't stop smiling.

"You could've told me he liked me."

"And ruin the surprise? Never!"

"I had a wonderful time, we danced and danced and danced. Ben is something else." She smiled to herself.

My eyes got big, "you didn't?"

Unique blushed, "it's not a big deal. I felt beautiful! He kept telling me how beautiful I was! It has been a minute."

"Tavio will kill him!" I covered my mouth.

"It's not like that, I really like him. And we appear to be very compatible." She raised her eyebrows at me.

I felt like she punched me in the stomach. "So now what? Where do we go from here?"

"He wants to talk to Tavio, we didn't plan for the night to end the way it did. Alaina, I really like him. Tell me everything you know about him."

We sat on that park bench talking for hours. Remembering when I first started hanging out with Ben and Tavio took me back to so many memories. I remember how in love Tavio was with Eva. How sad he was when they broke up. I silently wished that he met someone that he could have those same feelings with. Someone who made him think about future, instead of just for now. I suggested that we plan a big dinner where we could all interact and have a good time. Unique's eyes got big with excitement as she rapidly agreed.

Royce

Mandy was full of tears and wimpy sadness. I didn't want to ask her what was wrong, but she wasn't going to stop until I asked. So I took her in one of our conference rooms. Her stomach was starting to grow, it was barely there. I knew it existed so to me it was colossal. "What's up Mandy? You're bringing the morale down around here."

"I thought he would've been happy but he's acting weird ever since I told him. He didn't come home last night and when I asked him where he was he said he was out screwing some girl from the gym. We had a fight and then he started accusing me of cheating on him." My heart dropped; please don't be going with this story where I know she's going. "I told him to stop being rude. He keeps saying that the baby can't be his. I think he's just nervous about being a father."

I put my hands on my head, I counted out loud backwards from twenty then I looked at her. "He's trying to tell you something and your dumb behind isn't getting it."

Mandy jumped because of my tone. "Royce I am not dumb!"

"It sounds like he's telling you he can't have kids."

"What?" She looked at me like I was crazy.

"Look at the facts," I wrote on her notepad. "He's said no to having a baby and yet you were never protected. He said he didn't want a family, but he didn't do anything to stop it from happening. As soon as you tell him you're pregnant he knows you've been cheating on him. WAKE UP!"

"Plenty of guys say they don't want a family but they do nothing to prevent it. Then they act like you're doing something to them."

"Is your man that way?"

"I didn't think so, but I guess he is."

My head was pounding so hard. "The condom did rip a little that one time. It's possible Mandy!"

Mandy put her hands over her mouth. "No! NO! Not you! No!"

"Get rid of it Mandy!"

She grabbed her stomach. "NO! I've waited my entire life for this."

"Is a child worth losing your man over?"

Mandy started crying hard! "Royce, I've waited my entire life for this. What if this is my only chance?"

"Some people wait their entire lifetime waiting for a man to love them like yours does. He didn't beat you, or put you out. He's hurt but he'll get over it as long as you don't have that baby. You will lose your man, is that what you want?"

"Why would I choose a man over my child? He could leave me tomorrow and I would have no man and no child to show for it. NO!"

"Mandy, you can't do this to me. Think about the family that brought on your attraction to me. You want to be the reason my family is broken?"

"I can't worry about them if you didn't. You knew as well as I did the risk we were taking. I still don't believe that this baby could be yours. There's just no way!"

I sunk further in my seat; this idiot is going to be the death of me. "I can't believe this! You can't do nothing right!"

"What?" She looked at me.

"You've been messing up big time since you found out about your kid. Working out with you had me out of shape and whack. I start doing my routines on my own and look at me! You're an idiot and I can't cover for you anymore."

Mandy stood up, "I QUIT!" Then she stormed out of the conference room. She grabbed her things and then she left.

I explained to my boss that she was upset about the mistakes that I pointed out to her and so she quit. No one was even bothered that she left. I was the only person internally falling apart about it.

Alaina

I came up to the office to swap out my current laptop for a new one. My boss asked if I was considering coming on full time any time soon cause they wanted me to come in as a supervisor when I did. They were planning a small team for me to manage, and we would be doing a lot of reporting and analytical stuff. I told them I would let them know as soon as I was ready. My boss promised that they would work around my school schedule. My money from my job at the bank goes into a savings account in a totally different bank. Although I know Royce doesn't have access to accounts in the legal department. Knowing that Tavio used to look at mine, and I still look at his. I felt it was safer to have that account with another bank. Money goes in that account, and nothing comes out. I had a nice little savings account balance, but that was only because I was too afraid to touch it and risk Royce asking where I got the money.

As I walked out of my Boss' office I heard a familiar laugh. I looked at my boss and asked her if that was Mandy? She said Mandy came back a couple of months ago. Royce didn't mention anything about her not being his assistant anymore. When I walked out on the floor Mandy was talking to someone. The person smiled at me and Mandy spun around. I noticed her little bump immediately. I smiled and gave her a very excited congratulatory hug. Mandy asked what I was doing here, and I told her I come talk to our boss from time to time. I couldn't risk her telling Royce while they worked out. My boss was the only person who knew I still worked here. Everyone else thought I was only visiting whenever I came. I asked Mandy how she was feeling and she said not so great. She said her pregnancy has been flagged as high risk by her doctor. I asked her why, Mandy always eats clean, and she works out more than anyone I know. Mandy sadly said that she and her man are going through a tough time right now. The IT guy went into my Boss' office and then they called me to go in as well. I told Mandy I would be back.

They swapped out my laptops and then I put it in my purse and headed out. Mandy was going to lunch so she said she'd walk out with me. We were silent in the elevator since we weren't alone. Then we walked slowly out to the parking lot. Mandy said her boyfriend is insisting that the baby isn't his. I couldn't believe it. They've been together since I met her. She swallowed and then she said she did have a little affair, but she's sure the baby is her man's and not the other guy's. I asked her if she would get a DNA test to be certain after the baby's born. She said she keeps going back and forth. She said she really doesn't want anything else to do with the guy she cheated with. She said he's a jerk and they were never supposed to be anything other than a fling. She said she got lost in the idea of him. I asked her how come she doesn't work with Royce anymore. She said the guy was out there, and she just couldn't go back to San Francisco anymore. I told her Royce didn't mention anything about her leaving. She said she left so abruptly he was probably mad that she left him hanging.

****

I laid in that bed trying to contain my anger. I don't think I ask for too much. I don't even require him to be at home like he needs to be. He's constantly pushing for another child but he's never here for the one he has. He may take him out on the weekends. WHAT ABOUT ME! I get a kiss or two in passing. A butt pat to let me know he looked at me. The once every blue moon sex is whatever since I'm not into it anyways. Then he harasses me for the next however many weeks about being pregnant. His clock is ticking, and I'm waiting for it with my hammer so that I can smash the life out of it. Although he hasn't technically asked in the last couple of months, my point does not change!

He didn't give me a card, a rose or anything. He completely forgot about our anniversary! I don't ask for a lot, but my goodness would it kill this man to honor me? Royce rolled over and then he jumped when he opened his eyes and I was staring at him. "What is wrong with you?"

"You have the **NERVE** to ask me what is wrong with me?"

"Alaina please, don't stress me. I'm stressed enough as it is."

"Don't stress you? Don't stress you? I cannot believe you Royce! Look at the doggone calendar!"

Royce strained his eyes to look at the calendar across the room. When that didn't work, he walked over to it. Royce turned pale and then he looked at me as he swallowed. I reached in my nightstand and I threw his present at him as hard as I could. "You wonder why I keep refusing to have any more children with you. Stuff like this! I don't ride you about being out until all hours of the night. Missing in action with my son around your mother who only spreads poison. I don't say anything about anything, and then this is how you show me that you appreciate me? I've made our home a palace. Your son is more than prepared for preschool, HE READS! AT TWO I MIGHT ADD! I work my butt off around here, and you couldn't give me a funky rose. A card or nothing?

You come home and pass out! I'M SO DONE!"

Royce stood there looking like a defeated idiot. "Alaina, I'm…"

"SHUT UP! You don't care anymore! Then neither do I! We're strangers anyways, this just makes it official!" I grabbed jeans and a short sleeve t-shirt. I went to the guest bathroom and showered. Royce was sitting on the corner edge of the bed looking pitiful. He might've even been crying, but I didn't care. I put on my shoes, grabbed my purse and jacket and then I left. I went over Wesley's but he had company. Chareca didn't answer the phone, I hesitated and then I called Tavio. He answered on the second ring. I asked him if it was ok for me to stop by. He asked me why I called first, and I told him I stopped dropping by on him once I was pregnant, I didn't want to impose on him and Sabrina. He told me to come on. When I got there Lil T was patiently waiting for his mom and stepfather to pick him up for the weekend. They had a ton of plans that he was excited about. Tempest gave me a hug, chatted with Tavio real quick and then they left. I plopped on the couch then Tavio sat in the recliner. "Ok MAC what's up? You're up early and angry."

I finally broke down, "Royce forgot our anniversary. I know the Flintstones made fun of it all of the time. This is not funny in reality. I'm tired of caring, I'm tired of considering him when he doesn't consider me. I'm tired!" I cried into my hands.

Tavio looked into the kitchen, "hold on." He picked up his phone. "Hey… MAC is here too… MAC How you like your eggs?"

"Over hard."

"Bacon or sausage?"

"Crispy Bacon."

"Yeah she wants over hard, crispy bacon, and sourdough toast…. Lil T brought some in this morning… I'm getting to it right now…. jeez… ok, see you in a minute." Then he hung up. "Unique is coming over to talk to me. Come in the kitchen while I juice these oranges."

"Should I leave?" He patted a stool for me to sit on. He whistled while he got everything ready. "You don't have anything to say to what I just said?"

He shrugged, "you love him. You need to cool down. He knows he messed up royally and now he gets to sweat it out all day. What else is there to say?"

"You get on my nerves? It's that simple?"

"You don't function in complicated." He went back to whistling, and then he tied his hair back. Hair envy was all over my face. Tavio smiled at me then he went back to the task at hand. I opened the door when Unique rang the doorbell. I opened it to find Unique and Ben with arms full of food. I smiled and quietly welcomed them in. Tavio was cutting oranges when they walked into the kitchen. His eyes went to Ben and didn't leave, "what's this?"

"Our first family appearance as a couple."

Tavio shook his head, "it's always the sister!"

"Tavio, you had one job. Why isn't the juice ready?"

He took a deep breath as he looked from Unique to me. "You two are pulling on my self-control this morning."

"What does that mean?" I asked.

"What I said," then he focused on juicing his fruit.

Unique talked on while Ben watched his friend most of the morning. "Are we cool man?"

Tavio looked at Ben like he wanted to hurt him. "We're cool, but remember this is my sister and I didn't introduce you two for a reason."

"What reason?" Unique asked full of sass.

"Both of you are emotional, of course he'd like you. You're beautiful and just as driven as he is. I'm just thinking about the fireworks when you two blow up at each other."

"Well that's not fair." Unique darted her eyes at me. "I would never say that you and Alaina could pull off being friends. Your attraction for each other is obvious. I would've thought you two were having an affair years ago. Who am I kidding; I did think that until I got to know Alaina. I don't trust you to control yourself."

I looked at Tavio knowing that he was going to object to her statement, you know put her in her place. Tavio didn't look phased by her comment. "You are my little sister, I'm supposed to be overly protective of you."

Ben smiled at me when my face dropped cause he didn't address what she said. "Remember MAC back in the day, little nice Christian girl without all of the Christian surrounding her."

"What does that mean?" I frowned.

"You've always been sweet and respectable. Any man would have to be crazy not to be attracted to that."

Tavio smiled, "that's right. You were crushing on MAC back in the day."

"WHAT?" I almost choked on my orange juice.

"Right before you started dating that crazy guy, I was going to ask you out." Ben laughed, "you could be married to me. Making me chicken wings and making me fat."

Tavio and Ben had a good laugh about that. I looked at Unique who wasn't laughing either. "I haven't had my morning run, you want to join me?" Unique asked.

"I can't run in this." I pulled at my shirt.

"I have something for you." We left Ben and Tavio to talk and be silly on their own.

Unique handed me stretchy pants, a sports bra, and a tank top. My eyes got big as I looked at the clothes. I asked her where we were going to go running and she said on the Refugio Valley trail, which was just outside of her Hercules condo. I've always wanted to put on regular exercise clothes and just run with it. I knew Royce would have a fit. There's no way he'd show up out here, and if he did so what, I'm mad at him anyways. I came out of the bathroom feeling so naked. Unique said my butt looked amazing in my pants. I looked back at it and then I smiled. She paid my awkwardness no mind. She gave me a water bottle and told me to come on and stretch with her. We stretched outside and then we were off.

I cringed every time we passed someone or a car drove by. Unique was completely fine so I told myself to be like her and to stop tripping. When we got to the bottom we sat on a bench and drank our water. I expected her to ask me about Royce or something, but she didn't. She talked about anything other than the men in our lives.

The way back was hard. We were running up hill at about a two incline and in some places a four. I was so concentrated on my breathing I couldn't be embarrassed by my body. It was so much easier running in these clothes though. They weren't heavy and they didn't hold in heat making it impossible to breathe at times. Normally I would've stopped on the run down. I made it down with no problem. On the way up it burned and I was tired, but I kept pushing and made it all the way. Unique and I took pictures celebrating our triumph and then we took turns in the shower. When I came out of the shower I put her clothes in the washer. Unique had a green smoothie waiting for me. It was so good, my greedy behind accidentally spilled some on my shirt. Unique told me which drawer to go in to get another shirt. I was frustrated; all of her shirts were V-necks. Royce hates them so I don't own any. I told myself he's in the doghouse so I could wear what I wanted. I put on the t-shirt and I said hello to my cleavage. When we went back to Tavio's he noticed my shirt right away, but he didn't say anything. Every so often his glance would land on my V. Eventually he told me I looked nice.

Royce

I opened the small box and there was a wedding band. I exhaled as I looked at it. Alaina had been asking me about rings for some time. I never paid her questions any attention cause she normally asked them while I was focused on something else. When I put the ring on the un-smoothness of the inside made me take the ring off. I felt like garbage already. "The only man for me" was inscribed on the inside of the ring. That did it, tears started to form in my eyes. Alaina had put a lot of thought and planning into my gift and I couldn't take her out to dinner? I have been so distracted.

Mandy disconnected her number, and I only went to the gym a couple of times before I cancelled our membership and went to a new gym. I was really hoping that she would call me and say that she was messing with someone else or Her theory about her boyfriend flipping out was actually accurate. All of the logical possibilities say it's me though. There is no rebounding from this. I told Vanessa about it. I was freaking out too much not to tell her. She was mad, but she got over it. Something tells me that Alaina would not be so chill about the whole thing.

I called Rachel and I asked her to help me. I told her that I've been stressed about everything and I totally forgot about my anniversary. Rachel came over, she hadn't been to our house since we initially moved in. She told me it was time to grovel. I was in the doghouse, but I could redeem myself. We went on the computer and she pulled up every local romantic place she could think of. Nothing sounded good, a long car ride would mean we'd have to talk. She was madder at me than I've ever seen her before. Last thing she was going to do was be happily stuck in a car with me for a couple of hours. When Rachel exhausted all possibilities she turned to me. "Look baby brother I'm going to suggest Napa again. It's right over the bridge. As long as you keep her drunk off wine she might find a way to like you again." She had a point. I booked the most expensive honeymoon suite they had, and I added on every luxury I could think of. Rachel agreed to stay with Jerrell while we were gone. I only needed to call into work and tell them I would be working half days and telecommuting at that.

As it got later and later, I realized Alaina was going to play dirty and draw this out. I told Rachel I would call her tomorrow to let her know what time we were leaving. Around 10pm I called Ken who gave me a hard time about being a stranger. This was everybody hates Royce day. At first I was trying to get to the point of my call until I realized that Ken was really angry with me. He told me I've been in my own fantasy world while everyone else has been waiting for me to wake up. He got on me so badly about Alaina. I wanted to get mad and tell him to mind his own business. My pride was already damaged and he was just taking me lower and lower. By the time he was done with me my head was hanging low. I asked him if he's heard from Alaina at all today. That was the point of my call not all this negativity. He said no, I asked him to ask Chareca if she's heard from her. Chareca said Alaina's phone has been off all day and she figured that we were out celebrating.

Then Ken and I had some serious words. Our argument got so bad; I could hear him and Chareca wrestling for the phone. And then it hung up on me. Did I just lose my best friend since we moved out here? I couldn't even worry about that. I took a deep breath and I called Wesley. He said he talked to her briefly in the morning but he hadn't seen her all day. Then he hung up in my face. I called her father and he was very short with me as well. I can't believe Alaina told all these people our business. That's her problem; she's going to have to deal with all of their mouths when we make up! She was either with Ben or she was with Tavio. I'm willing to put money on her being with Tavio. I looked at the clock, she got one more hour before I go over there.

Alaina

Everybody was into the movie and I was getting antsy about the time. It was getting later and later, and every time I acted like I was going to go, they gave me a hard time. At some point I was going to have to go home to my husband. I guess no one cared about that part. Not that I really did either. It was kind of nice to be a rebel. Around two o'clock Unique said it was time to go. I stood up with her and walked towards the door. Tavio walked all of us out.

Royce was waiting outside his car against my car. It was cold out here and he didn't seem phased by the cold at all. I was so happy the four of us were walking out together; at least it didn't look like I was doing something else in there. Tavio walked with me to my car. I looked at him like he was crazy; I didn't know what he was doing. "Do you have any idea how late it is?" Royce ignored Tavio.

"Yes, but what difference does it make? Neither one of us have curfews. You come home when you please so can I. At least you know where to find me."

"You can go back in your house now." Royce said dismissing Tavio.

"You can roll up off my street with this nonsense." Tavio said dismissing Royce. He looked at me, "you can come back whenever you need to. He better be happy I didn't call the police on him. He's been sitting out here for the past three hours. I didn't want Jerrell seeing his father in that light. A black man already has to deal with too much in their life."

"Alaina! Get in your car!" Royce said firmly to me like he was talking to Jerrell.

Tavio frowned at him and then he looked at me. "Look! You don't come to my friend's house thinking you have the right to command anything of me."

"You can tell me how much you hate me when you get home. I'm not going to do this out here. You want to be the loud ghetto couple in the middle of the night?"

I didn't want to have some big ole dramatic scene in the middle of the night in front of Tavio's house. He lives in a nice neighborhood. One of the few neighborhoods in Richmond that is still nicely integrated. Tavio is the youngest homeowner here. "Thank you Tavio for everything." I could see his disappointed look without looking at him.

Royce started walking to his car where my baby was sleep in his car seat in the backseat. Tavio came in for a hug, "next time do what you have to do. Don't worry about my neighbors." Then he kissed my cheek.

Royce missed all of that as he got in his car, but Unique was sitting with her mouth hanging open and Ben was laughing in the driver's seat of Unique's car.

Royce

I followed Alaina home. I wanted to snatch her out of her car. I had to get Jerrell out of his seat while she strolled in the house like there was nothing wrong. I laid Jerrell in his bed and then I slightly left his door cracked. I walked in the bedroom as Alaina took her jacket off. I saw bare chest and I went off. I asked her what she was wearing. She looked like she forgot she was wearing that shirt with her business hanging all out. I thought I was going to apologize and we were going to make things better before daylight. We argued hard all night long. She complained about me never being home, and when I did come home I would go right to sleep. I complained about her wanting to make household decisions while we were in the bed. She countered with that was the only time she saw me. "Pack your bags, we're going away for a couple of days."

"NO!" She tried to pull back her panicked look.

"No? I'm trying to fix this."

"I have responsibilities here Royce. You can't spring a trip on me at the last minute. And that's so cheesy!"

"Rachel is going to stay with Jerrell."

"He's not my only responsibility. My Granny Shane and I do our grocery shopping on Mondays. You don't eat here so you don't notice anything."

"Can't someone else take her?"

"Not at the last minute, NO!"

"Alaina, I can't give the hotel 24-hour notice of our cancellation. I will be out over $2,000!"

Alaina smiled, "not my problem. You can't spring trips on me. I had to do something around here to fill my days since you don't want the family you forced."

"Like I ever have to force you to open your legs."

"Like you would know, you haven't been between them in forever. What was that by the way? A tease? I forgot you had skin! Having your body back is nice, but what's the point if I can't enjoy it."

"Kind of like your breast?"

Why did I say that? Alaina was almost foaming at the mouth. "If you can't understand that I can't have you on my breast while I'm feeding my son, I don't know what to tell you. You got all these rules about how much skin I can show, but you can't understand that one?"

"What about me?"

"It's always about you Royce! It's always about what you want and what you don't."

I was tired of arguing; apparently we could do this all night and day. In the end, Alaina just wanted more love and attention. About four hours ago I saw her notice that I was wearing the ring. She softened a little when she noticed it until I said the next dumb thing. "You're right, I'm sorry." Alaina waited like she knew I was tricking her. "I get it. I've been so busy working that I've neglected our beautiful family. I'm sorry Alaina. It's just been a lot going on. My workload has picked up and the gym has been my way to let off steam and stress from the day. I will make my time at the gym shorter and make a better effort to be here."

Alaina yawned real hard which made me yawn as well. "Fine! I'm going to bed."

"What about Jerrell?"

"Deal with it dad!" Then she got in the bed.

I called the hotel to cancel my reservation. Some of the add-ons had 24-hour notice so I could cancel them without charge. I still lost the money I told Alaina that I was going to. I called Rachel and I asked her to come pick Jerrell and I up. I was delirious. She took me to Tiffany & Co in Walnut Creek. Rachel helped me pick out the biggest ring I could afford. I smiled at the ring as I told myself I did good. Rachel agreed to keep Jerrell overnight and away from our mother. I put the ring box on the nightstand on Alaina's side. Then I got in the bed and passed out.

Chapter 16

Tavio

I completely forgot that Sabrina was coming early Sunday morning so that we could drive out to Gilroy. Her cousin is getting married and she promised to be on best behavior.

I was knocked out sleeping real good when she rang the doorbell. At first I thought she was MAC and I was wondering why she didn't use her key. By the second and more aggressive round on my doorbell I jumped up. Sleep still in my eyes, halitosis kicking like crazy. I opened the door completely caught off guard. Sabrina looked annoyed but she didn't say anything. I already knew what I was wearing so I jumped in the shower. I was ready to go in record timing. When I walked into the living room where Sabrina was impatiently waiting she looked at my hair, which was down. "You're not going to put your hair up or tie it back?"

I glanced at myself in the mirror. "I look good, what's your problem?"

"Nothing!" She threw her hands up. "Can we take your new car?"

"I'd rather put the miles on the other car if you want me to drive." It didn't really matter to me. However I saw the dollar signs in her eyes when she saw it for the first time. I know she just wants to show off and maybe it's because I'm tired but I don't feel like indulging her.

Sabrina exhaled loudly, "please Tavio! You owe me! I didn't say anything when you opened the door."

"Right, and I hadn't planned on driving. My other car is nice why are you tripping?"

"Never mind! Forget it! Can we just go?" She folded her arms.

When we pulled up in my older by a few years car her family and friends were acting like we pulled up in a Bentley. The fact that I'm employed was enough to impress a lot of them. When people would ask me what I did for a living I would say, "I work at an agency that acts as a go to for athletes."

Clearly this was too simple of an explanation for Sabrina so she would correct me and tell them that I'm an associate at one of the top sports agencies in San Francisco. Then she'd tell the ones who knew sports who a couple of my clients were. The wedding was nice, but Sabrina was here to show me off and start her bidding. I decided to let it go and pay it no never mind.

Sabrina looked very pretty and some of her family were actually cool. On the car ride home Sabrina entertained herself by telling me how many females commented on how handsome they thought I was.

On my way to work Alaina called me. She didn't go into detail, but she said she didn't get any sleep Saturday night cause she and Royce argued really badly. Then she told me that she was going to send me a picture of the ring Royce got her. When she sent it I told her he better had pulled out the big guns. He was about to lose his wife. Alaina hesitated then she changed the topic.

****

"Tavio, come here son," Mr. Barton called me over to walk with him. We were at the park playing basketball when he stopped our game to talk. My dad and everyone else continued on with the game. "Man to man, what's going on with you and my daughter?"

"Sir?"

"A couple of weeks ago her husband called me looking for her. I know she was with you. Before I go off the deep end I'm coming to you."

"Alaina is a very good friend and I love her very much."

"You're in love with her aren't you?"

"Yes!" That's right! I'm man enough to admit it.

"My daughter is married, for better or for worse. What are you going to do? Spend your entire life waiting for her to leave her husband?"

"I wouldn't do that to her. I've been holding back all these years. One day I'll get married myself."

"There's things you don't know about my daughter. She's been through an awful lot in her short lifetime. She acts more like me than she does her mother, but her mother is still in there." He looked frustrated, "her mother let guilt consume her and it took her away from us."

"Mr. Barton, Alaina has no reason to feel guilt behind me. I don't and I won't disrespect her marriage."

"The flesh is weak son." Then he stopped walking. "I like you, I like your family." He looked at my dad. "Even though we're broken I tried to give my kids a family like you grew up with. You're a decent person, and I see why she's drawn to you. I'm too afraid to lose her like we lost her mother." He burned me with his eyes, "you understand what I'm saying to you?"

"That's what Alaina and I have in common, parents who believed in us. You gave her the right foundation. She's a dedicated and loyal wife, even if it is to Royce."

Mr. Barton tried to pull back his chuckle but it escaped. "I like you, but I want my daughter to stand by her vows. Marriage is not a state of eternal happiness. There are rough patches."

"Shouldn't there be some smooth patches?"

"Yes that's what brings you together. Being honest, for some there's more rough than smooth. For a very select few there's mostly smooth. My daughter won't leave Royce."

Royce

"Mr. Chambers, this is Dolly your realtor."

"Oh yes, how are you Dolly?" I said looking over documents.

"I've been keeping an eye out for what you've been looking for and I think I may have found it."

I stopped working, she had my full attention. "Did you now?"

"Yes, it just went on the market yesterday. When would you like to see the property?"

"One moment," I pulled up my calendar. My morning was good, but I had meetings this afternoon. "Can we meet in an hour? I can take Bart out to Walnut Creek."

"Sounds like a plan, I will pick you up at the Walnut Creek station in an hour. You know my car."

The house was everything that I always envisioned Alaina and I having. The house was huge with five bedrooms and four bathrooms. Three-car garage, and newly renovated. The neighborhood appeared to be nice enough. I told Dolly to make an offer right away.

Eva

I shut Vanessa's door and dramatically posed in front of it. I didn't say anything I just stared at her. Vanessa blushed and then she put her eyes on the desk. "What?"

"It's your ex isn't it?"

"Don't judge me Eva!" She warned me.

"You said you hated him. I saw you slap him into the next week. What happened?"

"I can't talk about this right now."

"I don't care! You're going to. You've been avoiding me! If I have to break your legs right now you're talking to me."

Vanessa exhaled and then she started clicking on her keyboard. I sat down and waited. Pain was all over Vanessa's face. "What do you want to know?"

"How come I never see you anymore? We don't fly out or home together. When we're there you run out at quitting time. It's either him or," I covered my mouth as I gasped. "Or Kid?"

"No! Although I'm sure she wouldn't mind." She adjusted in her seat, "we're back together. Royce and I."

"Ok so why are you..." I looked at her guilty expression. "He's married?"

"Don't judge me Eva! We're grown! Just look away!"

She was extremely defensive about the topic but I couldn't let it go. "You obviously feel bad about it."

"To an extent, I feel caught up. I don't know what I'm going to do or how this plays out. I don't have any answers. I've told no one about this, and I wasn't going to tell you either. All of a sudden you want to be all up in my business. You never ask so many questions before."

"You've never dodged my questions before."

"How are things with my cousin?"

"Fine," I said sinking into my seat.

"Fine," she mimicked me, "now you know you're going to have to do better than that."

"Colby was the third guy, I've ever been with. I find myself," I moved my hands. around looking for words. "Not ready, does that make sense?"

"How is Kiev responding?"

I shrugged, "I don't know. We haven't mastered each other's communication style just yet."

"That's probably cause he got used to out spoken Faye. At least you never had to guess with her. She was in your face about everything."

"Right and I'm not anything like Faye."

"Um! That's a matter of opinion. I remember you with Colby, and watching you in these meetings. You'd never think your grandmother walks all over you like she does. Were you like that with your ex? What was his name something about cheese."

I laughed, "his name is Tavio. He kept calling that girl MAC."

"All I know is they looked cozy. Any who, how were you with him?"

"Same as I was with Colby."

"Well you knew both of them for years before you were a couple so maybe that has something to do with it." Then she tapped her desk. "So, since this project will be wrapping up in a few months, and we're not closing the California location, I'm thinking about moving back."

"For that guy? What if he blows you off again?"

"He can't," she moved around in her seat.

"You're grown, just like you told me. I hope you truly think it through. What about your mother, your brothers, your father and stepmom. Most of your family is here."

"It's only a thought right now."

Then there was a knock at the door. Mrs. Singleton and Katrina walked in with the baby. Katrina immediately handed little Selah to me. She's so tiny and precious. I felt the same way holding her as I do every time I hold Quinn. Selah gave me a gummy smile as soon as she looked at me. "I figured you were here when you weren't in your office." Katrina said as she sat next to me.

Mrs. Singleton walked over and looked out the window. "Mrs. Singleton you've been losing weight."

Mrs. Singleton turned around and tried to smile at us, "lack of Sunday dinners."

Vanessa bucked her eyes at me as I swallowed. "I don't know why you all can't continue without me there?" I kept my eyes on the baby as I feared her answer.

"We'll reconvene once you and Colby figure out what you're doing." Then she exhaled like she was trying very hard to keep her composure.

Katrina leaned in to me like she was defying her mother. "He's dating some chick. A nurse from his hospital."

"Katrina! Don't do that!" Mrs. Singleton warned her.

Katrina bumped my chair like she'd tell me more later, "yes mom."

"I want to talk to the both of you, but not on the clock. Can you have dinner with me after work?"

I was supposed to see Kiev, but he should be used to me cancelling on him. "Yes." I looked at Vanessa.

"Yes of course."

"Good, come to my house at 6:30." Then she walked out.

My body temperature went up, "she's going to chew me out about Colby isn't she?"

"I don't know, but she didn't invite me."

I looked at Selah who was watching my face. "So Colby's dating?" I felt guilty for wanting to know.

"Yep, I went over his place and she was there. In only his shirt cooking."

"What she look like?" Vanessa asked leaning all over her desk.

"Light skinned, long weave, her body was.... Whew! You could tell she works out. She was nice enough."

"Did he look happy?" Vanessa asked the questions I wouldn't allow myself to ask.

"He didn't look excited, but they looked fine."

"It's not too late Eva. Go get your man back before it gets serious."

"Now you sound like my grandmother. He's not my man anymore. I wish Colby the best, he deserves happiness."

Katrina sucked her teeth, "I found a nanny so I will be coming back to work just in time."

"In time for what?" I asked.

"I'll join you two in California for a couple days. I won't be out there all week. The teams out there will be under the five of us. I'm reading my emails now, but I'll be caught up by the time I come out."

"You're going to leave Selah behind?" I asked.

"Nope, the nanny and Selah are coming with me."

"Great!" I forced a smile while Vanessa looked out the window.

******

Vanessa pulled up to the Singleton home about five minutes after I did. The maid showed us to the dining room where a huge table was set up, but only three places were set. Vanessa sat across from me. Mrs. Singleton came in the dining room in jeans and a T-shirt with a big smiley face in the middle. I relaxed a little but not by much. She asked us why we didn't change. We said we came straight from the office. The cook brought salads to us and he placed the dressing options on the table. We quietly ate our salads, and then our soup came. We quietly ate as the cook poured wine and water. The maid cleared the table as we waited for our main course. Mrs. Singleton asked us what's going on with each of us. She said we started out strong and then I took my sister out to California and I've been guarded ever since. She said I've been so uptight that I broke up with her son. She light weight sounded upset about it.

Then she said my employment isn't dependent upon my relationship status, however I've been so short with everyone and they're complaining. As she gave me time to respond she turned her attention to Vanessa. She told her she did not send her to California to hook up with some guy. She told her it was unacceptable that she would send her across the country so that she could telecommute from her hotel room. Mrs. Singleton told her to get it together. She told us that she is so proud of our accomplishments, however our youth was starting to show.

Then she reached for my hand and asked me why I wasn't going to be her daughter in-law. That's when I started crying. When I looked at Mrs. Singleton she had tears in her eyes. The cook started to come out with our food and he turned around and walked back in the kitchen. I let my head droop as I cried. Mrs. Singleton lifted my chin, "I know baby. I know it's hard. I am the first successful person from my family. It's a lot of pressure, and then checking yourself constantly to remain grounded is hard. My children have had to work hard for everything they have. It seemed only right that Colby should've had to work for the woman he loves. It's time for you to do the work. Let go of the past! Carrying all that baggage around isn't going to help you. It's only going to hurt you." Then she lovingly caressed my face.

No matter how hard I tried to pull back my tears they wouldn't stop. It was like Mrs. Singleton commanded my tears and they didn't want to disappoint. It did feel good to finally cry though, I just hated the lack of control I had over them. "Mrs. Singleton you can't repeat any of this." I said reaching for my napkin to blow my nose. Mrs. Singleton promised and so did Vanessa. I didn't go into major detail but I told them about my parents. All of my mixed emotions about everything. How I understood that our grandmother was protecting us. I didn't understand how she let us walk around feeling rejected.

Rickie has spoken with our parents who are begging us to include them in our lives. I can't talk to them, I just can't. I told them that Unique remembers seeing me bruised and with a black eye even. I don't remember any of it. I told them my parents blame my grandmother for their addiction, and I can't talk to my grandmother. I told them I don't want children and I couldn't deny Colby the opportunity to be a wonderful father to his future deserving children. Mrs. Singleton asked if we took any psych classes. I got my grade and got out of that class I didn't retain anything. Mrs. Singleton suggested some self-check and health exercises. First thing she told me to do was to stand and face the mirror behind me. She told me to look at myself and tell myself three nice things about myself. When I hesitated she told Vanessa to go first. Vanessa started crying out loud.

When we finally calmed down to sniffles and low sobs the cook brought our main course in to us. We ate a little but we mostly talked about people in the office like we used to do on Sunday's before I ruined everything.

As we walked out the door Colby pulled into the driveway and of course he blocked my car in. Vanessa waved bye as she hurried to her car, and Mrs. Singleton hurried back inside. I could tell he just got off work "what are you doing here?" He walked very fast towards me.

"We had dinner with your mother, we" he kissed me as if it was going to kill him not to. He massaged my head as he kissed me. After the kiss continued on, I pulled back. "Colby stop!"

"You've been on my mind all day, and then you're here. I want to pick you up and take you home." He said as he refused to take his arms away from around me.

"You have a girlfriend." I tried to wiggle out of his hold.

"I'm in love with you."

"You like broken wings then. If I couldn't get it together for Tavio, I can't do it for you."

"Tavio?" He released me. "Is that the problem? You've been comparing me to your ex?"

"Amongst other things."

"You're trying to pick a fight." He eyed me.

I started walking to my car. "Eva," I kept walking. "Eva!" I got in my car and waited for him to move his car. If I really wanted to leave I could've turned my car around. It's not like we were in a skinny driveway. I just sat there telling my body to calm down. In all honesty, I didn't want something new tonight. I wanted and needed a familiar touch. Colby stood there for a minute like he was decoding the scene. He got in his car and drove away. I followed him to his condo.

He changed all the furniture in his place. It was like I never lived here. I sat on his new bed as he walked down the hall. He came back with our box of treats. I guess he didn't want them in the bedroom as a reminder of me. I would've thrown it away, but I was so happy he didn't. We never spoke another word to each other.

Colby released me from my bonds to the bed. I waited until he fell asleep, then I quietly crept out.

Tavio

"This is Eva," her tone was all business.

"This may be, but I'm looking for Eva Graham who grew up on the Southside of Richmond, California."

"What do you want big head, I'm working." All professionalism left her voice.

"You got the nerve to mention heads when you don't even try to hide your massive dome?" I laughed.

"Yeah but you were drooling while you rubbed it so don't even try it."

"Well yeah, hair or no hair you still fine. You could've warned me though."

"Nope, what do you want? I'm working."

"My flight leaves tonight, I'm coming out your way. I want to see you." Eva hesitated, "I thought we were friends. Give me Rickie's number I'll call her," I teased her.

"We are friends, you just caught me off guard. Why are you coming out here?"

"Scouting, making moves and connections. Does it matter?" She replied no real slow. "Why are you acting weird? You pregnant or something?" I held my breath.

"Heavens no!" I released my breath. "You caught me off guard is all. I'm supposed to have dinner with a friend tomorrow night. I guess you could come."

I was quiet for a minute; "you're going to bring me on your

date?"

"I don't know what else to do." She whined!

"Eeewwwllll! You are freakier than I thought," I laughed.

"Can I call you back tonight with details?" She pleaded.

I gave her my number then I shut down my computer. My assistant confirmed my arrangements and information about my athlete. I don't always sign my clients right away, I develop relationships and I advise them. Some Agencies come to them with "better" offers than I have. However, eventually they learn why they want to be with me. My client list is rapidly growing. It's now to the point that potential clients are seeking me out. My mentor tells me she couldn't be prouder of me. She reminds me to pay it forward and once I've gotten a few more years under my belt to mentor someone else.

"Hello."

"Old Merry MAC!" I spoke over the car speakers.

"What do you want fool?"

"Dinner, I leave tonight."

"Oh yeah, that's right. The usual routine?"

"You know it. I'm leaving the city now. Meet you at my house in thirty minutes."

"Ok I'll pack up Jerrell and meet you there."

Alaina says that since their fight Royce comes home more often, but still not like he should. If I felt he was a faithful and attentive husband I'd feel guilty about demanding her time like I do, but I don't, because he's not.

When I turned on to my street I cursed when I saw Sabrina's car. I pulled into my garage and I met her in the driveway. "What are you doing here?"

"You're leaving tonight, I came to see you off."

I exhaled, "you're doing too much. I have a routine and you're messing with it right now."

She cut her eyes at me, "I'm your woman. Why can't I see you off?" Like clockwork Alaina pulled up to the house. "What is she doing here?"

"HI AVIO!" Jerrell excitedly screamed through the back window he cracked.

"How's my little man?" I said ignoring Sabrina.

Alaina couldn't get the door opened fast enough. As soon as she opened it Jerrell jumped out and ran to me. Alaina smiled as she watched Sabrina's face. Sabrina was giving me an evil glare. "Hey Sabrina, who stole your puppy?" Alaina asked trying to break the ice.

Sabrina sucked her teeth at Alaina and looked her up and down. She started to open her mouth, but I cut her off. "My family is here, I'll see you when I get back."

"Tavio! Un un! This isn't going to work! How are you sending me away to spend time with a married woman?"

"Give me my baby, you two need to talk." Alaina reached for Jerrell who was frowning at Sabrina. "I'll make sandwiches, you two want any?"

"You need to go home!" Sabrina snapped.

I grabbed her arm and pushed her towards the sidewalk and her car.

"Tavio," Alaina pleaded. "Please come here real quick."

"What?" I was beyond irritated.

Alaina approached Sabrina and I cautiously. "Don't be mad at her, she doesn't understand and she feels threatened. Put yourself in her shoes."

"Being rude is not how you get your point across with me."

"I know that, but does she?"

"She should, she's not new." I said starting to push Sabrina again.

"Yes, but she needs the opportunity to understand our friendship. Please cut her a break this time. PRETTY PLEASE!"

"MAC you are so annoying!" I smiled at her. Alaina blew us a kiss and then she went inside. I let go of Sabrina's arm. I took a deep cleansing breath. "Go home and I will talk to you when I get back. My relationship with MAC is not up for negotiation. You need to decide whether you want to continue or not. I'll call you when I get back." I gave her a hug while she stood there stiff as a board.

I walked into my garage. I stood there looking at her as my garage door closed. Then I ran inside, Alaina was taking out the bread. I told her to put everything back so we could go have dinner like originally planned. I ran upstairs to my bedroom; I put my toiletries into my already packed bags. Then Jerrell helped me put my bags in my fancy car.

Alaina stared at me as soon as she sat in the passenger seat. Whenever she's this close to me I can see her restraining herself from touching my hair. "What do you want?"

"Why was she mad?"

"Cause I didn't want her to come to see me off."

"She could've come."

"And then she sits in the passenger seat while you drive a car I barely let her ride in. Oh and then watch you lock up my house when she still needs to call before she comes over."

Alaina faced forward and exhaled. "Our friendship isn't healthy."

"MAC! Don't start!"

"Ok, so then say we're like brother and sister and all will be forgiven."

I glanced at her; "keep talking and I'll kiss you right now." Alaina didn't respond with her normal fire.

"What do I know," she said lowly. "Granny Shane thinks Royce is having an affair."

"So you're taking a poll to tell you what you know in your heart?"

"My grandmothers are a part of my daily life. Granny Shane is more realistic about life. My Grandmother comes from a religious place. She's all, stand by your man, God hates a divorce. Granny Shane is waiting to put my cousins on him if she's right."

"What do you know to be right?"

"I love my husband, I didn't get married to get divorced."

"I'm not saying he's cheating, but I'm definitely not telling you that he's not cheating. Your boy is selfish and stupid. Time will tell." Alaina sniffed, and I bit my tongue for a minute. "What is wrong with you? Please tell me you're not that weak."

Alaina looked back at her son who was playing quietly in his seat with the car I gave him. "Shut up! Try loving someone on this level and then talk to me about the commitment required."

"You have no idea what my heart goes through." Now she's getting on my nerves. "Just because you said some funky vows to some fool who never deserved them doesn't mean you're on some level I can't comprehend. Try loving someone and then watching them suffer. You think you know love just because you said some words in front of a bunch of people. That's the show, that's not love. Love is deeper than that." I adjusted in my seat and eased my foot off the gas. "Love is walking away from the first person to love you back just as deeply as you love them because you don't want to end up like you."

"Me?" She pointed to her chest.

"Stuck! Whether or not you two discussed the plan for your married lives is irrelevant now. Now you're stuck in a stupid tug of war. He wants more children; you agreed to have a family. The only power you have in your relationship is over your body. And you've chosen to shut it down instead of standing up to that man. So what if he doesn't like what you have to say. He'd respect you more for saying it."

Alaina didn't say anything she sat quietly for the rest of our ride. When we sat at our table, I happily looked at the menu knowing I was going to order the clay pot. But I look just in case they added something new to the menu that I might want to try. Jerrell was too happy about his crayons and kids menu. We gave our waiter our menu, I ordered an Adios! And Alaina only had water.

"You're going to go see Eva?" Alaina asked quietly.

"Yep going to have dinner with her tomorrow night."

"Before I forget, am I picking up T from Tempest's before I get you?"

"That would be nice if you wouldn't mind."

"So you're nervous about seeing Eva?"

I frowned, "no! Why would I be nervous about that?"

"Your little speech about love. You're right, I don't know what's in your heart. But your speech proved my point. You walked away, you let her go. I'm trying to stick to my husband, the first and only man to see me. We're going through a rough patch and maybe we are fighting for power right now. But we're fighting with each other neither one of us wants to walk. I'm saying when you're fighting to stay then you can lecture me."

Stupid! Stupid! Stupid! Love makes you stupid! She totally missed the personal application in my speech. I throw my hands up; I don't even know what I was fighting for. "Fine! You're right." I slurped down my drink and told the waiter to bring me two more.

At the airport, I said bye to Jerrell. Then I got my bags out of the trunk. Alaina stood in front of me looking like she was going to cry as soon as she drove away. Don't give in! You're done! This idiot is in love with an idiot! You've wasted enough time here! I put my arms out and Alaina rushed me burying her head into my chest as she usually does. I kissed her forehead repeatedly. When she looked up at me I kissed her lips. Alaina jumped and told me to cut it out. She said I had too many drinks. So I decided to blame the alcohol as I kissed her again. Her heart was pounding to the beat of mine. She pulled away before she got lost in our kiss. She asked me if she should wait to make sure they let me on the plane. She told me I was drunk. I told her I was fine as I let my eyes droop low. She walked back to the driver's seat. Great! Is this kiss supposed to carry me another ten years?

****

"Hey baldy!" I said rubbing Eva's head.

"Shut up fool!" Eva laughed.

"It snows out here, your head don't get cold in the winter?"

"I let it grow out some."

"What does that look like?" I smiled at her, it was good to see her. Even if I was tagging along on her date with some guy, I was just happy to see her.

"My hair is kind of like wool, it's thick but it doesn't curl much. So I put a texturizer on it to make it curl once it gets long enough and brushing it doesn't help."

I smiled and started laughing. "So now you walk around with a boar bristle brush?" Eva started laughing immediately. "Where is it? I get to throw yours away as pay back."

"Heck naw! I'm not letting you near my brush." Eva smiled real big at me. "It's so good to see you. Can we come back to this bar after dinner?" She said referring to the bar at my hotel.

"Of course." The valet brought her keys. "Nice car!"

"Thanks," she smiled as she got in the driver's seat.

"When did you get it?" I looked around at the features.

"A few weeks ago."

"Ha! You copied me! I have the exact same car in black."

Eva started cracking up, and then she reminded me that we always seemed to have the same taste in cars. The whole way to the restaurant we played remember when. I had a blast remembering some of the dumb stuff we did in the name of youth. When we walked into the family style restaurant Rickie was standing with a huge smile. I got excited and I felt relieved when I saw her. I was not looking forward to being the third wheel tonight. As I hugged Rickie, Eva's date walked in. He was immediately sizing me up. Eva introduced me as their childhood friend from California. Her friend was alright, I didn't feel an overwhelming feeling to bond with him. We were cordial, but that was that. He wasn't overly aggressive; he could've cared less. I did notice that he didn't have a car. And when we dropped him off, he lived in an interesting part of town. The place we dropped Rickie to was much nicer. Rickie wanted me to come see the baby, but Eva didn't want to deal with their grandmother. As soon as we were alone Eva asked me what I thought of her friend. I shrugged and said I couldn't tell her. Eva shook her head, "we can talk about stuff like this Tavio. Don't get all weird on me." I laughed, "I mean I sat there and watched you and your love interest shoot eyes at each other all night." I stopped laughing, "I need an honest opinion."

"Am I that obvious?"

"I know the look, you used to look at me like that."

"He's fine! Dang, I don't know what I'm supposed to tell you. I wasn't impressed, but he wasn't trying to impress me either. He's cool and laid back. Tell me something. How old is he?"

"41," she smiled.

"YIKES! You're almost thirty so I guess it works, but DANG!"

"He's almost perfect, he doesn't want any more kids."

That probably wasn't meant to be a dig, so I shrugged it off. "As in he has children? Take note of my plural question."

"He's divorced, and he has three. I haven't met them yet, but that's fine with me. We're still new."

"So then what's the problem?"

"Sometimes I find myself missing my ex."

"Eva, I'm flattered but…" I laughed.

"Not you big head! Colby and I broke up for the same reason you and I broke up. He's ready to be a father and I never told him that I refuse to give birth. He was about to propose and everything. My grandmother is so mad at me for breaking up with him. We just about argue on sight of each other. She don't like my hair, she'd never approve of Kiev, she doesn't like all the traveling I've been doing for work cause she feels it distracts me from getting back together with Colby."

"You love him?"

"I loved you too, but I'm not having a baby just to keep a man."

"You definitely don't want to do that." Eva pulled into a garage, stating that she wanted to show me her apartment. I hesitated for a minute, but I ain't no punk so I got out of the car. I whistled as I walked into her place. "You and Rickie are living large!" Then we laughed again.

"Wait I can still do the dance from the movie." Eva said waving her arms as she wiggled.

We continued to laugh as she showed me around her place. It was very nice. I was relieved when we left without incident and went back to my hotel to the bar. Eva asked me how business was going and I smiled really big. I shared my accomplishments and we kept telling each other that we were proud of each other. She said that before all of the traveling her ex kept them busy with efforts for the inner city kids. She said her ex's family is very big on giving back to the community and making sure that they invest in our communities.

I took a deep breath and I told her about Sabrina. We've been dating for years and I didn't feel like it was worth it to continue. I told her about the picnic I had at my house when everyone met Sabrina for the first time. I had her laughing about how we were all fighting over Alaina's food. After she stopped laughing she told me I was wrong for not supporting my girlfriend. I told her I did support her; I just wasn't letting those greedy monsters eat all the food up from me. I touched her hand, "when was the last time you talked to Unique?"

"It's been a minute, probably the last time we all had dinner why?"

"She's dating my friend from college. I kept these two apart for years. Leave it to MAC to unknowingly bring them together. When they came to me, I kept telling myself not to be a hypocrite. MAC's brother and apparently her father all know how I feel about her. She's the only one claiming not to know. They don't give me a hard time about it, but they're realistic. Eva, Unique is falling in love with this guy and it scares me."

"Since we're sharing," she ordered another drink for each of us. "Rickie and I found our parents. We've got two brothers and a little sister. They're still together, they're married even." Eva started fidgeting in her seat. "I don't know how to feel about anything. At first it seemed like my grandmother was this heartless monster. After talking to them with Rickie it turns out she was protecting us. Our parents didn't abandon us like I thought. She kicked them out one by one and then she uprooted us and moved us across the country to protect us. Our parents were searching for us, and they've been begging for us to forgive them.

Tavio, do you remember me having a black eye?" She searched my face like she wanted me to say no.

I touched her right eye, "yes. I remember. You were acting very weird the day you got it and until it healed."

Eva pressed her fingers against her temple. "Why can't I remember any of that? Rickie said it, I talked to Unique and she confirmed it without knowing what Rickie told me. And now you... I don't remember any of that Tavio. I can remember my father yelling at us, and cursing at us. I can remember my mother going through withdrawals, it was so scary. I don't remember getting beaten, or anything about any of that."

"Ok, but isn't that a good thing?" She waited for me to explain. "Are they the same people that you two remember?" She shook her head no. "So just start over. Maybe your amnesia is a good thing. Imagine how you'd be if you remembered. The things you do remember you don't let go of, and you let them shape your future."

"At first I was so mad at my grandmother, all I could think was if we never moved you and I would be married with how many kids right now."

"We'd be totally different people if you would've stayed. That doesn't mean we would've ended up together." I admitted.

"Are you kidding me right now? You know you would be so sprung off me still. But I wouldn't know Katrina or Vanessa. I never would've loved Colby." She looked off.

"Or be dating Kiev."

"Or dating Kiev's FINE behind."

I cut my eyes at her, "you didn't have to say all of that. I mean I'm being cool about all of this but don't go too far."

She sat up straight, "have you had better than me?"

I almost spit out my drink, "who asks that?"

"I do, you know you want to know."

"No I don't, that's too far Eva."

She bit her finger, "it is? I thought we could talk about anything."

"Eva, we're sitting at a bar downstairs from my room. We're drinking, and we know how competitive we are. If we're not agreeing that we were the best each other has had we're going to end up upstairs and ruining everything that it's taken all these years to have. I don't want to know, I might have a girlfriend when I go home, and you are developing a relationship with the new guy."

Eva chewed her finger some more, "ok. Truth?" I nodded. "I've already backslid with Colby. I guess I was hoping to prove that it didn't mean anything if we slept together too." I frowned at her. "What I mean is… If I'm the kind of girl who backslides then I can just say that's what I do. Since you're not cooperating you're forcing me to sleep with Kiev to prove to myself that I'm over Colby."

"Eva, SHUT UP! You're drunk and talking like a crazy drunk person." I took her keys. "You can't even hold your liquor. We're done here." I paid the bill and then I took Eva up to my room. I took her shoes off and put her in the bed. I slept on the pullout couch. I thought about Alaina and the kiss I stole under the guise that I was drunk. I can't continue like this, it isn't healthy. I hated myself for agreeing with her.

****

As I came down the escalator the boys were front and center. Tavio is getting tall, I noticed it the other day when I hugged him. The munchkin Jerrell was excitedly jumping around next to him. Alaina was over to the side looking through her phone. I hugged my boys and then we got my luggage from the baggage claim. As we approached my car Alaina walked a little ahead of me and then she reached for the driver's side door. I grabbed her wrist, "what are you doing?"

"You were drinking on the plane. I'm driving us home." She bumped me with her hip.

I smiled, "how you going to tell me you're driving my car?" I stood there tickled and laughing past the urge to kiss her.

"How's Eva?" She looked in my eyes.

"In love with her ex and lost about what to do about it."

"Are you two going to get back together?" Alaina looked everywhere but at me.

I started to say something but then I looked at her, "MAC. Are you jealous?"

"No, I'm just thinking about your future children. They would be beautiful coming from Eva. I told you Sabrina would give you weird looking kids."

"Who says Sabrina's eggs aren't all dried up and crusty? She is older than me you know."

"So."

"So, she's over 35. She may never have children."

Alaina put her hands on her hips. "I would like to know who decided that women were no longer fit to be parents after 35? Women have been having children sometimes into their 50's all throughout history. Now all of a sudden a woman hits 35 and she's supposed to give up hope."

"Until they dry up, women can have babies; it's just more difficult and the child may be at risk to be special needs is all."

"Every child is at risk to be special needs. You need to let those statistics go. If you love her and want funny looking kids that will be bullied, picked on, and teased, then have babies with her is all I'm saying."

"I love you too MAC." I said walking over to the passenger side of the car. I opened my carry-on bag and got the small presents for the boys out. They excitedly thanked me and I tried not to smile too much at Alaina as she drove my car home.

When we pulled around the corner, I saw Sabrina's car. Her windows were all fogged up so she had been waiting for a while. Alaina pulled into the garage and closed the garage door. When I asked her why she closed the door, she said she didn't want Sabrina seeing her getting out of the driver's seat. I told her that her car was outside and then suddenly we're all here. It doesn't take a genius to know that she drove my car. Sabrina rang the doorbell, and then Alaina hurried Jerrell out the door claiming she had to get him home.

Sabrina said hi to Tavio, and he responded respectfully. However, he's never shown excitement about her like he has since he was a baby about Alaina. I made a mental note to have a serious talk with him about Sabrina. I don't want to waste her time; cause I know her clock is ticking. The thing is mine is too. When it gets real bad I talk to my momma who always seems to talk my baby clock down into submission.

Tavio said he had homework to finish. I asked him if he ate, "MAC made dinner. There's leftovers in the refrigerator. Good night dad." Then he walked up the stairs without another word.

Even though I wasn't hungry a moment ago, now I feel like I haven't eaten in days. Sabrina followed me into the kitchen. I stopped before I opened the refrigerator. I turned around and grabbed her up into my arms. I laid the biggest kiss I could on her. Sabrina started pulling at my jeans, but I didn't have a condom down here. I told her to hold on, and then I started to lead her to my bedroom. Sabrina pulled away at the foot of the stairs. "We need to talk."

I cringed, "*now*?" I whined.

"Yes, I don't appreciate how you handled any of this. You are rude and disrespectful. It takes your friend talking you down for you not to end things with me. She's driving your car that I barely get to ride in.

When did she get a key to your house?"

"Long before you and I even knew each other."

"Why does she have access to you where I don't?"

"I'm with you, she's just a friend."

"Are you sleeping with her?"

I walked back to the kitchen. "You're being ridiculous."

"Are you?"

"No, and I never have to answer your next question." I smiled at the food as I took it out.

"There's something going on, just be honest with me."

I slammed the refrigerator. "Fine! You want to know the truth?"

"Yes, please tell me."

"I'm in love with her. She's married to an idiot who's cheating on her and she can't open her eyes to see it. We have only ever been friends. I gave her the key for when she watches over Tavio for me, it's easier on everyone if she can come and go as I need her to. She drives my car to pick me up from the airport, and to drop me off when I don't take a shuttle. Once she got pregnant, I knew there could never be an us cause he's always going to be in the picture, messing with her head, and putting drama in her life. I'm trying to be with you, but you're so spoiled. You came in competing when no one asked you to. I like you, no I care about you. I'm with you but you're so rude and disrespectful at times. Truth is you're too old to need this much work."

"That's because you're comparing me to her!"

"No I'm not! Alaina is Alaina and there will never be another her. I'm looking at you Sabrina. You disappear for weeks sometimes and then you resurface. I don't know what you do and who you do it with. I don't question you about it, because it's beneath me to play these games with you. So now you tell me, who's the guy you're seeing on the side?"

Sabrina debated with herself and then you could see her give up. "You are the side chick! There you happy now?"

"Cool!" I said putting my food on a plate to heat it up.

"Cool? You mean you're ok with that?"

I licked my fingers savoring the flavors of my food. I put time on the microwave and then I looked at her. "Yep." She got mad, "when have I ever had raw sex with you? I won't let you give me head without a condom. You won't suck my finger after I've touched you so why would I ever go down there? At least now you can stop pretending that there's more to us than there is. Are you and your main guy going to get married?"

Tears streamed down Sabrina's face, "I can't believe you! I was lying."

I blew air, "no you weren't. The truth is out and now you're free. I refuse to sleep with a married woman so, when you do get married do me the courtesy of going away."

Sabrina picked up her purse by the door and left. I tore up my leftovers like I hadn't eaten all day.

Eva

I had Quinn cracking up as I played with her. She was sitting in Rickie's lap and I kept making faces at her that made her laugh really loud. I was so distracted by my nieces' cuteness that I didn't notice my grandmother's car when she pulled up and started towards us. I didn't see her until she was standing over us. I frowned at Rickie who shrugged like she didn't know what to say. "You're avoiding me!"

"Yes!"

"Why?" She sat next to me on the bench.

"I don't need the lectures, or the guilt trips, or your flat out bullying about my life. Colby and I are done."

"Is it a crime to want something better for you girls than any of my kids had?" Then she pointed to Rickie, "Quincy has that good job at the hospital and he's making progress. You've got a beautiful family, and you have a good job too." Rickie nodded in agreement. "Eva you're a little go getter and who would've ever thought that someone so successful was in our family? You girls are doing pretty good from where I sit."

I looked at Rickie and her eyes pleaded with me not to, but she knew I was going to. "What about our mother? How's she doing?"

My grandmother jumped, "how would I know? For all I know she's a Jane Doe somewhere."

"No she's not, she lives in Richmond and she's married to our father. They've been clean for years now."

"If you believe that, you're a fool! She was always promising to get clean and then she always had some kind of excuse for why she fell off the wagon."

"You let us believe that they left us and never looked back."

"Where is all of this coming from?"

"Clifton Pearcy works for me indirectly. Once I found him things started unraveling."

Our grandmother stood up and stormed away to her car.

****

There was a knock at my door. I told the person to come in while I finished reading the email that one of my direct reports sent me. He has had several Human Resources issues with this person. He sent me the write up from HR. I could see two people from my peripheral vision. I told them to have a seat as I read making sure everything was covered. I finished reading then I typed my response quickly, I highlighted a few things and then I asked HR a question. I hit send then I stopped breathing. I was looking into my mother's face. I looked at Rickie with glassy eyes waiting for an explanation. Rickie looked nervous as she started talking fast. She said she flew our mother out so that she could clear the air with our grandmother. I stared at Rickie, I felt so betrayed in this moment. I asked Rickie where our mother was supposed to stay when she and grandmother started fighting? Rickie hadn't thought of that. Our mother stared at me while Rickie and I discussed her as if she wasn't there. Rickie said we needed to start healing and our state of existing had gone on long enough. She was tired of pretending like she didn't know about everything. I looked at our mother, "what?"

"Please don't take offense but your father and I were wondering if you're gay and that's why you wear your hair like that?"

I cut my eyes at Rickie who was looking at the wall like there was something interesting on it. "Would you have a problem with it if I am?"

She shrugged, "no."

"If it doesn't matter why ask me?"

She exhaled, "this is a beautiful office. I guess you're doing pretty well for yourself."

I felt like she was about to ask me for money so I ignored her comment. I opened a new email.

To: charlottesingleton@singlevisionenterprises.com

From: evagraham@singlevisionenterprises.com

Subject: Productivity KILLED

Mrs. Singleton my sister just walked into my office with our mother. As you can imagine, I am quite shocked, appalled, and disgusted. I need to shut down for now. I will log in tonight.

Eva Graham

Senior EVP of Strategies and Initiatives

It seemed like she knew because she responded right away.

To: evagraham@singlevisionenterprises.com

From: charlottesingleton@singlevisionenterprises.com

Subject: Productivity KILLED

Go NOW! LEAVE computer here. Call me in the morning.

Charlotte Singleton

Chairman & CEO

I took a deep breath, and then I did as I was told. As I stood, our mother opened a hard candy. Not that I wanted one but I noticed that she didn't offer. I told Rickie I would follow them to her place. I was angry with Rickie but for some reason I couldn't go off on her for this. I guess because I know she's not trying to hurt me.

Rickie parked in the garage next to our grandmother's car. Our mother got out of Rickie's car with her eyes stretched wide looking at my car. She asked me what kind of car it was but I didn't answer her. She put another candy in her mouth as she gawked at my car. Rickie got her suitcase out the trunk, and she didn't even try to get it from her. I walked over to Rickie and pushed the suitcase out of her hand. Rickie was going to say something but I gave her a look. That's when our mother got the clue to come get her bag.

She was looking around the garage like she was impressed by it. Rickie closed the garage and then we walked inside. Grandmother was sitting in the middle of the floor reading Quinn a story. Quinn was sitting attentively like a big girl listening. As soon as she saw us she smiled and started speed crawling to Rickie. Our grandmother smiled at me and then she slowly got off the floor making noise the whole way up. "Who did you bring with you?" Grandmother said not even recognizing her own child.

"Momma it's me," our mother said as she put her suitcase down.

Our grandmother was speechless for all of fifteen seconds. Then she started screaming at me. She got in my face pointing her finger and everything. She accused me of being conniving, manipulative, and evil. I didn't say anything, I stood there with my hands in my pockets as I cried and listened to what my grandmother truly thought of me.

When Rickie got her attention I walked out as I heard her tell our grandmother that this was all her doing. When I got in my car my body was tense as if I had been fighting. I caught myself as I started to call Colby. I was tired of fighting. I openly admitted to myself that I truly missed him, but I refused to call him. I pulled over on the side of the road trying to decide what to do and where to go. I didn't want to go home, cause once Rickie told her everything she was going to want to come and apologize to me. If I was home, at Colby's, Katrina's, or Mrs. Singleton's she would get some kind of satisfaction out of that and I refused to give her that. Normally I would've called Vanessa, but she spends most of her time on the phone with that guy. To be married he seems to have an awful lot of free time. I told the car to call Kiev. He answered after the second ring. I asked him if he wanted to come out with me. He said he was working on a picture but I was more than welcome to come over. I said ok, even though the thought of the safety of my car sitting outside his place did alarm me. I've never gone inside his place no matter how many times he's begged me.

When I pulled up to his place he was standing in his doorway. I felt better just looking at him. This is a man that I've chosen, and there was nothing she could do to change that. That's when I realized that a huge part of me was always holding back with Colby because she chose him. I hit my head on the steering wheel. I needed the OFF button on my brain. Kiev walked over to the car and opened my door once I unlocked it. "Are you ok?"

"No, but I don't want to talk about it," I said quickly. I got out of the car and hugged him hello.

I followed Kiev inside his place as I kept shaking my head. His place was a lot smaller than mine and he didn't have much furniture. He had more art supplies than he had anything else. He went in the kitchen and brought back a glass of water. He told me to drink it as he took my jacket and purse to his bedroom. I walked over to the easel to see what he was working on. Kiev said he wasn't sure what it was going to be yet. He said he keeps getting ideas and then they change. "Faye called me today." He looked forward at the blank canvas.

"How's she doing?"

"She claims to be missing me."

"You miss her don't you?"

"Only to a point, I don't miss her mouth." We laughed together. "You miss Colby?" He continued to look forward.

I didn't realize he remembered his name, "yes."

"You think you'll get back together?"

"We can't," I said taking a seat in the chair next to him. "He wants to have children, and I don't."

"You don't want a child of your own?"

"No!"

"Can I ask why and why with so much passion?" He picked up a piece of chalk.

His hand waited for me to talk. "My childhood sweetheart and I's plan was to go to college, get our careers going, and then get married. We wanted at least two kids." The memory washed over me like it was yesterday. " We had a plan, and in our young minds it was going to work." Kiev's hand kept stroking the paper as long as I spoke. Whenever I paused so did his hand. "Then my family had to move to Daytona. Our plan was still golden. I started hanging out with the wrong kind of guy. He did nothing for me. When I went to college he got me pregnant on purpose. He denied me when he felt like I was dependent on him. My ex unknowingly gave me the money to have an abortion. That whole experience took the life out of me. As my child died, something inside of me died as well." Kiev stopped drawing and nodded his head at me like he understood. "My ex had messed up and gotten someone pregnant anyways. He's a good guy so there's no way he was going to leave his child even though I wanted him to. Until then I had never loved anyone like I loved my ex, and as much as I loved him he couldn't bring that part of me back to life. I knew it, he knew it."

Kiev nodded his head like he understood. "My wife and I fell in love pretty young, and it seemed like we married right away. We had no idea what we were doing. I took the first job I could get and so did she. We blamed each other when she got pregnant, it was her fault then it was my fault. We fussed and fought over who had to stay home with the baby, cause we were both young and immature. When the next baby came the gloves were off and our fights were worse, like we didn't know where babies came from. Then her cousin lost her son in some nonsense. Seeing her cousin grieve woke both of us up. Life is a gift and it's precious. We were creating masterpieces and we didn't even appreciate it. Powers of Gods wielded by children who miss the point. I was feeling it in my heart and when I spoke on it she said she was going to talk to me about the same thing. That's when we made our daughter Isis. It was like she was our first child, she was our first girl so to me that made it different anyways." I couldn't take my eyes off of how fast and precise his hand was moving. He made it look effortless, but I knew better. "Children, Eva… I sometimes think about how through me three people fill this earth. They live and they breathe because of me. Because I loved a woman they're here. I may struggle to feed them, or provide for their wants, but they will never question whether or not their father loves them. Because of me they're here. Because of me they will be great. Children are amazing creations that live on when you're long gone. They're your legacy, your long lasting contribution to this earth. The first two times my ex told me she was pregnant it felt like something died in me. Like I lost control over everything that my life was supposed to be. I was angry and I'm not proud of the way I conducted myself. I'm just telling you that as strongly as you feel against it. If you wanted to, one day you could feel the complete opposite. I'm living proof of it."

"You want to have more kids?"

He smiled, "no." Then he laughed. "I should say, that it doesn't matter if I want to or not, I can't." He started rubbing his drawing and then he went back to drawing. I couldn't believe how it was coming together. "I got a vasectomy to piss my wife off. We had started on our whole spiritual journey together. Not in a denominational way, but our spirits were growing, recognizing that there is a higher power to be respected." His hand started moving faster and angrier. "I'm not a good provider. I can work and do a good job, but my heart is never in any of these pointless jobs. I do what I have to, to make ends meet. Living high on the hog will never be something that I could provide my wife with. I get it now that she wasn't asking for that, but it felt like it. We wanted to have more children, but I felt it was irresponsible to continue to have them; no matter how beautiful they are, if we can't afford them. We argued like we always did and then I got the vasectomy. Everything spiraled out of control." He exhaled, "she's a good woman and I'm happy that she's found someone that she can live out all of her life's fantasies with. Why did you break up with Colby?" His hand continued, and I watched him create a baby in the arms of a woman.

"He wants a family and I don't. Same disagreement different person."

Kiev smiled at me, "Colby's a good man. Do you think you're done with him?"

"Colby's great, but he isn't the man for me. Why did you and Faye break up?"

His hand stopped moving, "her mouth." Then he smiled and went back to working. "Naw, I mean it bothers me, but it doesn't bother me that much. I don't want her to give up her opportunity to create eternity just to live the here and now with me. She wants to be a mother. She wishes she could mother my kids, but they aren't always fond of her. Being a step-parent is not the same as creating and nurturing a child from their first breath of life onward. Children are forever and she needs her forever."

"So is this what you do, meet a woman talk up children and then kick her out into the world?"

He smiled at me, "you don't want children though. You're so firm in your conviction that you pushed two men away behind it."

"Right cause I don't."

"Eva, I'm looking at you." He said with his eyes facing his drawing.

It was ME! I slumped in my seat. I was holding a baby looking down at it with the look of a mother's love for her child, while the baby held my finger and smiled up at me. The picture was spot on, and it was like he took a picture of me and then transferred it on to this paper. "Kiev!"

"You want children, the husband, everything. You're just not ready yet. Which is perfect for us now, because I can't give them to you. Maybe you don't get back with Colby, but you will have this one-day. You've had two men who wanted to marry you and have a family with you when a lot of women don't have one opportunity. Pay attention to the next one."

"So no false expectations of forever between you and I?" I smiled at him.

"As much as I would like to lie and say that it's me and you forever. You have some creating to do and I won't stand in the way of that. I had my turn, one day it will be yours."

Kiev made a vegetarian dinner for us, that was actually really good. We drank wine, and then we had sex on the floor in front of his drawing. IT MESSED UP MY GROOVE! Kiev saw me looking at it and he put it in the kitchen. Sex with Kiev was different, it was good, but it was different. It wasn't love it was sensual and amazing, but it definitely was not love.

****

When I turned my phone on message after message hit my voicemail. Text messages screamed their tone. My grandmother and Rickie blew my phone up. I deleted all of my grandmother's voicemails without even listening to them. I deleted her texts as well. Rickie's texts were full of apologies. On my voicemail you could hear the chaos in the background as Rickie pleaded with me to call her. She was apologizing all over the place. I didn't care that it was just after 4am in the morning I called Rickie's cell. She answered immediately and she went back into her apology. Now that I was relaxed my tears bubbled up and I started crying. Rickie asked me to come back. I refused, and then she asked me to come rescue her and the baby. She said everyone had just retreated to their corners. When I agreed, she called back and asked if it was ok if Quincy brought them and slept on my couch until he had to go to work. I said yes as I pointed my car at my place. As I pulled up to my complex my phone rang again, this time it was Colby. "Your grandmother was stressed cause she couldn't find you. I'm just making sure you're ok."

"I'm fine, I'm pulling up to my place right now."

"Ok," he said getting off the phone with me.

I was a little disappointed when he didn't pry or show jealousy over where I've been. We both know he was feeling it otherwise why would he call me in the middle of the night? "Take care Colby."

"Love you," then he hung up on me.

When Rickie and her family got to my place I had the couch made up for Quincy, He said a grateful thank you. He took the baby and laid down immediately.

Rickie and I went into my room and shut the door. Rickie said our mother and grandmother wasted no time digging into each other. Rickie said she told our grandmother that she was responsible for bringing our mother out. She said our grandmother said she could afford to pay more for rent if she could afford to send for her mother.

Our grandmother demanded to know what slant of the story our parents chose to tell us. She said they were screaming at some points so badly that she couldn't understand. Our mother told our grandmother that she has hated her all her life because she looked the other way when our grandfather came after her. She accused our grandmother of creating the problem and then screaming that she was a victim. Our grandmother admitted that she was wrong for that. Our grandmother would not apologize for keeping us away from them though. She said we were her two successes out of her entire family. She called our cousins and siblings worthless and said it was pointless to even consider them. Our grandmother said that Rickie and I and her sister in Florida were all the family she needed and worried about. Rickie said our mother screamed, cried, and said every hurtful thing she could to our grandmother.

When our mother couldn't take it anymore she got on the phone and called our father. They recited some serenity prayers, and did some breathing exercises. She said that was when she started calling me. She said our grandmother panicked when Colby said I wasn't with him and it was late. She told Rickie to come by my place and to make sure I wasn't hiding in my apartment. She said our mother couldn't get over how nicely we were living out here. Rickie told our mother she just went back to work and her husband was still considered new to his job. Rickie said our mother had no shame asking her for money. Not to borrow but to have. Rickie told her she didn't have anything to give her. Which only meant if I saw her she was going to definitely ask me.

Rickie said that our grandmother had a boyfriend back home that she left without a word. He died a few years after we left but our mother said our grandmother killed her boyfriend by breaking his heart like that. I put my hand up and I recited what she told me about my idea to live with Tavio. Rickie said our mother kept telling our grandmother that she needed to live by the rules she imposed on everyone else. Rickie even said she thinks our grandmother was seeing someone in Florida.

Quincy thanked me for letting him sleep on my couch as he handed me his folded blankets. He gave Quinn to Rickie and he kissed her goodbye. For the first time ever I felt something watching my sister with her family.

I called Mrs. Singleton at 8am, and she answered the phone telling me to take the day off. She said they called her late at night looking for me. Then she simply told me to be strong. I thanked her and then Rickie and I went out to eat. Neither one of us had slept in 24 hours, but for some reason everything was funny. After we were fed we decided to check on our mother and grandmother to make sure they hadn't killed each other. We could hear them screaming at each other as we approached the door. They didn't stop when we walked in. Both of them had points to make regardless of anything the other person said.

Rickie gave me pleading eyes to do something. I gave her the baby then I walked in the kitchen. "ENOUGH! YOU TWO HAVE BEEN AT EACH OTHER SINCE YESTERDAY! You shouldn't have anything else to say to each other. Both of you are equally wrong; Rickie and I are the biggest victims here. I swear you keep arguing hoping to never have to deal with what both of you did to us. Grandmother you could've told us that they wanted us back. Even if you made the same choice to run away from California. That way we wouldn't have felt like rejects." Then I looked at our mother, "let me beat you to the punch. Don't ask me for anything cause I have nothing to give you! I'm pretty sure if you don't calm down and resolve something with your mother you'll be fighting a relapse once you go home. Our grandmother gave up her home to protect us. That's what a mother does for her children whether she does it completely right or not."

"I came out here to make things right with you two."

"YOU DON'T EVEN LIKE ME! YOU'VE NEVER LIKED ME! YOU'VE GIVEN ME BLACKEYES AND BEAT ON ME LIKE I WAS AN ANIMAL! To the point that I don't remember it all. What did I do to you?"

"You remind me of them! You look like my father and act like my mother!"

Everything went silent! "There is no bigger insult you could've ever given me, than to tell me I act like HER!" I pointed at my grandmother who gasped. Rickie walked up the stairs quickly. "You must want to fight me!"

"Eva!" My grandmother said.

"Take it back! I do not act like her!" I was really mad and ready to fight.

"Eva?" My grandmother said with her feelings all hurt.

"You act like her, that's why you two are still fighting after two days!"

Why did my mother start foaming at the mouth? "NO I DON'T! GOD KNOWS I'M NOTHING LIKE HER!"

"Oh yeah?" I smiled at the sight of seeing her unraveled like she just had me. "You mad cause she sold you to her husband, your daddy. Then you sold Rickie to the rock man! YOU AIN'T NO DIFFERENT!"

My mother lost it and started to charge at me. All while my grandmother was still calling my name like she was hurt that it angered me that her daughter said I was just like her. I backed up into the kitchen and I pulled a knife out of the block on the counter. "I HAVE NO PROBLEM STABBING A CRACKHEAD! YOU BETTER BACK UP!"

Rickie came running down the stairs, she put Quinn in her playpen then she ran in the kitchen and stood next to me. "YOU NEED TO BACK UP!" The bass that came from Rickie let our mother know that she knew how to handle herself. I'm not the fighter in this family.

"I don't know what I thought could come from coming out here?" Our mother said frantically opening candy and popping it in her mouth. Then she marched over to the phone and dialed her husband. She was screaming and crying into the phone. "HELLO? HELLO? HELLO?" She shook the phone like it could personally tell her what happened.

Rickie's phone started going off in her purse. She answered it, and then she put the phone on speaker. "Baby!" Our father's voice was too calm through the phone. "Take a minute and breathe! I need you to calm down. You did not go out there for stress. Find your closure with your mother, make peace with our girls and come home to us."

"I know! BUT you don't know all that has been said to me." Our mother cried.

"It doesn't matter, remember you can't control them. You can't control any of this. You only have control over you and what you do. Say it with me, God grant me the serenity to accept the things I cannot change; courage to change the things I can…." They said their prayer thing together and then they both took deep breaths. "Remember the principles and come home."

My grandmother sat there looking at my mother like she was crazy. Our mother stayed on the phone for a long time with him and she kept popping candy the whole time they were talking. "Eva," my grandmother said lowly. I looked at her, "you hate me?" She looked at me with tears in her eyes.

"You're a bully! It's very rare that you say or show your appreciation. You're always telling me what I am or I am not going to do. I can never forget all that you said yesterday."

"I'm sorry, I was speaking out of anger. I didn't mean it."

"You said it, you hurt me."

"I'm sorry baby, I'll do better. I promise, don't hate me." She wiped a tear. "You and Rickie were my chance to have a do over. Your grandfather messed everything up and I loved him so much I couldn't see beyond the mess he left for me to deal with when he died. All of my children hate me; I can't do anything to fix all of that. You two, look at how good you two turned out. Rickie's in a good marriage, she has a beautiful family, and despite your parents she knows how to receive and give love. I take all of the credit for that. Eva, you are extremely successful. I never dreamed this big for you. You surround yourself with successful people. I love watching your mind work. You're such a hard worker, and even though I didn't ask you to, you sent for me. None of my kids would've done that. They hate me so much that they would've enjoyed watching me be homeless. You were willing to sacrifice all of this to take care of me. I love you baby, and I'm so proud of you."

Rickie was moved to tears while our mother watched and our father was silent on the phone. My heart was still hurting by what she said yesterday which was the total opposite of today. "I invited our mother out to try to clear the air. I want to be ok with the fact that I tried." She looked at our mother. "Most times I can accept that your addiction had you. That your disease is why you couldn't value us. Like I told you I can accept your apology. I did not bring you out here for anything other than closure. I was hoping you and your mother could have closure as well. Hope is not a strategy. Quincy tells me that all of the time but I don't listen. I can call and change your flight information to get you out tonight."

"Thank you," our mother said.

Tavio

Wesley and I were sitting on the couch drinking beers. William's mom is getting married and we were having a real conversation about stepfathers and blended families. Wesley was having a hard time with the idea of someone else playing daddy to his son. I was trying to assure him that it's possible to have a positive experience. I was telling him it really depends on the person. I told him that Tyrek comes from a blended family himself, so he knows firsthand what to do and what not to do. He comes straight to me about anything concerning my son and he never tries to overstep his place in my son's life.

Then Alaina walked in the door. She seemed happy and refreshed. She got her morning run in and some errands. Mr. Barton told her to meet him here so he only had to make one stop when he dropped the boys off. We were all laughing and joking when Mr. Barton walked in the door with both of the boys. He and the boys were smiling big. "Momma I can swim!" Jerrell said jumping into his momma's arms.

Alaina and Wesley's smiles dropped immediately. Mr. Barton put his hands up like he knew they would be upset. "Listen, these boys need to know how to swim. Wesley you know how to swim, you shouldn't hold them back just because of the past."

Alaina was madder than I've ever seen her. "THAT ISN'T YOUR CHOICE! WHAT IF!" She was crying so hard she couldn't speak for a few seconds. "What if something would've happened?" She barely got out of her mouth.

"I took them to the Richmond plunge, they had instructors in the water with them. I was right there the whole time."

"IT'S NOT YOUR CHOICE! YOU DIDN'T ASK ME IF MY SON COULD GO! YOU ALWAYS DO THIS! YOU ALWAYS!" Alaina screamed.

I put my head down, I wanted to walk out of the room cause this was a family discussion between them. All of this was none of my business. If I got up it may stop the flow of the discussion they need to have because they remembered that I'm here. "Baby girl please calm down and hear me out."

"NO! NO! You always do this to me! It's always about what you want and not what's best for me. I don't want my son in any large body of water. He needs to stay as far away from it as he can!"

"Alaina sweetheart listen, I know you're terrified of water. Your son isn't, he doesn't know about the past. You've got to let him live."

"You're such a hypocrite!" She screamed.

"Here we go!" Her father threw his hands up.

"Everything moves on your clock, when you're ready. Today wasn't about our sons, it was about you. You're ready to move on, so you used them to do it. You didn't say that you got in the water, but you put our babies in there! You are so wrong!"

"I'm not lying, I'm not a liar!"

"YES YOU ARE!"

"No I'm not Alaina!"

"YES YOU ARE! ALAYSIA WAS THREE WHEN SHE DIED NOT ONE LIKE YOU AND YOUR WIFE HAVE TRIED TO TELL ME! YOU TOOK THE PICTURES DOWN AS IF I WOULDN'T REMEMBER MY SISTER! WESLEY KNOWS AND JUST DOESN'T SAY ANYTHING. WHY WOULD YOU TRY TO ERASE SOMEONE SO IMPORTANT AS IF THEY NEVER EXISTED? SHE TRIED IT AND THAT'S WHY SHE'S DEAD NOW!"

Mr. Barton walked towards the door; "I can't talk to you when you're like this."

"You never talk to me period."

He stopped at the door, and then he turned to Alaina with fire in his eyes. "It's difficult to be real with your children and to maintain boundaries. Even though the lines were never blurred look how you act. You try to tell me how I should be when I will always be your father, not your best friend, not your big brother, I am not your equal. I know you don't want to hear it, but you've got a whole lot of your mother in you. You act just like her, you look like her, and you even think like her. She was mad at her father for cheating on her mother. So she decides she's going to be the one to do it in our relationship. I will never love another woman like I love your mother. Our relationship wasn't healthy for me or her. But we loved each other through sickness and in health. You can pretend to be mad at me all you want, but you're mad at her. You look for any excuse to use what I may do as a reason why you're acting ridiculous. You are responsible for your actions. You are responsible for how you treat the people in your life. Stop pointing fingers, and look around and deal with the drama in your life. And you are right; I'm letting go of the past. My grandsons learned to swim today. My grandsons broke the barrier of my HUGEST fear. I've got to let all of that go. I didn't deserve to lose my child or my wife, but it happened. I'm moving on, and as soon as I'm ready I'm getting married again."

Alaina stood up and screamed, "NO!"

Her father walked out the door slamming it behind him. Wesley put his arms around Alaina as she cried the most heartbreaking cry ever. The boys were frozen in their places; I forgot they were in the room. I took the boys to William's room and I played with the toys with them as I heard Alaina still crying like her heart was broken. I asked the boys if they had fun swimming, and they happily said yes.

Eva

I sat on the couch watching Vanessa's stylist put the finishing touches on her hair. I could sit for hours and watch people get their hair done. I always love the final polished look. Vanessa smiled big in the mirror showing her approval of her shiny straight hair. As she reached for her purse I took note of her freshly done nails. She looked great, better than anyone would normally for just a business trip. Vanessa stood up and flipped her hair. It moved in one smooth velvet tidal wave. She smiled and asked if I was ready. I led the way as Vanessa watched all the mirrors as we walked out. We walked a couple of blocks over to Stallone's our watering hole. We found a table in the bar area. Vanessa asked what was new, but she had twinkles in her eyes. "Never mind me, what's going on with you?"

"I talked to Mrs. Singleton and she approved my move to California." I stared at Vanessa like she was crazy. "Please don't judge me. Just be my friend ok?"

"What happens if he leaves you again?"

"I'll kill him!"

"Realistically..."

"I'll figure that out if it ever comes up." Vanessa looked at me with sad eyes. "I love him, my heart won't let me move on."

"What about his wife?"

Vanessa shrugged, "I know all the things you could say about this. I've beat myself up about all of it. This is still where I end up." She fidgeted in her chair, "what's happening with you and Kiev?"

"When I see him, we have a great time together."

"Have you met his kids?"

"No, and we decided that I won't meet them," now I felt guilty.

"WHY?" Vanessa covered her mouth. She took a deep breath and then she asked, "why?"

"Kiev and I are only sharing a moment together. No pretenses of love or that we're going to end up together. The only way that we're compatible is in that he can't have any more kids and I don't want any. Our schedules are just about polar opposites. When we see each other we have fun."

Vanessa sucked her teeth, "Kiev is not just a fun time in bed."

"You said we're all grown. Kiev is more grown than all of us." I laughed at my own joke.

"I don't like seeing my cousin get used."

"You're not seeing anything and you won't. You're going back to Cali remember?"

Vanessa smiled at me, "I'm going back to Cali?"

"Yes," I didn't get what was so funny about that.

"I'm going back to Cali, Cali, Cali. I'm going back to Cali. Humph, I don't think so..."

"I HATE YOU!"? I laughed as that LL Cool J song played in my head. "I'm not going to lie and say that Kiev and I are going to get married. He still sees Faye, it's only a matter of time before they're back together."

"What about you?"

"What about me?" I didn't understand the point.

Vanessa looked uncomfortable. "Look, I was visiting with Katrina. Colby came by with his girlfriend. She said that she and Colby were looking at rings." I felt like she stabbed me but I didn't react. "You should've seen Katrina's face. I think she did a good job of keeping it together. The girlfriend had no idea of what she said to us. Katrina waited long enough and then she and Colby disappeared."

"She was probably chewing him out," I tried to laugh.

Vanessa touched my hand, "are you really going to let him go?"

"Stop that, I released Colby back into the wild a long time ago." My body was on fire and I needed this topic to change. "I'm happy for him. He was getting baby fever, so now he can have as many as he wants."

Tavio

"MAC!" I was excited to have signed the first draft pick.

"Hi," she sniffed into the phone.

"You sick?"

"No!" Then she started crying out loud. "Royce just told me he's putting my house on the market. He said he's tired of Berkeley, and he's moving us!" Alaina was almost hysterical. "He's tired? I'm tired! He's never home! All we do is argue! I can't continue to live like this!"

"What are you going to do?"

"Sabotage!" She spit with complete fire.

"MAC," I didn't know what else to say.

"He called me from work this morning with this junk. I'm not going!"

"So then where are you going to go?"

"Tavio! Don't poke holes in my anger right now. I'm too angry!" Her voice shook.

"I know what you should do," I smiled.

"What?"

"You should cook a delicious smelling dinner and then after you and Jerrell eat, pack up the leftovers and put them in my fridge. He'll come home, smell the evidence and be too prideful to ask you where the food is."

"It always comes back to food with you doesn't it?" Her voice lightened a little.

"ALWAYS! I came out here and did what I was supposed to do.

Now I would like to celebrate. November is too far away to be waiting for a full dinner."

"I'll see what I can do."

"Should I have my assistant arrange a car service for me?"

"No, Jerrell has been asking for Tavio. I'll get him after school as planned and we'll pick you up from the airport. Matter of fact, meet us at the ice cream shop."

"I'll confirm in the morning that you're still ok. Try talking to the man before you decide to battle with him."

"Ok."

****

I didn't know what to expect, I hoped she felt better, but after that I wasn't sure. Alaina depends on everyone for support while Royce has been acting up. If he moves them she will come after him for sure. "Hello," she sounded normal.

"How are you?"

"I'm better, not 100% but we talked last night."

"So you're still moving?"

"He wants to, but he said we would talk about it some more tomorrow. He has to work late tonight and then he's going to the gym."

"Ok so then you're picking me up?"

"Yep, meet us at the ice cream shop."

"Alright, see you then." I was happy to hear her sound a little better. She's been so high strung lately. You can see stress all over her. Her shoulders seem like they're always hunched and she's just not happy.

In the airport on my way down to the ice cream store I stopped at a gift shop and I got the boys little gifts. I know they expect it, and I like giving them gifts. I thought I saw Eva breeze past me, but this is San Francisco; there are plenty of chocolate Sistahs out here with baldheads. I shrugged it off and paid for my items. As I cascaded down the escalator I kept blinking my eyes. Eva was standing by Royce as he hugged someone.

When they kissed, I really blinked my eyes to make sure I was seeing what I was seeing. I reached for my phone and started snapping pictures. They were lip locked with his hands all in her butt. He's a bold fool to do this out in public like this. Immediately I started thinking about Alaina, ice cream saved the day otherwise this would be bad. They moved away from the escalator and I didn't see which way they went. My heart was pounding cause this was going to be bad no matter how it happened. I was standing in the middle of the floor looking stupid trying to figure out which way they went. "Jerrell picked out pistachio for you." Alaina said creeping up on me out of nowhere. "You ok? Why are you sweating?"

"I'm fine, thank you. Let's go to the baggage claim." I took the ice cream.

"Why are you walking so fast?" Tavio asked me as he hurried to keep up with me.

"I just need to get my bag, come on." I jogged to the carousel. The whole time I was looking for Royce and I didn't see him. I told myself to calm down cause I had pictures. I needed to think of a game plan on how to show Alaina. She was in a good mood, and I hated to have to kill her mood.

I was looking at my phone and not looking which way I was going. I ran right into someone. I grabbed her so she wouldn't fall, it was Eva. "Well knock me over Tavio Dang! Hello mister brick wall!" She laughed as she steadied herself.

"What are you doing here?" I said loudly, and then I looked for Royce.

"It's my week to be out here." Then she put her hands over her mouth, "look at how big you've gotten."

Tavio smiled at her but he had no idea who she was, "hi."

"You remember MAC, and this is her son Jerrell."

"Oh yes of course," Eva went in for a hug.

"It's good to see you again." Alaina said.

"Are you traveling alone?" I asked still scanning the airport.

"No, my friend and colleague flew out here with me. She was anxious to get to her boyfriend. So she ditched me. I'm on my way to my hotel to get ready for tomorrow."

"Your friend?"

"Yes, you remember Vanessa don't you?"

"Barely," that was the truth.

"Oh well, is Unique in town this week? Maybe we can all do dinner again? Maybe my friend and her boyfriend can come up for air long enough to join us." She looked from Alaina to me.

"Sounds like fun," Alaina said with a genuine smile.

I was looking around everywhere and I didn't see Royce. My mind started shifting to how to tell Alaina. We said bye to Eva as she walked towards the rental car desks. I was walking behind our group looking around and trying to think.

Tavio asked Alaina why she wasn't making us take the stairs like she normally does and she said her legs were still tired from her workout that morning but next time we were doing laps around the airport and all the stairs since he asked. They were laughing when the elevator doors opened. Royce and Vanessa where all over each other and all up under each other's clothes. I saw them and then I looked at Alaina. The shock of a man and woman making out in the elevator registered first and she covered Jerrell's eyes. She looked at me, the look I gave her made her look again. Rage poured over her as she grabbed Royce by his suit and moved his whole body to the other wall. They hadn't even noticed us until she grabbed him. Alaina started wailing as she punched on Royce. Vanessa backed up as soon as Royce yelled Alaina's name. She looked at the kids and then she looked at me as she fixed her clothes. Yep she was Eva's friend, but she still looked familiar to me.

"Wait a minute! Wait a minute! Alaina let me explain!" Royce said restraining her.

Jerrell was crying, so I picked him up and I told Tavio to stand next to me out of the line of fire.

"Explain to me how you're here, when you're supposed to be at work or at the gym?" Then she started kicking him.

"Ouch Alaina! Ok! Ok! Ok! Wait a minute!"

"All these years and your excuse for seeing her was the gym! I WANT A DIVORCE! I HATE YOU! I HATE YOU!"

"Alaina what are you doing here?" Royce tried to ask her as if he had some right to question her.

Alaina broke free from his grasp, she tagged him in the mouth and his lip started bleeding. I patted Jerrell's back and I wouldn't let him turn around. I asked Tavio what floor were they parked on and he pressed 6. When we got to the 6th floor I told Tavio to take my bag and Jerrell. I gave him my keys and I told him to strap the baby in his seat and I would be right there. That's when I noticed the anger in Tavio's eyes as he reluctantly did what I told him to. "MAC! Come on, let's go!"

Royce looked at me, "my wife is not going anywhere with you."

"Alaina busted your lip, try and stop me and I'll knock your head off. You're caught Royce, accept it and regroup."

Royce let go of Alaina to come at me, and Alaina went for Vanessa. Royce grabbed her right before she got to her. "You're protecting her?"

"Alaina please calm down!"

"I WILL NOT CALM DOWN! I'M THE ONLY PERSON GETTING THE RAW DEAL OUT OF ALL OF THIS! ROYCE, LET ME GO!"

Royce had to realize that as much as he wanted to argue with me he couldn't let Alaina fight Vanessa. He pushed Alaina to me, and she flipped and kicked him in the face and he fell backwards. I picked Alaina up and I carried her to the car while she screamed her head off.

Chapter 17

Alaina

First thing I did was call Wesley, and Ken. They came over Tavio's house right away. Wesley had to hold Ken back as he went off as he promised all kinds of harm to Royce. He kept saying that he told him he was messing up. He knew it was bad, but he didn't want to accept it. He kept telling me he didn't know about the affair. I knew he was telling the truth because Chareca tells me how they don't talk anymore and how upset Ken was about all of it.

Wesley was mad, but he kept asking me what I was going to do. I didn't know so I would talk past it. Wesley kept asking me what I was going to do. When I finally snapped on him, I asked him why he keeps asking me that. He said because he doesn't make a move until he knows for sure I'm not going to go back to him. It made me mad when he said that, but then Tavio agreed with him, and they got Ken to calm down.

Their calmness pissed me off. Regardless, I wanted Royce to hurt right now, and there was more than one way to skin a cat. Granny Shane had threatened before to put my cousins on Royce. It was now time to let them get him.

Royce

Vanessa went inside the hotel and checked in. Then she came out and gave my keys to the valet as she helped me walk inside. She had me lay on the bed as she went and got ice for my throbbing nose and mouth.

Vanessa was a mess, she said my son was screaming and it was all her fault. I told her it was all my fault, nobody's but mine. I sat there face to face with everything I've done. This all started when I couldn't open my mouth to tell my fiancé what I needed. When her loyalty to me meant more than my selfishness.

I hurt Vanessa and I've carried that guilt with me into my marriage with Alaina. I let her believe that there was anything she could've done to alleviate my guilt. Giving Vanessa what she only deserved from me helped with my guilt towards her, but now I'm hurting Alaina and our son who never asked to be here. Who's here because I decided it was time to bring him. I need to give Alaina time; she's going to be mad. She's going to be hurt, but my wife is loyal to a fault. Tavio may try to get at her, but he will never be me. Alaina will come back to me, I just need to be patient and not rock the boat.

Eva

Vanessa looked like garbage she was pale and not on the wings of love like she normally looks. I got my coffee and then we quietly walked to the rental car. "Have you talked to Tavio?"

I looked at her, "he was at the airport last night." Vanessa hung her head as tears started dropping from her eyes. "Um, I know I never said it. You do know he is off limits? It would be too weird for me."

"What is MAC's real name?" She said between tears.

I thought about it for a long time, "I forget he calls her MAC so much I think everyone has forgotten her real name. Why?"

"Royce's wife's name is Alaina."

"Ok," I said not understanding.

"Alaina is MAC!" She cried harder.

"NO!" I put my hands over my mouth. "This world is too small! How did you find out?"

"She found us acting like teenagers in an elevator at the airport. It was almost like everything was meant to happen that way. Tavio had to pick her up and carry her to the car. Royce is upstairs with a busted nose and mouth."

"Tavio beat him up?" Figures he would.

"No, MAC did that."

"WHOA! A woman scorned for real!"

"Their son was screaming and screaming and it was all my fault." Vanessa cried harder.

"You're not responsible for their child."

"My actions hurt their child, I am responsible. Then…" she cried some more. "I forgot last night with all this chaos going on that I stopped taking my pills last month. I didn't think about it until this morning."

"You want to have a baby with this joker?" Vanessa didn't respond she just cried. "Hopefully last night wasn't the night. At least wait until the madness has died down. Let him choose you before you're stuck to him forever."

Vanessa blew her nose and then she told herself to get it together. She turned down the mirror and looked at her face. She said she brought waterproof makeup and she was so happy that she did. She took deep breaths, and she told herself to handle business today, she could fall apart tonight.

When I got to my desk I called Tavio, I asked him how MAC was doing. Then I went into my whole speech about how I didn't know.

He said she's really upset, and she wants Royce to feel pain. I asked him how he was doing, and he got quiet. I know him, and although he didn't want Alaina to hurt like this I know he wants her. This is a very delicate situation and handled wrong everything could be ruined.

Alaina

I called my boss as soon as she stepped into her office. I told her I was ready for the full time position as soon as she could open it up for me. She didn't ask me what happened, she told me she'd talk to her boss and get back to me with a plan. My laptop for work was at the house and I didn't want to go there right away for fear that Royce was there and then I would go off again. When Chareca called me I swear she said everything her husband said and worse. No one was on Royce's side. They all said they thought he might've been cheating but they hoped they were wrong. How could I have been so blind? If he was sleeping with her why did I have to do it at all? I kept flashing between angry and pissed off.

It's been 3 days; I need to get my backpack for school and my laptop for work. Tavio told me to wait for him, but he won't get here until Royce could be home. I have no idea what his actual schedule is anymore. So I decided to go in the morning.

I dropped Jerrell to Wesley's early in the morning so that my father could pick him and William up from Wesley's. Then I went over Unique's, she gave me a warm and sympathetic hug. I asked her to go with me to the house so that I could get the things that I need.

When we walked in the door the first thing I saw were my school papers all over the floor. All of my books were ripped apart and scattered all over the living room, family room; my backpack was ripped apart in the middle of the floor. I didn't see my work laptop, and fortunately I didn't keep them together. I ran to his office and into the closet in the back corner on the side of his filing cabinet. My laptop was there still neatly tucked away. I could tell he went through the rest of the house looking for anything. Our bedroom was completely torn up. All of my drawers were empty. He even went in the attic and through my boxes. As if I was the one with something to hide. I got the things I needed for Jerrell and I, and then I left.

I picked Lil Tavio up from school, and he smiled at me and asked me if I was ok. I smiled at him and said I was ok. "MAC, Royce is stupid. You should marry my dad and then you could be my stepmom."

I touched his chin, "if only it were that simple. You're right Royce is stupid, but your dad is with Sabrina. He's probably going to marry her. I just need a minute to figure things out and then Jerrell and I will be out of your hair."

"Where will you go?"

"I don't know, a place of my own I guess."

"You could stay with us. I like coming home to you."

"Yes, but last night Jerrell was getting on your nerves. I don't want you two to fight."

"That was nothing, little kids bug out like that sometimes, but it's fine. We normally get along really well."

"Yes you do. What would you like to eat for dinner?" I decided to change the subject.

"Chili dogs and garlic fries."

"You've got to have some sort of vegetable with every meal. Salad?"

"If you say so." He smiled at me real big. "MAC, who was the lady with the bald head at the airport that night?"

"That was Eva, she was your dad's best friend when he was little."

"My dad had a girl best friend like me?"

419

"Oh that's right, Cara Mia is your best friend. I guess history repeats itself."

"I can't wait to tell her about this tomorrow."

Tavio pulled up to the house as Lil Tavio and I were getting out of the car. "MAC tell me you didn't go without me?" I smiled a guilty smile. He sucked his teeth then he pulled his car into the garage. "Park your car in here, you should drive my other car until I get you new tires."

"No, I can get tires tomorrow."

Lil Tavio chuckled and took the groceries inside. Tavio looked irritated, "come here." He waved me over, "bring it in MAC."

I frowned at him and stayed put. "What?"

Tavio walked over to me and put his arms around me. "You know you don't have any money. You had your little savings back in the day. Let me do this for you."

"I have to figure out what I'm going to do. I need to find a place to stay."

"Ahem!" He looked around his garage. "What's wrong with Casa Spellman?"

I tried to move out of his arms but he held on a little tighter. "Nothing, it wouldn't be right for me to stay. I'm not divorced."

"I like coming home to dinner. I don't want you to leave, but of course you aren't listening." He let me go, "you never do."

"I appreciate everything. Unique and Ben are talking about moving in together. She said she would love to rent to me if I'm interested."

Tavio walked back to his car. "I'll pay for your tune up and tires. You've had this car for over ten years it's time to start thinking about replacing it."

"You just told me I don't have any money now you're talking about spending money I don't have."

"As long as you got me you won't need anything."

Royce

I can't believe this! I mean what else has she been hiding? I can't believe she defied me and actually enrolled in school. No wonder nothing was getting better between us. The time she was supposed to be spending focused on us she was studying and putting it all into school. I called movers and I've arranged for them to come next week and pack up the house. I plan to go back after Vanessa leaves Saturday morning. By then Alaina should be calm enough to try to talk this out. I mean we both have secrets so we'll both have to humble ourselves in this conversation.

When I opened the door to Vanessa's room she was sitting at the desk clicking away on her laptop. "Are you going to change or wear what you're wearing?"

"To?"

"Dinner with Kid," she said as if she's mentioned this to me before.

"I'm not in the mood to deal with Kid." I sat on the bed.

"Why? What's wrong with Kid?" She raised an eyebrow.

So I told her about my encounter with Kid at the Bart station. Vanessa asked me to play nice, but she didn't give me the option to stay behind. Irritated I told her I didn't think it was a good idea for me to be going out in public just yet. Vanessa said we were having dinner in the city, not too far from Kid's place. She told me it should be fine, but if I didn't want to go I was welcome to go home and she'd see me later. Even though we both knew I was in no hurry to go home, I acted like there was something to think about.

When we walked down to the lobby her bald headed friend was waiting. Of course she'd go with us to meet up with Kid. She didn't smile; she was almost frowning at me as she watched me. "What is your problem?"

"MAC!" She watched my eyes.

I don't know this girl from nobody, how does she know Alaina? I was trying to remember as hard as I could. "How do you know her?"

Her friend stared at me like I was stupid and then she got the car keys from Vanessa and walked away. I looked at Vanessa as I waited for an explanation. When we got in my car she started directing me. "There truly is only six degrees of separation." I waited for her to explain. "I've met your wife before. She came out to dinner with us one night with her friends. Eva knows her friends from since they were kids. He called her MAC so much, why would I worry about her real name?"

"The bald headed girl's name is Eva?"

"Yes," she said like I irritated her.

"What's wrong with you? It's not like you ever introduced us. How am I supposed to know her name?"

"There's so much more to my friend than her lack of hair."

"Like? All I see when I look at her is that she has no hair."

"Because you're shallow like most people. I'm thinking about shaving my head."

"WHAT? You better NOT!"

Vanessa folded her arms and looked at me like I was crazy, when she's the one talking about shaving her head. "And if I do?"

"I'm not dealing with it!"

"Like you have a choice in what I do with my hair! I will do with my hair what I want when I want. If you're going to be a big baby about it you can go! I will be beautiful with or without hair. You can't define for a woman what makes her beautiful and what doesn't. I gotta deal with that beard you can deal with a bald head."

I stroked my beard, "what's wrong with my beard?"

"It looks fine, but I prefer clean shaven."

"Alaina told me to do it." I said rubbing my beard.

"Well at least let the hair go. Your hair is thinning. Go ahead start shaving your head. We could be twin baldies."

I rubbed my head, "I like my hair. The beard is for Alaina."

"So you think she's going to take you back?"

"I know she is, she's going to make me pay for this. She's coming back to me, I have no doubt about that."

"What about us?" She sounded sad.

"I can't live without you. You saw the change in me. You came back and I found balance. I feel like myself again."

"So this is it? I don't get to have a husband?"

"I already told you I'm in love with you. I don't know what else to tell you. Do you want me to lie?"

"Forget you Royce!" She folded her arms and looked out the window.

When Vanessa and I walked into the restaurant hand in hand Kid didn't even try to hide her anger. She hugged Vanessa while she mugged me. "He's married!" Kid said before we could sit down.

"I know, why are you mad about it?"

"You're ok with that?" Kid stretched her eyes at Vanessa.

"It's not ideal, what's with the third degree?"

"She was hoping to get another threesome or a twosome without me," I smiled.

Kid rolled her eyes, "yeah you wish. I'm very happy in my current relationship. My partner and I have been together for some time now."

"Yeah right! You approached me at the Bart station because you're happy."

Kid lowered her eyes at me, "I forgot how annoying you are."

I made kissy faces at her, and then she mellowed out. We actually had a nice dinner. Kid insisted that Vanessa meet her children. I was ready to go back to the hotel so I told Vanessa we could only stay for a little bit.

When we walked into the apartment a little girl was sitting on one end of the sofa under a throw blanket and a little boy was on the other end under a blanket. They were watching a movie and happy to see their mother. As Kid introduced us to her children Brooke walked into the living room in pajamas. "Royce? What are you doing here?"

I cringed, "No! No! No!" I fell into the chair next to me. "Can this week get any worse?"

"Nefertiti, how do you know my little brother?" Brooke asked.

"We were close in college," she smiled at me.

She pointed at Vanessa, "who is this?"

I rubbed my head like it hurt, "that's my girlfriend Vanessa."

"The Vanessa?" Brooke asked Kid. Kid shook her head very happily at her. "Kids, it's late. You can finish your movie tomorrow. Give your mom a hug and kiss, and then go get in your beds." They did as they were told and then Brooke told Vanessa to have a seat.

I pulled Vanessa into my lap while I looked at Kid. "So you

knew this was my sister?"

"Not at first, she barely talks about her family. Even now you don't talk that much or like that it would've been easy to know."

Brooke was rocking on the edge of the couch. "I swear! I swear!" She was trying to find calmness. "Eventually you figured it out and I'm finding out about it just now!" Brooke raised her voice a little. "I warned you, did you think I was playing with you?"

"I'm not proud of this, I was embarrassed." Kid tried to plead.

"This is just gross! You slept with my brother," Brooke spit.

"It's a part of my past it's not like I knew after we were together for some time. It's the past."

"You should've told me as soon as you figured it out." Brooke was calming down.

Now if I didn't think Kid is evil and riddled with issues I would've remained quiet. "So, when did you figure it out then?"

"Baby remember that time when we were looking at family pictures?" Brooke nodded, then she looked at me waiting for me to get to my point cause she knew I had one.

"Was that recent?" I asked.

"Years ago, but we had already been together a couple of years." Brooke said watching me.

"You love her?" I asked my sister.

Brooke opened her hands, "depends on what you say when you get to your point."

"It's not like anyone has spared me any heartache this week." I rubbed Vanessa's butt, "remember when you got flowers from me at work?" Vanessa nodded yes, "she approached me suggesting a threesome for old time sake. That's how I found out you were out here and still worked for the same company. She wasn't expecting me to remember."

"I'm done!" Brooke shot up and stormed towards their bedroom.

Vanessa stood up and looked at me with sad eyes. I peeked in the room and Brooke grabbed her clothes in one grab and slammed them into a bag. She cleared the dresser into another bag. She was moving at an impressive rate getting her stuff. That's when the thought occurred to me that Alaina could've not come home.

Brooke had suitcases packed and she told me to pop my trunk. Vanessa looked at me; Kid was in the bedroom crying as she sat on the bed. The children didn't even come to the door, kind of like the sound of this situation was normal for them. I can't imagine that they were sleep already. I picked up the bags Brooke didn't carry and I walked out to the car. Vanessa said she was going to say bye. "Are you sure you can walk away from the kids like that?"

"They're her kids, if she cared about them she wouldn't act like our mother." Brooke said, "this is just the final straw." She exhaled, and then she took her phone out and called someone. She told them she was done and she needed a place to stay for a month so that she could get her own place. Then she hung up, "can you give me a ride to Richmond?"

"Of course, let me drop my girlfriend off first."

"What happened to your wife?"

"I'll tell you after we drop her off."

I told Vanessa I had to take Brooke to Richmond and I'd be back later. Vanessa reluctantly said ok, Brooke got in the front and then I gave her the rundown of my week. I took her by the house and I said I'd tell Alaina that Brooke wanted to see our son even though it was way after his bedtime.

The house was dark and closed up like Alaina hadn't been home all day. I frowned when the papers and her ripped up backpack were still where I left them. She hasn't been home as long as I haven't. I couldn't pull it back; I know Tavio is in her ear trying to get at my wife. Alaina wouldn't do it right? I mean I did think she'd come home. The thought of Tavio pushing up on my wife sent anger through my body. I couldn't pull it back. Brooke ran behind me back to the car. I drove by Wesley's condo to make sure her car wasn't there and it wasn't. I sped to Tavio's, Ken's SUV was here, and the rental car that the bald headed girl and Vanessa shared. Alaina and my son were in there I knew it. When I got out of the car Brooke did too. She tried to ask me who's house this was, but I marched on. I banged on the door like I was the police. Ken answered the door with fire in his eyes. "What do you want?"

"You are supposed to be my boy! How you gonna answer the next man's door like you defending him?"

Ken pushed my shoulder back so I'd backup. "You haven't left me a choice! For the past almost three years you've dropped everyone for some female? Alaina is heartbroken for what? Your son is confused for what? Everyone is up at all hours of the night for what? So that you can get your rocks off with some female who doesn't matter."

"You don't even know the whole story, how are you going to take her side?"

"I HAVE DAUGHTERS! One day you will too! I don't want this for them and you shouldn't want this for yours. Your kids are more likely to follow your example then listen to your words. Why would you want this for your son?"

"So the fatherless child thinks he can judge me? Alaina is not an innocent helpless victim regardless of what she's told you. It takes two! One day you'll understand what I mean!"

Ken looked me up and down. "Your parents were no more in your life than my father is in mine. You probably forgot cause we don't talk anymore. Your family is in there hurting. You're not here to restore peace, you need to leave."

"So Tavio can push up on my wife? No!" I planted my feet.

"Tavio? Really? That woman is in there heartbroken, she's not thinking about Tavio! She's been married to you, and in love with only you for about ten years this summer. You really think she would use your behavior as an excuse to pass herself around? Not that you wouldn't deserve it, if that man is smart and I believe he is. He's not going to go for her right now. When you love someone how could rebound sex ever be satisfying?"

"You just said he loves her!"

"He respects her, you need to fix this."

"I'm having the Berkeley house packed up." I said looking at Brooke who was shamelessly listening to everything.

Ken frowned, "why?"

"I bought a house in Walnut Creek. I'm putting the Berkeley house on the market."

Ken shook his head; "you're digging a ditch for yourself. She loves that house, she took pride in each of the upgrades."

"I'm not going to pay both mortgages. ESPECIALLY when she's not even staying there!"

"You might as well file for divorce." Ken said like it was pointless talking to me.

"The Walnut Creek house is an investment."

"As if a house in BERKELEY isn't? You're only thinking about what you want. Think about what she's going through."

"You're supposed to have my back!" I wanted to fire on him.

"I could let you sit in the dark! I got your back, which is why I'm telling you anything. You're not hearing that you're right so you're getting mad. Go home Royce! Figure out how you're going to get your wife back."

Eva

I followed Tavio in the kitchen. "He's been with Vanessa all week."

"Walk with me, talk with me." He led me to the coat rack. He grabbed a sweatshirt and he gave me my jacket. Alaina and her friend were sitting on the couch holding hands while they watched television. Little Tavio and a little girl were playing a game at the table, but he watched his father and I walk out into the backyard. "How long has he been seeing your friend?"

"About a year and a half. She's been talking about moving out here to be with him."

"You think she loves him?"

"I know she does."

"You think he loves her?"

"Yes."

We walked in a circle in the middle of the yard. "MAC loves him and he's a fool. This is going to get ugly before it gets better, right?"

I shrugged, "I've never been married. I have no idea of how the letting go process works."

"Yeah you do, maybe we weren't married but our breakup wasn't easy."

I smiled, "we are a divorced couple who found the maturity to be good to each other even though we didn't work out huh? I feel so mature."

Tavio laughed, "yeah but at first it felt like death."

"Losing me does feel that way doesn't it." I bumped him; "I can't imagine having a child in the middle."

"Right! Can you believe he was demanding more? She wasn't ready for the one they have."

"How she get pregnant if she wasn't ready?"

"You're asking for more details than I care to know. I just know that babies can happen when you have sex."

"I've made it a point to avoid babies."

Tavio stopped walking, he looked in my eyes. "Why?"

"You know why, what do you mean why?"

He rubbed my shoulder, "relax. I'm not attacking you." I didn't realize I tensed until he said it.

"I felt so helpless and alone. That whole experience from discovery until the end was traumatic. And if I couldn't have a baby for you, what I look like having one for someone else?"

"Maybe that's it, you should never have a child for anyone. We were supposed to do it together. Look at Tempest and me. We weren't in love and yet we raise our son in love together."

"That's because you're an exceptional man," I smiled.

Tavio stopped walking and looked at me. "Eva you tried to get me last time I saw you. Are you trying to tell me you want to get back together?"

I bucked my eyes, "NO! I can compliment you without hitting on you."

He flipped his hair, "I thought the power of the locs was taking over."

"Besides you're in love with MAC, it's all over you."

"Am I that transparent? Why does everyone keep saying that?"

"It's all over you. The way you look at her. You're so gentle with her, and I know cause you used to be that way with me. Just remember to let her work this out before you get all intense. She needs to close the door on her relationship first. I mean she doesn't even know the whole story yet."

"What's the whole story?"

Ugh! I shouldn't have said anything. I felt like I was betraying my friend. At the same time, Royce is so wrong I don't even care. "Vanessa and Royce dated seriously in college. They broke up suddenly, and just as suddenly got back together. They were talking about moving in together when he disappeared for years. Then one day she spotted him at the grocery store. She went off and I thought it was left there. I guess that's when they started again."

Tavio was quiet for a long time. "Tell your friend to be careful. He's been at this longer than just her."

Tavio

Alaina has been a mess. Her brother has been waiting for her to say she's done. She told her Granny, and then Wesley had to talk their cousins down. Didn't stop them from trashing his car while it sat at the Bart station.

Wesley came by looking for Alaina. She was out with Chareca. I rode with him to the Bart station. The car was up on blocks missing all four tires. All the windows were busted. Both mirrors were hanging by cords. Trash was inside and all over the car. It looks like they tried to set it on fire as well. Police were all around the car taking pictures and things.

Royce was standing there looking beyond pissed as he spoke with the officers. Wesley asked me how Royce had this new fancy car and his sister was still driving the car her grandparents bought her before they got married? I doubted Alaina even cared about that, but naturally I agreed with Wesley. Shouldn't your woman be taken care of before you buy something nice for yourself?

That night Alaina was in the backyard arguing with Royce about his car. He was accusing her of doing it and she had no idea. I distracted Jerrell with hot chocolate. Lil Tavio and I played with him and put him to bed. Lil Tavio followed me to my room. "Dad, why aren't you doing anything?"

"Like what son?" I didn't understand what he was asking me.

"Why won't you go beat him up? Hurt Royce for hurting MAC."

"You think that's the answer?"

"If he was Cara Mia's husband, I'd beat him up for making her cry."

"Sometimes husbands make their wives cry. It's not anything to be proud of, but it happens."

"Tyrek does not make my momma cry. And if she's crying somebody's in trouble. I told you about that time that man thought my momma was alone and he started yelling at her. When I went over there, momma was holding me back and the guy was still yelling like I was nothing. Then Tyrek came out of nowhere. He knocked the guy out with one punch. When his friend came Tyrek was ready for him talking about nobody disrespects his wife." He told the story like he was telling the best story ever told.

"What did the friend do?"

"He didn't want nothing. He helped the idiot up as we left. My point is you don't let nobody make your woman cry. That's what Tyrek said and I agree with him."

"MAC is Royce's woman, she's not my woman."

"Oh," he stood there thinking like he hadn't thought of that. "But she's crying so she won't be his woman too much longer. Then she can be yours."

I started laughing, "it's that easy?"

"Yes, you guys are always together and you act just like my momma and Tyrek."

"So does this mean you're going to marry Cara Mia when you grow up. You two are just as close."

Lil Tavio started blushing, "no! Cara Mia is crazy! She tells me mean stuff all of the time."

"Like what?"

"She gets mad when I don't brush my hair, if I just ate she tells me my breath stinks. She makes fun of the girls I like. She gets mad at me all the time, she's crazy."

I laughed at my son's ignorance. "When you get older more things will start to click. Sometimes girls are not crazy, just crazy for you."

Lil Tavio frowned, "I don't even know what that means."

I laughed, "I know son." We talked a little more and then he got ready for bed. Alaina came in the door trying to pull herself together. Lil Tavio shot me a look like he wanted me to do something about her being so upset. He hugged and kissed her, then he went to bed. I took the bottle of Hennessy out of the cabinet and I set two shot glasses on the table. "Join me for a drink."

Alaina said a defeated, "ok." Tears were still pouring out of her eyes as she sat at the table.

"Alaina don't," I said as gently as I could.

She didn't understand, she reached for her glass as I poured a shot. "Don't what?"

I took my first shot and sat at the table, and poured another. "Don't let this consume you. It's very hard to mind my own business when I see you looking beaten down like this. You are not in the wrong here."

"He thinks we're even because I was in school and he didn't know about it. He says no sin is greater than any other sin."

"What do you think?"

She took her shot, "it's hard to think right now."

"Lil Tavio wants to beat Royce up. He's convinced like everyone else that Royce is wrong. Royce is the only one trying to convince you that you would ever do something as painful to him. He may not like that you were in school. Going to school did not affect your dedication to him. It did not compromise your marriage."

"According to him it did. He wanted me to figure out why I wasn't responding to him like a wife should. That was supposed to be the whole point of me staying home."

"Responding to him like a wife should?" I had no clue as to what she was talking about.

Alaina poured another shot, downed it and poured another one. "You know our friendship turns another corner once we talk about this. You can't hold this against me or treat me like a leper when I share." Her eyes glassed over.

"This is the safe zone, when we sit at this table. The shot glasses, the Hennessy, it's safe."

Alaina took her shot then she poured another one and stared at her glass. "I don't like sex."

I looked around the room so I wouldn't stare at her, not what I thought she was going to say. "Why?"

"It's not from a lack of trying, Royce tried everything. I can count on my fingers how many times I actually enjoyed it, and I don't know if the first time counts as sex." She held up five fingers.

"So how was staying home supposed to fix that? Were you supposed to jack off all day until you figured it out for yourself?"

Alaina's eyes bulged, "do what?"

"MAC!" I blushed, "am I even the right person to talk to about this?"

She drank her shot then she poured another one. "I guess I'm getting drunk tonight. I don't know what I was supposed to do. That's what he said and he left it to me to figure it out."

"Did you try reading a book or watching a movie?"

Her eyes got big again, "a movie? NO! What am I supposed to do take notes on how to make unnecessary noises? No thanks."

I blushed again, "when it's good there's no room for quiet."

"Awkward!" She said smiling at the table.

"Reading a book?"

She shrugged, "I wouldn't know what to read."

"I feel like we having a Shug and Ms. Ciely conversation. You's still a virgin. How you supposed to know if he don't show you?"

"I don't know," she looked around the room.

I sat there debating with myself on what to say next. "We need to stop drinking. I've got both, which would you like?"

"BOTH? You mean you watch videos?" I shook my head yes. "Why?"

"Why not?"

She giggled, "I don't know." Then she shook her head, "I don't know."

"MAC! Here's the thing, I could show you. Tell you things and be your guide on this. I won't do that to benefit Royce. He didn't appreciate your innocence. He doesn't deserve to know you otherwise. You are a very sexy, strong, and intelligent young lady." She shook her head as she looked down. "NO! Don't do that, this is yours own it and embrace it. That fool transferred his issues to you. You were excited about sex weren't you?"

She shook her head fast, "I really was. I thought it was going to be amazing and everything that I've heard about. Just like everything else in my life it was a disappointment."

"MAC!" I straightened up in my seat. "Making love is like an art form. First you got to learn how to hold your brush. Then you got to learn how to stroke. One day if you're ready for me, I'd love to teach you some moves."

Alaina gagged, and then she squealed. "You are too hilarious. You are not Bruce Leroy!"

"I CAN TEACH YOU SOME MOVES!" I laughed.

She exhaled and stopped laughing, "thank you for making me laugh. What am I going to do about Royce?"

"Stop letting him tell you anything. He's in the wrong, sneaking to go to school took nothing away from your relationship, it secured a parachute for you for when he did this. What if his whole reason for you not working and going to school was so that when this happened you'd have to accept it?"

Alaina sat there with her mouth open like she couldn't believe what I just said. She grabbed her head; "you're overloading me with information and messing with my buzz."

"Ok, so what are you going to do?"

"I'm going back to work. I'm going to take my time. I refuse to live in Walnut Creek! So, I don't know I'm just going to wait and see what happens."

"Sounds good."

"Tavio," she said like she was nervous. My stomach flipped at the sound of her voice. "I just want to see like five minutes of a video."

"Why?"

"Well because now I'm curious."

"Ok," I looked at my last shot.

"Will you watch it with me?" She looked embarrassed.

I cut my eyes at her, "why?"

"I'm going to have questions. I'll be too embarrassed to ask someone else."

"You are pushing the limits of our friendship. I just said I'm not going to show you anything to benefit Royce."

"You saw him, she's gorgeous! He's probably packing up as we speak. I WILL NOT MOVE TO WALNUT CREEK! I just wanna ask some healthy questions."

"This is nothing but trouble!" I got up, "come on."

My legs have never felt so heavy as I walked up the stairs. I secured the house, and set the alarm. Alaina followed me quietly. I shut my bedroom door behind her. The most irritating feeling is walking into a situation that you know will not end the way you want it to.

I told Alaina to sit on my bed. I put a DVD on, and then I sat on the floor across the room by my closet. Alaina grabbed my pillow as she sat on the edge of my bed with big eyes. I skipped scenes until I got to one I thought she could handle. Alaina's eyes were BIG as she stared. I tried not to laugh at her, but she looked like a little kid watching the scene. She buried her head in the pillow and raised her hand like she was in school. I paused the video and waited for her to look at me as I silently laughed hard at her. She was blushing so hard; she asked me if it looked like that when most people do it. I told her it depends on the couple. She kept blushing as she said she was done, and then she thanked me for showing her. That was only three minutes, but I guess she couldn't hang. She opened my door and then she turned to me. She asked me if it looked like that when I do it. I didn't say anything I just smiled at her embarrassment. Alaina went to the guest room and shut the door.

Royce

Alaina is dragging this out too long! I stood looking out my window to my new office. I miss my wife, I miss my son. This madness has gone on long enough. I'm at my whit's end, I don't know what else to do or say. My phone rang, it was our receptionist. "Hello?"

"Royce, there's a Mr. Byron Chambers here to see you."

I sunk in my seat, *what does my father want*? I don't need this right now. "I'll be right out." I locked my computer, and then I touched my pocket to make sure I had my wallet. My father was charming the receptionist as I walked out. She was his type, plus sized and pretty. I thought he had a girlfriend but I shrugged it off, I didn't care. "Let's go have coffee." I said ushering my father towards the elevator.

My father stared at me during the elevator ride. I didn't know what he knows so I decided to be quiet. We walked across the street to a little cafe where they offer tables with waiters. My father told them we wanted to sit outside. That means he's going to yell at me. Well forget that, I'm not a child. "There's a Sale Pending sign in your yard."

"I know, the house is in escrow." I sipped my coffee.

"Where did you move to?"

"Walnut Creek," I watched his eyes.

"Where's Alaina?"

"What do you mean?"

"She didn't want to move that far away."

"Walnut Creek is not far, it's on the other side of Tilden park."

My father looked at me like I was stupid. "Where is she?"

"She's been staying with her friends. It's temporary."

My father leaned back and looked me up and down. "You are your mother's child aren't you?"

"What does that mean?"

"For the longest time I wasn't sure if you were my son or his. You're feeling good about yourself aren't you? Or at least you were until the bottom fell out. Don't try to run game on me, be a man and speak your truth."

"Wait a minute, I'm not your son?" I felt like a fatherless child looking into the face of a stranger.

"I think you're my son, but it's not like I ever got you tested to know for sure. Your mother was never straight with me."

Suddenly that empty feeling had a name to it. "What do you mean?"

"You look like your mother. You could be anyone's child."

My eyes glazed over, "what? How you going to drop this on me out of nowhere?"

"Where's Alaina?"

"Dad!" I tried to control my emotions.

"See how you feel right now! Now think about how your son is feeling. He doesn't understand that his father is a selfish jerk. All he knows is he loves you. You're over here trying to strong-arm your wife into a life she doesn't want. She didn't want to have your child."

"She told you that?" My whole body was tense.

"She didn't have to, I could tell. Why do you think I coughed up the money for your house?"

"Because I'm your son."

"Because you're selfish! You always have been. If Alaina doesn't move in with you I want my money back."

"That money was a gift."

"You better look at my letter that you signed again mister lawyer." He took an angry sip of his coffee. "I told you she was too good for you, but you don't listen."

"Are you my father?"

"You're going to have to ask your mother. I honestly don't know." Then he watched me, "I want to see my grandson."

"Jerrell looks like you."

"Does he?" My father looked at me like I was an idiot.

I tried to control my anger. "Cut it out! You know you're my father. You're just trying to mess with my head."

"If I was? Why are you above being messed with? Your family is in turmoil."

"You automatically blame me, you don't even know what happened. How you know Alaina didn't do something that made it impossible for us to stay in Berkeley?"

He continued looking at me like I was an idiot. "I sent your wife to the gym to get you. Did you ever wonder why?" He paused to let me think about it. "Cause you're selfish and an idiot. I bet you were faithful until Jerrell. Once you felt like you had her you let your hair down. You showed up late to your own wedding because of some other female. Look at you now; you're all polished up like you're trying to catch. Alaina loved you even when you were fat an ashamed. A lot of good that did her. When she divorces your ungrateful behind make sure she knows I don't support your selfishness."

"Is this why you've always spoken down to me? Cause you never believed I'm your child so you didn't care?"

"I've always provided for you the same as Brice and Brooke, I stayed with your mother until you and Rachel were grown. I've never treated you differently. I also never sugarcoat when any of you are wrong. You and Rachel can't help being like that woman."

I rode with my father to Richmond. Rachel wasn't home, but our mother was. When she saw my face she immediately asked my father what he said to me. I asked her who my father was. My mother went off on my father. I sat there and listened as they went back and forth. My mother complained about the time he was deployed. How he wasn't there for our births. How lonely she was. He called her every kind of selfish whore he could think of. He said he never cheated on her until her boyfriend kept following them around. My father could relate to Alaina because he was Alaina in their relationship. Whoever this guy was, he was Vanessa. History really does repeat itself.

When I got back to the office I called Vanessa. I told her about my day, "Vanessa! I love you, and I can't deny that. I don't know what to do. I'm in love with my wife."

Vanessa was quiet for a long time, "I guess I need to go back on the pill."

My head dropped, "why would you get off?"

"We talked about a family don't act like this is out of left field."

"I know, I just didn't realize that we were going to do that now."

"I can give you a little time Royce, but I will not wait forever.

Eventually you're going to have to choose and I deserve someone who chooses me regardless of how I feel about you."

"I'm in love with you Vanessa."

"Then let her go."

"I'm in love with my wife."

Alaina

When my alarm went off I popped up. Today I felt great, I told myself to check in with myself in a year. I took my outfit for today out of the closet and laid it on my freshly made bed. I went in Jerrell's room and he was knocked out of course. I kissed him until his eyes opened. "Wake up sleepy head. Today is mommy's first day of work."

Jerrell smiled as his eyes slowly opened. I told him to put on his clothes while I got in the shower. As I walked towards my room after my shower Jerrell had his pants on but they were pulled all the way up past his belly button as if he was an old man. I laughed and I helped my baby. I made his bowl of instant oatmeal and then I got dressed while he ate.

As I drove down the long street on Refugio Valley Jerrell always says excited hellos when he spots "Bambi" every deer is Bambi. Unique said I would get used to seeing all kinds of wildlife around the condo since we were right next to the Tilden Regional Park that spans the hillside from Hercules through Berkeley.

When Ken told me that night that Royce was packing up the house I went back and got anything I wanted to keep. Then I left my keys on the kitchen table. He could sale the house I didn't care; I'm not moving to Walnut Creek, that much I knew. Unique's two bedroom was the perfect size for my son and I. Tavio and Lil T weren't happy about us moving out. So the plan I worked out with them is that they could come have dinner with us whenever they wanted. My father, Wesley, and William are going to take Jerrell to Disneyland in a week. Even though

I'm not talking to my dad, I told Wesley I would entrust my son to him since I don't trust my father to honor my wishes.

I gave Jerrell and William kisses then I thanked Wesley. I hurried to my car and I excitedly drove to the Emeryville office. There wasn't any room in the Concord office where my old team sits so they got space for me out here. All I could think about at first was how close I would've been to home.

When I stepped off the elevator I badged into the door. Balloons sailed high above our section. I was here on Friday setting up my desk, and putting gifts on my team of two reports' desk. My boss had to have come in over the weekend to do this. I was forty-five minutes early, but I told myself this was ok. I connected my laptop to my docking station as someone knocked on my cubical wall. "Welcome," he said as he smiled at me. His smile got wider when I turned around.

"Thank you," I extended my hand for a shake.

"Alaina?" He said looking at my nameplate. "That's pretty, I'm Kyle. My team has been in this location for six years. So if you have any questions feel free to holler."

"Thank you Kyle, who makes the coffee?"

"First to come in helps everyone else out by putting a pot on. I'll show you where everything is."

"If you wouldn't mind, can we wait until the rest of my team arrives so we can find out at the same time?"

"Not at all," he looked around my desk. "Is that your son?"

"Yes, my one and only, he's three."

He whistled as he pointed to my wedding ring. "It must be nice to be loved."

I held on to my smile even though I wanted to sit down and cry. "Are you married?"

"Divorced," then he smiled at someone approaching us. "Hello, I'm Kyle welcome to the Emeryville office." He extended his hand.

"Amir," he shook his hand as he eyed Kyle. "Thank you. Good morning boss lady."

"Good morning early bird, once Bill gets here Kyle's going to show us the ropes around here."

"Did someone say my name?" Bill walked around the corner.

Kyle introduced himself and then he showed us around the office. Where the supply cabinet is, where the coffee supplies are. He was very helpful then he went to his cubical. Amir teased me and said I was making friends really fast. I told both of them to hush, and then I retreated to my cubical.

My first day went really well, and by Thursday it felt like I had been working out here forever. Chareca and Kendall came to have lunch with me on Wednesday. When she saw Kyle she asked me who he was immediately. I told her what I knew. She asked me if I would date a white guy. I told her I hadn't thought of it then we both looked at my ring. She asked me what I was going to do about Royce and I told her what Wesley said. He told me to let my tenth anniversary pass before I filed for a divorce, fortunately it was coming up. I told her that Royce went to my father's house when he couldn't think of anywhere else I could be.

My father called himself trying to talk to me about how marriage is and how I needed to try to work things out with Royce. Which only led to another argument between he and I. My mother ran all over him because she knew she could. She knew he would only forgive her so why would she really mean it when she apologized? I've liked being on my own, being in my own space. Exercising in clothes I can breathe in. When I went shopping for a few things for work, I actually got nervous as I paid for blouses and dresses with V-necks. Things that Royce would have a fit about me wearing outside of the house.

****

This week flew by and I couldn't wait for this morning. I took Jerrell to my father's house so that Royce could pick Jerrell up from there. Then I excitedly drove to Oakland. I got excited as I parked in the garage. I reminded myself to walk as I paced myself and tried to take normal steps to the shop. When I stepped in the door there were two chairs and lots of mirrors. There were pictures all over the walls. A small love seat was in front of the room in front of the window and there were magazines on the coffee table. The door chimed when I walked in. A middle-aged woman walked in from the back. "Are you Alaina?" I smiled and said yes. "Nice to meet you, I'm Lena." She put my purse and jacket in the cabinet behind her. She told me to have a seat then she moved her hands through my hair. She was lightweight massaging my scalp, which felt so good. I washed my hair last night like she told me and I lightly blow-dried it just for old times' sake. I've been putting my hair away so long. I didn't realize how long it had gotten.

Lena asked me what was wrong even though I thought I was putting out happy vibes. So I told her the story about my locs. How I've wanted them for years, but my husband was against them. I told her he messed up and so now I was finally treating myself to my locs. Lena said I'd be surprised at how many preconceived notions a lot of people still have about locs. As she was working I could feel my locs dropping just above my shoulders.

I was looking in the mirror when the front door opened and Tavio walked in. He smiled as soon as he saw me. "Old Merry MAC is living the dream! Watch out world here she comes!"

"You're so silly!" I blushed.

"Ms. Lena how she looking?" Tavio asked walking behind me to look. "How come hers look all silky?"

"This is how yours looked at first too."

"Looking good MAC!" He sat in the chair across from me.

Lena's husband came from the back to tighten up Tavio's hair. Lena was good; she had me done faster than I thought. I booked my next appointment then I walked out with Tavio. He kept looking at my hair and smiling. He asked me how I felt. I told him I couldn't put it into words yet. He smiled at me and told me I looked good.

Royce

We filled up the conference room awaiting whatever announcement management was going to give us. Our legal team has grown quite a bit in the last year and quite frankly we're working on top of each other. My boss walked in the room, "I'm not going to pull your legs or beat around the bush. There will not be any layoffs," everyone sighed in relief. "We have too many team members in San Francisco. We've secured office space in one of our Concord offices. If we don't get enough volunteers to move to that location we will choose. Come back to this room at noon, we'll have lunch brought in. We will determine who's going at that time." Then he walked out.

"Royce, don't you live out that way?" One of our attorneys called out.

I frowned at her, "so."

"So... Don't you think that they'll send you even if you don't volunteer?"

I walked out and I went to my boss' office. He basically told me that I would be sent if I didn't volunteer. However, if I volunteer first I'd get an office, as long as I'm in the office twice weekly. When I asked which location in Concord we were being sent to, he said it was the same building Alaina used to work in.

I spent the rest of the day talking myself into what I volunteered for. When I got off of work I caught Bart to El Cerrito Del Norte instead of the Walnut Creek station where my car was parked. Brooke picked me up and then we went to Alaina's father's house to pick up Jerrell, so that

I could have dinner with my son. As the three of us ate Brooke was beating around the bush until she couldn't any longer. "How's things going with your Baby Momma?" She nodded to Jerrell to say she was speaking in code for his sake.

"She's still not talking to me, I haven't laid eyes on her yet. Why?"

"I've out stayed my welcome at my friend Breezy's. I need a little more time. I was wondering if I could bunk at your place for about a month."

"That's her name?"

"Her mom was a semi-hippie, free love and all that. She's a little off, but we've been friends since childhood."

"Why can't you stay with her?"

"She's bipolar and really needs to take her meds. When she takes them she's calm and even. You can have a normal conversation with her. She be smoking and it messes her up. The courts took her daughter away from her cause she's crazy. She was doing good for a minute otherwise I would've toughed it out with our mom. When her family comes around she gets off schedule and it's difficult to get her back on schedule. I'm not getting any sleep and the types of guys she messes with ain't cool."

"Let's be clear on how long you need to stay."

"To be safe let's say two months. What are you going to charge me for rent?"

"Save your money and leave as soon as you can."

"Ok," then she leaned in. "It's been months, you really think she's coming back?"

I looked at my son who was coloring on his menu with concentrated effort. "Yes, she's just mad at me. I know she loves me and she's going to come back to me."

"Royce, I'm going to be real with you. You broke her heart. School is never the same as an affair. You don't even have a pre-nuptial, and you're in California. She's going to take you to the cleaners."

"If she was going to do that, she would've done it already."

Alaina

Tavio paid for the process server to serve Royce with the divorce papers. Although he picks Jerrell up regularly, I haven't laid eyes on Royce since that day at the airport. I miss the husband he was when we first got married. The one who wasn't ashamed and a lot of fun. I wish we could've had more times like that one in the shower. It was like he did it to show he could if he really wanted to, and then nothing as good as that time after that. I bet that's how he was with her all the time.

When I pulled up to Wesley's condo he was standing with a woman by a car I didn't recognize. When I got out of my car the girl looked at me then at Wesley. Wesley waved me over and introduced me to Rebecca. The first thing I noticed were her big brown eyes that seemed like they were made to capture your attention. She smiled and said it was nice to meet me. She had a little girl in the car who looked like a miniature version of her.

The little girl was too cute, I said hello and then I walked inside to give them space. Wesley walked in blushing cause he knew I was going to ask. So he poured information. Their relationship was new, but he said he thinks she's the one. I sat down and asked him how did he know. He said she's so human he can't help but be drawn to her. He said she's an open book with him, and in turn he's found himself telling her things he never even told his ex-wife. He said that he gets along well with her daughter, and next he wants to introduce the kids. I asked him why was he moving so fast and he said it didn't feel fast with her. He said Rebecca is unlike any woman he's ever known and it feels right.

My father brought the boys, and then he said that Royce wants to get Jerrell for the weekend. I told him that was fine. Then I walked away before he could discuss anything else with me.

****

At work, I came across a bunch of blogs were people were sharing their divorce experiences. I felt so inspired that I decided to start one of my own. Who knows, maybe what I have to say could help someone else in what they're going through. I sat in front of my laptop on a Saturday afternoon needing to scream. I kept typing and then deleting.

Blog Title: My Atypically Average Life

By: ABC (Alaina Barton-Chambers)

I titled my first post "My Average Life." I don't know why it felt good to express everything about my life out to the Internet. My first post was an overview of my life in general.

Jerrell was still napping and I felt like sharing more. I looked at the keyboard and then I titled my next post, "*My Average Letter 2 My Twin*." As soon as I typed the title my eyes started to sting letting me know my tears were coming.

To my dearest Alaysia,

I miss you! Every time I look in the mirror I see your face. Every time my conscience speaks to me I imagine that's your voice attempting to steer me in the right direction. Times like today I wish it were me instead of you. They took all of my pictures of you and tried to paint the picture that we lost you a lot sooner than my heart knows that I did. Even though I was young I know the difference between hugging you and looking in the mirror to see your face.

I miss you sister! I need you! Our mom blamed herself for losing you. Dad tried to convince her it wasn't her fault. But it was her fault! Maybe if he wouldn't have protected her so much, I wouldn't have to look in the mirror to see your face. Or record my words to hear your voice.

Guess what I did? Come on guess! You're a terrible guesser so I'll tell you. I started taking swimming lessons with Jerrell. He's a natural in the water and he wants to be on the swim team.

I came to terms with my fear when Tavio wouldn't accept my simple answers when I refused to go near the Richmond Plunge. He told me that I can't let fear rule me. He has no idea of what all those words mean to me, to us. It took a long time for me to even be able to put my feet in the water. The first time I went under the water, I came up screaming your name and I cried for two days straight. Wesley came over and cried with me. He came with me to my next lesson. He hadn't swam since we lost you either. Wesley experienced everything I did getting in the water. Watching our brother go under for the first time had my stomach in knots as I cried like a baby. We stood over to the side of the pool crying as we held on to each other. We miss you Alaysia! Wesley swam laps and became reacquainted with the water that day. I found the strength to say that I would continue my lessons until I learn how to swim. My next water date is dedicated to you. I love you sister.

Love,

Alaina

I cried really hard after I wrote that post. I put my laptop down and went to the bathroom.

The next day I had a couple of comments on my blog post. That night I had a few more, people were thanking me for sharing. Those who weren't sure asked if my twin drowned. Most people were supportive and understanding. Quite a few of them had lost a loved one themselves.

The positive feedback encouraged me to continue writing. I was surfing through other blogs when the *Athletic Student* blog caught my attention. This blog had been around for years, and he had thousands of subscribers. I scrolled through this year's post and the *Proud Dad* post caught my attention. My mouth dropped open as a picture of Lil Tavio came up. His post was simple and full of pride for his son's achievements.

I quickly went to the archives, all the way to the beginning of Tavio's blog. It was time to secretly dive into the sick and twisted mind of one of my best friends. He never even mentioned that he has a blog. I leaned into my laptop like juicy secrets were about to spill out.

****

As soon as I parked my car my cousin walked up to my car. "Granny Shane said you filed for divorce." He watched my eyes.

"Hello, how are you? I'm doing ok." I said as I got out of the car.

Jermaine jumped around with the biggest smile on his face. "Oh snap! Look at you! First taste of freedom and the real you comes out! You look GREAT!" He gave me a big hug then he touched my locs.

"You like them?" I blushed.

"I love them! Freedom looks good on you."

"Thanks Manie," I blushed some more.

He opened the back door and got Jerrell out. "What's up little man, you remember me?"

Jerrell looked at me like he had no clue. "This is our cousin Jermaine."

Then a car pulled up behind us. It was one of my dad's sisters. Everyone was waiting for me to say I filed for divorce.

Granny Shane invited all her kids and grandkids over to watch old movies of our parents when they were young and of us when we were little. This was her way of getting us together as a family.

****

Tavio's blog is very addicting. I'm still in his early days, but I had no idea he was this in love with Eva. How could you love someone this hard and now only be friends with them? I don't get it, so I read on to try to find the answer to my question. He blogged about their childhood and how close they all were. His love of sports and of course his love of food. Each post has some reference no matter how small to food.

****

I am addicted to this blog; I see why he has so many followers. Sometimes the comments are as entertaining as the post. After all these months, I still come to this blog and read whenever I can. Who knew Tavio was this interesting? He didn't post about Lil Tavio until he knew the sex. I went to the previous post which was about him beginning college. Then he drops the bomb about his son. I can hear concern in his tone as he expresses his inexperience, and nervousness about being a parent. That's when I realized I didn't go through any of that. I mainly stayed mad at Royce my whole pregnancy. My heart and everything in my soul says he did it on purpose. Tavio sounds nervous. I laughed at how he recorded his mother's reaction to the news. I could see her throwing something at him.

The first picture of Lil Tavio was so precious. Tavio looked so young and different without his locs. I've gotten used to seeing him with them, I forgot what he looked like without them.

I was about to start the next post when Kyle knocked on my cubical wall. "Sorry to interrupt you, but the fire drill is going to happen in a few minutes. You're supposed to shadow me so that you can be a searcher." I locked my computer, and then I followed him. He showed me where the vest were kept, the signs, and bullhorn. When the alarm sounded, we went around the floor telling everyone to get going. I checked the women's bathroom while he checked the men's. We checked the floor and then we announced all clear to the other two searchers on the floor. We walked down the stairs and then to our meeting spot. We did a head count and then we waited for instruction. Kyle kept staring at my empty ring finger. As everyone started walking inside Kyle hung to the back of the group. "I'm not going to ask cause it's rude, but I am going to point." He pointed to my hand.

"Pointing is rude too."

"Your ring tan is barely there. Did you put it in the shop?"

"I filed for divorce," it felt weird to admit.

"Are you ok? This is totally my area of expertise." He smiled.

"I have a good support group behind me."

"That's good, how's your son handling it?"

"I don't think he's noticed all that much. My husband was barely home before I caught him in the act so, I guess he's fine."

"Listen to my next words carefully." I looked at him, "my number is on the manager list. PLEASE! Please call me whenever you need anything. Even if you just need to talk, CALL ME!"

I laughed, "why are you saying it like that?"

"You don't pick up on clues very well."

"Huh?"

"I like you Alaina, and I would love to have an opportunity to get to know you better." My mouth fell open, "I don't think I could be any more blunt than that."

"BUT! But why! But how? We're from two different worlds." I was trying to find a nice way to point out that I was black.

"I don't know what you mean by worlds, but I think you're sweet, beautiful, smart, and interesting. At least that's what I see from the distance I've tried to keep. The moment you're ready to date please think of me. PLEASE!"

"COME ON YOU TWO!" One of the other searchers called out from the sidewalk. I was embarrassed and blushing like crazy.

I walked fast and back to my desk. I did a little work and then I got back to my reading. I gasped after I read two of his post.

<u>THE BEST MAC N CHEESE EVER!!!!!</u>

I went to a work picnic today. As a starving student and adolescent father of course I would not turn down the opportunity to partake of free food. I went into this thing not expecting much. She brought it, it looked fine. Ben tasted it and raved over it. So let me see if I can explain it to you so that you can understand.

This Mac N Cheese is creamy, and cheesy gooey, and slightly crisp. I don't know how she did this! I must sample this dish again! I almost cried when I ate the last bite. I don't know how she did this, but somehow she pulled it off. This woman's name is MAC, partially because I forgot her real name, but also because her dish will haunt my dreams until I can have it again! I am forever spoiled!

I smiled at the memory. I guess you can't say he ever lied about his enthusiasm for my macaroni and cheese. I read along as he wrote about his son, and his trips to see Eva where he felt horrible about his secret. THEN.....

<u>Cucumber Melons</u>

So I had to have a conversation with my friend. I know he was crushing on MAC for a while, but now she's with some guy. She seems to be happy in her relationship; meanwhile I can't get enough of her fruity smell. I don't know what this girl has done to me, but I can't stop thinking about her. I get excited every time I smell her perfume. I'm in no way ready for this girl. I've got to break the news to Eva when I don't even know how. Then the ones that I spend time with to pass the time. There's something about MAC, I try to ignore this girl. Treat her like any other female friend I've had and it doesn't work. My son gets excited to see her; at least he can be real about what he feels.

So I had the talk with my friend, he laughed at me and said that he was finally over her. He guessed it happened just in time to watch me slide in his place. She's so innocent, and how in the world is she still a virgin? That's something very rare in this day and age…

I sat there speechless as I looked at pictures of all of us. Regular post about me and our friendship. I was so stuck I didn't realize that the time to go had come. Amir and Bill came by and said goodbye, that's when I forced myself to shut down my computer and go home.

Royce

At the office, Alaina's old boss looks at me with no expression on her face. I know she keeps in contact with Alaina, so I have no doubt that she knows my business. I smile and say hello anyways. I don't have time for that girl power sticking together garbage. I miss my wife and it's ridiculous that she refuses to see me. She filed for divorce and hides. Jerrell and Brooke were running around the house making animal noises as they played. My sister is very good with children, I wonder if she ever wanted to have her own. I tried to call Vanessa but my call eventually went to voicemail.

Frustrated, I told Jerrell we were going for a ride and I wanted him to show me how to get to his house. I know they stay somewhere in Hercules cause Jerrell said that his mom takes the Hercules exit when they go home. To be four he is very alert and I have no doubt that he could just as easily guide Alaina to my house, which is why I never bring

Vanessa here. I bought this house for Alaina, and it just doesn't feel right to have Vanessa in it.

Brooke sat nervously as she told me this wasn't a good idea. I told her I wanted to see my wife, it's been over a year and I haven't seen her. I miss her like crazy and I can't take any of this anymore. Jerrell told me to keep going as I drove up the hill. There was a pathway alongside the street and people were walking and running up and down it. "Go that way…" Jerrell pointed to the right from the back seat. I turned right into a condominium complex. "Now go that way…" then he pointed to the left.

Yep, real precise instructions he was giving me. I drove to the circle cluster of condos at the end of this street. "Right there!" Jerrell pointed to an end unit. Brooke and Jerrell got out of the car and he showed her their door and their garage.

I didn't see Alaina's car in the parking lot so I figured she probably parks in the garage when she's home. How can she afford to live here? Her brother can't afford this place and his life. Tavio's still paying his dues at his job last I knew. Her grandparents on her mother's side are well off enough, but they want us to get back together. Her Granny Shane is just a thug. I bet she got Alaina's cousins supporting her up here. Then again, I doubt it cause even though her father may be mad about my affairs he wants us to work it out. I rang the doorbell and there was no answer. So we waited in the car. A runner ran towards the parking lot. She stopped running and held on to her side as she walked catching her breath. Alaina had on stretchy pants, a tank top, and a scarf over her hair. I was caught between outrage and longing. I even missed the curve of her spine. I took a deep breath and asked my body to calm down. When she got close I stood up out of the car. Alaina was walking towards her place. She glanced at me, took a couple more steps then it registered that she was looking at me. She stopped in her tracks and stared at me. I waved hello, Alaina frowned, and then she flipped me off. Brooke started laughing hard. Alaina went inside her place and slammed the door hard. I jogged over to her door and rang the doorbell. When she decided to ignore it I laid in on the doorbell hard. I was at her door for a while when a male voice came from behind me. "Can I help you with something?"

It was one of her thugtastic cousins. I don't remember his name though. "You can't help me with nothing!" I spit at him.

"Leave her alone!" He said approaching me.

As soon as this idiot swings on me he's going up under the jail. I will take him for everything his granny got! "Whatever!"

Then Wesley walked up, "Royce man! She don't want to see you. Get in your car and leave her alone."

"She won't talk to me, we have to determine child support. I need to talk to her."

"Put it in a notarized letter, you got to go!"

"Call the police, I'm not leaving!" I said.

"That's a good idea because you're trespassing."

Brooke walked over holding Jerrell's hand, everyone backed down a little. "Hi!" He said happily.

"Hey little man, who's that?" Wesley said to him.

"My auntie Brooke," he said happily.

Wesley opened his phone. "He got his sister and Jerrell out here." He let her talk then she cracked the door open and called Jerrell.

As Jerrell entered I rushed the door. Her cousin grabbed me, but I was still trying to get in. Wesley helped his cousin, while Brooke fell trying to get me free. They carried me to the parking lot and dropped me. "That is my wife and child!"

"Not for long! Don't be stupid Royce, just leave." Wesley said.

Brooke walked over to me and told me to come on.

Tavio

Hope is smart, independent, and driven. I told Wesley I don't like setups, clearly he doesn't care. He invited me over to *kick it*. Neither of us had our sons this weekend and so we planned to go out. We agreed to make it a everybody night. Ken had a sitter for his girls. Unique and Ben are coming. Even Dakarai and his girlfriend. I asked Wesley why Alaina isn't coming and he said she wanted to spend her time with her son.

A few minutes after I get to Wesley's his girlfriend shows up with her friend. I asked Rebecca where her daughter was and she said she took her to Alaina's. I shook my head at Wesley cause he didn't invite Alaina so that he could have a sitter, and the only ones not paired up were me and Hope. Hope is pretty and all that I stated before. I just don't feel anything about her.

Unique and Chareca were looking at Hope funny right off the back. At the club we had a lot of fun. Hope drank and then exaggerated the effects of her liquor. I haven't had sex since Sabrina so I was overdue for a release. I took Hope home and I spent the night. Still not excited, but it was something to do.

Alaina

"So what if he asks you out?" Chareca asked laughing at me.

Butterflies hit my stomach. "I can't say that I've ever been on a date. I wouldn't even know how to act," I said shyly. "What if he thinks he's supposed to get some?"

Chareca busted up laughing, "do you even think you could handle that?"

"Alaina, you are grown. Whatever you want to happen will happen." Unique said.

"I.... I.... I don't know what I would want to happen." I rubbed my sweaty hands on my shirt. "I DON'T KNOW!"

I was glad that the two of them were amused by this whole situation. Once Unique stopped laughing she wiped her eyes. "You need a practice date. Like a guide of what to do and what not to do. My brother should be your guide." Chareca and I grinned at her. "What?" Unique looked so guilty. "I really think you need a coach who will tell you right from wrong."

"Won't his girlfriend have something to say about that? She don't like Alaina as it is." Chareca said.

"Just being honest, I HATE that girl! I could care less what she thinks she has the right to say. Once Alaina says yes, I might send her raggedy behind over there to see you two having a good time." Unique said angrily.

"What makes you think Tavio would ever agree to something like that? He's with her, he's happy." I said looking at the floor.

When I looked up, Chareca and Unique were smiling at me like I just said the dumbest thing ever. "It's never been my style to out my brother, but if I told him about this conversation he'd do it. All I need to know from you is whether you want to do it."

They leaned in for my answer. "Leave me alone, I'm not trying to break nobody up."

"UGH!" Unique fell backwards on the bed. "Ya'll gonna be the death of me." Then she pretended like she was praying. "Lord please guide me! Give me the strength to endure these two and their procrastination. I can't do it no more! I can't stand it!"

"Your brother and I are only friends, stop trying to make us into something that we're not."

"Something you're not? The only thing you two haven't done is slept together. I kind of thought it would happen while you were there. You two get on my nerves." She exhaled and looked around the room. She looked at Chareca who nodded at her.

"WAIT! You two have nonverbal cues now?" I couldn't believe how close they've gotten now that Unique and Ben are together. "I feel left out."

"Stop trying to change the subject. Can I plant the seed for Tavio to walk you through the dating process?"

I exhaled, "fine!" Chareca screamed and dove on me on the bed. Unique got up and ran out of the room. "Where is she going?" My heart started pounding, "she's not going to do it right now?"

Chareca rubbed my head like I was a little kid. "Ssshhhhh! This is for the best. Just relax and let it happen." She smiled at me.

"No!" I tried to get away from Chareca to run and lock myself in the bathroom. She grabbed me in this extremely tight grip. I couldn't move and I was trying. "How strong are you?" Chareca laughed but she wouldn't let me go.

Unique pulled Tavio in the bedroom. "I don't want to be in here. Unholy things happen in here." Tavio whined.

"Big brother I need a favor." Unique made her voice all sweet.

Tavio narrowed his eyes at Unique, "you better not be pregnant! I will go throw him off the balcony!" He said pumping himself up.

"Don't be crazy!" She hit his arm, "listen. There's this guy at MAC's job that is working up the courage to ask her out." Tavio's eyes burned me as she proceeded. I wanted to go hide. "Can you believe MAC has never been on a date?"

"Yes!" He cut his eyes at Unique.

"Can you show her how a date is supposed to go?"

"Prepare you for some other guy?" He cut his eyes at me.

"Never mind Tavio! I'll test the waters of single life on my own." I made my face all pitiful. "It's ok if I end up victim to another Royce in gentleman's clothing." I hung my head.

Tavio looked at Chareca, "this sounds like a good idea to you?"

"Why would I object?" Chareca batted her eyes.

"Because she's still married." I slumped.

"TAVIO! That's only on paper, and we all know he hasn't lived like he's married for years. He deserves this!" Unique said.

"Do I?" He shot back.

Unique frowned like she didn't understand. "Huh?"

He looked at me, "what if I take you out and you start digging me? I know you; he's not completely out of the picture. I think you should wait until your divorce is final."

"Technically it would've been final a long time ago, he's fighting me." It's not fair cause technically I would've been free by now. I batted my eyes. Since my grandparents are against my divorce they will not help. There's no way I could afford a lawyer on my salary. Tavio volunteered and has made sure that I've had excellent representation. Royce fought the legal separation, he's fighting everything.

"Technical is not actual."

"Fine! Never mind then. When Kyle takes me out, my naivety will show and if he's a bad guy he'll pounce." I said folding my arms.

Tavio stared at me and then he shook his head. "All ya'll females are too emotional. I expected more from you Chareca. You're a married woman."

When he walked out of the room, Unique shut the door. "He's going to ask you out in a day or two. He don't like being put on the spot, but he's going to do it."

"How do you know?"

"I know my brother," she smiled. "Now when he takes you out you should wear something nice but not too sexy."

"You're so sure?" I asked.

Chareca shook her head yes, "I'd put money on it and you know how easily I part with my money."

We went through Unique's closet as she explained why certain things were a good idea. I stepped out of the bedroom to get some more wine from the kitchen. Tavio followed me in, "who's this guy?"

"Kyle," I turned my back so he wouldn't see my big smile. I wanted to be nonchalant, but it was hard now that I can see jealousy on his face.

"What are you doing tomorrow?" I shrugged to say I had no plans. "I'm going to a party at a colleague's, would you like to go?"

"A party sounds fun. What should I wear?"

Tavio walked into my face, "something sexy." Then he kissed my lips. I got butterflies in my stomach.

****

I feel so stupid! I took pictures of everything and sent them to Unique and Chareca. Then we talked about what accessories I should pair with my dress. My dress hit just above my knees. It was black with a gold chain belt. The V-neck in the front showed just enough cleavage. The dress didn't stick to me, but it hung from my curves unforgivingly. Royce would HATE this dress! I paired it with gold and black strappy heels. The heel wasn't as high as I wanted but I can't walk in those shoes, and I don't know how long I would have to be on my feet. I pulled all my locs to the side in a ponytail and I did my makeup simply, but I made sure my lips looked juicy.

Tavio was right on time, and I smiled at him when I opened the door. He was nicely dressed. Tavio smiled at me and then he took my hand and twirled me around. "Alaina, you look beautiful!" Then he kissed my lips.

"Thank you," I smiled as he led me to the curb. A limousine was waiting for us. I gasped and looked at him. "What's this?"

"I told you we're going to a party. Everyone arrives this way." He held the door open for me.

I don't know why I had nervous jitters, but I was quiet at first. Tavio kept talking like he normally does and I relaxed. Then he opened a bottle of champagne and we drank that. The party was in Atherton; I had never been over here before. The houses were big and beautiful. The driver pulled up to the gate, then he gave Tavio's name to the guard. When the limo pulled around there were fancy lights shining in the house and people walking in.

Some of the females, Tavio called them groupies, were barely wearing anything. Tavio held my hand as I looked around completely impressed by his colleague's house. A lot of these guys were like big kids. One guy even pushed a groupie in the pool playing too much. Her weave and everything were completely messed up. There were all kinds of athletes and people in the business here. Music was playing like we were at a club. And there was an open bar. Tavio and I drank lots and lots of Hennessy and we danced a lot. Whenever someone came to speak to him he introduced me. Then a woman came up, she was petite, beautiful, and drunk. "Tavio!" She howled, "it's about time you showed up. How you doing baby?"

"Man! I was wondering where you were. I haven't seen you all night."

"I had to do my rounds, and now it's time to let go." She glanced at me then she did a double take. "You look familiar."

"Lisa, this is Alaina."

"WELL IT'S ABOUT FREAKING TIME!" She threw her arms up and hugged me. "ALL THESE YEARS TAVIO!"

I raised an eyebrow to Tavio. "This is my mentor, she's heard about you over the years."

I had no idea his mentor was a feisty little Asian woman. He never specified, but I always thought his mentor was a man. "It's nice to finally meet you too."

"You better cherish this teddy bear! He..."

"Thank you Lisa, you've said enough."

She put her finger up to her lips, "sssshhhh! Got it captain." Then she started talking to someone else.

Tavio tipped the guy serving appetizers. Then we went back to the dance area. The server came over with drinks for us. As soon as we finished, the server brought more drinks and took our old glasses. I was having so much fun. I had no idea Tavio lived like this. When I couldn't dance anymore Tavio asked if I was tired. I was but I didn't want to go home yet. He asked me if I wanted to go out by the pool.

The environment was calmer out there but I was scared. I grabbed his arm and buried my head into it. Tavio carefully guided me outside and we sat away from the pool in a lounge chair on the grass. Tavio sat first and I laid with my back against him looking up at the beautiful starry sky. Tavio said I shouldn't be this comfortable on a first date, but he'd let it slide.

I figured it was now or never. I took a deep breath as I looked up at the sky, then I looked at the side of his face. I told him I started a blog some months ago. He asked for the name and address so that he could look me up. I told him what my blog was about and then I admitted that I hadn't posted anything in months. He told me that was ok because I didn't have to update it unless I had something to say. I smiled at him and said I've been distracted with another blog. I told him this writer has a lot to say and he's been saying it for years. He didn't act like he understood what I meant. So I quoted him, *"my muse for both day and night fills me with the inspiration to conquer the world."* Tavio blushed hard but he didn't say anything. I told him all these years of being just friends and I didn't realize how he was taking care of me. I thought I was only filling a nurturing roll in his life. I had no idea his feelings ran deeper than that. Tavio continued blushing but he didn't say anything. "The night we watched like two minutes of the porn why did you let me walk out of the room?"

"You weren't ready for me, don't I deserve all of you? I think I've waited long enough to have all of you."

"I love you Tavio, can we go slow?"

"What do you mean?" He looked up at the sky and exhaled.

"From what I've read, you're ready for everything. Wife, family, and everything that means. I want to have the time to get on your level. I've loved you all these years, but it was always put on the back burner for me. It's so intimidating to tell you I love you and not hide behind our friendship. What if you've only loved me like you have because you couldn't have me? What if once we're together you change your mind? You're a good guy Tavio, and I want you to have the space to change your mind."

"Change my mind?" He looked at me.

"You're with Hope remember."

He smirked, "no I'm not. I called her last night. We broke up if you have to call it something. I never considered myself her man."

"Was she upset?"

"Does it matter?" He watched my eyes.

So I kissed him, I hadn't kissed or been kissed like this since high school. Tavio's kiss was strong and passionate. We laid in that chair kissing for a long time, and he asked me if I was ready to leave. I stood up with him and we walked hand in hand by the pool back into the house. Even my fear of the water couldn't take this good feeling away.

Every so many steps someone came to talk to Tavio, it took us about an hour to make it out of the front door. Tavio gave the person at the door his name and they called his limo from Regal Rendezvous over. When we got in the limo he told the driver to stop at my place and then take him home. I grabbed his leg and I told him I wanted to spend the night at his house. Tavio swallowed and asked me if I was sure, cause that wasn't going slow. I smiled and said I only wanted to fast forward to that part. "Driver?" His voice cracked and even the driver laughed. "Please take us to the original pickup location." Then he closed the window between us and him.

Once I started reading all of these open love letters on his blog, I started looking at everything he does and says differently. He's been telling me he loves me for years and I didn't see any of it. I could feel my heart pounding every time I read a new post. He never told me about it so it's not like he did it knowing that I would ever read his true feelings. Every kiss touched my soul in the sweetest gentlest caress.

Let me be honest, I'm so curious to know if it's truly me or if Royce was FULL OF IT! I got nervous when we got to Tavio's house. He settled the bill with the driver and then we both walked very slowly to his front door. I was a little scared as if this was my first time. Tavio turned the alarm off and then he put his key in the door. He stopped and turned to me. "You don't have to do this."

"Yes I do, I need to know."

He shook his head, "if at any point you want to stop all you have to do is say so. There is no such thing as the point of no return when it's me, ok?"

"Ok," I said feeling relieved and I don't know why.

Tavio locked the door, "would you like another drink?"

"No," I want to remember this as much as I can.

Tavio smiled then he looked at me. "MAC we never talked about sex except for that night you told me you were a virgin and the night with the movie. What do you like?"

I shrugged, "that's the thing. I don't know."

"What don't you like?"

"I want the light on, no covers, and I don't want to do it on the bed."

"What's wrong with the bed?"

"It's a dead zone for me."

"Anything else?"

"I don't know." Then I looked around cause I started to get nervous. "Maybe wine would be nice."

Tavio told me to have a seat in the living room and he'd bring a bottle in. Then he went upstairs. I did a complete freak out dance, did I really agree to have sex with my best friend. This is going to be so weird and awkward. I almost want to back out, but then I'm curious to know if it would be any different.

I walked into the living room, and then I decided to go in the family room. I turned on the television and then I sat on the couch. Tavio came in the family room with an air mattress. He blew it up and put a blanket on the couch. He changed his clothes, he was shirtless and he had on sweats that barely hung on to his waist. I kept looking at the mattress trying to see if my brain said that the mattress was a bed or not.

I watched Tavio when he walked back in the room; his lack of shame about showing skin was definitely a step in the right direction. He kept smiling at me as he opened the wine and poured our glasses. Then he stood me up and asked me how would I be comfortable? In my dress, in my underwear, or he could bring me a shirt. I told him I would be back. I went up to his room and I opened his drawers until I found his t-shirt drawer. I took out a wife beater and then I took my dress off and my bra. I left my panties on. I wanted him to take them off. Did I really just think that, I held in my nervous laughter as I looked at myself in the mirror. I asked myself if I really wanted to do this. Royce splashed across my mind and my body went dead. Then I remembered him with his hands all in that woman's stuff. His body pressed into hers, and I no longer felt guilty. I deserved this if nothing else.

I looked at myself in the mirror and I smiled, I was having fun already. Royce didn't even want me walking around the house like this. FORGET ABOUT ROYCE! When I walked into the family room Tavio was sitting on the couch with his legs open watching TV. He looked at me, he swallowed then he smiled. He told me I was beautiful. Then he stood up and asked me where I wanted to sit? I was nervous so I told him I would sit in the recliner for now. He smiled and said ok. We drank our wine and I noticed the condoms on the end table by him. I swallowed and went back to drinking my glass. Tavio started talking like normal, like we weren't about to cross every unforgivable line possible.

Once I relaxed and he had me laughing he stood up and walked over to me. He pulled my hips to the edge of the chair. He pushed my chest back slowly as he watched my eyes. Then he put his hands on my hips and slowly peeled my panties down. He asked me if it was ok, and I shook my head yes. He turned my hips forward and then he licked his lips and asked me if he could kiss me. His eyes suggested a place other than my mouth. I was stuck, Royce never even pretended like it was something he was in to. Tavio waited for my response. I shook my head yes, he licked his lips again and then he kissed me. I looked around the room wondering what I was supposed to feel and then his tongue made contact with me. My eyes bucked and then he did it again. He pushed my legs further apart and then he went crazy on me. His tongue, little nibbles with his teeth, and I think those were his fingers and I couldn't believe when I was moaning out loud. My moans seemed like they encouraged him. He wiped his face on my t-shirt and then he asked me if I was ready? I asked him if there was more? He smiled and then he said of course. I didn't know if there was anything else my body was supposed to feel cause his oral already surpassed anything I ever felt with Royce. He stood up and his sweats were sticking straight out. He grabbed a condom and then I watched him put it on. He hit the recline button on the chair and it laid almost all the way back. He grabbed my ankles and pulled my feet which made me fall back. Then he held my ankles as he watched my eyes as we made contact. He moaned and so did I. The sound of his moan was so erotic to me; I wanted to hear it again. A few strokes in and my body tightened up, I reached out for him cause it scared me and he looked at me like he knew it was going to happen. He told me to lay back and enjoy it. It felt like, like, **LIKE** we became the center of gravity and the point where we connected is where everything was being pulled. My body seized up on me, released, and then it did it again. Everything was happening so fast and oh so beautifully slow. Tavio was stroking me and he told me to say his name, when I did he moaned. I loved that sound it made me seize up again. So I kept saying his name which made him blow and my body go crazy.

Tavio fell back on the floor and then he got another condom. He took the one he was wearing off, and then he asked me how I felt. I looked at him and said, "there are no words!" He smiled and then he kissed me. When he started kissing on my neck he asked me if I could go again. I excitedly said yes, and then he said he had to get me ready.

Although he was still hard it wasn't as hard as it was before. I couldn't help it I stared at his dick. Royce was not circumcised, so Tavio's looked completely different to me. Tavio's seemed more stealthy and made for this job. Maybe it was just Tavio. Tavio sat back on the couch and then he told me to come, he was now at full attention again. He told me to straddle him and then he kissed me for a long time while his fingers teased the rest of my body. As I slowly descended on him he exhaled and I said his name again. He moved my hips showing me what to do and I cried out as I seized again. Tavio smiled then he grabbed a hold of my hips and he lifted himself just above the seat and started pumping me like crazy. I called his name as I exploded again and then he cried out my name, which took me to no man's land. He buried his head in my chest as he exploded. He picked me up and laid us on the air mattress. He changed his condom again and then we made slow love watching each other's eyes. I will never be the same.

Chapter 18

Tavio

Alaina's locs were all over and she's never looked more beautiful to me. I told the little voice in my head that was telling me this is bad to shut up. Alaina stirred and I closed my eyes trying to pretend I was sleep. When I peeked at her she was staring at my body like she was making a mental impression. I closed my eyes again and then she kissed me. "You ain't sleep," then she laughed at me.

I started laughing, "how do you know. I could've been sleep."

"You weren't snoring anymore." She smiled at me.

"I snore loud or something."

"No, actually it was just a little." She blushed as she looked at me again. "Good morning Tavio."

I blushed bigger, "Good morning Alaina."

"About last night," She put the covers over her head.

"Yeah?"

"I think we should talk about it." She said from under the covers.

"Ok, shoot."

She started giggling, "no. You go first."

"Did you enjoy yourself?"

"Un huh," she giggled some more.

"Why are you covering your face?"

"I'm embarrassed!"

"Why? You didn't do anything wrong."

"Yes, but I felt so stupid. I didn't know what to do at times, and I feel like you did everything for me while I did nothing for you. Are you even satisfied?"

"VERY!" I said pulling the blanket off of her face. "Last night was worth the wait." Then I kissed her nose.

"Next time I want to do more for you," she said still blushing.

"Next time? This wasn't a onetime thing," I teased.

"GET REAL!"

"Everyone's going to want to know how everything went last night."

"We're adults we can be honest." She looked around the room, "we didn't do anything wrong. You did everything right Mr. Spellman," she blushed again.

"So you really had a good time last night?" I watched her eyes.

"First of all, I've only seen you with your shirt off a couple of times. I didn't know the whole picture would be so beautiful. You are a walking piece of art. I love that you're not ashamed of showing it."

"I work out too hard to be trying to cover up," I smiled.

"Everything was new, everything felt so, so, so right. You didn't call me MAC once last night."

"You mean all night?"

"Yes, why?"

"I was supposed to be teaching you the ropes. Some other guy shouldn't have come out the gate with a pet name for you."

"You did."

"I also wasn't trying to push up on you. Last night was an Alaina and Tavio night. We can get back to MAC and T once we stop blushing and being bashful."

Alaina sat up, "are you hungry?"

"Yes, after last night I'm starving."

"Come on, I'm going to show you how to make omelets so that you can make me breakfast in bed one morning."

"That's what you like?"

"I think it's what I would like, I've never been pampered. Since you're the pampering kind, I figure I should show you what I like."

Alaina was completely naked and she got up and walked to the kitchen. She was impressed that I wasn't bashful; I was impressed that she didn't try to cover up either. She put aprons on us, and then she showed me how to crack eggs and make omelets. In the kitchen it was normal, fun times with MAC. Well until she turned around and her naked behind was showing. After we ate I asked her if she was sore, and she said she was a little. I told her I would make a bath for her. She was quiet for a minute then she said she normally takes showers. I asked her if she could soak a little for me now, so we could make love this evening. She blushed, and asked me to stay with her.

I ran a bath in my bathroom for her. Alaina stood there taking lots of deep breaths and then she grabbed my arm as she sat in the tub. I pulled her locs up so they wouldn't get wet. I did most of the talking while Alaina soaked. When she got out of the bath we laid on my bed and took another nap. I slept for a little bit but then I couldn't help it. I kept kissing her.

Alaina woke up and we laid there just kissing and kissing. For every time I looked at her and felt like I had to hold back, I kissed her again.

Alaina didn't even close her eyes; she kissed me back and watched me. Then she smiled and asked me what I was thinking. We talked about self-control and how it's been for me all these years. I told her about the things she did that made me want to be all over her and I knew she was choosing to be clueless. She didn't deny my charge, but she listened. We talked for a long time. "You're spending the night right? I realize I suggested it, but you didn't actually say yes or no."

"Of course, that was the point of that bath wasn't it?"

I kissed her again, "yes. We should get up go get your car and clothes for work tomorrow. Then we should go get our boys. We could have dinner together."

Alaina smiled, "sounds fantastic."

When we got to her place, I don't know what happened but I was overcome with desire, and I had to taste her in preparation for tonight. I laid her on her bed and sampled her juices. Alaina was calling my name as she held on to my head. When I stopped there, her eyes got big. She said she's never felt any of this before.

As I drove behind her, I noticed that her car was smoking. When we got to my house. She parked her car and I told her she couldn't drive that car anymore until we got it fixed again. I told her to use my nice car. And since our primary financial focus right now is her divorce, a new car would have to take the back burner. Wesley looked from Alaina to me to Alaina again. He said Rebecca called him yesterday about the conversation I had with Hope.

Alaina didn't say anything she just stood there. I looked in his eyes and asked him what he was asking me. He held back a smile as he said he wasn't asking me anything. He hugged his sister and asked her if she had a good time last night. Alaina said she had a blast and Wesley looked at me and said, *I bet you did.* He kept a smile on his face the entire time we were there. Jerrell talked our ears off about all the fun he had with his uncle and cousins, since Rebecca's little girl is already considered a cousin.

When we got to Tempest's house, she looked me in my eyes like she was looking for something. She asked me who was in the car? When

I said it was Alaina, she got excited and ran out of the door. Tyrek and I shrugged and we followed her out. Tempest had Alaina out of the car and she was jumping around with her arms around her. Alaina kept blushing and asking Tempest what was going on. Tempest told her not to try to play it off cause she could see it all over her. She kept hugging her and telling her she was happy it was her. Lil Tavio asked me what his mom was talking about and I shrugged and told him I didn't know. The three of us stood there looking at that crazy lady as she kept hugging and kissing Alaina on her cheek. When Tyrek had enough he told Tempest to come inside. Tempest was reluctantly going inside the house then she yelled out, "NOBODY LIKED HOPE! SHE WAS WORSE THAN SABRINA!" I laughed and Lil Tavio eyed me like he was trying to put together what his mom was saying.

When I got in the car we started bouncing restaurant ideas off of each other. We had narrowed down our options when the car said my momma was calling. I answered, "what are you doing?"

"I'm with MAC and the boys and we are about to go out to eat. What are you and dad doing?"

"I cooked dinner Dakarai is here with his girlfriend, and Unique and Benson are here. Do you all want to come eat with us?"

"Is there enough food?"

"Of course!"

"Do you have a dessert?"

"That's the one thing I don't have. Could you pick something up and come over?"

"Grandma how about pound cake?" He did that on purpose. He knew I would want something else but if Grandma was expecting something then you had to deliver.

"Of course baby that sounds wonderful, see you in a little bit."

Alaina crossed her legs and sat quietly in the car. In the store, Lil

Tavio took Jerrell ahead with him to the bakery. I told him to meet us in the ice cream aisle. I asked Alaina if she was ok. She said she was but I could see it all over her face. I stopped walking and looked at her. "I'm trying not to be a brat, but how long are we going to stay at your parents? We have things to finish." She bit her lip.

I couldn't help it, I fell out laughing. I had kind of forgotten about turning her on at her place setting the scene for her anticipation. "We don't have to stay all that late. T has school in the morning. We both have to go to work."

"Am I being too ridiculous?" She looked embarrassed.

"Not at all, I feel the same way. I'm just trying not to overload you." Then I kissed her lips.

Alaina turned her head and T was standing there with the cake in one hand and holding Jerrell's other hand. Both of them had their mouths completely open and their eyes bucked. Alaina and I started laughing, but the kids kept their shocked looks. I asked T if he was ok, he closed his mouth and then he smiled devilishly at us as he said yes. I asked T what kind of ice cream he wanted and he said it didn't matter he already got what he wanted, as he walked on with Jerrell who kept looking at us like he didn't understand. T kept his smile as he remained quiet the entire car ride. He kept staring at us like he was going to see something written on our faces.

Once the aroma of my momma's cooking hit his nose T forgot all about us. Unique was smiling when we walked in, when she looked at me and then Alaina she got giggly and she took Alaina out the door. Oh what I wouldn't give to be a fly on the wall for that conversation. Ben smiled at me and then a big grin spread across his face. "What's new son?" My momma said coming in for a hug.

I shrugged, "nothing much."

"There's something, you're glowing baby. Is it that girl, what's her name?" She was trying to remember. "Unique doesn't like her, but at the end of the day it doesn't matter who she likes." She snapped her fingers, "HOPE! That's right, that's her name Hope! Is it her?"

"No momma we broke up last night." Ben sat there cheesing at me while my momma analyzed my appearance.

"I've never known you to be so jovial after a breakup. What's…" Then Alaina and Unique walked in the door. Alaina was blushing and Unique was still cheesing. My momma looked at Alaina and then at me. "THANK YOU JESUS!" She yelled interrupting my dad and Dakarai's conversation. She hurried to Alaina and put her hands on her face as she kissed her cheeks. "I'M SO HAPPY!"

"Grandma! I saw them kissing!" T interjected before he put a forkful of food in his mouth.

Alaina's face drained of all color, while everyone else erupted into laughter. I started laughing, "and this is exactly why we can't tell ya'll nothing. Don't make a big deal out of this. Please give us space."

"SPACE?" My momma and Unique said in unison.

"BOY! Do you know how long I've been waiting for this!" My momma said putting her hands on her hips and getting in my face. I backed up.

"In fairness to your momma son, she has been saying for years that Alaina would be perfect for you."

"Thank you baby! Yes! I'll try not to get overly involved, and I'm happy to see you two are finally seeing things my way."

Unique put her hands out, "you can thank me with cash."

Eventually everyone calmed down as much as they could. When we left they all walked us out to the car, and everyone had cheesy grins on their faces. T sat forward and asked where we were going. He got excited when I said home. We put the kids to bed and then Alaina asked me if it was a good idea to be out all over the house when the kids could walk anywhere we could be? I said it was a risk we'd have to take later on. Alaina looked at the bed. She told me to leave the light on and no covers until we were sleeping. I agreed, and then we made love again. I hadn't felt this since Eva, I love the feeling and I never want to let it go.

Alaina

Getting up this morning was different. I wasn't at my place; I woke up in Tavio's bed. I woke up with butterflies and a feeling I've never felt before. I felt satisfied and I felt content. I wasn't on edge about what Tavio was going to say today, or like he was asking more of me than I knew how to give him. When I got in the shower, I took an extra five minutes in there to cry. I felt too good, and I've never felt this way. Immediately I started thinking of things that could interfere with my happiness.

As I put on lotion, Tavio finally stirred on the bed. He sat up and kissed my forehead. He looked at my eyes and then he asked me what was wrong. I said nothing and then I started crying again. Tavio pulled me into his lap in the middle of the bed. I wanted to protest that he was going to make me late, but I knew that wasn't going to save me. I sat there crying as I pieced together the words in my mind to explain what I was feeling. Tavio patiently waited for me to say. His mouth fell open as I declared that I was too happy and content. I was afraid that something was going to come along and ruin the feeling. Tavio listened and then he started laughing, I didn't expect him to laugh. So I stopped crying and stared at him like he was crazy. He said he was having the same thoughts last night. That's when I smiled and relaxed, I wasn't crazy. Tavio wiped my eyes and told me to embrace the feeling and enjoy the ride; he said that's what he told himself last night.

When I walked out of the room, Jerrell was eating a bowl of cereal and he was already up and dressed. He said T woke him up and poured his cereal. I thought my conversation with Tavio made me late, but T's help made me early. I gave T a hug and thanked him. He smiled big about my applause. I asked him what he wanted for dinner, and T's eyes lit up. He told me he'd text me this afternoon.

As soon as I got back in Tavio's car after dropping Jerrell off, my cellphone rang which rang over the car. It called out that Chareca was calling me. When I answered the phone she barely let me say hello. She told me to please tell her that I didn't call her all weekend cause my date extended over the entire time. When I sat quietly on purpose she screamed into the phone. I couldn't stop gushing about how much fun we had Saturday night at the party. I didn't say anything about the night; I just said that we went over his parent's for dinner on Sunday. "NOW YOU KNOW! YOU BETTER OPEN YOUR MOUTH BEFORE I COME THROUGH THIS PHONE!"

I didn't mean to but I started crying and hard, "I'M FOREVER CHANGED! HOW COULD I EVER GO BACK AFTER THIS? LIFE AS I KNEW IT IS OVER!"

Chareca was quiet for a minute, "it was that good huh?"

I didn't answer that directly, I just went on and on about how I felt. Chareca said she was pulling up to Ben's and she and Unique were going to spend the morning and probably all day talking about me. We laughed and then we got off the phone so that I could walk into the office.

I felt like I was floating, I brought up my computer. I made a cup of coffee and then I got on a conference call with my boss. During our call she told me she needed me to come by the office after my appointment tomorrow. My eyes went to my calendar, and circled in black was my mediation appointment with Royce. I've cancelled so many times. I do not want to see him! They had to just about threaten to take Jerrell away from me for me to give in and agree to tomorrow's date. I already took the class on parent alienation and all of that. I wouldn't talk bad about Royce in front of Jerrell. I remember how it felt when my aunty and my mother got into an argument. Even if the things she said was right, it hurt my feelings that she was talking about my mother. I wouldn't do that to my son no matter how much I hate his father. I told my boss I would come directly after my meeting and then I would come into the office from there.

****

I put on grey slacks and a peach colored blouse. I pulled my locs up on my head into a ponytail. Tavio agreed when I originally freaked out about the appointment to come with me. He buried his head in my bosom and told me he liked my blouse.

We dropped Jerrell off at Wesley's and then we made our way to Martinez. There was an accident on Highway 4, which almost made me late to the appointment. Tavio let me out in front of the courthouse and then he went to find parking. I hurried through the metal detectors just in time to hear the counselor call my name as if he had called it before.

I took a deep breath and then I followed him in to the room where Royce was waiting. Royce's eyes went to my hair and they stayed there for a long time. He didn't say anything but I know he wasn't happy, and I could care less. Royce sat back in his seat as he took in my whole look. His eye twitched as he looked at the small amount of cleavage that my blouse showed.

The counselor went over the paperwork from the courts. He told Royce the amount that he needs to pay me for child support. I asked the counselor if he had the numbers right. Royce didn't say anything. I guess I stopped paying attention to how much money he was making at the bank. I wanted to say that I didn't need his money, but that was not the truth and Royce knew it. I need to buy a new car, and with my current salary and even with the sweet deal that Unique made with me for my rent. I don't make enough to afford very much. I have to stick to my budget always. With Royce's money Jerrell wouldn't want for anything. My son deserves to be able to see a movie with me, or go to Chuck E. Cheese with me when he deserves it. I wanted to say no so badly, but I remained quiet.

The counselor moved to spousal support, and I quickly said I didn't need anything. Royce sat back in his chair and drummed his fingers on the table. When the counselor moved to visitation, that's when the argument started. Royce said he didn't want to wait until the weekends to see his son and then every other weekend at that. I said it didn't matter because he was only seeing his son on the weekends while we were married so I didn't know why it mattered now. Royce isn't a bad father when he's plugged in to being present. I just don't want to have to ask my dad to be the mediator or more than he's already been. I don't want to see Royce any more than I absolutely have to. Outside of his pop up at my house, I haven't had to see him or deal with his disapproving glare like the one he's been giving me since I walked in this room.

The counselor told me that sharing 50/50 custody with Royce wouldn't change the support I receive. That was the amount after the shared time split adjusted the amount. I REALLY have no idea how much money this man makes. I told the counselor that I don't want to see Royce. "What's wrong with seeing me? I'm not the one who's changed the way I wear my hair, and the way I dress. You couldn't wait to get those things in your hair could you? I bet you ran to the shop the day after you decided to pull all this nonsense."

"I want a divorce, I'm not your wife anymore. You can go marry that girl you were all over in the elevator!"

"I don't know what you're talking about." He looked me in my eyes.

I was so shocked I sat there looking at him like he had to be crazy. He slightly flared his nostrils. "Oh so now you're up to lying? I was wondering how you've drug this on for so long. You're lying about everything aren't you?"

Royce calmly looked at the counselor, "I love my wife. I want her to come back to me and to forget all this. She's normally very loving, nurturing, calm, and patient with me. She saw me with someone and then disappeared. She wouldn't come home or talk to me. We haven't discussed anything and then I get served with divorce papers. Alaina, I'm still in love with you. Please come home, and we can start over."

I looked at the counselor, "are we done here?"

"The court order is for joint custody. We need to agree to a schedule."

"How can you ask for him during the week? You're going to have him flip flopping in daycares? That would be too traumatic for him. My dad takes him to preschool for me and picks him up. If for some reason he's sick he stays home with my father because I have to work. I..."

"FINE ALAINA! I would like to regularly have dinner with my son on specific days of the week. Can you at least give me that?" Royce said like he was doing me a favor.

I looked at the mediator completely irritated. When we were done in that room I stood up and marched out. Tavio was waiting in the waiting area for me. Royce looked at Tavio but he didn't say anything. Tavio listened to me go off the entire way to the Concord Bart station where I dropped him off so that he could go to work. He kissed me and told me to do my best to be calm for the rest of the day and that we'd talk about it more when he got home.

When I parked my car, Mandy was getting out of hers at the same time. She said she had to take her baby to the doctor's this morning so she was just now getting to work. I tried to keep my irritation off my face. Mandy yawned loud and hard. "Girl, you know those things are contagious."

"Sorry, the baby has been sick. You remember how it is, sleepless nights and everything. My boyfriend is no real help with the baby either."

Royce was up during the nights helping with the baby so I couldn't say I know how she feels. "This time passes and it does get a little easier. What did you have again?"

"A girl, I named her Arianna."

"That's pretty, I like that."

"Thank you," then she got quiet. I was going to ask her what was wrong but our elevator ride was over. She hurried off the elevator towards her desk, and I went to my boss' office. We went over information and forms she wanted me to go over with my team. We chatted for a little while, and then I told her I was going to grab a bite to eat and then head to my office.

Royce

I sat in my car for a long time trying to get a grip. Alaina kept looking at me like I was nothing. There was no sparkle in her eyes for me. She wasn't looking at me like I was Royce her loving husband. No, I was Royce her baby daddy or something like that. Like I was a mistake from her past. Nothing about all that we shared. We used to have fun together and enjoy each other's company.

My singular decision to increase our family took us from a good place to this. I love my son; I wouldn't trade him for anyone. I wish there was a way we could've had him and been on the same page. I parked my car and then I slowly walked towards the office. I told myself to suck it up and I would try to think of a way to win her back. I'm not giving up; I love my wife more than life. I pulled change out of my pocket to get a soda from the vending machine before I went up to my office. I was counting change when I bumped into someone. Alaina gasped when she saw me and I immediately apologized. "Fine!" She tried to hurry past me.

"Alaina please!" I didn't know what else to say. There were no historical facts to pull from other than how much I love this woman.

"Please what? What do you want from me?"

"I want you!"

"I wasn't good enough, you had me and you still had to have her."

"I messed up, haven't you ever messed up before?" She didn't respond she just stared. People walked past us and noticed the obvious tension between us. "Please come up to my office."

"So that I can embarrass you by screaming at you?"

"It's a floor full of lawyers, we're all loud. You're screaming would blend in with the ambiance." Alaina hesitated, "please!"

She turned around and walked towards the elevators and my heart started pounding. I pressed the sixth floor and no one got on with us. I led the way to my office in the corner. My neighbor was out today. I turned the two chairs in front of my desk towards each other. Alaina looked around my office. She noticed my picture of Jerrell and then she walked towards my desk. I still had our family picture framed on my desk. She didn't mean to smile. I walked towards her. "That was a good day, you remember?" She nodded her head yes. I wanted to kiss her. "I like your hair Alaina. You were right they look very nice on you." She didn't say anything she just looked at me. I moved closer to her and she backed up. She backed up until she was against the wall. I took a step forward into her personal space. "Alaina I love you, and no matter what you will always know that's the truth. I messed up. I messed up big time. I couldn't blame you if you never forgave me, but I'm hoping that you do." Then I leaned in to kiss her, she turned her head and I kissed her cheek then I started sucking on it like I've always done.

"Stop it Royce!" She said weakly.

"I love you Alaina, I'm so sorry. Please give me another chance."

"I can't!" She took a deep breath. "Move!" Then she pushed me backwards. "It's over, fighting me in court is only making me madder. If you really love me let me go."

"NO! I can't do that! I know you; if I let go you will try to replace me with a lesser man. I want, no I need another chance." I followed her out of my office back to the elevators. Alaina crossed her arms and shut her ears. I followed her into the elevator. As she started to walk out to the parking lot she stopped and looked at me. "Tell me what to do."

"You said you love me, let me go."

"I can't!"

"No you refuse to relinquish the control you think you still have over me."

"That's not true, I just told you I liked your hair."

"What about my blouse? Is it too revealing?"

I wanted to say yes. Her softness was right there peeking at me all morning. Turning me on even though I tried to fight it. I even saw the mediator steal a look when she wasn't looking. Vanessa and I have had so many arguments about her clothes that I'm learning to pick my battles. "You look beautiful!"

"Go back inside Royce."

I looked around the parking lot. "Why is someone here you don't want me to see?"

"No! Nothing like that just go back inside."

"I'm not leaving until you do." I watched her get angry. She stormed off with me on her heels. When she chirped Tavio's car I frowned, "where's your car?"

"It needs to go into the shop, but you want to take all my money fighting this stupid divorce!" She looked guilty.

"Good thing you'll be getting child and spousal support." I caught the door before she closed it. "What are you doing here?"

"I came to talk to Karen, MOVE!"

"We're going to be a family again!" Then I moved out of the way.

Alaina

Tavio took the day off work so that he could take care of personal business. He volunteered to chauffeur everyone this morning. We took T to his school so that he and Cara Mia could assist in the office before school.

When we pulled up to Wesley's to drop off Jerrell so that he and William could go over my father's my dad's truck was outside. My dad got out of his truck slamming his door as he marched up to the car. He told me to get out of the car as if I wasn't doing that already. "SO IT'S TRUE?" His eyes looked crazy and he was almost foaming at the mouth. "YOU ARE A MARRIED WOMAN! WHY ARE YOU DOING THIS?" My father screamed at me.

"My marital status is just a technicality! I would've been divorced a long time ago if Royce wasn't playing all these games."

"YOU WERE NOT RAISED TO BEHAVE THIS WAY!"

Wesley hurried out of his front door as Tavio got out of the car. "Dad! I have neighbors, you can't do this out here."

"How can you think you have a leg to stand on mister been dating his girlfriend for years? You have no right to say anything about my life!" I said.

"It doesn't matter what I do in my life, I'm your father!"

"And I'm a grown woman who was miserable in her marriage. You don't care about how any of that affected me. You'd be happy as long as I stuck it out."

"Marriages go through rough patches. You may be having fun with him right now, and that's because it's all-new. Give it time and those same rough patches will appear again. What are you going to do hop from bed to bed? In search of the fairy tale? You need to honor your vows!"

"Mr. Barton..."

My father cut Tavio off, "DON'T YOU EVEN TALK TO ME! I CAME TO YOU MAN TO MAN! NO MAN WANTS THIS FOR HIS DAUGHTER AND STILL YOU LURKED UNTIL YOU FOUND YOUR OPPORTUNITY TO POUNCE ON MY POOR CHILD! NOW ON TOP OF EVERYTHING ELSE SHE'S COMMITTING ADULTERY AND YOU COULD CARELESS!"

"DAD!" I screamed at him! "LOOK AT ME! MY NAME IS ALAINA! I AM NOT ALLISON! SHE DIED YEARS AGO! YOU ARE SO TWO FACED! WESLEY CAN GET DIVORCED! WESLEY CAN DATE AND EVEN HAVE A CHILD OUT OF WEDLOCK AND YOU SAY NOTHING! YOU'LL ALWAYS BE THERE FOR HIM, LOVING AND SUPPORTING HIM! FOR ME YOU HAVE THESE RIDICULOUS DEMANDS!"

"WESLEY HAS BEEN THROUGH ENOUGH! HE DOESN'T…"

I cut him off, "LIKE I HAVEN'T? DADDY? SERIOUSLY? MY TWIN SISTER DIED! MY MOTHER DIED! MY FATHER WON'T LET ME LIVE! WESLEY AND GRANNY SHANE ARE MY ONLY REAL SOURCES OF SUPPORT! The rest of you all judge me like you could have the right to! Do you think because of Wesley's biological makeup that he's suffered more than me? We lost the same things, and we've suffered the same pain. You only validate his! I HATE YOU SO MUCH FOR THAT!"

"OH YEAH! WELL I HOPE YOU FEEL GOOD ABOUT YOURSELF, CAUSE NOW YOU'RE ACTING JUST LIKE YOUR MOTHER!"

Wesley had just gotten Jerrell out of the car when my father said that. As if he could feel my reaction before I did, he grabbed me by the waist as my body moved forward. I don't know what I thought I was going to do to my father. I think I was going to punch him, or kick him. Wesley grabbed me before I could do any of that. "Dad! Please leave!" Wesley said as calmly as he could.

"What kind of man are you supposed to be?" My dad said to

Tavio.

"Mr. Barton, I can see you're upset. Once you've calmed down if you would like to talk to me I'm all for it. You know very well the type of man I am. I don't respect the way you're talking to your daughter right now. You don't like her life choices, ok well that's fine. All this negativity is unnecessary and I will not have this around my woman."

"SHE DOESN'T BELONG TO YOU! YOU HAVE NO IDEA OF WHAT YOU'RE DEALING WITH!"

"Alaina is my woman, and that's the end of discussion. Come holler at me when you've calmed down." Tavio said standing firmly in front of my father.

"DAD! I've asked you nicely, now I'm telling you to leave!" Wesley said still holding on to me.

"HYPOCRITE! YOU'RE TALKING ABOUT ME! YOU'RE ACTING JUST LIKE HER! WHAT ARE YOU GOING TO DO NOW? GO HOME AND DO THE SAME THING SHE DID?"

"ALAINA!" Wesley shook his arms around my waist. Then he let me go and he picked up my son and walked back inside his place.

My father got in his truck and sped off. Tavio hurried to me, but I hurried inside Wesley's place. He turned on the television for the boys. William had no idea of what was going on. Jerrell was very quiet and sitting on the couch very still. "I'm sorry!"

Wesley looked at me with red eyes and then he walked towards the stairs. I followed him up to his room. He paced the floor; "this is not helping me today. Why Alaina? Why do you keep bringing up stuff that I don't want to think about anymore?"

"I'm not lying though, and he's not trying to squeeze you into a box like he does me. You can do no wrong, but I'm supposed to accept my husband cheating on me when I gave him everything in me and it was never enough. I am not the woman for Royce. For me he's all fat and unhappy, for her he's thin again and spending all of his time with her. I'm supposed to rollover and accept that? That's supposed to be my life?"

Wesley sat on his bed holding his head! "Stop fighting about mom, I can't handle it! I don't need flashbacks of finding her. Losing Alaysia, or watching them trying to convince you that Alaysia never was. Mom wanted to try again and dad didn't want to. She was too unstable."

"He couldn't control her so he tries to control me!"

"You both know he can't. Why do you argue with him? You like the drama?"

"No," I hadn't even thought about why I argue. "No one was listening to me."

"*Was* is the operative word. You're with Tavio remember. Stop arguing with him. Things got better between us once I stopped arguing with him. The way he thinks and does things isn't going to always agree with you. You don't have to argue about it, so what if he doesn't approve. You're grown so act like it. Reliving the past won't fix anything about today.

Eva

As soon as Rickie walked into my living room her eyes went to Kiev's picture of me. She silently stared at it for a minute. "That's an intimate picture." I didn't say anything. "Seems like he knows you pretty well."

"It's just a picture," I put my hands out for Quinn.

Rickie watched me hug and kiss Quinn. "Grandmother and I were going through pictures. Quinn looks just like you except she's got her daddy's lips, head shape, and ears."

"That's because this is auntie's baby." I kissed her again.

"Our mother called last night. Can you believe Quincy understands her crazy? He said I handled everything wrong. You and grandmother didn't have a choice. I threw you all together and then I expected a miracle. I made things worse because now you won't deal with grandmother at all."

"Now I know what she thinks of me. It came from her mouth. If I would've been responsible for our mother coming out would she still apologize for her words? She still would've been out of line."

Rickie sat down, "I hope you don't mind that I talked to Mrs. Singleton. I needed to talk to someone and she was the only sensible sounding board I could think of." I shook my head no. "She said this time is about us, more you than me. I'm at a point in my life where I want resolution. I want to take a generation picture for Quinn. I want her to know that despite all of our pasts we fought to survive and we are her legacy."

"You don't need me for that."

"I wasn't done," she smiled. "I want to take a family picture. Our parents are married and we have brothers and a sister. Brenda asks about you all the time. Uncle Clifton told her how important you are. You changed the scope of possibilities for all of them. Our mother told them about your office and this place. She says they're all dreaming bigger now. You escaped when all we see are limits."

"Then she asks you for money."

Rickie nodded as she deflated. "Look! Asking ain't getting. She can ask, she can't demand. My no doesn't stop her from calling me. Sometimes she calls me in the middle of the night crying cause she says she hears me screaming for her. Or she has a flashback of hitting on you. You wouldn't let them break you then. You were strong for me, I wanted to die and you wouldn't let me. So I'm not going to let you become Grandmother. She's not perfect; we've always known that. You used to let her roll off of you. Now you're letting her harden you. Their anger and their hate dies with them. This is not us! You can be guarded but you need to come to California with me."

"Grandmother agreed to go?"

"Well..." Rickie moved her hands. "When I tell her you're going she'll go. She said she would do anything to make up with you."

"She's just afraid I'll stop paying for things."

"Nope, she still has the money from her house. She plans to leave it to you and I."

"Leave me alone Rickie!" I whined.

"No I can't, I know you want to grow your hair back. I know you want to have babies. I know you still love Colby. Your resistance is your only sense of control."

"Please! You're so wrong!"

"So why you gotta go with me and Katrina to get our hair done?"

"I like to watch." I stuck my tongue at her.

"That picture and the way you are with Quinn and Selah."

"I love my babies, and that picture doesn't mean anything."

"Colby?"

"I didn't stop loving him. He wants a family I don't," I looked away.

"What?" Rickie waited for me to say.

"I had a dream the other night. Remember how I told you how everything hit the fan with Tavio's friend and her husband when we went out?" Rickie nodded yes. "We were outside talking. At one point Tavio asked me if I was trying to get back with him. At that moment I told him he was being ridiculous. I haven't been able to stop thinking about it. I mean Vanessa moved back to California, couldn't I move out there and see if there's anything to be rekindled with Tavio?"

Rickie's eyes got big, "but! BUT! Unique said he's dating the cheese girl. She said everyone is really excited about them being together too. Even his baby momma is excited. Why would you interfere?"

"He was mine first, and all of this began because of him. His son is growing and he'll be off to school soon."

"No! Eva! Come on!" Rickie got up in frustration. Quinn and I watched her walk across the room to my sliding glass door. She looked out at my view. "You are so afraid of being happy with Colby that you would sink to such a level. You said yourself that you know Tavio is in love with the cheese girl. Why would you do that to yourself or Tavio? You would ruin the friendship that you two have worked to have. Colby's with that girl and you keep trying to act like you don't care. Meanwhile time is ticking."

"I don't have some invisible clock that I'm marching to."

"YES YOU DO! You're going to play this game so long that you're going to be an old woman with regrets. STOP IT!"

Quinn looked at me like she was looking for a response from me. "Nope, since it bothers you so much, I will continue on." I stuck my tongue at her.

We hung out for a little while and then Rickie went home and I met Kiev downtown to help him get some of his supplies home. He seemed bothered, but he said he didn't want to talk about it. He put the canvas up in the middle of the room. Every time he would attempt to start he'd look back at me and stop. He did this for over an hour. "We're off!"

"Your problem is me?"

"You're holding back, I'm holding back. Let's have it out."

"I'm holding back?" I said pointing to my chest.

"Yes, we both are."

"Then you go first since I have no idea what you're talking about."

He started scribbling on his canvas. "You! You're letting anger, hurt, and confusion consume you. You don't love me, and yet you keep trying to force yourself to be here. Why do you do that?"

"I didn't realize that my being here was a problem. I can go." I stood up.

He started scribbling harder then he threw his chalk across the room. "Don't do that! Be straight with me! What's wrong with you?"

"Nothing's wrong!" I was looking for the shoe I kicked off earlier.

"STOP LYING!" He yelled from his gut.

I stopped moving and looked at this fool who was clearly upset or just crazy. "Since you know so much you tell me."

"You're all over the place. You want to eat, but then you're not hungry. You want to go out, but then you want to stay in. You make plans with me then you cancel."

"Not fair! You've always known that I work."

"Yes, but I do know the difference between when you cancel for work and when you cancel out of indecision. What are you wrestling with? I don't have time for this!"

"I'm not Faye who walks around bluntly telling everyone everything. I didn't realize I was sending you such mixed signals. I'll just…"

"TELL ME WHAT YOU WANT? WHAT'S WRONG EVA?"

"I DON'T KNOW!" I found my shoe.

Kiev picked up his canvas and threw it across the room. "YOU'RE DRIVING ME CRAZY! I HAD NO IDEA YOU WOULD

BE SO INSECURE AND UNSURE OF YOURSELF! WHAT
HAPPENED TO THE STRONG SEXY YOUNG LADY I FIRST LAID
EYES ON?"

It was like he was pouring salt on wounds I didn't even realize
were there. "GO TO HELL KIEV! This isn't all on me!" I pulled my
corporate calm tone as I took slow deep breaths. "You want to take me
out knowing you can't afford to take me out as much as you're asking.
You've had your panties in a bunch since your wallet got stolen that day.
Money is not an issue to me, but it appears to be to you."

"It's not an issue to you cause you got it. I have to work very
hard for the little bit I get. You drive around here in a spaceship wearing
clothes I've never heard of. Taking trips to Aspen and places like that.
You're black Eva, we don't volunteer to go to the snow!"

"Ooh! That is such a stereotype! You've never been on a ski trip
so how would you know? I've never asked you to buy me anything,
you're the one making a big deal out of it."

"I have nothing to give you!" He said getting to the root of his
issue.

"We aren't about money."

"Right, I'm supposed to be your Oasis away from everything,
but you're turning me into the problem."

"I'm turning you into, sounds like you're doing a lot of that on
your own buddy."

"I said we're both off."

"What else?"

"Faye, we've been talking and…" he took a breath. " She needs
me and I'm torn."

"We always talked about you two getting back together."

"Yes, but I don't want to leave you hanging. You need to get over this hurdle in your life so that you can start living again. It's time, don't you think it's time?"

"I don't know how."

Kiev put a new canvas on the easel, "come here." When I did he told me to take my shoes off. Then he stripped me down to my underwear and he did the same. He put chalk in my hand then he held on to my hand. "Which way would you like to stroke first?"

"I don't know how to do this." I said honestly intimidated by the blank canvas.

"I'll guide you, do one heavy line for the pain. It can be as big or as small as you want it to be." I slowly moved our hands across the canvas. "How did it feel?"

Tears burned my eyes, "all I see is a line." I said honestly.

"It's ok, I have different eyes, you'll see what I see in a minute. Next stroke, do you want heavy or light?"

"Heavy!" I made a slightly lighter line all crooked below the line.

"Just go, go until you can't." He held my hand as he made lines on the canvas like I was slicing it. I made chopped and symbolic gashes all over the place. Then I started crying, I didn't even know where the tears were coming from. "It's ok, what do you see."

"MY **BABY**!" I screamed and then I fell to my knees. Regret and pain were all over me as I cried from a place I didn't know existed. "Why? How could I have been so stupid? I killed all possibility of life! I died on that table! I don't deserve to be happy! I don't deserve to be loved! I don't deserve anything! My sister is the only person to love me, and I didn't even know how much. I thought she hated me and judged me. I never thought of her actions as protective. How can I love another child when I hated the one before?"

"Eva, plenty of women move on to have healthy families."

"I didn't lose my baby, I killed it! Tavio's situation was just as bad as mine and he made it work. His son is alive and well, he doesn't regret like I do." I screamed! "His son looks at me like he knows something."

"Eva, he doesn't know."

"I know you're right, but my heart hurts when I see him. My child would be a preteen."

"Eva, watch the board. I want to show you something." I cried as I looked at the easel. "All of this is your pain, look at it." I looked at all the angry lines all over the canvas. "Give me your hand." He took my hand with the chalk and he made waves to make most of it water. My angry vertical slices became flowers, reeds, and trees. My anger became a beautiful lagoon. With a paddleboat sitting in the middle. Kiev asked me who goes in the boat. Tears came to my eyes as I said my baby does. He drew a little baby looking over the side smiling at its reflection in the water. He signed it in the corner and then he told me to do the same and to date it.

I got dressed and then I hugged Kiev goodbye. He told me to call him when I got home. I didn't wait for framing on this one. I put my picture on the wall and I stared at it as I cried and cried. It was almost midnight, when I reached for the phone and I called Colby. I didn't know if he was at work, home, or what. He answered the phone wide-awake. I asked him if he was busy. He said he was at work. He asked me if he could come by when he got off. I hesitated and then I said yes. Colby came around four. I showed him my picture and I told him I was so lost. He stared at the picture for a long time. Then he said I was taking a step in the right direction. I told him I needed more time, and if he ended up married I understood. Colby kissed my forehead, and then he said he'd talk to me later.

Chapter 19

Alaina

T and I were at the grocery store, getting stuff for dinner when my cellphone rang. It was Royce, and although I didn't want to talk to him he had Jerrell. So he knew I would pick up, "hello?"

"I don't understand what Jerrell is telling me."

"What do you mean Royce?" I threw the bananas in the cart.

"Why are you telling Jerrell your last name is not Chambers?" I sighed but I didn't say anything. "YOU ARE STILL MY WIFE! STOP THIS NONSENSE!"

"Where's your girlfriend? Ask her to take your name. I don't want it."

"Where are you?"

"Out! What do you want?"

"Jerrell said he's ready to come home."

"Take him to Wesley or my dad, I'll get him in a little bit."

"He said he wants you!"

"He will have me, in a little bit."

Royce put Jerrell on the phone. "Mommy?" He sounded upset.

"What's wrong baby?"

"I want you!" He cried.

I looked at T who was watching my mouth. "Is daddy being mean?"

"No, I want **YOU**!" He cried some more.

"Ok, I'm coming. Put your daddy on the phone."

"Hello?"

"Why is Jerrell crying?"

"We were going over his homework and tracing his name when he started crying saying that you are not a Chambers."

"Where are you? I'm coming right now."

"Hunan Villa in Pinole, you remember. How long will it take you to get here?"

"Ten minutes," I said releasing the cart.

"I'll pay the check and meet you in the parking lot."

I told T we would come back to the store and we needed to go. "Baby do you ever want to go back to your mom's when you're with your dad?"

"No, I love being with my dad."

"What about when you're at your mom's?"

"No, I have my little brothers and sisters there. Plus I like spending time with Tyrek."

"Jerrell is too little to understand everything that's happening."

"Jerrell is crazy, he always makes girl toys beat up boy toys." T laughed.

I felt guilty cause I knew that is his reaction to seeing me hit his father. "They never get along?"

"Only when he's playing us. The roller is you, the domino is my dad, I'm the coin, and he's the boy. We're always in a car going somewhere. Sometimes he tells me I can't play with him. He likes to play that game by himself."

"What does that mean?" I shook my head.

"Nothing he's just crazy is all." T laughed, "MAC."

"Yes baby?"

"I love coming home to you. I don't like Royce! I want you and my dad to get married."

A heat wave hit me, "married?"

"Yes, you've always been like a mom to me anyways. My momma is so excited that she was telling my aunt about you and everything. My grandma and everybody is so excited. Cara Mia said when you and my dad get married that will make us cousins. Is that true?"

"Well, um! Uh! Uh!" My mind went blank for a minute. "Not by blood, you two could still get married."

"MARRIED?" His eyes got big and he looked how I felt. "Cara Mia is my best friend, I can't marry her!"

Now I started laughing, T didn't laugh he just looked at me. "I'm sorry baby, I was just saying." I guess he has no idea that Chareca and Ken refer to him as their future son-in-law.

T swatted the air like something tasted nasty. "Yuck!"

Baby boy did a good job of taking my mind off of the fact that I was going to see Royce. When we pulled into the parking lot Royce was holding Jerrell in one arm. With his backpack and jacket in the other. As soon as Jerrell saw T his face lit up and he wiggled until his father put him down. He ran to T even though Royce tried to tell him not to run in the parking lot. The car door opened and then Royce's father got out and hurried to me. As soon as I saw him I got excited and like Jerrell I ran to Mr. Chambers. He gave me a big hug and then a kiss on my forehead. He rubbed my back as he said he was sorry his son is an idiot. I didn't expect Royce to tell his dad, but I can't say I know what I expect from him anymore. "Who's car are you driving?"

"Oh that's Tavio's my car needs to go in the shop. As soon as that idiot stops fighting the divorce I can put it in the shop."

"So you've filed for divorce?" He looked at his son while he asked me.

"Yes, and he's not cooperating." I cut my eyes at Royce.

"Well now can you blame him, at least he knows you're worth fighting for." Then he looked at T, "how you doing son?"

"Hello," T said standing by the car listening to everything while Jerrell kept laughing and punching him.

"Where's Tavio?" Mr. Chambers asked me.

"He comes back tomorrow," I reached for Jerrell's things.

"Alaina, please come home."

"No! Can I have my son's things so I can get going?"

"What are you doing for money? You living off spousal support?"

"No I don't want his support, I have a job."

"Where?" Royce interjected.

I looked at Mr. Chambers, "I'll call you later."

Mr. Chambers' eyes turned sad, "Alaina." He looked at his son, "fix this!"

"Dad! I'm trying! She's not trying to give me another chance. She saw me talking to another woman and she flew off the handle."

I sucked my teeth; "you two were basically having sex on the elevator."

"Royce!" His voice sound so hurt. "You are your mother's child."

I looked at Royce and he looked like his dad just ran him over with his words. Royce always tries to suck it up, but his father's words hurt him no matter what. "I messed up, but she's not even trying to hear me out or work with me. She cut me off like she was done with me long before this."

"Were you?" Mr. Chambers asked me.

"No! The timing of everything. He up and puts my house on the market. He moves to Walnut Creek without a care about how that would affect me."

"Sell the house, come back! Why would you go with all of this happening?"

Royce walked closer with his hands out like he was approaching peaceably. "The house I bought for our family is way nicer than that Berkeley house. I want something nice and better for our family. I didn't put our house on the market until I was out of escrow for the new house. You know how you surprised mom with the house she has now, I was copying you. I knew once she saw the house she'd be in love, but then I messed up."

"Have you at least seen the house? Half of it is yours at least." Mr. Chambers looked at me.

"No," Mr. Chambers looked so sad. "I'll think about it."

Royce looked surprised then he smiled, "thank you."

Royce

"Dad! You have to be there when she comes!" I said excitedly in the car.

"No," he said weakly.

"WHAT? You have to be there! Alaina respects you, she will

listen to you. She won't listen to anything I have to say. You've got to be there."

"Did you ever stop to think that maybe I know her pain? That maybe the ONLY reason I asked anything of her tonight is for my grandson? You are selfish and a real piece of work. I see you trying to skate around what you did. You only partially admit to it because she caught you. You'll act just like your mother and try to deny the truth even when you're caught. I hung in there with your mother because I didn't want my kids bouncing off of emotions like Jerrell is. He didn't show happiness until he saw that little boy. You want your wife back? Be a good father to your son. The son you wanted! Even if she don't take you back, your son didn't ask to be here. He didn't choose such a father. Be good to him."

"I am good to my son." I rubbed my beard.

"Alaina was different, I don't know that you'll ever get her back. You obviously hurt her too badly." He was quiet for a minute. "Does that little boy come around often?"

"Yeah, Alaina would keep him for Tavio from time to time. Why?"

"Why was he listening to everything?"

"That nosey little punk is always listening like that."

"Listening and reporting back to his father?"

"Probably, it's not a secret to me or anybody else that Tavio has a little crush on Alaina. My wife is loyal, and as long as she's married to me she wouldn't take another man."

"That's why you're dragging out the divorce?" My father looked at me like I'm stupid.

"My wife is coming back to me!"

"She don't even like you, I don't know how you think she's

coming back to you!"

"She don't have to like me to love me. Love conquers all."

My dad smiled, "I liked her hair. She looks so free."

"You would like her hair. She's wanted those things for years. They don't look bad like I envisioned, they're just not my taste."

My father gave me the side eye, "you're an idiot you know that."

"Why do you keep talking to me like this?" I pulled into his driveway.

"Cause it's the truth! I am only agreeing to go because of my grandson. I'm not going to defend you, or help you try to trick that girl. Time is almost up; I will be coming for my money too. Don't make me take you to court."

When I got to Vanessa's place, she was in the kitchen with her mother unpacking groceries. They were talking about the pros to living in California. Vanessa kept pointing out the weather. Her mother kept pointing out the earthquakes. Her mother hadn't decided if she was moving out here or staying out there yet. So these debates were always the topic of discussion whenever I was around. "Baby please tell her about your pool."

"I have a heated pool, you can swim in it all year round." I smiled, and then I kissed Vanessa's lips.

"Vanessa keeps saying all these wonderful things about your house, but I haven't seen it yet."

"That's because it's still being remodeled. My sister stays with me to help out when she can. You'll see it soon."

Eva

My phone rang at two o'clock in the morning. My heart sped up;

cause calls at this time of night were never any good. "Hello?" I said trying to take the sleep out of my voice.

Rickie was crying, "Eva, I'm so sorry for calling you so late. Quincy's father is in the hospital! We need to go back to Daytona. Can you help us with emergency airfare?"

"Of course!" I sat up and then red alerts went off in my brain. "WAIT YOU CAN'T GO TO DAYTONA! JAMES IS OUT THERE!"

Rickie blew air, "please! We were homeless in Daytona, and we never saw James. No one is worried about him. Quincy is really upset about his dad."

Now I started crying, "Rickie! You're all I got!"

"Quinn is going to stay behind with grandmother, can you help her out in the evenings?"

"How long are you going to be gone?"

"Hopefully only a week."

"Please be careful Rickie, you're all I got." I started panicking.

I went over in the morning to take Rickie and Quincy to the airport. Quincy's eyes were puffy and he kept promising he was going to pay me back. I gave Rickie cash and I told her I transferred money to her account so that they could get a nice hotel room and rental car. These people who let my sister and brother in-law be homeless were not going to get a second chance to make them feel unwelcomed. Rickie hesitated like she wanted to tell me she didn't need it, but we both knew she did. She hugged me tight and said thank you. I went to work early since I was up and I needed to leave to have time with my niece. I called Katrina and asked what time she was leaving so that we could let the girls play together. She told me to come over whenever since she was working from home today. I texted my grandmother telling her I would pick up Quinn around 3.

I talked to Vanessa a few times about business and then we

chatted a little about things in California. I told her that we were all coming out shortly. I didn't think it was funny, but apparently it was funny to her how Rickie convinced me to go. She told me to give her dates and she'd make sure her mother was there so that we could have a big dinner together. "Is your boyfriend going to be there?"

"If he doesn't have his son he will be here, maybe his sister too."

"I don't like him, you could do so much better." I tried to pull back my irritation.

"We're grown Eva. I know it's somewhat of a conflict of interest for you. Please just be my friend." I exhaled, "and don't tell my mom." Then she laughed, I didn't.

"I'm not seeing Kiev anymore."

She was quiet for a minute, "why?"

"Our season has passed."

"What does that mean? Is he hurt? Did you break his heart?"

"Whoa! Whoa! No, nothing like that." I took a deep breath. "Faye just had a baby and she needs him."

"WHAT?" She screamed into the phone. "He can't have any more kids."

"Faye has a friend who wants children but he and his partner can't have children. So they're going to co-parent."

"What about financial support?" I could hear worry in her voice.

"Faye and her friend have that covered. Call your cousin and talk to him."

"You're really not going to be my cousin?" Vanessa sounded disappointed.

"Aw! Boo! We always gonna be family."

504

I zipped through the rest of my day and then I went to pick up Quinn. She was napping as I put her car seat in my car. My grandmother has stopped apologizing, now she waits on me to say what I need or want. I only talk to her when I need to. She told me to feel free to call with any questions if I needed to. When Quinn woke up she got so excited when she saw me. She wanted me to hold her immediately. I asked her if she wanted to go with me and she got excited. This is the first time I'd have Quinn overnight all by myself. I told myself to take it minute by minute. Quinn seemed up to the challenge.

When we got to Katrina's, Selah started laughing excitedly as soon as she saw Quinn. The two of them played nicely in the play corner with Selah's stuffed animals. Katrina said they were going to start trying soon for baby number two. We talked about work and as we talked Colby walked in the room. He immediately looked at his sister like she needed to explain. Katrina smiled at him until a woman appeared behind him. It was her! Everything everyone has said about her was true. She's pretty and seemed to have a bubbly personality. She smiled at me as she waited for an introduction. "This is Eva." Colby said plainly and her smiled disappeared.

Then she caught herself. "Hi I'm Corrine, it's nice to meet you."

"Likewise," I said watching her.

"I'll be back," Colby said walking out of the room.

Corrine stood there awkwardly for a minute. "So..." She looked around the room for a conversation piece.

"Come in," Katrina told her. "Have a seat, get comfortable."

"Where did Colby go?" I asked.

"Chauncey," they said in unison.

"I'm sorry, but we are nothing alike. I always assumed that you were like me and that Colby had a specific type."

505

Corrine stared at me like she expected a response. "You're looking to me to address your assumption?"

"When did you have a baby?"

I blank stared at her, "if Colby didn't tell you about her why should I?" Now I know I was being messy by leaving that open like that. Ask me if I cared, this light skinned Barbie walks in here like I could never be good enough to live in Colby's heart.

She looked at Quinn and then she looked at me, she sat there quietly. Katrina did her best to try and engage both of us. Just when I was about to say that Quinn and I were leaving Mrs. Singleton came over. She said hello to Corrine then she came and hugged me. She hugged me tight and started talking to me like no one else was in the room. Then she gave Selah and Quinn hugs and kisses. Not knowing about my insinuation earlier it did seem like Quinn received the same love that Selah did. I stepped just outside the room when Rickie called me to check in. She said they got their room and they've been at the hospital ever since. She said her father in-law is worse off than Quincy's family let on. Then she said thank you over and over for having the foresight to make sure they had their own accommodations. She said Quincy's brother is so rude and he's the reason they rather had slept in their car than be mistreated by him and the ones too weak to stand up to him. She said one of the first things out of his mouth when he saw them was that James had been asking about her. I felt a little dizzy. Rickie told me not to flip out cause everything was going to be fine. I told her to be careful about where they went cause word always tends to spread fast about negative things. She said ok, and then we got off the phone.

I walked back in the room just as Colby was picking Quinn up in his other arm. He took both of the girls to the opposite couch from Corrine and Mrs. Singleton and he sat down. He sat there smiling at them, since I don't care about Corrine, especially at this point, I sat on the same couch as Colby. He looked at me for half a second and then he went back to the girls. It was all over Corrine's face that she was not happy about me sitting so close to Colby but I didn't care. Mrs. Singleton looked away and started talking to Katrina who was watching us with big eyes. Corrine stopped talking and openly stared at me like I was crazy.

Finally Colby announced that he and Corrine were leaving. The girls were not happy to be separated from him. Quinn especially cried in protest. I smiled at Colby as I saw the girls pulling at his heart. As soon as they left, Katrina asked me what was going on. Mrs. Singleton showed no shame about waiting for my answer either. I told them things have been changing in my world. I finally told them about what I only told Colby. I told them what happened in college and Katrina said she didn't understand how I kept that from her. I told them how Colby and I have been talking on occasions and he's been helping me work through all of my many emotions around the whole thing. Mrs. Singleton smiled real big at me as if she could hear me say that I was coming around to the idea of a family.

After a while, I packed Quinn up and then we went back to my place. Even though I live in a high security building, and I park in a monitored garage. I felt vulnerable as I carried Quinn, her diaper bag and my purse inside. My arms were completely full and Quinn was dependent on me to keep her safe. When we got inside my place, I heated up the food Rickie sent over. Quinn and I ate then we sat and stared at each other. I smiled when my phone rang, it was Colby. "So, you're letting your hair grow back?" Colby asked me.

"Every day I debate whether I should just cut it or let it continue to grow." Quinn grabbed the phone and started talking as if she didn't see Colby earlier. "Are you two in for the evening?"

"YES!" I got excited.

"Can I bring you anything?"

"Maybe some popsicles."

"Ok, see you in twenty."

I got excited and I started dancing around which made Quinn laugh and get up to join me. When Colby came he played with Quinn, and then we all sat and watched TV together. Quinn fell asleep in my arms cuddling with me. Colby smiled down at her and asked me if I realized that the current events set me up, and then he kissed me.

Tavio

I heard Alaina moan my name and it woke me up out of a dead sleep. I looked around my hotel room trying to remember where I was. I sat there for a minute pulling myself together. Thoughts of Alaina flooded my brain and I had a good laugh at how sprung I felt even when I'm thousands of miles away from her. I looked at the clock and it was just before midnight here on the east coast so that meant it was just before nine, Jerrell is in the bed. I called Alaina as I sat on the edge of the bed in the dark. "Hello?" She said just above a moan.

My whole body came alive, "what are you doing?"

"Watching one of your movies thinking about you."

I wiped the drool from my mouth. "Wait a minute! How you gonna watch without me?"

"I was curious," she said shyly.

I turned on the light; I was looking for my laptop. "I need to see this, turn on your computer. Skype me."

"Ok," then she hung up. I dove for my laptop. I connected the power cord to make sure I didn't have any problems. I was completely turned on and excited. When Alaina's call came in she smiled shyly at me. "So you just want to watch me watching the movie?"

"Yep!" I traced the curves of her face on the screen.

Alaina's eyes were glued to the television like she was watching an action packed film. She blushed a few times and then she looked at me. She turned off the TV then she asked why I wasn't sleep. I told her that thoughts of her woke me. Alaina smiled and said she was thinking of me too. We talked for a little bit then she told me I needed to rest cause we couldn't have me missing my flight home in the morning.

******

I caught Bart to McArthur Bart Station and the Emeryville transit *EmeryGoRound* to Alaina's office. The guard downstairs gave me a badge and told me which way to go once I went up. Alaina was standing in the middle of the floor listening to someone talk. It was a friendly conversation, and then I saw the guy I was supposed to be the warm up act for. He was looking at me trying to figure out who I was. I knew it was him cause he was all in their conversation from his cubicle. Plus, he was the only person to notice me. He walked and extended his hand for a shake introducing himself. The sound of my voice saying hello caught Alaina's attention. She smiled with desire in her eyes. She walked away from the person she was talking to without ending their conversation. The woman stood there for a little bit frowning then she walked away. "Kyle this is my man Tavio," Alaina said proudly.

"Nice to meet you," then he walked away.

Alaina hurried to her desk and then she told someone she was going to lunch. She turned our five-minute drive to my house into a two-minute drive. We didn't even make it out of the garage. I could get used to this type of homecoming. Alaina kissed me and then she said she'd be home after she picked up Jerrell. I crawled up the stairs completely spent and I took a long nap.

I woke up to the sound of T coming in the front door. He came up the stairs and straight to the door. He stood still trying to see if I was awake. "Hey son how was your day?"

"Ok, how was your trip?" He looked concerned.

"It was good, come rap to me." I rolled over as I patted the bed. T came and sat on the bed. I focused my eyes and then I looked at my son. "What's wrong?"

He took several deep breaths. "Have you talked to MAC?"

"About?" I watched his face looking for a suspension, a broken window I have to pay for, something.

"So the other day, Jerrell was supposed to have dinner with his dad, but he started crying for his momma. MAC didn't want to go but Jerrell was crying. When we got to the restaurant Mr. Chambers was there."

I frowned, why was he being so formal? "Royce?"

"No, his dad!"

"Oh," I went back to listening.

"Long story short, Mr. Chambers got MAC to say she would go over Royce's house."

I frowned, "what she need to go over for?"

"I don't know, but I think he's going to try to kiss her."

"He better not even try it!"

"Did I do good by telling you?" He watched my face.

"Of course, thank you for the heads up."

"Royce thinks MAC is still his woman."

"You can't worry about what idiots think. Are you ok?"

"I wanted to say something but I didn't know if you would be mad."

"You did good, it takes a good amount of self-control to remain quiet when you don't want to. I'm proud of you."

"Can we have pizza for dinner?"

"Sure."

"Can Cara Mia's family come over?"

"If they don't have plans that would be fine." T shot up, "where you going?"

"I gotta clean my room." Then he called out from the hallway, "Cara Mia makes a big deal about my room."

I texted Alaina and I told her about T's plan. She asked me to get Jerrell and then she'd go to the store and get stuff for salad and things like that. I got to Wesley's place at the same time he did. We were standing by his car as he told me about his day at work.

We were out there for a while when his father pulled up. If looks could kill I would be dead. His father got out of his truck and let the boys out. Then he walked up on me with fire in his eyes. He asked me what kind of man am I supposed to be? I looked him in his eyes and told him he knew exactly what type of man I am. He said Alaina was not ready for me and he knew I knew it too. Wesley told him that he was assuming and the fact that we were together suggested that maybe she could be ready. He scoffed at us and said we were smarter than that. Neither one of us were new to relationships, and we know how the healing process goes. He said I stooped to being a rebound guy instead of the mister right. Wesley told his dad even if that was the case his behavior only made the situation worse. He asked his father to chill out and to stop flipping out. Especially while he was planning his own future with someone else. Mr. Barton told Wesley that he will never be their equal and he will always be their father. It didn't matter what he had going on in his life, he could still point his children to right and wrong. Wesley started breathing heavy, and then he said that thinking is exactly why they had problems when his mother died. He told his father to lead by example and if he couldn't then he needed to shut up. I took a step back but Wesley was beyond pissed. He told his father he needed to get the point, that no one would give credit to a hypocrite. He said his father could point out every wrong and have valid solutions but since he does not have freeness of speech no one will ever listen to him. He said Mr. Barton is acting like he kept Alaina in the middle of a congregation. The death of his mother revealed a lot of their hypocrisy. He said that Mr. Barton should be happy Alaina allowed him to control her during her formative years. He said he needed to approach her as a young woman who's been married to someone who did not make her happy. You keep trying to strong arm her and you're going to lose her forever doing that. Mr. Barton fussed some more then he got in his truck and drove away. Jerrell and William played in the grass by Wesley's door. Wesley took a deep breath then he told me to be careful.

When Jerrell and I got to the house we heard T whimper. We raced up the stairs to T's room. It was tore up worse than when he began. He was standing in the middle of the room looking overwhelmed. I asked him what happened, and he said he decided at the last minute to change his room around and everything got out of control. Jerrell volunteered to help him and his little self-got to work immediately. T started moving faster with the help of Jerrell. I walked away cause I didn't want anything to do with all of that.

I heard the garage, and then there were voices. I opened the door to the garage and Chareca was coming in with her girls and Alaina. Chareca kissed my cheek hello and then she said Ken was coming straight from work. Cara Mia and Kendall went upstairs and you could hear Cara Mia fussing as soon as she saw T's room. I explained what happened to the girls and they started laughing. We were all in the kitchen sipping when Alaina's phone started ringing. It was next to me so I handed it to her. The Caller ID said that it was Royce's father. Alaina answered the phone and then she excused herself and went out to the backyard. "So…" Chareca smiled at me. "How are things?"

"Great! How about you?"

"You know what I'm talking about." She smiled bigger at me.

"I thought girls talked about things like this."

"We do, but you know I'm supposed to probe and then report everything you say."

"Well in that case, I could use more sex and more food."

"I thought you two were at it all the time?"

"We are, but does an addict ever get enough?"

Chareca blushed, "I am so happy for you two. Ken is having a hard time with all of this. Just an FYI."

"Why?"

"He understands why and all of that, it's just that even though Royce hasn't been much of one over the last few years. Ken still considers himself a friend to Royce. I guess he feels stuck in the middle."

"Right is right," I said.

"Sometimes right is determined by perspective."

Alaina came back inside as the doorbell rang. She went to the front door and let Ken in. They hugged and then they came into the kitchen. I asked Alaina if everything was ok. "Yes, Mr. Chambers wants to spend time with Jerrell and I tomorrow." She had a guilty look on her face.

"What are you going to do?" I asked waiting for her to tell me how Royce fit into this.

"Probably talk about his son. I told him we'd spend the day with him. He's going to pick us up in the late morning tomorrow."

"Where are the kids?" Ken asked looking around.

"Upstairs in Lil Tavio's room, you don't hear Cara Mia barking orders?" Chareca asked Ken as she watched his face.

Ken stood behind the counter next to his wife. "Let me say my peace and then I'll leave you all alone."

"Hold on, let me order the pizza first." I said flashing a smile. I ordered a bunch of pizzas to make sure everyone's topping preference were represented. I got Ken a shot glass and then I told him to relax and then speak his mind.

Ken had two shots, "I'm not trying to be a kill joy. I'm caught up in a conflict of interest here. Alaina and I are friends, and over the years Tavio we've become friends as well. Before all of you were even known to me I was friends with Royce. We've been close since he moved out here. I know he hasn't been right for the past few years, but one thing I do know beyond a shadow of a doubt is how much he loves you. He's going to be devastated once he finds out about all of this."

"If he loves me so much why did he do it?"

"I don't know Alaina, remember I was in the dark just like everyone else. I don't know what he was going through." Ken looked at me, "how far is all of this going to go?"

I looked him in his eyes, "as long as she'll have me, we're going all the way."

Alaina gripped the counter, "don't make me have to choose between my childhood friend and you."

"You already have," I said plainly waiting for him to get it.

"SON OF A…" Ken caught himself right as Cara Mia walked into the kitchen.

"Hi daddy," the joy of catching her father slip up was all over her face.

"Hi angel, how was your day?" Ken looked so guilty everyone snickered to hold back their laughter.

"It was good, Tavio's room will be done in a little bit. Everyone has their orders and I told them I would be right back to inspect their work." Then she looked at me, "Big Tavio. Can we have some water bottles because we're going to be thirsty in a little bit?"

"Of course," I gave her what she needed. Then she looked at her father and smiled before she went back up the stairs.

When the pizzas came, the kids came down and ate. Kendall was determined to keep up even though she was littler than Jerrell. The kids went upstairs and the girls talked us into watching a chick flick. Chareca and Ken were on the love seat and Alaina and I were on the couch. When the guy was all messed up in his head and unintentionally stringing the girl along, Chareca sat up and looked at Ken. "Baby thank you for never doing that to me. You've always made it clear how much you love me and our family. You've always been here for me, and you didn't leave me guessing ever about your love for me. Thank you for always being faithful to me, and to our family. I love you so much!" Then she kissed him and their kiss went on and on.

Alaina picked up the pillow by her feet and threw it at them hitting both of them in the head. "Get a room! Nobody cares!" She laughed.

"Hater!" Chareca said as she laughed.

"I got one better," then she paused the movie. She sat up and looked at me. "Tavio I will always be your MAC! I had no idea that you could see the average me that I've always been. Looking through your eyes makes me feel like I've been more than who I've always been, just an average girl from Richmond. You have freed me of the enslavement of average and you've given me the best any woman could ever have. Peace, faith, hope, love, patience, and orgasms." Ken slumped, "deal with it Ken. Your friend is evil! I'm FREE now, and you're friendship has done that for me. I can now relate to Chareca and Unique about their feelings for the men in their lives. I never thought I would ever feel anything like this. I love you Tavio, thank you for never agreeing to be my brother. That would make all of this so wrong!" Then she kissed me.

"We can't let them have all the fun!" Ken declared as he stood up and made Chareca stand up with him. "I knew from the moment that you flowed right with my crazy and accepted my application to be your man that I had to have you. Girl! The first time you let me in I felt like my head was going to pop off. Every time we do it is like the first time for me. You're still as crazy today as you were when we were kids, and even when I try to act like I don't like it I love it. Being with you has grown me up so much, you made my relationship with my momma that much tighter for me. You're my baby momma, my wife, my lover, and my best friend! Tonight we're pulling out all the stops, you will be walking funny tomorrow."

Chareca got excited, "YOU PROMISE?" We all laughed so hard. Then they kissed with Ken's hands all in Chareca's butt. "It's your turn," Chareca said to me.

"How could I ever follow up something like that?" I searched my brain for a minute. "You notice that I rarely call you MAC since our date?" The realization spread all over Alaina's face. "MAC was my friend that I had to hold back with. Alaina is my woman, Alaina is my lover, Alaina is my heart. I love you more than any words could ever express, so I'll just express my love with a kiss, and a smack, and an orgasm." I kissed her lips, smacked her butt, and then I nibbled on her neck.

"OK, time to go you guys!" Alaina announced.

"The kids aren't done, I'm ready to go! Trust I'M READY!" Chareca lovingly cut her eyes at her husband. "We are on the first thing smoking as soon as they eat dessert.

Everyone sat down twirling their fingers. Alaina looked at me and blushed. We watched the rest of our movie and then the kids announced that they were done. We made them eat dessert while we went up to look at T's room. His room was cleaner than I've ever seen it. Cara Mia told T he never knew when she was going to pop up, and when she did she wanted to see his room looking just like she left it. Ken and Chareca left shortly after that. T took a shower and Jerrell passed out, I put him in his bed. T said good night, and Alaina and I ran to my room.

In the morning, she was up early stating that Mr. Chambers was coming to pick her up. She said she had to go home and get something to wear, and then he'd pick them up from her place. She kissed me and hurried out the door. I tried not to feel irritated or anything else that she didn't mention that she was going over Royce's.

Royce

I ran around all morning getting all of Alaina's favorites for the house and dinner. I had the housekeeper come the day before to make sure everything was perfect. I was hoping that she would be so Wowed by everything that she'd be swayed to come out here.

I was running around so much and time seemed to fly by. I got to the house thirty minutes before my father was supposed to arrive with Alaina and Jerrell. My father is always on time so I knew I had to book it around that house. I walked in the door with plastic bags in both hands from multiple stores. I didn't want to go back and forth to the car so I loaded up to make it in one trip. The splash in the pool and sound of fun caught my attention at first. The clothes all over the floor by the sliding glass door enraged me. Brooke was in the pool with someone having a good time. "WHAT ARE YOU DOING?" I yelled.

Brooke looked confused, "this is my friend Breezy and her daughter Danyale. I asked you if they could come over today to swim two weeks ago."

"No you didn't!"

"Yes I did, I wanted them to come last weekend, but you told me to have them come today. What's wrong with you?"

CRAP! I remembered now, I was so excited about Alaina I forgot all about this. I cursed. "Well come get these clothes, none of that excuses making my house a pigsty!"

Brooke came inside and looked at me. "What's wrong baby brother?"

"Dad is coming with Alaina and Jerrell in minutes. I forgot about your company."

"Alaina's coming here? What about Vanessa?"

"What about her?"

"I thought you were happy with Vanessa?"

"I am for the most part, but no one replaces my wife."

Brooke stared at me, "this is exactly why I don't do men. You all are so confused."

"Whatever Brooke, you don't like men because you don't like men. You go through the same drama in your relationship that anyone else goes through. Your girlfriend of many years slept with your little brother and never told you. Same drama different spin on it. You're not making a better choice by choosing women."

I put the preordered food in the oven to keep it warm. I opened the red wine to let it breathe. Right on time the doorbell rang and I hurried to open it. Jerrell was at the door and he was excited to come inside. He jumped on me and hugged me. Alaina walked behind my dad looking around at the house. She was impressed even if she didn't say anything. Immediately her sundress made my body stiffen. Why does she keep wearing all these revealing clothes? Her sundress had spaghetti straps and her skin was glowing. It stopped above her knees showing off her muscular thighs, and beautiful legs. Her hair was down, but I noticed the band on her wrist like she planned to put it up at some point. Her cross body purse was cuffing her right breast, I looked at the sweater she had draped over her purse, to divert my eyes. My dad gave me a look to say he tried but it was hopeless. Alaina backed away when I tried to hug her, and that irked me but I accepted it for now.

Brooke came to the door dripping wet to hug my dad. He was so surprised to see her, he didn't care about getting wet he hugged his daughter. Alaina stood there looking around the kitchen. I told her to come on as I gave her a tour of the house. I showed her the guest room (that Brooke occupies), my office, and bathroom downstairs. The living room, dining room, laundry room, and she saw the kitchen already. Then Jerrell led the way down the hallway to his bedroom upstairs. Alaina smiled real big at his room that still had basically the same design she had in the Berkeley house. The only thing is this room was bigger and better. I showed her the other rooms and when she entered the master suite her eyes got big and she asked me how much money I made. I told her whether she believes me or not, I was working very hard to provide all of this for us. Alaina sucked her teeth then she walked out of the room. Her dress softly caressed her butt as she walked, and my eyes couldn't stop watching as she walked and she jiggled a little. I hurried and gently caught her arm. "Alaina please forgive me, look at all this that I'm working for. We have more than enough room to have more children now. I can afford this without you working."

Alaina snatched her arm and then she held out her dress. "Do you like it? I wore it especially for you!" She narrowed her eyes at me.

I swallowed then I looked at her, "you are very beautiful no matter what you wear."

That wasn't what she expected me to say, and I really wanted to tell her to cover up while my dad was here. However, I was trying not to rock the boat. "Do you like my dress?" She unbuttoned the top button to reveal more cleavage.

"What are you doing?" I swallowed as my mouth filled up with desire.

"Asking you a simple question. Do you?" She unbuttoned the next button.

I closed the bedroom door as I stroked my beard, "Alaina stop playing."

"I'm not playing, I'm proving a point." There went the third button as she reached for the fourth button I could see her bra and my brain was turning to mush.

"What point, that you can still turn me on?" I said glancing at the tent in my pants.

"That you haven't changed, admit it. The sight of me walking around in a normal dress, skirt, blouse, or anything turns you on and that's why you always wanted me in clothes too big for me and covered up like I had no curves."

I wanted to pick her up and lay her on the bed. "Alaina," I got on my knees and scooted in front of her. I clasp my hands together and pleaded. "Please come home! I love you, and I will do better. I go to the gym during the day now. I only work a little over time when my review load warrants it. I will be more present. We can have more babies. Please!" I rubbed her soft thigh.

Alaina looked down at me unaffected by my pleading or my arousal. "I'll think about it."

I reached under her dress and touched her panties, they were bone dry. The site of my arousal used to turn her on, now it was like she could care less. That hurt me, but I wasn't finished. Alaina backed up from me and started to walk towards the door. "Your dress," I said as she got close to it. She re-buttoned her dress except for the top two buttons and then she walked out of the room. Ok, now I was annoyed. I followed Alaina down the stairs as my father was introducing Jerrell to the little girl with Brooke. The little girl was not well looked after clearly. It was sad, because she could be a cute little girl if someone just put the effort forward. Good thing kids don't notice such things. The little girl asked Jerrell if he could come swim with them, and Alaina said a quick no. My dad looked at the expression on Alaina's face and he hurried to her. He asked her what was wrong. She said she doesn't like pools. Judging by her reaction, I knew better than to tell her that Jerrell swims like a fish regularly in that pool. I asked everyone if they were hungry and Jerrell said yes. At the mention of food the little girl came inside eager to eat as well. Brooke and her friend were lounging on noodles in the water not paying us any attention. Jerrell got excited when he saw the barbecue. My son is a meat eater like his dad and he gets excited about all the stuff we eat whenever we're together. I tried to take him to that Chinese spot in Pinole and he was not feeling it. We sat at the table and I kept watching Alaina. She mostly watched Jerrell making sure he had what he needed, and the little girl. Every time our eyes caught she looked away.

Something in her eyes was different. She didn't look at me the same way she used to. I know I cheated, but how could that immediately wash away all the love we shared. My dad sat at the table with us, and he got us laughing about stuff that happened years ago. Back when it was just Alaina and I. We sat at that table for hours while Jerrell and the little girl played with his toys nearby. We were two and a half bottles in to Rombauer feeling good and laughing. Alaina relaxed a lot and so did her left strap on her dress. It wouldn't stay up on her shoulder. It looked so soft and I wanted to kiss it so badly.

Brooke and her friend finally made their way inside. Alaina stared at Brooke's friend, I looked at the friend, and she didn't look familiar to me. Brooke was showing her the food. Alaina wouldn't take her eyes off the girl and I wanted her to look at me and tell me what was going on. Brooke and the girl came to the table. The girl looked at everyone and then she sat down. Alaina continued to look at her. Brooke introduced Breezy to the table. Brooke and my dad started talking, the girl took a bite of her ribs, and then she looked at Alaina. Alaina sat up like she was preparing herself to stand up quickly. She chewed like she was trying to remember something. She chewed some more then suddenly she stopped chewing and she looked at Alaina. Alaina stood up fast and backed away from the table. "WHERE IS TAVIO?" She screamed at Alaina.

"What is that?" Brooke asked this clearly crazy girl.

"The guy who got me fired and ruined my life!" She barked at Brooke.

"Tavio didn't get you fired no more than he convinced the court to alter your DNA results."

"HE DID! HE LEFT ME TO RAISE THIS BABY ALL BY MYSELF!"

"Breezy, calm down! You said that other guy was Danyale's father." Brooke said calmly.

"What guy?" Her eyes looked extremely crazy and like she was high or something.

"The one that is in jail, the one who was waiting in your house that night after your date. You said he got you so high you didn't know whether you were coming or going." Brooke said like this wasn't the first time she's reminded her.

"Chris?" She said as a tear fell out of her eye.

"Yeah, whatever he had you on that night messed you up for good. Calm down, Tag-it-toe ain't Danyale's daddy so calm down and sit down and eat." Brooke said taking another bite of her food.

"Where is Tavio?" The girl asked Alaina.

"He's in his skin, I would never tell you where he is. You're crazy!" Alaina said still standing.

"Oh yeah sister-in-law she is crazy. Breezy did you take your medicine today?" Brooke teased.

"Alaina come sit down, this girl ain't going to do nothing to you." My father said giving the girl a look.

"Why are you asking her about Tavio?" I asked the girl.

"Cause I saw her with him." The girl said.

We looked at Alaina, "Tavio and I were working out when she came over hollering about her DNA test. After security came and we started to walk away she grabbed me by my hair!" Then Alaina slapped the mess out of her. "I OWED YOU THAT!"

My father and I jumped, the girl scrunched up her face and then she moved it around. "Yeah alright, fine! I still yanked your butt up by your hair. What I care about your slap?" The girl went back to her food.

Brooke asked who the guy was to Alaina. Alaina sat down slowly keeping her eye on the girl, so I explained that Tavio was Alaina's friend. Brooke looked at Alaina for a long time then she looked at me. He's her friend, she asked me while staring at Alaina who was still not responding. I said yes, but I took in Alaina's whole demeanor, which was different. She's a grown woman, she can't be hitting on people and thinking that she can get away with that. I decided to let it go for now, but as soon as we're back together she has to know all of this behavior has to stop.

Alaina remained on guard the rest of her visit. Jerrell was so happy having both of us in the same place. At one point while we were at the table he walked up to us and hugged Alaina and then he hugged me as he said, *my parents*. I felt like mud and so did Alaina. She started trying to be nicer after that. We took out the monopoly board and things got serious. Alaina was kicking major but. Maybe I didn't notice before, but this aggressive side is all new to me. My dad and Jerrell played the same hand, and the girl and her daughter played together. Brooke, and I were on our own. Alaina took over Boardwalk and once that happened she dominated the board. My dad would tell Jerrell to butter Alaina up so that she would let them pass or pay a lower rent whenever they hit her real estate, which quickly became the whole board once she took all the Railroads from everyone. My dad was very tickled behind Alaina's behavior all I could think is, *my wife has changed*.

That strap wouldn't stay up and eventually the other one joined in its lack of structure and support. Those two buttons were still unbuttoned. I was trying to decide if I was going to deal with blue balls or if I was going over Vanessa's once they left. Alaina's hair wasn't that bad after all. I guess she could keep it after we got back together. Jerrell was delirious and Alaina asked my dad if it was time to go? He told her he was ready when she was. Alaina and I helped Jerrell pick up his toys. In Jerrell's room, I decided to go for it and I called myself kissing Alaina. She wouldn't open her mouth and her body was stiff. She didn't melt into me like she used to. Defeated, I exhaled and let her go home with my dad. I walked them out to the car and I told Alaina that I enjoyed her company. Jerrell gave me a big hug goodbye, and then I watched them drive away.

Brooke was explaining that Alaina was my estranged wife when I walked back in the house. That girl said she thought that Alaina was with Tavio because he was protective over her like she was.

Tavio

T and I entertained ourselves with silliness and deep conversation as we waited outside of Alaina's place. I didn't care what time it was, I was going to be right here waiting when she pulled up. T and I played basketball until we couldn't move anymore. Covered in sweat we ate left over pizza and talked about father son stuff. T said he liked how Cara Mia rearranged his room. He said they argued a little bit about where some things should go, and he moved a couple of things around after she left. Overall he liked her direction. T didn't understand why I was laughing at him, but he's too young to get it.

He's way more innocent than I was at his age. I'm so thankful for that. I've always been curious about girls and what they felt like, given the opportunity I was always looking under Eva's dress. Unique was more like a little brother than a sister. Eva was a girl and I wanted to see what made her different. Then I wanted to see what it felt like and how good that part felt rubbed up against me. At T and Cara Mia's age I was stealing kisses, grabbing Eva's butt, and telling her that she was going to be my wife. That's kind of how I talked her into most things; I would tell her that we were already married so it was ok. T is so innocent he honestly looks at Cara Mia as a best friend. Cara Mia is going to have to be the one to tell him that they're going to be together, and I'm thinking that's a good thing.

It was almost ten when a car pulled around to the circle. T and I were standing out in the open to make sure we were seen. The car stopped by us, and then Alaina got out. She asked what we were doing here, and I didn't say anything. I walked up to her and kissed her long and hard. Jerrell was yelling hi to us from the car. Alaina looked drunk from our kiss as she smiled at me. A little worry spread across her face as she bent down to speak to Mr. Chambers. I walked over to the driver's side of the car and waited for him to roll down the window. "Good evening sir how are you?"

"I'm so confused right now, when did this start?"

Alaina looked embarrassed and annoyed, "fairly recent. It's good to see you again. You need to come over and hang out with us when you find the time."

"Ok son, ok." Mr. Chambers said showing the rejection of his sorry son all over him.

Alaina hugged him goodbye through the window then he drove away. Alaina asked me what I was doing here, and I asked her why was she annoyed. I asked her why it was a secret that she went to Royce's house. Jerrell was so happy to see T that he asked Alaina to turn on his game so that they could play.

I followed Alaina into her bedroom; I asked her how things went. She didn't answer me instead she said she wasn't ready for Royce to know about us yet. She said he acts like her going to school was the end of the world. She said he was going to blow us way out of proportion and make her life miserable behind it. I told her he can't harass her unless she allows him to. I didn't like any of her arguments for why she didn't want Royce, a guy who is beneath me to know about us. Maybe now he'd let the divorce happen. Let him go and let's move on.

Eva

Colby spent the night last night and it looks like he's spending the night again. We had a nice day with Quinn at the park. This little girl loves the swings; I wish I liked anything as much as she loves the swings. I was getting a real workout running around that park after little Quinn. I told myself I'd think about joining a gym in a week. Quinn got excited and scooted up next to me in the bed. She had the biggest smile on her face as she snuggled into me. Colby looked at her and laughed. "So how's parenthood been for the last few days?"

"It's not so bad," I said under my breath.

Colby put his hand up to his ear. "Can you say that again, I'm kind of hard of hearing."

"It's not so bad, BUT! This is different. I know that if it gets too difficult all I have to do is give her back. It's different when it's yours."

Colby rubbed my arm, "you wouldn't be alone." Then he looked around the room. "What do you think of therapy?"

"Physical therapy?" I asked sarcastically.

"You know what I mean, baby you've made great strides. Looking at all the original artwork you have around here, I feel I owe our artist friend a world of thanks. But, you need more help."

"What makes you think I need help?" I was trying not to get defensive.

"Seeing a therapist doesn't make you weak. I see one from time to time, especially lately." I watched him walk to my bathroom.

I rubbed Quinn's back as she got sleepy. "Why do you see one?"

"My job is stressful and it's strongly recommended." He called out from the bathroom. "I ran back when we broke up."

I sunk into the bed, "I'm sorry."

"I know it's not your fault. If I thought you were trying to hurt me or string me along, I would've kept moving." He walked back into the room. "The million dollar question is, do I break up with Corrine now or wait?" I opened my mouth. "You're not a part of this decision. Corrine has been good to me and resistant to the fact that we can't go any further. Can you blame her though?" He smiled at me.

"She doesn't understand why you're attracted to me."

"That's her problem, she doesn't know you." He exhaled, "I've liked you since Katrina introduced us."

"Why?"

"You're beautiful, and when no one's looking you show that all you want is to be loved. Plus you're a freak and the only person to keep up with me."

I blushed, "you're always testing limits. How could we have all of that and rug rats running around? We couldn't just run out to the strip club at the drop of a hat anymore."

"There's nothing a stripper could teach me. Nowadays they're only recycling each other's moves." He smiled at me, "you learn anything new?"

"I haven't done anything like that without you."

Colby smiled and then my house phone rang. The Caller ID said it was Rickie. "Hey…" I said with a smile in my voice.

"How's Quinn?" Rickie sounded upset.

My body tensed up and I pulled Quinn in a little closer to me. "She just fell asleep, she's right here next to me. Colby's still here. What's wrong?"

"Do you have a minute to talk?"

"Yes! Yes! What's going on?" I said as calmly as I could so that I wouldn't wake Quinn.

"James," just the mention of his name made me feel like I was drowning. I gripped the phone as I whispered *Rickie*. "Quincy's stupid brother made sure he ran his mouth about us being out here. His brother is just evil and hateful!" It sound like she hit something in the background.

"Where are you?"

"My hotel room," then I heard Quincy saying something in the background. "Is it ok if I put you on speaker?"

"Of course, I'm going to do the same." Colby sat at the foot of the bed and he started massaging my feet.

I put the phone on speaker, "so he was running his mouth

thinking it wasn't going to come back on him. Long story short, James shot Cherard because he thinks Cherard told him the wrong hotel on purpose. When Quincy told Cherard the wrong hotel cause he didn't trust him. Cherard is going to be ok, but they got James on attempted murder. And then the gun he used on Cherard was dirty and he's going to county right now. He's got a lot of enemies in there, he's not coming back."

I started crying as silently as I could. "He's gone?"

"Sis, he is gone. You will never see him again. Plus the girl he was living off of came to the police station with a black eye and everything else. Assault and battery on top of everything. There won't be some ghetto fabulous ending to his story. He's gone and he's irrelevant to your life from now on." Quincy said like he understood without ever talking to me about what happened.

Colby watched my face as I sobbed tears of release. "So let me get this right, your brother being a jerk has benefited all of our lives for the positive?" Colby smiled at the phone.

"Yes brother in-law. You can see the news report on it if you search my brother or James' name. Oh, and my father's surgery went well. We should be home as scheduled," Quincy told Colby.

"Maybe when you all come back we can have Sunday dinner." Colby watched my eyes.

I could see Rickie's smile through the phone, "that sounds wonderful."

Royce

My dad was calling me as Brooke and I picked up the house. "Did you forget something?"

"I'm only telling you this because as your father I couldn't live with myself if I didn't tell you. I honestly believe you deserve every bit of this but I can't know and not tell you." He paused as he took a deep breath, "Alaina is gone son. Give her the divorce and cut your losses."

I frowned at the ceiling, "what? What did she say?"

"It's not what she said. Tavio and his son were at her place when I dropped them off tonight. Tavio greeted her with a kiss and under no uncertain terms did I misunderstand what I saw."

I dropped everything in my hands as I cursed. "WHAT?"

"You heard me, she's with Tavio."

I heard him; I didn't want to believe it. "No she's not, Alaina is loyal she wouldn't do that to me."

"Do what to you son, she's been fighting you for her freedom all of this time. She doesn't want you, and hasn't wanted you for some time. Think about your interactions today. She wasn't the same, now you know why. There's no room for you in her heart anymore, let her go."

"NO! Dad NO! You misunderstood. Tavio isn't half the man that I am that I became. Alaina is in love with me and he sits on the sideline looking…" I couldn't get the rest of the words out of my mouth. I hung up the phone.

Brooke looked at me but she didn't look concerned or surprised. She didn't even ask me what was wrong. "So I guess Vanessa gets to come over now?"

Alaina

"You don't get to decide when my life unravels! I just don't want Royce in my business period."

"I will yield and show respect to your father because he will always be your father. I could care less about Royce or his father. I have a right to claim you."

"Claim me? I'm not a piece of property for you to show off. You just wanted to rub Royce's nose in all of this."

"Even if I did, why do you care? You're over him remember? Besides its ok for you to claim me as your man at the office, but in front of your ex's father you want to back pedal? You're living in fear of Royce is going to cause problems between us."

My cellphone rang and it was Royce, "and so it begins! I don't want to deal with this Tavio!"

"Give me your phone!" He put his hand out.

I didn't want to, but the look in Tavio's eyes was on the crazy side so I did as I was told. "Hello… We're busy, she will call you back…" and then it went downhill from there. I watched Tavio curse Royce out and the two of them go back and forth. Lil Tavio and Jerrell came to my door knocking. I opened it and I told them everything was ok, and that Tavio was having a grown conversation. Lil Tavio whispered asking me if it was Royce. I caught myself before I asked him why he told his father about the other night. If I had thought about Lil Tavio saying something to his dad I would've said something or whatever. I just didn't want this scene. I didn't want to hurt…. That was weak; Royce didn't care about hurting me. I took a deep breath and I waited for Tavio to finish his conversation. Royce hung up on Tavio and Tavio called him right back. He told him to man up and deal with the fact that he lost a good woman and to let it go. When Tavio got off the phone he told me I better never pull a stunt like today again. He told me he needs to be able to trust me, and he needs me to be open and honest about everything no matter how ugly the truth may be.

Chapter 20

Royce

What did she do, trade phones with Tavio? Every time I call my wife he answers the phone talking about she's busy. I became obsessed with ringing her phone. I didn't care if I was being petty and annoying, I wanted to talk to Alaina. I knew I shouldn't have listened to Ken and left her alone. Look what happened! I called my lawyer and I told her to contest the spousal support. I told her to use the fact that Alaina has been having an affair with her *friend*. She asked if I still planned to continue to deny Alaina's claims of me having an affair? I told her it was my word against Alaina's. Tavio would support her claim because he obviously would lie for her. Every once in a while my lawyer gives me looks or I can hear her disapproving tone in her voice. She's very good at her job so I let the looks slide. I picked up the phone. "Baby brother what are you doing?" Brooke said like she was talking to a child.

I stared at her like she was an idiot. "I'm trying to call my wife!"

"Well, you're clearly losing it. I called Brice and Rachel over you need an intervention."

"I need everybody to shut up. Listening to other people is how this happened!"

Brooke reached out slowly and put her hand on my phone. "Just hear us out, then you can go back to being a crazy person."

Then the doorbell rang, I sat in the same seat in the kitchen that my wife sat in not even twenty-four hours ago. No one smiled they sat at the table and then waited for the other person to go first. "I don't get what's supposed to make Alaina so special? Does she deep throat you or something?" Brooke blurted out.

I lowered my eyes at her, "don't talk about my wife like that!"

"Ex-wife!" Brooke yelled at me.

"We are still married!"

"You're the only one who believes that!" I started to stand up, Brooke grabbed my knee. "Don't leave listen to reason Royce."

"Look at the facts, Alaina caught you red handed. It's not like she heard it from someone else. Besides you were fat on her time, and as soon as you start messing around you go back to the old you? Insult!"

Rachel chimed in, "I'd sleep with someone else just to hurt you for that. I honestly thought she was going to get fat with you. What do I know?"

"Your mother brainwashed you! Are we done?" I got up and the three of them got up and followed me. "Leave me alone!" I went into the living room and sat down in the chair since they wanted to follow me.

"Baby brother, I don't understand. Why do you want Alaina back? You're always with Vanessa and you seem happy with her. Vanessa don't take your crap either." Brooke smiled like the memory pleased her.

"Who's Vanessa?"

"The same chick he was creeping with. She's actually pretty cool, I like her."

"I married Alaina for a reason." Anger turned in my stomach.

"Why?" My brother asked calmly.

"You've seen us together, Vanessa's fine, but she'll never be Alaina!"

"So give up the Vanessa chick and do right by Alaina." Brice said like it was so easy. I shook my head cause he didn't understand. "Royce you are a very intelligent man. This palace is evidence of this. Why are you being so stupid in this situation? Alaina never said she would forgive you if you cheated. She didn't even suspect it; you basically came out of left field with this. I would be suspicious if she did come back after all of this. You're the only one who's crazy enough to believe marriage works period. Look at mom and dad, get out while you can."

"Brice! How can you say all that? Outside of this, Alaina has always been good to me. This is just her pain talking. This is not a reflection of who she is."

"I still like Alaina, considering the problem you two were having..."

I cut him off, "DON'T BROADCAST MY BUSINESS!!"

Rachel smiled, "what problem?"

Brice and I were locked in a stare down, "did it get any better?"

"GET OUT!!" I stood up ready to swing on my brother.

"Whether I leave or stay it won't change anything. Whether you share or not, that's not going to change what has happened."

I charged Brice and he kicked me in my chest. I fell backwards holding my chest. It felt like I couldn't catch my breath. When I caught my breath and stood up again. Brice was going to tell them anyways; at least I could release my frustration by hitting him. Brice and I tussled all around that living room. Rachel laughed while Brooke broke us up. Then Brice told them, "he's just mad because he couldn't get her off. You know somebody else went in and probably turned her out." I stuck him in his jaw. That started our fight all over again. "Still doesn't change anything. Give it up Royce!"

"I'm not listening to none of ya'll! Listening to ya'll is how she ended up laying with Tavio!"

Brice got excited and put his fist up to his mouth as he laughed hard. "Tavio hit it! YOU AIN'T EVER GETTING HER BACK!" He laughed hard at me. I threw my lamp at his head and it just missed.

"Why do I know that name?" Brooke snapped her fingers trying to remember. "The guy Breezy was hollering about last night?" Brooke turned to our siblings, "I was wondering why Alaina slapped the mess out of Breezy! Now I got the full picture. You're not willing to fight over a random person or hookup. He must've blew her back out!" Everyone started laughing.

"A! Brooke, Tavio is not some ill-informed little boy. He definitely knows his way around a woman!" Brice said to get under my skin. I looked for something else to throw at him.

"Royce calm down, Brice stop teasing him." Rachel said trying to be the voice of reason.

"Look at my eye! I will tease him until I get tired!" Brice said pointing to his face.

"Just your eye, your whole face is jacked up! A smart person would leave me alone."

"To be so smart you are heck of dumb. How you gonna keep the girlfriend and then beg your wife to come back? Why would she agree to that? Alaina caught you and bounced. You had to have been putting that girl through it. What woman doesn't give her man a chance to fight for her unless she's done? Just like you told me to stop chasing after Erica cause she didn't want me. I'm telling you the same thing. You can't make someone love you, either they do or they don't."

"ALAINA DOES LOVE ME! SHE WOULDN'T HAVE MARRIED ME IF SHE DIDN'T!"

"Ok! Ok!" Rachel put her hands up in surrender, "we're going about this the wrong way." She crossed her ankles and looked at me. "Does Vanessa know about Alaina?" I shook my head yes, "ok well at least you listened to me there." She pointed to the chair that I was sitting in before it got turned over when I dipped Brice. "Have a seat baby brother. You're going to fight until you can't anymore. That's admirable. You want your wife back, then you need to listen to me." Brooke and Brice frowned at her. "You guys can try to tell him until you're blue in the face that it's over. Clearly you see he's not accepting the truth. We got to support our brother, right or wrong." Then she looked at me, "how do you feel about her sleeping with this guy?"

I turned the chair over and plopped down in the chair. I hadn't allowed myself to think about how I felt about it. I wanted to talk to Alaina and hear her tell me it wasn't true. I rubbed my temples trying to hold back the sting of my tears. "I don't know."

"You don't know?" Brice said like my comment was ridiculous. "You know it's messing with you. Tavio is a good looking cat!" Brooke and Rachel flashed him looks, "I'm man enough to admit it. You've got to face all the facts here. They've been friends since before you got married. They were close at that. Where did he come from? I don't remember her having any guy friends in high school."

"They met when we broke up but, that's my point. If he's all that like you're saying how did I come back without any problems? She kept him in the friends' zone and she married me."

"Royce you're asking about the choice Alaina made as a little girl. Ten plus years later things change."

"Not that much! We were fine until I forced the pregnancy. That's when things got really rocky between us. My wife had never told me no so much in our lives."

"You forced the pregnancy, do I even want to know how you did that?" Brooke asked almost like she was disgusted with me.

"No, I thought it was time, and clearly it wasn't. Everything went crazy after that. I love my son! I do not regret him. I look at him and I see us."

Rachel pointed, "use that. Be the best father you can be to Jerrell. Go over and above. A woman cannot resist a good father! Don't question her about this guy either. You're going to have to play the understanding roll. You're going to have to tell yourself you deserved it until you believe it. Then when you talk to her don't even bring it up. Just be the loving attentive guy she fell in love with."

"How do I do that? She won't talk to me."

"Hear me out," Rachel put her hands out. "Stop fighting the divorce Royce. Give her what she wants. That will make her put her guard down. Every time you look at her convey your love for her in your eyes. Pull at every sensitive bone you got, and run out of things to do. Put on some Babyface, Raheem Devaughn, some real sensitive man stuff and let it be your guide. No matter how *hard to get* a woman plays. Seeing her Alpha Male go humble in regards to her is a turn on." I nodded in agreement. "And then you gonna have to be smart about your girlfriend. No public outings! You need a phone just for her, if you have to contact her outside of work hours. Got it?"

"Well dang! I didn't know you were this manipulative!" Brooke said shaking her leg.

"What can I say, I am my mother's child." Rachel made a face like our mother would.

"Did dad ever tell you that he's not sure if you and I are his kids?" They gasped the same way. Brooke covered her mouth but tears still came to her eyes. "He even took me with him while he tried to confront her."

Brooke hurried and sat next to Rachel as they cried while they hugged. They kept apologizing to each other while they cried. Brice and I patiently waited for them to explain. Brooke said they used to tease each other about their differences. When they got older they questioned their differences and even asked mom. She got so mad at both of them and that's when Brooke and mom fought. I sat back in my seat, I assumed dad was being paranoid. Brice stared at me and I stared back. "I would compare our faces but I can only see out of one eye right now."

Alaina

Every time my phone rang I shot Tavio an, *I told you so look*. After a while Royce stopped calling, and I finally calmed down. I made an early dinner and we sat at my table and ate as a family. Jerrell was eating it all up. Royce was never home to eat with us, so it was only he and I unless someone came over or we went over their house.

Tavio sat at the head of the table with his locs down looking delicious. I had to decide how long I was going to play upset. I don't really care what Royce knows as long as he leaves me alone about it. All of the men were shirtless at the table which I love. Tavio would walk around naked if I asked him to, and I love that about him. Tavio is just everything Royce isn't.

536

I chuckled when I thought about all the years I would've died if I thought about Tavio beyond a kiss. Now all I can think about is the sex. I surprise myself with how much I want it. All those years where Royce really had me believing that there was something wrong with me. Orgasms are glorious! I was in my own world thinking about all the things Tavio has done to and with me. Then I heard all of the men laughing and I knew it was at my expense. I asked them what was so funny. Lil T asked me what I was thinking about and I blushed and looked away. Tavio smiled at me while chewing his food. Kill me! I wanted to disappear for a little bit. I smiled at Tavio then I asked him to step into my office. When he smiled and said *no* my legs gave out and I plopped into my seat. WHAT? I blinked at him because I know I heard him wrong. Tavio smiled then he licked his lips and said *no*. "WHAT?" I yelled which made both of the boys jump and look at me like I was crazy.

"You heard me, I said no." He continued to taunt me.

"Don't play with me! I will cut you!"

"Threats?" He laughed at me.

"Nothing's funny!"

Tavio stood up and started clearing the table. "We're going to clean your kitchen, then T and I are going home."

I frowned at Tavio; I folded my arms and stood up. I no longer had an appetite. Jerrell watched me walk to my room and pout. I slammed my door and then I sat on my bed. I looked at myself in the mirror. Was I really this sprung that I'm over here having a fit because he's not putting out. I mean I'm still irritated with him pissing all over me in front of Mr. Chambers, but I was willing to put my feelings aside so that I could get some tonight. I took off my tank top that very loosely covered my sports bra. I pulled at my very short shorts and wondered why he didn't get the memo? Tavio says he loves my body and how I'm not ashamed to walk around naked in front of him. I love the same thing about him, but if he only knew how uncomfortable I was the first time. No amount of running is going to give me back my un-stretch marked skin. Mrs. Spellman told me to try Shea butter, and coffee scrubs for cellulite. All of that helped, but I still know the difference. Tavio says I have a real body and he loves it. I don't know how many Barbie dolls he was with, but Unique, Chareca, and I know Sabrina had a boob job at least. I mean her breast sat up perky without a bra and she had to have full C-cups.

As I admired my hard earned legs Tavio walked in the room. He smiled at me and then his eyes went up and down my body. He hesitated for a minute, swallowed and then he shut the door behind himself. Well at least I knew he wasn't completely rejecting me. I spread my legs, planting my feet on the floor as I looked him up and down. Tavio smiled and mimicked my stance. He pursed his lips at me, so I did the same. "You really wanna go here with me? I was married, I know how to go without sex."

Tavio laughed, "that's cute. You're still mad about last night. So until that's resolved and you admit that I handled everything right you not getting none of my nookie."

"Seriously Tavio? I mean, you fine, but you ain't all of that. This argument may never be resolved. Are you prepared to hold out FOREVER? **FOREVER**!" I put my hands on my hips and walked into his face.

Tavio chuckled, "being right is more important than caressing your softness."

"My voluptuous softness?" I pecked his lips.

"Your voluptuous and ample softness is no match for my stubbornness." He pecked my lips back.

"FINE! FINE! I'm sorry, can we do it already?" Then I jumped on the bed and stuck my butt out at him.

"You being sorry doesn't resolve this. How you going to go over there without telling me where you're going? You acted like you were sneaking. Why would you sneak unless you were really trying to sneak about something? And I know how controlling he is, your little dress was all to taunt him. Don't play these games with me Alaina, these types of games damage trust."

I sat in the middle of the bed. "Of course I wanted to rub his nose in everything. My hair, my clothes, and the fact that he couldn't tell me what to do about anything. Last night was exhausting, he called every thirty minutes. He's going to start harassing me, and I didn't want that."

"He's been harassing you. Admit it, you were afraid of him knowing about us."

I exhaled and slumped; I swear it sucks sometimes when someone knows you inside and out. "Fine! I didn't want him to know."

"My question is why?"

"What if he thinks we started before we actually did? I was faithful to him, I was in love with him and devastated by his betrayal."

"Who cares what he thinks? He doesn't own the right to question anything about your life." Then he looked at me, "I knew you weren't ready. We should've waited."

"What are you talking about?" His accusation made me angry. It felt like he was saying he regretted me.

"Everybody was sitting on their hands waiting for us to get together. I drug my feet because I know you. You're not ready."

"I told you I needed to go slow!"

"Yeah slow, not backwards."

"Forget you Tavio! Last thing I need is to be judged by you!"

He walked over to his clothes. "I'm not judging you, I'm stating facts. When you still feel like you have to rub your ex's face in anything you're not done. You're looking for a reaction out of them." Then he pulled his shirt on, his stomach flexed and unflexed with his movements.

"I'm sorry! Don't leave Tavio! I learned my lesson whatever it is." I smiled at him.

He laughed then he plopped on the bed next to me. "Alaina, I am in love with you. Do you even understand what that means?"

"That you love me."

"I am overly sensitive to everything you do. Going over your ex's who's still pining over you without telling me about it makes you look suspicious. It shines a light on every vulnerability and insecurity I could possibly have with you. I know it's not fair that you asked for us to go slow and then I'm having a hard time managing the pace. So I'm trying to keep that part on my own, but you can't do stuff like this. I'm calm this time because I'm giving you the benefit of a doubt. Next time prepare yourself for the wrath."

"Why would there be a next time?"

"Because that's how you learn." I kissed his lips, pulled away just a little. "MAC please don't break my heart."

"You could break mine, why you always putting it off on me?"

"I'm all in, the ball's in your court."

****

My boss Karen's boss, was in town. So Karen told me to bring my team so we could have lunch. We met in downtown Walnut Creek. Amir and Bob volunteered me to drive so that they could ride in Tavio's car. They were oohing and awing everything that I've become accustomed to. I've forgotten what it was like in my car with the squeaky brakes. We were first to arrive so we waited in the lobby. Mandy and the new girl on Karen's team walked in and Mandy's face changed. She probably heard about my divorce and has an opinion like most people. I smiled and hugged her tightly letting her know I didn't want to talk about it. I asked her how the baby was doing and she said she was fine quickly then she changed the subject.

As soon as we sat down, all my old teammates wanted to see pictures of Jerrell. I proudly whipped out my phone and passed it with his picture on the screen. Mandy looked over the new girl's shoulder. Her smile fell a little and then she tried to smile at me and say how handsome my son is. I know Jerrell is handsome so I don't know what her problem was. Mandy sat down and she was quiet for a while. Until someone brought up weight loss after having a baby. The ones who weren't there couldn't believe how much weight I gained while I was pregnant. Before Jerrell, my workouts were not life and death like they became after he was born. Royce's mom was so happy to finally see me gain weight. I got irritated at the memory. Someone said Mandy was all stomach during her pregnancy. "It's not like I had a choice. I couldn't look like a had a baby walking out of that hospital."

"Why would you put that kind of pressure on yourself?" Karen asked Mandy as she bit into her burger.

"My boyfriend is into fitness, and I volunteered to be a part of his advertising. It was fine before the baby, but pregnancy made everything difficult. Everyone was watching to see what was going to happen after the baby. Plus I didn't want him feeling like I changed."

"Did your husband put pressure on you to lose weight?" The new girl asked me.

"No, I actually put us on diets. Then he acquired a desire to exercise on his own." I took a deep breath to keep everything even.

"Her husband used to be one of my boyfriend's clients. You should've seen how much he gushed over his wife and child," Mandy added.

I forgot all about that, "does he still workout with him?"

"No, Royce left our gym a long time ago. I guess it wasn't a good fit cause he's reached his goal wherever he's at now."

"Why did he leave?"

Mandy shrugged, "I don't know." She broke out in a little sweat. She grabbed her glass and gulped down her drink. "Waiter! Can I have another water?"

"Both of you look great. My wife and I love her new body. After she had the third baby it changed. She thought I would be upset or turned off. We've got three kids; I don't expect her to look like she did when we were young. I don't look the same either. My love for her has only gotten deeper." Amir said from his heart.

"How long have you been married?" Bob asked him.

"Fifteen years this year. She was best friends with my sister. She was like family already."

Mandy frowned, "well that's just nasty." Everyone looked at her, "she was like your sister then you kissed her? Why didn't that feel wrong to you?"

Amir looked confused, "be-cause she's not my sister."

"But at one point you looked at her like she was a sister, shouldn't kissing or at least the first kiss shouldn't it have felt wrong?"

"No," Amir looked at her like she was stupid.

"That's like kissing your best friend. Just nasty!"

The only people who knew Royce and I were getting a divorce is Karen and my team. My team are the only ones who know that I'm with Tavio now. "That's a matter of opinion Mandy. Your spouse is supposed to be your best friend."

"That's not the undeniable recipe for a successful marriage. Alaina and Royce are closer than close and last I knew she was best friends with that guy Tavio."

"Oh yeah, how's Tavio?" One of our teammates asked me.

"He's fine."

"How's he doing, I haven't talked to him in ages." Karen said smiling really big.

"He's no longer a junior agent, he was promoted to agent. His clientele roster has been growing and he's making quite the name for himself." I said as evenly as I could.

"He was always such a people person. Sounds like he's in the right career." Karen said then she took another bite of her burger.

Eva

I wanted to throw my alarm clock into the wall. It screamed at me telling me to get up and get going. My shuttle was going to be here in an hour. My bags were packed and waiting for me by the door. I showered, dressed, and then I went downstairs when the driver called to tell me he was outside. I gave him my luggage and then I got in the shared shuttle.

Vanessa's mom, Rickie and of course Quinn, Quincy, and my Grandmother were already inside. We said our hellos and then we were off. We had breakfast at the airport. My grandmother was quiet as she looked around in the Oakland airport at all the things that had changed since she had been here last. I remember the first time I came back, everything was different but it was all the same.

Quincy drove the rental SUV while Rickie navigated for him. We checked into our hotel and then we went straight to Vanessa's condo. The building was very upscale; we were on the list at the guard station to enter her complex. When we parked, Vanessa walked out in shorts and a tank top. Looking every bit like the stereotypical California girl. She went straight for Quinn, and she hugged her up. We were all standing around, and it took a minute before I asked why were just standing outside. Vanessa laughed nervously and then she started walking. I mean I already knew her stupid boyfriend was going to be here. I guess she wasn't sure about what was going to come out of my mouth. Her boyfriend and his sister were inside when we walked in. Vanessa's mom has no idea of how much of a jerk this guy is so she was very happy to see him. Quincy and my grandmother said hello when introduced, but they were vibing off of us. After a little bit Vanessa said she wanted to show us around the complex. She took us around to the tennis courts, the pools, the saunas, this complex had four gyms full of equipment, and two rooms for group classes like Zumba and Aerobics. As we entered the last clubhouse I noticed that everyone was hanging back and Vanessa was pointing me inside. When I looked through the glass I saw Colby. I snatched the door open as he stood there smiling at me. "What's going on?"

"You didn't think I'd let you go through this week alone did you?"

I jumped on him, "your schedule is impossible! I didn't think you could come so I didn't even ask." I kissed his cheeks, "thank you for coming. I can do this now." I squeezed him tight. "When did you get here?"

"I was supposed to land an hour before you did, but my flight got delayed. I was ducking and dodging you at the airport." He smiled at me, "are you surprised?"

"Completely," I kissed his lips. "Corrine's not going to be mad about you being gone all week?"

"I broke up with Corrine as soon as you started opening up to me." He watched my eyes.

I kissed Colby with everything in me. "I love you, I'm sorry."

Colby smiled, "I know."

When Colby and I walked out together Rickie ran to us and hugged Colby. Quinn got just as excited and ran over too. We went back to Vanessa's place and I took in her decor of mostly silvers and grays. Even her carpet was gray. Then she added pops of color in the pillows and artwork on the walls. Her place was very trendy and nice. Her man and sister played bartender.

Royce was mister personality and I guess now that I've mellowed out I could see how good they were together. Vanessa looks happier than I've ever seen her. I may not agree with how they came to be, but it's obvious that they're good together. Royce kept touching his face and I thought I was the only one who noticed until Colby asked him why he kept doing it as well. Royce explained that he had a beard for years and he's so used to stroking it. He said Vanessa convinced him to let go of the past and move on. So as a step in that direction he shaved his beard. I forgot he had a beard until he said it. I still felt the need to be guarded with Royce, but I decided to mind my own business and be cool for my friend's sake.

Rickie and my grandmother were having a good time. Royce was charming them and Vanessa's mother all over the place. Royce's sister kept looking at Quincy and me. Quincy was over to the side being quiet and talking to Colby mostly. I guess she was trying to figure everyone out, who was who and things like that. When it was time to go, Vanessa hugged me tightly and thanked us for coming to see her. Her hug kind of felt like a goodbye, so I looked at her trying to get her to tell me what was going on. Vanessa gave me a guilty smile and said she'd call me later. She told me she loved me and then she walked back inside.

Colby brought his luggage into my room, and then he asked me to join him in the shower. I hadn't experienced Colby's touch since that night I ended up at his place. I was eager but something inside of me didn't want the whole experience. It had to be nerves. We showered, but I told Colby I was tired and I wanted to sleep. He seemed a little disappointed, but he held me all night and that was better than any extreme love making session that he is guaranteed to provide.

When I woke in the morning I laid there staring at the wall. I felt completely numb and I knew it was a little bit of anxiety about taking our family pictures today. We were meeting at the portrait studio, and then from there we were going to have an early dinner. Rickie said this way when everyone argued it wouldn't affect our pictures.

Colby kissed my cheek as if he knew I was awake and then he ordered room service for breakfast. I wanted to get up; I wanted to make love to my man. The man who has loved me even when I pushed him away. The man who has loved me with all of my faults. Instead I laid there unable to really move. I don't know why today is hitting me like it is but it's hitting me hard, heavy, and fast. I ate a little breakfast but I didn't have much of an appetite. Colby kept looking at me like he understood what I wasn't saying.

When it was time to start getting ready, Colby reminded me that I had to do my hair, so I needed to get started earlier. I keep forgetting about my hair and to factor in more time in my get ready time because of it. My hair is now in a short-stacked bob. Long on top and short on the bottom. It creates this stacked look that I love. I go to Vanessa and Rickie's hairdresser. She keeps telling me how pretty my hair is, something no one has ever told me. She says my hair is capable of doing so many things. She promises to show me everything. I'm in love with this style for now. After looking at myself with a baldhead for so long I forgot that I'm beautiful with hair as well. I think I started to feel like I could only look right with no hair. It shocked people and then it held their attention. As soon as I decided to grow it out, it seems like my hair grew faster than it ever has in life. I keep getting it cut to maintain this style a little longer because I like it so much.

I laid my clothes out on the bed and then I got in the shower. When I walked out the bathroom naked and ready for lotion Colby was ironing my skirt. He said my shirt needed the iron and then he tisked at me. He knows I hate to iron, and because of my hatred. I never really learned how to do it properly. At home I throw my clothes in the dryer if they're wrinkled. And when I was on the road all of the time I bought a fabric spray that would release the wrinkles.

I thanked Colby and then I looked at his almost matching attire. I smiled and asked him if he was joining our portrait. He said yes as if I was silly for asking. I smiled and embraced my feeling of relief. Colby's calmness and tenderness gave me the strength to face whatever was bugging me.

Rickie called to see if we were ready. Nervousness was in her voice. I told her we were ready and on our way down stairs. Quinn's voice was the only speaking voice in the car. She kept talking to my grandmother mostly. Making her respond to her. As we approached the portrait studio Quinn started laughing. She laughed hard; her little contagious laugh was just what we needed in that moment.

When we got out of the car Rickie told the girl at the desk that we were the Graham party, and the rest of our group was due to arrive shortly. The girl welcomed us and then she brought us water. She said Studio B was setup for our group photos and then we would go to the other studios to take our smaller group photos. Colby took my hand and we sat down in the lobby while Rickie and Quincy talked quietly amongst themselves. Quincy was calming Rickie and trying to help her with her nerves like Colby was doing for me.

Five minutes later my little sister hurries in the door too excited to see us. She looked around the room with a big smile and then she hurried over to Quinn who was running in circles by my grandmother. She hurried over to Quinn and immediately started playing with her. My grandmother stared at her granddaughter that she's never met, but she didn't say anything. Our brothers walked in next and they came to me and Rickie offering hugs. They were dressed in white tops and black bottoms like Rickie had instructed. They had fresh haircuts and they seemed like they were a little nervous too. I introduced them to Colby; he was in full bedside manner mode. I could see my brothers relax as he greeted them and immediately got them to open up about themselves. I thanked Colby with my eyes. Outside of the window my parents, aunties, uncle, and their spouses and other children were kind of huddled like they were encouraging each other to come inside.

"Are you my grandmother?" My little sister asked my grandmother.

Everyone looked at my grandmother for her response. "Yes baby I am."

My little sister smiled real big and then she hugged my grandmother really tight. "You're even prettier than I imagined!"

I saw the coldness melt away from my grandmother as she let

their hug take over her mood. She hugged Brenda back and told her she was beautiful as well. My little sister started talking about all the pictures she made for her as soon as my mom told her about her.

When our parents and aunties and uncles and other cousins and their families walked in the door they came in like a mob. Everyone was looking at my grandmother without smiles. They brought tension in the room and made the air thick. Brenda smiled at everyone and announced that her grandmother was prettier and nicer than she could've ever imagined and then she told everyone to come get their hugs. Brenda's little announcement hit all of them like it had hit us moments ago. At least our cousins stepped forward and hugged her and introduced their families. The three photographers assigned to our group took all of us to studio B so that we could get started.

They positioned all of us on the tiers. My grandmother sat in a chair in the front of our group with her grandchildren and great grandchildren all around her at the bottom. We took a few pictures that way. And then the spouses all moved and only her children, grandchildren, and great grandchildren were in the next set. At the family level the group split up and amongst the smaller studios. We took all girl pictures, and boy pictures. When it was time to take the family picture with our parents heat hit my body. Colby grabbed my hand and Rickie grabbed the other. The photographer asked me to stand next to my mother. I could smell the candy she sucked on as we stood. My parents smiled so big as they took the picture of our family.

Colby and my father, and brothers stood over to the side talking as my grandmother sat down holding Quinn. The photographer had us stand around them and we took Rickie's picture. Her generation picture that she wanted so badly. Rickie got emotional as soon as the photographer stopped snapping pictures. Our grandmother was called to the other studio for more generational pictures with her other children, grandchildren, and great grandchildren. I hugged Rickie as she cried. Brenda said, *AW!* and she ran to us and hugged us as well. Little Quinn followed suit, as our mother stood to the side popping more candy and watching us.

Once we were done, I was just happy that no one had killed anyone. Everyone was on their best behavior. Then our uncle informed us that they had food waiting back at the house and he expected to see us there in a few minutes. I took a deep breath cause I knew that meant at some point the argument was going to happen. Rickie answered for us and said we were following him. Again, everyone was silent in the car especially when Quinn fell asleep in her car seat. I held on to Colby and thanked him with a kiss for coming.

Everybody was smiling and pleasant except for our mother of course. She kept watching our grandmother and everything she did. Everyone else kept engaging her in conversation. My aunts and uncle were even nice to my grandmother. It seemed like they were surprised by her calmness and humble demeanor. The food was delicious; everyone brought a dish, which resulted in a huge spread of food. Colby was sharing with everyone how we used to have Sunday dinners and all of the dishes my grandmother introduced him and Katrina to. Everybody was talking about the dishes she makes that they loved and how some of them adapted her recipes to make their own versions. Everything seemed to be going well until… "ALL OF YOU MAKE ME SICK! ACTING LIKE YOU AREN'T JUST AS MAD OR HURT BY THE STUFF SHE DID! STOP ACTING!" Our mother blurted out in the middle of the floor.

"Nobody's acting, just like you've changed. So has she, look at how calm and quiet she is. She's isn't judging anyone, throwing her opinions around. She's being quiet and giving everyone what they need." My uncle Clifton said.

"I know I've hurt you all, and I haven't done everything right. All I can say is I'm sorry. I got all these grandkids and great grandkids that I don't know any more or some at all. I know you all have reasons to hate me forever. The fact that you showed up today and you did all this for each other gives me a reason to be thankful. You all got families and you proved me wrong about all the things I assumed about you. I understand if you're mad at me, I'm mad at myself. I'm learning that everyone doesn't need someone to be overbearing in their lives sometimes. I left Eva alone and look at her. She's growing her hair back,

549

the man that's meant for her is by her side, Rickie and Quincy worked things out." I looked at Rickie and shot her a look like what is she talking about? "Everyone is strong, and all I need to do is be the grandmother and in some cases the great grandmother. I'm sorry I didn't realize this sooner."

"We can see that, and there's not a person here who hasn't made more than their fair share of mistakes. We're moving forward Ruby. This is a fresh start. Embrace it and move on."

"YOU AIN'T CHANGED! WATCH AT THE MOMENT YOU LEAST EXPECT IT THE OLD HER IS GOING TO POP OUT! THEN YOU'LL BE HATING HER JUST LIKE YOU ALWAYS HAVE!"

"Well you can sit over there holding your breath if you want to. The rest of us are moving on with our lives." Uncle Clifton told my mother. Colby went over and hugged my grandmother and she held on to him apologizing lowly for everything. I could hear her taking responsibility for our breakup and everything. Colby told her it was not her fault and we needed to get our houses in order before we moved forward. "So young man, you're the young fella who has captured our little Eva's heart. What do you do for a living?"

"I work at Boston General hospital with Quincy."

"Does Eva's success bother you?" My uncle asked assuming Colby worked side by side with Quincy.

"Not at all, I've always supported her in her success and achievements."

"How did you feel about her when she shaved her head?" Everyone waited for Colby's response as if he was going to say he hated it.

"I loved her hair cut. I was with her when she got it done. Eva can do no wrong as far as I'm concerned." Everyone smiled like he just made the best speech ever.

******

My phone said it was Unique calling. "Hello sweetheart."

"Hey doll face! Let me know if you don't want to. BUT!" Unique was excited, "I told Tavio we were supposed to come meet your man, and he got jealous. He wants everyone to come over his house. He wants to meet Colby and see your brother in-law again if that's ok with you. My parents want to see you all and your grandmother again too."

"Sounds like you got everything worked out already, is there any point in saying no?"

"Nope, I'll text you Tavio's address in case you forgot how to get there, come at 1. Love you much ta-ta for now."

I rolled over and Colby was looking at his phone and checking emails. "You feel up to meeting Tavio today?"

Colby smiled at me, "feel up to it? Of course I want to meet the only other man that you love. I need to know who's image I'm competing with."

I frowned, "what do you mean? You're not competing with his image."

"Maybe you don't realize it, but you compared everything about me with him."

I smiled, "I asked him who his best sex was."

Colby started laughing, "did he fall for that?"

"Fall for what?"

"You were trying to bait him weren't you?"

I blank stared at Colby, "am I that transparent cause he said the same thing."

Colby started laughing, "guess he knows you as well as I do."

"He was there first," I smiled.

"Doesn't matter, I'm here last." Then he kissed me.

I texted Rickie and told her about the change in plans. I told her to meet us in the lobby at 12:30 so we could go. She's been avoiding me since our grandmother's comment. She has to talk to me eventually. When my grandmother and Quinn came down to the lobby, as usual Colby took her under his arm and loved her up. It was silence in the car and then we pulled up to Tavio's house. Rickie said she loved it already.

Unique opened the door for us, and she excitedly said everyone was in the backyard. Unique introduced us to her man and their friends Ken and Chareca. MAC warmly greeted us and introduced a little girl named Kendall to Quinn. The two of them started playing just like Quinn and Selah do. I told MAC I loved her locs and I told her she looked really good. Her smile was big and she looked so happy and content with herself. Tavio was playing grill master and he invited Colby and Quincy over with the rest of the men.

Rickie and I sat next to Unique catching up, Unique was excited and gushing about her man. She told us to prepare ourselves to be bridesmaids. I wanted to know, but I didn't want to ask. So Rickie asked how MAC was holding up. She said she looks fabulous. She said she loved her locs and she looked happy and content. Unique explained how Royce had been fighting the divorce until recently. She said he's just trying another approach cause now he's trying to play nice and mister wonderful. Trying to find any way he can to be in MAC's ear. I asked if she thought MAC was falling for it? She shrugged and said she didn't know, she said she keeps telling Tavio to point it out. She thinks Tavio wants her to choose him so he doesn't say a whole lot. I could see the effects of me on his relationship. I chose control over us, and I guess now he's hoping that MAC will be the one to choose him like he deserves to be chosen.

Rickie interrupted my thoughts when she said Vanessa and Royce deserved each other. Rickie held my hand as she told us how Vanessa and Quincy messed around once. I looked at my sister in shock.

Unique looked Rickie in her eyes and asked her how did it feel when Rickie punched her in her face? Rickie said it was all a mistake and it got out of control. She said that Quincy came to her immediately begging for forgiveness. She said he told her everything and how Vanessa didn't want him to tell and that she just wanted the whole thing to be swept under the rug. I asked her how she could go over Vanessa's house the other day knowing all of this. I asked her why she didn't tell me. She said she went to prove to herself that it was over and that she had made the right choice. She said she didn't tell me because it was over and she and Quincy were moving forward. She said I've been going through so much, she didn't want to burden me with anything else. I mentioned how Vanessa said goodbye, it was like she was saying goodbye for good. Now I understood. Now her move to California made even more sense. I looked at Colby and I couldn't help it. I wondered if she ever tried to sleep with him. She was the one who was always telling me how much of a freak my man is. I tried not to feel uncomfortable about the idea. I watched Colby from across the yard. Eventually he looked up, and my expression; I guess made him come over and ask me to come with him. We walked over to the far side of the yard and I locked on his eyes. "Do you know about what happened with Vanessa?"

He watched my eyes as he took a drink from his red cup, "yes."

"Did she ever try to sleep with you?" Colby didn't say anything, he watched my eyes. "Did you sleep with her?"

"No," he didn't move his eyes.

"But she tried?" I was getting mad.

"That girl has low self-esteem. She didn't try very hard, she created the opportunity but I didn't go for it." Then he took another drink, "what happened between her and Quincy was an accident."

"How do you accidentally sleep with someone?"

"We were out, we were drinking. I left when I had enough, not remembering to check for Quincy and how he was doing. His heart was heavy about a lot of things and he had drunken more than he should've.

Alcohol, low self-esteem, heavy hearts, stuff happens. Neither one of them intended for it to happen. And if there had been some sobriety present it never would've happened. Quincy went to Rickie right away, it's over."

"You went to her place without me knowing that she has a thing for you." I crossed my arms.

Colby smiled, "I love it when you get jealous over me." Then he kissed my lips. "I went, her boyfriend was there the entire time. I knew you were coming and that's all I cared about. Besides we weren't technically together when she tried it. You swore you were done with me."

"Are we technically together now?"

"Eva," he took another drink. He looked around then he took a deep breath. "Will you marry me? Will you have my baby? Will you spend the rest of your life as my sex slave?" He smiled at me as he gently stroked my cheek.

"You know I'm scared of all of that."

"Yes, but I also know that you love me. And if there was anyone you would say yes to it would be me." He picked up my hand and kissed my palm.

"But if I said yes, it would just prove my grandmother right about everything."

"We both know she's not right about everything, but she can be right about us. I'm perfectly ok with that one."

My eyes caught Tavio at the grill CHEESING hard at us like he knew what we were talking about. Like he coached Colby on what to say or something. "I love you Colby, but…" Colby closed his eyes and prepared himself for however I was going to reject him next. "I don't want to get married in Boston. My family can't travel all the way out there."

Colby's eyes popped open and he gave me the most surprised expression. "Did you say yes?"

"Kind of, I want a real proposal and some real effort put into it. Tavio's backyard is not my idea of romance. Just know that when you ask me for real, I'm going to say yes."

Tavio

Royce is on my nerves! He isn't fooling me! I know what he's doing. This may be the smartest route that he's decided on. I pulled Alaina into my lap as she unknowingly paraded herself around my bedroom, as we got ready to take the kids. T is going with his mom, and Jerrell is going with his dad. Tomorrow night we're going to one of my client's games. I kissed Alaina's neck and she was automatically ready for more. Sex is not the problem in our relationship. Alaina has lived with hypocrites her entire life. So she doesn't always notice the hypocritical things she does. Like she will DIE if she thought there was ever a reason to doubt me. So I'm completely open with her. She has access to my everything. Somehow she's forgotten to give me a key to her place, or her phone. She doesn't get it when I allude to it so I let it go for now. Because a key or a passcode don't affect my happiness. "So, about tomorrow night."

"Un huh?" Alaina moaned as she enjoyed my kisses.

"Check in with me if you feel uncomfortable or anything like that. The women hanging around are looking for someone to take care of them."

"Groupies," she said as she caressed my head.

"Yes, groupies, vixens, and Blaque Widows." I continued kissing her.

"Blaque Widows? What's that?"

"They're the women who will suck the life out of you. They

555

aren't satisfied until you're dead."

Alaina lifted my chin to look at her, "you ever hook up with any of them?" I didn't say anything, I let my silence speak. "Any that are going to be there?" I didn't say anything again. "Let's get going." Then she got out of my lap and walked out the room.

T was talking to Jerrell when I came downstairs. Jerrell had a cold and he was on his way back to normal. He still had a little cough, but our little soldier was improving. Alaina worked from here so that she could stay with Jerrell all day. She didn't want to send him to his dad's while sick. Of course this was the perfect opportunity for Royce to get her on the phone. I will say that he's always shown his son love, and he's always been excited about him. It's just the way he does things now. I can see what he's doing, anything to make him look good. If he only knew how done Alaina is with him he'd stop trying.

Alaina was telling both of the boys she was going to miss them. Jerrell was eating it up of course; I could tell T was trying to play it cool. But I could see him soaking up Alaina's words. We went to Mr. Barton's first. His fiancé opened the door and greeted Jerrell. Alaina handed her Jerrell's bag, hugged him, and then she walked back to the car. Tempest came running out to the car. She's the most excited about us being together. Tyrek always laughs at first and then he gets tired cause the girl will keep us here if she could. On the way back to my house I picked up Alaina's hand and kissed it. I told her that I've been thinking that it only makes sense for her and Jerrell to move in. Alaina started sweating immediately. I didn't say anything; I waited for her to gather her words. Alaina looked out the window as she said, "you agreed to move slow."

"I didn't propose, I'm saying it doesn't make sense for you to pay rent at Unique's when you're always with me."

"This is too fast, next you'll be pressuring me to marry you."

"Why would I have to pressure you? Either you love me or you don't." Her silence irritated my soul. "Look Alaina, I honestly don't know why you feel like you need to pump your breaks with me on everything except our sex life. I don't know what game you're playing. Either we move forward or we break up before you devastate me. I'm not going to beg you to be with me. It's beneath me to stoop to such a level." Alaina didn't say anything she continued to stare out the window.

This is not the way I envisioned our evening going. Normally when the kids are gone we have sex anywhere but in my room. I look forward to it and I know Alaina does. Her little silent act is costing us valuable time. Just agree with how much you love me and let's move on with this.

"Tavio my head hurts. Suddenly I'm flooded with emotions I don't understand." She said locking the garage door behind me.

"Talk to me, cause I'm feeling like I don't know you after all this time."

Alaina went to the kitchen and got two shot glasses and the bottle. She took them upstairs and I followed her. She put the glasses on the dresser, and then she took off her clothes like they were bothering her. She stripped to her underwear and then she poured two shots, she took both of them. Then she poured two more and brought me one. "I hate my mother! I hate her so much Tavio! I don't expect you to understand because your mother is wonderful. Your mother tells Unique real things. Your mother isn't happy about Unique and Benson living together, but is she acting like the world's coming to an end? Is your father? Your parents are giving them space to figure out their relationship. My mother pumped up my head with all this nonsense about how a family is supposed to be. She made us all go to service regularly and put on happy faces while we were there. Then she'd come home and be so depressed. She'd put on her housecoat and just sit or lay in the end. The only time she came alive is when it was time to be fake. I think she loved my father at some point; he was always protecting her even when she was wrong. He still protects her! She was in love with Wesley's father. After Alaysia died he wouldn't see her. He was traumatized, but who wasn't? I felt so trapped being married to Royce! I was constantly telling myself I'm not my mother. One time you were tipsy and you kissed my neck. You didn't even know you did it. I wanted to jump your bones right then and there. I sucked back all my want for you, because I did love my husband. And I felt like I needed to prove to myself that I was not her. It's like there's this battle inside of me. I feel so torn, part of me agrees with my dad. This is wrong and I shouldn't be here. Like I should try to work things out with Royce now that he understands that I'm not taking his nonsense anymore." I felt myself stop breathing. "The rest of me doesn't want to be without you. I want to have something new with you." Her eyes watered up, "you don't try to control me. I get to be free with you. Look at my hair! Look at me! Royce didn't even want me walking around the house comfortable. In the end he was never home, otherwise he would've seen me doing it for attention even if it was an argument." She drank her shot, "you want the wife, the kids, the family. What if some weird retardation happens and I want to go back to Royce? I come from some of the most dysfunctional people. At this point I don't even trust myself."

"What would make you want Royce back?"

She thought about it for a long time. "If he was like the Royce in high school, the one who noticed me when no other boy was looking at me. The one who made me feel special, and loved."

"Does that guy even exist anymore?"

She was quiet for a long time, "when he came back. He came back different. I thought it was all the wedding planning."

"Do you think I'm going to change up on you?"

"Yes," she lowered her head as a tear fell.

That was not the answer I was expecting, "how?"

"I'm going to hurt you and then you're going to hate me!"

"How are you going to hurt me?"

"I don't know, I just know I'm toxic. That's what my dad is screaming about. Like no matter what, I'm going to mess everything up and then my inner Allison will end it all in the bathtub like that's some romantic way to die or something. She let us walk in on her like that. She couldn't wait until my dad was home, coward!" She shook her head, "Wesley's dad refused to see her. He said he was done with married women. It was never about her children, she only cared about herself. She wanted to make sure he knew she was gone. She killed herself to punish him." She looked at herself in the mirror, "I lost her!" She pointed to herself, "the only person who could understand what we were going through. The only person who could've helped me fight back. It was my dad's fault. I viewed him as a victim until he made himself my enemy!"

"Your dad is not your enemy, he loves you very much. He…"

"He went along with her when she screamed at me telling me that there was no Alaysia. He let her spank me for holding on to my twin's memory! Granny Shane gave me the only pictures I have of my sister when my mother died. She told me to put them away from my dad. I knew I wasn't crazy! I just learned not to speak my sister's name."

"Parents handle things wrong sometimes. There's no manual for how to be parents."

"Says the guy with perfect parents."

"My parents are far from perfection. My dad is a sore loser, and my momma don't care. One time their competition turned into an argument and the argument turned into screaming. I just remember hearing slapping noise, and I ran to protect my mom. Police were called; my dad was taken to jail. We all had to go through family counseling, and reconnect. I was angry with my dad for a long time after that. I felt like I had to protect my momma from any side eye he'd give her. I nominated myself as the protector of everyone."

Alaina stared at me with big eyes. "You never told me this."

"It's not anything that I'm proud of. My family isn't perfect, we all have our stuff. Just because my father had to learn how to control his temper doesn't mean that my temper will throw me into a violent rage. I have a bad temper, I know this about myself. You are not your momma; don't let anyone tell you that you will repeat her mistakes. You married Royce and that was a mistake, but it's not like you could've known that.

Despite my attempts to change your mind you married Royce and you were faithful to him. He's the only idiot who would try to convince you that you didn't do your part. That's your past; your present is with me. I am the love of your life. I want to move warp speed ahead! But I'm trying to be fair."

"I do love you Tavio."

"Are you in love with me?"

She exhaled as she looked down, "I don't know!" Ouch! That hurt my pride. How could she not know? "This isn't fair to you."

"Fine, I'll stop pushing." I said heading to my closet. I stripped then I got in my bed. I don't care what she does she's not getting none tonight.

Alaina

Tavio has been one word answering me all morning. It's bad enough that he went to bed with his pillow in a chokehold. I tried to touch him and he shrugged me off telling me to leave him alone. Even though I was irritated, I figured that I'd make a big breakfast in the morning. Normally as soon as he smells food he comes down excited. He eventually came downstairs with his grey sweats hanging off his morning erection looking sexy as all get out. He didn't say anything to me, he opened the cabinet and pulled out a cereal box, bowl, spoon, and he got the milk out of the refrigerator. He took two steps and I lost it. I snatched the cereal box out of his arms and sat it on the counter. Tavio sat at the counter trying to pretend my breakfast wasn't good. I waited for him to take a taste. He closed his eyes and I smiled at him, then I went upstairs. As I climbed the stairs he called out that I could've apologized.

I got my phone and I went in Jerrell's room and shut the door. I stared at my phone, who was I going to call Chareca or Unique? If I called Unique Chareca wouldn't forgive me for not calling her first. And of course I'd loop around and call Chareca anyways so I called her first. I was praying that she and Ken weren't snuggled in and doing the whole no phones thing. Sometimes they disconnect from everything and everyone. They make me sick how they get lost in each other and have all these love fests. When Chareca answered on the second ring I got excited. I asked her what she was doing and she said that Unique and Ben just got to their place and they were about to get out and into their day. I asked her to take Unique into her room and to put me on speaker. When they did, I spilled everything. My conversation with Tavio last night, his attitude this morning. Both of them were quiet for a long time, the silence was eerie. "You are not your mother! Tavio is a good man and all he wants to do is love you. Everybody doesn't get a second chance at love. They may get a second chance at companionship, or intimacy. Real True LOVE! No! Everybody doesn't get that. You're letting things that didn't hold you back from a man who deserved every kind of hold back, hold you back from a man who deserves every goodness you have to give. I'm not saying that just because he's my brother, but because it's true."

"Right, and speaking as someone who's been here since the beginning. You're doubting yourself Alaina. You're letting your father and everybody else get in your head. Royce is trying to manipulate you into thinking he's changed. He's not going to change, he may love you. No I know he loves you! But it's not the love you need. If you were to ever go back to him, realize what you're going back to. **WEAK SEX!** Let me say that first! His overly controlling ways, and eventually he's going to be missing in action again. Trying to blame you for it all."

"Plus, when Eva came out she told me that Royce is still with her friend." That hurt, I fell on Jerrell's bed and stared at the floor. "Do you want the whole story?"

"Of course, as much as you know I need to know. I don't know why you didn't call me immediately."

"I didn't think it mattered, I thought you moved on." Unique took a deep breath. "That last year and a half he was seeing Eva's friend. He went after her and pursued her. They dated in college up until the night before your wedding."

I suddenly remembered coming out of the bathroom nervous as all get out on my wedding night. Royce was knocked out in the middle of the bed. No matter what I did to wake him he wouldn't. Now that I know better that's how he was whenever he was tired, there was no waking him up. "He was cheating on me while we were engaged?" I could barely get out of my mouth, I was crying hard with Jerrell's pillow over my mouth.

"Yes, baby I'm so sorry. He's no good and he ain't ever going to be no good. If he were truly sorry and about to change wouldn't he let Eva's friend go? At least, while he's trying to convince you that he's changed, and that he's worthy of you taking him back?"

"Chareca, you knew this and didn't say anything?"

"No, I'm sitting here with my mouth open. Ken can't know about all of this, he would be so done with Royce. I bet Royce was always feeling guilty and that's why he was the way he was. All short tempered at times and moody."

"Unique, how do I fix things with Tavio?"

"Tavio is your man and he's in love with you. Do what you need to do so that you can fall just as in love with him."

"Ok, so I'm scared. Tavio's always been my best friend. I don't even allow myself to think about that when we're doing *it* cause I don't think I ever would've if I did!"

"GROSS! TMI ALAINA! **TMI**!" Unique screamed which made Chareca and I crack up.

"Sorry, I'm just saying. Everything I feel for him is based off of our friendship. I haven't allowed myself to feel the relationship side of things. That's system overload. I just get stuck and it's like I can't vocalize any of it."

"You need to do something otherwise he's going to believe that you're rejecting him."

There was a knock and then it sound like the door to the bedroom opened. Ken asked what they were doing. They said they were talking to me in unison. Ken told them to get off the phone so that they could go. Ken's voice was all deep and no joking in it at all. Chareca said, "I love you gots to go!" and then she hung up on me. I cried some more then I took a deep breath. I stood up and wiped my face. When I walked back into the bedroom Tavio was back in the bed, laying on his stomach, with the covers pulled up around his neck, but his bottom half of his body was outside of the covers. His sweats were low almost showing off his butt. He was texting someone and completely into his phone. I walked over to him and took his phone out of his hands. He sucked his teeth as he looked at me. I yanked the covers off of him and then I laid next to him and kissed him. He tried not to kiss me back at first but I kept coming for him. I rolled him on his back and then I took his sweats off. I took my shorts off and then I straddled him. I took him in before he had a chance to reach for a condom. Tavio gasped and then he told me to wait. I started working him as hard as I could. Tavio's eyes rolled back as he kept saying wait, wait, wait. When he moaned we both lost it and I would not slow down for anything in the world. Condoms are fine, but there's no better feeling than being skin to skin. Tavio started cursing as he started exploding. Which made me explode right along with him. "I FORGIVE YOU!" He yelled as he gave in to me.

****

There were groupies everywhere just like Tavio said. Girlfriends, wives, managers, agents, all kinds of people. Everyone was dressed up, and I had on a nice dress. But I felt so underdressed because all of my business wasn't hanging out. They were either dressed like vixens or businesswomen. Tavio told me I looked beautiful before we left, but now... All these fake and catty females looked at me and then they looked me up and down like they were trying to figure out why I was here. Tavio asked me if I wanted anything to eat, there was a buffet table to the back full of food. I shook my head no. He said he was going to get us some drinks, which meant he wanted me to go sit. I stood up straight and walked towards the seats in the front of our skybox. These females looked me up and down over and over. You could see the evilness that

563

was going to spill forward as soon as one got the courage. "You're here with Tavio?" One said like she couldn't believe it. "He never brings anyone."

"I am," I said taking a seat in the front row.

"Wait until he sees," one girl said like she couldn't wait for some kind of drama to unfold.

"Didn't he used to date a girl named Hope?" One girl said leaning forward with a messy smile on her face.

"Probably, why should I care?" I started looking out at the court like something amazing was happening out there. I wanted them to leave me alone.

Tavio walked over with two drinks, "ladies." He said dryly.

"Hey Tavio, we were just saying how you never bring a date to any of the games you come to. Who's this?"

"Oh I know right, but this is my wife Alaina." I didn't flinch when he said it, but my body temperature went up. I mean it was only a matter of days before my divorce was final, but goodness. The wife label already.

"WIFE? As in you married HER?" One girl said with so much venom in her voice.

I turned around to say something cause she was on my nerves. "Yep, and you know what. You're irritating me. Why don't you and anyone else who has a problem with it leave this box or the game altogether. I don't want your negativity all up in here." Then he shot her a look. The girl got up irritated, she grabbed her purse, and then she flipped Malaysian Remy over her shoulder and walked out of the box. The other two girls looked like their sister just got beat and they didn't want none. They sat back in their seats and tried to remove any expressions from their faces.

"You can kick people out of here?" I whispered.

"This is my box," then he kissed my forehead.

We watched the game, which was really good. The things I didn't understand Tavio quickly explained to me. At the intermission I excused myself and went to the bathroom. I was walking back to the box when the girl who got kicked out was pointing to me as she spoke to someone. The girl had a baby in her arms and then she looked at me when I looked at her. It was Hope. My eyes quickly went back to the baby trying to figure out how old the baby was. Hope looked at me, she smiled an evil smile then she started bouncing the baby. I smiled and kept walking. Tavio was talking to someone when I walked back in the box. I walked up to him and put my arm around his. Tavio asked what was wrong. The person walked away. I told him I saw Hope in the corridor and she had a baby in her arms. He frowned and repeated my words. Tavio and I walked back to the doorway, Hope was gone. He said we'd see her before we left he was sure of it. I asked him if the baby could be his, he said not that he knew of. The rest of the game Tavio was talking to people who dropped by the suite. Each time he was introducing me to someone and being his normal charming self. I couldn't wait for the game to be over. At the end of the game, someone came in the suite and handed Tavio a print out with his players' stats on it. He was looking over everything as I tried to wait patiently for him to get up. Tavio held my hand as we walked out of the suite. We kept descending down and down until we were next to the locker room. There was Hope and the main messy girl. Tavio said a happy hello to Hope, and then he congratulated her on her baby. She said thank you, then she pushed the blanket from around the baby's face. Tavio looked surprised then he smiled, "when did you and Josh get together?"

"How do you know this is Josh's baby?" Hope asked.

"WHO ELSE HAS EARS LIKE THAT?" Tavio laughed so hard it made me chuckle.

"We got together right after you dumped me." She said like that would have any effect on Tavio.

"I'm glad you found love or whatever. Tell Josh I said

Congratulations." Then Tavio asked me if I was ready to go.

Royce

Rachel has been obsessed with the idea since I mentioned it. She wanted to know the truth. I mean I wanted to know as well, but it didn't bother me like it bothered Rachel. Rachel called me and told me she turned on the locator app on our mother's phone. I told her that was kind of illegal and I couldn't be a part of it. Rachel said she would do it alone, but she wanted to give me the option to be there and know for myself. Rachel decided that she was going to wait until she knew for a fact that our mother was with this guy and then she was just going to show up. She said our mother goes to mostly the same places. And the main one was a house in Berkeley. Curiosity wouldn't let me let it go. So I finally broke down and told her I would go with her. After I dropped Jerrell off to his grandfather, I picked Rachel up. The only words Rachel spoke to me were the directions on which way to go. The rain seemed like the perfect backdrop to this craziness. The house didn't look great at all. This house needed to be upgraded and fixed up. It had character, as Alaina would say when we were looking for houses. This is the type of house Alaina would've liked. In hindsight, the way she upgraded our old house was amazing. It looked like a completely brand-new house by the time I sold it. Her upgrades made the value of the house skyrocket.

"Royce! Pay attention! What's wrong with you?" Rachel was annoyed that I wasn't listening.

"What?" I snapped annoyed with her annoyance.

"Are we just going to walk up to the door and ask for our mother? What should we say?"

"I don't know, I say we wing it." Then I got out of the car. I hurried across the street and on to the steps out of the rain. Rachel was right behind me. I knocked on the door and she started fussing saying she wasn't ready. The door opened and our mother opened the door looking stuck. "Is he here?" I said walking into the house.

"What the? What are you two doing here?" Our mother said trying to pull herself together.

Jazz was playing, a fire was lit and there were two glasses of wine next to the rug that he was lounging on. The guy stood up waiting for us to say something. He didn't look like Rachel, or me but he looked like Jerrell. Or Jerrell looked like him. He looked more like him than he did me. I slumped a little. "IT'S TRUE!" Rachel screamed as she looked at him. "MY NEPHEW LOOKS JUST LIKE HIM!" Then she fell to her knees and held herself crying as she rocked.

"Rachel, get up." He said, and both of us looked at him like he was crazy. He knew who we were.

"Get out of here! Nobody asked you to come here!" Our mother said above her tears.

"What's done in the dark always comes to the light." He said to our mother. "I just can't believe it took this long."

I couldn't say anything, for the first time ever; there was nothing I could say.

Chapter 21

Eva

It's only been months and I feel anxious about it all. Like if my anxiety settles I might change my mind or something.

We had the best time at Tavio's. His son's family came over. It took a minute to place his mother, but I remembered her from high school. Tavio did a wonderful job of making sure everyone got along. Rickie said Tavio is good at what he does. She pointed out that his first, baby momma, and current girlfriend were all in the same space getting along without a drop of tension in the air. I didn't even have to ask Colby if he liked Tavio, those two got a long like old friends. I promise it seemed like they talked about Colby proposing. Tavio kept shooting me goofy smiles. At the end of the night, Unique's man got down on one knee in front of everyone. I got goosebumps thinking about when it would be my turn.

When we got back Colby put his condo on the market and he moved in with me. This man is so excited to be a father. If a baby comes across the screen while we're cuddling he's all over me. When we made the decision to let nature take its course it's like it has been his personal challenge to see how quickly he can knock me up.

Our plan is to buy a house, ceremony directly following, baby in the mix whenever it happens.

******

Colby and I walked around the house taking in everything about it. Five bedrooms and four bathrooms, the square footage on this house almost made me too afraid to see it. This house wasn't far from Colby's parents and Katrina. Colby smiled at me as he looked at the structure of the architecture of the ceiling and walls. I knew he liked the house, where I loved it. For once I wanted to do my own decorating. I could see our family here and all the love in our home. The backyard was huge; as I stood in the window I decided that would be the location of our wedding. Everyone would have to fly out after all. That is whenever this man gets around to asking me.

"What do you think?" Colby asked me.

"I can see our wedding in the yard."

"Our children exploring the yard."

I smiled, "right."

"I liked how your friend had everyone over scattered throughout his yard relaxing and enjoying each other."

"That was nice wasn't it? You would want to do that here?"

"I can see your grandmother and Rickie trying to finally teach you how to cook something during one of our Sunday dinners." That was his way of gently pushing me to deal with the idea of my grandmother.

My grandmother seems to be our only argument that we have these days. He wants me to forgive her, and every time I think of her it pains my soul. She was mean and vicious in the things she said to me. "Right."

"So folks, what do we think?" The realtor said announcing his arrival before he turned the corner. I can only imagine the embarrassing moments he's walked in on.

"We'll take it." Colby told him.

The realtor looked surprised and excited. "Excellent, would you like to place an offer today?" He was a young guy, who's probably been in the business a year or two. Colby liked his vibe even though he isn't as seasoned as we're used to dealing with. Colby said we're giving him a learning opportunity. The Singleton's are very big on supporting black owned businesses. This young fella fit the type. Young, driven, ambitious, and the list goes on and on. When Colby called him with the MLS number for this property, Colby said the guy was silent for a minute. We had to give him an extra day to get the key to show us this place.

"Yes, but we'll have to hurry. I have to get back to the hospital." Colby said extending his arm to me so that we could leave.

When we walked out of the door Colby's parents and family were waiting out front for us to say whether we liked the house or not. As I walked down the stairs I saw Rickie and Quincy. I walked a few steps towards them. The goofy grins on their faces made my heart race. I turned to look at Colby and he was on one knee. He dramatically dropped his head and held out the ring box. I clutched imaginary pearls matching his dramatic posture. Everyone laughed at our play. "Eva, you like this house. That means I love it! I've been in love with you since the beginning. I look forward to the rest of my life with you. Just say yes so we can get on with it." He kissed my lips.

"Yes Colby."

Alaina

I didn't recognize the 925 area code number that was calling me on my work phone. "This is Alaina."

"Alaina," Royce's voice was heavy and he sound like he was on the verge of tears.

"What?"

Royce was breathing heavy, "he's not my father, Byron Chambers is not my father." He kept breathing heavy. "I'm not Royce Chambers. I'm... I'm... I don't know who I am anymore!"

"What happened?"

"Rachel wouldn't let it go, and I didn't want to believe it. We traced my mother to the man she's truly in love with. He's my father."

I immediately thought of Wesley. "You aren't responsible for what your mother has done. Besides unless you get tested how could you know for sure?"

"Jerrell looks like him. Like the parts of him that don't look like your dad." I didn't know what to say to that. "I'm going to have lunch with him. Can you come with me?"

"Royce, I don't... I don't know about that. I need to discuss it with Tavio."

"What am I going to do? Kidnap you? You're still the closest person to me whether you want to be or not. This affects our son and his sense of reality."

My mouth suddenly got dry. I picked up my water bottle. "Is this your work number?"

He exhaled, "yes."

"Let me call you right back." I said as I wrote his number down.

"Fine, please call me right back. I'm over here going crazy."

I took my cellphone and I walked out the door. Down the stairs, and to the parking lot. I pressed Tavio's work number. "Good morning beautiful."

"Hi," I said chewing on my nail.

"Uh oh, I thought after last night you'd be too weak for anything to bother you."

"Royce just called me."

"Oh," is all he said.

"He just found out that Mr. Chambers is not his biological father. He said Jerrell looks just like this man. He asked me to go with him to meet with him for lunch."

"You want to go?" He didn't even try to hide his irritation.

"Yes," I thought about offering an excuse. At the end of the day I wanted to go to be nosey and I didn't want to feel like I was sneaking.

"That's his business not yours, why do you need to go?"

"I just want to, and I need you to be okay with it."

"At some point you're going to have to start letting go."

"Please trust me with this. I need to know you trust me."

"As your friend I understand, as your man I don't like it. You know there's nothing between me and Tempest, but if you said anything about her, made you uncomfortable I'd change it all. Royce still thinks he can get you back. He's still trying. I know this is devastating to him and any amount of sympathy he can pull from you he's going to try to get.

His main objective hasn't changed."

"Baby, that's why I need you to trust me."

"This time Alaina, he needs to understand that you're mine."

"Thank you, your faith in me to do this is all I need." I took a deep breath, "I'm in love with you Tavio. I need him out of my hair." There was absolute silence on his end of the phone. I looked at my phone and our call was still going. "Tavio?"

"Huh?"

"Why are you so quiet?"

"I'm resisting the urge to run screaming through this office." Then he lowered his voice, "it's all your fault. You have successfully turned me on and there is no off button!" He laughed wickedly. "It took you long enough girl! I was thinking about bopping you upside the head or telling you in your sleep."

I blushed as Tavio continued to make me laugh. When I went back to my desk I asked Royce when they were going to lunch. He said he'd pick me up, but I told him I'd come out to his office. Out of habit I looked at myself in the mirror in the bathroom. Royce was going to hate my pencil skirt and cleavage showing blouse. Tavio was trying to convince me to be late once I got dressed. Honestly I was still tired from our night. Or else I would've taken him up on his request.

I told Amir I'd be back later and then I drove to the Concord office. I went to Karen's office and I told her I was having lunch with Royce. She looked like she wanted to tell me no and not to do it. She stifled her response to a sigh and then she asked how much longer until I was completely free. I told her we were in the homestretch.

I texted Royce and I told him I was in the lobby as I waited. Mandy came rushing through the lobby. She looked upset as she hurried past me. I don't think she even realized she was looking at me. "What's wrong?"

"You look amazing," she said sadly.

"What's wrong," I asked again.

"My daughter's sick again. They're trying to get her medicine right. How's your son?"

"He's good thanks for asking. Is she going to be ok?" I rubbed her back.

Royce looked like he saw a ghost as soon as his eyes landed on Mandy. "What is she doing here?"

"You didn't know she's been working in this building all these years?"

"NO!" He stayed back like she had the plague.

"Glad to see the hate is mutual!" Mandy spit at him. Then she started walking towards the elevator.

"Wait a minute, why do you hate him?" I said holding Mandy's arm.

"He's an insensitive jerk!"

"How am I all that?"

"You fired me!"

"No I didn't, you quit."

"Because you were going to fire me!"

Royce flared his nostrils letting me know he was about to lie. "No I wasn't."

"Why did you quit?" I asked Mandy who was trying to reach for the elevator button.

"We got too comfortable knowing each other's business. He knew my man, I know you. When I told him I was pregnant, he felt the need to support my man's indifference about the whole thing. I crossed the line telling him how much of a control freak he is and how he'd end up losing you if he didn't get it together. I guess he listened to me about something, like I said you look amazing."

I felt sorry for her. "You wanna know why I look amazing?" Mandy frowned, "we're almost divorced. I'm free from all of his nonsense," I smiled.

"Why are you telling her that? Don't spread my business!"

A wide range of emotions scrolled over Mandy's face. "But you're his everything!"

"Apparently I wasn't enough, caught him and his mistress red handed." I smiled at myself. I could finally say it without crying or snapping.

"Mistress?" Mandy's head almost snapped off when she cut her eyes at Royce. "You were supposed to be different Royce! That's why I liked you!"

"A lot of good that did me!" He burned her with his eyes.

"I need to think," then she pressed the button for the elevator. As she stepped on the elevator she turned towards Royce. "You're going to pay for this!" Then the doors closed.

Royce was pissed and lost in his thoughts. I watched him as guilt washed all over him. "Alaina I..."

"Yes! Yes! You're sorry; you didn't mean to hurt me. Can we go?"

His eyes swept over my outfit. "What are you wearing?" Then he swallowed.

I twirled, "this is my outfit of the day. Didn't know I was going to see you."

He groaned, "let's go." When he held the door open for me he kept looking at my body. "You remember that time in the shower when we made love?" He called out from behind me.

"Which way is your car?"

"It's on the left," he continued to hang back. "I thought for sure you were going to be pregnant."

I stopped walking, "and then what? You were so disappointed when I wasn't that you stopped trying? Oh wait! That's right, you were singing Whitney Houston and you were saving all your love for her!"

"You didn't like sleeping with me. It wasn't a shared experience." Pain was all over his face.

"Should I drive my own car? You're too emotional."

"No," he walked next to me. "We should've went to therapy together."

"It's not too late for you to go. Matter of fact therapy sounds like it should be in your near future with all of this."

"Will you go with me?"

"Nope, ask your girlfriend."

Royce flared his nostrils, "what girlfriend?"

We rode in silence to a restaurant in Orinda. Orinda's a small city right next to the Caldecott Tunnel on the other side of Berkeley. Royce parked on the street and then he pointed to where we're going. I've never been here; he probably brought his mistress here regularly. He told the host we'd like a table on the patio that was somewhat on the sidewalk. The crowd of people here mostly looked like they were on business lunches. Everyone spoke in low voices and minded their own business. I wondered how many different things were happening in this one room. Royce pulled out my chair then he moaned in agony as I bent over to sit. "Alaina, I've always told you how beautiful you are."

"If only that would've been enough."

He sat next to me and scooted his chair closer to me as he faced me. "I'm using every ounce of self-control I can muster. You are smart, sexy as hell, and the most beautiful woman I will ever know inwardly. I don't want to give you this divorce. I will never love another woman like I love you."

"She should be so lucky," I said biting on a breadstick.

Royce got close enough to my cleavage, where I could feel his breath on me. "You are killing me in this outfit."

I smiled, "you like my hair boo-boo?"

Royce went back to his seat now annoyed by my lack of enthusiasm about his words. "It's becoming on you, I told you that."

"That doesn't mean you like it." I sang and then I took another bite. "My man loves it," I chuckled a little.

"Don't piss me off," then he waved someone on. An older gentleman walked through the restaurant and to our table. He kept staring at me like he was trying to place me. "This is my wife Alaina."

I smiled and stuck out my hand, "soon to be ex-wife. How are you?"

He held on to my hand, "you remind me of someone." Royce has his eyes, they held the same pain.

"More bed hopping with married women," Royce snapped at him.

"I'm Ralph, what has he told you about me?" He stared hard at my face.

My son looks like him, "just that somehow you slept with his mother. I don't understand how, she should've scared you into impotency."

"Why are you looking at her like that?" Royce didn't try to hide his jealousy.

"Would you like to order?" Our waiter asked. Royce and I ordered while his father stared. His hand shook a little as he asked for herbal tea. He asked the waiter to bring it out immediately.

"You're not cold?" Ralph asked Royce.

"No, it's nice out. Why?"

"I just can't afford to be cold." Ralph said hurrying to drink some of his tea. "Where are you from?"

"Richmond," he put his cup down as I said that. "What?"

He looked at me with stretched eyes. "Allison?" He said like that was my name.

"Alaina, Allison was my mother. How do you..."

"WHAT ARE YOU DOING?" Wesley's voice stole my attention. He was angry and stepping over the little gate separating us from the actual sidewalk.

"You knew about this?" Ralph pointed towards Royce and I.

"Knew what?" Wesley asked with disgust in his eyes.

"That they were married, this is your sister right?"

"Of course I know who she was married to."

"She's my kid!"

I sat up straight, "WHAT?"

Wesley and Royce held the same expression. "WHAT?" They said in unison.

"Your sisters are mine too!"

My mouth watered, I put my hand up to stop the vomit. The room started spinning as I grabbed the table to steady myself with my free hand. I shook my head no, "you're.... not.... my.... father!"

"You're not her father! My stepdad is!" Wesley said walking up on Ralph like swinging on him would change anything. A few customers looked at us."

"Stop acting like you're from Richmond and sit down." Ralph told Wesley with a look that said they were about to tussle if he didn't sit.

Wesley sat down, but he was angry. "Wesley, who is he to you?" Royce pleaded with his eyes.

"This is the punk who slept with my mother while she was married to my real father and created me."

"Mr. Barton is not your father?" Royce turned green.

"Not biologically!" Wesley looked at Royce, "why?" Sweat broke out on Royce's forehead then I saw it, he was as sick as I was. He hopped up and hurried to the bathroom. Ralph was gripping his head as he shook it talking to his self. I kept counting backwards as I tried to calm myself. 20, 19, 18.... Every time I gagged I started over. "You never told Royce about us?"

"It wasn't any.... Of his business..."

"But you told Tavio?" I didn't look at him to answer his question.

Royce returned completely sweaty and looking like he would blow again. "Is he?" He pointed at Ralph.

"How do you even know him?" Wesley was still angry.

"He's my father!" Royce said putting his napkin over his mouth.

Wesley gagged, "NO!" He groaned from deep inside. He looked at Royce like he could see it! He shook his head as tears fell down his face. "You are not Alaina and Alaysia's father. My dad got Alaina tested after our mother died to make sure he was her father."

Royce yelled in relief, where I was still sick. "You're still my brother!"

Royce shook his head as he calmed down. "But this is different."

"Only for you! My brother's brother is my brother! This is wrong!" I said as I told my legs to carry me to the bathroom. I made it into the bathroom stall just in time. I stood over the toilet cursing my mother. I HATE her so much! Fortunately this bathroom is really clean. I washed my hands and then I rinsed my mouth.

As soon as I walked out of the bathroom Wesley was standing there with his arms folded. As soon as he saw me he grabbed me, kissed my forehead, and hugged me tight. He rubbed my back as he said this is a gigantic mess. When I walked back to the table Royce had my food wrapped up to go. Ralph the man with the older version of my son's face was standing and looking concerned. Ralph started apologizing immediately, talking about when you're young you don't think about consequences. I didn't want to hear anything he had to say. I was now sick to my stomach and I wanted to get away. Royce told Ralph to stop talking. Wesley walked with me as Royce stayed behind to pay the bill. I asked Wesley what he was doing here. He said Ralph asked him to come meet his son. I looked Wesley in his eyes and I asked him how he knew Dad got me tested? He said Granny Shane demanded it when the truth came out about our mother. Wesley kept hugging me and telling me I was going to be ok.

Royce looked sick and ran down, as he walked to the car. He looked at Wesley like he was looking for traces of himself. "I don't see it, do you?"

"Nope, but maybe this explains why I wouldn't let my family kill you like they wanted to."

"Right," Royce ignored Wesley's comment cause he don't know Granny Shane like that.

"Are you going to be home later, I'll come by." Wesley asked me.

"We moved in with Tavio, I've been meaning to tell you."

Royce collapsed against the car then he got in. "You moved and I didn't have to lift a finger?" Wesley smiled big, "thanks. I'm coming by later."

"Ok!" We hugged and then Wesley walked away.

As soon as I sat in the car Royce went off. "YOU ARE MY WIFE! HOW ARE YOU GOING TO BE LIVING WITH ANOTHER MAN? HAVE MY SON LIVING IN HIS HOUSE! PRETENDING THAT ANYONE COULD EVER REPLACE ME!"

I looked at him with my stomach still a little nauseous. "Even after all of this you can't be serious!"

"I'm serious as a heart attack! You are not my sister. You are my wife!"

I put my hand on my stomach, I tried to calm myself. "Even if we erase this lunch I couldn't ever get back with you. You broke my heart Royce! I let you hold me back from being me. I was not free to be myself with you. Neither one of us were happy. You were fat, and I was wrapped up like a mummy."

"I was happy with you. I was just carrying all of this on my back. Something's were off and I couldn't put my finger on it."

"How's the house sale going?"

Royce tightened his jaw. "It's in escrow."

"Where are you going to live once the house is sold?" Royce was quiet, breathing irritation and frustration. "Look, one day you're going to realize that you moved on from me a long time ago. You don't love me like you think you do."

Royce sucked his teeth and then he turned his body towards me. "Alaina," he gently touched my cheek like he always has. "I'm in love with you. It wasn't always bad between us. Don't focus on just the bad stuff."

"Did you break up with that woman? Do you still see her?"

Royce froze, his nostrils flared. "We... We're not together... We..."

"You're lying!"

"Weren't you cheating on me with Tavio?"

"No, never! He was only my friend. I went after him after you drug out our divorce for the first two years."

"I don't believe you!"

"That's your guilty conscience. You know how you did me and now you're reaching. I was good to you and I took more crap from you than I should've. If you love me like you claim then let me go. Be happy for me."

"I'll be happy for you when you're with me."

I exhaled; I was too tired to talk about this anymore. "I need to talk to my boss and go home. I don't feel good."

Royce started the car, "you went to school behind my back. When did you start working for the bank again?"

I waited until he started driving. "I don't want to get in to the hows and whys. I didn't give up my job."

Royce shook his head, "but I'm the sneaky one?"

"My secrets didn't take away from our family. Just your sense of control."

"A lie is a lie, you hid the money and everything."

"You didn't tell me how much money you made. I found out in court documents that you have way more money then I knew. You tried to break me, make me move out here away from the eyes of my family and friends so that you could run around with that woman and act like there was nothing I could do about it. Well your plan backfired buddy. I landed on my feet and I'm just fine without you." Royce gripped the steering wheel. "I don't want to fight, I'm just…"

"Where was all this fight when we were together? You wait until I can't touch you to do this to me. Maybe if you would've had all this fight during our marriage I wouldn't have done what I did. You never knew nothing, how you wanted your eggs, how you wanted me to love on you… Nothing! I only know what I know, and if you don't tell me how am I supposed to know?"

"That's not fair!" I crossed my arms telling my tears to back off.

"It was frustrating trying to figure out what you would like and what you wouldn't. I loved you and am in love with you despite the fact that you don't know what you want. I tried Alaina; I tried for years to figure out what was wrong. Didn't I ask you?"

"Yes," I said sinking in my seat.

Royce pulled into a parking spot. "I'm not saying I'm perfect or that I did everything right. YOU KNOW I LOVE YOU! You never have to question whether I did or I didn't. Look at today; look at all that happened today. I mean I was close to my mom for a long time. It came down to you and me or me and her. I chose you over my mom. I now see what her problem was, or is. Look at where I come from. I tried and I'm still trying. We could take Jerrell and move anywhere you want to go. We could start over. I don't want to leave, but I would give it all up without a second thought for you. My wife."

I picked up my purse and I was nauseous again. I got out of the car and stood in the doorway. "You're probably only saying that because her job can be transferred anywhere you go. I'm not your wife anymore, I'm in love with Tavio." Then I slammed his door shut. I looked back at Royce and he was sitting in the car madder than I've ever seen him. I hurried onto the sidewalk and inside so that if he suddenly decided to jump the curb in a crime of passion, hopefully I could out run him and make it into the building. When I stepped off the elevator Mandy was standing by the elevator tearfully talking to Karen. Both of their eyes got big when they saw me. I told Karen I felt sick and I needed to go home. She told me to come with her into her office.

Royce

I wanted today out of my head. I wanted to end this scene so badly. Maybe I reminded Alaina too much of Wesley and that's why our sex life never went anywhere. I can't do the lawyer thing today. Mentally I can't do this. I'm falling apart and losing the will to fight anymore. In the back of my mind I could hear food calling me. Foods that didn't even sound good to me. My phone rang with Vanessa's ringtone. I barely got sound out of my mouth. "Hello?"

"You ok?"

"NO!" I looked around the parking lot.

"Should I cook?"

"If you and Brooke want to eat, I'm not hungry."

"What is it?"

"Today has been straight from hell. I met with Ralph, and Wesley shows up."

"Wesley?"

"Alaina's brother."

"Ok, but why?"

"Cause Ralph is his father!" My mouth started watering again.

"WHAT? Say that again!"

"I can't say it again."

"Baby, I'm sorry." Vanessa was quiet for a minute. "Royce, do you need me to come get you?"

I exhaled, "no. I'm going to go get my laptop, and then I'm going to go home." Vanessa was saying something when Mandy walked out of the building. She was trying to find me I could tell. "I GOT TO GO!" I hung up and then I got out of my car fast and moved quickly so that Mandy wouldn't see what car I got out of. I hurried over to the left while she was looking to the right.

As soon as Mandy saw me she started marching to me. I walked towards her as well. "I hate you so much! My boyfriend is not the father. He packed up his things and left last night." Mandy started crying hard. I couldn't say anything because she just shot me with her words. I mean I had a feeling, but now… "My daughter has sickle cell anemia. We're trying to get her medicines right."

"Is that supposed to mean something to me?"

"I don't have sickle cell."

"Neither do I. My son doesn't have it either."

"All I know is she has it and it's a genetic disease that doesn't run in my family."

If it wasn't for Ralph I could stand here for certain and know that there had to have been another guy. If it wasn't for Ralph maybe lunch would've gone differently. If it wasn't for Ralph… I wouldn't be alive. Right or wrong, I wouldn't be here if my mother was the faithful kind of woman. That's a hard pill to swallow. Frustration swelled in my stomach. "YOU'RE AN IDIOT MANDY! I TOLD YOU! I TOLD YOU FROM THE JUMP THAT THIS WAS GOING TO HAPPEN AND YOU ROMANTICIZED BEING A MOTHER!" My anger made Mandy nervous and she started hurrying back inside the building. When she went through the doors I grabbed her shoulder and made her spin around to face me.

Alaina

Karen's eyes were big as I told her everything. About my relationship with Tavio, and my lunch with Royce. At one point Karen grabbed her stomach like my story made her feel as sick as I felt. "Go home Alaina. In the morning go to the office and get your laptop, you can work from home."

"Thank you for understanding," I said wiping my eyes.

"Girl your life is like a soap opera."

"And you know I hate soaps. How did this become my life?" I picked up my purse to go.

"Get some ginger ale for your stomach, matter of fact. I'll walk down with you, I need some for mine too." Karen said grabbing her wallet out of her purse. "Do you think he'll do anything to try to hold up the divorce again?"

"I've asked my lawyer to make sure he can't, but I honestly don't know." I said as I walked ahead of her. "I just want this all behind me, you know what I mean?" I said stepping onto the elevator. There were people on the elevator so we stood silently waiting. The people got off on the second floor. As soon as the elevator doors to the lobby opened we could hear arguing. I rolled my eyes cause after the day I've had I didn't want to hear it. Karen pointed to say that the voices were coming from around the corner where the exit doors were. I rolled my eyes and followed her to the cafeteria. We got our canned sodas and then we walked back into the lobby. As I extended my arms to hug Karen the female voice told Royce to shut up. I wondered if it was his girlfriend. Karen lowered her head, it looked like she was praying, when I started to walk she grabbed my hand and told me to stand still. Then she put a finger up to her ear telling me to listen. I guess she wanted to hear whatever ridiculous thing he and his girlfriend could be arguing in public about.

Royce was frustrated I could hear it all in his voice, "I don't believe you! I need a blood test."

"A blood test? Really? Like I'm just some kind of whore you screwed randomly one night?"

"Were you only with me?" His girlfriend didn't respond, "exactly! So that's why I need to be sure. You're about to turn my whole world upside down and you want me to just take your word for it?"

"You were the one trying to tell me that the baby was probably yours in the first place."

"I wasn't taking ownership, I was saying there was a possibility. Look at the day and age we live in, if your name is not Alaina why would I take your word for it?"

"You're a pig! I hate you so much! You have ruined my life!"

"I ruined your life? So I came at you with this? You were the one walking around basically naked doing everything you could do to entice me. Alaina was supposed to have been your friend." My shoulders dropped, and Karen grabbed my wrist cause she knew I was about to walk around there. Who was he talking to? I wasn't friends with his girlfriend. We met a time or two, but we weren't friends.

"I wasn't trying to hurt Alaina, I got caught up in your stories about your family. Everything got out of hand, and I didn't mean to do it."

"You can't BS me! I'm a lawyer! You are so full of it. You came after me because your life was lacking, and I stupidly let you. You arranged everything, and you initiated it all. How do you think Alaina would feel about you if she knew?"

It was quiet for a minute, "how do you think she's not going to find out? If nothing else your son will tell her when he meets his sister."

"MANDY! I SWEAR TO GOD…" Karen released my wrist to cover her mouth, and I took off around the corner. Karen's eyes got big as she tried to grab for me to come back. It felt like I was running in slow motion even though I was running as hard as I could. Royce and Mandy jumped when I came charging around the corner. "ALAINA!" Mandy put her hands over her head to brace herself. I threw my can of soda as hard as I could and it exploded when it hit Royce in the head and he fell down. I grabbed Mandy by her weave and yanked her towards the ground.

I hit Mandy twice when Karen grabbed me and pulled me back. She had the busted can in her hand. The building security guards were rushing towards us; Karen put the can behind her back. I would not let go of Mandy's hair even though Karen was moving me backwards. One guard grabbed me and the other grabbed my hand and told me to let go of Mandy's hair, but I refused. "Why would I ever come back to you? Just when I thought there was no other way you could hurt me, you devastate me!" Royce was holding his head and blood was dripping from his arm.

The guard that had me told the other one to call the police. Royce was trying to talk, but everyone only paid attention to the fact that he was bleeding. Royce told them it wasn't necessary to involve the police. The guards said they had to fill out an incident report, and then they asked him who hit him. Royce held on to his head as he said no one hit him and that he fell. Mandy told them I threw a can at Royce's head. Royce said she was lying. The police asked Karen and she said all she knew is she came around the corner and Royce fell, she didn't see a can get thrown. We went back and forth with the police for hours. An ambulance came and took Royce to the hospital because he was going to need stitches. It was Mandy's word against ours, and the female officer wasn't going to take me to jail for pulling Mandy's hair when I found out she was sleeping with my husband. I texted Tavio and I asked him to pick up Jerrell for me. He asked if everything was ok, and I told him I'd explain when I got home. "Why would you sleep with my husband?"

Mandy exhaled, "I got caught up. He came to the gym wanting to better himself for you. All he did was talk about you and how excited he was about your son. He didn't come on to me. I made everything happen and was the one to keep things going."

I'm sure she thought her little speech was supposed to make me feel better, but it hurt like she was shooting me. "Where did it happen?"

"It wasn't planned, it's not like we had a hotel room or something."

"Spontaneous rendezvous?"

"Yes, but..."

"You should be proud of yourself. He gave you something he refused to give me." Mandy's mouth fell open with regret. I guess she thought she was supposed to be making things better. "He gave you and that other girl freely what he refused to give me. I guess as long as he was controlling me he didn't have to control you all." I looked at the officer, "are we done here?"

"Yes, you're free to go."

I turned to Karen; "I'll call you later. I think I need to find another job."

"I'll call Kelsey, maybe she can do something. This is a big bank Alaina."

I cried all the way home. I was putting the timeline together in my head. As far as I know it was only Mandy and Eva's friend. That's still two women and a child too many. I called Chareca crying into the phone. She screamed *WHAT*! When I told her that Royce has a child by my coworker. Ken took the phone from Chareca; I guess he needed to hear for himself. They didn't know about Ralph or any of the things I had to say.

Tavio was standing in the doorway when I pulled into the garage. He had concern all over his face but he was trying to be calm. I hugged Jerrell and Lil Tavio then I walked to the bedroom with Tavio on my heels. "I almost got arrested." Tavio frowned cause that wasn't what he expected me to say. "Wait let me backup. Royce and Wesley are brothers! That same slithering snake is both of their fathers."

"Wait a minute, wait a minute!" Tavio put his hands on his temples. "Start over, I'll be ready this time."

I started from the beginning, I let every tear fly. I said everything on my heart. I told Tavio how much I hated my mother. I expected him to try to talk me down or tell me not to. Instead he rubbed my back and told me he empathized with me. He told me about the feelings he experienced when he hated his father. They were for different reasons, but the emotions were spot on. We sat in the middle of the bed talking. Tavio understood what I meant which made me cry. My tears were cleansing and curing what aches inside me the most. Tavio made me some chamomile tea to soothe my nerves and my stomach. When Wesley called, he said I wasn't home when he was going to come. I explained the rest of my day to him. I told him I needed to rest cause I didn't feel good. Wesley gave me a hug over the phone, and he said he'd check on me in the morning.

Tavio

Alaina finally calmed down and fell asleep when her phone started vibrating. An unsaved number was calling. I pressed the button so it would stop buzzing. Two minutes later the phone signaled that she had a voicemail. Twenty minutes later it rang again. I pressed the button again. Alaina was finally calm and no longer puking every two hours. I was right there with her. If I found out my ex was my brother's sibling it would upset me too. That's too close to home. I mean Jerrell is a crazy little kid, but that's too much. I was starting to doze when my phone rang. It was the same number that had called Alaina's phone. "Hello?"

"Tavio," the female voice was jittery. "This is Vanessa. I've been trying to reach Alaina. Can you have her call me? It's an emergency."

"Hold on," I took the phone off of my ear. I gently rubbed Alaina's shoulder. "Baby, the phone is for you."

Alaina barely opened her eyes as she took the phone. She moaned then she said a sleep heavy, "hello?" She listened then she frowned, "who is this?....... My father?..... How do you?..... Wait a minute! Wait a minute!" Alaina sat up and wiped the sleep from her face. She shook her head, and then she put the phone back to her ear. "Ok, I'm awake. Start over!..... What hospital?.... Why would he call Royce?.... I'm on my way!" Then Alaina handed my phone back to me. "My dad and that woman were in a car accident. My dad called Royce cause Wesley hasn't answered his phone. Royce can't drive so Royce's girlfriend snuck and called me." Alaina went to the bathroom.

I got up and started pulling on my clothes. She paused when she came out of the bathroom. "You're in no position to deal with this on your own. T can keep Jerrell home tomorrow or today actually. Let's go find out how serious this is." I went in T's room and told him to call me if anything happened.

Alaina nervously bounced her leg as I drove. "Why is this day still going? Stop the madness already." She looked out the window. "Pull over!" She covered her mouth. I did and she threw up the tea I made her earlier.

"Baby you've got to calm down. You're working yourself up too much."

Alaina grabbed napkins out of the glove compartment. "Is this nerves?" She let her question linger.

I got lightheaded, "well... wha.... wha... What else could it be?"

Alaina was still looking down clearing her mouth. "Would it be the end of the world if I was pregnant?"

My body temperature shot up and sweat beads formed on my forehead. "Uh, um nope. I mean no. It wouldn't be the end of the world, we just hadn't discussed babies. You just came out the closet less than twenty-four hours ago."

Alaina was calm and slightly irritated. "Let's talk!" She turned off the radio. "My life has been full of other people's expectations. Everyone else's wants and ideas for me." She looked at me, "today. I mean yesterday last night sealed it. I'm over it all. Tavio I love you, I'm in love with you. I can't even believe that I trust you like I do after everything that I've been through. I want to climb into your lap right now. I want everything with you. Let's have a baby."

"Can your divorce be final first?"

"Do you want to get married?"

"Yes!"

She took deep breaths, "I'd do it for you. What would be different between now and then?"

I could tell she was going to tell me that marriage wasn't necessary. "You would be Mrs. Spellman, the highest honor I could give you. You'd be entitled to everything that I am, and the same for me."

"What's the difference between that and now?"

"Right now we allow each other that space. Do you love me?"

"Yes."

"Do you trust me?"

"Yes."

"Then you should trust me to be your husband." I parked the car, "kiss me." Our kiss went on and on. It escalated and I didn't intend to escalate. However I ain't no punk neither. We went from the front to the backseat. I didn't mean to act like a teenager in this parking lot. The more we escalated the more excited Alaina got. Alaina orgasmed so hard I thought her head was going to explode. Alaina kept grunting "I do! I do!" until she couldn't talk. She opened her mouth like sound was supposed to come out, but her screams were inaudible. The slightest movement took her back to the top of her orgasm. It took us an hour and a half to get out of that car. And at that point it was more or less like we had to get out before we never did. Alaina grabbed my hand as she shivered. We walked into the hospital completely calm and relaxed.

Mr. Barton and his girlfriend were waiting in the waiting area. His face turned angry as soon as he saw us. "You aren't even trying to spare my feelings!"

Alaina peacefully put her hands up. "Look Dad! It is what it is. You don't approve, oh well. We're in love and we're going to be together. If you don't want to be a part of my life just say it. You won't see me anymore. But you don't control me or my life anymore. Throwing tantrums about the things you can't control won't help you either. You would rather I be as miserable as you were while you were married to my mother. Suffering behind my love for someone who would never love me back."

"Royce loves you!"

"No, he loved the control he had over me. You know who called me tonight? The woman he lied to me just yesterday about. He said he broke up with her and all this nonsense. Then I find out he has a daughter, a Babygirl! And he was laying in the bed of the woman he denied nursing a concussion. I will NEVER get back with Royce! Look at me daddy! I'm free! I'm happy! I'm content! I'm exactly where I deserve to be. With a man who loves me and has no desire to control me. Tavio and I are going to have a family and a whole happy life. If you can't accept me, fine. You won't know your grandchildren, and you can go on being a hypocrite."

The girlfriend looked embarrassed, "how did the accident happen?" I asked assessing their injuries. Mr. Barton hit his head, while his girlfriend's face was banged up on her right side. Her right arm was in a sling, it looked like she suffered the most damage.

"I blinked," he said angry.

"You blinked? You fell asleep?" Alaina asked.

Mr. Barton's girlfriend looked irritated as Mr. Barton tried to dance around the answer. She put her hands up like she had enough. "My head was in his lap and he couldn't handle it." The look of betrayal on Mr. Barton's face was priceless. "She's right! I've told you for years that you're wrong and you're too stubborn to get it."

"You got in a car accident while your girlfriend was giving you head and you want to say something to me!"

She held up her hand, "wife. We've been married almost a year."

"Ooh! I'm telling Granny Shane!" Alaina smiled with the satisfaction of getting her father in trouble.

"Please Alaina, I'm grown."

"So am I, but you seem to believe that I still answer to you. I know my granny don't know about this, cause she would've said something."

"Alaina please don't."

Alaina looked at her father, "you've been horrible to me like I did something wrong in my marriage. Royce cheated on me with not one but at least two women! He even has a daughter to show for it, and you wanted me to rollover and accept that. You've shown me no loyalty or concern for my heart. I'm telling and I hope you get a whooping too!" Alaina put her phone up to her ear.

"It's the middle of the night, wait." Mr. Barton said taking his hands out of his pockets.

"So!" Alaina said sticking her tongue at her father. He wasn't expecting her to do that. "Granny, I just wanted to let you know..." Mr. Barton started charging Alaina telling her not to say anything. Alaina took off running while she spoke above her laughter. Alaina sang like a canary while her father chased her. Alaina's stepmom stood there laughing at them. Mr. Barton finally snatched the phone and started explaining.

Alaina

Tavio and I waited on one side of the waiting room, while Royce waited on the other. He openly stared at us, and I ignored him while Tavio stared back. "Alaina Barton and Royce Chambers?" The person called from the door.

I stood and Royce looked annoyed, I know he saw in the divorce papers that I was not keeping his name. We barely sat at the table but Royce started flapping his gums. "You hate me that much that you can't wait to change your name back?"

"Yes," what would be the point of sugar coating things for him?

"Alaina, you've never sat down and talked to me. One on one just you and I. It's not too late to save our marriage."

"I hate to interrupt folks, but the purpose of this mediation appointment is to map out your custody agreement. I..."

I cut him off, "let me say this and then we can get to the point of this meeting. Royce, you and I will never get back together. Mister recorder man you can document this promise. The only way I would get back with you Royce is so I could kill you in your sleep. You're a liar, which makes you perfect for your profession. I asked you directly about your girlfriend, you lied and said you broke up with her. She called me that night cause you were incapacitated." Royce frowned at me. "She didn't tell you in the morning?"

"You're lying," he tried to shrug me off.

"My father was in a car accident and he called you after he couldn't get in contact with Wesley to ask for a ride. She called me to tell me where he was. I guess that was her way of letting me know she was standing by you regardless." Royce looked like he didn't believe me. So I opened my phone and called out her number. "Check the call log and date." I held my phone in front of his face. "We are never getting back together! Deal with it!" Then I looked at the mediator. "Now we can move on!"

Royce

I stood at the mailbox staring at the two envelopes. What are the odds that my divorce documents and the paternity results would arrive on the same day? My father made it clear that his loan for our previous home purchase was to be paid to him out of my portion of the proceeds from the sale of my house. I didn't even care.

I opened the envelope from the courts showing the finality. I'm divorced, once again single and feeling so lost. Even though it was an overcast day, the sun shined in my eyes and made them water. I rubbed my eyes and put the envelope under my arm. I opened the DNA results and the first thing I saw after the colors from the grid was the 99.99% results of the DNA test. I cursed! I can't stand Mandy and now this! When I walked back inside the condo Vanessa and Brooke were laughing about something at the kitchen island as they cut up fruit. Their smiles dropped when I walked in the door. "99.99%!" I dropped the letter on the counter and then I went to the bedroom. I shut the door and then I sat on the bed.

Vanessa came in the bedroom and then she put her arms around me. "It's going to be ok. This changes nothing you hear me?"

"Alaina hates me!"

"Of course she does, you lied to her. Made her believe that you were someone else. You didn't own the drama you brought to your relationship. You weren't ready to be the man she needed you to be. You can sit here and beat yourself up about the past or you can move forward with me. Ralph is going to be here in a little bit. Let's tell Mandy to bring Arianna over as well so you can meet her. If Mandy isn't reasonable then we'll go to court. I'd rather get the introductions out of the way before I'm too tired to deal with anything." Then she kissed my lips. Vanessa picked up the phone and called Mandy. She gave her directions and then she told her to come as soon as she could.

"Thank you. I appreciate you not falling apart about this."

"All of this is our past, we're leaving all of our painful and selfish behaviors behind us and in the past. You hurt Alaina, and I've hurt my only friends." Vanessa lowered her head and I saw tears drop.

I lifted her chin, "it's all my fault. You didn't deserve what I did to you. I took you outside of yourself. I can see now that I have that effect on women. I got women cheating on their long time boyfriends. Running away from the state broken hearted. Sleeping with my sister to get back at me for breaking their lovers heart! It's time for me to man up. It's just hard you know?" Vanessa shook her head yes. I stood her up and then I caressed her stomach. "It's a totally different experience when both of you want it."

Vanessa kissed the top of my head, "I love you Royce. We're going to find a new normal and move forward."

Then the doorbell rang. I took a deep breath, everything was happening. I could hear Rachel introducing someone. Vanessa came out of the bedroom and Rachel was with someone. She introduced us to her boyfriend. This guy was about our age. She always described her boyfriend as older and less African American than this guy who could've grew up next door to us. I put my hands out asking the unspoken question. "This is Tevin, I finally decided to give a good guy a try. I don't want to be like her."

"Nice to meet you Tevin, this is my fiancé Vanessa, I'm Royce."

There was another knock at the door. Vanessa answered and introduced herself and then I heard Mandy's voice. When she walked in the door she was holding the hand of the cutest little girl I've ever seen. I looked at her and I saw Jerrell immediately. "Royce?" Rachel and Brooke said at the same time.

"That's my sister Brooke and my sister Rachel." Mandy waved as she said hello. "This is my baby's momma Mandy."

Rachel bent down next to the little girl who looked around while holding her mom's hand. "What's your name little lady?"

"Ari-ya-ya," her little precious voice said.

"I'm your Auntie Rachel, can you say Auntie Rachel?"

"Auntie… Ray-bell."

Everyone laughed, "and I'm Auntie Brooke. Can you say Auntie Brooke?"

"Auntie Book," Arianna said like she was proud of herself.

"Let's go talk for a minute, excuse us." Vanessa said directing Mandy and Arianna towards the home office. "Come in, have a seat." Vanessa held the door open for them as I followed in the very back. Mandy sat on the love seat and she sat Arianna next to her. Arianna was so little and so cute. Her little ponytails dangled just above her ears. And her mother had her hair in a bunch of ponytails with barrettes all over that matched her little outfit. Mandy seemed nervous and Arianna was picking up on it. She looked from her mother to us. "So like I said over the phone, we got the results of the DNA test today."

"Wait a minute, who are you? I mean I know you introduced yourself as his fiancé over the phone when you called with the arrangements to get the test. But who are you?"

Vanessa and I turned our chairs to face them on the couch. I sat in front of Arianna and smiled at her. She smiled a little as she looked me over. "I'm Royce's fiancé."

"You were the mistress?" Mandy said getting to the point.

"What you need to know is that I am going to be his wife." Vanessa picked up papers off the desk. "Here's what we plan to pay for child support. We would like to have Arianna the same weekends that we have Jerrell, which currently stand as every other weekend. We'd like the kids to know each other and bond as siblings should."

"The whole weekend?" Mandy looked like she was going to have a fit.

"Yes, we'll all need to adjust to everything. Do you have any questions?" Vanessa had her business hat on. She was speaking matter of factly and Mandy was all emotion.

"Yes, what is all of this?" Mandy shook the papers at Vanessa.

Vanessa exhaled then she pointed to the papers. "This is the amount we're going to pay you for child support. We will need her social security number to put her on Royce's medical and life insurance plans. We need to know about your expenses for her so that we can split them in half with you. Now Royce told me that Arianna has sickle cell, have you accumulated medical bills behind hospital trips?"

"Of course, but we finally have her medication right."

"Give us the bills and we'll pay them off. In the future, we'll make sure that she has everything she needs."

Mandy looked at me teary eyed. "You're still trying to be mister wonderful?"

I ignored her comment, I know Vanessa's plan to make both households equal was going to make her feel like I was saving her. When she thought the world of me before that was how everything started. "You can thank Vanessa, she put all of this together just in case." I didn't take my eyes off of my…. my baby girl. "Arianna, do you know who I am?" Arianna shook her little head no and her ponytails shook. "I'm your daddy."

Arianna looked surprised, "I have a daddy again?" She looked to her mother to tell her the truth.

"Yes baby, this is your real daddy." Mandy said as tears ran down her face.

"Can I have a hug?" I put my arms out. Arianna shimmied her little body off the love seat and took the two steps to hug me. I picked her up and sat her in my lap as I kissed her cheek. "Guess what else, you have a big brother and his name is Jerrell. He's going to be here in a little bit."

"Alaina's coming here?" Mandy looked worried.

"Only to drop Jerrell off, she never comes inside. She doesn't even come to the door. Most times her boyfriend walks Jerrell up."

"Do you have any questions about the paperwork?" Vanessa asked Mandy.

Mandy smiled, "you are the girlfriend aren't you?"

"In a little bit I will be his wife." Vanessa looked irritated.

Someone knocked at the door and then Brooke popped her head in. Being nosey and everything else. "Jerrell's here."

"Send him in here." Then Jerrell walked in the door, he looked at Arianna sitting in my lap like she was crazy. "Jerrell this is your little sister Arianna. Come say hello."

Jerrell's face lit up, "I have a little sister?" He hurried over and said, "hi. Do you want to go play with my toys?"

Arianna shook her head yes, and then I put her down. Jerrell held her little hand as they walked out the room. I was smiling thinking about my children having each other like I have my siblings. When I turned around Mandy was looking at me and smiling. I looked at Vanessa who was looking at me too. "What?"

"Children are so simple." Then Vanessa looked at Mandy, "are we going to have a problem?"

Mandy shook her head no, but I could see that look in her eyes. I exhaled cause I don't want nor need any more problems. Mandy cleared her throat then she sat up. "Let's be realistic, if I'm reading my audience properly I think we'll be fine. If... You know how to share Vanessa."

I gasped then I looked at Vanessa to see how she responded. If looks could kill Mandy would be dead. "Share?"

Mandy smiled then she leaned forward. "He wasn't yours in the first place. You got him by default. You were already sharing. I'm not some random stranger, share with me every once in a while and there won't be a problem."

Vanessa crossed her legs and then she rubbed her stomach before she thought about what she did. "I don't know what you think this is, but Royce and I are about to be married."

"Different marriages are made of different things. I saw you check me out; you know what's up. Royce and I had fun, and he knows I get weak in the knees when he does the knight in shining armor bit. "Vanessa looked at me like she was trying to read what I hadn't said. " You didn't share that part mister lawyer?" Mandy smiled.

Vanessa looked me in my eyes, "you manipulative slithering snake!"

"Hey! Wait! I didn't even remember all of that. I wasn't plotting, I swear Vanessa. I've been honest and forthcoming about everything. Why would I play dumb now?" Vanessa looked at me as she tried to calm herself.

"And now it's my turn to be honest. I don't want a full on relationship, but I have no intentions of being celibate. Royce you were a superb lay, and seeing everything you plan to do for our daughter has moved me into a non-hate section. I'm using everything in me not to jump on you right now." Vanessa was breathing hard. "Look at it this way. You'll know where he is, and he knows if he wanders beyond me we will ruin him."

Vanessa was frustrated, "SAY SOMETHING!"

I sat there trying to grab words out of the air. "Mandy, no" I shook my head no. "I mean I'm flattered, but I can't. Being selfish is how I lost my first wife. I don't want to ever get divorced again."

"Uh huh," Mandy gave me that smile like she wanted to jump on me. "Vanessa, he'll do it if you say yes. I guess we're all about to be best friends. After you have that baby maybe we can all hangout."

"Calm down Mandy," Vanessa looked at me as if I betrayed her and told Mandy about our past. "I need everyone to calm down. Mandy stop messing with Vanessa like that."

Mandy took her jacket off, "it's cool if I hang around right? Arianna has only spent time with my mother and I. She needs time to adjust."

"Royce go talk to your sisters, or check on the kids. I want to talk to Mandy."

I went to Jerrell's room. He was showing Arianna one of his toy planes. He was explaining that the people inside the plane never fall out no matter which way you turn the plane. For some reason this made Arianna very happy and she laughed which made Jerrell laugh. Then he took the plane on a flight that made Arianna laugh harder. Their laughter was like music to my ears. I always knew Jerrell would be a good big brother. I just never imagined that child wouldn't come from Alaina.

Vanessa can act mad all she wants, but I know she needs to feel like she's seducing someone or she'll go stir crazy. I didn't expect Mandy to dive in. I thought the topic would come up, but much later. If I can't have Alaina shouldn't I get everything else? Bet she'll think twice about going around me to make phone calls from now on.

I watched my children play peacefully for a while. The doorbell brought me back to the room. I took a deep breath then I opened the door. Ralph was taking the same deep breath as I opened the door. I invited him in and his eyes landed on my sister. "Brooke, I always knew you'd be a beautiful young lady."

Brooke looked at me, "why does he know who I am?"

"I've known your mother for a very long time." Then he looked at Rachel and smiled, then his smile lessened as he responded to the look on her face.

"Can you act like you're just meeting us? You may know all this background information about us, but we don't know you. This is hard enough without you acting like you just know everything."

"I understand, I'm sorry. It's just that you have no idea how hard it's been for me to stand down and watch you all from a distance and you had no idea who I was."

Rachel bit her tongue, "whatever. This is my boyfriend Tevin, Tevin this is Ralph."

"Nice to meet you," they said in unison.

"What do you want my kids to call you?" I said before going to get them.

"Plural? I thought you only had one?"

"We're waiting on the story too," Brooke said.

"I cheated on Alaina. There's your story. What do you want my kids to call you?"

"Gramps is fine," Ralph said taking a seat on the couch.

"Come on kids there's someone I want you two to meet."

Ralph's eyes got really big when he saw them. "They look like me!"

Vanessa and Mandy came out of the room looking normal and like they reached an agreement. They stood on either side of me, and then Mandy rubbed my butt on her side of me. Once everyone left and Brooke went to bed we were going to have to discuss rules.

Eva

I took several deep breaths and then I got out of my car. It seemed like forever ago that I even lived here. I rang the doorbell, and I heard Quinn's little feet running to the door. My grandmother opened the door and then she looked at me with surprise, but she didn't say anything. "I talked to my mother today and she said that you two have been talking, more like arguing, ever since we came back from California." My grandmother nodded, then she sat down on the couch. I picked up Quinn and I gave her a hug. "You've apologized enough so I'm not here for that. Somehow in the process of falling in love with me, Colby fell in love with the idea of you as a grandmother. He's threatening to hold up everything if you're not invited to our wedding." My grandmother tried to hold back her smile. I took a deep breath, "so will you give me away during my ceremony?"

"OH BABY YES!" My grandmother exclaimed as she gave way to tears.

I can't stand Colby sometimes, when I asked him if he set the date with the caterer he dropped the bomb on me that there would be no nothing without my grandmother there. I was prepared to hold my ground until he successfully held out on me that night. I mean I pulled out all the tricks, everything I could think of to get him to give in. He wouldn't let me touch him or anything. When he turned down everything I knew he meant it. So I decided to have her give me away to one up him since he thinks he's so smart.

My grandmother hugged me and squeezed me tight as she cried. Quinn looked from each of our faces.

****

We could hear the music all the way upstairs in the attic. Unique looked out the window as she admired the grounds of our home. Our house came with plenty of land around it, a lot like Colby's parents. Our ceremony chairs were set up facing the gazebo. And we had a tent So many feet away for our reception. The tent was very thin so that at night we could see the stars and look up heavenward during our celebration. Unique has been in love with our setup since she and her fiancé arrived the other day. Her ceremony is next month on the heels of ours, she is just bubbling over with excitement.

Our mother and Grandmother were fussing as usual behind me. We've all come to understand that fussing is what they do. Sometimes they're not even mad, but they fuss with each other even when they're enjoying each other's company. We had to learn to tune them out and let them express their relationship in their way. If my grandmother says yes, then my mother has to say no. That's just how they are and there's nothing that anyone can do to change that.

Rickie and our little sister stood to the side as my hairdresser put my veil on. Both of their eyes got big the same way. Rickie got emotional as she said I looked beautiful. My hair was pulled back into a bun. My headpiece was beaded and dipped at my forehead to give me a widow's peak. My long veil was pinned to my head below my bun. When I turned around they stopped fussing. My mother popped hard candy in her mouth then she fell out into dramatics about me. Telling me how beautiful I looked and how much she loved me. I looked in the mirror and I felt like a chocolate goddess.

I was happy this day was finally here cause I was sick of exercising and watching what I ate so that my dress fit. Unique's man designed and made my dress. Unique offered me up as a peace offering because she didn't want him to make hers. She told him she wanted him to be surprised when she walked down the aisle. She said it was torture because he pointed out all the things he liked about my dress as if he was showing her what she should be looking for. Unique and I are two different body types. I'm curvy and she's athletic. I'm pleasantly plump and she's lean. After we did all of our gasping and almost crying Rickie called the coordinator and told him we were ready. Mrs. Singleton gave me the biggest hug and kiss on my cheek. Then she walked out to start the procession. Katrina gave me an excited hug as she told me I was legally her sister now.

There was a moment when only my little sister and I were waiting in the attic for the cue to move forward. She stared at me with innocent big eyes. "Come here baby," she smiled and hurried to me and hugged me. "I love you so much, I want you to remember something." She shook her head yes as she looked up at me. "Our parents do not define us, they simply remind us of where we come from. You can be whatever you're willing to work hard to be. Hard work is as good for you as eating and drinking. Don't let one person and a series of persons close your heart to everything you deserve. You are going to be the real success of this family. You are going to be the one that everyone brags about your accomplishments. Do you know why?" She shook her head no, "because you're the strongest."

"I'm not stronger than you Eva, nobody is."

"Not true, do you know how I know you're stronger than me?"

"How?"

"You live with our parents, and all of our family and you still smile. You might not think much of that now, but when you get older you will realize that what I'm telling you is true. I want to be like you when I grow up."

That made her laugh, "thank you Eva."

Our Grandmother walked into the room. She said it was time. My sister picked up her basket full of fresh rose petals. Then we carefully walked down all the stairs. When we walked out of the sliding doors all one hundred and fifty of our guests stood for me. My grandmother held out my hand as if she was presenting me to everyone. When we passed Tavio and MAC they were smiling and holding hands. I looked at my family and friends feeling complete. Colby had the goofiest grin on his face as he watched my grandmother and I walk to him. When we met him in front of the gazebo we practiced walking up the stairs, but instead Colby met me with a kiss that made me almost forget where we were. People were applauding him and saying that's right and stuff like that.

During our first dance as husband and wife Colby held me close as he whispered I love you's in my ear. I kissed his cheek and stroked the back of his head as I ate it all up. So I decided to whisper a sweet nothing of my own in his. "I think I'm pregnant." Colby squeezed me tighter as he tried to keep his composure.

Alaina

Chareca showed no shame as she assisted the Pleasure party associate. She offered true testimonies to some of the items. We couldn't stop laughing as some of Unique's friends laughed, gasped, and giggled. Chareca called herself being funny as she passed me the lube and asked how many should she put me down for. I smiled and said I didn't need it as I gave it back to her. Then I took a sip of my wine. Chareca passed the tube to someone else but I knew that meant she was going to loop back around to it later. We played tons of games, and then we went into the bedroom with the consultant and placed our private orders. At the end of the night, it was Chareca, Unique, Eva, and her sister Rickie, and I. We were still light hearted from the evening and all of our drinks. "So how's married life?" Unique asked Eva.

"Wonderful!"

"I know Saturday is Unique's day, but I have to ask. Why aren't you drinking?" Rickie asked smiling at her sister.

Eva looked at Unique as if she was asking for permission to speak. Unique smiled real big and told her to tell us. "I'm just a little bit pregnant."

Everyone screamed congratulations to her. Then Chareca gave me an evil grin. "So come out with it. Why you trying to act like you're too good for the lube?"

"All I said is I don't need it." I don't know why I was embarrassed.

"If you don't need it, then you don't need it." Unique said not understanding the significance of it.

"How you don't need it now?"

"Everything is completely the opposite with my man. I don't need help with the things that come naturally with him."

"What does that mean?" Chareca asked.

Eva smiled at me, "so you're saying that you're getting it good now so you don't need the help you needed before."

"Right," I said then I looked at Chareca. "Fine, listen I don't need lubes anymore. Turns out that I create more than enough lubrication naturally. I was looking at it at the store one time, and Tavio asked me what I thought I needed it for. I explained, and then he explained to me why we needed to change the bed sheets every time. Then he pointed out why we didn't need it."

"Un huh, so what are you saying?" Everyone was leaning in to hear my answer.

"TMI CHARECA! GOD!" I put my hand up from embarrassment.

"MY GIRL! Welcome to the club!" Eva said excitedly. "My man is an absolute freak and once we hit that level it was completely over for both of us."

"How come I still need help sometimes?" Rickie asked sounding like a child who really wanted to know.

"A lot of women need help every once in a while. Only a small amount of women don't need a little help every so often." Eva explained everything as we all sat around listening with our mouths open. She gave them all homework, things to try.

When I got home, Jerrell and T were still up. Jerrell wanted to make sure he was walking right so every moment he got he was practicing his wedding march. They had their showers already and T explained that time got away from them. When I walked in the bedroom, Tavio had paperwork all over his side of the bed. He was watching someone's film and he had fallen asleep. When I turned off the television he jumped. The boys said goodnight as they walked past the door. "More research?" I smiled.

"This kid has amazing potential, I guess I got so caught up in the ideas that I fell asleep. How was the girl's night?"

"It was good, we had a good time." I helped Tavio put his papers away. "Is it weird to you when I hang out with Eva?"

"Not really, it would be if you made it weird though."

"Are there any similarities between me and Eva?" I watched his face.

"You're both black women."

"Besides that of course."

"At different times in my life I was or am in love with either of you." He looked at me like he was clueless.

"That's it, nothing else about us is similar?"

"You want to shave your head? I don't know about that, you see Jerrell's dome. I don't know if you have the right head shape for something like that."

"Ha! Ha! Ha! Very funny." I took my pajamas out of my drawer.

"Wait whoa, what did I do to deserve to get the pajamas?"

"Nothing, I'm tired." I said walking to the bathroom. I showered then I went to get in the bed. Tavio wasn't sleep, he had music playing and he was waiting for me. I took a deep breath and told myself to be strong. When I got in the bed I turned my back to him and pulled the covers up to my neck. Tavio scooted in close and then he kissed my neck. My body's immediate reaction told me this wasn't going to end the way I wanted it to. I moved my shoulder to fan him off. Tavio's hands went everywhere as he kissed all over my back. When he came back to my neck it was over for me. My resolve to hold out completely vanished and I kicked the covers onto the floor. Tavio asked me how I thought I was going to hold out on him? I didn't say anything, I couldn't. It was like he imprinted in my mind that any time I tried to turn him down this is what I would be missing out on. It was so good that the memory of our session knocked me out.

In the morning, Tavio was working in his home office and I took the boys to school. When I got home, I sat on the couch in the living room searching the Internet for anything about female ejaculation. Some sites said it was a myth, and they down played it a lot. Then I found women's testimonials. Tavio came downstairs and found me in the corner in the living room completely involved in my screen. He scared me when he touched me. He asked me what I was doing, and I told him it was none of his business. Tavio wasn't even curious; he said ok and walked to the kitchen. Ben called him going over something for the wedding. I decided to make a breakfast sandwich for myself. As I took everything out I asked Tavio if he wanted one. He was silent, when I asked again I realized he was probably in the living room looking at my laptop. I ran and he was smiling as he looked at my screen. I tackled him and told him he was too nosey. Tavio asked me why I was looking at all of that. I told him about Chareca offering me lube and how I told them I didn't need it anymore. "Have you experienced this with anyone else?"

"Sabrina, that's how I knew what it was."

"She was the only one before me?"

"It's not a common occurrence. Why you think she and I were together as long as we were?"

I don't know why I needed to hear him say it to feel ok with it. I didn't want to feel like there was something that Eva had over me. I know I shouldn't think of her like that. She's clearly happy with her new husband, but every once in a while your mind drifts. "I really didn't know." Saved by the bell I ran to answer the phone. It was my old boss Karen's boss Kelsey. I couldn't believe how much these two ladies liked me and fought for me to maintain my independence and work experience. Kelsey said she had a position that she thought I would be a good fit for. She explained the job and the part I loved most is that I would work from home and there would be minimal travel required. The money was better than my manager position. I only pay the utilities as it stands, but I want to contribute more. Knowing Tavio he'll make any additional contributions about food. Kelsey asked if I could meet them for lunch tomorrow, and I said I would be there.

****

"Alaina Barton, this is Nohemi Sindell-Hughes." Kelsey said as she introduced us.

"Nice to meet you, you come highly recommended," Nohemi smiled.

"Thank you, it's nice to meet you as well."

I immediately liked her; she put me at ease by sharing things about her family with me. She's happily married with four kids. One in college, two in high school, and one on their way to high school. She said she and her husband have plans to travel and just enjoy each other once all the kids are gone. She shared that her husband has his own equipment rental company. She said he started out leasing farming equipment, and now he has construction equipment as well as anything else we could think of. She was so proud of her husband; you could definitely see her love for him as she spoke. So I shared that my boyfriend and I plan to expand our family as soon as we agree on when. She assured me that time with my family was important to her since she has one of her own. Nohemi explained the position and what her managing style is like. Kelsey told me I'd get an offer letter in the mail by end of next week.

****

Unique was freaking out, and we were trying to calm her. All this time she was dead set on picking out her own dress. Her dress is beautiful, but now an hour before her wedding she's having second thoughts about it. Rickie, her maid of honor, was the best at calming her. Eva ran to get her mother; but Unique was completely melting down. Mrs. Spellman came into the dressing room with her eyes stretched. "What happened, you were happy when I left."

"WHAT-IF-HE-HATES-MY-DRESS? WHAT-IF-THE-WHOLE-TIME-HE'S-THINKING-HE-COULD'VE-MADE-IT-BETTER?"

Mrs. Spellman put her arms around Unique and rubbed her back. "Does Benson love you?"

"Yes momma he does."

"How do you know?"

"He takes care of me, he protects me, he shows and tells me all of the time."

Mrs. Spellman put her hands on Unique's face, "then what are you really falling apart about? Huh? If you're sure about his love for you, what's the tears about?"

"I don't know if I'm good enough to have all of this. I've always had my eyes on the scoreboard, it helped me not to focus on the boys who weren't beating down my door. I was always too strong, too competitive, and too tall to have anything real. I'm scared momma, what if he gets tired of me?"

I sat down in the nearest chair as Unique asked her mom all the questions I needed answered. Eva, Rickie, Chareca, and her other friends looked away and busied themselves while I sat there openly staring at them. "Baby you can't run your life worrying about what someone else may feel or do? You are an amazing woman, and that's why he needs to tell the world that you belong to him. As women get older, we get better. Everything you are today will only get better tomorrow and the next day and the next day. If he ever becomes foolish and decides to walk, you hold your head high because there will only ever be one you. One unique you in this world. Most fools come to their senses, but even if he doesn't he misses out on you. You can't worry about what he will do, he needs to be worried about never being that dumb." Unique hugged her mom, and then Mrs. Spellman told me to come over. "Come get some of this." She said holding out her arm for me to join their hug. Unique thanked her mom and then the makeup artist fixed her makeup that she just about ruined. Mrs. Spellman told us to calm down cause weddings never start on time.

When everyone was finally ready we walked out in the procession order. Rickie walked with Tavio since he was the best man and she was the maid of honor. Tavio kept smiling at me during the ceremony. Ben kept telling Unique how beautiful she was and how much he liked her dress. That brat acted like she knew he would love it and the whole melt down didn't happen. During the slow dance Tavio spoke in my ear, "I know you had the big wedding before. Would you humor me and have a big wedding for me?"

I exhaled, "you still want to get married?"

"I want to have a baby, but I would like to be married before that happens."

I put my head on his shoulder. His brother Dakarai was talking in his girlfriend's ear, probably having the same conversation we were. "You deserve to have all of this too."

"Do you love me?"

"Tavio I told you, I've never loved anyone more than you. I can be myself with you, you understand and know things about me that even Chareca doesn't know. I am completely and totally in love with you."

He looked at me and then he smiled, "how many babies you gonna give me?"

"Let's start with two, and if you're game for more we can have as many as you can afford." I kissed his cheek.

"Should I get that in writing?"

"No, our children will be the first that either of us has chosen to have."

"I spoke with your father the other day." I looked at him, he reached into his pocket. "He actually bit my diamond to make sure it was real." I gasped, "that's why he had an emergency dental visit." Tavio stood there cracking up while my eyes were plastered to the thing that sparkled in his hand. "As his wife rushed him off to the dentist, he gave me permission to have you as my wife." Tavio took my hand and slid the ring on my finger, "Alaina Barton. Will you be my wife from now until forever?"

"Yes, from now until forever!"

Tavio

It seems like putting that ring on Alaina's finger changed her entire thought process about our wedding. She went from simple and intimate, to Grand and large. When we met with the wedding planner, she helped Alaina bring her ideas together. When Carina gave us the estimate my eyes bulged at the price tag. We had to be realistic and pull back.

We bought a new house in Albany on the border of Kensington. The best thing about the house was the breathtaking view of the Golden Gate and Bay bridges. The house needed a lot of work. With Alaina's favorite pastime in hand, we had to rethink a lot of our choices. Since we decided to make our home our palace we had to be realistic about our ideas for our wedding. Alaina's creative juices started flowing as she started mapping out how we should renovate the house. She wants to tear down walls, add square footage to the house. Alaina enlisted the help of my momma and Ben.

Granny Shane has been Alaina's main supporter while her mother's parents were all stuck in their feelings until they realized that with or without them Alaina's life was moving on. Granny Shane has welcomed my family and she makes sure they're invited to the planning of anything she can think to make a fuss about for Alaina. Granny Shane called me over her house so we could talk one on one. "Now Tavio, you've been around for a long time. I know we've never talked on our own, but I think it's about time we clear the air don't you?"

I didn't know there was air to be cleared so I agreed. "Yes ma'am, the floor is all yours."

"Thank you baby, sit down, sit down. You're making me nervous standing over there like that." I sat on the couch next to her. "Now I never sat that fool down and spoke with him. Those other grandparents hijacked everything, fancy trips to New York just to spend thousands on a dress that in the end did not matter." She laughed, "that's what they get though." She laughed a little more and then she exhaled. "I'm so happy it's you. I've always liked you. You're a good kid, you come from good parents, and you make my baby so happy. Be patient with her, she got some of the most messed up parents. My son let his misapplication of the good book almost get him banned from the only daughter he has left's life. He was so young and to lose his child and his wife like he did. I didn't want to stress him too much. He stood up and did right by Wesley. You'd never know from my son that Wesley isn't his actual son. I admire that type of dedication in him. Maybe if he would've been honest about his new wife from the beginning Alaina never would've married that fool."

"But then Jerrell wouldn't be here. Can we even imagine life without him?"

Granny Shane hugged me, and then she kissed my cheek. "You are a good man, and my baby is so free with you. I bet you let her freak flag fly too don't you?" She raised her eyebrows at me. I wanted to crawl under this house and die. My expression made her laugh, "it's ok baby. I was young once upon a time. I just wanted to have some alone time wit cha and shoot the breeze."

I sighed in relief, "you had me a little worried when you said we needed to clear the air. I didn't know the air was stuffy around us."

"Oh no, I just wanted you to know that the day you decided to break your foot off in Royce's behind my grandsons got your back."

I laughed, "thanks but Royce knows he can't beat me. I doubt he would ever be that stupid."

Her eyes got big as she smiled, "did you beat him up before? Don't leave anything out, tell me everything."

"Royce is too sneaky to come at me directly. Let's just say that every time we played ball, any type of ball, he got his feelings hurt.

****

Ben made Alaina's dress, and he had the girl in his mentorship make the bridesmaids dresses. Alaina was nervous about giving a student such a major task. Chareca eased Alaina's mind when she shared how highly recommended Nellie came. Nellie beat out hundreds of other candidates for the opportunity to work with Ben. I met her a couple of times and she was so focused on her task, I knew that we were in the right hands.

Our wedding day was beautiful and exactly the way I imagined it. Alaina was the most beautiful bride. Lil Tavio and Jerrell stood next to me during the ceremony. Lil Tavio put the ring on Alaina's finger, and Jerrell gave me my ring. Before we sealed our vows with a kiss we hugged our sons and promised to love them forever. They were just as much a part of this union as we were.

At the reception, Mr. Chambers introduced us to his new wife. I thanked him for everything he has done for Alaina and I. When Royce attempted to try to withhold Jerrell from our special day. Mr. Chambers was the one to step in and deliver Jerrell from Royce's clutches. Royce has been impossible during this whole time. We've managed to keep the drama away from Jerrell, but it's only a matter of time before he catches wind to his father's shenanigans. There are certain choices I don't feel a child should have to make. Like which parent they're going to stand by. I remember how it felt to be in that position. How it changed the way I saw my father from that point onward. My father and I may be fine today, but it took a long time to get there. I don't want that for Jerrell. Tyrek has no patience for Royce and has offered to handle him for me as if I would need the help. I had to calm my baby-daddy-in-law down before someone got hurt. I don't know who has a worse temper, him or me.

Alaina and I took the kids on a family vacation during the first leg of our honeymoon. Then we spent a week locked up under the covers in Jamaica. We saw a little bit of the island, but this girl drained me of all of my juices. She kept calling me *juicy*. We had so much fun making each other laugh and being silly. At one point Alaina cried as she said she couldn't believe how happy she was.

******

I told Royce to have a seat. Royce as usual didn't try to hide anything, his demeanor was angry. "I asked you here today in hopes that we would be able to clear the air and get along for Jerrell's sake."

"That's not going to happen, you are exactly who I thought you were."

I smiled at him, "oh Royce. I didn't know you thought about me. Now that we're here I can admit it. I thought about you too."

"I'm not playing!" He slammed his fist on the table. "You stole my wife!"

"I didn't steal your wife, you lost your wife."

Royce shook his head, probably trying to hold back tears. "I would give it all up to have her back."

"Royce, you're always living with regrets. When do you embrace your present and move on gratefully?"

"I'll never love anyone like I love Alaina." He looked down at his hands, "she's my everything."

"Why did you cheat on her?"

"I wasn't good enough for her. My inability to make her feel complete was a constant reminder of how I was lacking. They filled that void."

"From what I've been told, you were always so guarded with

616

her."

"Do you have any idea how difficult it is to be vulnerable with someone so perfect? I mean I know she wasn't perfect, but she loved me unlike anyone ever had. Letting her in to every insecurity in my mind and soul… I haven't given that to anyone. Alaina was the closest. I mean I wanted to tell her everything, but she would've called off the wedding. It would've hurt her as my wife. She would've left me a lot sooner, and there would be no Jerrell."

"That's why you were fat, cause you were holding back?"

Royce leaned back in his chair; "you supposed to be my therapist now? I hate you, and I'm only here for Alaina."

"I'm trying to understand what makes you tick. I don't care that you hate me, I don't like you either. You did a number on Alaina, and I have to live with the after effects of you." Royce smiled like he liked the sound of that. "Like her addiction to orgasms. She never had them before me, and from what she tells me you failed to get her to the finish line. I could be evil and thank you for being such a loser. However, I'll stop with the enjoyment of watching that ridiculous smile drop off your face." Royce flinched like he wanted to fight. "You could try it, but you know you are no physical match for me." I took a deep breath trying to release some of my testosterone.

"Orgasm!" His voice was hurt and angry.

"Focus Royce! Jerrell! We're here for Jerrell."

Sweat broke out on Royce's forehead, his eyes turned red. He looked like he was about to blow. "This is pointless! I hate you! I hate you so much! You stole my wife! You can't steal my son! The moment I can, I'm taking my wife back!"

"You're gonna die trying. Alaina is not going anywhere. You will never be me, and if you would've been honest with yourself in the first place she would've been my wife all along. Doesn't matter about the time she wasted with you. All that did was make her love and appreciate me more."

Royce got up and walked away.

****

Alaina picked me up from the airport with her normal excitement to see me. I played in her locs as she eagerly drove us home. She was telling me about the events of the house of the past few days while I was gone, as if we hadn't discussed any of this over the phone. Then the car called out that Royce was calling. We let out the same sigh of exhaustion at the same time. "Yes Royce." She didn't even try to pretend that she wanted to be cordial.

"How are you doing?"

"What do you want?"

"Alaina can't we at least be kind to one another? Why do you have to sound like that every time I call you?"

"What do you want?"

Royce paused trying to hold back his irritation. "I wanted to let you know we picked dates for our trip to Florida. We decided we would go right after Jerrell's parent teacher conference."

"Perfect! You know, I could go to the conference and you all could just go. I'd let you know if there was anything you needed to know."

"I'm going!"

"At least bring your fiancé. One day when you let her set a date she could actually fill in for you. I actually like talking to her more than you or Mandy."

"If she can manage I'll let her know she can come." He was quiet for a minute, "does this mean you're bringing Tavio?"

"Of course I'm going to be there, what you think was going to happen?" Alaina smiled at me.

"When are you going to come clean about the affair you two were having behind my back? It's in the past now, why not tell the truth?"

I smiled at Alaina cause she was about to lose it. "Fine, you want the truth? Alaina and I realized we had feelings for each other before you got married. We had a dumb fight just before your wedding and that's when she convinced herself that marrying you was the right decision. The first time she came to work with that look of disappointment I laid her down and showed her what it felt like to lay with a real man. We would go at it, in closets, abandoned offices, her car, my car, you name it we did it there. We even had sex in your bed. While you were sleeping in it. Right next to you. You don't remember?"

Royce let out a deep breath, "you're always playing. How in the world can you take him serious?"

"Stop asking dumb questions. You know Alaina was faithful to you, otherwise you wouldn't continue to hold her up on a pedestal."

Royce got angry and proceeded to curse us. He went for every sensitive spot he could think of. Alaina looked at me and smiled and I smiled back. When we busted out laughing Royce hung up. I leaned over and I kissed Alaina's face. She told me she wanted to show me something before we went home. That was surprising, cause normally she couldn't think straight until we've connected whenever I come home from a trip.

When she pulled up to our house I smiled really big. This is why she always had excuses for why we couldn't come check on the progress. They finished the remodel ahead of forecast. I smiled up at our palace. Alaina got out of the car very excited as she told me they finished the night I left. The landscaping needed to be done next, but we could move into our house now. I couldn't keep my hands off of Alaina as we walked through the house. She transformed our little house into this masterpiece before us. The contractor explained in detail that the original flooring could be saved and they went over the plan of attack. It added more money to our bottom line, but as I walked through our house it was definitely worth it. We didn't even make it to the master suite, we broke in the house from the hallway and then eventually we made it to our huge master suite.

We agreed to move in immediately and officially move on with our lives together. Alaina was so proud of our house; we planned to have a housewarming party right away as well. Everything felt so perfect!

****

I held Alaina in my arms as I kissed her neck, "I love you Mrs. Spellman."

"I love you Tavio, I always have and I always will."

"How has life as Mrs. Spellman been treating you?"

Alaina smiled, "this is how I imagined married life would've always been." Then she rubbed her stomach as she breathed slowly.

The door opened and the doctor walked in smiling, "how's my favorite couple tonight?"

"We're ready for this little princess to make her debut."

The doctor washed her hands and then she put her gloves on. The nurse hurried around the room getting everything ready. As the doctor broke down the bed she smiled, "do we have a name for the princess?"

"Tera," we said in unison.

The doctor smiled, "that's pretty. Let's get her out here so all those people in the waiting room can come and say hello."

The door opened slowly and then Granny Shane and Alaina's Grandmother walked into the room. "You should already know I was coming in here regardless." Granny Shane said.

The doctor looked at us, "is that ok with you?"

"It's fine," Alaina said rubbing her stomach as she breathed through her contraction.

Alaina's grandmother and Granny Shane held on to each other as Tera was born screaming. When the doctor laid her on Alaina's chest Tera stopped crying and looked at both of us. Alaina cried as she kissed the baby and said hello. I have a daughter, a little girl. I'm married to the woman of my dreams, and our family is expanding. Alaina looked at me with tears pouring out of her eyes. "She looks like Alaysia," then she kissed her.

"Alaysia Tera instead?"

"You don't mind?"

"Of course I don't."

"Look at all of that hair. Are you going to make her wear dread locs too?" Alaina's grandmother asked.

"If she wants to loc her hair I will be all for it, but we'll let her decide when she's older."

"She's beautiful you two." Granny Shane said as she rubbed the baby's back.

"We'll go get the boys, as soon as you're cleaned up we'll bring them in." Alaina's grandmother said as she held on to Granny Shane's hand.

After they cleaned her up, they put Tera in my arms. This little girl was going to have to learn how to answer to both her names. Alaina thinks she looks like Alaysia, but I happen to think she looks like me. Alaina watched us with a smile on her face. "So, when do you want to try again?"

"Whenever you're ready is fine with me. Look at how beautiful this little girl is."

"Six months tops."

I looked at Alaina to see if she was joking. "You're serious?"

"Nothing about this experience was traumatic. I can't wait to do it again."

I bent down and kissed my wife, "I'm so happy I waited for you. I don't think I could be any happier than I am right now. I love you Alaina Barton-Spellman."

"I love you Mister Tavio Spellman, until forever."

"Now until forever and ever!"

Author's Closing Thoughts

Hello all, and thank you for allowing me to entertain you for a few hours with another story about life and love. Can I share some things about this story with you?

The story you just read was actually my third attempt at telling Alaina, Tavio, and Royce's story. In each version Alaina did not have her biological mother. In one version her stepmother came along suddenly when she was a teenager. She immediately inherited a stepbrother and her stepmother ran things. Tavio had a blog in that version and he was a world famous writer in the beginning. For the NaNo WriMo 2015 challenge I started fresh on November first and that attempt was golden.

Let me think, how did the other version go? Oh dear, now I can't remember, and I'm patting the bed looking for my phone to look at my original draft. Oh well, just know that it was totally different.

The only similarities were the character names and the fact that Royce always loved Alaina, but some how he lost her. I guess I was playing time machine against myself. (No matter how I tried to save Royce, he always fell short.)

What did you think about that ending? (BIG SMILE!) How many times did you have to read that part to make sure you got it? Royce's father and his brother, what a triangle right! My beta reader said she almost threw her phone... Can I tell you there's no greater joy than making someone express their dramatic reaction by throwing their device or book. It's really just the simple things you know. LOL!

What did you think of my first "standalone" after the Wallace's? Did you notice the *Easter eggs* that I placed inside this story that connect the Wallace Family Affairs stories to this one? I know, I know... I can't help it. You have no idea how hard it was to ask the Wallace's especially Darryl to stay out of this story.

It was during this story that I decided that the Final Together We Are Strong Season would wrap up the Wallace's direct story line. Don't worry, I promise to include little mentions and updates about them in future stories. Malcolm, Amber, and the whole family will randomly pop up from time to time. Why? Because they're real, and they continue to live. At least in my mind they do.

Right after I finished writing this story I lost a family member who was very dear to me. I tried to be angry, because I hate being sad about something I can't control. I struggle with Chantel moments all of the time. You know how she used her anger as a protection until she saw the negative results of it. Well sometimes I forget and find myself going back to old habits. Using anger as a way to deal. Instead, I guess I'll do what I've done before and use this emotional time to write something else. I'm not sure if this book will release before or after Novian and Torrie's book. However, now that I'm finished with Alaina's story it's time to write Novian's. I guess I will use this energy to craft that story. Please be sure to tell me how I did. I hope you don't mind me sharing on such a personal level. I feel like Tavio, sometimes you have to just put your emotions out there to the world and hope that if someone reads it that they understand where you're coming from.

Again I just want to say thank you for hanging in there with me, and until we meet again Ta Ta for now. Muah!

ABOUT THE AUTHOR

Thank you for allowing me to entertain you. If this is your first time reading any of my work, please check out the Wallace Family Affairs Series. If you have not read any of the books within this saga, please checkout the list below. Each book outside of *Present* and *Together We Are Strong* can be read as standalones. Stay tuned for more to come shortly. Follow my Author Pages on FaceBook www.facebook.com/careythewriteranderson Instagram www.instagram.com/author_careythewriteranderson to keep up to date with my new releases and be sure to check out Carey's Corner Carey Anderson.

At Last
Tracy's Complications
Distorted Mirrors
Sometimes Love Isn't Enough
Love Is Just Enough
Just A Friend
Abandoned
Invisible
Look Beyond Your Eyes
No Regrets
First You Laugh Then You Cry
A Heart That's Taken
Last Words
Present
I Knew You When
What Comes Next
Second Chances Retold **Standalone**
Secret & Lies Standalone
Looking Into The Sun **Standalone**
Face Of A Stranger **Standalone**
Scorned – Refuting the Truth **Standalone**
Paisley Clouds Over Paris **Standalone**
Letting Go (Coming Soon)

www.ingramcontent.com/pod-product-compliance
Lightning Source LLC
Chambersburg PA
CBHW020604040726
47498CB00003B/631